Chloe Walsh is the bestselling author of The Boys of Tommen series, which exploded in popularity on TikTok, Goodreads, and Amazon. She has been writing and publishing New Adult and Adult contemporary romance for a decade. Her books have been translated into multiple languages. Animal lover, music addict, TV junkie, Chloe loves spending time with her family and is a passionate advocate for mental health awareness. Chloe lives in Cork, Ireland with her family.

To find out more, visit
www.chloewalshauthor.com.

REDEEMING 6
CHLOE
WALSH

PIATKUS

PIATKUS

First published in Great Britain in 2023 by Piatkus

15

A CIP catalogue record for this book
is available from the British Library.

ISBN: 978-0-349-43930-3

Typeset in Garamond by M Rules

Printed and bound in Great Britain by
Clays Ltd, Elcograf S.p.A.

Papers used by Piatkus are from well-managed forests
and other responsible sources.

Piatkus
An imprint of
Little, Brown Book Group
Carmelite House
50 Victoria Embankment
London EC4Y 0DZ

The authorised representative
in the EEA is
Hachette Ireland
8 Castlecourt Centre
Dublin 15, D15 XTP3, Ireland
(email: info@hbgi.ie)

An Hachette UK Company
www.hachette.co.uk

www.littlebrown.co.uk

Redeeming 6 *is dedicated to the boys I went to secondary school with, whose shenanigans, friendship, banter, hilarious antics, and blind loyalty inspired the characters of Johnny, Gibsie, Feely, and Hughie.*

Walshy, Slash, Al, & Madden: the OG Boys of Tommen.

(And, yeah, I married the first one.)

Glossary

Bluey:	Porno movie.
Jammy:	lucky.
Jammiest:	luckiest.
Corker:	beautiful woman.
St. Stephen's Day:	Boxing Day/ December 26th.
Bonnet:	hood of the car.
Boot:	trunk of the car.
Pound Shop:	Dollar store.
Burdizzo:	castration device
Messages:	groceries.
Mickey/Willy:	penis.
Spanner:	idiot.
Feis:	a tradition Gaelic arts and culture festival/event.
Hole:	often said instead of ass/bottom.
Solicitor:	lawyer.
Daft:	silly.
Daft as a brush:	very silly.
Poitín:	Irish version of moonshine/illegal, home-brewed alcohol.
Wheelie Bin:	Trash can.
Jumper:	sweater.
Cracking on:	hooking up.
Runners:	trainers/sneakers.

Wellies:	rubber boots worn in the rain.
Fair City:	Popular Irish television soap.
On the hop:	skipping school.
Cooker:	Oven/Stove/Hob.
Rolos:	Popular brand of chocolate.
Eejit:	fool/idiot.
Gobshite:	fool/idiot.
Lifted:	arrested.
Sap:	sad/pathetic.
Rebel County:	nickname for County Cork.
Primary School:	elementary school – junior infants to sixth class.
Secondary School:	high school – first year to sixth year.
Leaving Cert:	the compulsory state exam you take in your final year of secondary school.
Junior Cert:	the compulsory state exam you take in third year – midway through your six-year cycle of secondary school.
Playschool:	pre-school/nursery.
Junior Infants:	equivalent to kindergarten.
Senior Infants:	equivalent to second year of kindergarten.
First Class:	equivalent to first grade.
Second Class:	equivalent to second grade.
Third Class:	equivalent to third grade.
Fourth Class:	equivalent to fourth grade.
Fifth Class:	equivalent to fifth grade.
Sixth Class:	equivalent to sixth grade.
First Year:	equivalent to seventh grade.
Second Year:	equivalent to eighth grade.
Third Year:	equivalent to ninth grade.
Fourth Year:	Transition Year: equivalent to tenth grade.
Fifth Year:	equivalent to eleventh grade.
Sixth Year:	equivalent to twelfth grade.

GAA:	Gaelic Athletic Association.
Culchie:	a person from the countryside or a county outside of Dublin. Usually used as a friendly insult.
Jackeen:	a person from Dublin. A term sometimes used by people from other counties in Ireland to refer to a person from Dublin.
Dub:	a person from Dublin.
Frigit:	someone who has never been kissed.
Gardaí Síochána:	Irish police force.
Garda:	policeman.
Shades:	police.
Hurling:	a hugely popular, amateur Irish sport played with wooden hurleys and sliotars.
Camogie:	the female version of Hurling.
Scoil Eoin:	the name of Johnny, Gibsie, Feely, Hughie, and Kevin's all-boys primary school.
Sacred Heart:	the name of Shannon, Joey, Darren, Claire, Caoimhe, Lizzie, Tadhg, Ollie, Podge, and Alec's mixed primary school.
St. Bernadette's:	the name of Aoife, Casey, and Katie's all-girls primary school.
Grinds:	Tutoring.
Fortnight:	two weeks.
Chipper:	a restaurant that sells fast food.
Craic:	fun.
Gas:	funny.
Mope:	idiot.
The Angelus:	Every evening at 6pm in Ireland, there is a minute silence for prayer on the television.
The craic was ninety:	Having a lot of fun and banter.
On the lash:	going out drinking.
On the piss:	going out drinking.

Swot:	nerd/academically gifted.
Spanner:	idiot.
Yolk:	nickname for an illegal drug.
Hatchet craic:	Great fun.
Langer:	idiot.
Fanny:	Vagina.
Scoring:	Kissing.
Shifting:	Kissing.
Shifting Jackets:	Lucky piece of clothing, usually a jacket, when trying to pick up a girl.
Langers:	group of idiots and/or to be extremely drunk.
Tog off:	change into or out of training clothes.
Child of Prague:	a religious statue farmers place out in a field to encourage good weather. (An old Irish superstition.)
Rosary, Removal, Burial:	the three days of a Catholic funeral in Ireland.
Spuds:	potatoes.
A slab of beer:	a box of 24 bottles of beer.
Get your hole:	have sex.
Ridey:	a good-looking person.
Strop:	mood-swing/pouting/sulking.

Name Pronunciations

Aoife:	E-fa
Aoif:	(like reef without the r)
Sean:	Shawn
Gardaí:	Gar-Dee
Caoimhe:	Kee-va
Sadhbh:	Sigh-ve
Sinead:	Shin-aid
Neasa:	Nasa
Eoghan:	Owen
Tadhg:	Tie-g (like Tiger but without the 'r' at the end)

Author Note

Redeeming 6 is the fourth installment in the Boys of Tommen series, and the second book for Joey Lynch and Aoife Molloy.

Some scenes in this book may be extremely upsetting, therefore reader discretion is advised.

Because of its **explicit** sexual content, graphic violence, mature themes, triggers, and bad language, it is suitable for readers of 18+.

It is based in the South of Ireland, set during the timeframe of 1999 to 2005, and contains Irish dialogue and slang.

A detailed glossary can be found at the beginning of the book.

Thank you so much for joining me on this adventure.

Lots of love,

Chlo xxx

PART 1

PART 1

Still trying

JOEY

"You're fierce quiet, Joey son."

"I'm grand, Tony."

"Are you sure? You're as pale as a ghost and haven't had a whole pile to say for yourself all week."

"It's all good."

"You and Aoife haven't ..." He let his words trail off, but kept his worried eyes on me, waiting for an explanation.

"We're grand, Tony." I fed him the lie he wanted to hear before turning my attention back to the rachet in my hand. "Everything's grand."

"Thank Jesus for that." Relief flashed in his eyes. "Then you wouldn't happen to have any idea what's after getting into her? She's walking around the house with a face like thunder."

"No clue." *Liar.*

"Really?" He scratched his jaw in confusion. "You're usually the first to know when there's drama."

"Think she had a fight with Casey over the Christmas."

"Did she now?"

I couldn't explain why the words 'we broke up' refused to come out of my mouth. Or worse, why I lied and placed the blame on her best friend instead, but I did it. "Yeah." I nodded, following through on my bullshit. "I think I heard something about that."

"Jaysus, it must have been one hell of a fight," he stated, watching me from the other side of the car we were working on. "She's been hysterical for days now. Crying herself to sleep most nights."

Fuck. "She has?"

Her father nodded.

My heart sank into my ass. "Jesus."

"You should have a word with her," he added, turning his attention back to the task at hand. "She listens to you. Get her to patch things up with young Casey before she floods the house with tears."

"Yeah, I'll, ah, I'll call her after work," I managed to squeeze out, though it was hard to breathe let alone talk.

Because this was on me.

Molloy's tears were on me.

This whole damn mess was a result of my inability to resist the pull of my fucked-up DNA.

Feeling like my heart was constricting to the point of explosion, I set the rachet down and moved for the back door. "I'll be back in five."

"Pack those damn cigarettes in for the new year," he called after me, but his tone was jokey enough.

Either way, we both knew that I wasn't going to quit.

Not when I had already given up so much.

Slipping out back, I placed the cigarette balancing on my ear between my lips and grabbed a lighter from the pocket of my coveralls.

Sparking up, I inhaled a deep breath and sagged against the wall at my back, feeling a million different emotions rushing through me.

Exhaling a cloud of smoke, I fought an internal battle with myself to *not* throw in the towel and do exactly what I knew I would. In the end, it was only a matter of minutes before I grabbed my phone – the same phone that I had to pry from my brother's fingers this morning.

Blowing out a frustrated breath, I unlocked the screen, declined another call from Shane, brought up the name *Molloy* in my contacts, and pressed call.

She answered on the fourth ring but didn't greet me.

I didn't blame her.

I didn't deserve to be greeted.

If anything, I deserved to be hung up on.

"It's me," I said quietly, taking another drag of my smoke. "Can you talk?"

The hustle and bustle in the background let me know that she was at work.

When it grew quieter on the other line, I knew she must have moved to someplace quiet.

"Okay," she finally said down the line. "I can hear you."

"Are you at work?"

"*No*," she bit out, tone laced with venomous sarcasm. "I'm out on the town with my new boyfriend."

Taking her bitchiness on the chin, I took another drag of my smoke before asking, "And how's he treating you?"

"A hell of a lot better than the last asshole I made the mistake of falling for," came her smart-ass response. "What do you want, Joe?"

"I just . . . " Shaking my head, I blew out a pained breath before saying, "I wanted to check in on you."

"Why?"

"You know why, Molloy." Shrugging helplessly, I concentrated on a spot of dirt on the path. "I didn't flip a switch and turn my feelings off—"

"Don't," she choked out, emotion overtaking her sarcasm. "Not when I have three more hours at work to get through."

Retracting my words, I bit back a pained growl and steered the conversation in another direction. "Tony said that you've been crying."

"And?"

"*And?*" I shook my head. "It fucking guts me to hear that. I don't want you to cry, Molloy."

"Well, unfortunately, that's usually what happens to a girl when her boyfriend sacks her off."

"Stop." I flinched, hating both the words and the pain in her voice. "I didn't sack you off."

"You broke up with me, Joey," she replied, tone thick. "You can wrap it up as sweetly as you want, but in the end, that's exactly what you did."

"I still love you."

I heard her sudden intake of breath, but she didn't say anything for a long beat. "Don't."

"I fucking love you, Aoife Molloy," I repeated, focusing on an oil stain on the back wall of the garage. "I always will."

"Then take it back."

"I can't." I shook my head, feeling like my heart was splitting clean down the center. "I'm not good for you."

All I wanted to do was sprint over to The Dinniman and wrap her up in my arms, but I couldn't afford to make another mistake with this girl.

Not when I'd already crushed her.

"Are you clean?"

I closed my eyes and nodded weakly. "Yes."

"Since when?"

"I haven't touched anything since that night."

"Because you're turning over a new leaf?"

"Because I'm fucking ashamed of myself," I came right out and told her. "Of what I exposed you to. How I treated you."

There was a long stretch of silence, where I swear that I could hear the sound of my own heart thundering in my ears, before she spoke again. "So, two weeks without anything, huh?"

I nodded again. "Yes."

"Yeah, I'll be back in five," I heard her say. "I'm owed a cigarette break ... Yes, Julie, I know I don't smoke, but I cover for you at least seven times a day when you take yours, so I'm having one." The line was muffled for a few moments before she returned. "Okay, I'm back. Julie's just being a greedy bitch."

"Picking fights with co-workers, Molloy?"

"No more than usual." There was a bite to her tone that she didn't try to conceal. "And Shane Holland? How many weeks have you been *clean* of him?"

"The same."

"How can I believe you?"

"I don't know." I exhaled a heavy sigh. "All I have is my word."

"I want to believe you, Joe," she whispered down the line. "So badly."

But you can't. "I get it," I replied, roughly clearing my throat. "We both know that I haven't been the kind of fella you could put your faith in."

"You didn't call." The accusation was there in her voice. "Not once."

"I couldn't." Grimacing in what felt like physical pain, I forced myself to give her my truth. "I only got my phone back this morning."

"From who?"

"From Tadhg."

There was a pause. "Why did Tadhg have your phone?"

"Because I needed to *not* have it."

"Because?"

I grimaced. "You know why."

"Joe." She breathed heavily into the phone, and I didn't have to be there to know there was a tremor running through her body. I knew because the same tremor was running through mine. "You're really clean?"

"Yeah, Molloy." *For you.* "I really am."

"Then what are we doing here? Why am I here and you're *not*?"

"I need more time."

"To do what?" she snapped. "To fuck around?"

"To get myself straightened out," I corrected gruffly, narrowing my eyes. "Don't even fucking go there when you *know* that I'm not looking at anyone else."

"Well, if you're clean, then why can't we just ... " Stopping short, she blew out a shaky breath and said, "You know what? Forget it. I won't beg you again. If you're not calling to get back together, then hang up the phone."

"Molloy."

"I mean it, Joe. Don't call me again. Not unless you've changed your tune."

The line went dead, and I let my head fall back against the concrete wall.

"Fuck."

Breathing hard and fast, I resisted re-dialing her number and giving her exactly what she wanted.

The only way I was able to stop myself from doing just that was with the knowledge that while she might want me, she certainly didn't need me.

Not now.

Not yet.

Not at all if I couldn't get a handle on myself.

Serving pints and pricks

AOIFE

Ending the call, I shoved my phone into the front pocket of my black apron and shook my hands out, desperately trying to get a handle on my emotions before they got the better of me.

One whole week had passed since I landed on Joey's doorstep on New Year's Eve, and I was still a walking mess because *nothing* had changed.

We were still over.

He was still gone.

I was still shredded.

Keep it together, Aoife.

You're at work.

You can cry when you get home.

Don't you dare embarrass yourself!

Refusing to give into the overpowering urge to slump in the corner of the smoking area and rock, I pushed my shoulders back, tipped my chin up, and sauntered back to the bar.

I might be crumbling to pieces on the inside, but I would do it with dignity, dammit.

He's just a boy.

Just one boy.

You can survive this.

"Mind the bar," Julie muttered, skulking past me when I returned to my post. "I'm going for a ciggie."

Since turning eighteen last September, I'd stepped in enough times behind the bar, and pulled enough pints, to know my way around a tap. When the orders started trickling in, I handled it with ease, flirting and smiling and sticking out my chest, like the pro I was.

Unfortunately, one of those orders just so happened to come from a man who made my skin crawl.

"Jameson straight, no ice," Joey's father demanded from his perch at the bar.

Forcing myself to keep my smile in place, I quickly set to work on preparing his drink, forcing myself to repress a shudder when I felt his eyes on my back.

"What?" Teddy taunted when I set his drink down on the beer mat in front of him. "No sweet talk for me?"

"That will be three euro please," I replied, jaw aching from the effort it was taking to keep my smile in place.

Reaching into his jeans pocket, he grabbed a fistful of loose change and smacked it down on the counter in front of me, causing pennies and coppers to spill everywhere. "You can count, can't ya, girl?"

"I sure can," I replied, unwilling to let him entice me into an argument, as I used my finger to slide the coins towards me. "Enjoy your drink."

"I'd enjoy my drink a lot more if you popped a few buttons on that blouse."

Now I *did* shudder. "Don't you have a wife at home to be looking after, Teddy?" Moving to the cash register, I tallied up his drink and dropped the coins inside the till drawer before snapping it shut with a clatter. "A *pregnant* wife."

I wasn't unfamiliar with being propositioned by punters. It came hand in hand with the job, but this was Joey's father.

As far as he knew, I was his son's girlfriend.

This wasn't his first attempt to lure me out back for a quickie, but that didn't make it any less disturbing.

The man set my teeth on edge in the worst kind of way, and being in his presence was the ultimate form of unsettling.

Dutifully ignoring his comments, I cleared away glasses and wiped down the bar, doing pretty much anything I could to get away from him.

"Tell me something." Shifting on his stool, he folded his arms across his chest and gave me a heated look. "What are ya doing with him?"

"I presume you mean Joey?" I answered, knowing that he wouldn't let up until I did.

Like I said: not my first time serving this creep.

Nodding stiffly, he never took his cold brown eyes off me.

Fully aware that any admissions from the heart would be wasted on this man, and unwilling to lose my job over him, I slapped on a smile and said, "I told you before. That son of yours is more than able to keep me satisfied."

"He's a kid."

"And what am I?" came my dry response. "A middle-aged woman?"

"If I was your father, you wouldn't be working behind a bar."

"You're certainly old enough to be my father."

His nostrils flared. "You don't know what you're missing."

"Okay, you need to stop." My smile faded and I gave him a hard look. "If Joey knew that you were speaking to me like this, he would—"

"What?" he cut me off with a threatening lilt to his voice. "He would do what, girl?"

"He would break your fucking neck," I bit out, keeping my tone low. "So, back off."

"Well, I don't see that young fella of mine anywhere, do you?" Elbows resting on the bar, he leaned closer. "What time do ya get off work?"

"A freckle past a hair."

"What's that code for?"

"It's code for never," I snapped. "As in, it's never going to happen. Not in your wildest dreams. So, why don't you finish your drink and clear off across the road to another pub, because whatever you're looking for, you won't get it from me."

"Prick-tease."

Beyond repulsed, I wandered to the far end of the bar, putting as much space between us as possible. The man made my skin crawl, and the sooner Julie came back from her break, the better.

A few minutes later, he crooked his finger and pointed to his empty glass.

Biting back the urge to scream, I begrudgingly returned to his end of the bar and gave him a blank stare.

Teddy slammed another fistful of coins down on the bar. "Another."

Counting his coppers, I moved to the till and tossed them inside before pouring him another glass of his poison of choice.

Whiskey.

"You know he's a disaster, don't ya?" Teddy slurred, nursing the glass I set down in front of him. "Can't help himself. It's in his blood."

I knew that he was talking about Joey, but I refused to play ball with him. Regardless of our current relationship status, or how badly Joey had hurt me by walking away, I was prepared to die on my hill of unwavering fealty to him.

"The boy is fucked in the head," he continued, taking a sip from his glass. "Always has been. Been a problem from day one."

"I wonder why."

He glared at me with those cold eyes. "You think you know everything, don't ya?"

"I know enough," I held my ground and replied.

"You know fuck all." A cruel smile spread across his face. "He's either going to end up killing himself or someone else."

"Then let's hope it's you."

My response surprised him, and he rose a brow. "You're not afraid of me, are ya, girl?"

"I don't fear men," I tossed back, meeting his stare head-on. "Because the man in my life knows how to treat a woman."

"Already told ya that young fella of mine is still a boy."

"He's more of man than his father."

Realizing that I had no intention of giving into his oppression, Teddy dismissed me from his presence with a flick of his wrist, muttering something unintelligible under his breath.

More relieved than angry, I once again moved to the other end of the bar, sighing in relief when my eyes landed on Julie returning from her smoke break.

"Oh good, he's still here." Setting her pack of cigarettes under the bar, she fluffed out her hair and smiled. "Something to look at for the evening."

I knew she was referring to Teddy and the thought made me want to hurl my lunch up.

To the untrained eye, it could be assumed that he was a beautiful man.

He was tall and blond, with golden skin, and a strong, muscular physique, but once you knew who he was, once you got a glimpse of the evil lurking beneath the surface, you could never mistake his looks for beauty.

How he fathered five pretty epic humans was beyond me, but he had, and all four of his sons bore an uncanny resemblance to him. Shannon was the exception to the gene pool, clearly taking after Marie in appearance.

My mind drifted back to Joey and the resentment weighing heavily on my shoulders significantly lightened.

Being in the presence of his father, a man Joey had to endure his entire life, caused my skin to crawl and my resolve to weaken.

How could I be angry at him for trying to fight against turning into the piece of shit propping up the bar?

He was terrified of us becoming his parents, of becoming the man at the end of the bar and had taken drastic measures to stop that from happening.

To protect me.

Telling me that he loved me on the phone earlier wasn't right, he should be keeping that shit to himself, but I'd be a liar if I said it didn't soothe the ache in my chest.

Just a smidge.

"Are you pregnant?" was the first question my mother asked when I walked through the door on Friday evening after work.

"Am I *what*?" I asked, dropping my bag on the kitchen table, and turning to gape at my mother.

"Pregnant," she repeated, setting her iron down. "You can tell me if you are, Aoife." Wiping her hands off on her trousers, she stepped around the ironing board and closed the space between us. "I won't shout at you, love, I promise. But I would rather know now than later on."

"No, I'm not *pregnant*," I snapped, shrugging off my coat before hanging it on the back of the kitchen chair.

"But you *are* sexually active."

"Oh my god," I groaned, kicking off my heels. "What are you going on about, woman?"

"You're having sex."

I gave her a look that said, '*how dare you even suggest such a thing*', before adding, "And even if I was having sex, which I'm absolutely not, I'm on the pill, remember? You took me to get it when I was fourteen."

"To help with your heavy periods," she reminded me. "Not because I was giving you the green light to have sex with Paul."

"And I didn't have sex." Shrugging sheepishly, I added, "With Paul."

"But you are now." She offered me a supportive smile. "With Joey."

I snorted. "*No.*"

Mam cocked a brow. "Do you think that I came down in the last shower? It's not your father that you're talking to. Don't try to pull the wool over my eyes, young lady. I know well what happens when that boy sleeps over."

"Oh my god."

"If you're sexually active with young Joey, then there's no need to hide it from me," she continued. "You've been together for a while. I'm not mad, love. I'm just concerned. "

"And so what if I am having sex with him?" I choked out, blushing. "I'm not fourteen anymore, Mam. I'm eighteen, remember?"

"That's fine," she replied, voice strained. "Thank you for telling me."

"You're . . . welcome?"

"Now, are you being safe?"

"I'm *on* the pill," I repeated slowly. "How much safer can I get?"

"Condoms."

I scrunched my nose up in awkward discomfort.

Mam's eyes widened. *"Aoife."*

"What?" I threw my hands up. "We're being safe."

"So, you've been taking your pill at the same time every day?" she pressed, tone laced with concern. "Religiously?"

I balked. "Why are you even asking me all of this?"

"Because you're moody, you're spending all of your time holed up in your room, you're eating like a horse, and you look like you're seconds away from bursting into tears at any given minute."

"And that makes me pregnant?" I demanded, hands on my hips. "What's next; are you going to tell me that I've put on weight, too?"

"Aoife."

"No, Mam, Jesus, I'm not pregnant." Shaking my head, I stalked over to the fridge and swung it open. "I had a period before Christmas."

"You did?"

"Yes."

"You're sure?"

"Yes, Mam." I rolled my eyes. "I specifically remember because I'd been out shopping with Casey that week and didn't buy this really cute white skirt from The Modern to wear out for Katie's birthday – even though it was a total bargain at a tenner – because I knew I couldn't risk wearing it."

Relief flooded her eyes. "Oh, thank god for that."

"Thanks for the vote of confidence, by the way. I really appreciate how much faith you have in my ability to not ruin my life." I waved a hand around aimlessly. "I hope you plan on giving Kev the same supportive pep-talk, because he's a moody bastard who rarely leaves his room, either."

"Don't be daft." Mam batted the air like it was the most ridiculous thing she had ever heard. "Your brother can't bring a grandchild home to me in his belly."

"And you think that Joey and I are thick enough to?"

"I think that you've both been swept up in the throes of first love."

Both her eyes and her voice softened when she added, "And I think that a lot of mistakes can be made when emotion takes the driving seat over logic."

"Well, that shows what you know," I replied, slamming the fridge closed. "Because Joey and I aren't even together right now."

"You're not?" Her eyes widened. "Oh, I didn't know, love."

"Well, now you do," I said flatly, moving for the door. "I'm nursing a broken heart, Mam, not your grandchild in my belly."

"Aoife?" she called after me. "Wait, pet, we can talk about it if you want? I'm here for you, love."

"I don't want to talk about it," I tossed over my shoulder, as I thundered up the staircase.

I can't.

Turf war

JOEY

"What the fuck are you on?" Podge demanded, as he chased me around the pitch at the GAA pavilion on Saturday afternoon, with his hurley in hand. "I haven't seen you this pumped since we won the county final in third year."

"Nothing," I panted, narrowly side-stepping him, to hook the sliotar with my hurl and tap it back to him. Tony had closed up early, something that left me with my hands hanging, which had led me to text the lads to meet me for a puck around. "I haven't been out since Christmas."

"Then what the fuck did Santa put in your stocking?" Alec wheezed, chopping down hard on Podge's hurl, and robbing the ball. "Speed?"

A reality check. "Nothing."

Podge narrowed his eyes in disbelief. "Then what the hell is going on with you?"

"Nothing." I shrugged, breathing hard and fast. "I'm just done with the bullshit."

"Meaning?"

"Meaning I'm done fucking around."

"Meaning he's too busy getting his hole off sexy-legs to even think about getting high," Alec snickered. "Jesus, her pussy must taste like ambrosia or whatever it is the gods eat – ow, Jesus, fuck, don't hit me with that." Clutching the side of his head, he groaned, "Dammit, Joe, you're lucky I'm wearing a helmet. You could have given me brain damage."

"No, *you're* lucky you're wearing a helmet," I shot back, still wielding the boss of my hurl precariously close to his throat. "Next time you even think about my girl's pussy, I'll take the head clean off your shoulders, ya hear?"

"Give it a rest, Al," Podge snapped, dragging my attention back to him. "What does this mean, Joe?" His attention was riveted on my face. "When you say that you're done fucking around, do you mean with Holland and his crew?"

I nodded stiffly. "I mean with all of it."

"Yeah?"

"Yeah." Shrugging in discomfort, I hooked the sliotar onto my boss and broke off on a solo run before deftly lobbing the ball over the bar of the far end goal.

With sweat trickling down the back of my neck, I retrieved the sliotar from behind the back of the goal before sprinting off again, desperate to burn the tension out of my body.

I couldn't remember the last time I'd gone this long without anything in my system.

But I was still here, still trying, still hanging in there.

For her.

"How long has it been?" Podge asked when I returned with the ball.

"How long what?" Alec piped up.

"A few weeks," I replied, using the hem of my jersey to wipe the sweat dripping from my brow. "It's nothing to sing home about, but it's a start."

I had this horrible anxious tremor rolling through me, one that no amount of exercise could settle.

I knew why, of course.

My body wasn't craving exercise.

It didn't want food or water, and it wasn't satisfied with a smoke.

It wanted *more.*

I was fucking ravenous.

But with two weeks of hell put down to get where I was today, I was strong enough to let it starve just a little while longer.

One more hour.

And then another after that.

Keep fucking going, lad.

"Well, shit." Podge's brows shot up in surprise and he quickly laced the sliotar down the pitch before telling Alec to go long. "Am I wrong in thinking that Aoife has a fair bit to do with this sudden change of lifestyle?" he asked when Alec was out of earshot. "She's a good influence on you, lad."

"We're taking some time out," I forced myself to admit out loud to quite possibly the only person I trusted aside from the two girls in my life.

I had managed to work an entire week with Tony without disclosing as much as a drizzle of information on my relationship with his daughter. It hadn't been easy facing him, and the unknown, but to his huge credit, the man treated me exactly the same as always.

"You and Aoife?" Podge asked, eyes widening, and I quickly realized that he wasn't going to do the same. "Since when?"

"Since I pulled my head out of my ass long enough to see what I was doing to her."

"Are you serious?"

"Come on, Podge." I shrugged, deciding to go with the truth for once. "It's fairly obvious that the road I've been travelling down isn't exactly aligning with the one Aoife's on, lad."

"And that matters to you?"

"She matters to me."

"Are you broken up for good?"

His question caused my heart to plummet into my ass, and my mind to scream *fuck, I hope not*. "It depends."

"On what?"

"On whether or not I can get my shit together."

"Which you apparently have."

"And now, whether or not I can *keep* my shit together," I forced myself to add. "Which, let's face it, lad, I don't have the best track record of doing."

"So, this time out was her idea?"

"No." I shook my head. "It was mine."

"So, does this time out mean that you guys are seeing other people?"

"No," I balked, feeling sick to my stomach at the thought. "I don't want to even *think* about another girl, lad."

"Is she?" he pushed. "Thinking about other lads?"

"She should," I muttered. "But no. I don't think so."

"And if she does?"

I bit back the urge to roar. "Then I won't hold her back."

"Jesus, you really love her, don't you?"

More than life.

"So what if I do?" I bit out, immediately on the defensive.

"Nothing, lad, nothing," he was quick to placate. "It's just that I've known you since junior infants, since we were four, and I've never heard you admit your feelings for anyone."

I shrugged, uncomfortable with this line of questioning.

"Obviously, I noticed that weird chemistry the two of you have the second we walked into first year, but I never realized it was that deep." He shook his head before admitting, "I always figured the infatuation you had with her had more to do with pissing off Ricey than anything else."

"Ah, yes." I smirked to myself, thinking back to the countless times down through the years when Ricey had caught us bantering and lost his shit. "That was an enjoyable perk."

"Could you have pucked the sliotar any further?" Alec panted, jogging back over to us, ball in hand. "I had to climb into the bushes to get it back."

"Sorry, Al," Podge chuckled, and then turned back to offer me a wink. "Keep on keeping it together, Joe."

"That's the plan."

"Keep on keeping it together? The plan?" Alec shook his head and groaned, "Why do I always feel like you two are speaking in riddles around me?"

"Because you're perceptive," Podge shot back with smirk.

"No, no, I'm not," Alec grumbled. "I know what you two fuckers are doing. Don't deny it."

"He said you were perceptive, Al," I laughed, pucking the ball towards him. "Do you know what perceptive means?"

"Of course I know what it means," Alec huffed, catching the sliotar mid-air. "It's when you're second guessing everything, and don't trust a word of what's being said around you."

Podge threw his head back and laughed, while I scrubbed a hand down my face before muttering, "That's paranoia, Al."

"It *is*?"

Podge chuckled, "Yeah, lad. It's a whole different word with a whole different meaning."

"Maybe I did hit you too hard before," I offered dryly.

"Paranoia." Alec frowned. "Then what's perceptive?"

"Something you'll never be accused of being again," Podge laughed.

"Right, lads, spread out and we'll have another puck around before it gets dark," I instructed, jogging backwards. "We've a match against St. Fintan's next week, and I have no intention of letting those fuckers knock us out of the playoffs."

"So, the school board got back to you with their decision?" Alec asked, tone hopeful.

"Yeah, they phoned Mam the day before yesterday," I replied, jumping up to catch the sliotar mid-air. "Apparently, I'm on the last of my nine lives."

"So, you're not getting expelled?"

I grinned. "Not this week."

It was closing in on five in the evening when Podge nudged me in the arm, alerting me to the fact that we had company.

Squinting in the semi-darkness, I tried and failed to put names on the faces watching us from the far side of the pitch, as my hackles rose, and my body tensed up at the unknown threat.

"They're definitely watching us," Podge muttered.

"I think they're from Tommen," Alec noted, rubbing his jaw. "I've definitely seen that big fella in the local paper playing rugby."

"Yeah, they drink in Biddies."

"The fuck are they doing here?" I bit out.

"Yeah. Wrong pitch."

"Wrong side of town, more like."

We continued to puck the sliotar around for another five minutes until it was clear that they weren't going away.

"Give me a sec," I snapped, throwing my helmet off. "I'll sort this." Pissed off and irritated, I stalked towards the group of rich pricks huddling at the sidelines of my goddamn pitch.

"Don't lose the head, Joe," Podge warned, hurrying after me.

"Yeah, lad," Alec muttered in agreement. "There's like six of them over there."

"Got a staring problem, assholes?"

"Ah, Jesus," Alec groaned, clutching the back of my t-shirt. "We're going to die."

"Are ye deaf?" I demanded, shaking him off, my entire focus on the lads watching me. "I asked ye a fucking question!"

"Yeah, that's the one," one of the lads said, before taking a safe step behind an even bigger lad. "You do the talking, Gibs."

This one had a familiar look about him, with blond hair and a goofy as fuck smile. "Howdy, friend."

"I'm not your friend," I seethed, closing the space between us, hurley in hand. "And the last time I checked, the rugby club was on the other side of town," I reminded them. "You have no business here."

"Oh, Jesus." The blond lad's silvery grey eyes lit up with what I could only describe as playful mischief when he chuckled, "Are we about to have a turf war?"

I cocked a brow. "A turf war?"

"Yeah." He nodded eagerly. "Like the T-birds and the Scorpions in *Grease*."

"*Grease*?" I gaped at him. "What the fuck are you talking about?"

"Don't mind Gibsie," another one of them said, and this one was definitely familiar. "He's a fair bit dysfunctional."

"How do I know you?" I demanded, eyeing him warily.

"I'm Hughie Biggs," he was quick to offer up, holding his hands up, the universal symbol of peace. "Our sisters are friends."

"Yeah," the big one chuckled, waving a tissue in front of him. "We come in peace."

"Shut up, Gibs," Hughie muttered, shaking his head. "Jesus, lad."

Taken aback, I unfurled my fists, and forced myself to simmer down. There was no threat here.

I needed to get my body to register that.

"What are you doing here, Biggs?" I asked, addressing Hughie, and ignoring the big ape of muscle he had standing beside him. "What do you want?"

"Looking for you, actually."

Now, I was on alert again. "Why?"

"I sort of need a favor."

"I don't do favors for strangers."

"Our sisters are friends," he repeated, tone hopeful. "Which means we're sort of friends, or acquaintances, maybe . . . no? Okay then."

"I don't do friends," I repeated coldly, sizing up each and every one of the overgrown bastards, with their designer clothes, and expensive haircuts. "And I don't do favors."

"*Hey*," Alec huffed, folding his arms across his chest in outrage. "Thanks a fucking lot, friend. What am I? Dog shit?"

"Shut up, you dope," Podge grumbled. "Let Lynchy handle this."

"Fair enough," Hughie replied, with a shake of his head. "Clearly coming here was a bad idea."

"Clearly," I bit out, staring him down until he looked away. "See ya."

"What?" the big fella demanded. "No, no, it was a brilliant idea, and I'm not leaving until I get what I came for."

"And what was that exactly?"

"We're looking to take a trip to the spliffs of Moher, if you get me?" he chuckled, waggling his brows.

I stared blankly back at him.

"We need drugs."

"Jesus, Gibs," Hughie groaned, dropping his head in his hands. "Tact, lad. *Tact*."

"Drugs?" I cocked a brow. "And you came to me because?"

"Because we've heard the rumors," another one said.

I arched a brow. "Rumors?"

"From Hughie," the big lad offered up.

Hughie groaned loudly. "Jesus, Gibs."

"He said you're off your trolley on drugs and I really need to borrow some of those."

"Thanks a fucking bunch, Gibs," Hughie spluttered, taking a safe step back.

I locked my gaze on the big one. "And you thought that I could help you with that?"

He nodded brightly.

"Look at me, asshole." I gestured to my training gear. "Do I look like a dealer?"

When he didn't immediately say no, I narrowed my eyes. "I'm not a fucking dealer."

"But you *do* have contacts, right?" he offered back, tone coaxing. "You know, friends in low places and all of that jazz? You are from Elk's Terrace, aren't you?"

"One: I'm not your friend. Two: the fact that you're insulting me to my face by insinuating that I'm from a lower place than you, deserves a smack in the mouth. And three: I'm not doing shit for you. Now, clear off."

"I accept all three of those reasons as being fair and true," the big fella replied. "And I honestly would oblige you by clearing off, but I really need those drugs for my captain."

"Your captain."

"Yeah, my captain." He nodded eagerly. "He's having a hard time right now – a really fucking hard time. He had this procedure before Christmas, you see, and the poor bastard is as stiff as a poker from it. All I'm looking for is something to help relax him."

"Gus, is it?" I asked calmly. "Is that your name?"

"Gibsie," he corrected with a sheepish grin. "It's Gibsie, although my mother calls me Gerard—"

"I don't give a shit what your mother calls you," I interrupted, leveling him a warning look. "And as for your captain and his *procedure*? Tell him to go to a doctor and get a prescription like everyone else." Turning back to Hughie, I added, "Don't come back here, Biggs." I pointed to the big ape beside him before adding, "And especially not with him."

"But he can't write me a prescription for weed!" the big lad blurted out. "Please? Come on, man, it's just a little weed?"

"What part of *I'm not a dealer* are you having trouble with?"

"I know, I know, you're not a dealer, blah, blah, blah. I heard ya," he reeled off. "But if you could make an exception just for tonight, then I would really owe you one."

"You already owe me," I muttered. "The last five minutes of my life that I'm never getting back."

"You can come to our party tonight," he tried to coax. "It's at Hughie's gaff. It's 90's themed—"

"No, it's not, Gibs."

"Yes, it is," the big lad argued before turning back to me. "His folks are in Portugal. Free drink all night – oh, and sausage rolls, too."

"Free sausage rolls?" I feigned excitement. "Well, why didn't you say that earlier? I'm in."

His eyes widened in delight. "Really?"

I rolled my eyes. "No, not really, you langer."

"We can pay," another one said, and this one had dark hair. "We have money," he added, standing slightly back from the others. "Whatever you want. It wouldn't be an issue."

"Shit, Feely, lad, don't say that," Hughie groaned. "We only have two hundred."

Now, I *was* listening. "Two hundred?"

"Yeah," he replied, withdrawing a wad of twenties from his jeans pocket. "Is that enough?"

I glanced at Alec, who was dutifully trying not to burst out laughing. He might be a thick fucker, but he was streetwise enough to know that they had enough cash to supply their rugby team *and* our hurling team.

"How much are you looking for?" I heard myself ask.

"Lynchy, can I talk to you real quick?" Podge interrupted, before dragging me away from them.

"What are you doing?" I hissed, shrugging his arm off.

"What am *I* doing? What are *you* doing?" he demanded, when we were out of earshot. "I thought you were done with Shane Holland and all of that bullshit?"

"I *am*," I bit out, glaring at him. "I don't need to go anywhere near Holland for this."

"How?"

I shrugged. "I have an eighth back at the house."

"I thought you were done with all of that?"

"I *am*," I repeated, pissed off. "I haven't used."

His eyes bulged. "Weed *is* using."

Mine narrowed in response. "*No*, it's not."

"Yes, it is."

"No, it's not."

"Cannabis is a drug."

"Cannabis is a *plant*."

"It's against the law in this country."

"So is taking a piss on the street," I shot back. "Rules are stupid. What's your point?"

"Jesus, Joey," Podge groaned, rubbing his face with his hand. "It's like two steps forward and ten steps back with you."

"Bullshit. It's prescribed by doctors for pain in half the world."

"So is Oxycontin and the dozens of other prescription meds I've watched you ram down your throat since primary school. They're prescribed for pain, too, Joe, but you know only too well what happens when they fall into the wrong hands."

"I told you that I haven't touched anything in weeks."

"Except *weed*," he reminded me, tone exasperated.

"Don't act all high and mighty about it," I shot back defensively. "Not when you've passed around many the spliff in your day."

"There's a big difference between having a smoke and hustling a bunch of naïve rich boys out of cash."

"Hey, don't fucking judge me," I warned, narrowing my eyes at him. "Two hundred quid, Podge. *Two hundred.* And they're waving it around like it's monopoly money. That might be pennies to guys like them, but for the likes of me, that's serious fucking money." I threw my hands up in frustration and spat, "You might be in the privileged position of being able to turn your nose up at it, but I sure as hell can't afford to. Do you have any idea what that money could do for me?"

For my mother.

For my siblings.

It would mean the difference between my brothers living off cold baked beans and butter sandwiches for the next week in the freezing cold of winter until Mam or I got paid or having a hot meal in their bellies and a warm fire to heat them before bed.

There was no choice to make in this instance.

"And what about Aoife?" he demanded, cutting me where it would have the biggest impact. Right in the heart. "How happy do you think she'll be when she finds out—"

"Don't bring her into it," I warned, cutting him off. "Don't you dare throw her in my face." Shaking my head in warning, I held a hand up and took a step back, regretting ever confiding in him. I couldn't trust a goddamn soul. "You *know* why I can't turn this down, you fucking *know*, Podge, so don't twist the knife in deeper."

Guilt flickered in his eyes, and he shook his head. "If you need money for your family, I can—"

"I don't want your charity," I spat, shaking because of how horribly fucking exposed I felt. "I can handle it myself."

He stared at me for the longest time before relenting. "Fair enough."

He threw his hands up in defeat. "I won't say another word, only to say that I think this is a bad idea."

"I accept that," I replied with a stiff nod. "Now, you can either stay here on your high horse and judge me, or you can come with me to their fancy-ass party, and eat your weight in sausage rolls." Turning around, I strode off in the direction of the lads from Tommen. "Either way, bad idea or not, I'm doing this."

This is the closest thing to crazy

AOIFE

"We're staging an intervention," Casey announced later that evening, throwing my bedroom door open and sauntering into my room like she was practicing for the catwalk. Dressed to the nines in a short denim mini, stilettos, and that cute white gypsy blouse I bought her for Christmas, she planted her hands on her hips and glared at me. "That bastard dumps you on Christmas Day and you don't *call*!"

"Smooth, Casey," Katie cringed, following her into my room. "Your mother called us," she hurried to explain, tone laced with sympathy. "She's really worried about you, Aoif."

"We all are."

"Ugh." Groaning, I rolled onto my back and starfished the bed, knocking countless empty sweet wrappers off in the process.

"Okay, you need to turn the song off," Casey ordered, moving for my stereo. "And climb out of your misery."

"No, this is the best part," I choked out, wailing along to the lyrics of Katie Melua's 'The Closest Thing To Crazy'. "I'm fine," I sobbed. "Really, I am."

"*Sure* you are," Casey shot back, arching a brow. "That's why you have chocolate smeared all over your chin."

"I'm trying to process here," I mumbled pathetically, around a mouthful of M&Ms. "God, is that so terrible?"

"Then process by getting mad," she instructed, stalking over to swipe the half-eaten packet out of my hands. "Hell, get *even*. But don't get *fat*."

"Casey," Katie spluttered out. "You don't say things like that."

"Well, sue me, because I said it," Case shot back unapologetically. "And I'm not going to sit back and watch my best friend self-destruct because her asshole ex dumped her at Christmas. I mean *Christmas*?"

Her tone was incredulous. "After a year together? Who the hell even does that?"

"Joey didn't dump me," I huffed. "We're taking time out."

"Decided by who?"

"Him," I strangled out, feeling my heart splice open.

"For how long?"

As long as it takes for him to get his crap together. "I don't know."

"I really hate when boys pull this stunt," she growled. "He doesn't have the balls to knock it on the head, so he leaves the girl hanging in limbo, stringing her along for weeks until she finally comes to her senses and sees that the *space* that he desperately needed wasn't really space at all, but a new girl to bury his dick inside."

"Casey, please," Katie snapped. "You need to tone it down."

"You are worth ten of that dickhead," Casey continued to grumble, as she set her duffel bag down on my bed and unzipped it. "And I plan on reminding you of it."

I eyed the bag warily. "What are you doing?"

"The question you should be asking is what are *we* doing," she replied, dragging out a mountain of clothes, make-up, CDs, and a bottle of that cheap Prosecco we both loved. "And *we*, my dearest, oldest, most gorgeous friend in the whole wide world, are going to a house party."

"No, no, no." I shook my head. "*You're* going to a house party. I'm not going anywhere."

"Yes, you are," she chimed back, ignoring my protests. "Katie's fella has a free house, and he's throwing this huge party before school starts back on Monday. They're having an actual DJ, with a mountain of free booze. It's going to be packed to the rafters with all of his buddies from the rugby team, and you *are* going to come with us."

"No," I vehemently protested. "I am absolutely *not*."

"Did you not hear me?" She gaped at me like I had lost my mind. "I said it's going to be filled with rugby players, Aoif. Big, hot, sweaty, sexy rugby players."

"I don't care."

"Best of all, it's a Tommen party, so you don't have to worry about bumping into anyone from BCS," she quickly continued, ignoring my wishes entirely. "And by anyone, I mean that good for nothing asshole."

"Casey, if you told me that the entire Irish rugby team was going to be in attendance, I still wouldn't come." Reaching for a pillow, I hugged it to my chest and sighed heavily. "Do you remember the Cadbury's advert that used to be on the television when we were small; the one with the woman devouring a square of dairy milk while 'Show Me Heaven' played in the background?"

"Yeah, so?"

"Yeah, well, I'm the woman in the ad and Joey's the chocolate bar."

"So, you're saying that he's the only flavor you want to taste?" She shook her head. "That's so stupid when he's the only flavor you've ever tried. He dumped you, Aoif. He cut off your chocolate source. So, get off your ass and come sample something from the luxury menu with me instead."

"I'm not interested."

"Get up."

"I'm too sad."

"Which is exactly why I'm not leaving this room without you. Now, Katie, go and turn on the shower for our girl here," she ordered, "And put this on," she added, tossing Christina Aguilera's *Stripped* album into Katie's hands. "Track two."

"Is it really that kind of an intervention?" Katie asked, hurrying over to the stereo. "You're bringing out the big guns?"

"I think I need a new haircut," I mumbled, pulling on my long braid. "I need a change."

"Oh my god, it is," Katie yelped, quickly switching discs.

"You can bet your ass it is," Casey replied. Christina's 'Can't Hold Us Down' blasted from the speakers a moment later, and Casey nodded her approval before turning her attention back to me. "If you chop off those long locks, I will use the strands to strangle you with. Now, get up."

I shook my head. "No."

She narrowed her eyes. "Get your ass up, Molloy."

"Never."

"Don't make me climb on there and get you."

"You wouldn't dare."

"Try me."

After a ten second stare down we both dove for my duvet at the same time, arms flailing and legs kicking.

"If you're not ready to get over your ex by getting under one of those fine-ass rugby boys, then I will take one for the team and do it for you," she growled, wrestling the blanket out of my hands, as she straddled me. "But you're *still* coming with me to be my wing woman."

"Never," I protested, trying and failing to knock her off by bucking my hips. "How are your thighs so freakishly strong?"

"It's called using my mam's thigh-master, bitch," she shot back, pinning my arms to the mattress. "Now, do you relent, or do I need to kick your ass some more?"

"Case . . ."

"Do you *relent*?"

"Fine." Releasing a pained groan of defeat, I stopped fighting her. "I relent."

How the other half live

JOEY

Spending my Saturday night inside of a house that could have easily accommodated three of the one I'd grown up in, and surrounded by a bunch of people from Tommen College, was *not* something I had ever anticipated happening.

The closest I'd ever come to their elite school was when I walked past the big iron gates on my way to a match. Now, somehow, I found myself slap bang in the middle of their fucked-up inner circle, watching on as a bunch of privileged private school boys got fucked up on high-grade skunk.

The captain these lads had been hellbent on loosening up hadn't bothered to show up tonight, but it was clear from most of their red-eyed, goofy-as-fuck expressions, that all thoughts of their captain had long since dwindled.

Clearly, there was no limit to the levels that I was willing to stoop for a couple of hundred quid.

Jesus.

The fact that my sister was supposed to start school with these people on Monday morning didn't exactly sit well with me.

Especially the big blond fucker with a penchant for dope, debauchery, and his friend's baby sister.

"Put her down right this instant, Gerard Gibson," Shannon's curly-haired pal, Claire Biggs, instructed, as she stood on the last step of their impressive staircase, dressed up as the blonde from the Spice Girls, and pointed a finger at the big bollox attempting to waltz to the Vengaboys' 'Boom, Boom, Boom, Boom!!' with a pampered looking cat. "Don't you dare hurt my—"

"Pussy?" he offered, and then made a ridiculous purring noise with his tongue. "You know that I would never hurt your pussy, Claire-bear."

Yeah, he was a few crayons short of a full box.

"I told you not to call me that in public," she protested with a huff.

"And I told you not to wear that pink dress," the big lad shot back with a wolfish grin, as he set the cat down on the couch and prowled towards her. "But I'm so fucking thrilled that you didn't listen to me."

"Avert your eyes from my sister, fucker," Hughie warned, appearing from thin air to intercept his friend before he reached the staircase. "What did I tell you about keeping your dick on the other side of the street."

"Contrary to the many rumors going around about my magical dick, it doesn't yet possess the ability to un-attach itself from the rest of me, lad," he shot back, brows waggling, as he bopped and rocked around in a pair of pink board shorts and a Hawaii themed, floral shirt. "So, if I'm here, my dick's here."

"Then go home."

"No way," he laughed. "This 90s party is my lovechild."

"It's not a 90s anything, Gibs. It's just a party, so tell that asshole on the decks to play something decent."

"No. It's my party and he'll play what I want him to play."

"It's my house."

"It's my playlist."

"Then at least go home and change your clothes. You look like a tool."

"Are you mental? Look at me. I make a beautiful Ken."

"Beautifully deranged, more like. Nobody else is dressed up, lad."

"My lover is."

"Your *lover*? Are you well? She's my sister, not your *lover*, asshole."

"I take it all back," Podge slurred, distracting me from their antics. Leaning heavily against my shoulder, he tossed back another shot of Jameson and grinned. "This was a fantastic fucking idea."

"Where's Alec?" I asked, roughly shrugging him off. I fucking hated being touched, and this drunk asshole knew it. I also detested the smell of whiskey. It did shit to my head. Made me feel on edge.

"He went upstairs with some posh girl with a huge rack," Podge replied with a huge grin, still leaning heavily against me. "Lad, these rugby-heads know how to throw a party." He waved a hand, gesturing to the mob of bodies surrounding us. "This is unreal, Joe." He pointed to where some older lad with speakers and decks set up in the far corner of the room had switched songs to 2Pac's 'Changes'. "I've never seen so much drink and food in my life."

"It's easy for them to have it," I replied bitterly, still nursing the same bottle of beer I'd been handed when I walked through the door. "When they have their fathers' wallets to pay for it."

"Ah, loosen up, Joe. It's not their fault they've got a few bob in the bank," Podge chuckled, looking like something a Christopher Lee Dracula movie shat out with the big bloodshot eyes on him. "You did good tonight."

No, I did what I had to do to feed my family.

"Have a smoke and relax," he encouraged, handing me another bottle of beer from a nearby table. "A few drinks and a smoke won't hurt."

I arched a brow and set it back down. "Coming from the fella who almost pissed himself when I told him that I was still smoking."

"Yeah, well." He grinned at me and shrugged. "I've been reminded of the perks of being your best friend."

"Yeah." I smirked. "Damn straight, asshole."

"Stay out of their medicine cabinet, though, ya hear?" he warned, holding a finger up. "And don't go losing the run of yourself." He reached up and slapped my chest. "If you get tempted to score, just think about the girl whose name you've got tattooed over your heart . . . "

"Best friend or not, if you put your hands on me again, I will rip your arm off," I warned, batting his hand away. "And if I wanted to get fucked up, that's exactly what I would be doing, but I'm not. So, I don't need any lectures or advice from you, and I don't need any reminders of what's at stake, either. I'm a big boy, Podge. I can handle my own shit. I've been doing it my whole life, so don't start trying to mother me, ya hear?"

"I hear you, Joe," he chuckled good-naturedly, holding his hands up as he backed away. "I hear you, lad."

Jaw ticking, I watched as he slipped into the crowd, feeling pissed off and on edge.

This wasn't easy for me, and I needed him reminding me of that like I needed a hole in the head.

Fuck.

Depressed and on edge, I finished my bottle and set it down, refusing to pick up another. I didn't need the complications that I knew would follow.

"Because he's only using you," I heard someone say, and I turned my attention to where Hughie was in a heated discussion with another familiar blonde.

This one wasn't his sister Claire.

No, this girl was Shannon's other little friend.

I couldn't remember her name, but I had a feeling it was Lilly.

Or maybe it was Izzy.

Either way, she was standing near the doorway, with her arms folded across her chest glaring up at Hughie Biggs, who was glaring back at her, while he flailed his arms around in obvious exasperation. "You can't seriously be considering going upstairs with him."

"Like you give a shit," she continued to say. "At least Pierce doesn't act like I'm invisible when he's with his friends."

"You know I give a shit," he was quick to counter. "If I didn't care, I wouldn't—"

"You wouldn't what, Hugh?" she cut him off by hissing. "You wouldn't treat me like an afterthought? Because, newsflash, asshole, that's *exactly* what you've been doing."

Taking it all in with sober eyes, I briefly considered telling them that if they were trying to conceal a hook up, then they were doing a pretty terrible job, before remembering these assholes were not my monkeys and this was *not* my circus.

Shaking my head, I stepped around them and headed through the impressive kitchen until I found the back door.

Slipping outside, I ignored every other asshole in the back garden, and wandered over to the far end of the yard, sparking up a cigarette as I went.

Temptation was all around me and I needed to keep my head.

I had two weeks of torture put down and I sure as hell didn't plan on throwing it away for a piss-up with a bunch of people who, in any other given circumstances, would cross the road to get away from me.

"Got one of those to spare?" a female voice asked, and I turned around to find Shannon's friend that had been fighting with Biggs moments before. "Remember me?"

"Just about," I replied, rubbing my jaw. "Lilly Young, right?"

"It's Lizzie," she corrected, unblinking. "So, can I have one?"

"One what?"

"A cigarette."

"No."

Her blue eyes narrowed. "Why not?"

"Because you don't smoke," I replied coolly. "And I don't share."

She gave me a hard look, one I was only too willing to return, before relenting with a heavy exhale. "I hate parties."

"Then why come?"

"It's complicated."

"Fair enough."

"That's it?" She eyed me curiously. "You're not going to ask me why?"

"No."

"How come?"

I shrugged. "Because I don't care about your answer."

"Hm." She tilted her head to one side, studying me with her blue eyes. "You don't belong here either."

"No shit, Sherlock."

"Then why'd you come?"

I smirked. "It's complicated."

Her lips begrudgingly tipped up in a smile. "You know, I used to have an epic crush on you when I was younger." She didn't blush or blanch when she said it either. Girl had an impressive pair of balls on her. "Most of the girls in our class had. You even overtook Leo DiCaprio for a bit – and that was during his *Titanic* superstardom stage." Shaking her head, she released another sigh before adding, "Which only proves that I've always been attracted to the worst kind of wrong for me."

Frowning, I inhaled a deep drag, held it there just long enough to take the sting out of the pain in my chest, and then exhaled slowly, while I tried to think of what to say to this girl who, even though she clearly had a sharp tongue, didn't look like she could handle another kicking. "For a kid, you sound awfully cynical."

She narrowed her blue eyes. "I'm *not* a kid."

"Maybe you're not." I shrugged and took another drag. "But you *are* friends with my baby sister, which means that you could be forty and you'd still be a kid in my eyes."

"If this is your attempt at letting me down gently then save your breath," she was quick to counter. "I said that I *used* to have a crush on you, as in *past* tense, as in not currently."

"Wise decision," I chuckled, amused by her bitchiness. "Best to stick with Leo."

"Funny." She rolled her eyes, tone flat. "Besides, I know you hurl for Cork, and I don't like athletes anymore."

"And yet you're attending a party being thrown by your school's rugby team." I nodded. "Makes perfect sense."

"I'm here for Claire."

"Bullshit," I corrected with a snort. "You're here for her brother."

Her eyes widened. "What are you—"

"Let me guess," I interrupted, amused. "You're fucking Biggs, and he won't commit, so you've gone off with one of the lads on his team to get back at him?"

"I don't ... It's not ..." Her mouth fell open and she gaped in horror at me.

"You need a better poker face."

"You have it all wrong."

"I don't think I do."

"Joey, please—"

"Don't worry," I cut her off with a wink. "I don't talk."

"There's nothing to talk about." She looked truly terrified now. "Because like I said, you have it all wrong."

"*Sure* I have."

"Oh god. Please don't say anything, Joey." Swallowing deeply, she pressed a hand to her brow and groaned. "He has a girlfriend, and I have a . . ."

"I'll tell you what, Lilly."

"It's Lizzie."

"Lizzie." Taking pity on her, I pulled a cigarette from my box, put it to my lips and sparked it up, before holding it out for her. "You keep an eye on Shannon when she starts at your school next week, watch her back and keep any assholes who think about targeting her in line, and I'll forget everything you think I have *all wrong*."

"I was planning on looking after Shannon, regardless," she replied, taking the cigarette and putting it to her lips.

"And I was planning on keeping my mouth shut, regardless," I replied evenly. "So, it looks like we both win."

"I'm not a bad person," she was quick to point out, tone defensive. "I'm not a slut, either."

"I never said you were."

"Yeah, but I know what you're thinking."

I arched a brow. "I really doubt that."

"You're thinking I'm a horrible snake to even consider going there with another girl's fella, but you have no idea what's really going on," she mumbled, red-faced. "It's really, *really* complicated. And messy." She exhaled a ragged breath before muttering, "And a million other things."

I shrugged. "It's not my business."

"So, that's it?" She eyed me warily. "That's all you're going to say?"

"What else is there to say?" I replied with a shrug. "The way I see it; you're not the first to get tangled up like this, and you won't be the last.

Either way, I'm no priest, so no need to offer your confession up to me. Not when I've done plenty worse than you."

She arched a brow, reluctantly intrigued. "When you say *worse*."

I smirked. "You'd need a bishop to take my confession."

Jolene was a blonde with a death wish

AOIFE

Groomed to within an inch of my life, and with three quarters of a bottle of Prosecco in my system, I leaned back on the couch in Katie's boyfriend's living room, feeling like I had taken a trip back in time.

Whoever was on the decks clearly had a hard on for 90s music, because Bloodhound Gang's 'The Bad Touch' was just the latest in a long list of songs from the previous decade.

Feeling buzzed, I watched as Casey backed her ass up against some dark-haired boy from Tommen and feigned a stagger.

I rolled my eyes when he grabbed her hips to steady her, which was exactly what she wanted.

She was *so* predictable.

"Thanks," Casey said, beaming up at him.

"No problem."

"What's your name?" she asked, stepping closer.

"Patrick," he told her, offering her a shy smile. "What's yours?"

Run, Patrick, run, I felt like shouting, *she's going to eat you alive, you poor, innocent fool.*

"I'm Casey." With one hand curled around his neck, she fisted his shirt with the other and tugged his big body close against her. "So, Patrick." Trailing her hand from his neck to his cheek, she pulled his face down to hers and beamed up at him. "What year are you in?"

"Fifth year, you?"

"Sixth year."

"At BCS?"

"Uh-huh. Do you play rugby, Patrick?"

He nodded. "I'm an inside center."

"Excellent."

Yeah, my best friend was the meaning behind that *small but fierce* saying.

She needed a wing woman like a fish needed rollerblades.

"That's Patrick Feely," Katie explained in my ear. "He's good friends with Hugh."

"And that's Hugh's younger sister, right?" I asked, pointing out the stunning blonde with a head of to-die-for curls, who was sitting on the couch opposite us, dressed as Baby Spice.

I watched, completely invested in the animated conversation she was having with an equally beautiful blond boy dressed like a Malibu Ken doll I used to own back in the day. They were all smiles and hands flailing as they talked and laughed and touched each other.

"Yeah, that's Claire," Katie replied. "She's probably one of the sweetest girls that you'll ever meet."

I narrowed my eyes as recognition flickered through me. "Wait a minute. I think I know that guy she's talking to."

"Everybody knows Gerard Gibson," Katie chuckled.

"He offered Joey a condom in Biddies once."

"Sounds very Gibsie-like." Katie bit back a laugh. "He's, uh, well, let's just say that he's one of a kind. He sort of lives in his own world."

B*Witched's 'C'est la Vie' started to play and I swear to God, this Gibsie boy all but levitated from the couch with excitement, dragging Claire along with him.

"She clearly lives in that world with him," I mused, feeling myself smile for the first time in weeks, as I watched them.

Bopping around and throwing shapes like nobody was watching, Gibsie and Claire danced around the living room to what was clearly their jam. Him spinning her out and then pulling her back to his chest as they stumble-waltzed to the music.

"I'm guessing they've been together since forever, am I right?"

"They're actually not together at all."

"Bullshit." I pointed to where they had moved to the middle of the makeshift dancefloor. "Look at that boy. He's clearly besotted with her, and she's staring at him all gooey-eyed like he hung the moon." I shook my head. "Nah, K, they're clearly doing the deed."

"I swear," Katie laughed. "They're really not."

I cocked a disbelieving brow as I watched them break into an impressive Irish dancing set jig. Completely in sync with each other's bodies, and with their entire focus on the other, they laughed and danced it out to the beat, uncaring that a huge portion of their schoolmates were watching them.

"No way," I choked out a laugh. "Boy moves like lord of the dance."

"Pretty sure his mam made him take Irish dancing lessons in primary school," Katie giggled. "There's a bunch of medals on display in the cabinet in Hugh's front room from Feis competitions that they competed in."

"Who? Gibsie and Claire?"

She nodded.

"Aw, they *danced* together?"

"Uh-huh." Katie laughed. "Until he hung his dancing shoes up for rugby boots."

"You're honestly trying to tell me that those two aren't in love?"

"I never said they weren't in love." Chuckling, she added, "Only that they're not together."

"Hm." I eyed them, entirely unconvinced that they weren't. "Well, they look gorgeous together. And I love the color of her hair," I added, secretly envious. "Those curls are amazing."

"The color and curls are totally natural," Katie offered, sounding just as wistful as I felt. "Hugh's hair is the same."

"Joey has curls, too, but he keeps them chopped off. He always keeps the sides and back of his head shaved tight, and leaves a bit more on top, but if he doesn't cut his hair for a few weeks, it grows all wild and curly on top like Seany-boo's. It's so adorable," I heard myself say, and then scrunched my nose in despair. "Sorry."

"Don't be sorry, Aoif," she replied softly. "I'm honestly surprised you came tonight. I know Casey practically dragged you out, but I wouldn't have blamed you if you didn't come." Releasing a heavy sigh, she hooked her arm through mine and said, "I know you've been in love with him since forever, and feelings don't switch off overnight, so if this gets too much for you, or you want to go home at any time, you just say, and I'll get one of Hugh's friends to drive you."

"Thanks, Katie," I replied, resting my cheek on her shoulder. "So, they're really not together?" I asked, inclining my chin to where Gibsie and Claire now resembled something straight out of a Gene Simmons tribute act, as they jammed it out to Robbie Williams and Kylie Minogue's 'Kids'.

He was strewn out on the flat of his back, singing to his heart's content into his imaginary microphone, while she straddled his hips and joined him.

"Uh-oh," Katie snickered, watching as her boyfriend came thundering towards them. "Hughie's going to freak."

Holding a hand up to warn her brother off, Claire continued to bop her head and drum one-handedly to the music, while Gibsie folded his arms behind his head and grinned sheepishly up at her brother.

"Oh crap," Katie groaned then, dragging my attention back to her.

"What?" I asked. "He's hardly going to lose it over his sister dancing with his buddy."

"Not him," Katie strangled out, pointing towards the doorway that led to the kitchen. "*Him.*"

Craning my neck, I followed her line of sight, only for every muscle in my body to lock tight when my eyes landed on *Joey*.

"Oh my god." The air escaped my lungs in a breathy rush and I quickly jerked my gaze away. "What's he doing here?" Panic-stricken, I looked to my friend for help. "Katie, what is *he* doing here?"

"I don't know," she choked out, shaking her head. "I have no idea."

"Oh, Jesus." Dropping my head in my hands, I groaned loudly, while my stomach twisted up in knots and my knees started to bop nervously. "You said he wouldn't be here."

"He shouldn't be," she protested. "I know that Claire is friends with his sister, but I didn't think that he and Hugh were friends."

"Oh my god." My stomach churned and I felt faint. "I need to get out of here."

"No, you don't have to," she hurried to soothe, wrapping an arm around my shoulders. "It's okay. Just calm down and take a breath."

It was at this exact moment that Casey burst through the crowd, squealing, "He's here, he's here, oh my Jesus, he's here!"

"Does he look okay?" I heard myself strangle out, peeking between my hands at my friends. "Is he fighting?" My heart seized in my chest and I forced out the words, "Is he high?"

"I'm not sure," Casey replied, voice slurred. "He's definitely not fighting, but he's too far away to tell if he's buzzed or not." She craned her neck to see better and, a few seconds later, let out a furious growl. "So, apparently Dolly was wrong when she said Jolene was a redhead." Inclining her head towards the kitchen, she hissed, "It turns out she's a blonde with a death wish."

"Oh god," Katie groaned, sounding queasy. "Please tell me he isn't?"

Heart hammering violently in my chest, I forced myself to inhale a few steadying breaths before daring to glance in his direction again.

Dressed in dark jeans, and a fitted navy shirt, with the sleeves rolled up to his elbows, Joey leaned against the kitchen island.

With his arms folded across his chest, he stared down at the floor, looking mildly amused, as the blonde, who was sitting on the island beside him, swung her feet back and forth as she talked to him.

Pain.

It hit me so hard and fast that I honestly thought I would crack down the center.

"Oh no, guys, that's only Lizzie," Katie was quick to point out. "She's in third year at Tommen. She's best friends with Claire."

"Maybe for now," Casey corrected hotly. "Soon, she'll just be known as the girl I went to prison for killing."

"You're drunk, Casey. Put your claws away," Katie snapped, before turning her attention back to me. "She's probably friends with his sister, too, and that's why he's talking to her," she offered calmly. "They're only talking, Aoif. It looks completely innocent."

"Oh, please," Casey slurred, swatting the air like it had offended her. "Don't be so naïve, Katie. There's nothing innocent about that Mischa Barton wannabe."

"I know you have nothing but good intentions, but right now, you're causing more harm than good," Katie grumbled. "Aoife doesn't need this. She doesn't need to hear your inner running commentary, Case."

"Maybe she doesn't," Casey declared before bounding off in the direction of the kitchen. "But he's going to."

"Oh, this is so bad, Katie." Jerking unsteadily to my feet, I pressed my fingers to my temples and watched in horror as Casey rounded on Joey in the kitchen. "You know what she gets like. She can be a messy drunk at the best of times."

"Then you need to go over there."

"I can't," I choked out, feeling starved for oxygen at the prospect of having to face him again. "I'm not nearly drunk enough to jump back in the ring with him."

"You have to," she urged, pushing me towards the doorway. "They're arguing over you. You need to get in there and diffuse it."

"No."

"You go and get Casey, and I'll find Patrick Feely. He's not drinking tonight, so he'll give you guys a spin home."

"I can't go over there."

"You don't have a choice."

"No."

"Yes, Aoife.

"Okay, okay, fine!" Exhaling a ragged breath, I shook my hands out and sucked in a deep, calming breath, before forcing myself to walk into the kitchen to face him.

The road to hell is paved with good intentions

JOEY

"And then there's Ronan McGarry. He's a little shit, but he's relatively harmless," Lizzie said, reeling off the last on her list of potential troublemakers that Shannon might run into at her new school. "Honestly, though, aside from the odd gossiper or queen bee, it's pretty mellow at Tommen. Of course, there's Bella Wilkinson to contend with."

"Who's she?" I asked, standing in the kitchen alongside her, mentally taking notes. "Would I know her?"

"Doubtful," she shot back. "You're hot, but you don't have the pedigree to get on her radar."

I cocked a brow. "Wow. Thanks."

"Sorry, but you don't." She offered me a half-hearted shrug. "You're a BCS boy from a council estate, and she's a money starved, fame-hungry whore," she explained, scrunching her nose up in disgust. "You might be the next big thing for the GAA, but unless you come with all the trimmings – and when I say trimmings, I mean money, a flashy car, and a future playing professional rugby – then she won't look sideways at you."

"I'm distraught."

"Yeah, you really sound it." Lizzie laughed, slapping my arm. "Put it this way; she would get up on a razor blade if said razor blade came in the form of one of the Academy boys. But she's in sixth year and really doesn't bother with anyone from third year, so Shan shouldn't have any issues with her. Besides, none of the lads in our year are impressive enough to be on her radar. She's more interested in the older lads, the big-time rugby-heads with godlike status."

"Like Johnny Kavanagh?"

"Exactly." Lizzie nodded. "Or Cormac Ryan. They're both in The Academy."

"I've seen them both play," I mused, rubbing my jaw. "That Kavanagh lad is seriously impressive, but that Ryan kid isn't going any further than The Academy."

"Want to hear a fun inside scoop going around the rugby circle?"

"Not really."

"Well, I was forced to hear it, so you can, too."

"Please don't."

"Apparently, Bella's been sleeping with Cormac since before Christmas, even though she's meant to be with Johnny Kavanagh, but he's out on injury."

"Oh, the scandal," I replied flatly. "What life changing information I have been given about three people I couldn't give one single fuck about. How will I ever contain my excitement?"

"You're sarcastic and blunt to the point of being cruel." She threw her head back and laughed. "I love it."

"Well, it didn't take you long to jump back into old habits," a familiar voice sneered, and I turned my head to see Casey Lordan glaring up at me. "Having fun with your new sidepiece, asshole?"

I narrowed my eyes. "What are you talking about?"

"You," Casey hissed, pointing a finger between us. "And this little slut."

"Did you seriously just call me a slut?" Lizzie interjected. "Are you insane?"

"If the dick fits, sweetie," Casey sneered, giving Shannon's little pal one of those withering looks, and sloshing wine over the rim of her glass in the process. "And it sure looks like it does."

"Don't call me *sweetie*, bitch," Lizzie warned, hopping down from the island. "Because you don't know who the hell you're dealing with."

"Pack it in," I warned, quickly stepping between my sister's best friend and my girlfriend's one. "Whatever you think you know, you don't," I said, addressing Casey. "She's my baby sister's friend."

"Yeah, *sure* she is."

"Yeah, I am," Lizzie argued from behind me.

"You," I ordered, turning back to face Lizzie. "Walk away."

"But . . . "

"Walk *away*," I barked, waiting for Lizzie to storm off, before turning my attention back to Casey. "As for you," I snapped, tone laced with disgust. "I don't know what's after coming over you, Case, but you need to get your head out of the gutter."

"I saw you all over her!"

"She's a *child*," I bit out. "Have a bit of cop on, will ya? Jesus! And keep your goddamn nose out of my business while you're at it."

Doing the complete opposite, she reached a hand up and slapped me across the cheek, and fuck if it didn't sting.

"Or what, huh?" She pushed at my chest with a surprising amount of force considering she barely reached my chest in height. "What are you going to do if I don't, asshole?"

"Casey," I warned, backing up a few steps, only to have her close the space between us. "Back off."

"Why'd you do it, Joey?" she demanded, pushing and shoving at my chest until she had me cornered with nowhere to go. "You could have left her alone," she slurred, wobbling in her heels, and I, for some unknown reason, reached a hand out to steady her.

That's right; I was the eejit who stopped the girl who was attacking me from falling over.

As a thank you, she slapped me again.

Lovely.

"Listen here, you good-looking son of a bitch," she slurred as she poked me in the chest with her finger. "I don't care how slick you can move your hips on a pitch – or on a mattress, for that matter – we both know that you are punching *way* above your weight with my girl."

"What the hell are you talking about?" I demanded, feeling my temper rise. "You sound like a headcase."

"I'm talking about you breaking my best friend's heart," she hissed, poking me again. "Aoife is worth ten of every other girl at this party, and you're a stupid asshole if you can't see that."

"You think I'm fucking around?" I gaped at her. "Are you insane?"

"Oh, I *know* you are. I just caught you red-handed."

"Talking," I spat back. "You caught me red-handed *talking* to my sister's childhood friend."

"Deny it all you want. I know what I saw."

"You're deluded."

"And you're a dickhead," she continued her rant. "Aoife was *fine* with Paul. She was *okay*. Her life was stable. It was consistent. He was *good* for her. But you just couldn't leave her alone, could you? No, you just had to keep chipping away at her heart, until she threw it all away for you. And look where it got her."

"Now, you listen to me," I seethed. "If you so much as think about trying to sink your toxic claws in Aoife, and twisting this into something it's not, then I swear to Christ, Case, I will lose my mind."

"You lost your mind the minute you decided to break my best friend's heart," she snapped. "Aoife Molloy is the single *best* thing that's ever happened to you, Joey Lynch, and everyone knows it. She *loves* you, asshole, despite your reputation and all of the horrible things you've done in your past, and instead of treating her with the love and respect she deserves, you trample all over her with your bullshit."

"You don't know a damn thing about it," I snarled, furious. "You have no clue of what's happening between us, so don't start harping on to me about shit that doesn't concern you."

"I know that you fed her some asshole line about needing space, and then sauntered off without a backwards glance," she replied, sounding just as furious.

"Casey, stop it!" Molloy's achingly familiar voice echoed through my head, causing every hair on my body to stand on end.

"Stop it right now," she ordered, dragging her friend away from me. "Don't do this."

"He deserves it."

"You don't know anything about it, now stop."

"I know he hurt you."

"Casey! I mean it. Let's go."

Struck fucking dumb at the sight of Molloy in a skin-tight, backless, red dress, I could do nothing but watch as she completely ignored me, focusing on her friend instead.

"But he hurt you," Casey continued to slur, pointing her finger in my direction. "You're so sad, and eating all that chocolate, and it's all his fault."

"It doesn't matter," Molloy bit out, wrapping an arm around Casey's waist and pulling her towards the door, never once looking at me the entire time. "Come on," she continued to say, coaxing her bitchy gal pal away. "I'll get us a spin home."

"Molloy?"

"Not right now, Joe."

My heart bucked wildly in protest. "Molloy."

"No," she choked out, before hurrying out of the kitchen with Casey draped around her. "I can't do this right now, okay?"

No, it wasn't okay.

It wasn't fucking okay at all.

My legs were moving after her before my brain had a chance to catch up.

"Patrick Feely is outside with the car," her neighbor told her, as she looped an arm around Casey and helped Molloy cart her outside to a nearby running car. "He'll make sure that you guys get home safely. He's one of the good guys, Aoif. You can trust him."

"Thanks, Katie," I heard Molloy reply, as she opened the back door and maneuvered Casey inside. "Sorry about this."

"It's totally fine, girlie," Katie replied, giving her a side hug. "You didn't do anything wrong."

"I don't want to go home," Casey slurred, slumping into the back seat. "I'm having fun."

"Yeah," Molloy growled. "Ruining my life."

"Don't be mad at me," her friend whined. "I'm trying to mind you."

"I can mind myself, Case."

"But he made you so sad."

"Just scoot over and let me in. We can talk about this later."

"Molloy," I interjected, grabbing ahold of the door when she moved to climb in beside her friend. "Don't leave yet."

"I have to."

"Why?"

"I'm playing by your rules here, Joe," she croaked out, still averting her gaze from me. "You do your thing and I do mine, remember?"

"Yeah," Casey slurred from her perch on the back seat. "Leave her alone, asshole."

"Casey, it's grand, stop," Molloy muttered, cheeks flushed. "Just leave it, okay?"

"Don't leave," I repeated, ignoring the evil eyes her friend was giving me. "Don't go, Aoife."

"I have to," she replied quietly. "She's drunk and I need to make sure she gets home."

"I'll take her home, Aoif," Katie offered up, and I instantly knew which one of her friends was my favorite. "If you want to stay and, uh, talk things out or whatever, then I'd be happy to go with Patrick and drop her home."

"Thanks, Katie, but that's putting you out."

"I don't mind," Katie was quick to counter. "I think you should stay and talk to him." She offered me a smile – albeit a warning one. "*Nicely.*"

"Hey." I held my hands up, letting her know that I was fully prepared to comply with her wishes.

"No . . . " Casey whined. "Don't do it, Aoif, he'll only feed you more bullshit."

"Shush, you!" Katie snapped, quickly climbing into the back seat alongside Casey before swiftly closing the car door.

Moments later, the car pulled away from the path, leaving us standing in a thick, strained silence.

"So, you were just going to leave without speaking to me?"

"I don't want to argue with you, Joe," she whispered, arms moving to wrap around her waist protectively. "I'm too tired."

"I don't want that, either."

She nodded stiffly and continued to stare down at her stiletto clad feet.

"Are you going to look at me?"

"Not right now."

"Why not?"

"Because it hurts too much."

My heart constricted in my chest. "Baby."

She swiftly changed the subject by asking, "So, what are you doing at a Tommen party, Joey Lynch?"

"Believe it or not, I was invited."

"By who?"

"Hugh Biggs," I replied before quickly turning the tables. "What are *you* doing at a Tommen party, Aoife Molloy?"

"I was invited."

"By who?"

"Katie Wilmot."

I thought about it for a moment before awareness dawned on me. "Wait, your next-door neighbor, Katie, is with Hugh Biggs?"

"Yeah," she mumbled. "You already knew that."

I had a vague recollection of Molloy telling me about her friend having a boyfriend on the rugby team at Tommen, but I'd been too strung out to pay much heed to the conversation at the time. "No, no, no, you told me her name was Katie Horgan." That, I *did* remember.

"She's Katie Horgan-Wilmot," Molloy replied. "Her parents aren't married, remember? Her mam's Horgan and her dad's Wilmot. She has a double-barreled last name, but she mostly goes by her dad's name."

"So, *Katie* is with Hugh."

"Yeah, they've been together for a while now."

"Well shit." My thoughts reverted back to the conversation I had with

Lizzie, and a pang of sympathy hit me in the chest, before I abruptly stripped all memory of that conversation from my mind.

Not my monkeys, not my circus.

"Why's she at Tommen again?" I asked, searching my mind and coming up empty. "She's from Rosewood. Her folks aren't exactly flush with cash." Without trying to sound like too much of a dick, I asked, "Shouldn't she be at BCS with us?"

"You know why she's at Tommen, Joe," she muttered, kicking at a stone with her foot. "I've told you all about it before, remember?"

Yeah, but I was on another planet and couldn't hear you.

"Oh, yeah," I lied, disgusted by just how many ways I'd let this girl down. "I remember."

"Have you been drinking?"

"I've had one drink the whole night."

"Wow," she said softly. "That must be a personal best for you."

Ouch. "I deserve that."

"I didn't say that to hurt you," she squeezed out, shaking her head.

"I wouldn't blame you if you had."

"Yeah."

Another strained silence settled between us, and it made me feel uneasy.

"You do know that Casey was completely off the mark earlier, right? That girl I was talking to back there is a friend of Shannon's," I heard myself hurry to explain, heart gunning in my chest. "You get that, right?"

"Yeah." Her voice was barely more than a whisper when she said, "Katie mentioned something about that."

"So, you're okay then?" I pushed gently. "You know that there was nothing going on."

"No, I'm not *okay*," she choked out, voice thick with emotion now. "I haven't been *okay* in weeks." This time she did look at me, and it cut like a knife when I saw the tears pooling in her eyes. "But you seem like you're doing a lot better, so clearly this break-up is working for one of us."

"Are you serious?" I took a step back, feeling like she had just knifed me in the gut. "You think I'm not hurting?"

"I don't know how you feel anymore."

"In love," I bit out. "With you."

"Don't . . ."

"Nothing's changed for me, Molloy," I interrupted, needing her to know. "*Nothing*."

"I can't do this," she admitted, voice torn. "I can't."

"Can't do what?" I asked, feeling panicked. "Can't talk to me?"

"Be here with you and not be *with* you," she strangled out, pressing a hand to her forehead. "It's too much. It's too hard." Shaking her head, she turned to walk away. "I can't."

"Aoife." A fucked-up combination of guilt and fear coursed through me as I watched her leave. "All I'm trying to do is protect you."

"No—" Swinging around, she stalked back to me, looking mad as hell. "No," she repeated through clenched teeth, pointing her finger at me. "This is not protecting me, Joey. Walking away is *not* protecting me. Leaving me is *not* protecting me, dammit!" Furious, she blinked back her tears and glared up at me. "That is *not* how you treat the person you love, which goes to show that you never loved me the way I loved you."

"Never loved you?" I gaped at her. "Are you fucking *crazy*? You're the only person on this planet I *do* love!"

"No," she snapped, shaking her head. "You don't get to do that. You don't get to come back and wreck me." Placing her hands on my chest, she pushed me back when I reached for her. "You don't get to tell me you love me and then go right back to breaking my heart!" She choked out another pained sob when I cupped her cheek. "You don't love me, Joey." Eyelids fluttering, she leaned into my touch and sniffled. "You don't know how to love anyone."

"Maybe I do it badly," I strangled out, as my heart splintered apart. "But I do love you."

"You're a shithead."

"I know."

"I can't live like this."

"I know."

"No, I mean it, Joey," she breathed, jerking away from me with a shiver. "I can't take another second of it." With that, she turned on her skyscraper heels and marched back inside the house, tossing the words, "It hurts too much," over her shoulder as she went.

I knew that I should turn in the opposite direction and walk my ass away from her, but that wasn't what I did.

No, because like the sick, masochistic fuck-up I was, I followed her back into the Biggs' house, knowing that Molloy wasn't one to take being scorned lying down.

There wasn't a doubt in my mind that she had every intention of making me pay for not giving her what she wanted, which, just so happened to be exactly the same thing as I wanted.

Fuck my life.

Don't get mad, get even

AOIFE

Several rounds of shots later, and I had swiftly moved beyond the point of tipsy and was teetering closer to the verge of intoxication.

Shaking my ass with Katie, who had returned from chaperoning Casey, we danced around the makeshift dancefloor with Ken and Baby Spice, while I dutifully ignored the asshole passing around a joint in the kitchen.

So much for being clean.

Asshole.

"You do know that Hughie is going to kill you, don't you, Gibs?" Katie asked, dragging my attention back to the present, to where Gibsie Gibberson, or whatever his name was, had stripped down to his jocks to Aqua's 'Barbie Girl'.

Shameless in the act of debauchery, he had thrown his dance partner over his shoulder, and was drumming on her ass to the rhythm.

Squealing in delight as he bopped around the floor with her dangling haphazardly in the air, Claire held onto his biceps for dear life.

Giving Katie a wolfish grin, the big lad continued to dance with his little gal-pal, either unaware or just plain uncaring of the *many* longing looks he was receiving.

To be fair, it didn't take a genius to figure out why the girls from his school were looking. The boy was built like a brick shit house, with both nipples pierced, and more muscles on his body than he had common sense in his head.

Common sense or not, the big man certainly seemed to have his priorities in order, placing his curly-haired queen in a firm first place position. While the rest of his friends had long since abandoned their girlfriends and dates, Gibsie hadn't taken more than three steps away from Claire all night.

"Honestly, they're not doing it," Katie offered, seeming to read my thoughts, as she rolled her eyes. "They're always like this. Like two weird little unicorn magnets drawn to each other."

Laughing, I nudged her and said, "Well, when they fuck, there's going to be fireworks."

"If it ever happens, then it'll be on their marriage bed," Katie snickered. "Because Claire Biggs isn't opening her legs for anything less than a big fat diamond and the promise of forever."

"Good for her," I replied, and then offered her a teasing grin. "Sounds like she's taking her cues from her future sister-in-law."

"Hey." Katie's face flamed with embarrassment. "There's nothing wrong with wanting to be good."

"True," I mused, slinging an arm over her shoulder. "But being bad is so much more fun."

"Speaking of bad." Catching ahold of my arm, she leaned in close and asked, "Are you going to go over there and talk to Joey?"

"Nope."

"Oh, stop it," she growled. "You're hurting and I get that, but pretending like you don't want to go over to him is just silly."

"It's not, actually," I lied. "I'm perfectly content staying here with you."

"God, you're both as stubborn as each other."

"No, *he's* stubborn," I shot back. "*I'm* protecting myself."

"Come on, Aoif, don't cut off your nose to spite your face." She sighed heavily. "It's pretty clear why he's still at the party."

"Yeah? If it's so clear then why isn't he over here?"

"Because he already tried to talk to you," she reminded me. "You walked away from him."

"Because he broke up with me, Katie." Feeling a lump bob in my throat, I quickly forced it down before hissing, "He *dumped* me. What am I supposed to do? Stick around for another verse of *it's not you, it's me*?"

"Well, break up or not, it's obvious that he's not looking to replace you," she replied, pointing a finger in the direction of the kitchen. "Gretta Burchill is the sixth girl I've watched crash and burn with him tonight."

Reluctantly, I turned around and peered through the archway to see Joey leaning against the marble kitchen island, rollie in hand, as he chatted to a group that contained Alec, Podge, Katie's boyfriend, Hugh, the designated driver, Patrick, Shannon's friend, Lizzie, and a few others I didn't recognize.

White hot fury scorched through me when the leggy brunette who was sitting on the island next to him, sidled closer and whispered something in his ear.

She was all flirtatious smiles and not-so-innocent petting, as she hooked an arm around *my* asshole's neck and dragged him backwards to rest between her legs. Keeping her hand on his chest, she rested her chin on his shoulder and whispered something else in his ear.

Oh, hell fucking no.

"Stem the crazy, Harley Quinn," Katie coaxed, gripping my wrist when I moved to go cut a bitch. "Just watch."

Not missing a beat, Joey caught ahold of her hand and deftly slipped out from under her arm, shaking his head when she moved to pull him back to her.

"See?" Katie called over the music. "He's not interested in any other girls, Aoif."

I was too far away to hear what was being said, but the hand he held up to warn the brunette off, not to mention the bemused expression etched on his face, momentarily mollified me and sated my thirst for blood.

The girl held her hands up and said something to Joey, and whatever he said in response caused them both to turn in my direction.

The girl had the good grace to blush when our eyes met.

Meanwhile, Joey gave her a smug look that said *see, I told you.*

Narrowing my eyes, I glared at her until she scrambled off the counter and away from my man, retreating from the kitchen with her tail between her legs.

Our eyes met, green on green, and he winked at me from across the room.

And just like that, I was *ruined*.

"Go on," Katie urged, giving me a little shove in the direction of the kitchen. "You're Aoife Molloy. Since when did you start letting a boy call the shots on your life?"

"I don't," I mumbled before snapping my attention back to my friend. "I *don't*."

"Exactly." She smiled. "So, go on over there and claim that incredibly sexy and incredibly *scary* boyfriend of yours before anymore girls try to snatch him up."

"Damn straight I will." Narrowing my eyes, I turned on my heels and marched straight for the beautiful pothead himself only to swing back at the last minute and grab Katie's hand. "But you better take your own advice and come with me because that moody-looking pal of Shannon's is looking like she wants to eat that posh boy of yours up."

"Who, Lizzie?" Katie laughed, trailing after me. "No way. She's in their super elite inner circle at school. She's just a friend."

"Uh-huh." I rolled my eyes. "Rule one, my innocent little neighbor. Never trust a girl who looks like *that* around a boy who looks like *that*."

"Wah-hey, sexy-legs," Alec cheered when Kate and I joined their little circle of smoke in the kitchen. "How's my favorite girl?"

"Don't push your luck, lad," Podge chuckled, ribbing Al with his elbow. "You're looking well, Aoife."

"Cheers, Podge," I acknowledged, feeling awkward when Katie moved straight for Hugh, leaving me standing alone in front of a group of boys who, normally, I wouldn't bat an eyelid at chatting to.

But this is different.

"Molloy."

Heat flooded my belly when he spoke my name, and I forced myself to face him. "Joe."

I cocked a brow and watched as he exhaled a cloud of smoke.

"On the straight and narrow?" I rolled my eyes. "Yeah, asshole, it sure *smells* like it."

His brows furrowed in confusion, while Podge let out a very loud *ha*.

"A smoke doesn't count, Molloy."

"Yes, it does."

"Since when?"

"Since always." Frustrated and weary, I rolled my eyes and gave him my back, unwilling to fight him on this. "Hi," I said instead, giving the scowling blonde my attention. "I'm Aoife."

"Lizzie," she replied, giving me a half-hearted smile, shaking her head when Alec held the joint out for her. "Your friend was wrong earlier, just so you know. I wasn't trying to get with your boyfriend."

"It's not my business who Joey gets with," I replied, achingly aware of how close he was standing behind me. "He's a free agent, and so am I."

"Like fuck we are." His hand came around my waist, fingers flexing against my flesh, as he pulled me backwards into his embrace. "Pack it in."

"Woo," Alec spluttered through a fog of smoke. "Is there trouble in paradise I'm sensing?"

"What's the matter, Joe?" I taunted, resisting the urge to shiver and sag against him. "You want to be done, then deal with the consequences."

"Molloy."

"Shush." Keeping my ass pressed against the front of his jeans, I flicked my long hair over my shoulder and smiled at the stranger taking a hit from the joint. "Are you planning on sharing that, blue-eyes?"

Offering me a flirty wink, the lad held out the joint for me.

"What are you doing?" Joey's tone was hard. Releasing a frustrated growl, his big hand splayed across my belly. "Put that the fuck down, Molloy. Now."

Not having a notion of what I was doing, I balanced it between my fingers, pressed it to my lips and sucked in a deep drag, willing myself not to splutter my lungs out, as my head swam and my eyes burned.

"Molloy." Twisting me around in his arms, Joey glowered down at me. "I'm not fucking around here."

Forcing myself to exhale slowly, I beamed up at him. "What's the saying, Joe? If you can't beat them ... "

"Join them," Alec cheered, drumming his hands on the counter at his back before quickly quietening down when he was met with a death glare from Joey. "Or not?"

"No," Joey deadpanned, turning his attention back to me. "No."

"What's wrong, Joe? You can have fun, but I can't?" I taunted, putting the joint to my lips once more and taking another eye-watering hit.

"Molloy!"

"Lynchy, just relax."

"She's only having a bit of craic, lad."

"I said no," he snapped, snatching the joint out of my hand and handing it off to the stranger standing behind him. "I said *no*, Aoife."

"You can't tell me what to do, Joe," I growled, feeling a combination of drunk and dizzy. "You don't own me."

"Well, that's bad fucking luck on my account, because you sure as shit own me!"

Drunk or not, his words hit me like a wrecking ball to the chest.

Feeling the air whoosh from my lungs, I glared up at him, feeling a torrent of emotions crashing through me. "Why would you say that to me?"

"Because it's the truth."

"Since when?"

"Since I was twelve."

Showing hearts

JOEY

Nobody served up karma quite like Molloy.

Watching her do something as mundane as taking a hit from a joint had caused something inside of my heart to flip the fuck out.

Because this wasn't her.

She didn't dabble in weed.

Hell, the only time I'd seen her put a cigarette to her lips in the six years I'd known her was at a disco back in first year, when she'd taken a hit off Rambo's blunt at the back of the Pav, only to unceremoniously spew up the contents of her stomach afterwards.

I was the fuck-up in this relationship, not her.

Molloy played her ace card tonight, though, and in doing so, had forced me to fold, with nothing but hearts on display for everyone around us to see.

"Nicely done, baby." Blowing out a frustrated breath, I clamped a hand on her hip and pulled her close. "You win this round."

My life was unpredictable, and my future was bleak, but I had no doubts that wherever I ended up, this girl would forever have a hold over me.

"This round?" Defiant as always, she looked up at me with those ridiculously sexy green eyes and arched a perfectly groomed brow. "I *always* win, Joe."

Yeah, she did, even when it wasn't good for her.

Her body was pressed against mine, causing her tits to brush against my chest every time she breathed. It was entirely too much in this moment, and I was having a hard time keeping my head on straight.

I could hear murmurs of a conversation happening around us, but I couldn't make out a single word of it, because my entire focus was on the girl who'd been successfully tormenting me from the first day we met.

Because I loved her.

Because every part of me loved every part of her.

The good, the bad and the ugly.

I fucking reveled in all of it.

She had my heart in knots, and my head spinning.

Never once taking her eyes off mine, she trailed her long red nails down my stomach to my belt buckle and tugged me closer.

Fuck.

She knew exactly what she was doing when she took the hand I had on her hip and placed it on her peachy ass.

Reaching up on her tiptoes, she curled a hand around my neck and pulled my face down to hers. "You're an asshole."

"I know."

"You crushed me."

Pain. It hit me square in the chest. "I know."

"Bad boy." Her breath was laced with alcohol and so fucking warm on my face when she whispered, "Tell me you're sorry."

Pissed off and agitated, I gave in without a fight, too weary and too damn in love to fight my feelings. "I'm sorry."

"How sorry?"

"Very sorry."

"Good boy." Her tongue was on my ear then, her body pressed flush against mine. "Now, tell me you love me."

"I love you." The words flew off my tongue in record time.

"Say it again."

"I love you."

"How much?"

"A lot."

"Hm." Taking my hand in hers, she led me onto the dancefloor and like the habit of a lifetime, I followed after her, knowing that this girl was by far my greatest addiction. "What are you doing?"

"You broke my heart," she told me, moving my hands to her hips, as she curled her arms around my neck and stepped closer. "The least you can do is dance with me."

Too weary to argue and too damn weak to resist, I pulled her close, thankful for the vodka in my stomach, because I was in no way comfortable with dancing, but this girl, well, I seemed to do just about anything she asked.

Drunk on vodka and regret, I kept my hands clamped on her hips, feeling her curvy body press against mine as she ground her hips against me, while the melancholy sound of LIVE's 'Lightning Crashes' drifted around us.

As my brain processed the lyrics, a horrible weighted energy settled on my shoulders.

"What's wrong?" Molloy asked, instantly noticing my discomfort.

"Nothing."

"Joe?"

"I just . . ." I shook my head again and blew out a pained breath. "It's the song."

"What about it?"

"Reminds me of her."

"Who?" Her green eyes softened. "Your mam?"

With my jaw clamped tight, I forced a nod. "Fucked-up, I know."

"It's not fucked-up." Reaching up, she cupped my face between her hands and pulled it down to hers. "Look at me."

It hurt to look at her.

To feel how deeply I felt and know that I wasn't good for her.

"Look at me," she repeated, green eyes burning through me as the song played around us. "Keep your eyes on me." Shivering, she kept me close and said, "Make this song about us instead."

With a dull ache in my chest, I forced myself to comply. To give this girl whatever she wanted. "I love you."

"I know."

"I don't want to hurt you."

She stroked my cheek. "I know that, too."

Exhaling a pained breath, I let my brow sag against hers. "You're all I want, Molloy."

"Then prove it," she whispered, fingers gliding over my skin. "Because you can't keep me hanging in limbo like this."

"That's not what I'm trying to do."

"Maybe not, but that's what you're doing."

Pain struck me in the chest. "I'm trying to protect you."

"Stop trying to protect me and start making me happy," she countered, eyes locked on mine. "Because it's time to pick your poison, Joey Lynch."

Don't say it if you don't mean it

AOIFE

"It's time to pick your poison, Joey Lynch." Trembling, I stood in front of the only boy I had ever loved, with an ultimatum hanging heavily in the air between us.

What I said was true.

I genuinely couldn't live another day feeling like this.

I needed to know where I stood with him.

I couldn't cope with the unknown.

It *terrified* me.

"There's no decision to make," he blew my mind by saying, green eyes blazing with heat. "You already know it's you."

His response caused a shiver of delight to roll through my body, but my heart was still wary.

"No, I *don't*," I choked out, heart racing violently. *Because if I did, I wouldn't be standing here, putting my heart and pride on the line.* "I *don't* know, Joey."

"Then let me be very clear about it," he replied, reaching up to cup the side of my face. "It's you, Molloy." He tipped my chin up, forcing me to look at him. "It's you."

"Don't say it if you don't mean it."

"It's you," he repeated gruffly, fingers tightening on my waist. "I pick you. Every single time."

"I mean it," I warned, shaking my head. "I'm a big girl and I knew what I was getting myself into when I kissed you that day outside your house. You have this warped notion that you need to shield me from your life when *nothing* about your life has come as a surprise to me. I walked into this relationship with my eyes wide open, and guess what; my eyes are still open, and I still want in."

"I still want in, too," he replied gruffly. "I just ... " He blew out a ragged breath. "You mean the world to me," he confessed, voice pained. "I know I have a fucked-up way of expressing myself, and I don't show it like I should. But it's true. I *don't* want to do anything to hurt you, yet most of the time, that's exactly what I end up doing."

His words, his touch, his scent, it was all too much in the moment. "Joe."

"I'll love you the right way this time," he whispered, and his breath fanned my cheek. "If you show me how."

My hand shot out of its own accord, knotting in the front of his shirt and pulling him closer when I needed to push him away. "Joe."

"What I did at Christmas? How far I went? It scared the *shit* out of me, and all I could think about was if I didn't get you away from me, I would end up destroying my world, because that's what you are to me, Aoif. You're my whole goddamn world wrapped up in one girl. So, yeah, maybe I've gone about it entirely the wrong way, but all I've ever tried to do is protect you."

"See, that's a huge part of our problem right there, Joe, because I've never needed your protection," I croaked out. "I'm not your mother or your sister. I'm not another girl who needs something from you. I'm the girl who whole-heartedly *wants* you. I'm the girl who wholeheartedly *loves* you. The hurler. The mechanic. The boy. The protector. The asshole. The lover. The addict." Sniffling, I added, "All of your versions. All of your shapes and colors. I accept them all. So, I don't care how fucked up in the head you get, or how bad of an idea you decide you are for me. If you can't be with me, warts and all, then walk away now, because I won't go through this again with you."

"I hear you, Molloy," he replied, tone strained, as he rested both hands on my waist.

"Do you?" I implored him with my eyes to be honest. "Do you really hear me, Joe?"

He nodded slowly. "I hear you, baby."

"Good." Trembling, I clenched my eyes shut, losing the battle with both my emotions and my pride, as I dropped my forehead to rest against his chest. "Because you can't take it back this time, Joe. Do you hear me? You don't get to walk away again for any other reason than you don't want to be with me, and trust that I will do the same."

"Okay." His hands slid from my waist to my shoulders, and then moved to cup my face, hands tangling in my hair, evoking a shiver of pleasure from my body that only he could. "I can do that."

Illicit sensations and feelings roared to the surface when he stroked his nose against mine, nuzzling me with the kind of affection I knew he held only for me. It was empowering and terrifying all in one breath. "I love you."

He said it so easily now that it sounded foreign to my ears.

A shaky breath escaped my parted lips.

"I love you," he repeated slowly, leaning in to give me an innocent, sweet, soul-destroying kiss.

"No more walls, Joe." My arms came around his waist, fingers digging into the fabric of his shirt, as I clung to him like a prayer. "No more secrets and coverups, okay? We're way past those. Because I've never been your enemy," I squeezed out. "I've always been your teammate."

He stilled for a moment before releasing a heavy sigh. "Then in the spirit of full disclosure, I should probably tell you that I didn't just come here because I was invited."

"Okay ..." I narrowed my eyes, instantly suspicious. "What did you do?"

Shaking his head, he caught ahold of my hand and led me outside to a quiet part of the garden. "Don't flip out."

I folded my hands across my chest and glared up at him. "Don't give me a reason to flip out and I won't."

He scrunched his nose up before muttering, "I sold Biggs an eighth."

"Of *joy*?"

He squirmed in discomfort. "Of weed."

"Jesus, Joey!"

"I didn't go to Shane," he was quick to offer up. "I haven't gone near him since that night."

"Then where'd you get it?" I demanded. "Your personal stash?"

He offered me a sheepish shrug.

"Jesus." I shook my head. "What am I saying? *Of course* you have a personal stash."

"That's all I have, I swear."

"Don't lie to me—"

"I'm not," he interrupted. "That's all I had. That's it, Molloy. I swear."

"Why?"

"Why what?"

"Why'd you do something as incredibly stupid as selling weed to a bunch of private school kids?"

He eyed me warily, but didn't answer.

"*Why?*" I repeated, not backing down.

"Because they asked me to?"

I gave him a look that said *wrong answer.*

He released a frustrated growl and tried again. "Because I needed the money."

Now we were getting somewhere. "For?"

"My family."

"Because?"

He looked up to the sky and shook his head before saying, "Because my old man blew every penny my mother had, and when he was finished spending her money, she handed him mine."

"Are you serious?"

"It's my own fault," he replied in a resigned tone. "I always give her half of my wages at the end of the week to help with the bills, and a few extra quid at Christmas to get what she needs for the kids." Frowning, he added, "Your father gave me an extra couple of hundred in my wage packet for Christmas this year, and I was either too stupid or too high to consider the repercussions when I handed it over to her."

"You gave her all of your money?"

"Every cent," he admitted before quickly backpedaling with a frown.

"I got those slouch boots you wanted for Christmas first. They're under my bed."

My heart squeezed in my chest. "Joe."

"I've been staying out of trouble, Molloy, really, I have," he urged. "Hughie Biggs approached *me*. He and his friends were looking for a smoke and throwing around more cash than sense." He shrugged before adding, "I took the opportunity with both hands, and I won't apologize for it. I needed that cash for my sister and the boys. For the baby. I couldn't see Seany go without." He shook his head, eyes awfully full of regret for a guy who refused to apologize. "I'm not a dealer, Molloy – you know I'm not. But I couldn't turn my nose up at a one-time offer like that. I couldn't afford to."

"Why?" Curiosity got the better of me and I asked, "How much did they offer you?"

"Two hundred euro for a bag that cost me sixty."

"Are you serious?" My mouth fell open. "Do you know how many hours I have to work at the pub to make that kind of money?"

"I know." He nodded, wide-eyed. "It's the same for me at the garage. That's exactly what I thought. See? This is why I love you. You get it."

"Yeah, I get it, but that's not the point," I hurried to add, giving him a warning stare. "That shit stops." Narrowing my eyes, I said, "Never again, do you hear me? If you so much as consider—"

"Don't worry," he was quick to interject. "I've made the mistake of handing over my wages to a bum for the last time."

That was a lie.

The minute his next wage packet landed in his hands, Joey would go right ahead and hand it over to her again.

It was one of the reasons I loved him so much.

And a huge reason why I despised his mother.

"So, I'm sort of freezing out here," I told him, gesturing around us.

"Shit, yeah," he muttered, reaching for the hem of his hoodie, only to realize that this was one of the rare occasions in which he wasn't wearing one. "Do you have a coat?" he asked, pulling me in close and splaying his big hand across my bare back.

"No, but I don't need one," I replied, just about done with all of the heavy. "Because I have an unlimited supply of free alcohol to warm my belly, and this asshole guy I'm sort of in love with to warm everywhere else."

He smirked. "Is that so?"

"Uh-huh. Come on, Tony Soprano." Wrapping my arm around his waist, I slid my hand into his back pocket leaned in to his warm side. "This time, you can look after me."

No more walls

JOEY

Molloy laid her cards on the table, gave me her ultimatum, and I'd never been more grateful.

I'd never been the kind of person that took being cornered, or told what to do, lying down, but I didn't feel the usual need to fight her on it.

It had taken years to happen, but my body and mind didn't automatically slip into attack mode when she called me out on my bullshit anymore.

I didn't shift into defense mode either, because something deep inside of me recognized her as an *ally*.

My teammate.

It had never happened before.

Not with a single other human on this planet.

Not even my sister.

But something about this girl settled something deep inside of me.

I couldn't understand it, much less explain it, but when I was with her, I felt like I was drowning and breathing all at once.

I felt like I was riding this thrilling wave and it didn't matter if I fell or not because I could only land on softness.

I wasn't going to get *hurt* this time.

Because Aoife Molloy, and it had taken me six long years to accept it, was not going to harm me.

When she told me that she loved me, she *meant* it, and it was as unsettling as it was addictive, because if she only felt a fifth for me of what I felt for her, then I was one lucky son of a bitch.

"Do you know what yesterday was?" Molloy asked, several hours, and countless drinks later. We were still at the party, still in the same position we'd been in for the past hour; with my back pressed to the living room wall, and her body pressed flush against mine.

"What was yesterday, Molloy?" I indulged her by asking, keeping one hand clamped on her hip while I took a swig from my bottle with the other.

She was loaded, while I had somehow managed to remain in control of my impulsive nature. After nine bottles, I was mildly buzzed, but I had built up a tolerance level that could rival a horse. Unlike my lightweight drinking buddy, it would take a lot more than a few beers to take me down.

"Yesterday was the seventh."

"The seventh?"

"Uh-huh. Our anniversary," she announced, cheeks stained in that adorable pink shade that always came out when she was drunk. "One year ago yesterday we had our first kiss."

Well shit. "I didn't know that."

"Yep," she breathed, leaning heavily against me. "Exactly one year ago yesterday, you stuck your tongue down my throat."

"That's a little fumble with the truth," I teased, grinning down at her. "If my memory serves me correctly, it was *your* tongue that entered my mouth first."

"Only because you were too pussy to make the first move."

I laughed. "I was building up to it."

She arched a brow. "For five years?"

"What can I say?" I pulled her closer. "I had to be sure."

"Of what?"

"That you wouldn't run."

"And now you're sure?" She watched me closely. "Now you trust me?"

"Yeah, Molloy." Nodding slowly, I leaned in close and brushed my lips against hers. "I trust you."

"Wow." She expelled a shaky breath. "I think that means more to me than when you finally admitted that you love me."

"How'd you figure?"

"Oh, please. You've been in love with me since forever. It's *so* obvious," she replied, without a hint of self-doubt or shyness, and I fucking loved it. "But I was never sure if you could ever truly open yourself up in that way to anyone."

"Not anyone, Molloy," I told her. "Just you."

"You know I've got your back, right?" she breathed, hands moving under the hem of my shirt to press against my bare stomach. Her nails gently scraped my skin, causing an immediate response from my dick, as she leaned up on her tiptoes and pressed a kiss to the curve of my jaw. "I am so down for you, Joey Lynch."

Snaking one hand up to cover the tattoo on my chest, she used the other to move the hand I'd been resting on her hip to her tattooed ass cheek. Leaning back, she looked me right in the eyes and whispered the words, "Ride or die, Joe."

Fuck me . . .

A shiver rolled through me and I couldn't stop myself from grabbing her ass and dragging her body roughly against mine. "Ride or die, Molloy."

Her lips crashed against mine, and it was in this very moment that I knew I would never be able to untangle myself from this girl.

Not in this lifetime.

Bambied

AOIFE

"We've . . . talked . . . about . . . this."

"I know, I know . . ." Moaning, I tried and failed to keep my thighs open, as I balanced precariously against the side of a fancy, cast-iron, oval-shaped bathtub, with my back bowed, and my arm stretched out to grip the other side of the tub. "I'm sorry, I just . . . uh, I can't!"

"You have to." With one leg hitched over his shoulder, Joey knelt on the floor, with his face buried between my thighs. "You're going to . . . strangle me."

"Stop talking, Joe, I'm so close," I cried out hoarsely, back arching when I felt his tongue flick my clit. "Oh, Jesus!"

"Molloy," he growled, reaching up and pushing my thigh away from his head. "Spread these goddamn ladders for legs."

"No!" I wailed in despair as the feeling I had been chasing quickly receded. "Why would you do that to me? Why would you *stop*?"

He glared at me. "Ah, maybe because I require oxygen to breathe, and you're choking the very fucking essence of my being out of me with your *legs*."

Bang. Bang. Bang.

"Ignore them," I instructed, breathing hard, as someone knocked on the door. "This house has more than one bathroom." Frowning, I added, "And I thought you liked my legs."

"I love your legs," Joey agreed, hair all mussed up and sexy, as he looked up at me from his perch. "But if you don't start remembering to keep them open when my *head* is between them, then they're going to be responsible for my death."

"It's your fault," I huffed, feeling both defensive and aroused. "You and your devil tongue."

"Keep these legs open, ya hear?" he warned, pointing a finger at me. "Last warning."

"Or what – oh my god!" Eyelids fluttering, I reached a hand between my thighs and knotted my fingers in his hair. "You're so good at that . . . "

"Molloy!"

"Sorry," I strangled out, forcing my thighs apart. "Don't stop."

Bang. Bang. Bang.

"Fuck off," I screamed at the inconsiderate bastard banging on the bathroom door.

Bang. Bang. Bang.

"She said fuck off!" Joey roared; a hell of a lot louder than me.

Bang. Bang. Bang.

"That's it," he snapped, tone furious, as he climbed to his feet and moved for the door. "If that creepy blond bastard is on the other side of that door again, I am going to fuck him up!"

"But you've been so good," I replied, choking out a laugh, as I hurried to intercept him before he could open the door. "Don't fuck him up," I purred, sliding between him and the door. "When you can fuck me instead."

His eyes blazed with heat. "Molloy."

"I promise I'll feel better." Reaching up, I quickly slid the sleeves of my dress down my arms, letting the fabric pool at my waist, before hitching the skirt up to join the rest of my dress. "So, what's it going to be, Joe?"

"Fuck." His heated gaze moved straight to my bare breasts and he released a low growl. "Me."

Feeling empowered, I quickly led him over to the sink. "Good boy."

He arched a brow. "Don't mock me."

Smirking, I reached for the button on his jeans and flicked it open before undoing his fly and roughly dragging his jeans and boxers down his hips to free his hard erection. "Big boy."

"Molloy!"

"Shutting up now," I breathed, reaching a hand between us to stroke him.

"It's been a while since we were together," he admitted, closing the space between us, as he reached for my waist. "I'll probably go off fast."

"That's okay." Giving him my back, I leaned forwards and gripped the sink, gaze locking on his in the mirror in front of me. "Just keep your eyes on me."

"Jesus." With a shake of his head, he stepped closer, encouraging me to spread my legs, as one hand smoothed down my back, settling on my hip, while his used the other hand to slowly feed his big dick inside of me, inch by delicious inch.

Bang. Bang. Bang.

This time when the intruder pummeled on the door, Joey was too wrapped up in pummeling me to care.

"Don't stop," I cried out hoarsely, clutching the porcelain sink for all I was worth, as I forced my legs to hold their ground against his deliciously addictive thrusting. "Make it hurt."

"Christ, Aoif," he bit out, breathing hard. With eyes locked on mine in the mirror, he continued to thrust his hips at a furious pace. "You're so tight."

Bang. Bang. Bang.

"Then stretch me," I moaned, struggling to keep eye contact, as my entire body shook and trembled. "Make me yours."

"You're already mine," he told me, reaching a hand between my legs to thumb my clit. "Every inch of you."

Bang. Bang. Bang.

I was so wet that I could feel him sliding in deeper with every thrust. He was so big, pushing so deep inside of me, that it was borderline painful, but when that familiar pulsing of heat and pleasure grew stronger with every thrust of his hips, I found myself begging him to take me harder.

Bang. Bang. Bang.

It was only when Joey leaned in close and covered my mouth with his hand that I realized I was screaming.

"Shh, Molloy," he warned, keeping his eyes on mine in the mirror. "Quiet, baby."

Ah Jesus . . .

I couldn't take it.

My body couldn't handle another jolt of pressure.

My cries were muffled by his hand as my orgasm tore through me, hitting so fucking deep, that my body clamped up tight, and my legs threatened to give out beneath me.

"Fuck!" Breathing hard and fast, Joey sagged against me, as his erection pulsed inside of me, flooding me with heat. "You good?"

"Uh-huh," I laughed, breathless, as I leaned heavily against the sink. "You?"

"Yeah, Molloy." Chuckling, he squeezed my hip as he slowly pulled out and moved to sort himself out. "I'm good."

"I think you broke me a little bit towards the end there." Staggering unsteadily on my feet, I clumsily cleaned up and readjusted my dress before taking stock of my disheveled appearance. "Look at those shakes," I said, pointing to the very obvious tremor running through my legs. "I think you bambied me."

"Would you look at that." Thoroughly amused, Joey closed the space between us and knelt down at my feet. "Come on, Bambi," he chuckled, helping me to step back into my thong, and then pulling the fabric up my thighs. "Let's make you decent."

A few moments later, when Joey swung the bathroom door open to let us out, we were greeted by a roaring cheer.

"You fucking stallion," some random lad declared, as he held a hand up for Joey to high-five. "My Jesus, for a minute there, I thought we were going to have to call an ambulance for your lady friend!"

Joey gave him such a withering look that the lad physically shrunk away from him, quickly taking his outstretched hand with him.

"The hell is wrong with these people?" he muttered, slinging an arm over my shoulder. "Every one that I meet is stranger than the last one."

"Who cares," I replied breezily. "Let's go eat and drink eat our weight in their generous offerings."

Joey nodded his approval. "I saw this seriously expensive looking bottle of champagne in the fridge."

"Yeah, I saw that, too."

"I've never tasted champagne before."

"Me either," I told him. "But I have a purse in the living room big enough to smuggle a bottle back to my place."

He stopped in the hallway and turned to face me. "Should we, though?"

"Someone's going to end up drinking it." I shrugged. "Why shouldn't it be us?"

He studied my face for a long moment before making his decision.

"Get your bag," he instructed. "I'll get the bottle."

"Already on it," I replied, bumping his fist with mine, as we moved in opposite directions.

It was my turn to look after you

AOIFE

When I peeled my eyelids open the following morning, it was to the hangover from hell, and a hand probing my face.

Blinking awake from the sticky intrusion, I quickly studied my surroundings to find myself twisted up in the sheets of a familiar bed, while an equally familiar toddler poked at me with his slobbery little fingers.

My body tensed for the briefest of moments, as my bleary-eyed gaze took stock of the wide-eyed child staring back at me, and the lap in which he was perched on.

Shirtless, and propped up against the wall his bed was aligned against, Joey had his head tilted sideways as he slept.

He had one hand balled into a fist at his side, while the other hand hung limply around his brother's waist.

Protecting him even in sleep.

"Hi, Sean," I whisper-croaked, trying to conjure up a smile for him, not an easy feat considering even my lips ached.

"E-fa," he whispered back, and then shyly clambered back to the safety of his big brother's arms. "O-ee." Wrapping his small arm around Joey's neck, he snuggled closer, and buried his face in the curve of his brother's neck. "O-ee."

"You're grand, I promise," Joey mumbled, eyes still closed, as he tightened his arm around the little guy, and my heart squeezed tight at the sight. "Just close your eyes, Seany-boo."

"O-ee, poos."

Those two words had Joey practically vaulting off the bed, with his baby brother tucked under his arm.

"Fuck my life," he muttered, stalking over to his door and one-handedly dragging the chest of drawers out of his way before unlocking and yanking the bedroom door open. "You can wipe your own ass this time," he warned the little guy in his arms, as he disappeared into the landing. "But good job for telling me, kid."

Frozen in place, the throbbing in my head assured me that I couldn't move if I wanted to.

A few minutes later, Joey strolled back into his room, this time clutching a can of Coke instead of a sibling.

"Morning." His eyes danced with amusement as he closed his bedroom door behind him. "How's the head?"

"Morning," I croaked out hoarsely, as I made a feeble attempt to drag myself into a sitting position. "And terrible." I blew out a pained breath and clutched my temple. "I think I'm on the way out."

Closing the space between us, he sank down on the edge of the bed. "Nah, you'll live," he chuckled, thrusting the ice-cold can into my hands. "Drink."

"I can't," I groaned, and then physically gagged at the concept of putting another drop of liquid inside my poor stomach. "Seriously, I think I'm dying here."

"You're not dying, but you *are* in trouble."

"Ugh," I groaned. "Why? What did I do?"

"Smoking." He gave me a hard look. "Not cool, Molloy."

"Yeah, okay," I snorted. "Like you can talk."

"I'm serious." His green eyes were full of sincerity and concern. "I know why you did it, and it worked, but don't ever do it again, okay?"

"Don't worry," I moaned. "I have no plans to."

"Good." Shaking his head, he reached over and cracked the can open and gently pushed it towards my face. "Now, drink up or you'll feel worse."

Reluctantly, I took a small sip from the can, and when it didn't kill me, I took a bigger one.

Suddenly realizing just how parched I was, I quickly gulped down half the can, my eyes never leaving his as I drank.

Nodding his approval, Joey reached into the pocket of his grey sweatpants and withdrew a small packet of paracetamol, and from the other pocket, he produced a packet of salt and vinegar crips.

"Trust me," he was quick to coax when I eyed him warily. "It'll work."

"Fine." With a resigned sigh, I popped two painkillers and quickly drained the rest of the can before reaching for the crisps. "I thought we were going back to my place?" I mused, unable to piece the events of last night together through the hazy fog in my mind, as I munched on the crisps.

"So did I," he agreed. "But you insisted that I take you back to my place."

"I did?"

"Yeah, you did."

"Huh." Swallowing down a mouthful of salt and vinegar goodness, I titled my head to the side and considered his cure, feeling my stomach settle second by second. "Sugar, salt, and paracetamol? I have to say, this is a pretty strange hair of the dog, Joe, but it's a good one."

"Family recipe," was his wry response. "Perks of growing up with an alcoholic for a father, and a mother with a penchant for benzos."

"And a messy drunk for a girlfriend," I offered, wincing when my eyes landed on the notable sick bucket next to *my* side of the bed. "I'm guessing that was for me, right?"

Joey smirked and I dropped my head in my hands.

"Oh god," I groaned. "You had to clean up my puke."

"It was the champagne," he replied with a chuckle. "Or so you told me in between spraying us both in chunks in that Feely lad's car on the way home."

"I did?"

"Yeah." He inclined his head to his t-shirt that I was sporting. "I had to put you in the shower when we got back here."

"Oh, my sweet baby Jesus," I wailed, mortified. "Stop laughing, Joe. It's not funny. It's horrifying."

"It's not a big deal," he laughed, pulling my hands away from my face. "It's not like you haven't returned the favor a time or ten for me." Shrugging, he added, "It was my turn to look after you."

"That's different."

"How?"

"Because you're my boyfriend."

"So? You're my girlfriend."

"Girlfriends are supposed to be sexy."

"Molloy, I can assure you that you are insanely sexy."

"I am?"

"Absolutely," he replied and then choked out another laugh. "Especially when you have champagne bubbles coming out of your nose."

"Oh, fuck right off," I snapped, grabbing a pillow from behind my back and smacking him over the head with it.

"I did the best I could with your hair," he added. "But I've never washed hair as long as yours before, so if I screwed up, don't hold it against me."

My heart squeezed. "You *washed* my hair?"

"I sort of had to," he replied. "You sprayed your ponytail with chunks, too."

"Oh god." I pulled my damp hair over my shoulder and took a sniff, instantly recognizing the shampoo scent as the one he used. "That's quite possibly the most romantically disgusting thing anyone's ever done for me."

"Come on," he said, shaking his head. "I'll make you a cuppa."

"Isn't that against your rules?" I reminded him, throwing the covers off and climbing out of bed. "I mean, don't you prefer us to stay in your room when we're here?"

"Yeah, well, that was before."

"Before what?"

"Before last night," he replied gruffly. "Before I opened my ears and actually listened for a change."

"So, boys *can* listen," I mused, readjusting the waistband of his boxers he clearly dressed me in last night. "I thought that was just a myth."

"I heard you, Aoif." Reaching for my hand, he pulled me close. "And I meant what I said about trusting you."

"Yeah?"

"Yeah." He nodded slowly. "This is my world. It's fucking horrible, but I'm willing to show you, if you're willing to stay."

"Always, Joe," I whispered, wrapping my arms around his waist. "Always."

Braless beneath his white t-shirt, and with only his black boxers to cover my ass, I piled my hair into a make-shift bun on top of my head, and trailed downstairs with Joey, too hungover to care that I looked like something the cat dragged in.

Fully aware that much of last night's make-up was still smeared across my face, I checked my vanity at the kitchen door, and let him walk me inside.

"Joey," his mother said from her usual perch at the table. Her gaze flicked to me and I felt a sudden shift in her mood. "Aoife."

"Morning." Acknowledging his mother, Joey walked us over to the kettle, keeping my back pressed to his front as he set to work on making coffee.

The need to conceal his hard-on that was digging into my back was no doubt the reason for keeping me close.

"The two of you woke half the house up last night, making all that racket when you came in."

"Hi, Marie," I replied, offering her a smile, even though she did *not* look happy to see me. "Sorry about that."

"Yeah," Joey called over his shoulder, while poking me in the rib. "She'll puke quieter next time."

"Asshole," I grumbled under my breath, trying and failing to stamp on his foot with my heel because the asshole had the reflexes of a cat.

"Oh," his mother said, watching us warily from her perch. "When you didn't bring Aoife around over Christmas, I thought you two might have gone your separate ways."

No such luck, bitch.

"I'm afraid I'm here to stay." I gave her an extra wide smile, as I spooned sugar into my mug. "Coffee?"

"No. Thank you." She turned her attention to her son. "I've agreed to take on Betty Murphy's cleaning shift at the hospital this afternoon. You'll be here to watch Sean, won't you?"

"No."

"No?" Confusion filled her blue eyes. "What do you mean no?"

"I mean no." Stepping around me now that his morning wood was under control, Joey moved for the fridge and grabbed the milk. "I have plans."

"What plans?"

"Just plans, Mam," Joey replied, pouring a dollop of milk into both of our mugs.

"With who?"

"With Aoife," he replied, winking when he handed me the mug.

My heart thudded in victory.

"Can you change your plans?" his mother pressed. "I already told Betty that I would cover her shift."

"No, I can't," Joey replied slowly. "Sunday is my only day off and I'm spending it with my girlfriend."

Ha-ha-ha-ha! Giving her a sweetly smug fuck-you smile, I leaned up on my tiptoes, and pressed a kiss to her son's cheek.

"We need the money."

"I don't know what to tell ya, Mam."

"Well, what am I supposed to do with Sean?"

Joey shrugged but didn't answer.

"Shannon is at Nanny's getting her uniform altered, and your father has taken Ollie and Tadhg to that hurling blitz at the pavilion."

"He's your son," came my boyfriend's quiet reply.

"I know that, Joey, but I need you."

"Mam."

"You have responsibilities."

His nostrils flared. "I'm well aware."

"We can stay here and mind Sean for your mam, Joe," I decided to say, thrilled that he was trying to put me first, but knowing that his guilt would only serve as a downer on his mood for the rest of the day. "It's not like we have anything better to do."

"You sure?" Uncertain green eyes landed on mine. "You didn't sign up to spending your Sunday babysitting my brother, Molloy."

No, but I definitely signed up to be with you.

"I'm sure." I gave him an enthusiastic nod before turning back to his mother. "We'll watch your son."

Joey's mother didn't like me, didn't want me anywhere near *any* of her sons, but I had her over a rock, and she could do nothing but nod stiffly and say, "Thank you."

"You're welcome." Still smiling, I caught ahold of Joey's hand and practically dragged him out of the kitchen. "Let's go."

"Did you see the look on her face?" he chuckled, following me up the staircase, trying to balance both steaming mugs of coffee. "She's raging."

"Because she doesn't want me in her house." Closing his bedroom door behind us, I turned the key in the lock and prowled towards him. "Distracting her perfectly trained, busy little worker bee."

Setting both mugs down on his windowsill, Joey turned back to me and gave me a heated look. "Call me a bee again, and I'll have to sting ya."

"Sounds tempting."

Reaching for the hem of the t-shirt I was wearing, I quickly whipped it over my head and laughed when he groaned. "Fuck."

"Come on, Joe." Hooking my fingers into the waistband of the boxers I was wearing, I pushed the fabric down my thighs. "I have the perfect place for you to put your stinger."

"Your mind is so messed up," he laughed, pushing his sweats down his narrow hips. "You can make filth out of anything, Molloy."

"You love my dirty mind."

"You're right. I do," he agreed, as he closed the space between us and reached for me. "And I love your ass." Hoisting me up, he pushed my back against his door and leaned in close. "And these lips."

Kissing me deeply, he growled into my mouth and rocked himself against me, causing the thick head of his cock to probe my clit.

"Do it, Joe," I encouraged, hooking my legs around his waist, as I slipped a hand between us and fisted his shaft. "Take me."

"Have me," he whispered against my lips, as he slowly rocked into my touch. "Put me inside you."

Oh, Jesus.

Shivering against his lips, I tilted my pelvis, aligning my body with his, and slowly fed him into my body, breathing hard as he filled me to the point of pain. "You stretch me so good."

"Keep talking and it'll be over before it starts," he warned, hips gyrating against mine, as he slowly built up a delicious rhythm that involved making minimal noise against the door frame while making maximum impact on my body.

"You like my pussy, Joe?"

"I love your pussy."

"How much?"

"Molloy."

"Come on, Joe. Talk to me."

"I can't." Releasing a pained groan, he dropped his head on my shoulder. "She's right downstairs."

"So?" I breathed, pulling his face back to mine and kissing him hard. "Since when do we care about what she thinks?"

"We don't," he agreed, lips meeting mine for a glorious kiss, while he rocked into me. "But this is her house—"

"This is your room," I interrupted, thrusting myself against him. "And in your room, you *fuck* me, Joey."

Heat flooded his eyes.

"I'm yours," I whispered, giving myself entirely to him. "You can have me anytime, anyplace, anywhere because you *own* me."

"Jesus."

"Every inch of me," I breathed, chest heaving against his as our bodies collided. "So, take what's yours."

Releasing a feral growl, Joey claimed my lips with his and did just that.

PART 2

Back to bullshit – I mean BCS

JOEY

I was a bundle of nerves.

I couldn't fucking breathe out of concern for the girl in the bathroom.

Today was Shannon's first day at Tommen, and she had been locked inside the bathroom for so long, that I was beginning to consider the possibility that she might have washed herself down the drain.

I mean, in all honesty, there wasn't much of her there to begin with.

It wasn't that hard of a stretch to imagine.

Unable to take another second of the not knowing, I threw my door open, padded into the landing, and rapped my knuckles against the bathroom door.

"Shan? Hurry up, will ya?" I knocked again, lying through my teeth when I added, "I'm bursting for a piss."

"Two minutes, Joey," she called back and I leaned an ear against the door, listening as she muttered positive affirmations to herself from behind the closed door.

Poor kid.

"You can do this," I heard her tell herself over and over again.

Jesus, I sure as hell hoped it was true, because I was over eighteen now, a legal adult, which meant that the next time I had to intervene on her behalf, I would be heading straight for Cork prison.

When the door finally swung inwards, and I was faced with the sight of my baby sister clad in a *private school* uniform, it took me a moment to process my thoughts. "You look . . . " I let my words trail off, shaking my head when I took sight of the blazer. A blazer? Who wore a fucking blazer to anything besides a wedding and a funeral? I didn't understand any of this. The world she was about to enter was one I would never belong to.

"Lovely," I forced myself to tell her, and it wasn't a lie. Besides from the fact that she looked skittish and terrified, she really did look the part. "The uniform suits you, Shan."

"Do you think it'll be okay?" she asked, voice small, eyes wide with barely contained fear. "Do you think I'll fit in, Joey?"

I don't know, but I hope so.

I really fucking hope so, Shan.

"I'm so fucking proud of you," I said instead, struggling to keep my emotions in check. "You don't even realize how brave you are."

It was the truth.

Where she saw weakness, I saw strength.

Where she saw fear, I saw resilience.

Where she saw timidity, I saw courage.

Unlike me, Shannon didn't need to alter her mind to survive the world we lived in.

She thought she was the weakest link in the family chain, when it couldn't be further from the truth.

My sister was titanium.

"Hang on," I said, hurrying back to my room. "I've got something for ya." Retrieving my wallet from the pair of jeans strewn on my bedroom floor, I withdrew two fivers and returned to the landing to hand them to her. "Here."

"Joey, no," she was quick to protest, staring down at her hand in horror. "I can't—"

"Take the money, Shannon," I instructed. "It's only a tenner. I know Nanny gave you the bus money, but just have something in your pocket." Shrugging, I added, "I don't know how shit works in that place, but I don't want you going in there without a few quid."

She eyed me uncertainly. "Are you sure?"

"Come here." Hooking an arm around her bony shoulders, I pulled her in for a hug. "You're going to be grand," I told her, and I wasn't sure which one of us I was trying to convince; her or me.

Trembling, she hugged me back for all she was worth.

"If someone gives you even the *hint* of shit, then you text me, and I will come over there and burn that school to the ground, and every posh, rugby head fucker in it."

"It's going to be fine," she strangled out, clinging to me for dear life. "But I'll be late if I don't get going, and that's so not what I need on my first day."

I let my arm fall from her shoulders, but she didn't move.

Instead, she continued to cling to me like a baby monkey would its mother.

She has to do this, I mentally chanted, *and you have to let her.*

Feeling panicked when she finally worked up the courage to release me and shrug on her coat, I busied myself with scratching my chest, anything to stop myself from throwing her over my shoulder and locking her in her room where I could keep her safe.

Picking her schoolbag up, Shannon hoisted it onto her small shoulders and offered me a hopeful smile before hurrying down the staircase.

Let her go, I silently commanded myself, *stay put and let her do this.*

"You text me," I couldn't stop myself from saying, as I hurried after her. Stopping midway down the staircase, I watched on helplessly as she opened the front door. "I'm serious. One sniff of crap from anyone, and I'll come sort it out."

"I can do this, Joe," she replied, turning back to look at me. "I *can*."

"I know you can." I forced myself to smile back at her. "I just ... " Blowing out an anxious breath, I said, "I'm here for you, okay? *Always* here for you."

The face I'd spent most of my life protecting looked up at me with such wide-eyed innocence that I felt my heart crack.

With a small, reaffirming nod, she turned and walked away, quietly closing the front door behind her.

The minute it clicked shut, I heard the air whoosh from my lungs.

"Fuck."

Pressing a hand to my chest, I leaned against the banister and allowed myself to sit with my anxiety for a moment, reeling in the potential problems she might encounter and a million *what ifs*, until I felt I might explode.

Only then did I turn around and jog back up the stairs, calling out, "Tadhg, Ols? Let's go, lads. It's time for school," as I shifted into daddy mode and got the rest of my brood sorted.

I need him like water

AOIFE

My relationship was back on track, my hair was on point, it wasn't raining, and I didn't have work tonight.

All in all, I considered this to be a successful first day back at school.

All was right in the world of Aoife again, and I was basking in the cold January afternoon, taking in the sight of thirty or so boys, kitted out in the school colors of both BCS and neighboring town St. Colum's, as they knocked the living shite out of each other with hurleys.

Sighing in contentment, I leaned against the school wall at my back, balancing my ass on my school bag, as I watched Joey own the pitch and everyone on it.

Gifted was the only word to describe the level of talent he displayed.

He literally oozed skill and flair by the bucket full, without even having to try.

He played center back on the team, and wore the number six jersey, but in all fairness, he could play in any position on the team and excel. The boy was beyond gifted.

At best, he was putting a mere sixty percent effort into this match, and still managed to outclass every other lad on the pitch, coming up trumps with three goals and six points for our school.

The speed in which he could break free of his opposition number, and whizz down the pitch on a solo run, weaving and twisting through St. Colum's defense, was second to none.

The fact that several of Teddy Lynch's school team pictures, ranging from 1976 to 1981, still hung proudly on the walls of our school was something that I hated for Joe, but not nearly as much as I hated the comparisons that he had to endure.

For six years in the late seventies and early eighties, his father had commanded BCS's hurling team, earning him a lifelong tenure of adoration from both past and present members of the school faculty.

For years, I witnessed the bullshit. It never mattered what Joey achieved, or how many championships, titles, and medals he won for our school, because his father had achieved it all first, and boy was everyone and their mother just waiting in the wings to remind him of it.

Said comparisons were made to Joey, both often and loudly, and every time it occurred, his mental health took another irreparable blow, because the voice of paranoia that he lived with on a daily basis, the one that assured Joey that he was just like his father, pushed him back towards a place he had spent his youth residing in.

Addiction was a consequence of being raised by street thugs and dealers, where the only substitute available for a mother's love came in the form of a line of cocaine, or worse, a needle in the arm.

Joey had somehow managed to survive his childhood and early teens by replacing the lack of his mother's affection with the warm, enveloping embrace of ecstasy, and his father's constant stream of mental gaslighting and physical abuse with the mind-numbing dexterity of opioids.

It wasn't right, the complete opposite, but I could understand it.

I could understand *him*.

From the tender age of nine or ten, Joey Lynch had been knocking on Shane Holland's door, treating him like his own personal doctor, seeking help and finding it in the worst form.

And, like a black-market pharmacist, Shane had been more than willing to take advantage of a vulnerable child from a broken home.

The fact that Joey was even attempting to break free from the hold drugs had on him, from the blanket of security that they provided him, only proved to me further that he was worth every sleepless night and tear I had shed over him.

"Would you look at the speed of him," Casey said, joining me.

"I know," I mused, eyes locked on Joe. "He's a bullet, isn't he?"

"He's something alright." Dropping her school bag on the ground beside me, Casey sank down on it and stretched her legs out. "I bet he fucks as fast as he runs," she teased, nudging my shoulder with hers. "Better still, as hard as he plays."

"Too far, Case," I sighed, shaking my head. "And too much."

"Really?" she laughed. "That's too bad because I originally planned to go with 'does he last a solid sixty minutes under the sheets like he does on the pitch' question, but decided to tone it down."

"You're a lot of personality for one tiny person."

"True," she agreed with a chuckle. "So, on a scale of one to ten, how mad are you at me for my epic jump to the wrong conclusion on Friday night?"

"Me?" I offered. "A lukewarm one and a half, but I'm not the one you slapped across the face."

"Yeah." She smiled sheepishly. "How mad do you think he still is at me?"

"Oh, you mean after you assaulted him and accused him of sleeping with a girl the same age as his baby sister?"

She nodded.

"It's been three days, so I reckon he's come down to a stony seven."

She scrunched her nose up. "I went a tad too far, huh?"

"Just a smidgen," I replied with a smile. "You were over the top, and out of line, but I love you for having my back."

"Good, because I'm not sorry."

"Case."

"What? I'm not. My delivery might have been wrong, and I shouldn't have slapped him, but he deserved the wakeup call."

"Well, wakeup call or not, don't do it again."

She laughed. "Okay, *Mom*."

"I'm serious." I gave her a meaningful look. "Don't put your hands on him again, Case."

"Okay, Aoif," she replied, hearing the plea in my tone – and the warning – as she held her hands up. "It won't happen again."

"Not ever, okay?"

She nodded slowly. "Okay."

Blowing out a breath, I turned my attention back to the game.

"You guys seem like you're back on track," she offered. "He was all over you in school earlier."

"We are," I confirmed, relieved that the weight on my shoulders had lifted. "It's all good."

"He seems a lot more stable than he was before Christmas break," she added cautiously. "He's doing better?"

"Yeah." Nodding, I released a heavy breath. "Thank god."

"Is that seriously all you're going to tell me about it?" she whined. "Come on, Aoif. I want details. You've always told me everything about your life, but when it comes to him, you're a closed book. I mean, you didn't even tell me that you guys had broken up. I had to hear it from your mam – two weeks *after* the event."

"Well, we're not broken up anymore," I replied. "So, there's not much to say."

"Aoife."

"Casey."

"I know that you love him," she said. "And I'm happy for you, Aoif. Hand on my heart, I am. But don't make him the be all and end all of your world, because, like you've already experienced, if it goes pear-shaped, you'll have nothing to fall back on."

"That's not what I'm doing."

"Isn't it?"

"It's not that I don't want to tell you things," I tried to explain. "It's just … I'm just … and he's so … Our relationship is just really … "

"Intense?" she offered gently.

"Oh, it's a whole lot intense," I agreed with a breathy sigh. "But it's also a whole lot of complicated and private and—"

"Not up for discussion?" She winked. "Gotcha."

"You know I love you," I tried to placate, hooking arms with her. "You're my best friend."

"But so is he."

I shrugged, helpless. "Is that such a bad thing?"

"It's an *amazing* thing," she encouraged in a sad tone. "When he's not off his rocket."

"Casey."

"Just be careful, okay?" she hurried to say. "I know you love him, Aoife, and I know what you and Joey have is about as real as it gets, but so are his *issues*."

"He's doing better," I heard myself defend.

"For now."

"He's doing *better*, Casey," I reiterated thickly. "I don't have a crystal ball to show me the future, so I'll take a 'for now' as a win."

"Fair enough." She sighed heavily before adding, "Just don't let yourself get swallowed up in him again."

The referee blew his whistle before I could answer her, signaling the end of the match, and I turned my attention back to the pitch just in time to see Joey yank his helmet off.

Breathing hard and fast, he used the hem of his jersey to wipe his face and the move gave me a glorious glimpse of his toned stomach, while his teammates celebrated the win.

The moment he noticed me watching him, a slow smile spread across his face.

Cupping my hands around my mouth, I called out, "Nice abs."

"Nice legs," he called back with a wink, and just like that, I was ruined.

"What am I saying?" Casey declared with a resigned laugh. "Of *course* you're going to get swallowed up in him again."

Same shit, different school

JOEY

My day had consisted of seven hours at school, followed by a match, followed by a further four hours at the garage.

By the time I walked through the door a little after eleven that night, I was bone weary, and in dire need of a mattress to collapse onto.

However, the look on my mother's face assured me that sleep was the last thing I would be getting.

"What's wrong?" I asked, dropping my school bag, gear bag, hurley and helmet in the hallway before making a beeline for the kitchen. "Mam?"

"It happened again," she choked out, tears streaming down her face, as she dropped her head in her hands. "Shannon's in hospital."

My heart sank. "No."

Mam nodded in confirmation and I thought I might explode from the sudden rush of blood to the head.

"Why?" My breath caught in my throat. "What *happened*?"

"She has a concussion," she explained, slumped in her usual chair. "They're keeping her overnight for observation."

"A concussion?" I gaped. "How? Where? What the fuck?"

"Some boy in one of the senior classes hit her with a rugby ball during practice, and she took a terrible fall at school." Sniffling, she reached for the torn fabric in front of her and held it up. "Ripped her skirt in the process, apparently. I can't remember his name," she strangled out. "But he was an older boy around the same age as you."

"On purpose?" Fury roared to life inside of me. "Mam, did he do it on purpose?"

"He swore blind to the principal that he didn't mean to hurt her," she replied, tone dripping with disdain. "He brought her inside when she collapsed and was sitting with her outside of the office when I arrived, but you know what they're like," Mam sobbed. "I thought this time would be different for her. Better. She needs better, Joey. She needed a fresh start and it's ruined."

"What's Shannon saying about it?"

"She swears it was an accident, too," Mam replied wearily. "But you know how she lies."

"Well then, maybe it was," I offered, allowing myself to be hopeful for once in my life. "If he took her to the office after it happened and stayed with her until you came."

"I expect that kind of naivety from your brothers and sister, but not you," Mam snapped. "You know better."

Yeah, I did, but for once, I didn't want to.

For once in my life, I wanted my mother to show me the same consideration that she so willingly showed the rest of my siblings.

It wouldn't happen, of course.

Because my feelings weren't meant to be spared.

They were meant to be bulletproof.

Or nonexistent.

"What's Dad saying?"

Her shoulders slumped, but she didn't reply.

"What's he saying about it, Mam?" I pushed.

"That it serves her right for thinking she was better than the rest of you."

"Prick," I muttered, rubbing my jaw. "He doesn't have a goddamn—"

"Please don't start," she cut me off with a sob. "I've already heard all that I can handle tonight from your father."

"Mam," I began to say, but she shook her head, silencing me with her dismissal.

With a sniffle, she rose from the table, pressed a hand to her growing stomach, and walked straight past me, with scorn and disappointment wafting from her in waves.

The kitchen door closed behind me, and I felt that familiar swell of frustrated desperation rise up inside of me. It was the same feeling that was never sated until I forced it away with whatever I could get my hands on.

Helpless, I stood in the kitchen, with my hands hanging limply at my sides, as I absorbed the horrible fucking sensations and feelings rushing through me.

Unwilling to unlock my muscles out of fear of what I was capable of doing, and even more unwilling to detonate the self-destruct button on the life I had barely managed to get back on track, I bowed my head and breathed in deep and slow.

It doesn't matter, I tried to soothe myself by mentally chanting, *none of this matters, because you don't care, remember?*

You don't care.

You don't care.

You don't fucking care!

The night visit

AOIFE

It was a little after midnight when I was roused to the sound of my bedroom window creaking open and then closing shut.

My heart accelerated in my chest when muffled footsteps followed, and then I felt the mattress dip beside me.

Remaining silent, I rolled onto my back, and turned my head to look at my boyfriend.

Because I just *knew* that it was Joey.

Fully clothed and body rigid, he lay on top of my covers, with his hood up, and his hands resting on his stomach, as he glared up at my bedroom ceiling.

He was breathing in excessively deep and slow, letting me know that he was dealing with something in his mind, and instead of running to Shane, he had come here.

To me.

In the darkness, with only the hue of the moon shining through my window to illuminate us, we laid side by side. My body cloaked in warmth, and his in coldness.

Mirroring our lives.

Without speaking a word, I reached out and took one of his big hands in mine and lifted it to my mouth.

He needed to process.

He needed to make the next move for himself.

I couldn't do that for him.

Pressing four soft kisses to each of his scarred knuckles, I cradled his hand to my chest and waited.

After what felt like an eternity, he exhaled a pained breath and entwined my fingers with his.

He turned his head to look at me, so I did the same.

"I needed Tommen to be better for her."

"Shannon?"

He nodded stiffly.

Heart sinking, I covered our joined hands with my free one.

"She looked at me like it was my fault."

"Your mam?"

Another stiff nod.

My heart squeezed.

I knew that he didn't need me to bombard him with questions, much less did he want my pity or comfort, so I just stared at him, watching as his clear, green eyes focused on my mine.

"She hates me," he finally came out with, his words a pained admission. "You should see the way she looks at me."

Pain encompassed me and I rolled onto my side, facing him. "What do you see when I look at you?"

He flinched. "That's not the—"

"What do you see, Joe?"

"You," he whispered brokenly. "I see you, Molloy."

"You see love," I corrected softly, releasing his hand to cup his stubbly cheek. "You see acceptance."

He swallowed deeply, but didn't reply.

"We're mirrors, Joe," I told him, taking his hand and placing it on my cheek. "Everything you feel for me is reciprocated. It's mirroring back at you."

"Molloy."

"Your mother might be foolish enough to disregard you, but that will never happen from me," I whispered, shifting closer until our noses were brushing. "I will *never* reject your love."

He exhaled and whispered, "I'm really fucking drowning here, Aoif."

"Don't worry, Joe. I won't let that happen," I replied, nuzzling his nose with mine. "I won't let your head go under."

"Promise?"

I leaned in and pressed a kiss to his lips. "I promise."

"I love you."

"I love you back."

"I'm going to get this right, Molloy."

"I know you are, Joe."

"You're really sticking around, aren't ya?"

"Afraid so." I smiled in the darkness. "For the ring. The white dress. The white picket fence. The whole nine yards."

"Jesus," he chuckled. "Don't push it."

"I always push it, Joe."

"Understatement of the century, Molloy."

"When we get engaged—"

"We're not getting engaged."

"I want a ring the size of my fist."

He snorted. "Good luck with that."

"And when we get married—"

"We're not getting married."

"I want a big house in the country, with a huge four-poster bed, and one of those giant flatscreen televisions hanging on the wall."

"And where am I going to find the money for that?"

I beamed at him. "I thought you said we weren't getting married."

"We're not." He turned to face me. "We can't because I'll be in prison for robbing a bank to pay for that fist-sized ring you have your eye on."

"And when we have babies—"

"We're not having babies."

"They'll be blond and green-eyed and just like their dad."

"You're insane."

"I'm in love."

"I'm not having babies, Molloy," he whispered, giving me a lonesome look. "I can't be a father."

"Joe."

"It's a hard limit for me."

"Okay." Giving him a reassuring smile, I said, "No babies. We'll have a fur-baby instead."

"Hm." Turning back to stare at the ceiling, he inhaled a deep breath. "You might want to lower the bar with the mansion in the country, too."

"Why?" I laughed. "What have you in mind?"

"Don't know," he admitted. "I never think about that kind of stuff."

"The future?"

He nodded. "Yeah."

"Well, you better start thinking about it," I teased. "Because you're in mine, and I always get what I want."

"Yeah." He squeezed my hand. "I know."

"So, do you want to keep talking?" Springing up, I reached for the hem of my t-shirt and whipped it off. "Or should we get naked and screw?"

"Jesus Christ." Chuckling softly, Joey mirrored my actions and pulled his hoodie and t-shirt over his head. "Where did I find you?"

"Your dreams." Reaching for the waistband of my knickers, I quickly shoved them down my thighs and clambered on top of his lap. "Hey, stud."

"Hey, queen."

"Queen?" My eyes danced with delight as I reached for the waistband of his sweats. "Now you're talking my language."

Lifting his hips, he pushed sweats and boxers down, freeing himself and giving me a close-up of his big damn dick. "I've never had this."

"What?"

"This," he whispered, kicking off his clothes, and hooking an arm around my back to pull me close. "Us." Pressing his lips to mine, he reached a hand between us and aligned the head of his thick cock against me. "You."

"Well, good." Shivering, I lowered myself down on him, reveling in the wonderful way he stretched me to the point of pain. "Because I'm completely yours."

My eyelids fluttered when he rolled his hips upwards, pressing deep inside of me in the best kind of way.

"I'm completely yours, too." The words were a quiet, barely spoken admission, but they meant so much to me because I knew it all but killed him to expose himself to me. "I always have been."

"I know, Joe." Cheeks flushed and body burning in heat, I wrapped my arms around his neck and pressed my forehead to his as I rocked on top of him. "God, I could have you inside me forever and it wouldn't be long enough."

"I know what you mean," he bit out, cheeks just as flushed as mine, as he gripped my hips and thrust into me in a delicious rhythm. "I want in you constantly."

"Have you ever had that before?" I asked, breathless, as our bodies rocked and thrust together. "Mm . . . "

He shook his head and pressed a kiss to my lips. "Just with you."

"Don't leave me again, Joe."

His thrust faltered. "Molloy."

"Mm . . . don't."

His hands tightened on my hips as he deepened his thrust. "I won't."

"Mm . . . good." Blowing out a breath, I bit back a moan and buried my face in his neck. "Because I've got serious wifey feelings for you."

"Jesus, baby." Flipping me onto my back in one swift movement, he was back between my legs, pushing inside me. "Don't play with me."

Breathless, I spread myself open for him to have me. "I'm not playing, Joe." Taking his hand in mine, I pressed it to my chest and looked up at his flushed face. "I feel *everything* for you."

"You can have whatever you want from me," he whispered, thrusting deep inside of me. "It's yours." Dropping down on an elbow, he leaned in close and crushed his lips to mine. "Because I'm only doing life for you."

Engineering class

JOEY

"Oh my Jesus!" Alec ripped off his protective helmet and tossed it on top of my leaving cert project, causing me to burn a fucking hole right through his helmet. "Am I dead? Have I gone to heaven?"

"I don't know about dead, but you're definitely thick," I snapped, turning off the valve on the welder in my hands, and quenching the flame, as the stench of burning plastic filled my senses. "I could've taken the hand clean off ya. Put your fucking helmet back on before you go blind, asshole."

"I'm already seeing stars," he replied, pointing towards the front of the room when I removed my welding hood.

Donning a white lab coat over her tiny scrap of a school skirt, and with protective goggles perched on top of her head, Molloy looked like something out of medical porno. The top two buttons on her shirt were undone, and her tie was nestled between her tits like a glove.

"It's actually disgusting how lucky you are."

"Yeah," I wholeheartedly agreed. "I know."

She was all flirtatious smiles and banter with our teacher, Ballsy Goggin, who was lapping up the attention.

It didn't matter that the fucker was old enough to be her father.

He was looking just like every other asshole in the room.

"Jesus," Alec groaned from beside me. "I know you'll kill me for saying this, but I would do pretty much anything to get between those—".

"You're right. Finish that sentence and I *will* kill you." Setting the torch down, I pulled off my protective gloves and made a beeline for my girlfriend, while mentally taking note of every cheeky bastard wolf-whistling. I would settle those scores later.

"Hey, Joe," she acknowledged when I reached them. "I was just asking

Mr. Goggin if he could spare a student for twenty-minutes to help me out with my practical in Biology."

The fuck?

I frowned at her.

She returned my questioning look with a smile that said *go with it.*

"We're dissecting cow hearts today. Everyone's already paired up in class, sir, and I'm all alone at my station with no one to help me. I'm so nervous to dissect anything, that my teacher said I could have a student from another class accompany me in case I faint," she continued to say, batting her big green eyes at old Ballsy, who was falling for her bullshit hook, line, and sinker.

"Of course, Aoife, of course," he replied, slapping a hand on my shoulder. "Take young Joey here."

"Are you sure, sir?" Molloy beamed at him. "I'm not disrupting your class too much, am I?"

"Not at all," he replied, giving my shoulder another clap. "Will he do?"

"Yes, he'll do just fine, sir," she replied, flicking her hair over her shoulder, as she caught ahold of my hand and practically dragged me out of the metal work room. "I'll bring him right back once I'm finished with him, sir."

"What the hell are you up to?" I laughed when we were in the corridor. "Biology? Fainting?" I stared at her. "They'd be hard stretched to find another girl in school who loves gory shit more than you, Molloy."

"Yeah, well, you're working this afternoon and I'm working tonight."

"So? I'll call over after."

"So, I want time with you *now*." Snatching my hand back up, she dragged me down the corridor before pushing me through one of the many do-not-enter doors scattered around school that were intended for emergencies only.

This particular door led to a dimly lit stairwell that, once followed to the end, led onto the pitch. "Here or my car?"

"What?" I laughed, allowing her to pull me flush against her. "You do know that I was in the middle of something back there."

"Wouldn't you prefer to be in the middle of my legs?"

Jesus.

She claimed my mouth with hers and pushed me roughly against the wall at my back, while her hands moved for my belt buckle.

"You're crazy," I growled, hips thrusting towards her, without an ounce of protest, as I watched her unzip my pants, yank my boxers down, and drop to her knees.

"Wait, wait, wait. Your car. We should definitely do this in your—" My eyes fluttered shut when her tongue circled the head of my dick. "Mm . . . never mind."

"Mm . . ." Purring like a kitten, she took me into her mouth, while she pulled on my shaft with her hand.

"You're a dangerous fucking girl," I choked out, hissing out a sharp breath when she gave my nuts a warning squeeze. "You're a perfect fucking girl."

"Mm," came her approving purr as she deep throated me like the champ she was, choking and gagging and coming back for more every time.

Knotting my fingers in her hair with one hand, I used the other to wipe a rogue tear from her cheek. "Don't choke yourself, baby."

"Mm," she gagged, and the pressure was fucking unreal on my shaft. "Mm . . ." Unwilling to slow her pace, she upped the ante, pulling on me harder and quicker while she choked on my cock.

"I'm going to cum."

"Mmm."

"Pull back."

"Mm-mm."

"I'm going to cum in your mouth, Molloy."

She grabbed my ass and sucked me in deeper. "*Mmm . . .*"

"Oh fuuuuck . . ." Feeling everything inside of me tighten to the point of pain, I let my head fall back and fucked her mouth until the pressure in my balls released with a sudden jerk. "Watch the teeth."

"Mmm."

Hips bucking wildly, I came hard in her mouth, as my thighs shook from the instant relief. "Jesus . . . "

"Woo," she breathed, flopping back on her heels, as she dragged in several mouthfuls of air. "That's a personal best." Wiping the corner of her mouth, she climbed to her feet and readjusted her ponytail, while giving me devilish wink. "Feeling better, stud?"

"Yeah." All I could do was lean against the wall and nod at the powerhouse of a girl, who could suck dick like a hoover. "Uh, thanks?"

"Meh." She shrugged and waved a hand around. "I figured I owed you a blowy."

"I, uh . . . " Shaking my head to clear the lusty haze in my head, I reached down and put my dick away, feeling a swell of heat at the memory of her mouth on me. Instantly, I was sporting a solid-semi. "Sorry for the, uh, for the mess."

"Oh please." She rolled her eyes. "If I didn't want you to cum in my mouth, I would have stopped you, and if I didn't want to swallow, I wouldn't have."

Fuck me.

What was I supposed to say to that?

"Thank you?" It seemed like the appropriate phrase given that she had blown my world with her tongue. "Seriously, thank you."

"Such good manners," she teased, reaching up to pat my cheek before moving for the door. "Don't worry, pookie. I plan on cashing in my love chip later."

"Love chip?" Chuckling, I followed her back into the hallway. "Should I know what that means?"

"It means you should neck a few Red Bulls before you come over tonight," she replied, fist-bumping me before skipping off in the direction of the labs. "Because you won't be getting much sleep, my friend."

Weighing scales and Ouija boards

JOEY

"What the hell are you doing?" I asked, standing in Molloy's bedroom doorway, as I took in the sight of her standing on her mother's bathroom weighing scales, in a skimpy red bra and grey granny knickers.

"Oh good, you're here." Huffing out a breath, she stomped over to the door and dragged me inside her room before closing her door and locking it. "I'm having a crisis."

"You're having a crisis?" I couldn't stop my eyes from trailing over her glorious body. "*I'm* having a crisis just looking at ya."

"Well, simmer down, stud, because I'm having a serious problem here."

"What's the problem?"

"I've put on weight."

"No, you haven't."

"Yes, I have," she argued, blowing a blonde strand of hair off her face. "I've ripped the ass out of my jeans."

I pressed a fist to my mouth to stop my laughter.

"It's not funny." Narrowing her eyes, she slapped my shoulder. "Don't say anything about the size of my ass."

"I love your ass," I tried to coax, holding my hands up. "Your mother probably shrank your jeans in the tumble dryer."

"*No*, because when I asked her about it, she said she dried them on the clothes *line*," my girlfriend cried dramatically. "And then Kev said that I've an ass like a blowfish's face."

Now, I did laugh.

Loudly.

"Oh my god. You're such a turncoat!" she screamed, spinning on her heels and stalking back to the weighing scales in the middle of her bedroom floor.

"Oh, come on, Molloy." Groaning, I dropped my gear bag on the floor and walked over to her bed. "You're not turning into one of those self-conscious girls, are ya?"

"I gained weight, asshole," she shot back. "I never said I wasn't beautiful."

"There's my vain baby."

"Seven pounds, Joe," she declared, arms flailing wildly, as her gaze flicked from my face to the mechanical scales she was standing on. "I've gained seven pounds since Christmas! Can't you see it?"

Yeah, I could see it.

I'd been with the girl long enough to know every inch of her body, every freckle, scar, and curve, so the fact that she was recently sporting a few extra pounds wasn't something that skipped my attention.

Her clothes, when she decided to wear them, clung to her hips and thighs in a way that they hadn't a few months ago, but I sure as hell wasn't complaining – especially since those pounds seemed to have shifted directly to her tits and ass.

To be honest, I thought she looked sexier than ever, but I wasn't nearly suicidal enough to bring her weight up in conversation.

Especially when I was already skating on thin ice.

Whether it was to compliment her or not, I knew my role in this relationship, and had my lines rehearsed off by heart . . .

Hey, Joe, have I put on weight?
Where? Your imagination?

Hey Joe, does my belly jiggle?
You'd have to have a belly for it to jiggle, and you clearly don't.

Hey Joe, you think she has a better figure than me?
Nobody has a better body than you.

Girls were dangerous creatures with hidden meanings behind every word they spurted, and Molloy was no exception to the rule.

She might be my best friend, and there was very little I held back from her these days, but I had enough of my balls still attached to know that there were two crucial no-go topics that should be avoided at all times.

The first was weight – *her* weight, to be exact, because apparently, she could comment on my appearance to her heart's content, and suffer no such consequences.

The second, and most crucial, topic of conversation to *never* enter into was the one about previous relationships; or in my case the girls I had fucked in the past.

Yeah, that was a huge no-no.

Again, it didn't matter that I had to sit in a classroom with her old boyfriend, knowing that, at one point in time, he'd had his fingers and tongue inside her.

No, being pissed about the four-year relationship she had shared with another guy was totally unreasonable, but so much as acknowledging a girl I'd been with, regardless of it being a one off, was a mortal sin.

Because you put your penis inside her, was the excuse I was given any time I pointed out the double standards.

You put his penis in your mouth, I felt like shouting back, but I had the wherewithal to keep my mouth shut and not open that particular can of worms.

"There's nothing there, Molloy." I leaned back on my elbows, thoroughly enjoying the floor show, as my girlfriend pranced around in her underwear. "You're fucking gorgeous."

"Yeah, I know that," she huffed, catching ahold of my hand and dragging me over to the weighing scales. "But now I'm carting an extra seven pounds of gorgeous around."

"The scales are wrong."

"Three times?"

"You do realize this floor is uneven," I tried to placate. "You're never going to get an accurate reading up here, Molloy."

"I'm not?"

"No, you're not," I coaxed, continuing to fill her up with the bullshit she needed from me. "I should know. It was fucking awful trying to measure these rooms for wardrobes. This whole house is out of alignment."

She looked up at me with a hopeful expression. "Really?"

"Really, really." Nodding, I hooked an arm around her waist and lifted her off the scales before setting her down. "Now, let's get rid of this bullshit."

"I'll check one more time—"

"No, you won't," I warned, snatching up the scales and moving for her door. "Don't let me catch you fucking around with this thing again." Unlocking her door, I stepped into the landing and shoved the scales on the top shelf of the hot press before returning to her. "I swear those damn things do more damage to girls than Ouija boards."

Molloy laughed. "How can you compare a weighing scale to a Ouija board?"

"Easy." I shrugged. "They both summon demons."

"I am completely fuckable, though, aren't I, Joe?" she asked, hands on her hips. "You still think I'm the business, right? A few extra pounds or not?"

"Oh, you are beyond fuckable," I coaxed, closing the space between us. "And your business is the only business I want to get caught up in."

"Smooth." Grinning, she hooked an arm around my neck and pulled my face down to hers. "Give me a kiss."

"Speaking of getting caught up in business . . ." I trailed my hand down to the waistband of her big-ass granny knickers and pinged the elastic. "Please tell me these aren't what I think they are."

"Afraid so." She laughed against my lips. "I'm spotting, which means . . ."

"You're due on," I groaned, letting my head fall back. "Fuck my life."

"Come on, stud." Reaching for my hand, she tugged me over to her bed and winked mischievously. "I'm sure we can be inventive."

"You know, sometimes I really," I breathed, trailing after her. "Love my life."

Late bloomers

AOIFE

Late night visits and secret rendezvous became the norm for us, and as the days turned into weeks, and the winter made way for spring, the mile-high wall that Joey had spent a lifetime erecting around his heart continued to lower.

It wasn't that his home life had become any easier; the opposite would be a closer comparison. The fights with his dad had significantly worsened, resulting in deeper mood swings and darker bruises, but his eyes remained clear and his head focused.

Most of the time, that intense focus seemed to remain honed in on me, and I wasn't complaining. He spent every second of his spare time with me and having him close settled my anxiety.

Because when he was with me, I could keep him safe.

When he was with me, he was sober and unharmed.

"What the hell are you doing?" my brother demanded when he walked into the living room on Sunday night.

Mam and Dad had gone out for a drink, and Joey and I were thrown down on the couch, watching *You're A Star* on RTE, and arguing over who we thought should win the singing competition.

I was rooting for the siblings from Westmeath, while Joey was rooting for an aneurysm to put him out of his misery, or so he continued to tell me.

Secretly, I think he liked the siblings, too.

"What?" I stared at Kev in confusion before looking down at myself. Dressed in sweatpants and a baggy t-shirt, with my legs sprawled over my boyfriend's lap, I couldn't be accused of being too revealing. "What did I do?"

"It's not what you did," Kev groaned, pointing at the plate of food balancing on my lap. "It's what you're eating." He shook his head in disgust. "Nachos and chocolate spread?" He gaped at me in horror from across the living room. "Oh my god, are you mixing the chocolate with *mayonnaise?*"

"Hey, don't knock it until you try it," I replied, tossing back another mouthful of deliciousness. "So . . . good."

"You are sick." He looked to Joey. "Are you responsible for this?"

"Nothing your sister does surprises me anymore, lad," Joey mused, stretching his legs out on the coffee table.

"So, you don't think what she's doing is beyond sick?"

"Hey." Joey shrugged noncommittally. "Whatever she wants to put in her mouth is fine by me."

"You *would* say that," Kev replied, repressing a shudder.

I snorted. "Spare me the cynicism, Kev. I'm eating nachos, not sucking his dick."

"Again, fine by me," Joey interjected with a smirk.

"You two are sick," Kev muttered, turning on his heels, and stalking out of the room. "Sick, I tell you."

"Put it there." I raised my bare foot in the air, and Joey scowled at me for a long moment before relenting and indulging me with a high-five to the sole of my foot.

"So, you'll never credit what happened while I was at the pitch with the kids yesterday."

"*Ooh*, gossip." I grinned wickedly. "Tell me."

"Shannon went out with friends for the day."

"For real?"

"Yeah." He nodded. "Apparently, she went off yesterday afternoon and didn't come back until late. Spent the day with Claire and Lizzie."

"I'm guessing this rarely happens?"

"Try never," he replied, snatching up the remote and flicking through the channels. "The old man went batshit when she came home last night. Apparently, she'd only arrived back when I walked in the door from work."

"Which explains this," I whispered sadly, fingers grazing the fresh bruising on his neck.

"Don't worry," he was quick to placate. "I handled it. Shannon's grand."

"I wasn't worried." *About her, at least.*

"She has *friends*, Molloy," he said then, sounding as close to content as ever I'd heard him. "An actual social life. She's not hiding behind her bedroom door, listening to music and burying her nose in books. She's going out."

"So, Tommen *is* suiting her." I smiled. "All of that worrying was for nothing."

"We'll see," he replied, gaze flicking briefly to me, before returning to the match on TV that he had so smoothly switched on. "It's still early days."

"Or could it be possible that your baby sister is growing claws?"

"Christ, I hope so."

"Yeah." *Me, too.* "You have to remember that she's almost sixteen now, Joe," I reminded him. "With hormones, and feelings, and a mind of her own." I ruffled his hair and smiled. "It was bound to happen at some stage."

"I was worried it wouldn't," he admitted gruffly.

"All flowers bloom, Joe, even the late ones," I told him. "And sometimes, it's the late blooming flower that makes the biggest impact."

Rolling in the hay

JOEY

It was almost midnight on a Friday night, and instead of doing something productive, like sleeping in an actual bed, I found myself slumped on top of a stack of bales, with my girlfriend nestled between my legs, and a pink, fluffy blanket slung over us.

The majority of our classmates from Sixth Year 3 were crammed into Podge's hay-shed, having been smuggled onto his parents' farm on the back of a tractor trailer.

To be fair, we had no business being here, but when the idea arose in class this morning, a haphazard plan was thrown together and here we were.

The rain was pelting down on the tin roof, the drink was flying, the tunes were pumping from Neasa's Murphy's battery operated boombox, and the craic was ninety.

Most of us here had endured one another's company five days a week for almost six years now, and there was a definite sense of comradery between us.

We'd grown up together, suffered through all of the teenage bullshit, fights, bitching and hardships.

Hell, a good portion of those in attendance knew each other on an intimate level, but being here now almost felt like we had come full circle.

Knowing that in a couple of months, we would all go our separate ways should have made me feel some semblance of sadness and anxiety, but it didn't.

The rest of my class could shoot off in whatever direction they wanted after the leaving cert, just as long as I got to keep the girl in my arms.

"I bet you've never spent a Friday night rolling in the hay, devil-tits?"

"You'd be surprised how I've spent my Friday nights, Al," Casey laughed, readjusting her woolly hat before accepting the naggin of vodka he held out for her.

"Jesus, lad, could you be any more conspicuous?" Podge demanded, gesturing to the hi-vis coat that Alec was wearing. "You're not at your Saturday job, Al. You could have left the construction site jacket at home."

"Ooh, get you and your big words," Alec grumbled, sparking up a rollie. "Fuck off, ya swot. I haven't a notion of what you're talking about."

"Conspicuous," Neasa chuckled. "It means you're not being very discreet, Al."

"Discreet about what?"

"About the fact that we're not meant to be here," Podge argued. "And you can't be smoking in here, either. The bales are dried out, lad. One rogue flame and this place will go up like a Christmas tree."

"Don't mind you, farmer fucking John with your big words and laying down the law. If I want a smoke, I'll have one."

"Could you be any more of a townie?'

"Better a townie than a farmer with a big culchie head up on him."

"Hey now, there's nothing wrong with farmers," Casey chimed in with a wink. "Plenty of money hidden under the mattress."

"Plenty of sheep, too."

"Actually, we're tillage and beef farmers."

"So?"

"So, we fatten bullocks, asshole, not sheep."

"Joe, I feel sick," Molloy declared, distracting me from our friends' antics. She thrust her half-empty can of Dutch Gold into my hand and groaned. "Seriously, my stomach is turning."

"Well, take it handy," I replied, snaking an arm around her waist and pulling her closer. "Don't mind what the rest of these assholes are doing." My lips brushed against her ear as I spoke. "It's a marathon, not a sprint."

She looked fucking adorable in her puffy white coat and pink bobble hat, scarf, and matching gloves, with her long blonde hair braided in two plaits that reached the middle of her back. The epitome of fashion, regardless of the venue, she donned a light blue tracksuit she liked to call her knock-off juicy, whatever the fuck that meant, and a pair of black wellies.

"My stomach's not turning from drink," she grumbled, twisting around to look up at me. "It's turning from having to look at those two."

My gaze flicked to where she was pointing and a deep shudder rolled through me.

"Jesus."

From where we were sitting, we had a perfect view of Ricey and Danielle.

"I can't decide if he's trying to kiss her lips or eat them?" I mused, ignoring my phone as it vibrated in my pocket.

"Both," Molloy laughed. "Uh, Joe, it's so bad, huh?"

"Yeah, it's pretty bad, Molloy."

"He has this really wide tongue," she continued to tell me, like this was important information her current boyfriend needed to know about her ex. "Which would be a pretty great asset if the boy actually learned how to use it." Snickering, she added, "But he's one of those 'three flicks of the bean and I'm done' kind of guys."

"What a lovely mental image to inflict upon me," I drawled, tone laced with sarcasm. "Ricey's wide tongue on my girlfriend's pussy."

She threw her head back and laughed. "Trust me, it was never a pleasurable experience."

"Do you want me to puke?" I accused. "Because I'll puke, Molloy."

"Oh please," she snorted, digging me with her elbow. "Like you haven't had your dick in half of the females in attendance tonight."

"Who?"

"The girls in our class."

"Which girls?"

"Take your pick. You've been with most of them."

"When?"

"Joey." She gave me a hard look. "Don't piss down my back and tell me it's raining."

What could I say to that?

Nothing that wouldn't result in her going full-blown drama queen on me, so I sensibly kept my mouth shut and took a sip from her can instead.

"Ha. See? You can't even deny it. You're such a slut," she accused, snaking a hand under my hoodie to pinch my nipple. "Did you lick her out, Joe?" Her eyes narrowed. "What am I saying? Of course you did. Nobody is as good as you are at giving head unless they've been around the block a time or thousand."

I knew better than to respond to that, too.

I remembered all too well how Molloy had reacted when I admitted to having sex with Danielle back in third year.

I'd been given the silent treatment for weeks and we had only been friends at the time.

I was a quick enough learner to know that it would be less painful to chew my own arm off than willingly wade back into that kind of dangerous territory.

It was a trap, nothing I said could benefit me, so I took a mental vow of silence and kissed her cheek instead.

"Hm." Huffing out a breath, Molloy cupped my cheek with her glove-covered hand and gave me a hard look. "It's a good thing I love you."

Yeah, it was.

She cracked a smile then and leaned in to kiss me, smearing the sticky lip-gloss on my lips.

"I hate that stuff," I grumbled, trailing my tongue over my bottom lip and tasting *her*. "You don't need to wear any of it. You look good, baby."

"I know I do." She grinned back at me and tapped my nose with her glove covered finger. "I wear it for me, not you."

I shrugged. "Fair enough."

"So, are you doing okay?" Twisting sideways so that she was sitting on my lap, Molloy hooked an arm around my neck and snuggled into my chest. "You good, stud?"

I knew what she meant and I nodded slowly. "I'm good, queen."

"Are you going to answer that?" she asked then, alluding to the phone that was still vibrating in my pocket. "It's been going off all night."

It didn't take a genius to know that it was my mother calling, and it sure as hell didn't take any guesses to know what she wanted, either.

"No," I replied, knowing that if I did answer my phone, there was a very big chance that I would have to cut and run.

Surprise flashed in her eyes. "No?"

"No," I confirmed, tightening my arms around her. "I'm here with you."

"Oh." She beamed up at me. "You are *so* getting the good loving tonight."

"Is that so?"

"Uh-huh." Hooking an arm around my neck, she pulled me close and stroked her cold nose against mine. "Then what would you say to having a little roll around in the hay?"

"I'd say you're a bad influence on me," I laughed against her lips.

"Really?" she purred. "Because I'd say that I'm an even better influence when I'm *on* you and you're *in* me."

"If you're trying to make me hard, then mission accomplished, Molloy."

"I'm trying to get my hole, Joe."

"Jesus, your mouth is terrible."

"What was that?" she teased, eyes twinkling with mischief as she climbed off my lap, reached for my hand and pulled me up. "You want to do terrible things to my mouth?"

Grinning like a dope, I slid off the bale we'd been sitting on and trailed after her, ignoring the wolf-whistles from our classmates, as she led me behind a stack of bales until we were out of sight.

"Now." With her back to a heaving stack of bales, she pulled my body flush against hers and grinned up at me. "Where were we?"

"I was behaving myself." Hips thrusting against her, I cupped her neck and pulled her face up for a kiss. "*You* were trying to lead me astray."

"Don't behave yourself, Joe," she breathed against my lips, as she removed her gloves and reached for the waistband of my sweats. "I like you so much better when you're bad."

"I'm always bad, Molloy."

"Which is exactly why I'm so in love with you." She slid her hand into my jocks to grip me. "Well, that and your big dick."

Caught red-handed

AOIFE

"Aoife Christina Molloy. I know you're in here, bitch. Your school bag is on the floor."

"Oh shit." My eyes widened in horror and I sprang upright, colliding with the steering wheel in front of me. "Is that Casey—"

"Shh." A warm hand clamped over my mouth, and I was yanked backwards to rest against my boyfriend's bare chest. "Less talking, more fucking, Molloy."

"But she's right out—"

My words broke off when he claimed my mouth, and continued to pump me from behind, thrusting deep and fast.

"Oh, Jesus," I moaned, tearing my lips away from his, as I sagged against the steering wheel, gripping it tightly, while my hips bucked restlessly on his lap. "Don't stop."

Reaching a hand between my thighs, he located my clit like the champ he was and thumbed it with just enough pressure to make my toes curl. There were no fumbling fingers from this boy. He knew *exactly* where to touch me, and how much force to use.

"Hey, assholes, the windows might be tinted in this fancy-ass Range Rover, but it's still rocking."

"Go away, Case," I cried out, breathless. "I'm ... busy."

"Yeah, busy getting your hole, you little whore," my best friend grumbled. "We were meant to go shopping after school, remember? I waited at the bus stop for an hour—"

"Fuck *off*, Case!" Joey bit out, as he cupped my breast in his free hand and quickened his pace. "Jesus, baby. Your friend is a fucking disaster."

"Ignore her," I cried out.

"How?" he demanded. His thighs were shaking, sending vibrations shooting through my body, which was a sure way to tell that he was close. "She's got her face pressed to the window."

"Omigod, Casey, go away!" I screamed out, chasing my release as my body grew more frantic with need. "*Please*."

"Okay, fine," I heard her call back. "Tony's just after pulling up in the tow-truck, but whatever."

"Aw, shit!"

Joey was out of me in an instant, literally throwing me off his lap and onto the plush leather passenger seat, as he scrambled to pull his clothes back on.

"Your old fella went to Skibbereen for a catalytic converter for Johnny Crowley's Subaru," he panted, breathless. "He shouldn't be back for at least another hour."

"You could've finished," I laughed, slipping my bra back on and fumbling with the buttons of my school shirt before reaching for my skirt. "She's only messing, Joe. My dad's not outside."

"Hello, Casey, love," I heard my father say. "Strange seeing you at the garage."

We both froze.

I locked eyes on Joey. "Oh . . . "

"Shit," he finished for me, eyes growing wide as saucers.

"Hey, T-Daddy. I was just looking for Aoife."

"Ah, she'll be over at The Dinniman around this time of the evening. Any sign of young Joey around the place?"

"Aw *Jesus Christ*," Joey practically whimpered, as he hastily slid his arms back into his overalls and fell out of the driver's door and swiftly slammed it shut behind him, leaving me hidden behind the tinted windows. "I'm here, Tony."

"What were ya doing in John Kavanagh's old doll's pride and joy, boyo?"

"Just, ah, getting a feel for it." There was a brief pause before he added, "Closest I'll ever get to sitting behind the wheel of a Range Rover."

"I know the feeling, boyo."

"You're back early."

"I only went and forgot my wallet, didn't I?"

"Disaster."

"Not completely. Come on into the office for a cuppa, and let me tell ya about this old doll I met broken down on the road."

A few moments later, the passenger door swung open and I was faced with a grinning Casey. "Okay, the coast is clear. Daddy took baby-daddy to the office."

"Baby-daddy?"

"It was a joke, babe. Chill."

"Not funny, Case."

Blowing out a shaky breath, I readjusted my skirt and scrambled out of the car, hunching low as I crept towards the exit, resisting the urge to tumble and roll in my bid to escape.

"I thought you were joking about Dad." A relieved laugh escaped me when we reached the footpath. "God, that was close."

"You know," Casey mused, falling into step beside me. "I should be mad at you for blowing me off to blow him, but I'm going let you off the hook this time, since he has such a pretty cum face."

"You didn't see his cum face."

"Maybe not, but if those flushed cheeks are anything to go by, then I can use my imagination."

"Casey," I warned. "Don't be looking at him like that."

"Like what?" She laughed, holding her hands up. "Like he's the epitome of sex on legs? Because, news flash, Aoif, the boy is divine."

"The boy is mine," I warned. "So, find some other epitome to admire."

"Oh, retract the claws." Hooking an arm around my neck, she pulled me in for a side-hug. "You know I would never ever, *ever*, in a million years go there."

"Hm." Reaching into the pocket of my skirt, I withdrew a lollypop and tore off the wrapper. "It just irks me sometimes, you know?" Sticking the pop into my mouth, I dropped my head to rest on hers, and mumbled, "He's been with a lot of girls from school, Case. A *lot* of them."

"So, he enjoyed himself," she said. "Name one boy in our year that hasn't?"

"There's enjoying yourself, and there's spreading yourself thin, Case."

"Babe." Sobering her features, she gave me a sympathetic look. "Don't let those kinds of thoughts in. They'll only screw up your happy, little love bubble."

"Yeah, I know."

"Do you?"

I shrugged.

She rolled her eyes. "You're dumb."

"How'd you figure?" I laughed.

"Because you should be deliriously happy," she explained. "Not worrying about who he's been with in the past. Those girls are in the past for a reason, Aoif." Waggling her brows, she added, "Besides, I sincerely doubt Danielle Long ever rocked his world in the front seat of a Range Rover."

I smirked. "True."

"Besides, Danielle might have been his first bang, but you're his first love," she added, bumping hips with me. "Trust me, that leaves one hell of a residual mark on a boy."

"Well, he's left his mark on me, Case."

"Yeah," my best friend agreed, giving me a peculiar look.

"What?" I asked, unsettled by the way she was looking at me. "What's with the face?"

"Nothing, I just thought you had more to add," she replied, still looking intensely at me. "Because you can tell me anything, Aoif."

"I know." I smiled. "Right back at you, Case."

Ho ho ho, Joe

JOEY

"Who's up for a Chinese?" my father announced in a jovial tone, when he sauntered into the kitchen late Saturday evening, with two brown paper bags in his arms. "My numbers came up at the bookies and there's plenty for everyone."

With the plastic peeling from a shop-bought frozen lasagna in my hands, I watched as my mother and siblings all filed into the kitchen after him.

"Come on, boy," he said, slapping the bags down on the table, while my mother hovered close by with a stack of plates. "Throw that shit away," he commanded, waving a hand towards me. "There's a chicken curry in here for you, too."

Doing the complete opposite, I walked over to the bin, tossed the plastic inside, and then returned to place my lasagna in the oven, ignoring the swell of bitterness that rose up as I watched the rest of my family – Shannon included – line up with their plates, like a scene straight from 1840's Ireland.

Don't be so fucking weak, I wanted to scream, *his soup kitchen has consequences.*

"Didn't ya hear me, boy?" Dad barked, as they all took up position around the table like a big happy family.

"I heard you."

"Then what are you waiting for?" He kicked out a chair for me to join them. "Grab a plate and sit down."

"I don't want any."

"Ah, go on, will ya? You need to bulk up a bit, boy."

"I said I don't want your food."

"Why not?"

"Because it comes with strings attached and I'd rather starve."

"Joey." Mam dropped her fork and sighed. "Please. Don't start trouble. Your father is trying."

Yeah, that's what I'm afraid of.

Folding my arms across my chest, I glared at him when I said, "I don't know what you're angling at, old man, but you're not fooling me with your bullshit."

"If you don't want to eat with your family, and you can't be civil to your father, then you can leave," Mam instructed, reaching across the table to place a calming hand on my father's balled fist.

The other four were rigid in their seats, with their heads bowed, and their attention on anything but our father.

"I'll go when my food's ready," I bit out, jaw clenched.

"Just leave it, Marie. There's no pleasing that fella. Eat your food," Dad ordered, and like a well-trained soldier, my mother fell into line, obeying his every command by dropping her gaze from me and shoveling a forkful of rice into her mouth.

Shoulders bunched tight with tension, I turned my back to them, concentrating on my food in the oven, instead.

Twenty minutes later, there was a knock at the door, and I felt my body both tense up in anxiety and sag in relief at the same time.

Molloy was supposed to be coming over tonight. I didn't want it, at least, I didn't want her *here*, but I was working really hard on keeping the lines of communication open, and putting momentous effort into *not* shutting her out.

That was all she wanted from me.

Honesty was only thing she ever asked me for.

It seemed to be working in my favor, too. The more I let her in, the more she rewarded me.

Sometimes, I felt like a fucking dog bringing her a stick just for a belly rub, but I had grown too addicted to her affection to slam the brakes now.

Knowing there was a ninety-nine percent chance that I would find her on the other side of the front door, I moved before anyone else could, hurrying through the hallway and swinging the door inwards.

"Shh." She pressed a finger to her lips when I opened my mouth to greet her.

Grinning devilishly, she unhooked the belt of her long black coat and pulled the lapels open and winked.

My eyes quickly trailed down her body, taking in the sight of what she was wearing – or should I say the lack of what she was wearing.

Suspender stockings, a frilly garter belt, lacey, barely-there thong, and matching bra all in the color of crimson greeted me on what was, by far, the man up stairs' greatest creation.

She was shaped like every fella's wet dream, with this narrow little waist that curved out into a pair of thick hips and a round, peachy ass. She had legs for days that the red stockings enhanced further. Her hair was poker-straight, loose, and reached the frilly garter belt that was hugging her in all the right places.

And her tits? Jesus, don't even get me started on her double-ds, as they strained against the scrap of a bra attempting to contain them.

Donned up to the nines with a face full of make-up, and crimson painted lips, she looked like she belonged on the cover of a fucking magazine, not a doorstep in Ballylaggin.

The miniature-sized Santa hat perched on top of her head was the icing on the cake.

I shook my head, at a complete loss. "What. The. Fuck."

Beaming back at me, she waggled her brows and purred, "Ho, ho, ho, Joe."

"Christmas was two months ago, Molloy."

"I know. But I found it on a sale-rail in the city today and couldn't wait to try it on!" she squealed, clearly delighted with herself, as she did a little dance in her skyscraper black stilettos. Hitching her coat up, she twirled around to give me a 360 view, not giving two shits who saw her. "Fifteen-euro, Joe. Down from eighty-five! Can you believe it?"

I heaved out an impressed breath, that had nothing to do with the price tag, while my dick grew hard enough to cut diamond. "Jesus Christ."

"Well?" she gushed, giving me – and half the street – another twirl. "What do you think, huh?"

"There's only one head doing the thinking for me now, Molloy, and it's not the one on my shoulders."

She threw her head back and laughed. "Exactly the reaction I was looking for."

"Jesus Christ." Stepping outside, I quickly grabbed the lapels of her coat and yanked it shut, before glancing over her shoulder to see if any fuckers from my road were lurking.

If they were, then my girlfriend had just given them a glorious fucking peek-a-boo.

"I'm willing, I'm waxed, and I'm raring to go," she declared, hooking an arm around my neck, and pulling me in for a kiss. "Seriously, I was listening to Mazzy Star's *Fade Into You* on the drive over here, which, FYI, is our second song, and now I'm in the mood to get *naked* with you."

"Are *you* high?"

She rolled her eyes and gave me a *you wish* look. "I'm just happy. I had the best day shopping with the girls, and now I'm here with you. And besides, we never got a chance to have that un-Virgin Mary sex for your birthday."

"Fair enough—"

She kissed me again, deeper this time, fingers knotting in my hair. "But first, I need you to feed me."

"My dick?"

"Later." She laughed against my lips. "But first, fuel me up, because I'm *starving*."

"I've something cooking inside."

"What?"

"Lasagna."

"I *love* lasagna."

"I know."

"Where's it from?"

"Supervalu."

"Their own brand?"

"Only one I can afford."

"That's my favorite one!"

"Yeah, Molloy, I *know*."

"So, you cook, you clean, you change nappies, you fix my car, you give me unlimited orgasms," she teased. Stepping back, she snatched up her little Santa hat and slipped it into the pocket of her coat. "Keep this up and I might just have to hang onto you, Joey Lynch."

"Whatever you say, Molloy," I chuckled, shaking my head. "Come on." Grabbing her overnight bag from the ground, I threw it over my shoulder, and led her inside. "Fair warning; he's in rare form."

You'll always have me

AOIFE

Back in the early days of our relationship, the only hatred I had felt towards any member of the Lynch family was Joey's father.

However, as the months rolled into years, and Joey opened up further, giving me exclusive access to his life behind closed doors, not only had I found my disdain for Teddy reach extraordinary heights, but the animosity I felt towards Marie had shot off the charts.

Joey's mother made me feel stabby, which frustrated me on a number of levels, because I had been raised to show compassion to the less fortunate.

And in truth, Marie Lynch deserved to be pitied.

Problem was, the way she treated her second born, the disgusting way she favored Shannon and the younger boys above him, had slowly caused any ounce of compassion I had for the woman to disintegrate.

I was in love with her son.

Joey was, in my biased opinion, the best thing to come out of Teddy and Marie Lynch's fucked-up marriage, and the fact that his own *mother* couldn't see beyond his jagged edges, made me furious.

Because if she only took the time to peel back the layers, she would see what an incredible human being she had brought into the world.

Sure, he was reckless and brash, stubborn and short-tempered, but he was also selfless and thoughtful, determined and dedicated.

He was loyal to a fault, and even though he tried his very best to hide it from the world, my god did he have a heart the size of the moon.

My boyfriend's biggest mistake, and I included his drug abuse in this statement because I was a firm believer that both were significantly connected, was that he offered unconditional love and fealty to a woman who would never deserve it.

I had no doubt that, given half a chance, Joey would have zero qualms about throwing his father under the bus – both physically and proverbially – and then take the greatest of pleasure in pissing on his grave.

Teddy Lynch was a scumbag, rat-bastard, without a single redeemable bone in his body, but he wasn't the parent that Joey couldn't walk away from.

Marie was the only one with access to that particular pedestal, and instead of doing the right thing for Joey – for all of her children – she kept him chained to this house.

Teddy was the house in which they were stuck inside, and Marie was the key that refused to the turn in the lock and *free* them.

Because, despite his shortcomings, Joey Lynch held the morals of a *good* man.

His morals would never allow him to leave his siblings, and his loyalty would never allow him to leave *her*.

Therefore, when it came to feeling sympathy for Marie Lynch, I was the Sahara Desert.

Bone dry.

Shaking my head to clear my thoughts, I slapped on my brightest smile, and followed Joey into the kitchen, in awe of the mammoth effort I knew it had taken him to let me through the door. The atmosphere inside his house was always malignant and void of happiness. Unease settled heavily on my shoulders every time I stepped over the threshold, but it was important to me that Joey knew that I accepted every part of him. He had nothing to be ashamed of, and he never needed to hide a thing from me.

His family were sitting around the kitchen table when I walked into the room, and the coldness I usually received from his parents felt particularly arctic tonight.

"Hey, Aoife," Tadhg and Ollie both chimed, while Shannon offered me a timid wave before quickly bowing her head, eyes trained on the table. Poor little Sean didn't say a word, but his wide-eyed expression assured me that he felt incredibly confused. *And frightened.*

"Hey boys," I replied, forcing myself to smile and keep my feelings in check, as I kept my back to the fridge, and my eyes trained on the table. "Hey, Shan."

"H-hi," she whisper-croaked, hiding her face behind a mountain of brown hair.

"Aoife," Marie acknowledged with a small nod, her anxious gaze flicking from me, to Joey, before settling on her husband, who was heading up the table and making no secret of his obvious ogling of my body. I had a full-length coat on, but I may as well have been naked for all the good it did me around this man. "I didn't know you were coming over this evening."

"I invited her," Joey was quick to intercept the conversation and say, thumb smoothing over my knuckles before he released my hand and moved towards the oven. "She's staying over tonight."

"It would have been nice to be told that we were having a visitor," his mother said quietly.

"I pay my way in this house," was my boyfriend's cool response.

"Your father and I were hoping to make this a family night."

If she was trying to make me uncomfortable enough to offer to leave, then it wouldn't work. I had no intentions of going anywhere without her son.

"That sounds nice," I replied, giving her a false smile. "We're having a date night."

"Date night," his father scoffed. "And you're cooking dinner for her." He shook his head in disgust. "Are ya completely pussy-whipped by this one, boy?"

"As opposed to just plain whipping her?" Removing a tray of lasagna from the oven with a tea towel, he quickly set to work on plating it up. "And as for Aoife staying over, I wasn't aware I needed to ask your permission for shit."

"Don't get lippy, boy," his father warned, never taking his beady eyes off my legs. "This isn't a whore-house."

"It's not?" Joey drawled, tone dripping with cynicism, as he handed me a plate of food and a fork. Reaching around me, he grabbed a couple of cans of coke from the fridge and slid one into each pocket of his sweats. "Well, shit, you could've fooled me, considering it produces just as many unwanted pregnancies."

"Joey!" his mother snapped, looking mortified, while I bit down on my lip to stop the smile from spreading across my face. While my heart cheered *go on, baby, you tell those bastards.*

Tadhg made the mistake of laughing, which earned him a, "don't fucking start, boy," warning snarl from their father, as he slammed his fist down on the kitchen table, and extended his power.

Like dominos, I watched as five heads dropped in submission.

Or fear.

Not my one, though.

Not *my* Lynch.

Like a lone wolf standing on the outskirts of his family pack, Joey refused to bend or cower to the alpha.

"Don't start getting too big for your boots, boy," Teddy warned, glaring daggers at my boyfriend. "I have no problem knocking you back down to size."

"You want to throw down, old man?" Setting his plate down, Joey gestured for him to go for it. "Then fucking try it. I'm right here."

"Joey," Marie tried again, tone admonishing. "Stop trying to provoke trouble."

"Save your breath, Marie," Teddy said, eyes still locked on his son, but making no move to leave the table. "That little cunt isn't worth the energy."

"Thought not," Joey replied hotly. Shaking his head, he turned his attention to me. "Come on, Aoif." He gestured to the door. "Let's leave them to their *family* night."

I knew that Joey would erupt the minute we were alone, so it came as no surprise that, as soon as his bedroom door was closed behind us, he kicked it twice, released a pained roar, and then gave it a further four kicks before tossing his plate and our cokes on his dresser and running his hands through his hair.

After abusing his bedroom door, the same door he regularly fucked me against, he yanked it open and stalked out, returning a few minutes later with my overnight bag, a jar of mayonnaise, and a regenerated thirst for pummeling his door.

Smiling when he handed me the mayo, I padded over to his bed and sank down, letting him do his thing and process, while I occupied myself by scoffing down every morsal of food on my plate.

When his knuckles were aching, his breathing was ragged, and his anger was spent, only then he did he slump down on the bed beside me, with his plate on his lap, and a dejected look on his face.

When he made no move to eat, I stabbed a piece of his lasagna with my fork and held it up to his mouth.

He stared at it for the longest time before finally accepting my offering and taking a bite.

I repeated the move another seven or eight times, feeding him when he wouldn't, until he shook his head, shoulders slumping in defeat.

Setting our plates on the windowsill next to his bed, I shifted closer until our shoulders were touching and leaned my cheek on his shoulder.

After a long beat, he exhaled a resigned breath and rested his head on top on mine. "This is the part where I go out and lose my mind."

Taking his hand in mine, I entwined our fingers and gave him a reassuring squeeze. "I know."

"I don't know how much more I can take," he admitted quietly, head bowed, gaze trained on our joined hands. "How much more he can push me until I snap and throw it all away."

"You've got another night in you," I told him, pressing a kiss to his shoulder. "You can hold on for one more night."

"Can I?"

"You've got this, Joey Lynch." I reached up and cupped his chin between my fingers and thumb, forcing him to look at me.

The lonesome look in his eyes almost broke me, but I forced myself to remain strong, allowing him to absorb all of the comfort, strength, and whatever else he needed from me. Because, God knows, the bastards downstairs would never give it to him.

"You've *got* this," I repeated, imploring him with my eyes to both *hear* me and *believe* in himself. "And I've got you."

"Yeah?"

I nodded. "Yeah."

His lips were on mine then, hands pulling at the opening of my coat and tearing the fabric from my body, as he chased the physical connection he needed to ground himself in this moment.

Breathing hard, he tossed my coat on his bedroom floor and quickly reached for his t-shirt, whipping it over his head in one swift move.

Trembling with feelings and anticipation, I lay back on his bed, giving him unlimited access to my body.

When his big body came crashing down on me, pushing me deeper into the mattress, I felt myself slip deeper into his world, as I drowned in the love I felt for him, and he drowned in the physical affection that he had spent a lifetime being deprived of.

"Roll onto your back."

"Hm?"

"I didn't get all dolled up to be hidden in the sheets." I pushed at his chest. "I want you to see me."

Complying without objection, he rolled us over until he was underneath, with me perched on his lap. I grinned down at him and trailed my freshly painted red nails down his bare stomach. "Hey, stud."

His fingers flexed on my waist. "Hey, queen."

"Do you want to know a secret?"

He laughed. "I don't know, Molloy, do I?"

"I think you do."

"Okay." He nodded. "Tell me."

I crooked a finger. "You need to come closer."

He pulled up on his elbows. "Well?"

"Closer."

"How close do you need me?"

"This is perfect," I said approvingly, wrapping my arms around his neck when he sat straight up, with his chest flush against mine. "First, give me a kiss."

"Jesus, Molloy, just tell me already—"

"Ah-ah-ah. I want a kiss."

"Pain in my hole," he grumbled, hands moving to cup my ass, as he leaned in and pressed a drugging kiss to my lips.

"Mm." Pulling back before I lost myself in his lips, I used my thumb to wipe my smeared lipstick from his lips and smiled. "I have a peephole."

"A peephole."

"Uh-huh."

"This is your big secret?"

Grinning, I nodded. "You want to see?"

Joey stared at me for a long moment before blowing out a breath and shrugging. "Yeah, fuck it. I want to see."

"It's down here." Taking his hand, I placed it between my thighs and laughed when his fingers grazed me there. "Feel it?"

"That's not a peephole, Molloy," Joey muttered, pulling back to get a better look. "There's nothing there."

"I *know*." Clapping with delight, I lifted up on my knees to give him a proper look. "Crotchless knickers, Joe. What an incredibly useful invention, huh?"

"You know, sometimes I don't know if you use me as a soundboard for the crazy shit that goes on in your head or an accomplice," he admitted, thoroughly investigating my ensemble. "I'm down for either, by the way."

Thrilled that I had managed to coax him out of his bad mood, I took my chance and capitalized. "Want to know something else?"

"Hm?"

"You're a diamond, Joey Lynch." Cupping his face between my hands, I leaned in and kissed him tenderly. "You're one in a million."

"Oh Jesus," he chuckled against my lips, as he reached up and knotted his hand in my hair. "Should I be worried about where this is leading?"

"Nope." Shaking my head, I exhaled a contented sigh and pushed on his shoulders until he flopped down on his back. "Just wanted you to know that you're someone's favorite person in the world."

"Don't get soft on me, Molloy," he teased, but I could hear the emotion he was trying to hide in his voice.

Smiling, I leaned in close and kissed him again. This time, I wholeheartedly let myself get caught up in the moment, in the feel of his lips on mine, his hands on my body, skin on skin.

"You're someone's favorite person, too," he whispered a little while later, when he rolled me onto my back and settled between my legs.

"Oh really?"

He nodded. "Don't want to do this whole life gig without you, Molloy."

"You won't ever have to," I replied, reaching between our bodies to free his erection. "You'll always have me, Joe."

"I'm going to hold you to that," he whispered, pushing deep inside of me.

Food runs and future discussions

JOEY

It was Sunday night, Molloy was naked in my bed, sleeping soundly, with her head on my chest, and one of her legs draped over my thighs, and all I could think was; *I can't get deep enough inside of this girl.*

It was a strange way to feel, considering I hadn't spent much time out of her since last night, but I felt it anyway.

She had one of her random mix-CDs playing in the background, and as I listened to The Goo Goo Dolls' *Iris*, I found myself considering something I'd never given much thought to before.

The future.

With one arm behind my head, and the other cupping her cheek, I stared up at my bedroom ceiling, deep in thought.

We had a little more than three months until we sat our leaving cert exams.

Afterwards, there would need to be a discussion, where we both laid our cards on the table and decided if they aligned with the others.

Would her plans for the future match up with mine?

If they didn't, could we make it work?

Would she want to?

Would I?

I had wanted her since I was twelve years old, and now that I finally had her, I quickly realized that I would never stop *wanting* her.

I used to feel like an insect trapped in the unyielding web of lies my parents had spun around my life, but I now knew that the web my parents spun never held a flame to the one Molloy had weaved around my heart.

I was also achingly aware of the fact that there was a baby coming early in the summer.

Another Shannon.
Another Tadhg.
Another Ollie.
Another Sean.

And as much as I despised myself for it, I knew deep down that I couldn't do it again.

I *couldn't* raise another one of his children.

I wanted a life of my own.

More than that, I *wanted* a life with the girl in my bed.

She joked about rings, and weddings, and babies, but I didn't know if she was serious – or if it was something I was capable of giving her.

I didn't want marriage or babies, but the thought of her having those things with someone who wasn't me made me want to die.

The thought of her, years into the future, with another man's ring on her finger, or worse, another man's child in her stomach, made me want to burst into flames.

Deep down inside, I knew that it all came down to what I could and couldn't live with.

So, could I live with marriage and babies if that was what her future consisted of?

Could I live with it?

All I knew was that I couldn't live without her.

It wasn't an option.

Jesus, I was so fucking snared by this girl.

When the song ended, and Mazzy Star's *Fade Into You* drifted from my stereo, I felt her stir against my chest.

"Mm. I love this song." Snuggling in close, she draped an arm around my stomach and pressed a kiss to my bare skin. "I love you."

Wondering how the fuck I had managed to get this girl in the first place, let alone keep her around, I tilted my head to study her.

Naked as the day she was born, and with an aura of contentment floating from her in waves, Molloy didn't move to cover herself up.

Confident in her skin, and in my feelings for her, she arched her back like a kitten stretching and let out a sexy, moaning yawn.

Her blonde hair was splayed over our bodies, and I twisted a strand around my finger aimlessly, as I pondered my next move.

She made it for me when she declared, "My stomach is growling like crazy."

"Is that your way of telling me to get my ass out of bed and go to the shop for you?"

"Yep," she agreed, nuzzling my chest with her cheek. "You know what I would love, Joe?"

"What would you love, Molloy?"

"A Loop the Loop ice pop, and a packet of salt and vinegar crisps."

I reached for my phone and unlocked the screen. "It's half ten."

"Centra on main street is open until eleven."

"And there's nothing I can tempt you with from the kitchen?"

"Does the kitchen have Loop the Loop ice pops and salt and vinegar crisps?"

I sighed in resignation. "Fine, let me up."

"You're the best." Grinning victoriously, she rolled onto her back and sighed in contentment. "You can take my car."

"You can bet your ass I'm taking your car," I replied, pulling on my clothes and reaching for her keys. "Is there anything else the queen would like?"

"No, I think that's all, my noble steed," she shot back, without missing a beat.

"I'm not a horse, Molloy."

"Maybe not in real life, but metaphorically speaking, you're an absolute stallion in the sheets."

"Fuck off."

"Sure thing, *stud*." She waggled her brows. "See what I did there."

"Hilarious." I shook my head and pocketed my wallet. "Lock the door behind me. I'll be back in half an hour."

"Will do. Oh, and go ask Shan if she wants something," she called out as I closed the door behind me.

I knocked on the door next to mine.

"Come in," my sister called out, and I pushed her door inwards to find her sitting cross-legged on her bed, with her schoolbooks laid out in front of her. "What's up, Joe?"

"I'm going to the shop. Do you want anything?"

"You are?" She offered me a small smile. "Where's Aoife?"

"In my room."

Sticking her pencil behind her ear, she flicked through the pages of her textbook.

"Is she staying over?"

"Yeah," I replied, impatient. "Do you want something from the shop or not? It's closing soon."

"Why are you going to the shop so late?" She eyed me curiously. "What do you need that's so important?"

Deciding it would be more fun to fuck with her than admit my girlfriend had sent me out on a food run, I grinned and said, "do you honestly want me to answer that?"

"No," she groaned, thoroughly sickened with me. "Go away."

Laughing, I closed the door behind me. "Night, Shan."

"Be safe!" she called after me. "I'm too young to be an auntie."

"No fear of that happening," I grumbled, repressing a shiver.

"Tampons!" My bedroom door flew inwards, and Molloy's head popped out. "Get me a box of tampons, too, Joe, will you? I'm really bloated, and I'm due on any day now. I didn't pack any in my bag, and your mam doesn't have any in the bathroom."

"Wouldn't Shannon have—"

"No, I've asked her before. She's not there yet."

"Fine." There went my plans for the next week. "Do you want the sticks or the pads?"

"Sticks?"

I shrugged. "You know what I mean. The blue box of sticks. Is that what you need, or is it the ones with the sticky stuff on the back?"

"Whatever you can find is fine, Joe," she replied with a laugh. "You're the best."

I was a fool for her, that's what I was.

Jesus, the old man was right; I *was* pussy-whipped.

I'm always careful

AOIFE

"We need to talk," Casey announced on Monday morning, as she stood in the middle of the empty girls changing room at school and glared at me.

We had a double class of PE and I was sitting on the wooden bench, last as usual, attempting to tie the laces of my football boots and catch up with the rest of my class.

Meanwhile, Casey was fully kitted out in her training gear which consisted of a jersey, white GAA shorts, socks and boots.

She had her hurley in one hand and her pink helmet –something I hadn't realized they sold in that color – in the other.

"I've tried to keep my nose out," she added, planting her hands on her hips. "Really, I have. I figured that you'd tell me when you were ready, but it's starting to get obvious now."

"I'm a little lost here, Case," I admitted, adjusting my football socks before reaching for my hurling helmet – a staple item in every school-going Irish person's cupboard across the country.

"Listen." Sliding onto the bench alongside me, she set her hurley and helmet down before reaching for my hand and giving it a reassuring squeeze. "You know that I love you, right?" She gave me one of those supportive smiles. "And there's nothing on this planet that you can't tell me."

"Obviously."

"Good." Another hand squeeze incurred. "So, if there was anything that you wanted to get off your chest, you would tell me, right?"

"What's this about, Case?" I asked, brows furrowed in confusion.

"You tell me."

I stared blankly back at her. "I have no idea."

"Come on, Aoife," she urged, eyeballing me with what I presumed was meant to be a meaningful stare, but only made her look psychotic. "It's *okay*. I'm your best friend. I won't turn my back on you in your hour of need."

"Turn your back on me for *what*?" I laughed, at a loss, but finding her amusing just the same.

"Does your mother know?" she demanded then, huffing out a breath. "I presume Joe knows. That's a given – oh my god, does Katie know? Because I can understand your mam and Joey knowing, but I swear if you told Katie Wilmot before me then I'm going to be seriously pissed. I don't care if she's your next-door neighbor, I'm the one who's had your back from the dawn of time, bitch."

"Case, you're going to need to tell *me* what the hell you're talking about, because I'm genuinely lost here, babe."

Casey stared at me for the longest moment before her blue eyes widened and her brows shot up. "Of *course* they don't know," she mumbled, pressing a hand to her brow like she had a sudden migraine. "Because *you* don't know."

"Don't know what?"

"Aoif." My best friend shrugged helplessly, before saying, "I think you might be in the family way."

I took in the sight of her comical expression and burst out laughing.

"Aoif, I'm being totally serious here."

"I know you are," I agreed, still laughing. "That's what makes it so funny."

"Aoife."

"Oh my god, no. I'm not pregnant, Case," I choked out, trying to sober my features. "Why would you even think that?"

"When was your last period?"

I gaped at her. "*What*?"

"Your last period," she urged, tone serious. "When was that exactly?"

"I'm due on," I told her.

"No." She shook her head. "No, you're not."

"I think I'd know when my period is due," I replied, tone defensive now, as the funny side of this conversation quickly faded.

"You would think," she muttered, pressing her fingers to her temples. "Listen to me. Since first year, we've always been in sync. The third week of the month. Like clockwork."

"So?"

"So, you're either two weeks late on last month's one, or two weeks early for this month's one."

"I'm . . . no, that can't be right." Shaking my head, I reached into my bag and grabbed my phone. "I'm due on." Tapping furiously on the buttons of my shiny new Nokia 3510i, my secret Santa Christmas present from Nana Healy, I searched through the calendar notes, panic rising in my chest at a rapid speed. "I'm not late – oh, thank Jesus!" Exhaling a ragged breath when I found what I was looking for, I handed the phone to her and physically sagged in relief. "See?"

"What am I looking at here?"

"I knew I wasn't late," I told her, pointing at the saved note. "I had a switch up a couple of months back, where it came early, but I'm fine, see? My last one started on the fourteenth."

"Yeah, that was December, Aoif."

"What?" I shook my head. "No, no, that was January."

"No, babe," she corrected, tapping her long nail against the screen of my phone. "It was December."

"That can't be right."

"Tell me that you had a period last month?" she begged, voice holding a note of anxiety similar to the feeling rising up inside of me. "Aoife, please. Tell me—"

"I did," I strangled out, snatching my phone back up, and furiously checking through every calendar note and outbox message I could find only to come up empty. "Of *course* I did. I had one at the end of January . . . except . . ."

"Except what?"

"Well, it was weird," I strangled out, feeling my anxiety rise. "It was super light and only lasted a day or two. It was like some light spotting that just tapered off."

"Dear Jesus," Casey cried, slapping the heel of her hand against her forehead. "That could have been implantation bleeding."

"What the hell is implantation bleeding?" I demanded, eyes wide and full of terror. "Implantation of what?"

"Of Joey's strongest fucking swimmer!" Casey strangled out. "Seriously, I know what I'm talking about. It's like this teeny-tiny period like spotting that can trick you into thinking you're having a period. It happened to my cousin Lisa. You know Lisa, with the twins?"

"Yes, Jesus, I know Lisa," I wailed. "But that's not happening to me."

"You had a lot going on back at Christmas." My best friend gave me a worrying look. "You know, with Joey going off the rails and stuff. Maybe you missed a pill or something?"

"I'm not pregnant, Casey!" I practically hissed, feeling the blood rush to my head at record speed. Heat encompassed my body, flooding my cheeks, and making me want to run at top speed as far away from this conversation as I could get. "I'm not, okay? I can't be. And I *never* miss my pill. *Never.*"

"I know you don't," she was quick to soothe, reaching out to place a hand on mine. "I believe you." She exhaled heavily before continuing, "It's just that you and Joey were going through all of that crap in the new year, and your head was a little screwed up. Maybe, it slipped your mind."

"No," I snapped, rejecting any other thoughts. "Nothing slipped my mind. I'm careful, Case."

"Were you on antibiotics?" she offered then. "Because certain types can mess with the pill and make it ineffective? Because that's how my own mam ended up with me."

"No," I strangled out, feeling weak. "Nothing like that."

"Were you sick? Have you had any bugs?"

"Casey!"

"Because your period has deserted you, you've been eating like a horse for the past two months, and your boobs have definitely gotten bigger ... " Words trailing off, she reached for the hem of my jersey. "And I mean, no offence, babe, but you do look like you've packed a couple of pounds on your lower belly."

"Stop it!" I cried out, holding a hand up. "Just stop, okay?"

"I'm trying to be supportive here, Aoif," she defended.

"Well don't," I cried out. "I did the right thing, Casey. I followed the rules. I waited for the right guy. I took my time. I took the damn *pill*. This is not supposed to happen to me. Seriously, this is all a big mistake."

"Maybe?" she offered with a grimace. "Or maybe, you need to consider making an appointment with your doctor, because whether you want to believe it or not, Aoif, it's looking a lot like—"

"Shh. Don't say it. Just start praying."

"To who?"

"St. Anthony," I strangled out, dropping to my knees, and clasping my hands together. "He's the saint we're supposed to pray to when things go missing, isn't he?"

"I don't think St. Anthony can help find your missing period, Aoif."

"You never know."

"Mr. Ryan sent me to tell you both that you need to get your asses out on the pitch," Danielle interrupted, stalking into the changing room. "Or he'll save you both a seat in detention at lunchtime."

"We're coming," Casey mumbled, making no move to get up, eyes still glued to mine.

"He said now."

"We're coming," I snapped, springing up and hurrying for the door, needing to get as far away from this conversation as I could.

"Aoife," Casey called after me. "Wait."

I didn't wait.

I didn't answer her, either.

I couldn't.

Not when my fear was paralyzing me.

Don't do me any favors, asshole

JOEY

We were in the middle of picking teams in PE when Molloy finally decided to grace the rest of our class with her presence.

Looking adorable in her helmet, with her long ponytail swinging as she moved, she hurried onto the pitch, hurley in hand, with Casey chasing after her.

"Aoife," Ricey, the bastard, called out, picking my girlfriend for his team.

Ignoring him entirely, Molloy walked right over to my team, which earned several laughs and cheers at her ex-boyfriend's expense, not to mention an evil-eyed glare from Danielle who had re-joined his team.

"Fine," he relented with a huff. "Casey, you're with us."

"No, I'm not," Casey shot back, making a beeline for Molloy. "I'm with them."

"Then the teams aren't fair," Ricey complained, glaring. "This is bullshit."

"Aoife, you're on Joey's team," Mr. Ryan instructed. "Casey, you're on Paul's."

"But—"

"No buts," our teacher barked. "Move your ass, Lordan. Now."

"Be careful," Casey warned Molloy before reluctantly joining the opposition.

Once everyone was allocated a team position, our teacher blew his whistle, and the class filed out onto the pitch.

"You good, Molloy?" I asked, nudging her shoulder with mine, as she joined me in midfield, looking nothing like the smiling girl I'd woken up next to this morning.

"Yeah, I'm good, Joe," she replied, sounding like the complete opposite, as she stared off, distracted.

"Yeah?"

"Yeah." Shaking her head, she fell into position, flanking me, as I took up the front for the clash of the ash. "It's all good."

"Don't worry, Lynchy," Ricey drawled, taking up position next to Molloy. "I'll be really gentle with our girl here."

His comments earned him a hurley to the shin, courtesy of *our girl*. "Don't do me any favors, asshole."

Yeah, she didn't need my protection.

My girl could handle herself on the pitch.

Molloy possessed all of the skills and temperament to make her a proficient hurler. With a hurley in her hand, and a stony expression on her face, it was as clear as day that Ricey was fucked.

"Stop shouldering me, Aoife."

"Stop being a little bitch, Paul."

"Keep it up and I'll knock you on your ass."

"Try it and I'll ram this hurley up the highest part of your hole."

Smothering a laugh, I turned my attention back to Alec, who I was marking, and waited for Mr. Ryan to blow his whistle.

"Take it handy on me," my friend grumbled, shouldering me to get in a superior position. "I'm nursing one bastard of a hangover, Lynchy."

"No bother, Al."

The minute the whistle was blown, and the sliotar was thrown in, it was on.

"I said take it handy," Alec complained, losing his hurl in the clash, as I secured the sliotar for our team, breaking free on a run. "Show off!"

Half an hour later, and our team were running away with the game, having gone clear out of sight on the scorecard, and causing Mr. Ryan to make the decision to switch up positions. "Joey, swap over with Alec."

"That's bullshit," Podge argued, throwing his hurley down. "He's our best player, and that lazy bastard over there is barely moving."

"Hey! I told you I had a bad pint last night," Al huffed.

"Exactly," Ryan snapped. "Let's make it a fair game."

"I resent that," Alec panted, breathless. "My hole is like a volcanic onion ring. You're damn lucky I'm even kitted out."

"Paul, take Alec," our teacher instructed. "Joey, take Aoife."

"You're putting him on a *girl*?" Podge choked out, outraged. "How in the name of Christ is that fair?"

"Don't be sexist."

"I'm not being sexist."

"Yes, you are."

"It's fair because that girl is *his* girl."

"Oh!" Podge's eyes lit up. "I take it all back, sir. You're a genius."

"Don't even think about going easy on her," Ricey warned, jogging past me to take up position next to Alec.

"Get fucked," I called back, jogging over to where my girlfriend was standing. "Molloy."

"Joey," she acknowledged. "Nice moves."

"Nice legs."

"If you ever want to experience them wrapped around your waist again, then you'll back down."

"That's blackmail," I teased, narrowly avoiding a sneaky swipe of her hurley across the shins.

"Hm," she muttered, pushing me with her shoulder. "I prefer when we play with your other stick."

"Lynchy, head's up!"

Paul pucked the sliotar in my direction, and I raised my hand up to catch the ball mid-air, only to miss my target entirely when Molloy grabbed me in a precarious fucking spot.

"That's my ball, Joey Lynch," she warned, squeezing my nuts just enough to let me know that she was capable of doing damage. "And so are these."

"Jesus," I strangled out, throwing my hands up in surrender, as my blonde-haired nemesis secured the ball for herself, and whizzed past me, cackling evilly.

Molloy made it about fifteen yards up the pitch before being blown clean off the ball with a hard shoulder.

Flattening her like a pancake on the grass, Ricey scooped the sliotar back up and passed it back to me. This time, when I didn't catch the ball, it wasn't because I was distracted. It was because I was too busy ridding myself of my helmet, as I stalked up the pitch towards them.

"I'm grand," Molloy was telling Casey, who was fussing over her. "I said I'm fine, Case." Taking her friend's hand, she climbed unsteadily to her feet and adjusted her helmet that had been knocked sideways. "Relax, will you? I'm okay."

"What the fuck is wrong with you?" I roared, closing the distance between us, fury rising inside of me. "You just mowed her down!"

"It was a fair tackle," Ricey called back, retreating several steps. "Besides, what are ya complaining about?" He smirked. "We're on the same team, remember?"

"It's okay, Joe," Molloy called over. "I'm fine."

"No, no, no," Mr. Ryan interjected, swiftly coming to block me. "You heard Mr. Nyhan, Joey. You're on your last strike, son. No more fighting. He *will* expel you."

"Like I give a fuck," I roared, pushing against the hands that were holding me back. "You saw that. You *saw* what he just did to her."

"Three months," Mr. Ryan, who I reluctantly had to admit was my favorite teacher, implored me with his eyes to listen to him. "That's all you have left, Joe."

I presumed his motives for trying to keep my ass in school had a lot more to do with the upcoming hurling championship we were competing in more than anything else. However, aside from Mrs. Adams, he was the only other teacher to ever show an interest in me in the six years I had attended BCS. He'd spoken up for me on many the occasion down through the years, and, for that, I respected him.

"You've come so far," he continued to coax, as he slowly walked me backwards off the pitch, and away from trouble. "You've been doing so well since Christmas. You're so *close* to finishing this out. Don't throw it all away for a punch up over a girl."

"She's *not* just a girl," I bit out, feeling my body burn with heated frustration, as I ran a hand through my hair and stared over his shoulder to where Molloy was brushing herself down. "It's like you said earlier; she's *my* girl."

"I know."

"You don't know shit."

"Listen to me. I'm a teacher, Joey, I'm not immune or blind to the rumors and gossip that spreads through the halls," he explained, tone coaxing. "I've heard all about the on-going issues you have with Rice. So, think about just how nicely it would suit his narrative if you were to go and get yourself expelled from school. It would suit him down to the ground to have you off the team and out of the way."

I gave him a hard look. "What are you saying?"

"I'm saying don't give the little shit what he wants," he replied. "He's playing you. He can't compete with you on any level, so he's pushing the one button he *knows* will make you trip yourself up."

"Aoife."

"Aoife," he confirmed with a knowing sigh. "Don't prove him right, kid. *Don't* give him the satisfaction."

Doing the math

AOIFE

"That house party we went to back in the new year?" I whispered in my best friend's ear, as we huddled together at lunch, heads bent over the table, food untouched. "The one the boys of Tommen threw before Christmas break ended?" Feeling a frantic flurry of panic attack my insides, I added, "I had *way* too much to drink and spent that entire night and following day spewing my guts up. That's the only thing that I can think of."

"And Joey?" she asked, leaning in close. "You were with him that night?"

"Yeah." Flushed, I blew out a breath. "We had epic make-up sex that night, and we were together *a lot* that weekend."

"Did he wear a condom?"

I shook my head.

"Shit," Casey expelled a breath. "That's not good, Aoif."

"But I didn't miss my pill," I tried to defend. "I took it at the same time on both days."

"That wouldn't matter."

"Don't say that, Case," I strangled out, clutching her hand. "Please don't say that."

"I'm sorry," she whispered, squeezing my hand. "I don't want to upset you, but I can't lie to you either." She gave me a worrying look. "It's not looking good, babe."

"Oh Jesus." My lungs heaved and I bit down on my lip before asking, "The vomiting? Do you think that might be what happened here?"

The way she winced in response assured me that she did.

"I can't be pregnant." My eyes welled up with tears, and I shook my head, feeling utterly blindsided. "I can't be."

"It's going to be okay."

"How?" I choked out, feeling my windpipe tighten. "*How* is it going to be *okay*?"

"Because it just will be," she assured me, looking as uncertain as I felt. "We'll go to the pharmacy after school and get a test, and at least then you'll know for sure."

"I don't want to know."

"You kind of have to, Aoif."

"No." Dropping my head in my hands, I clenched my eyes shut, feeling the tears dampening my lashes. "No."

"Don't panic," she instructed, placing her hand on my back. "We'll figure this out."

"Case," I strangled out, chest heaving. "Tomorrow is the first of March. If that wasn't a period I had last month, then I'm . . ."

"Eleven weeks tomorrow?" She sighed heavily and rubbed soothing circular patterns on my back. "Yeah, Aoif, I've already done the maths."

"This can't be happening," I groaned, feeling sick to my stomach, as I pressed the heels of my hands into my eyes. "This *isn't* happening."

"What's wrong, Molloy?" an achingly familiar voice asked, and I clamped up with tension when Joey sank down on the table in front of me. "Were they out of Rolos in the tuck shop?"

Forcing myself to steady my nerves and look at him, I leaned back in my seat and smiled weakly. "How'd you guess?"

He tossed a packet onto my lap and winked.

My heart flipped in my chest as I stared down at the packet.

"Joe." My throat felt like sawdust. "That's so sweet."

He rolled his eyes at my overly dramatic reaction to his kindness and turned his attention to his friends, who were all joining us at the table.

"Fuck no, he didn't," Alec announced, laughing at something Podge had said. "Not a hope in hell does he have a chance of making the under 20's."

"I'm telling ya, lad, he's a shoe-in for the summer tour," Podge pushed, wolfing down a sandwich, as they discussed some rugby player. "Maybe even the senior team."

"Bullshit," Alec argued, tossing his crisp packet on the table. "He's younger than us." Turning to Joey, he asked, "What do you reckon?"

"You know my view on Kavanagh," my boyfriend said with a shrug. "He's going to make a fucking fortune."

"*Thank* you," Podge said before turning back to Alec with a smug expression etched on his face. "I rest my case."

Reaching over, Casey gave my hand a reassuring squeeze, and mouthed, "it's going to be okay."

I couldn't return her reassuring smile.

I couldn't even breathe.

As my gaze flicked between my best friend and my boyfriend, I felt the walls of the canteen close in around me.

This isn't happening.

This can't be happening.

And yet, here I was on the verge the unspeakable, and the brink of a mental breakdown.

"Hey." Joey's voice broke through my frantic thoughts, and I felt his fingers on my chin, tilting my face up to look at him. "You good, queen?"

"Yeah." Releasing a shaky breath, I leaned my cheek against his hand, reeling in my panic and the warm feel of his touch on my skin. "It's all good, stud."

His green eyes were clear, focused and full of unconcealed affection.

The way he looked at me now was worlds apart from the way he used to.

I could see the trust he had for me. He didn't try to hide his feelings from me anymore and seeing all of this in his eyes only made my stomach knot up tighter.

He turned back to his friends, chatting and laughing, but he kept his hand on my cheek, as his thumb traced the curve of my jaw, and I was grateful for the contact.

Shifting closer, I leaned my other cheek against his side, and clenched my eyes shut, inhaling his scent and taking comfort in the sheer strength of his body.

In the moment.

Because I knew that once I told Joey, the moment I conveyed to him his biggest fear, then everything we had worked so hard to build would go clean out the window.

His trust.

His communication.

His sobriety.

No.

Clenching my eyes shut tighter, I repressed the urge to sob.

I couldn't let this happen.

PART 3

Mood swings and Mister Rugby

JOEY

I was having a very weird week, in which some of the females in my life were acting strange as hell.

Molloy, who had never been short of something to say a day in her life, had barely spoken more than a few sentences to me since yesterday, and her little sidekick, who had been just as blessed with the gift of the gab, had spoken even less.

When school finished, she couldn't get away from me fast enough, mumbling some shit about having a hair appointment before burning off in her car with said sidekick in tow.

I wasn't stupid.

Clearly, I had fucked up somewhere between yesterday morning when I left her outside the changing rooms for PE and today, but I was struggling to pinpoint *where* exactly.

I kept my hands to myself during PE yesterday and *didn't* get myself expelled. Christ, I'd even slipped out of Construction early to snag her a packet of Rolos in the tuck shop. Sure, I had a smoke behind the shed with the lads at lunch today, same as always, but it was a cigarette and *not* a hit from Rambo Regan's perfectly rolled joint, tempting as it had been. All in all, I thought that the first two school days of the week had been productive.

I didn't even get detention.

However, the way Molloy had all but catapulted herself away from me the minute the final bell went yesterday, and then again today, and the two text messages I sent her that had gone unanswered, assured me that I had indeed fucked up along the way.

"I don't know what to tell ya, Trish," Tony snapped, stalking into the office with his mobile pressed to his ear. "I'll have a word when I get home. Yeah, right. Bye, bye, bye."

He ended the call and released a strained growl.

"Everything okay there, Tony?"

"I don't know, Joey, lad, I really don't," he grumbled, shoving his phone back into his pocket. "There must be something in the water today."

"How'd you figure?" I asked over my shoulder, as I spooned sugar into two mugs of coffee.

"That wife of mine," he said, brows furrowed, as he took the mug that I held out for him. "That's the fourth time today that she's phoned me up to give out. If it's not the dog shitting on her flower bed, then it's the tap leaking, or the socks I left on the bedroom floor, or that young one of ours slamming doors and giving her cheek."

"Aoife?"

He nodded and took another sip of his coffee. "On the warpath since yesterday, apparently."

I knew it.

I fucking *knew* she was in a bad mood.

"Doesn't she have an evening shift at the pub on Tuesdays?"

He nodded. "According to Trish, she almost took the front door off its hinges when she left for work."

"For real?"

"Do yourself a favor, Joey, lad," he said. "And steer clear of my house for the evening. Sounds like both of the women who live there are on the warpath."

"Jesus," I muttered, rubbing my jaw.

"Good lad yourself," he said, giving my shoulder an approving squeeze. "Best to keep a wide berth when one of my girls is brewing up a storm."

Unease filled me, followed by a wave of concern.

Molloy didn't keep shit from me.

That was not how she rolled.

When she had a problem, I was the first one to hear about it – especially since I was usually the problem.

"I'm going out back for a smoke," I told her father, grabbing my phone off the counter before heading for the door.

"Don't do it, son."

"Do what?"

"Put yourself in the eye of the storm by phoning my young one," he called after me with a chuckle. "By the sound of it, she won't think twice about swallowing you whole."

Jesus.

Still, like a glutton for punishment, I stepped out back, sparked up a cigarette, and dialed her number, ignoring the dozen or so messages I'd received from Shannon.

My sister could wait.

My girlfriend came first in this instance.

When it rang out, and went to voicemail, my unease spread.

Redialing, I held the phone to my ear and took a deep drag of my cigarette.

Five rings in and she finally answered. "Hello?"

"It's me."

"Yeah, I know." Her tone was clipped. "Your number came up."

"What's wrong?" I came right out and asked her. "You're pissed." No point in beating around the bush. "Tell me why."

"Nothing." She sighed down the line. "Everything's fine."

"Don't bullshit me." Taking another drag, I exhaled a cloud of smoke and said, "I know something's up, Molloy."

"Joe."

"Tell me."

"There's nothing up."

"Liar."

There was a long pause and the sound of cutlery clattering filled my ears, before her voice came back on the line. "Listen, I need to go. I'm at work."

"What time are you finished?"

"Half ten," she said quietly.

"I'll walk you home."

"I have the car."

"Fine. I'll walk over to the pub and drive you home."

"You finish at nine."

"I'll wait."

"Joe, I need a night to myself, okay," she said, tone strained. "I've, ah, well, I just do, okay?"

"Are you mad at me?" I asked, hating the helpless feeling eating me alive. "Did I do something to upset you?" I swallowed down a growl before asking, "Are you pissed that I didn't do something when Ricey knocked you over in PE yesterday? Because I wanted to, Molloy. I was fully prepared to kick the shit out of him for putting his hands on you."

"Are you kidding? No, I'm so proud of you for not reacting. It was only a push, no big deal, and I swear you didn't do anything, okay?" she hurried to soothe. "I love you, Joe. I'm not mad at you, I promise. I'm just dealing with something and I need a night to myself."

"I love you," I heard myself admit, tone gruff. "Do ya hear me? I love you, Molloy."

"I know you do, Joe," she replied, tone thick with emotion. "I'll see you at school tomorrow, okay?"

"Yeah." I bowed my head. "Okay."

"Bye, stud."

"Bye, queen."

"That's the start of it," Tony chuckled, joining me out back. "Keep pandering to that young one of mine, and you'll be in big trouble, boyo."

I'm already in trouble.

"Yeah, well, it's a quiet life I'm after, Tony," I replied with a shrug, as I took another drag of my smoke and scrolled through my phone, counting at least twenty-five call-me text messages from Shannon. "The hell is wrong now?"

"What's that?"

"My sister," I explained, dialing her number, feeling a different sort of panic rise up inside of me. "She's after blowing up my phone with messages."

"Is she alright?"

"Shannon," I demanded when she finally answered. "What's going on? Are you okay? Did something happen at school?"

The sinking feeling in the pit of my stomach assured me it had.

My blood pressure was rising at a rapid pace and I had to take a second before I could speak again.

"If one of those posh fuckers did something to you, I will—"

"I'm fine. I'm okay. Calm down. I missed my bus and the next one's not until quarter to ten tonight," she explained down the line, sounding eerily calm for someone who had blown up my phone.

Was she hurt?

She didn't sound it.

Was she lying?

It was close to impossible to tell.

"It's already dark and I don't want to walk in case . . ." She paused, and the sound of rustling filled my ears, before she spoke again, "Are you with Aoife? Can you guys come pick me up? I'm really stuck, Joe. I wouldn't ask you if I wasn't desperate."

"I'm working until nine," I heard myself say, pressing the heel of my hand to my forehead. "And Aoife works until half ten on Tuesdays." Not that I was about to ask the girl who asked me for *space* to collect my sister. "Did you try Mam?"

"She's working the late shift, and I'm not calling Dad."

"No, Jesus, don't call him," I agreed, shaking my head. "Look hang up and give me a few minutes. I'll call around a few of the lads, and see if anyone can pick you up." Surely Podge or Alec would drop her home for me. "I'll call you back in a few."

"No, don't do that," she was quick to say. "The school stays open late. I can wait here until my bus comes – oh no, no, no, that's okay."

I frowned. "Huh?"

"You don't have to do that," she said – obviously not speaking to me.

"Do what?" Curiosity piqued, I eyed Tony, who wasn't even pretending to not listen to the conversation. In fact, he had stepped closer. "Shan, what's going on? Who are you talking to?"

"Oh, ah, just this guy from school."

"Guy?" Tony's brows shot up at the same time as mine. "What guy?"

"Just a guy I know," she replied, all coy and shit. "Honestly, it's fine. You don't have to drive me home."

'Drive her home?' Tony mouthed, pointing at the phone. *'She's a baby.'*

'I know,' I mouthed, before turning my attention back to my sister. "Hold up, who's driving you home, Shannon? Why are you talking to guys old enough to drive you home?"

'Tell her she's fifteen,' Tony mouthed with a thumbs up.

"You're fifteen," I heard myself say, feeling like a fucking hypocrite. If he knew the half of what I wanted to do to his daughter when she was fifteen, he would be shitting rocks.

"I know what age I am, Joey," Shannon snapped and I cocked a brow, hearing the rare spark of fire in her voice. "Look, relax. I'll wait here until my bus comes."

Like fuck she would.

I wasn't born yesterday.

And if she's anything like you, it won't be the front seat she'll be climbing into.

Jesus.

"Put him on the phone," I ordered, shuddering.

"What?" Shannon asked. "Who?"

"The lad who's just a guy you know with a car."

"Why?"

"Because I want to talk to him."

"Why do you want to talk to him?"

I gave Tony a knowing look and said, "Because I want to talk to the fucker offering to take my baby sister home in his car, that's why."

He nodded his approval.

"Hey, this is Johnny," a male voice with a thick Dublin accent, came down the line a moment later.

'That's no boy,' Tony mouthed accusingly, gaping at the phone, *'That's a fucking man's voice.'*

'I know,' I mouthed back, *'shut up and let me think.'*

Tony held his hands up in submission.

"Johnny," I said coolly, making an effort to use my most threatening tone of voice. "I hear you know Shannon."

"Yeah, I know your sister," he replied, tone impeccably polite.

"So, is it just Johnny from Tommen, or do ya have a last name?"

"Kavanagh."

"The rugby player?" Tony and I both asked in unison.

"Yeah, that's me."

'Well shit,' my boss mouthed, eyes wide with excitement, *'the lad from The Academy?'*

If this hotshot fucker had taken time out of his rigid schedule to drive her home, then my baby sister had made more than just waves at Tommen.

She'd summoned a goddamn tsunami.

"I saw your last game with the U18's," I heard myself say. "You were class."

"Thanks, it was a strong performance all round," he replied – again, with the polite bullshit.

"You're heading for the U20's tour with the Irish squad in May, aren't ya?"

"Probably."

'Ask him for a few tickets,' Tony mouthed, nudging my arm.

'I can't do that,' I mouthed back, glaring at him.

'Do it.'

'No.'

'Ask him.'

'No.'

'Do it for your boss.'

'No.'

'Fine. Do it for your future father-in-law.'

I gaped at him.

He grinned back.

"Ah . . . is there any chance of a few tickets?" I closed my eyes when the words came out of my mouth, feeling like an asshole for asking. "My girlfriend's father is a big fan."

"Yeah, I'll see what I can do," he replied, like it was something he was asked on the daily. "Home games only, though, and the tickets don't go on sale to the public until May. Shouldn't be a problem, though."

'Well?'

I nodded.

'Get fucking in there!' Beaming at me, Tony held both thumbs up. *'I always knew you were worth the trouble.'*

Rolling my eyes, I turned my attention back to my phone call. "You do realize she's fifteen, right?" I said, tone serious. "My sister Shannon? She's only *fifteen*. So, I hope you don't have any notions because she's a good girl."

"I'm well aware, and no, I don't," came his cool response and for the first time, I heard a crack in his polite bullshit exterior. Clearly, I'd hit a nerve. "We're, uh . . . "

"Friends?" I offered, amused.

"Yeah," he answered, sounding flustered. "We're friends."

I smirked. "*Just* friends?"

"Obviously."

"What kind of a license do you have?"

"A full license."

"Is your car safe?"

"Yes."

"How old are you again?"

"Seventeen."

"So, you're a lot older than her."

"I know that," he replied before adding, "I get it."

"I hope you do, because there's a big difference between a fifteen-year-old girl like her and a seventeen-year-old lad in a position like yours."

"Yeah," he bit out, still not backing down or rescinding his offer. "I'm aware of the difference."

"Alright, Mister Rugby, she's all yours," I said with a shrug. "Don't get her killed in that car of yours, ya hear?" *And for the love of Christ, don't hurt her.*

"I won't," I heard him say before the line went dead.

"Well, thanks a fucking bunch for that, Tony," I said, sliding my phone into my pocket. "The lad offers to drive my sister home, and I end up bumming tickets for a game."

My boss chuckled. "Ah, sure if he ends up coming through with the tickets, you know I'll take ya with me."

Two pink lines
AOIFE

When I got home from work on Tuesday night, my mother was sitting on her bed, pairing socks, and all I wanted to do was curl up in a ball on her lap and cry.

I felt sick to my stomach as I hovered in the bedroom doorway, trying and failing to come up with the words needed to express just how terrified I felt in this moment.

"Back for round two?" Mam asked, flicking her gaze to me, referencing the blazing row we had this afternoon over her walking into my room unannounced, of all things. "Or are you finally ready to tell me what's wrong with you?"

Mam, I'm scared.

Mam, I'm in trouble.

Mam, I need a hug.

"What's troubling you, Aoife?" she pressed, concern filling her eyes. "You've been standing in the doorway for ten minutes now, clearly trying to work up the courage to tell me something? Out with it."

"I . . ." the words wouldn't come out, and I shook my head, trying again, "I . . ."

Again, nothing came out.

"I'm sorry," I finally managed to squeeze out, voice strained. My cheeks were flushed, my skin was on fire, and the plastic stick I had tucked in the pocket of my coat caused my heart to seize up with dread. "For taking your head off earlier."

"That's not you, love."

"I know."

"Is it Joey?" she asked then, setting down a pair of socks and giving me her full attention. "Are you two having trouble again? Because I thought you sorted everything out with him."

"I did," I replied, expelling a harsh breath. "We're fine."

Mam frowned. "Then what's with the lonesome face?"

"I'm just .... I'm ..." Shaking my head, I cleared my throat and mumbled, "Tired. I'm just really tired, Mam."

"Are you sure that's all it is?" She didn't look convinced. "Because you know you can tell me anything."

"I'm sure." Forcing a smile, I nodded and slipped away, moving straight for my room.

Closing my bedroom door behind me, I made a beeline for my bed and dove under the covers, fully clothed, shoes and all.

With the duvet over my head, I slowly withdrew the pregnancy test from my coat pocket, the one that had taken me twenty-four hours to work up the courage to use.

The two glaring pink lines in the display box hadn't faded one bit since their original appearance in the bathroom at work tonight.

And there it was.

Staring me right in the face.

My life was over.

Your sister's a whore

JOEY

I knew I was walking into trouble before I stepped foot through the door after work. I could feel it in the air around me.

Everything was all wrong and out of kilter.

I was also achingly aware that today was children's allowance day. A windfall day on the first Tuesday of every month, where our father got paid by the government for having children, and then drank every penny, before beating the living shit out of said children.

Sometimes, I thought that monthly allowance was the reason he continued to reproduce so many of us.

"How's it going, *family*," I said, tone laced with derisive sarcasm, when I stepped into the kitchen.

The minute I walked inside, I could smell the whiskey permeating off the old man, as he hovered unsteadily in the middle of the room.

"Joey," he acknowledged warily.

"Boys in bed?"

Our father nodded, keeping his eyes on mine the entire time, watching me like I was some dangerous predator that would strike at any given minute.

He was dead on the fucking money.

I could feel the fear coming off my sister in waves as she cowered by the sink, with her small hand pressed to her neck.

Shannon's face was all blotchy, and her eyes were bloodshot.

I wasn't stupid.

It was as clear as day that I'd walked in at the right time.

Trying to keep my head, I reached for a can of Coke from the fridge, knowing that I had to be careful here. "Where's Mam?" I asked, taking a swig. "Still at work?"

"Your mother's at work and this one here is late home again," Dad slurred, glaring at Shannon. "Missed her fucking bus, apparently."

"I know," I replied coolly, giving Shannon a wink. "How's it going, Shan?"

"Hey, Joe." She swallowed deeply and attempted to smile at me. "Nothing. Just hungry. I was getting a snack."

Getting a smack more like.

Walking over to her, I playfully nudged her cheek with my knuckles, but it was only so that I could get a better look at the marks on her neck.

Bastard's fingerprints were imbedded on her skin.

Fuck.

"Did Aoife stay long after she dropped you home?" I threw her a lifeline by asking.

"Uh, no." Her eyes widened in awareness and gratitude as she hurried to say, "She just dropped me off and went straight home."

Offering her a small wink of approval, I grabbed a packet of biscuits from the press and tossed them to her. "Here. No doubt they were what you were looking for."

They weren't.

She would never touch a thing on the top shelf that I stored my shit on, but *he* didn't know that.

"It's not a halfway house," Dad snarled.

"This is my food, old man." I turned back to glare at him. "Bought with *my* money. From *my* job."

"This is my house."

"Given to you by the government," I drawled, unwilling to back down an inch from the piece of shit in front of me. "Because of *us*."

"Don't get smart with me, boy."

"Shannon, why don't you head on up to bed," I told her, knowing that shit was about to go down, and needing her out of the firing line.

Shannon moved for the door, but he stepped in front of her, blocking her way. "I'm not done talking to her."

"Well, she's done talking to you," I said, tone deathly cold, as I shouldered him out of the way of the kitchen door, giving my sister an escape route. "So, get out of her way, old man. Now."

Thankfully, Shannon took the opportunity to bolt out of the room before he could catch ahold of her ponytail.

"Don't fucking think about it," I warned, blocking the doorway, when he made to move after her. "She's not your fucking punching bag."

"Did ya see this?" Grabbing a newspaper, he tossed it at me. "Did ya see this carrying on, boy!"

Smoothing out the page, I stared down at a picture of my sister with none other than Mister Rugby himself.

"Well, shit," I mused, reluctantly smiling at the sight of *my* baby sister tucked under the arm of the rising star of Irish rugby. "Maybe he *has* notions."

"You think this is funny?" Dad snarled, ripping the newspaper from my hands and tearing the page in half. "Your sister's a fucking whore, and all you can do is smile about it?"

"Clearly, our definitions of the word whore are very different."

"That doll you're fucking around with is another one," he told me. "Little blonde whore, prancing around my house with her tits and legs and hole on full show. She's looking for it, that one. I'm telling ya, boy, she's looking for a good seeing to—"

His words broke off when I leveled him with a fist to the face. "You keep your goddamn eyes off her!"

"Eyes?" He threw his head back and laughed. "I'll put more than my eyes on her the next time I see her."

And that was all it took to unravel months of hard work and preservation.

Losing my absolute shit there and then, I ploughed into my father, both throwing and receiving punches, as we crashed into kitchen table, knocking chairs over as we brawled.

"Was she a virgin before ya broke her in, boy?" he continued to torment me by saying. "Did she bleed all over ya? What am I saying?" he laughed cruelly. "There's nothing between your legs to break her in with."

"I *will* kill you," I roared, straining against the beefy hand he had wrapped around my throat, as he pummeled his fist into my face. "If you so much as *think* about putting a hand on her—" Breaking free of his hold, I threw my entire weight at him, propelling us both forward until his legs gave way beneath him and we crashed to the ground. "If you look at my girlfriend again," I roared, fists flying with a flourish. "If you fucking breathe too close to her, they'll have to take you out of this house in a body bag!"

"Joey!" Mam's voice filled my ears, and I looked up to find her standing in the kitchen doorway, cradling her round stomach, and looking at me like I was the monster in our story. "Get *off* your father."

The clever bastard beneath me let his hands fall to his sides, feigning innocence, as he groaned in pain. "He's killing me, Marie."

"Get off your father," Mam repeated, tone hardening, as she staggered into the kitchen. "And get out of my sight before I say something we'll both regret."

Disgusted, I released my hold on his shirt and climbed to my feet.

With blood smeared on my knuckles, I pointed a finger at her and spat, "You're a fool if you think you're not next," before stalking out of the kitchen.

Taking the staircase two steps at a time, I grabbed a wad of toilet paper from the bathroom before storming into my room, slamming the door shut behind me.

Stripping down to my jocks, because that man's hands had touched my clothes, I sank down on the edge of my bed.

Resting my elbows on my thighs, I sagged forward, and pressed the tissue to my mouth.

If I could peel the skin from my bones in this moment, I would have.

I didn't want his hands anywhere near my body.

I couldn't fucking bear it.

"Joe?" My bedroom door opened inwards and I saw my sister standing in the doorway. "You okay?"

"I'm grand, Shan," I bit out, wiping the blood from my mouth. "You should go to bed."

"You're bleeding."

No shit.

"It's just a busted lip." Impatient, and just about done with the whole fucking lot of them, I grumbled, "Go back to your room."

She didn't move.

Instead, she continued to hover in the doorway, until I relented and patted the mattress beside me, giving her what she needed.

"I'm sorry," she strangled out, hurrying towards me. "So sorry," she continued to cry, as her small arms came around my shoulders, putting more weight on me than I could handle.

It felt like my life was on a constant loop of reruns, repeating the same scene, the same pain, day after day, year after year, until it broke me.

Still, I went through the motions of comforting my little sister, and assuring her that it wasn't her fault, which was true.

Tonight wasn't on Shannon.

None of the previous nights of our past were on Shannon.

It was all *them*.

All of it.

After reassuring her a couple of hundred times, I gave up on any hope of having some alone time.

The tremors rolling through her assured me that she wasn't leaving my room.

Fuck my life.

Giving up my bed, I took the floor and settled down for the night, as the topic of conversation – and my sister's focus – shifted from our father to a boy she was intent on feigning indifference towards.

Johnny Kavanagh.

When she told me that he was responsible for her concussion that first day, I felt something settle inside of me. Because I finally had the confirmation that what happened to her that day, *had*, in fact, been an accident. The lad was almost mechanical in his rigidity, with impeccable manners. The academy had him groomed into the perfect gentlemen.

No way would he risk a future as bright as his on a childish stunt.

I could smell the bullshit a mile off every time she denied her very obvious feelings, and smiled to myself as I listened to her ramble on about who I thought might be her very first crush.

Being one of those asshole older brothers I *never* wanted to be, I heard myself warn her off, but not because I didn't want her to find someone.

I did.

I just didn't want to see her get her hopes up on a fella with a future as bright as Johnny Kavanagh's.

I had no doubt that she would be watching him from the television in a few months, and call me a protective asshole, but I didn't want to see my sister get *hurt*.

You have to tell him

AOIFE

"It's been over a week," Casey exclaimed, sliding onto the stool next to mine at our workstation in Biology on Friday. We were early for class, and, with the exception of a few stragglers at the other end of the lab, we were thankfully alone. "You *have* to tell him, Aoif."

Keeping my eyes trained on my pencil case, I didn't even try to stop my hands from shaking. They hadn't stopped since my world fell around me. "I know."

"And you have to go to the doctor."

"I know."

"I can make the appointment and go with you."

I shook my head. "No."

She sighed heavily. "Aoife."

"I'm not ready, okay?" The tremor in my hand increased to the point where I couldn't open the zip of my pencil case. "I'm just not."

"You still have options, you know," she said softly, reaching over to open my pencil case for me. "Fuck this country. There's always England. We can get on a boat to Liverpool in the morning, if that's what you want. If you want it to be over, then it can be."

"I know," I whispered, biting down on my lip.

"So, you *have* thought about it?"

"Of *course* I've thought about it." Blinking back my tears, I nodded slowly. "It's the best thing for both of us. I'm not stupid, Case, I know it's what's best in the long-term, but it's too late for that."

"It's not too late," she was quick to point out. "If we leave tomorrow—"

"No, no, it is for me, okay." Exhaling a ragged breath, I dropped my head in my hand and buried a sob. "I've thought about it and I can't do it, Case. I just *can't*, okay?"

"Okay," she conceded, tone soothing "Okay, Aoif."

Slowly exhaling, I concentrated on keeping my breathing even, deep and slow, and not giving into the panic clawing at my throat.

"So, you're going to go through with this?" she said softly. "You're really going to have Joey Lynch's baby?"

Words failed me and I clenched my eyes shut, barely managing to nod my head.

"And keep it?" she asked cautiously. "You're going to keep it?"

"Yeah," I squeezed out, hand moving to rest on my stomach, only to think better of it and grip the desk instead. "I guess I am."

"Then you have me," she said, sliding her arm through mine, as the lab started to fill up with other students. "And I've got your back. Always."

"We're supposed to be going to the cinema tonight," I told her in a shaky tone, eyes trained on the front of the room. "He texted me about it earlier."

"Then maybe you guys can have a conversation afterwards," she offered in a hopeful tone.

"He won't be able to handle it, Case," I whispered, teeth chattering from nerves. "He'll go off the rails again."

"You don't know that."

"I do." Knees bopping anxiously, I blinked away another batch of tears. "It will wreck him. He's been doing so well. Better than I could have imagined. And this? This will *ruin* him."

"Either way, he has to be told," she replied gently. "You know that, Aoif."

"Yeah, I do." I nodded weakly. "But my world is already collapsing around me. Can you blame me for wanting to delay that for him?"

"Well, don't delay it too long," she mumbled. "Because you're starting to show."

Those words were all it took for everything inside of my stomach to come rushing back up.

Bolting off my stool, I ran out of class, not stopping until I was on my knees in the girls' bathroom, with my head in the bowl and my life in pieces around me.

I'm really scared

JOEY

"Are you sure you're not hungry?" I asked Molloy on Friday night, as we took our seats in the middle row at the cinema.

She shook her head.

"Thirsty?"

Another headshake.

She had been banging on about going to see *Boogeyman* for weeks now. I'd finally managed to get a night off work to take her, and she couldn't look more miserable if she tried.

She wasn't talking.

She wasn't eating.

She wasn't smiling.

The girl sitting next to me was not the same girl who climbed out of my bed last week and I was really starting to worry.

"So, I heard a rumor this evening," I decided to go with next, knowing that Molloy could never resist some juicy gossip. "According to Mack, that Johnny Kavanagh lad from Tommen kicked seven kinds of shit out of Ciara Maloney's fella in Biddies this evening."

When she didn't reply, I continued to ramble on, hoping to stir some sort of reaction from her.

"Apparently, Ciara and Hannah were giving Shan shit as usual, and yer man Kavanagh absolutely lost it. Knocked over a table of drink and everything. Gave that Murphy lad a right kicking," I added, stuffing a handful of popcorn into my mouth. "I reckon there's something going on there; between Shannon and Kavanagh. She'd never admit it, of course, but I'm not thick. I mean, first he's driving her home from school, then he's taking her to the pub, and now he's publicly defending her honor and settling scores with a bunch of bitches that have been hounding her for years? Sounds a little more than just friends, if you ask me."

A half-hearted, "Oh?" was all I got for my troubles.

At a complete fucking loss at what to say or do next, I drummed my fingers on the armrest and decided to concentrate on the screen in front of me.

It wasn't coming easy, though.

Not when I could literally feel the anxiety wafting from my girlfriend.

"Joe?" Molloy finally whispered, an hour or so into the movie. "I need to tell you something."

"Hm?" I turned to look at her, relieved that she was finally making conversation. "Yeah?"

"I'm ... " Her green eyes were wide and full of panic. "I'm ... "

"You're what, Molloy?"

"Scared." Exhaling a shaky breath, she shook her head and reached for my arm, draping it over her shoulders as she leaned into my side. "I'm really scared."

"It's just a film," I whispered, tightening my arm around her. "It's not real life. Don't let it freak you out."

"I know." Shivering, she buried her face in my chest, and fisted the front of my hoodie in her hand. "I'm just ... I'm still scared."

Confused, I looked down at the way she was clinging to me and felt even more uneasy than before.

The way she was acting was all wrong.

None of this sat well with me, because this was the same girl who loved gore and horror in movies.

"Do you want to leave?"

She shook her head.

"I can take you home."

Another headshake.

"You're clearly miserable."

"I don't want to go home."

"Then what do you want from me, Molloy?" I asked, feeling helpless. "What can I do here?"

"You can stay," she squeezed out, and a shudder rolled through her. "I want you to stay with me, Joe."

"I'm staying," I replied, expelling a frustrated breath. "I'm not going anywhere."

Later that night, as I drove us home from the cinema in Mahon Point, I watched from the corner of my eye, as Molloy stared out the passenger window, clearly lost in thought, as Bell X1's 'Eve, The Apple Of My Eye' played on the local radio station.

"I'll drive you home," I told her, breaking the silence. "And I'll walk home from your place."

She swung her gaze to me. "You're not staying the night?"

"Not tonight."

"Why?"

"Because if I wanted to get the cold shoulder, then I can get plenty of those at home," I replied, hand tightening on the wheel.

"It's not like that, Joe," she croaked out. "It's not."

"Then what's it like, Molloy?" I demanded hoarsely. "Huh? What's happening with you?"

"Nothing," she whispered, retreating back to her perch of staring out the window and ignoring me. "I love you, Joe."

"Yeah, and I love you back," I admitted, feeling frustrated and pissed off and anxious all in one breath. "But I don't understand what's happening here. With you. Between us. I don't fucking like it."

"Don't go home tonight," she said, after a long stretch of silence. "Please."

"I'm not staying at your house."

She turned to look at me. "Why?"

I shook my head. "I already told you."

"Then can I stay at your house?"

"Molloy." I released a pained sigh. "Don't."

"Please." Reaching across the console she placed her hand on my jean-clad thigh. "I know I'm holding back, okay? I know. I'm just . . ." Releasing a pained growl, she shook her head and reached a hand up to swat what I presumed was a tear from her cheek. "Ugh, why am I such a fucking girl?"

"Are you crying?"

"No."

"Molloy?"

"I'm being stupid."

Throwing on my indicator, I waited for a break in traffic before pulling off to the side of the road and throwing on the hazard lights.

Killing the engine, I turned to face her. "Okay, you need to start talking to me."

"Really, I'm fine," she sobbed, batting tears left, right, and center, as they dripped onto her cheeks. "I don't know why I'm crying," she half-laughed, half-sobbed, as tears continued to fall from her long lashes. "See?" Wiping her eyes with the back of her hands, she smiled across the seat at me and said, "I'm totally fine."

"Jesus. No, you're not." Pushing my seat back as far as it went, I unfastened my seatbelt and reached over to unfasten hers before pulling her into my arms. "Come here."

"I'm fine," she full on cried now, sobbing uncontrollably, as she buried her face in my neck. "This is ridiculous."

"You're not pregnant, are ya?" I joked, wrapping her up in my arms.

"Could you imagine?" she joked back, still crying.

"Fuck no," I chuckled. "I think I'd rather open the door and lie down in the traffic."

"Then it's a good thing I'm not," she replied, laughing almost manically, before another batch of sobs racked through her. "It's probably just period hormones or something."

I'm an addict, you're a bitch

AOIFE

My pitiful attempt at telling Joey about our little situation had resulted in him indirectly admitting that he would rather play with traffic on the M8 motorway than father a child with me.

Joking or not, it wasn't a risk that I was willing to take, especially when Friday night traffic was so heavy.

By the time we made it back to his house, I was fresh out of tears and he was fresh out of patience.

"I don't know, Molloy," he said, parking the car, after I finished giving him a detailed rundown of the woes of womanhood and premenstrual syndrome, literally anything to buy myself more time from having to tell him the truth. "It's not my area of expertise, but surely they can give you a prescription for that."

"You think I need a prescription for mood swings?"

"No, not a prescription, per say," he hedged, climbing out of the car. "More like a light tranquilizer."

"Well, you'd know all about those," I huffed, stepping out and slamming my door shut. "Wouldn't you?"

"Forget about it being light; a horse tranquilizer should do it," he muttered, slinging an arm over my shoulder. "Come on, cranky."

Sighing, I slid my hand into his back pocket, leaned into his side, and said, "I'm sorry for being such a bitch to you."

"Meh. I'm an addict, you're a bitch," he mused, pulling me close. "No relationship is perfect."

I laughed. "It works, though, right?"

"Right." Grinning, he leaned down and kissed me, as we rounded the garden wall and walked up the driveway. "Two of a very fucked up kind."

"Hey, guys." Shannon greeted us in the doorway, with a sobbing

Sean on her hip, and I felt my boyfriend stiffen when his eyes landed on her face.

Her very black and blue face.

"What happened?" Joey demanded, moving straight for his siblings. Scooping Sean into his arms, he quickly led his sister into the house, while I hurried after them.

"He lost it," Shannon explained, cracking her knuckles anxiously. "Over that picture in the paper of me and Johnny Kavanagh. He wouldn't stop, Joe. No matter how much I begged him." With her small hands trembling, she walked over to the cooker, and retrieved a small foil-covered plate. "Mam came in and pulled him off me," she whispered, sniffling, as she removed the foil and put the plate in the microwave to heat up. "But then he hit her, too."

"He hit Mam?" Joey's voice was deathly cold. "She's five months pregnant."

"I know," Shannon sobbed, rubbing her swollen cheek. "When he left, he took everything with him. He filled up the car with everything he could get his hands on – he even took the television in the sitting room."

"I paid for that," Joey bit out, body thrumming with tension, but trying to steady himself, as the small toddler in his arms clung tightly to his neck. Rubbing Sean's back in small, circular motions, he looked at his sister and asked, "Where's Mam now?"

"The boys are in bed," she hurried to tell him. "They eventually passed out, but I can't get this little guy to stop crying long enough to go to sleep."

"I'll sort him," Joey replied before repeating, "Where's Mam?"

Shannon flinched. "Joe . . . "

"Where's *Mam*, Shannon?"

"Gone," she squeezed out. "She left us."

"Left you?" He shook his head. "Left you how?"

"She packed a bag and climbed into a taxi," his sister confessed, jumping when the microwave pinged behind her. "About an hour after

Dad left." Shivering she opened the microwave door and withdrew the heated plate of spaghetti. "That was around half past six, and she hasn't called or answered her phone since."

"So, what?" Joey demanded. "Mam just left you here alone with the boys? No explanation or anything? She just upped and left?"

She offered her brother a sad smile and set the plate clearly meant for him down on the table. "Here; I saved you some dinner."

"Shannon."

"You should eat it before it gets cold."

"I'm not hungry. Answer me."

"Are you sure?"

"Shannon!"

"Yes," she admitted quietly. "I suppose she did."

"Why didn't you call me?"

"Because you were going to the cinema."

"Shannon!"

"I didn't want to trouble you again." She cringed, cheeks burning. "I feel like that's all any of us do these days."

"Because I'm your *brothe*r," he snapped, closing the space between them and tucking her under his arm. "That's what I'm *supposed* to do."

I watched as both Shannon and Sean clung to Joey, a lot like I had earlier in the car.

"You call and I come running," he told them in a gruff tone, but his eyes were locked on mine as he spoke. "Every time."

Daddy duties

JOEY

Once again, I found myself up shit's creek without a paddle – or a parent to show me the way.

My father was gone, my mother was missing, my sister had been beaten to a pulp, my brothers had been abandoned, and my girlfriend had been possessed by some demon bastard called premenstrual syndrome.

And here I was, in the middle of the carnage, trying to stay clean and keep my head on straight.

Im-fucking-possible.

Shannon was at home with Sean, and I was supposed to be in the city, at a minors training session of my own, but I was here, in Ballylaggin GAA Pavilion, with my attention switching between each of my brothers' underage matches.

Reverting to the life-learned pattern that had led me down the path that Molloy had dragged me out of at Christmas was not an option, so instead of drowning out the noise by self-medicating, I settled for a smoke instead.

Sitting on the grassy slope, away from all of the other parents and supporters flocking the GAA grounds, I rolled a joint, while I waited for the boys to finish competing in their underage hurling blitz.

With my arms hooked loosely around my knees, and my hood up to conceal my face, I took a deep hit, holding it there just long enough to feel the burn in my lungs and the haze in my mind, before exhaling slowly.

Hurling wasn't Ollie's cup of tea. He struggled with the concept of the game in the same way Shannon used to struggle with Camogie before she gave it up.

Tadhg, on the other hand, seemed to have the gene that had been passed down from our father in droves.

Hurling came naturally to him and, when you watched him play, you knew you were looking at something special.

At *someone* special.

I had a feeling that, given the time and space to hone his craft, providing our father didn't suck all of the joy out of the game for him like he had for me, that Tadhg would become the best one of all of us.

Ols was a trier, but the kid just didn't have the hand-eye coordination, dexterity, or cut-throat attitude that went hand-in-hand with the sport, which was fine by me. I couldn't care less if any of my siblings played or not.

To me, it was a game, just a game, but to our father, our ability to hurl was a rite of passage that couldn't be skipped over or avoided.

From the age of four, a hurley had been thrust into each one of our hands, and we had been marched over to this very pitch, handed over to the underage trainers and coaches, with our father's full permission to bend, break, and shape us into the best we could be.

It was our own personal baptism of fire.

Smart but not insolent, confident but not arrogant, brave but not audacious; Darren had always fit the mold of golden boy to perfection. All of those characteristics, along with his mild-tempered mannerism and perceptive nature, were the primary reasons why he had always been our mother's favored son, and up until he learned of his sexual orientation, our father's favorite, too.

Most importantly of all, Darren had been both a skilled and proficient hurler, but he had never been a *phenomenal* one. He had never taken the shine off our father, and, because of this, the old man had never felt threatened by him. Because, in our father's eyes, the better hurler you were, the better son you were, unless you were *better* than him. Then you were a threat to his legacy, and he loathed that more than if you couldn't hit a ball straight. He wanted us to be reminded that he had been one of the greats and *not* the other way around.

While I had never been the son our mother could be proud of, lacking the silver tongue my older brother possessed, I *had* managed to fit the stereotypical prototype required to be accepted and praised by our father. Until, at the tender age of eleven, when I made the unforgivable error of coming under the radar of the county selectors, something my father hadn't managed to achieve until he was thirteen, and Darren fourteen. After that, our relationship went downhill fast, shifting from tempestuous to downright intolerable.

The more I played, the more he hated me, and the more he hated me, the harder I played just to piss him off further. It was a vicious, never-ending cycle of toxicity that resulted in me resenting the game almost as much as I resented him.

My father hated *me* because I played the game better than he ever had, and I hated my father because he had morphed me into his own personal living, breathing clone.

He taught me everything he knew and then resented me for using it, while I loathed him for instilling inside of me a gift that would never be *mine.* For the rest of my life, whether I was better than him or not, he would forever be credited with my achievements. I still played, though, because, in all honesty, I didn't have a whole host of other skills.

"I haven't seen you in a while," a familiar voice said, as a tall figure sat down on the grass beside me. "How've you been doing, kid?"

Immediately tense, I balanced my smoke between my lips, and turned my head to look at him. "What are you doing here?"

"Daddy duties." Shane inclined his head towards where a minis game was going on. "You see that young fella over there? The big lad with the ball?"

"Yeah?"

"His ma is an old doll of mine from back in the day," he explained, holding his hand out. "Resurfaced lately, with a habit and her hands hanging. Apparently, he's meant to be mine, or at least she says."

Inhaling one more drag, I passed him the joint and exhaled a cloudy breath. "So she says?"

"When it comes to women like her," he paused for a moment to take a hit before continuing, "labeling that kid as mine holds as much merit as her falling into a bunch of nettles, and being able to pick out the one that stung her."

I winced. "A stab in the dark."

"A very fucking wild stab in the dark," he agreed with a chuckle, exhaling a cloud of smoke.

"Well, shit," I muttered, not knowing what else to say.

"So, how've you been, lad?" he asked, taking another hit. "Haven't seen you around in a while."

"Keeping busy," I replied, disappointed with how his appearance had killed the mellow buzz I had been enjoying.

Now, I was on edge again.

On edge and overthinking.

The old saying *out of sight, out of mind* clearly held some level of merit, because, over time, the more space I had managed to put between myself and my old life, the easier it had become to stay away.

But now that old life was sitting beside me, I realized just how quickly old longings could resurface.

"You still knocking around with that barmaid?"

"She's a waitress."

"Waitress," he corrected, exhaling another cloud of smoke. "I saw your old man in town the other day."

"Like I give a fuck."

"Fucking some barmaid at the side of The Dinniman."

I stiffened.

"Looked an awful lot like that waitress of yours."

I turned to glare at him. "What's your angle here, Shane?"

"No angle," he replied, holding his hands up. "Just doing a good deed for a friend."

"It wasn't her."

He shrugged. "I could be wrong."

"You are."

"Still, though," he mused. "You know what those barmaids are like—"

"Waitress. She's a *waitress*, and I'm not listening to this." Rising to my feet, I turned to look at him. "I told you before that she's a hard limit for me."

He shrugged. "I'm only looking out for a friend."

"Except that I'm *not* your friend, Shane," I told him. "I'm just the fool that halved his wages with you since he was old enough to earn it."

"Sit down, Lynchy."

"No, I'm not interested."

"Sit the fuck down," he warned, tone low and menacing. "*Now*, kid. I'm not finished with you."

Wishing more than anything that I was still blissfully ignorant of what he was capable of, I reluctantly sat back down, knowing there was no level he wouldn't stoop to in order to prove a point.

My baby brothers were a stone throw away from where he was sitting.

I couldn't afford to be reckless.

Because as dangerous of a *friend* as he was for me, making an enemy of him would be infinitely worse.

"Your doll is a hard limit for you," he said calmly, nudging my shoulder with his. "I didn't hear you before, but I hear you now."

Body rigid with unease, I nodded stiffly.

"She's off the table," he offered. "How's that?"

"What do you mean?"

"I mean I remove her from my mind," he replied breezily. "Meaning that I forget all about her. Where she lives. What she looks like. Where she works. Her old man's garage. All of it. Erased."

Bullshit.

The very fact that he was saying this meant that he was using her against me.

He was letting me know, in no uncertain terms, that he could and *would* go after my girlfriend if I didn't play by his rules.

The only problem I had was that I didn't know what game he was playing. "What do you want?"

"Nothing."

More bullshit.

I arched a disbelieving brow.

"Fine," he conceded with a chuckle. "I want you to come and see me again."

In other words, pick back up where I left off.

"No." Struggling to contain my emotions, I shook my head. "I'm done with that shit."

"Are you?" he asked, tone coaxing. "Or is your doll doing the thinking for you?"

Shoulders slumping, I let my head fall forward, desperately trying to keep my head and not fuck this up.

The maze I had managed to lose myself in was virtually impossible to navigate my way out of.

Every time I tried to escape, I got dragged back down another dead-end path.

"That supply issue I was having is all cleared up now." Reaching into his pocket, he withdrew a baggie, and thrust it into my hands. "Your usual."

"Shane." With my chest heaving, I stared down at the bag of oxy in my hand. "I *can't.*"

"Tell you what," he said, rising to his feet. "This one's on me. If I don't hear from you again, then no hard feelings."

He walked away before I could say another word, leaving me alone with my self-control hanging by a tether.

Revelations and rugby boys

AOIFE

Neither one of Joey's parents had returned to the house by the following night.

Alone to bear the huge weight of responsibility they had unceremoniously dropped on his shoulders, I had tried to help as he, once again, parented his siblings with a proficiency a grown adult would envy.

Going from hauling them around to their extracurricular activities, to cooking and cleaning up after them, and then bath-time to bedtime; it was exhausting watching him go through the motions.

No wonder he would rather throw himself into traffic than have a child, I thought to myself, *he already has four.*

When Joey eventually did sit down, a little after eleven, looking bone-weary and close to breaking point, the very last thing I wanted to do was give him that push.

Slumped at the kitchen table, he let his head rest in his hands and exhaled a heavy sigh. "Pretty shit date night, huh, Molloy?"

"Oh, I don't know." Walking over to where he was sitting, I set two mugs of coffee down and wrapped my arms around him from behind. "I wouldn't say it was that terrible," I replied, pressing a kiss to the side of his neck. "I mean, the company's pretty epic."

Grunting in response, he reached a hand up and gave mine a squeeze.

"So." Taking the seat next to his, I reached for my mug and blew the rim before taking a sip. "What's the plan?"

"I don't have one," he admitted honestly, reaching for his mug. "I have no idea what I'm doing, or how long I'll have to do it for."

I thought about what he said for a long time before saying, "I think you're quite possibly the most incredible human being I've ever known."

He shook his head and chuckled. "Fuck off."

"I've never meant anything more in my life," I urged. "Who you are? What you do? The knocks you've taken? The blows you continue to receive? How hard you love those kids? How much you sacrifice so that they don't have to?" I shook my head. "It's mind-blowing, Joe. Your selflessness is staggering."

"Don't say shit like that, Molloy," he muttered, taking a swig of his coffee.

"Why not?" I pressed. "Are you afraid someone might hear me and realize how amazing you are, too?"

"I'm far from amazing," he replied quietly, brows furrowed. "Seriously. Don't put me on a pedestal. I wasn't built for one. I'll only end up letting you down."

"I'd say you're doing a pretty good job of doing the opposite," I offered. "I'm so proud of you, Joe."

"Don't be proud of me, Molloy," he bit out. "Don't be. Because I'm not better. I'm not cured." He blew out an agitated breath. "I'm just . . ."

"Trying?"

"Yeah." Shoulders slumping, he nodded slowly. "Trying."

"That's enough for me," I told him, voice thick with emotion. "*You're* enough for me."

"I need to talk to you about something," he said then, expelling another frustrated breath. "Something important that happened today at the GAA grounds."

"Yeah," I agreed shakily. "I need to talk to you about something important, too."

"Hey, guys."

It was at that exact moment that Shannon walked into the kitchen, causing us both to turn away from the other in relief.

"How's the face, Shan?" Joey asked, eyes trailing over the bruises. "Jesus."

I looked at her, taking in the sight of her black eye and winced, feeling sick to my stomach.

"It's okay Joe," she told him, offering him a weary smile. "It looks worse than it feels."

"I'm so fucking sorry, Shan." He dropped his head in shame. "I should have been here."

"It's not your fault," she told him before I could. "None of what happened last night was your fault. You're entitled to have a life, Joey."

Yeah, he was, but that didn't make it any easier for him.

"Did you manage to get Sean to go back to sleep?" I asked, tone soft.

"Finally," Shannon replied. "Tadhg and Ollie are out for the count, but Sean? God, he's in an awful way over Mam. He was sobbing his heart out for hours. He ended up crying himself to sleep."

"Fucking cunts," Joey choked out, vibrating with tension again.

"Joe," I whispered. "Don't say that."

"Say what?" he argued "The truth? Because that's what they are; a pack of fucking cunts."

"She's still your mother," I said, not because I didn't feel the same way as he did. I simply knew that his words, no matter how true or sincere, would haunt him later, because his mother held power over him in a way that I could never understand.

"She's worse than him," he snapped, running a hand through his hair. "Leaving those kids here on their own. She could pick up the phone and talk to the boys, but no, like always, she runs and buries her head in the sand."

Yes, she *was* worse than him, but Joey didn't really feel that way.

He was anxious and frightened, and feeling cornered.

He was reacting to his trauma by using his words as bullets.

Same as always.

But those bullets were made of buckshot that splintered and ricocheted through him, too.

"Let's see what we're dealing with," he said then, emptying his pockets on the kitchen table. "I don't get paid again until next week. Which leaves us with exactly . . . " His voice trailed off as he counted his cash and stacked a few rogue coins. "Eighty-seven euro and thirty cents for the next six days."

"That's good, right?"

"It should work."

"You know I'd help if I could," Shannon blurted out, looking guilty. "But he won't let me get a job."

"Stop. Don't even think about taking on blame for this, Shan," Joey warned, holding a hand up. And then, with a wince, he added, "Check the fridge for me, will ya?" When she obliged, showing us that it was completely bare, I watched as my boyfriend balled his hands into fists and growled. "Fucking cunts."

"The cupboards are the same," Shannon said quietly. "Mam usually does the shopping on Saturday."

"Usually," Joey sneered, hands in his hair as he slumped over the table, staring down at the stacked coins.

"She wouldn't leave like this, Joe," Shannon offered quietly, worrying on her lip. "She'd never leave us without the shopping."

"Well, she did," Joey shot back, tone hot and full of resentment. "Fuck it; it's grand. We'll manage."

"Yeah?"

"Yeah."

"Okay," his sister replied, looking upset and sounding unconvinced.

"I'll give Mark a buzz in the morning," Joey offered then. "He has a conservatory job lined up in the city next week. I'll ask if he needs a laborer."

"No way," I argued. Mark was one of Dad's clients that used the garage. Every time he came in for a service, he tried to poach Joey to work construction for him. It drove my father crazy. "You can't miss school. It's the leaving cert."

"No," he replied, tone hard and unyielding. "I can't let the kids go hungry. And God only knows when that bitch will come back."

"Joe, I can help with—"

"I am not taking your money, Aoife," he all but spat, looking mortally offended at the very thought. "So, please don't offer."

"Joey." I shook my head, feeling at a loss. "I *want* to help you."

"And I love you for that, but I'm not taking handouts from my girlfriend."

The look on his face assured me that the topic of conversation, for him, was over and done with.

"Do you know where she is?" I asked instead. "Your mam, I mean?"

"I presume she's gone to find him," Shannon replied, looking so small and lost.

"Okay, don't bite my head off for this," I said, choosing my words carefully, fully aware that I was poking a bear. "But should you maybe think about calling in the authorities?"

Joey glared at me.

Shannon gaped in horror.

"They can't keep doing this to you," I tried to persuade, feeling sick to my stomach, and hating the look of betrayal in their eyes as they looked at me. "And you're both here alone looking after three small children." I shook my head. "It's not right or fair on any of you."

"No, it's not right or fair on us, but Shannon and I have been down that road before and there's no fucking way that we're going back there," Joey blurted out, stunning me.

Back there?

Back where?

"Joey!" Shannon hissed, horrified that he spoke so freely around me.

"Look at us, Shan," he replied wearily. "She can already see how fucked up we are!"

"What do you mean?" I asked, giving my boyfriend my full attention. "Back where? What are you saying, Joe?"

"When we were small, before the boys were born, when it was just Darren, Shannon, and myself, the three of us were put into care for six months," he blew my mind by revealing.

"Oh my god." My heart seized in my chest. "You never told me that."

"Yeah, well, it's not something I go around talking about. Besides, I was only six at the time," he muttered, dragging a hand through his hair. "Shan was three. Mam placed us in voluntary care – said she was too *sick* to care for us at the time." His tone was dripping with disgust as he spoke. "Dropped us off and walked the fuck away. Shannon and I got lucky. We were placed together with a nice family. Darren was eleven at the time and wasn't so lucky."

"Joe, please don't," I heard his sister say, pleading with him to block me out of their world.

"He was sent to a care home where things happened to him," Joey continued, giving me his truth. "Things that aren't supposed to happen to children."

"Are you saying he was . . . " He nodded.

I felt my hand shoot up to cover my mouth; a knee-jerk reaction to hearing something so incomprehensible. "Oh—"

"Don't," he warned, holding a shaky hand up. "It didn't happen to me."

"I know," I choked out, reaching for his hand. "I just . . . it's awful."

"Anyway, when Mam's health improved, she went to court and managed to get us back," he explained, brushing my sympathy aside. "It all came out in court about what had happened in that care home to my brother, and because she'd voluntarily given us up, because of health problems, she was somehow re-awarded custody."

"Oh my god."

Joey shrugged. "Darren was never the same again, and neither was our father." Brows furrowing, he scratched his chin before adding, "He actually wasn't too bad of a guy before that. But after it all came out about Darren; the old man lost his fucking mind. He couldn't get over it and turned to the drink worse than ever. Got this ridiculous fucking notion into his head that what happened to Darren had somehow turned him." Joey shook his head. "Had he paid an ounce of attention to us growing up then he would have known better."

Reeling.

I was completely reeling.

It all made sense now.

Jesus.

"I don't know what to say," I confessed.

"It's not right what happens in this house," he said, clearing his throat and drumming his fingers on the table. "But it's better than what's out there in some of those care homes. There's no fucking way I'm letting my sister and brothers go into care. No goddamn way. At least when they're here, they're all in one place, and I can keep them somewhat safe."

The irrational fear he had about the authorities finding out the truth wasn't so irrational after all.

It was totally justified in his mind.

In all of their minds.

Because the Lynch children had been let down by both the state and their parents in all of the worst possible ways.

"Do you guys have someone you can call?" I heard myself ask. "A relative or family member?"

"Nanny is eighty-one," Shannon explained. "She's too old and fragile to—"

"Myself and Shannon have each other," Joey cut her off, tone flat. "That's it."

"Not anymore," I replied, squeezing his hand. "You have me." I looked at his baby sister and smiled sadly. "All of you."

They were both quiet for a long moment before Joey snatched my hand up. "Christ," he muttered, pressing a kiss to my knuckles. "I love you."

This was the first time that Joey had ever openly admitted his feelings in front of another person, and I felt the gravity of his admission in the deepest part of my heart.

"Okay." Standing up before I collapsed in a heap and cried in sadness for them, I clapped my hands together and smiled brightly. "I am *starving*, and I know you both must be, too. So, I'm going to make a food run to the chipper and it will be my treat."

"Aoife," Joey began to say. "I told you—"

"*My* treat," I warned, cutting him off, and casting him a warning glare. He could fight with me about everything else, but not this. "Now, are you coming with me?"

"Yeah, I'll come," he muttered, rising to his feet. "You're not driving around town in the middle of the night by yourself."

"Well, at least you're finally eating again," Joey noted, half an hour later, as we sat in one of the empty booths at the local chipper, scarfing down a monster-sized bag of chips. "You had me worried for a while there."

"Believe me, Joe, taking into account the amount of crap going on in your life right now, my appetite is the least of your worries," I assured him, dabbing a chip in mayonnaise before popping it into my mouth.

"Kev's right," he mused, eyeing me curiously. "This new-found love of mayonnaise is weird as fuck, baby."

Cheeks flushing, I averted my eyes from his, both unwilling and unable to delve deeper into the origins of my new-found cravings.

That was a conversation for another day.

A day when your boyfriend's life isn't unraveling around him.

"Should we head back?" I asked, changing the subject. "To the kids?"

He shrugged. "Probably."

"What?" I asked, eyeing him warily when he continued to stare at me, making no move to leave. "Have I got something on my face?"

He shook his head slowly. "I'm just thinking."

Oh shit.

"About what?"

"How different you look."

Oh, double shit.

"Different how?"

"I'm not sure," he mused, tilting his head to one side, studying me with razor-sharp eyes. "But you do."

"Is that a bad thing?" I chuckled nervously.

"Nothing about the way you look is ever bad, Molloy," he replied, tone thoughtful. "You just look sort of shiny."

I swallowed deeply. "Shiny?"

"Yeah." He nodded. "Kind of like you're glowing."

That would be your baby.

"That would be my halo," I joked, as I quickly stood up and grabbed all of our empty food wrappings. Walking over to the bin, I tossed our rubbish inside and quickly wiped my hands together. "It's shinier than yours, remember?"

"It's a good look," he assured me, pulling me close to give my ass a squeeze, before leading us out the door. "Very sexy."

"Joe." I couldn't repress the illicit shiver that rolled through me if I tried. "Don't."

"Don't what?" he purred, pushing me up against the wall outside. "Don't tell my girlfriend that I think she's sexy as fuck?" Pinning me with his hips, he cupped my face in his hands and kissed me hard. "You drive me crazy," he growled against my lips. "You twist me up in knots, queen."

"Right back at you, stud," I breathed, relinquishing all power over to him, as I wrapped my arms around his neck and pulled him closer.

"How do you feel about getting naked tonight?" he said against my lips.

"Joe, I'm . . . " I exhaled a ragged breath. "I'm—"

"Whatever it is, I don't care," he cut me off by saying. "I need in you so fucking bad, Molloy."

"I don't know who you bleeding are!" A nearby voice boomed, and we both turned our heads in unison to see an absolute giant of a boy slumped against the glass front of the chipper, talking *at* his phone, while he inhaled an abnormal number of burgers. "I don't know any bleeding King Clit!"

"Well shit," Joey mused, stepping back. "That's him."

"Who?"

"That's the lad Shannon has her eye on."

"The one you said beat up Ciara Maloney's boyfriend?"

"That's the one."

"Well, go Shannon," I said, taking in the sight of the ridiculously attractive boy, who was making a ridiculously *unattractive* attempt at swallowing a quarter pounder in two bites. "He's a little ridey, isn't he?"

Joey snorted in disgust.

"Don't worry," I teased, patting his chest. "The steroid-head look doesn't appeal to me."

"No?"

"Nope." Grinning up at him, I added, "I'm more into the lean, mean, cocaine snorting machine type."

He smirked. "Funny."

"Let's go say hi."

"What?" Joey gaped at me like I'd grown three heads. "Why would we say *hi*?"

"Because he could be your future brother-in-law."

His brows furrowed. "Like fuck."

"Come on," I laughed, catching ahold of his hand. "Live a little – but be nice about it. Don't even think about scaring him off your sister."

"She could do better."

"She could do a lot worse," I laughed. "Go on, Joe. Go and say hi to him."

He gaped at me. "Why me?"

I shrugged. "Because she's your sister, not mine."

"So?"

"So, shut up and do it already!"

"Why am I constantly being ruled by the women in my life?" Joey muttered, trailing after me. "Johnny Kavanagh?"

"No pictures tonight, kids," the boy replied, shoulders slumped. "Johnny's on a time-out."

Joey gave me a look that said *what a dickhead*.

I gave him an encouraging nod.

"I spoke to you on the phone the other week," Joey offered then, giving me a pointed look. "You know my sister, Shannon. You dropped her home."

The boy's attention quickly sparked to life at the sound of Shannon's name, and I watched the fog dissipate from his steel blue eyes.

"You're the hurler." Johnny straightened his brick shithouse shoulders.

"Joey." Smiling proudly to himself, he added, "Shannon like the river, and Joey the hurler."

Joey gave me a *what the fuck* look.

I choked out a laugh in response. "Like the river?" I grinned. "God, how much have you had to drink?"

"A river load by the looks of it," Joey said dryly, nudging my shoulder with his. "Do you think you should head home? You look fairly well oiled, lad."

"Would if I could," Johnny grumbled, looking a little lost. "No taxi."

I opened my mouth to speak when Joey shook his head, giving me a warning look that said *don't do it.*

"Sure we could give you a lift home, couldn't we, *babe*?" I said, doing it anyway, and reveling in the *fuck you* expression on his face. "We're only parked down the road."

"That would be great," Johnny replied, voice slurred, but eyes full of relief. "Thanks."

"Yeah, sure," Joey said flatly. "No *problem.*"

I snickered.

Joey glared at me.

I beamed back at him.

This would be fun.

"I'm Aoife Molloy, by the way," I said, amused at how this giant of a boy tried and failed to walk a straight line down the footpath towards the car. Rounding the car, I yanked the door open and snickered, "Joey the *hurler's* girlfriend," before climbing inside.

"Nice to meet you," Johnny replied, manners impeccable, even though he was having a hard time keeping himself upright.

"Three-door," Joey explained, gesturing for our passenger to maneuver over his seat to get into the back. "You're going to have to climb into the back."

"It's fine, lad," Johnny replied ever so politely.

And then I watched as, quite possibly, the biggest boy I'd ever seen in my life tried and failed to wedge himself into the back seat of my poor Opel Corsa.

Rolling his eyes, Joey shoved him into the back seat with an impatient "for fuck's sake" growl.

"Christ," Johnny muttered when he was inside, taking up the entire back row of my car with his shoulders alone.

Climbing into the driver's seat, Joey shoved his seat back as far as it would go, causing the big lad in the back to wheeze out a breath. "You good?"

"All good," Johnny strangled out, clearly crushed. "Thanks again for the lift."

"No problem." Joey leaned in close and mouthed the words *you're dead* before brushing a quick peck to my lips. "Where are we heading?"

"About four miles the other side of Tommen College," Johnny slurred. "Head out the main road for the city. I'll call the turn offs when we get to them."

Joey had just pulled onto the road when he had to slam on the brakes when a big, blond bastard all but threw himself on the bonnet of my car.

"What the fuck?" we both roared in unison, gaping at the lunatic hugging my car like he was superman.

"Get off the car, asshole!" Joey roared, rolling down his window.

"You're stealing my center! Give him back," the boy called out, coming around to the side of the car to poke his head through the driver's window. "Hey, Cap, how's it going?" he said then, smiling into the back seat at Johnny. "I've been looking everywhere for you."

Joey and I looked at each other, instantly recognizing the mad bastard as none other than Gibsie Gibberson or whatever his name was from the Tommen party.

"And this clown is?" my boyfriend asked, knowing full well who he was. The look he gave me told me to *go with it.*

"He's my flanker," Johnny replied with a groan, as he leaned between the seats and hissed, "Gibs, what the fuck are you doing, lad? You're supposed to be gone home with Hughie."

Joey and I looked at each other again, and I knew he was thinking the same thing I was when we mouthed the word *champagne* in unison.

Aw crap.

"The Gards pulled him over for tax and insurance," Gibsie declared, clearly intoxicated, as he staggered and swayed on his feet.

"So?" Johnny hissed. "Hughie's above board."

"He looked at me, Johnny! He shone his big fucking torch right in my eyes," Gibsie slurred, wide-eyed. "I panicked and jumped out of the car. I've been running around town ever since. I tried to call you but you kept cutting me off.

"You're *King Clit*?"

"Oh yeah. I forgot about that."

"What's Hughie down as?"

"Ginger pubes."

"He's blond."

"His girlfriend isn't."

"Jesus Christ, Gibs."

"What do you want me to do with him?" Joey asked, sounding bored, while I was thoroughly amused by their antics.

"I should probably bring him back to my place," Johnny muttered, rubbing his jaw. "Or to a secured hospital."

"See what bullshit you got us into?" Joey told me under his breath, before throwing the door open and climbing out to move his seat forward.

With none of the grace or consideration his friend had shown for the shocks of my car, Gibsie threw himself into the back seat, sprawling out on top of his friend's lap.

"Fuck!"

"Shit, man, did I get your dick? I'll get ice for your balls when we get home."

"Get. Off. Me."

"Christ, this is the tightest hole I've been inside for months."

"I hope there's no more of ye," Joey muttered, climbing back into the driver's seat and pulling off. "The car's weighing down in the back."

"Sorry," Johnny replied, clearly embarrassed.

"It's his fault; the fat bastard," Gibsie declared and then turned his attention back to his buddy and asked, "Hey, is your dick okay, man? I'm really sorry about that. I hope I didn't squash your balls."

"Go fuck yourself, Gerard."

"I was being sincere, Jonathon. For that, you can get your own ice tonight . . . hold up! You traitor! You went to the chipper!"

"Yeah, I did, and it was fucking delicious, and I have no regrets."

"What did you have?"

"A few cheeseburgers and a curry-chips."

"How did it taste?"

"Better than sex."

Joey snorted and muttered, "Clearly, he doesn't have a clue about sex, if he's willing to trade pussy for a burger," under his breath.

"Be nice," I scolded, slapping his shoulder.

"I wouldn't trade you for all the steak in Ireland."

I grinned. "Flattery will get you everywhere."

Winking, Joey turned his attention back to road.

"We're supposed to be on a diet," Gibsie accused, dragging my attention back to their banter. "Did you get me something?"

"Yeah, I got you a burger."

"Thanks, Johnny."

"And then I got hungry, so I ate it."

"You're a *monster*!"

"You two are so weird," I laughed, shaking my head, as I turned back to my boyfriend. "Aren't they funny, Joe?"

"They're something alright," he muttered, shaking his head, letting me know that he was entirely unimpressed with his future-bro-in-law's antics.

"Hey." Gibsie sprang forward between the seats to gape at us. "Who the fuck are you guys?" he asked, though the expression on his face assured me that he knew *exactly* who we were.

'*Not a word about the weed,*' he mouthed, begging me with his eyes to keep schtum. '*He's the captain I tried to drug. He'll kill me!*'

"Johnny's friends with my boyfriend's sister," I threw him a lifeline by offering.

"Sister?" Now, Gibsie really did frown in confusion. "What sister?"

"Shannon," Johnny chimed in.

Gibsie's eyes widened to saucers. "Shannon?" He gaped at the back of Joey's head and mouthed, *'Oh, Jesus, that's his sister? Cap's obsessed with his sister!'*

Snickering, I nodded.

"Yes, *Shannon*," Johnny bit out.

'Oh shit,' Gibsie mouthed before turning back to his buddy.

They fell into a blatantly obvious double-meaning conversation then, where the only people in the car that they were fooling were themselves.

"Oh, yeah." I leaned close and whispered in Joey's ear. "That big gorilla of a boy definitely wants in your baby sister."

"Jesus Christ, do you want me to crash the car?" Joey choked out with a shudder. "That is a hideous thing to say to me, baby!"

"It's true, though," I mused. "Maybe they've already done the deed."

"Molloy."

"She's so tiny, and he's so big—"

"Aoife!"

My sister needs a friend

JOEY

Manipulated into driving miles out of the way on the insinuation that I might get my dick wet afterwards, had me driving through an impressive ten-foot cast-iron gate, and up a mile-long private country lane that led to a house straight out of the films.

Seriously, in any other circumstances, I would be shot on target for trespassing on a property like this.

In fact, I half expected to see a guard of some sort jump out of the bushes with a shot gun.

I had to steel my features when I pulled up outside what I could only describe as a stately fucking mansion.

This was where Kavanagh *lived*?

I looked to Molloy who was gaping at the house not unlike the way I was.

"And I thought his friend's house was a palace," she mumbled, face pressed against the window. "Holy crap, Joe."

"I know, Molloy."

These people owned acres of land and grounds.

They were sprawled out everywhere.

Christ.

After helping Kav deposit his ward onto the couch in a living room that looked like it could have been a ballroom before it had had been renovated, I stopped at the front door, unable to walk away until I addressed the elephant in the room.

"Listen." Rubbing the back of my neck, I turned to face him. "About Shannon."

Kav seemed to straighten, as he stood in the entryway of his impressive as fuck house and inclined his chin for me to get this conversation over with. "What about Shannon?"

He didn't back down or shy away.

Instead, he just braced himself for what I had to say.

"She's fragile," I heard myself tell him. "Vulnerable."

"Yeah. I already guessed that."

"What I'm trying to say here is that I appreciate you looking out for my sister. She's had a hard few years, and Tommen seems like a good fit for her."

He gave me a clipped nod. "It is."

Reluctantly impressed, I gave him a hard look, taking his measure to see if he would slip or falter.

Blue eyes stared back at me, unyielding, and unwilling to bend an inch.

Well, shit.

This fucker was going to stand his ground.

Not wanting to meddle in whatever my sister had going on with this lad, but needing to let him know that I wasn't going to sit back and let him fuck her over, either, I said, "So, I guess I'm hoping that you continue keeping an eye out for her at school. You know, make sure that no one is giving her any hassle."

He nodded once. "That's no problem."

"She seems to be settling in at Tommen, and she keeps telling me that the kids are nice to her, but I'm at BCS so I've no way to tell if she's okay or not." I shook my head and sighed. "And she never tells anyone what's going on in that head of hers until it's too late."

"Too late?"

"Bitchy girl shit." I hated the feeling that I was baring my neck to this lad, but I didn't have any other hand to play. He was the one at school with my sister. He was the one with the ability to do what I couldn't. He was the one going around handling her bullies. He had the upper hand in this situation. "My sister has had a target on her back since she was in nappies."

"Jesus Christ." Raw, unrestrained emotion flashed in his eyes then, and in his voice, letting me know that he wasn't quite the robot he had been programed to be. "That's pretty messed up."

"Kids are cruel," I offered, giving him the perfect opportunity to tell me about the altercation he and Shannon had at Biddies.

"They sure are," was all he offered in return.

No bragging.

No pissing contests.

No explanation.

Just stoic silence.

Well, shit.

"Are you going to tell me about it?"

Silence.

"Ciara Maloney's boyfriend," I mused, lips twitching when he made no move to comply. "Some fella from Tommen beat the shit out of him in town yesterday."

"Oh?" He shrugged noncommittally. "Is that so?"

I smirked. "Yeah, it is."

"Well, I hope he fucked him up," he finally offered, folding his arms across his chest. "Heard his girlfriend's a bitch."

"I heard he was in a bad way," I replied evenly. "Broken nose, and a few stiches."

"How awful." Kav's tone was dripping with disdain, his eyes void of any empathy – or regret.

"Anyway, I just wanted you to know I appreciate that my sister has someone looking out for her when I can't."

"No problem."

"A friend," I said slowly, watching his reaction. "My sister needs a *friend*, Kavanagh. She doesn't need to be getting her hopes up on a guy who'll be gone come the summer."

Or her heart broken.

"I won't hurt her, Joey."

The sincerity in his voice, and the vulnerable look in his eyes assured me that not only was my sister's heart on the line here, but so was his.

Poor fucker had gone and caught himself some big old feelings.

For my sister, of all people.

Go figure.

"I think you're right about them," I said when I climbed back into the driver's seat.

"I usually am," Molloy mused, as she looked through the stack of CD cases in her hands. "But indulge me anyway."

"That big, overgrown fucker?" Fastening my seatbelt, I started the car, and turned to look at her. "Yeah, I'm fairly sure he's banging my sister."

"No way?" Throwing her head back, she laughed. "Go Shannon."

"She's fifteen."

"Oh please." She rolled her eyes at me. "Like you're in the position to throw stones."

"Exactly," I bit out, driving down the tree-lined lane towards the road. "We all know what a shitshow fifteen was for me. Shannon should be learning by my mistakes, not following in my footsteps."

"She's sixteen tomorrow," she reminded me.

"Worse still," I groaned. "Sixteen was another trainwreck of a year for me."

"Hey!" Molloy folded her arms across her chest and huffed out a breath. "I take offense to that statement."

"Why?"

"Because I was in your life for both of those years."

"Ah, but I didn't get naked with *you* until seventeen," I reminded her, winking. "Seventeen was a far more productive year for me."

"No, you didn't get naked with me until you were seventeen," she agreed with a sudden bite to her tone. "Because, if I recall correctly, you were too busy sticking your dick in most of the girls in Ballylaggin and at least fifty percent of our friendship circle at school."

"Funny. Because if *I* recall correctly, *you* were in that four-year relationship with one of my teammates."

"Three and a half years," she corrected with a growl. "And that was totally different."

"How?"

"Because I never *slept* with Paul. *I've* only ever been with *you*."

"Yeah, and I never *loved* any of the girls I slept with, because *I've* only ever loved *you*."

"So, I get your heart, while you get my heart *and* my virginity?"

"Sounds about right."

"That's not a fair trade."

"Tough shit."

"Joey!"

"What do you want me to say?" I demanded in exasperation. "I can't go back in time and *un*-stick my dick in the first girl I slept with, Molloy."

"How about just the first fifty?"

"Now, you're being ridiculous," I muttered, running a hand through my hair. "I haven't been with *fifty* girls. I don't even *know* fifty girls to begin with."

"Well, I can name at least ten girls from school that know *you* on an intimate level," she was quick to point out. "And those are only the girls from BCS, Joe." She finally decided on a disc then, one of her older burner-CDs, labeled *JL 4 AM 1999* in black sharpie ink, and popped it into the stereo.

A few seconds later, 'Joey' from Concrete Blonde drifted from the speakers.

"Turn it off," I warned. "I mean it."

"No, I like it, and don't change the subject," she argued. "We were talking about the fact that you've made your way through half of the girls at school."

"How did a conversation about Johnny Kavanagh's sex life switch into a fight about our previous sex lives?"

"*Your* previous sex life, Joe," she corrected hotly. "My entire sex life, past, present, and future starts and ends with you."

"And my sex life, present and future starts and ends with you."

"But not your past."

"I don't know what to tell you, Molloy."

"How about the truth?"

"The truth about how your mood swings are on another fucking planet?" I bit out, jaw clenched. "Jesus Christ, what is *wrong* with you lately?"

"It was Danielle Long, wasn't it?" she pushed, ignoring my very accurate assertion. "I know you slept with her. *Multiple* times. But she's the one who took your virginity, isn't she?"

"Why are we even talking about this?"

"Because I want to know."

"What does it even matter?" I growled, knowing full well that whatever I said or didn't say, could and would be used against me in the court of Aoife Molloy. This was a dangerous fucking conversation, one that I had deftly managed to avoid until now, and one I could never in a million years win. "The past is in the past for a reason."

"Yeah, I know."

"Then *drop* it."

"Alright. Fine."

"Well, alright then."

"Fine."

"Good," I replied, nodding. "Glad that's settled."

She shrugged. "You're still a huge whore, but whatever."

"Really, Aoif?" Fresh out of patience, I flicked my attention from the windscreen to her. "You want to get salty with me over something I can't change?"

"Nope," she replied all snippy, with her nose in the air. "Just stating facts."

"You're absolutely right; I do have a past," I agreed, pissed off. "One that doesn't include you. One where, yes, I did have sex with other girls. One where I've made some questionable decisions. I am no fucking angel. I've never pretended to be."

"But was it her?" she asked, chewing on her lip, when we pulled onto Elk's Terrace. "Danielle? Was she your first?"

I didn't want to answer these questions.

"Tell me, Joe."

"No good can come from this conversation."

"Please."

"Yeah, she was my first," I reluctantly admitted, as I pulled onto my street and parked up outside my house. "I was young and thick, and desperate for a bit of affection." Killing the engine, I turned in my seat to look at her. "It meant nothing, and I remember even less about it."

"So, she had you first."

"Aoife." I blew out a weary breath. "I can't change my past."

"Who else?" she asked. "How many others?"

"No." I shook my head. "I'm not doing this."

"Why?"

"Because I don't want to," I snarled, losing my cool. "Because I don't fucking remember. In case you forgot, I've spent most of secondary school off my goddamn head. So, I can't give you a number, Molloy, and I can't give you names, because I don't fucking remember." I blew out a harsh breath before adding, "I'm sorry about that, okay? I know that this must be a fucking horrible thing for you to have to hear, because if the shoe was on the other foot, and you were the one saying all of this to me, then it would *shred* me." I shook my head, feeling at a loss. "But it's the truth."

"You were right, Joe." Flinching, she exhaled a shaky breath, and clutched her stomach, looking physically sick. "No good can come from a conversation like this."

"It's only been you," I heard myself tell her, even though I knew that no amount of damage control could repair tonight. "Since we've been together? Since the day you put your lips on mine? It's *only* been you, Aoif."

"Yeah, but you've been off your head for most of our relationship." I watched as a tear trickled down her cheek. "And if you can't remember the girls that you were with before me, then how can you be sure—"

"Because I am. Because I know." Reaching across the car, I grabbed her hand in mine, flinching when I felt the tremor rolling through her. "Because I'm sure about you."

"And I'm sure about you," she strangled out. "But I've spent most of my life watching my mother forgive my father for countless affairs." She shook her head when she said, "I *won't* be that kind of person. I won't become her. It's a hard limit for me."

"And you think I'd do that to you?" I demanded. "You think I'd risk our future for a cheap fuck?"

"No," she admitted, sounding pained. "It's just . . . "

"Listen to me." Leaning in close, I tucked her hair behind her ear and said, "I'm not Tony, and you're not Trish, okay? I would never do that to you," I promised as I cupped the side of her face with my hand, and resisted the urge to shake this sudden onslaught of irrational fear and neediness out of her. "Do ya hear me? I would *never* cheat on you."

She reached up and covered my hand with hers, as her green eyes searched mine for a reassurance that she'd never needed from me before.

"Because, you see this face?" Leaning in close, I rested my brow against hers and stroked her nose with mine. "Your face right here is the only face I've been seeing since I was twelve. Because no matter how off my head I've been over the years, no matter how far from reality I've let my mind wander, I have never lost sight of this face."

Shivering, she exhaled a shaky breath and grabbed my face between her hands. "Really?"

"The only face," I confirmed with a small nod. "The only girl."

"Future," she whispered shakily, and then her lips were on mine. "You said future, Joe."

"No," I mumbled against her lips. "I said *our* future."

She pulled back to look at me. "You want one of those?"

I watched her carefully. "Don't you?"

"With me?"

"Who else, Molloy?"

She looked genuinely stumped. "But you *never* talk about the future."

I shrugged. "Never used to think I had one."

"And you do now?"

"You sound surprised."

"Because I am." Her eyes searched mine, as she continued to hold my face between her hands. "You want a future with me, Joe?"

"I know that I don't want one without you, Molloy," I replied, leaning in to brush my lips against hers. "So that narrows shit down, doesn't it?"

"I guess it sort of does," she breathed, thumbs tracing over my cheekbones. "So, do you have any idea what this future might look like?"

"Well, it won't look like a mansion in the country."

"I don't care about that," she whispered, eyes full of urgency. "Tell me, Joe."

"I suppose it looks a bit like us finishing out school," I offered with a shrug. "You'll get into that hairdressing course in St. Johns, and I'll take the apprenticeship at the garage with your dad."

"Uh-huh." Her eyes twinkled with excitement. "Keep going."

Maybe the night could be saved after all.

"And then we'll attempt to save up for a flat," I said, amused by her sudden perkiness, and playing along to make her happy. "That I'll end up paying for because you'll blow every cent you earn on clothes and make-up – which is nothing new there."

"For real?" she squealed, bad mood forgotten now, as she shimmied around in the passenger seat. "You see us moving in together?"

"Don't get your hopes up," I warned. "On an apprentice's wage, it'll end up being a shitty one bed apartment at the end of Elk's Terrace, with leaky pipes, and a mouse infestation problem."

"Psssh." She waved her hand like those details were unimportant. "That's why plumbers and mouse traps were invented." She grinned at me. "What else does this future of ours consist of?"

"Aside from all of the wild sex we'll be having in our shitty flat?"

"The *constant* wild sex," she agreed approvingly. "On every surface."

"Which we'll soon run out of because it's so small."

"And mouse infested."

"And damp."

"And unbearable." She smiled. "Keep going."

"After a while, we'll upgrade to a two-bed."

"A two-bed?"

"Yeah," I chuckled. "Somewhere for my sister and the boys to hide out. Otherwise, they'll end up emotionally scarred from all of the wild sex we'll be having."

"Okay," she laughed. "So, we're adopting your siblings now, are we?"

"What can I say?" I grinned. "It's a matter of buy one and get four free."

"Maybe we should just permanently evict your parents and keep the house," she joked. "We'd save a fortune in subsidized rent from the council."

"Don't tempt me," I groaned, reluctantly smiling. "So, now that we've established a future with me consists of slumming it up in a flat in Ballylaggin and becoming parents at eighteen."

Her eyes widened. "Parents?"

"Yeah." I nodded. "Buy me and get four kids free, remember?"

"Your siblings."

"Who else?"

"Right," she laughed. "Good one."

"So, any cold feet?" I mused, tucking a tendril of hair behind her ear. "Any changes you want to make to our future plans, or are we all set?"

"No cold feet," she replied, burying her face in my neck, as she hugged me tightly. "I want that future with you."

Be here with me

AOIFE

Joey said all the right things, made all the right moves, and I found myself, once again, snared to his mattress, with his big body on top of mine.

With our clothes cast aside on his bedroom floor, and our lips a crazed frenzy against the others, he moved between my thighs, burying himself deep inside of my body, filling me to the point of pain, and shattering any hope I had of ever surviving a life without him in it.

His family was falling apart around him, and instead of me supporting him, he was supporting *me*.

Genuinely feeling like I was losing my mind one hormonal imbalance at a time, I clung to his shoulders, my fingertips digging into his skin, as he built up a rhythm with his hips that directly aligned with the glorious heat building up inside of me.

Pulling up on his knees, he grabbed my hips and moved faster, as each thrust of his hips became more intense – more feverish.

Even now, as my body reveled in the wonderous feelings he could evoke from me, all I felt like doing was bursting into tears; consumed by emotions, by my fear of the future.

All I wanted him to do was hold onto me and never let go, because the unsteadiness of my life, as I balanced precariously close to the edge of the precipice that was parenthood, was *terrifying* me.

"You good, queen?" His words were a breathless pant, as his chest landed heavily on mine, and he hitched my thigh around his hip, deepening the angle. "You still with me?"

"Yeah." Nodding vigorously, I pulled his face down to mine and kissed him deeply. "I'm with you, stud."

"I love you." His lips were back on mine, his tongue in my mouth, as he fused his body with mine.

"I love you," I cried out between kisses, as my body burned in pleasure and my heart seized with dread.

He loved me now, but would he love me tomorrow, or the next day, or the day after that, once the truth came out?

When he realized that I had taken his future from him?

The one he spoke about earlier?

It would never happen for us now.

Whether he tried to mask it or not, his resentment would be undisguisable.

His entire life was one long sequence of shouldering heavy responsibilities, and birth control had been one of the few things I could take care of for him.

It was a responsibility that I had gladly taken on my shoulders; empowered by the level of trust it had taken him to relinquish that control.

I was the one who vetoed a condom our first time; too caught up in my feelings to think about the consequences.

He was the one who suggested we use both the second time – and the third time, and the fourth, fifth and sixth.

I was the one who had naïvely assured him that we were protected every time it came up.

The pattern we had since fallen into had been built on the foundations of *his* ability to trust *my* ability to protect us from the very thing we were now facing.

"Get out of your head," Joey grunted softly, nose brushing against mine, as he pressed another kiss to my lips, and pulled me back to the moment. *To him.* "Stay with me," he instructed, green eyes locked on mine. "Be here with me."

"I am," I whispered. "I'm with you, Joe."

With my eyes wide open and focused entirely on his, I forced my fears to the back of my mind, letting my body take over the thinking for me, as I drowned in my feelings for him.

*

Several hours later, long after he had fallen asleep beside me, I slipped out from under his arm, and quietly grabbed his hoodie and grey sweatpants from the corner of his room, throwing them on, before creeping downstairs, phone in hand.

It was 03:30 in the morning, and his house was in a rare state of silence. I padded into the kitchen, and dialed the phone number I knew off by heart, knowing that regardless of the early hour, my call would not be rejected.

"Hello?" My mother's sleepy voice came down the line. "Aoife, love, are you alright?"

"Hi, Mam." Closing the kitchen door out behind me, I exhaled a shaky breath and leaned against it. "No. I'm not."

Concern immediately filled her voice when she asked, "Where are you?"

"At Joey's."

"Are you alright?" she demanded. "Have you two had a fight?"

"No." I shook my head. "Nothing like that."

"Okay." Relief flooded her voice. "It's half three in the morning, pet."

"I know, Mam." I chewed on my nail anxiously. "I just . . . " I exhaled a pained breath. "I needed to hear your voice."

There was a long stretch of silence and I heard the ruffling of bedclothes, followed by footsteps padding.

"Okay, I'm in the kitchen alone," she said a few moments later. "Your father's upstairs in bed. We can talk."

Trembling from head to toe, I exhaled a cracked breath. "I don't know where to start."

"Start at the beginning."

"I'm in trouble, Mam." I heaved out a sob and let my head fall forward. "And I'm really scared."

"Okay?"

I shook my head, unable to get the words out.

"Aoife." She sighed heavily down the line, and I could hear the kettle bubbling in the background. "What kind of trouble?"

"The late kind," I strangled out, lowering myself to the floor, dizzy with anxiety and fear. "I'm *late*, Mam."

"Late?"

I nodded weakly. "Late."

"How late?" she asked evenly. "A few days? A week?"

Shaking, I hooked an arm around my knees and choked out, "Almost thirteen."

"Thirteen days?"

"Weeks."

"Jesus Christ." I heard my mother's sudden intake of air, and it caused a flurry of panic to skyrocket through me. "Aoife."

"I didn't know, okay?" I clenched my eyes shut as I sobbed down the line. "I didn't realize. I had my last period on the fourteenth of December, and then everything happened between me and Joey, and I just ... I lost track, Mam. I had a period at the end of January? Except it wasn't like a normal period. It was like a little bit of spotting, but I just put it down to hormones, but Casey said that vomiting can affect the pill, and that wasn't really a period at all and was something called implantation bleeding. I was sick in the new year, Mam. When me and Joe were together? I was really sick for a couple of days, and I'm sorry, Mam. I am so sorry! Please don't hate me."

"I don't hate you, love, I could never hate you," she was quick to soothe, as the sound of a chair scraping off tiles filled my ears. "I just need to sit down and think about this for a moment."

"Okay," I sniffled, nodding aimlessly, as tears trickled down my cheeks. "Take your time."

"Have you taken a pregnancy test?"

"I've taken four."

"And?"

I choked out a sob. "All positive."

"Oh, Aoife, love."

"Yeah." I shrugged, helpless.

"Have you told Joey?"

I shook my head.

"Aoife, does Joey know?"

"Not yet," I breathed, chest rising and falling quickly. "And don't tell Dad either, okay? Or Kev – or Nana. Not yet. Not until I talk to Joe."

"And when do you plan on talking to Joey?"

"I don't know." I felt my shoulders slump. "I tried to earlier, but I'm so scared."

"Aoife, this is Joey's burden just as much as it is yours. I know you're frightened, but the boy has a right to know."

"I know, Mam, okay?" I snapped, chest heaving. "I know. God! I'm trying to work up to it."

"He's a good boy," she was quick to assure me. "He is, Aoife, he's one of the few good ones, if that's why you're avoiding telling him."

"How can you be so sure?"

"Because your father and I have known that boy since he was twelve years old," she replied. "Joey might be rough around the edges, but he's never been one to shy away from hard work or responsibility. It's not in his nature."

"Yeah, Mam, but this is different," I squeezed out, blinking away my tears. "This is a baby."

"He won't turn his back on you," she promised. "Trust me. I'm your mother. I was put on this earth to worry about you, and when you told me you were late, a million different fears and worries flooded my mind. But never once did I worry about that boy's willingness to stick by you."

"Maybe you're right," I choked out, resting my head on my knees. "But I just . . . I need some more time before I tell him."

Mam was quiet for a long time, clearly reeling in my revelation, until she finally spoke again. "Look, today is Sunday. There's not much we can do today. I'll phone the GP first thing in the morning. We'll get you an appointment as soon as possible, and we'll go from there."

"No, no, no, I can't, Mam," I cried hoarsely. "I'm not ready."

"You're going to have to be," she stated in that no-nonsense mothering tone of voice that held no room for arguing. "You need to have your bloodwork taken, and have a dating scan. You need to meet with a consultant and put a hospital plan together." Mam sighed sadly again.

"Because, whether you're ready or not, there's a baby growing in your belly who won't wait for anyone."

"Mam."

"*Talk* to Joey," she pushed. "Talk to the boy, Aoife. I promise, you'll feel a lot better once you do."

"Are you disappointed in me?" I dared to ask, and then held my breath out of fear of her answer.

"I'm not disappointed in you, sweetheart, I'm disappointed *for* you," she replied gently. "You're eighteen years old, with a big, bright future laid out in front of you, and now it's ... going to be changing course. You're going to have to grow up way too fast, and I hate that for you, but your father and I will be there every step of the way."

"Dad. Really?" I flinched. "He's going to hit the roof, Mam."

"Let me handle your father," she replied. "You don't have to worry about him or Kev. You are our daughter, and you have a home with us now and always." She paused for a beat before adding, "And you have my unconditional support."

"I'm so sorry, Mam."

"Me too, Aoife," she replied sadly. "I'm so sorry, too, love."

Ending the call, I slid my phone into the pocket of Joey's sweatpants that I was wearing, only to still when my fingers brushed over a small plastic baggie.

Tensing, I withdrew the small bag from my pocket and stared down at the tablets in my hand.

It took my eyes a moment to make sense of what I was seeing, and my head a little longer to register the magnitude.

Trembling, I slowly unsealed the bag and poured the contents into the palm of my hand, counting thirty or so small pills, in a several different shapes and sizes.

The majority of the pills were stamped with little numbers: *512. D5. 325. M30. K9.*

Beyond horrified, I shoved them all back in the bag and resealed it, before shoving it back in my pocket.

Bunching the sleeves of his hoodie up to my elbows, I sagged against the kitchen door at my back, breathing escalating to the point that I was on the brink of a panic attack.

No.

No.

No, God, please no!

Staggering to my feet, I opened the door and quickly hurried back upstairs to his room, heart racing wildly, as I struggled to restrain my fear from overtaking me.

When my eyes landed on Joey, sprawled out on his back, with his arm slung over his face, still sleeping, I released a shuddering breath and quietly closed the bedroom door behind me.

Fingers trembling, I reached for the hem of his hoodie and quickly dragged it over my head before kicking off his sweatpants.

Desperate to get it away from my body, I threw them back in the corner of his room where I'd found them, before sinking down on the edge of the mattress.

With my hands knotted in my hair, and my elbows resting on my thighs, I sagged forwards, and breathed deep and slow, forcing myself to get a handle on my emotions.

It doesn't mean anything.

The bag is clearly untouched.

He's clean.

He's still trying.

Don't freak out.

He's always with you.

You would know if he was using again.

There's a reasonable explanation for this.

There has to be . . .

Groaning in his sleep, Joey rolled onto his side and reached for me. "Molloy."

Shivering, I let him pull me back into his arms and press a kiss to my temple. "Hm?"

"Don't run," he mumbled in his sleep, as he draped his arm around my body and spooned me from behind. "Stay, baby."

"I'll stay, Joe," I whispered, clutching onto his forearm for dear life. "If you will."

Sweet sixteen

JOEY

The following morning, when I finally woke a little after ten, it was to an empty bed and a childless house.

The note on my bedside locker, in Molloy's familiar scrawl told me all that I needed to know.

Hey stud,

If you're wondering why I'm writing this down instead of texting you, it's because I'm out of credit. Oh, and if you're wondering why the house smells like bleach, and your money is all budgeted for the week in cute envelopes, it's because I've been up since 4am. Hope you don't mind.

Anyway, Sean woke up and came into your room around 6am, but you looked so exhausted, and it's the first time I've seen you actually get a good night's sleep, that I decided to take him and the boys out, and let you have a lie in.

We've been to the shops to grab a few supplies. It's all unpacked and in the cupboards.

We're going to the GAA pitch now. Tadhg wants to show me his 'mad skills' and Ollie wants to hit the playground afterwards.

I'll bring them back around 1pm before my shift at work.

Don't forget to give Shan her birthday presents. And give her a big squishy sweet sixteenth birthday hug from me.

I know you're really busy, but could you swing by my house after the kids are in bed tonight? There's something I really need to talk to you about.

I love you,

Aoife. x

P.S: don't stop trying, Joe.

The house was spotless, the fridge was packed, the cupboards were full, and I felt sick to my stomach over it.

Good intentions or not, it wasn't my girlfriend's job to look after my family and put food on the table, it was mine, and I didn't need her taking on my shit for me.

Especially since I was having such a hard time trying to make sense of why she would even want to.

Any other girl would have run for the hills the minute they felt the full weight of my excess baggage.

Not Molloy, though.

No, instead, she waded into the middle of my bullshit with bags of shopping and budgeting solutions. And then she slapped coats and hats on three quarters of said baggage and took them to the fucking playground.

She'd left both her car *and* twenty quid from her purse behind for me to take Shannon out for a birthday breakfast.

I didn't understand her actions, and I understood her reasons for said actions even less.

Shannon, on the other hand, wasn't one bit surprised by my girl-friend's weird as fuck behavior. On the contrary, she reveled in my discomfort, finding it absolutely fucking hilarious that I had somehow come under the thumb of a girl with bigger balls than I had. Taking delight in my discomfort, my sister goaded and tormented me with notions of wedding rings and forever, making it perfectly clear that she was a solid fan of my girlfriend.

Her smug grin wasn't long evaporating when a phone call from Gibsie had us driving back to lover boy's house to return the phone he'd left in the back seat last night.

Yeah, Shannon's tune had taken a drastic change by the time I parked up outside the manor, and it was my turn to revel in *her* discomfort.

Refusing point blank to get out of the car, I gave up on trying to convince her otherwise, and left her to it.

Strolling into a mansion of a foyer, I followed the sound of voices down an impressive hallway, and finally found both lads in the kitchen, looking a little lost for wear, and a lot hungover.

"You should have a tour guide at the front door," I said, walking into his kitchen, phone in hand. "This house is like a museum."

"That it is," Gibsie agreed, giving me a friendly wave, from his perch in front of a fancy-ass range stove. "Welcome to the manor."

The manor was right.

He could sell tickets to an open viewing of this place, and folks where I came from would arrive in throngs.

"Thanks for this." Kav stood up and walked over to where I was standing in the doorway. "Appreciate you driving all the way over with it," he said, polite as ever, as he pocketed his phone.

I shrugged. "Yeah, well, I was promised food."

Taking his measure in the clear light of day, I begrudgingly admitted was a lot less appealing.

Clocking in just under 6'1, I had plenty of height to play with, but this fucker was simply enormous. Clearly, whatever his mother had fed him growing up, looked a lot different to the menu I'd been eating from.

"And King Clit was very persuasive," I drawled, amused by the name Gibsie was stored under on his phone. "How's my food coming along, chef?"

"Faster than a whore at a brothel, good sir," Gibsie called over his shoulder, not missing a beat. "Egg?"

"Lad." I shook my head, taking in the state of him – and the grease splattered tiles around him – as he attempted to fry a few rashers on a griddle pan. "Are you old enough to use the cooker without your mammy?"

"I doubt it," he replied honestly. "It's my first time."

Another splatter of grease flew at his face, causing him to yelp like a wounded dog.

"Give me that thing before you hurt yourself," I ordered, taking the spatula from him. "Fucking private school boys." Mopping up the splatters with a nearby tea towel, I slung it over my shoulder, and worked to salvage the meat disintegrating on the pan. "Used to having everything done for ye."

"Shit, Kav, I was wrong," Gibsie chuckled, hovering over my shoulder like a child waiting for a slice of birthday cake to be cut. "This fucker right here is the daddy."

"Give me some plates," I instructed, annoyed by how close he was – literally breathing on me. "And some personal space."

"On it," he chuckled good-naturedly.

What a strange bastard.

"Do me a favor, will ya?" I said then, looking over my shoulder at Kavanagh. "Go and check on my sister, will ya?"

He was instantly alert now, hangover forgotten. "Shannon?"

"Yeah." Nodding, I took the plate that Gibsie was holding out for me, and started to pile the rashers on it. "She's out in the car."

"Why would you leave her in the car?" he demanded. "It's *freezing* outside."

"Because she wouldn't come in for me," I replied calmly. "You can try to get her to come inside yourself if you want, but she's not budging."

He didn't answer me.

Because he was too busy diving for the door.

I smirked.

"Lad," Gibsie snickered, nudging my shoulder with his. "I think my best friend is a small bit obsessed with your sister."

"What did I tell ya about personal space?" I snapped, and then waited for him to take a safe step back, before cracking an egg into the pan. "But yeah, I reckon my sister is a small bit obsessed with your best friend, too."

"Aw shucks," he mused, eyes dancing with mischief. "Isn't young love fun?"

"Hm," was all I muttered in response.

"Yeah, well, word of warning, Joey the hurler," he chuckled. "If shit gets serious between them, which I have a feeling it already is, then your shy baby sister's world is about to turn on its axis."

I didn't like the sound of that.

Not one fucking bit.

"Explain."

"Kav doesn't ride waves unless he's sure of the tide."

"Okay; explain in *plain* English."

"Alright." Gibsie grinned. "Kav clearly wants your sister. Your sister clearly wants Kav. Maybe there's a little more than just wanting each other going on here. Who knows? Either way, he's someone whose intentions you take seriously."

"Seriously?"

"Yes, seriously," Gibsie confirmed. "Everything about Kav's world is serious, stable, and selected since birth. His future is set in stone, and his plans are cemented in front of him, without an inch of moving space. So, if he's moving shit around to make space for her, if he's even considering putting her slap bang in the middle of those plans, then it's not an accident. He's about as spontaneous as a dustpan and brush, lad. So, if he decides to go there with your sister, you can be sure that he'll have put together an entire thesis of the pros and cons of making such a move beforehand. Johnny's careful, lad, and he's stable, and when he makes a decision, it's done intentionally and with permanence in mind."

I listened to what he was telling me, and had a feeling that, in Gibsie's own fucked up way, he was trying to let me know that I could trust his friend not to hurt my sister, and that no harm would come to Shannon when she was with Johnny.

"And this is the same fella you thought you could get to smoke a joint," I joked, tone laced with amusement. "This serious-thinking, predictable, unspontaneous giant of a lad is the one you and Biggs thought ye could loosen up?"

"I said that Kav was a serious-thinker," Gibsie chuckled, holding his hands. "Me? I'm spontaneous as fuck, lad."

"You're a strange one," I said, and then had to, once again, ward him off with the spatula. "Would ya step back?"

"Why?"

"I don't fucking like people breathing down my neck."

"I wasn't breathing down your neck," he replied. "I was admiring your cooking skills."

"Well, admire from a distance," I warned. "At least three feet would be preferable."

"Fine," he grumbled. "Are you heading back into Ballylaggin town after eating?"

"I live in town," I deadpanned. "So, that's the plan."

"Could I bum a lift?"

"Where to?"

"Biddies. I left my car there last night."

"Yeah, grand."

"Good man yourself," he replied, hovering again. "And that bacon smells fucking excellent." He leaned in over my shoulder to sniff the pan. "Jesus, I'm starving."

"You're doing it again," I bit out, roughly shrugging him off. "Don't fucking touch me, lad. I won't tell you again."

"What?" he huffed out defensively. "I can't help it if I'm friendly."

"Well, I'm not."

"Not what?"

"Friendly."

"Ah, I don't know about that," he laughed. "Given a bit of time to get to know each other, I think we could be the best of friends."

"That will *never* happen," I warned, glaring at him. "You're a mad, posh bastard, with a personality that, quite frankly, unsettles the fuck out of me." Switching off the stove, I grabbed two plates, laden down with food, walked over to the nearby island, and set them down. "Meanwhile, I'm a short-tempered asshole, with neither the patience nor the temperament to handle a person such as yourself in my life."

"Well, I think you're wrong," Gibsie replied, handing me a fork, and taking up position on the stool next to mine. "I think we could love each other."

I gaped at him. "You're a *freak*."

"Oh, relax," he chuckled. "I meant like brothers."

"I already have four," I said flatly. "Don't need anymore."

"See," he chuckled, tearing a rasher in half and stuffing it into his mouth. "You're already opening up to me about your family. We're bonding."

"We aren't bonding," I argued, stabbing my fried egg with my fork. "We will *never* bond."

Thankfully, Kav returned to the kitchen then, and what do you know, he had my little sister in tow.

"Hey, it's little Shannon. Did Johnny manage to coax you inside or was it the smell of my fucking amazing cooking that drew you in?" Gibsie joked.

"It's raining," Shannon mumbled, sidling exceptionally close to a fella she considered to only be a *friend*.

As I bantered back and forth with the strange one, I watched as Kavanagh fussed over my sister, and I had to admit that he was the first person I had ever seen put a genuine smile on her face.

They looked fucking ridiculous together, with her barely reaching his chest bone in height. They were worlds apart and polar opposites, but the way they were looking at each other assured me that neither one of them gave one iota of a shit for the small details.

Yeah, I could smell the sexual tension from here. It was almost as bad as the god-awful wet dog smell coming from her.

Apparently, she'd been knocked on her ass outside by his dogs.

Deciding to fuck with them a little further, I asked lover boy if he had a change of clothes she could borrow, and to watch a lad, who pummeled grown men into the ground on a weekly basis, turn bright red like that was fucking hilarious.

"Johnny, she can take a shower here, can't she?" Gibsie, who was equally amused by what was unfolding before us, decided to ask.

"What?" Shannon squeaked, wide-eyed and red-faced.

"Uh, yeah, I guess," Kav replied, clearing his throat several times before adding, "If she wants."

"Good idea," I joined in by adding. "Wash that wet dog smell off ya before we have to drive home in small confines."

"I don't smell."

"You stink," we replied in unison.

"Fuck off the pair of ye, and leave her alone," lover boy came to the rescue and warned. "She doesn't smell bad at all."

"You don't smell it because you're immune," Gibsie explained. "He lets the mutt sleep on his bed every night."

Johnny narrowed his eyes, outraged. "Call my dog a mutt again and you'll be wearing that frying pan."

Gibsie held his hands up and laughed. "My sincerest apologies, lad. I never meant to insult your precious pooch."

"I am so sorry about this," Shannon choked out, looking up at Kav like he hung the moon. "I don't have to shower in your house—"

"Ah, yeah you fucking do," I interrupted, earning a snicker of encouragement from Gibsie. "I meant it when I said you're not getting into Aoife's car like that. I could run a drag off ya with the state you're in."

"For fuck's sake," Kav muttered, catching ahold of my sister's hand, before the pair of them disappeared down the hallway.

"Ah, that was brilliant," Gibsie sighed in contentment. "He's probably up there shitting pebbles because this wasn't part of his concrete plan."

A reluctant smile breached my lips and I shook my head, concentrating on clearing my plate. "So, what's the story with you and your buddy's sister?"

"Who?" he asked. "Claire?"

I nodded.

"She's my intended," he came right out and said, without a hint of embarrassment.

"The fuck?"

"It's true," he urged, eyes wide and full of sincerity. "We're betrothed."

"Since when?"

"Since she was four and I was six, and I promised her that I would marry her."

"So, in other words, you signed your life away on a child's promise?"

"What can I say?" He shrugged before adding, "I'm a man of my word."

I gave him a curious look. "Explain."

"Hugh and I were in first class over at St. Paul's, an all-boys school, so Claire was sent to the mixed school across town."

"Sacred Heart Primary School," I filled in with a nod. "The same one myself and Shannon went to."

"I remember it like it was yesterday," he said, smiling fondly at the memory. "It was Claire's first day in junior infants, and she had come home in floods of tears. I was out front kicking a ball around with Hughie when she stumbled off the school bus at the end of our road, and all I could see was a mountain of blonde curls, as she raced up the driveway towards us."

"Why was she crying?"

"Apparently, some little shit in senior infants told her that she had to be his girlfriend." Gibsie threw his head back and laughed. "And when she told him that she didn't want to be his girlfriend, he pulled her hair and told the class that she ate bogies."

"What a little prick," I chuckled.

"She was so upset, lad." Gibsie laughed. "Honest to God, you've never seen devastation like it."

"What did her brother do?"

"Hughie told her to tell him to fuck off."

"I'm guessing that's not what you did?"

Eyes twinkling with mischief, Gibsie opened his mouth to answer me when Kav came bulldozing into the kitchen, with a face like thunder.

"I've a question, Joey the hurler."

The sheer fucking condescension dripping from his tone had my back up in an instant. "Go for it, mister rugby."

"I need a minute, Gibs," Kav snapped, and without a word, his dopey pal strolled out of the kitchen, closing the door behind himself. "Now." Kav folded his arms across his chest and glowered at me. "Who the fuck is putting their hands on your sister?"

Well, shit.

No one ever had the balls to ask such a forthright question.

Nobody ever asked because they didn't want to get involved, and, even if they did ask, they didn't want the truth. That's how it had been for as far back as I could remember. With teachers, trainers, neighbors, hell, even the Gards didn't want to know.

The only person in our lives that had ever taken the time to dig deeper, to push further, was Molloy.

Until now.

"Yeah, you heard me," Kav pushed, unwilling to back the fuck down like I was used to. "I found her on her hands and knees at school on Friday, throwing her guts up," he continued to say. "Something's happening to her, and I want to know what it is."

"Why?"

"Because I want to fix it."

"Why?"

"Because no one should be putting their goddamn anything on her!" he snarled, losing that perfectly polished exterior. "Fuck!"

"What did she tell you?"

"That she fell over Legos." He threw his hands up in frustration. "Fucking *Legos*."

"If Shannon says that's what happened, then that's what happened."

"No – *no*!" he as good as roared, losing his cool completely, as he held up a hand and battled to control his temper. Something I was all too familiar with. "Don't give me that shit. This isn't the first time I've seen her with marks. What's *happening* to her?"

Leaning back on my stool, I studied the lad who had injected himself into my sister's life – and potentially all of our lives.

He was standing in front of me, asking for the answers I couldn't give.

The helpless tone in his voice struck a chord with me.

Because I knew that tone.

I knew that desperation.

I felt it daily.

"Who is hurting your sister?" he repeated, as desperation and frustration fused together inside of him.

This fucker cared.

He cared an awful lot.

"Is it those pricks from school?" he pushed. "Was it them? Those girls?" His voice cracked and he took a deep breath before asking, "Is she hurting herself?" His eyes hardened like blue steel when he hissed, "Are you hurting her?"

All I could do in this moment was arch a brow.

He had some pair on him to say that to my face, and the only reason I wasn't gunning for blood for the hideous fucking accusation was because his feelings for my sister were written all over his face.

"Lad, you better start talking because brother or no brother, I will kick your ass."

He could try.

Johnny Kavanagh might have the upper hand in the physical stakes, but I had a feeling that a fella as stable and sound of mind as him, having grown up in a home like this, never had to fight for survival quite like I had.

He'd been raised like a fucking prince, with countless portraits and pictures of him adorning the walls of his family home, while I'd been born into hell and dragged up on the streets.

There was a killer instinct required to survive as far as I had, and that meant it didn't matter how much of an underdog I ranked in a fight. The only way that I would *ever* back down or quit was if my heart stopped beating. So, if he planned on throwing down with me, then he needed to be prepared to kill me because I would never stop getting back up.

Not for my father.

Not for him.

Not for any other fucker on this planet.

The fact that it was genuine concern for my sister that evoked his threatening behavior, had me keeping my head in a way that was unheard of for me. Still, something deep inside of me instructed me to do it.

He wasn't the enemy.

Not today, at least.

"You'll need to talk to Shannon," I finally said. "I can't give you the answers you want."

"*Yes*, you *can*," Kav shot back, imploring me with his eyes to speak up. "Just open your mouth and *speak*!"

"No." I shook my head. "I can't and I won't. If she trusts you enough, she'll tell you. If she doesn't, she doesn't. Either way, it's not my call."

"Not your *call*?" He looked incensed at that. "What the fuck is that supposed to mean?"

"Exactly what it sounds like," I bit out. "It means that it's not my call. But I can assure you that I have never put my hands on my sister. Or any woman, for that matter."

"I want to know what's going on here, Lynch. If she's being bullied or some shit like that, then I can *help*. I can fix this if you just *tell* me."

"*You* can fix this?"

"For her?" He nodded vehemently. "Absolutely."

"You like her." I tilted my head to one side, studying him. "Maybe even more than like her."

He didn't deny it.

Good.

Another tick for him.

"I want to know what's happened," he tried to reason. "I need to."

Maybe his buddy was right about this lad sticking around. His words certainly displayed a level of permanence.

"Listen, I'd love to tell you," I replied. "I'd have no goddamn problem laying it all out there for you. I have nothing to hide."

As I spoke the words, I realized that they were my truth.

Because something had happened inside of me, something fucking strange, and I was growing weary of lying.

Of covering up.

Of constantly watching my back and the backs of my siblings.

It was no life to live, and I didn't want it anymore.

I never had.

"But she won't want me to do that," I tried to explain to him. "Shannon would die if she thought anyone knew her business. After all the shit that went down for her at BCS, she *wants* that clean slate at Tommen – and I want that for her, too."

"So, she *is* being bullied," Kav choked out, missing the mark entirely, and looking physically sick at the thought. "Someone at Tommen." He shook his head, looking lost. "Or at her old school."

I sighed heavily. "Listen, Kavanagh, if you want to know what goes on in that head of hers, then be worth it."

"Be worth it?" He glared at me. "Be worth *what*?"

He knew exactly what I meant.

If he wanted in, like he so desperately seemed to, then he needed to earn that entry pass from Shannon.

I couldn't give it to him.

Even though, a weird part of me strongly wanted to.

Because, even though I'd long given up on protecting myself, and having spent years failing to protect my siblings, I was starting to come to terms with the possibility that I wasn't doing the right thing for them.

That keeping quiet wasn't the right thing.

Maybe I had taken too many blows to the head at the hands of our father, or maybe it was Molloy getting inside my head, but keeping my mouth shut was starting to look, in my mind, less like protecting my siblings, and more like enabling my parents.

Still, the memory of Darren's abuse continued to imprison me, keeping the fear alive just enough to keep my tongue at bay.

"You're a smart guy," was all I replied. "You'll figure it out."

Kav shook his head again. "I don't—"

My phone rang out loudly in my pocket, stalling him, and I quickly pulled it out, only for my heart to fall into my ass when I saw the name flashing across the screen.

Dad.

Fury enveloped me then and I held a hand up to warn Kavanagh to keep his goddamn mouth shut as I pressed the answer button and put the phone to my ear.

"Joey, it's me."

"What the *fuck* do you want?" I sneered, thoroughly disgusted that he even thought that mine was a number he could call.

The sound of his voice had every hair on my body standing on end.

It didn't matter to me that he sounded sober.

Everything about this man, drunk or otherwise, made my skin crawl.

I almost fell off the stool when I heard him say, "I'm phoning you to let you know that I'm coming home with—"

"No, you were told," I cut him off, pacing the kitchen, trying to keep my shit to myself all while I was losing the very same shit. *You were goddamn told there was no coming home.* "There's no coming back."

"What happened the other night was a mistake," I heard him say, tone level. "I didn't mean to hurt your mother. It was a heat of the moment thing. You understand."

He didn't mean to hurt Mam? I *understand*? What about Shannon? Had he meant to hurt her when he pummeled her face with his fist? Of *course* he fucking meant to.

Believing that he didn't mean to do something that he had repeatedly done throughout the course of our lives was the definition of insanity. "I don't give two shits how sorry you are."

"Would ya just shut that hole in your mouth and listen to me for a second—"

"No!"

The last time I sat down and listened to him attempt to absolve himself of any wrongdoing was more than eight years ago, shortly after witnessing him brutally rape my mother against the same table we were forced to eat at every day since.

I'd taken a hurley to him in my pathetic attempt to protect her, and the fight that ensued had been so loud and vicious that the neighbors called the Gards.

As a result, the social workers had been called in, and I had been forced by the very woman I had tried to protect to sit at that same kitchen table that still remained in our house, and listen to her abuser reel off a convincing tale of how the ring on her finger gave him dominion over her body and mind.

I had instantly called bullshit on that and was then treated to an indepth and graphic play by play of what happened to a small boy when he went into care by my father.

Darren, being the diligent and conscientious son, having endured the suffering had been spared the warning.

So was Shannon and the small boys.

Not me, though.

Not the black sheep of the family.

The liability.

The fuck-up.

I lost my childhood that day.

I'd never had much of one to begin with, but whatever innocence that had been there, all of my boyhood hopes and dreams, had been snuffed out in an instant.

Mentally and physically scarred to the point where I couldn't picture myself trusting another human being. Terrorized with grave details about what would be done to me if I didn't keep my mouth shut, or worse, what would happen to Shannon and Tadhg, I'd buckled under the pressure and lied through my teeth like the good solider I'd been trained to be.

From day one, my reluctance to commit to Molloy never had a thing to do with my ability to love her, and *everything* to do with the fear of loving her the *wrong* way.

The fucked-up part was that I couldn't see then what I was starting to see now, that I was trying to protect those kids from rapists, by *living* with one.

Because that's what he was.

He *was* a fucking rapist.

The things he did.

The pain he caused.

The lives he ruined.

No, I would *never* listen to another excuse that man made again.

"Your mother is in the hospital," Dad said, dragging my thoughts back to the present, and bringing with it a flood of panic. "She had a bleed the other night. A bad one."

I gripped the phone so tight; I thought the skin around my knuckles might crack. "She's *where?*"

"Are ya deaf, Joey? I said she's in the fucking hospital," he barked. "Placental abruption, apparently."

Jesus Christ. I felt faint as I pressed a hand to my brow. "When did that happen?"

"Friday night," he replied, confirming my worst fears. "The hospital rang me to come in to be with her."

My heart sank into my ass.

I was calling her a cunt while she was bleeding out in the hospital.

"She went in with bleeding, but when they went to examine her, her waters broke," he added, sounding genuinely human for once. "She, ah, she was in a bad way with the bleeding, so they took her down to theatre to sort it. According to the consultant, it can happen in older women who've had a lot of children, and your mother had a c-section on Tadhg."

"And the baby?" I heard myself squeeze out.

"What do you think, ya bollox?" he snapped. "It's fucking dead, isn't it? It wasn't much bigger than the size of my hand."

Jesus Christ.

"*It?*" I choked out, feeling my legs tremble beneath me. "*It?*"

"What do ya want me to call it; your brother?" he demanded.

So, it was a boy.

A baby brother.

Jesus.

"It's fucking gone, and that's that," Dad snapped. "No point in getting worked up over something we can't change."

I didn't know what I wanted him to say, but calling the baby '*it*' made me feel physically sick.

"Your mother's in a bad way here," he continued to say. "They're discharging her, but she won't leave the hospital" He exhaled a frustrated breath before adding, "She won't leave it."

Stop calling him it, I wanted to scream, but my current company caused me to refrain. "What the fuck do you want me to say?"

"Well, first thing's first, you can get rid of that sorrowful tone of voice," he snapped. "Why would you be sad? It's not like you were happy about it."

"Why would I be *sad*?" I shook my head in disgust. Was he *serious*?

"You didn't want her to have another baby, and now there isn't one," he bit out, tone accusing. "This suits you down to the ground, boy, so you might as well be honest about it."

Yeah, I didn't want them to have another child, but that didn't mean that I wanted my mother to *lose* her baby.

I didn't want my baby brother to *die*.

I would *never* want that.

But I couldn't stop myself from hissing the words, "It's a goddamn relief is what it is," down the line – and I meant it, but not for the reasons he thought.

The baby would be spared the pain of ever being carried through the threshold of hell that was our home.

The baby would never feel the sting of our father's slap, or the pain of our mother's lack of emotion.

There would be one less sibling to protect, to worry about, to feed, to nurture, and I would be a liar if I pretended otherwise.

As resentful as I had been about the pregnancy, that didn't mean that I wouldn't have loved him just the same as I loved the rest of them. My heart would have expanded, and my arms would have stretched that little bit further to fit him in.

"I need you to come over here and talk some sense into your mother," Dad continued. "You know what she's like. How her mind drifts away under pressure. You've always been able to bring her back when she checks out like this."

"Fine," I replied, tone tight.

"We're at St. Finbarr's in the city," he added. "You know where that is, don't ya?"

"Yeah, I'll be there."

"Grand," he said with a relieved sigh. "Because I don't know what to do with her. She's just crying and rocking and I can't be fucking handling her when she's in one of these moods."

"I just said I'd be there, didn't I?" I snapped, repressing the urge to roar when I found Kavanagh watching me like a hawk. "I'll *be* there."

"When?" Dad pushed. "How soon can ya be here? Because I'm not fucking around, boy, I'm close to losing my patience with her. I want to get home and have a shave and a shower. I can't be sitting here, watching her crying into a box."

"I'm on my way."

"Good lad," he said, tone approving. "Be quick about it—"

Numb, I hung up and slid my phone back in my pocket and looked at Kavanagh. "I need to take off."

"Take off?" he demanded. "Where?"

"I have somewhere I need to be," I mumbled, completely fucking reeling.

"Hold the fuck up," he warned, blocking the doorway. "Your sister is upstairs in my shower."

"Yeah." I shook my head and blew out a pained breath. "I'm going to need you to hold onto her for me."

"Hold onto her?" He looked at me like I'd just lost my mind. "You just want me to *hold onto* your sister?"

"That's what I said, wasn't it?"

"You're not saying anything," Kav hissed, furious. "That's the problem. You're not telling me shit!"

"I did tell you," I snarled, losing my cool now. I didn't have time for this shit. "I told you to *ask* Shannon!"

"So, you're what?" His eyes bulged in his head. "You just going to leave her here?" It sure beat the alternative. "For how long?"

"I don't know."

"You don't know?"

"Yeah, I don't fucking know," I snapped, just about done with his bullshit. "Is that a problem?"

"It's not a problem that she's here," Kav was quick to state, "It's a problem that you're leaving her here, and I have no goddamn idea of what to tell her."

"Fine," I lost my cool and spat. "Tell my sister that our *father* called. Tell her that our *mother* had a miscarriage on Friday night, and he's on the way home from the hospital with her now."

He had the good grace to flinch. "Shite."

"You have no fucking idea," I seethed, shoving past him and stalking down the hallway to swing the front door open. *No goddamn clue.*

"Do you want me to bring her straight home?" he asked, trailing after me, anger gone now, replaced with awkward sympathy. Fuck him. I didn't want his sympathy. I didn't need it either. "Or should I take her to the hospital to see your mother—"

"I want you to hold fucking onto her!" I roared, turning around to face him. "Can you do that, Johnny Kavanagh?" I clutched the front door with a death grip as I met his gaze head on. "Can you look after my sister for me?" *Or have I read you all wrong?*

"Yes." He nodded stiffly. "I can."

"Good." I nodded stiffly. Reaching into my pocket, I grabbed my phone and held it out to him. "I'll call you when I can to sort out picking her up. Just . . . just *keep* her until I can call you, okay?"

Without a word, he took it and added his number to my contacts.

I nodded stiffly and slid it back into my pocket before calling out, "Gussie, I'm leaving now if you want a spin into town for your car."

"Everything okay?" he asked, head popping around the living room door.

Too fucked up to think straight, I turned around and walked away, feeling like my feet didn't belong to me, as I somehow managed to trudge across the gravel and collapse into the driver's seat of Molloy's car.

"It's Gibsie."

I turned to watch him climb into passenger seat beside me. "What?"

"My name," he explained, fastening his seatbelt, and withdrawing a box of cigarettes from his pocket. "It's Gibsie, not Gussie."

"Right, yeah. Gibsie." I started the engine and tore off down the driveway, gratefully accepting the cigarette he had sparked up and was holding out for me. "Cheers."

"No worries, lad," he mused, sparking up a cigarette of his own. "Looked like you needed one." Shrugging, he added, "It's only nicotine, I'm afraid."

"That'll do."

"For now," he joked in a light-hearted tone.

"Yeah," I bit out, as that carnal urge of desperation and need reared its ugly head at the thought. "For now."

Little alpha

AOIFE

Surprisingly, spending time with the younger Lynch boys did wonders to clear the anxiety-weaved cobwebs in my head.

The oldest of the three was the living, breathing clone of my boyfriend back in the day.

The middle one could give me a run for my money in the talking stakes.

As for the baby of the family?

God, Sean was just so damn cute, it was ridiculous.

Too busy fielding the never-ending stream of questions that came from Ollie's wildly imaginative brain, while supplying endless cuddles to the adorable fingers-and-thumb-sucking three-year-old, I didn't have time to brood or ponder on my problems.

The sheer volume of prepubescent, alpha-male attitude coming off Tadhg in waves was impressive, and, if it wasn't for the fact that I had a first-class honor's degree in handling such a snarky little shithead, I might have felt overwhelmed.

However, little alpha proved that he was, indeed, his brother's double by eventually – and of course reluctantly – succumbing to my irresistible wit and charm. The fact that I could puck a sliotar hadn't hurt the cause, either.

By the time we made it back to their house a little before one o'clock, I was somewhat confident that, in the event of all-out war breaking out, I had earned myself three little allies.

The only thing to put a dampener on the day was that Joey and Shannon hadn't returned.

I didn't have any phone credit to contact Joey, and even though Tadhg and Ollie might have been fine on their own for a bit, I could never, in good conscience, leave them to their own devices, with a three-year-old to fend for.

I ended up waiting until half past one before knocking on their next-door neighbor's door to use her landline to call in sick to work for a shift that I should be starting at 2pm because Joey's landline could only accept incoming calls. I'd also used Fran's phone to try Joey's mobile, but it went straight to voicemail.

At first, it hadn't worried me too much, but after rummaging around in his room for music to entertain the boys – because their shithead father took their television with him – and realizing that the sweatpants containing that bag of pills was gone, I quickly changed my tune.

Clearly, Joe had thrown them on this morning before leaving the house, which meant that wherever he was now, he was walking around with his own personal ticking time bomb in his pocket.

"I'm a good dancer, huh?" Ollie asked, dragging me from my thoughts, as we bopped around the kitchen to The Bloodhound Gang's 'The Ballad of Chasey Lain' – courtesy of his older brother's ridiculously explicit music collection.

Yeah, I was a real stellar babysitter.

"So good, Ols," I laughed, watching as the little guy threw shapes like no one was watching.

Thankfully, he and Sean seemed blissfully unaware of the meaning of the song, too busy spinning and twirling around the kitchen to take any notice.

Meanwhile, little alpha was cracking up from his perch on top of the kitchen table.

Slugging a can of his brother's Coke, Tadhg almost choked to death on several intervals throughout the course of the song.

"Hold on, I gots a song. I gots one!" Ollie declared when the song ended, running into the sitting room and returning a moment later with a disc. "This is Mammy's music," he explained proudly, switching up discs on the small kitchen stereo. "I love it."

A moment later, Loretta Lynn's 'The Pill' drifted from the speaker.

"Oh, for fuck's sake," Tadhg groaned, slapping the heel of his hand against his forehead. "Really, Ols?"

"Uh-huh." Singing the song word for word, Ollie bounced around the kitchen with Sean's small hands in his. "Mammy sings this song to us."

"Really?"

"Oh yeah," Tadhg replied, giving me a knowing shake of his head. "Most kids, when they're small, get nursery rhymes." He shook his head and pointed to the stereo. "We got this."

"Well, shit."

"Joe gave her the album for Mother's Day a few years ago." He smirked before saying, "I think he might have been trying to tell her something with that song."

I laughed out loud, even though it was completely inappropriate, not to mention slightly hypocritical.

Grinning wolfishly, Tadhg hopped down from the table and sauntered over to the stereo to switch up discs.

After spending a few minutes flicking through tracks, he settled on Bowling For Soup's 'Girl All the Bad Guys Want'.

He gave me a cheeky wink and said, "This one's for you, blondie."

Well, shit.

I choked out a laugh.

Little alpha had moves.

I'm here to take you home

JOEY

"Thank Christ, you're here." My father greeted me in the hospital corridor.

He was holding a folder overflowing with paperwork in one hand and a plastic bag with what I presumed contained my mother's clothes in the other, as he closed the space between us.

"I can't deal with her, Joey, son. I can't." He clamped his hand down on my shoulder in a move that I could only presume was a show of relief at my presence, but only made me want to peel the skin from my bones. "I know that she's upset, but all that crying and carrying on isn't right."

"Yeah, well, suck it the fuck up," I snapped, roughly shrugging his hand off. "Because you're the one that got her pregnant. She's your responsibility, Dad. She's in this position because of you, so man the hell up and take care of her."

"Don't get lippy with me, boy," he warned, tone taking on a menacing lilt. He gave me a look that said *you'll pay for speaking to me like that*, but I honestly didn't care. "It's easy for you to judge when you don't know what I've been dealing with here."

"I don't care what you've been dealing with," I spat, reluctantly following him down the corridor until he stopped outside of a closed door. "Is she in there?"

He nodded. "I'll let you to it. I've a few things that need sorting."

Meaning, there was a bar stool waiting for him at his local.

"Fine." I jutted my chin out, unwilling to beg the bastard not to leave me to clean up his mess. *Again.* "Do whatever you want."

And then he was gone, and I was left alone, staring at a closed door.

A million different emotions rose up inside of me as I battled to steel my nerves and keep my head.

I didn't want to be here.

I didn't want to see what I knew I would see the minute I opened the door I was hovering behind and stepped inside her room.

Inside her turmoil.

Get a fucking handle on yourself, asshole.

With my hood up, and my hands shaking, I forced myself to reach out and knock lightly before opening the door and walking inside.

A pale blue curtain draped around the bed was the first thing my eyes took in, while my ears were immediately assaulted by the sound of low, almost feral keening.

It was a sound that I'd never heard before and never wanted to hear again.

It was the sound of a woman's heart breaking.

"Mam?"

The crying stopped for a brief moment, and I heard her drag in several gasps of air before she croaked out, "Joey?"

"Yeah." I nodded, trembling. "It's me, Mam."

"Joey," she cried out hoarsely. "My Joey?"

"Yeah, Mam," I replied, clearing my throat. "Can I open the curtain and see ya?"

A few moments later, the curtain was pulled back, and I was greeted by the sight of my mother's tear-stained face, as she staggered off the bed and collapsed in my arms. *"Joey!"*

"Shh, it's okay," I coaxed, catching her before she could hit the ground. "I'm here."

"He died," she wailed, fingers knotting in the front of my hoodie, as she clung to me, body limp and racked with grief. "The baby died, and they took him away. They took him, Joey. They took him away from me."

"I know, Mam," I strangled out, helping her back to the bed.

"He was so small," she cried, refusing to let go of my hoodie, as I stood helplessly in front of her, my hands hanging by my sides, as she took from me whatever she needed in this moment. "Twenty-one weeks," she continued to wail. "He was so tiny."

I couldn't tell her that I knew how she felt or understood her pain, so I just stood there, feeling useless and on edge.

"He's gone now," she said through her tears. "Your father let them take him."

"Take him where?" I forced myself to ask.

"Away," she wailed, crying into my chest. "They'll bury him in the hospital's angel remembrance garden."

"Is that what you want?"

"I don't know," she sobbed. "Your father said that's what's best."

I had nothing to say to that.

She released a shuddering breath before whispering, "Shannon. The boys. Are they okay?"

"They're grand," I was quick to soothe. "They're all grand, Mam."

"And you're here," she said weakly, still clutching me. "How are you here?"

"Dad phoned," I explained, slowly peeling her hands off my hoodie and taking a seat beside her on the bed. "He asked me to come and see you."

"He did?"

I nodded slowly. "Yeah, he did."

"Where's your father now?"

The pub, probably. "He had to leave." I inhaled a deep breath before adding, "Dad says the doctors have discharged you, Mam. I'm here to take you home."

"No, no, no." Her eyes widened with fear. "I can't leave him here. He doesn't even have a name! Just baby boy Lynch. That's what they called him."

"Mam," I sighed, trying and failing to come up with the right thing to say. I could hardly tell her that she had to. "You can't stay here," I settled on. "The boys need you at home with them."

"I don't want to," she wailed, dropping her head in her hands, and reminding me of a child trapped in a woman's body. "Please don't make me."

"I'm not going to make you do anything," I coaxed, eyeing the small pill dispenser on her tray, containing what I instantly knew was a fucking fabulous combination of valium and diamorphine. "Is this for you?" I asked, reaching for the tiny plastic dispenser with shaky hands. "Are you meant to take these, Mam?"

She nodded weakly. "But I get so sleepy."

"That's the point." I thrust the pills into her hand and then placed the small Styrofoam cup filled with water in the other. "Swallow them down and it'll take the edge off."

"Joey, I don't—"

"Take them or I will," I cut her off and warned. "And then we'll both be fucked."

Sniffling, she gave me a pained look before popping the pills into her mouth and flushing them down with a gulp of water.

A mixture of devastation and relief flooded me and I sagged forward. "Good girl."

"I want to see him one more time," she whispered, sagging heavily against my body. "Before we go."

"Okay," I replied, reluctantly slipping an arm around her frail shoulders. "I'm sure one of the midwives can organize that for you."

"Will you stay with me when they bring him back?"

I stiffened.

"Please, Joey," she sniffled. "Don't leave me alone."

"Fine," I choked out a resigned sigh. "I'll stay with you, Mam."

Get me out of this house

AOIFE

It was a little after eight when Ollie had somehow managed to coax Sean upstairs only to end up falling asleep beside him on Joey's bed.

Downstairs in the kitchen, I washed the dishes from dinner earlier, while Tadhg played a game of Snake on my phone in his bedroom.

All in all, I was pretty damn proud of how well I had managed to handle today, but that didn't stem the anxiety steadily rising in my chest at the lack of contact from Joey.

He hadn't come home and he hadn't called or texted, either.

Something was wrong, I was sure of it, but aside from sending out a search party, which I clearly didn't have the means to do, there was nothing I could do but sit and wait for him to return.

With my back to the kitchen door, and my arms up to the elbows in sudsy bubbles, I swayed my hips to the rhythm of The Cranberries 'Linger' as it played on the radio, foot tapping to the beat, and I hummed along to the music.

A few moments later, when the sound of the front door opening and then closing filled my ears, I visibly sagged in relief.

"About damn time, guys," I called over my shoulder, setting a plate on the draining board and shaking the water from my hands. "I thought you were dead or something." I moved to turn around then, but his big body was on me, slamming me roughly against the sink. "Jesus, Joe," I chuckled, with my back to him. "Miss me much?"

His hot mouth was on my neck then, but it didn't feel right.

His sharp wet tongue trailing down the side of my neck felt all wrong. *Wrong, wrong, wrong,* my body assured me.

It was at that moment that I took sight of my reflection in the window over the sink and my blood ran cold.

"Oh my god," I screamed. "Get the fuck off me, Teddy!"

I moved to twist away, but he wrapped his beefy arms around my arms and chest, keeping me pinned to the sink.

Fear spiralled inside of me at a rapid pace.

"Let go," I tried again, keeping my tone as hard and forceful as I could manage, when all I wanted to do was scream and cry. "Now, asshole."

"I've wanted a taste of ya since I first saw ya," Joey's father slurred, and the smell of whiskey that wafted from his breath was stifling. "Look at the body on ya." He hardened behind me and I felt like vomiting. "Wasted on my young fella."

His hand moved to my breast and that's when I flipped the fuck out.

"I said get your hands off me," I snarled, trying and failing to break free of his hold. "I swear to god, if you so much as think about—"

My words were swept away when he clutched my throat with his hand and squeezed.

Paralysed with fear, I dragged my feet against the tiles when he walked us over to the kitchen table.

"Here's how this is going to go, ya little cunt," he snarled, slamming the side of my face against the table. "You're going to keep your mouth shut and take what I give ya." Reaching for the waistband of my sweats, he roughly pushed them down my thighs. "Prancing around my house like you're god's fucking gift."

"Fuck . . . you," I strangled out, with my cheek pressed to the table, I clawed and tore at his hand, trying to inflict as much pain as I possibly could, while locking my legs together, desperate to protect myself while in this helpless position. "Don't touch me!"

"I always wanted to touch this hair," he slurred, releasing my neck, only to roughly twist my hair around his fist until the nape of my neck burned from the pain. "Smooth like silk. Mm. Fucking lovely."

"Please." My stomach heaved and I gagged and gawked in disgust. "Let me go!"

His hand moved to my knickers and he roughly dragged the fabric down, while keeping a death grip on my hair. "Open your legs."

"Drop dead!"

Hooking an arm around my waist, he forced me back up. "Open your fucking legs, cunt!"

"No – no!" I choked out, repulsed by the feel of his hands on my body, as he pushed his knees between my legs, forcing them open, leaving my vulnerable and exposed to him. "D-don't do this!"

I could feel the rough fabric of his jeans against my bare skin, and then the sound of a zip unfastening filled my ears.

"Don't," I cried, bucking to break free. "Don't touch me—"

The sound of the front door slamming followed by a familiar voice roaring, "Get the *fuck* off her!" had me collapsing in a heap against the table.

His hands were gone not a second later, and I crumbled to the floor, shaking violently, as I scrambled to pull my underwear and sweats back into place.

Through my tears, I could see Joey and his father fighting, smashing and crashing into the counters, as they literally tore strips out of one another.

They were shouting, but I couldn't hear a word of it.

The sound of ringing in my ears was deafening me, as I trembled violently, feeling violated.

"Aoife," Mrs. Lynch sniffled, eyes wide in horror, as she hurried towards me. "Are you alright?"

No, I wasn't alright.

How the fuck could I be alright?

Her husband had been seconds away from *raping* me.

"Don't touch me!" I screamed when her hand landed on my shoulder. Scrambling to my feet, I backed up as far away from these people as I could physically get. "Stay the fuck away from me, all of you!"

Unfortunately for me, the way out of this hellhole was on the other side of the kitchen, and while I was desperate to get out, I couldn't make my legs move, because moving forward meant passing *him*.

"Molloy." That was Joey. He was standing in front of me, with his hands on my cheeks, green eyes wild and frantic, and I was having none of it. "Aoife, baby—"

"Don't touch me," I choked out, yanking my face free from his touch. "Just get me out of here."

"Aoife." He moved for me again, and over his shoulder I could see the crumbled heap that was his father, twisting and groaning on the floor. "Please, just ... don't ... I'm so fucking sorry."

"I said get me out of here, Joey!" I screamed, dragging my hands through my hair, as I tore my eyes off *him* and forced myself to look at his son. "I want to leave *now*!"

My gaze once again flicked to the monster, who was now sitting up, while his wife held a damp tea towel to his cheek.

Was she serious?

Did she not see what he just tried to do to me?

"Get me the fuck away from these people, Joey," I spat, glaring at my boyfriend. "Now."

Heaving out a shuddering breath, Joey nodded and wrapped an arm around my shoulders, blocking my view of his father, as he led me out of the house.

The minute I was outside, I shrugged out of his hold and rushed for my car, gasping in mouthfuls of the cool night air, as I tried to make sense of what the hell had just happened.

"Aoife."

"Don't!" I strangled out, pushing away from him. "Don't talk. Just ... just take me home."

I was reeling.

My mind was blank.

My body was coiled tight with tension.

Joey opened the passenger door and I collapsed into the seat, breathing hard and fast, as my entire framed rattled and shook.

Coming around to the driver's side, he climbed in and looked at me with anguished eyes. "Molloy, I'm so—"

"No." Trying and failing to fasten my seatbelt, I gave up and bit back the urge to scream, pressing my fingers to my temples. "Just drive."

Wordlessly, Joey reached over and fastened my seatbelt for me before starting the engine.

With his hands rigid on the steering wheel, he bowed his head and sucked in several deep breaths before returning his focus to the road ahead and pulling off.

Biting down on my fist to stop myself from screaming, I tucked my hair behind my ear and then shuddered when I remembered the feel of his hand knotted roughly in it.

Striving for calm and coming up empty, my entire body buzzed with this strange, anxious energy, and I wasn't sure if it was my fear, my anger, or sheer adrenalin causing the upset.

Either way, I couldn't seem to control my limbs.

They had a mind of their own.

When Joey took a left at the end of the road, instead of the usual right turn that led to my estate, I started to get panicky.

When he pulled up outside the Ballylaggin Garda Station a few minutes later, the panic I'd been feeling quickly shifted into a full-blown anxiety attack. "What are you doing?"

He killed the engine and stared out the windscreen ahead of him, hands still wrapped tightly around the wheel.

"What are you doing?" I repeated when he didn't respond. My heart raced wildly in my chest. "Joey?" My eyes were wild with panic. "Take me home."

"I can't take you home, Molloy," he finally said, and his voice was barely audible. Keeping his eyes trained on the building that we were parked in front of, he slowly shook his head. "I need to make this right."

"What do you mean?" I demanded, voice cracking. "I'm not going in there, Joey. I won't, okay! I just want to go home and take a shower."

"We have to go in there," he replied, unfastening his seatbelt, and reaching for his car door. "He's not getting away with putting his hands on you."

"Don't!" Reaching across him, I grabbed the door and slammed it shut. "No. I don't want that. I just want to go home, okay? Just home. That's it."

"Molloy." Joey exhaled a pained groan and turned to look at me. The pain in his eyes, the absolute fucking devastation, seemed to mirror exactly how I felt. "He tried to rape . . ." His voice broke, and he shook his head before quickly looking away. He dragged in a pained breath, hand slamming against the steering wheel. "He tried to do that to you."

"I am *not* going in there," I warned, eyes filling with tears. "I am *not.*"

"You have to tell them what he—"

"No, all I have to do is go home," I cut him off and screamed, skin crawling with unease and shame. "That's all I want you to do for me. That's it. Just take me the fuck home."

"Aoife, please."

"This is *not* your call to make!" I screamed, pulling on my hair in sheer frustration. "You don't get to make this decision, Joey. I do. This is my choice, my decision, and I choose not to go in there, okay? I choose to forget about it. That's what I fucking choose. All I want to do is go home. I don't want anyone to know about it, okay? I just want to go home, erase it from my mind, and forget that I ever stepped foot inside of that house!"

Joey watched me for the longest time before releasing his hold on the door handle.

"Fuck!" he finally roared, slamming his hand against the steering wheel, and then sagged forward, wrapping his arms around the wheel and burying his face in them. "Fuck!"

"Where *were* you?" I heard myself croak out, delirious with pain and upset. "I had work! I wasn't supposed to be there, but *you* . . ." I stopped short of blaming him, knowing that it was my hurt talking and not the reality of the situation, and released a pained cry. "I was supposed to be at work." Tears blurred my vision, and I quickly pushed my hair back, not wanting to feel it touching my neck. "I wasn't supposed to be *there.*"

"I *know,*" he strangled out, looking like he was physically dying inside, as he banged his forehead repeatedly against the wheel. "Fuck, I know! It's just ... something came up, okay? And I forgot to call—"

"Something came *up*?" My voice rose with my incredulity. "Oh, that's fine then, isn't it? If something *came up*!"

"I'm sorry, okay." A distressed sob followed by an anguished roar tore from his chest and he pulled back to look at me. "Let me go in there." Tears were flowing freely down his cheeks, as he implored me with his eyes to give in. "Let me do this for you."

"No." I shook my head, refuting his plea, and roughly batted my tears – and then his hand – away. "Just take me home, Joe. *Please.*"

"I don't know what to do here, Aoif," he strangled out, chest heaving. "I hear you, I do, but it's not the right thing here."

"If you give one iota of a shit about me, then you will take me home," I warned, holding a shaky finger up. "I mean it. If you don't move this car, I'm getting out and walking."

When he made no move to respect my wishes, I pushed open my door and reached for my seatbelt.

"Okay, okay!" Joey quickly turned the key in the ignition and the old engine roared to life. "I'll take you home."

Sniffling, I closed the door, keeping my tear-filled eyes locked on the road ahead of us.

Releasing a heavy sigh, he pulled away from the Garda Station, taking me straight home without any more detours.

"Shannon," he finally said, when we were pulled up outside my house. He pinched the bridge of his nose before saying, "I left her at Johnny Kavanagh's house. I need to go back for her. I, ah, I can't leave her there. If they find out she's with him—"

"It's fine." Unfastening my seatbelt, I threw the door open and scrambled out of the car. "You can take the car."

Closing the car door behind me, I hurried across the road and swung my garden gate inwards, desperate to get inside the safety of *my* home.

"You could come with me?" he called after me, as he climbed out of the car and hurried across the road to reach me. "It won't take—"

"No, I'm going home," I repeated, slipping inside and closing the gate, effectively keeping him out.

"I'll bring the car straight back afterwards."

"It's fine, I don't need it."

"Fine. *I'll* come straight back afterwards," he offered, opening the gate and following me inside.

"No." I shook my head. "You don't have to."

"Aoife." His hand shot out and grabbed mine, and the pain in his voice was too much. "Please don't do this."

"I need to be alone right now, Joe," I just about managed to choke out, trying and failing to break free of his hold. "I can't be with—"

"I know what you want to say, but don't just . . . *please* keep it inside you," he begged, imploring me with his eyes to hear him. "Don't say it out loud. Not tonight, okay? Just . . . not tonight. Because if you say it out loud, then it becomes real, and I can't let it be real, Molloy, okay? I can't lose you."

I looked away and then I looked back at him.

He was rigid, watching me with fearful eyes.

I tried to say the words that would make him feel better, but I couldn't.

I couldn't comfort him right now.

I felt too damn broken.

"I need time," I finally whispered. "Some space to clear my head."

"I'm so fucking sorry."

"I know you are, Joe," I croaked out, feeling devastated. "I know, okay. I just . . ." Sniffling, I shrugged helplessly. "I need to *not* be near you right now, okay?"

"Aoife."

"Because every time I look at you, all I can see is—"

"Him," he deadpanned, immediately releasing his hold on me. "Got it." Nodding stiffly, he backed up to the gate, looking more crushed and broken than I'd ever seen him. "I hear ya, Molloy."

And then he turned around and walked away.

Unable to watch him leave, I hurried into my house.

Slamming the door shut behind me, I heaved out a huge, gut-wrenching sob, and collapsed in a heap on the floor.

"Aoife?" Mam's head popped around the living room door, and then she was there, on her knees with her arms around my body. "Did you tell him?"

Breath catching in my throat, I heaved out another pained sob and shook my head. "I c-couldn't."

"It's okay, pet," Mam soothed, wrapping me up in her arms just like she did when I was small. "Everything is going to be just fine. We'll figure it all out."

Bitter disappointment

JOEY

I thought the worst image I could see today was that of my mother cradling her premature, underdeveloped baby, followed closely by the screaming and keening and begging that had incurred when it was time to leave him behind at the hospital. It had taken me hours to get her to leave him. I thought that was the worst of it. The worst that could possibly happen.

I was wrong.

Walking into the kitchen tonight, and seeing my father with his hands on my girlfriend – with her bent over the table like a fucking dog, with her underwear around her ankles, and his jeans undone, was worse.

So much fucking worse.

Trembling violently in the passenger seat of the car, Molloy refused point blank to look at me, as she wrapped her arms around herself, knees bopping restlessly.

"Get me the fuck away from these people, Joey."

It didn't take a genius to decipher that she included me in that sentiment.

She couldn't bear to look at me and I didn't fucking blame her one bit.

Jesus Christ.

It had finally happened.

The bullshit that was my life had finally broken her.

The look in her eyes?

Fuck, she had looked at me like I was the enemy, too.

"I was supposed to be at work . . . "

*

"I wasn't supposed to be there . . . "

"Where were you..?"

She blamed me.

She didn't say it in so many words, but I knew she did.

This was *my* fault.

I was on my own until Molloy.

She came into my life and all of a sudden, I had a partner, a friend, a true equal who was willing to go down in flames with me.

Someone to pull me to safety.

Someone on my side regardless of whether I was right or wrong.

And my father took that away from me.

He took *her* away from me.

I could still smell her on my hoodie, in the car, all around me, and the scent was too fucking much for me to take in this moment.

The fuck was I doing thinking that I could have a normal, healthy relationship when my life was the polar opposite?

Feeling utterly dead inside, I phoned up Kavanagh, much to his disgust, and told him that I was on the way to collect my sister.

When he threw open the front door a few minutes later, he looked like he was ready to throw slaps. Shannon appearing in the doorway quickly put to rest any notions of that.

"Joe?"

"It's time to go, Shan."

"It is?"

"Yeah. Mam needs a hand with the kids."

I watched as resigned sadness settled in her eyes. "Okay."

"She can stay," Kavanagh argued and then turned to my sister. "You can stay."

"No, we need to go," I bit out, too fucking worn out to handle another argument, as I led my sister to the car. "Thanks for your help, Kavanagh."

"Thanks, Johnny," Shannon croaked out, looking over her shoulder as we walked away. "For everything."

"Shannon, you don't have to—"

"Come on, Shan," I cut him off and snapped. "We need to get home."

I didn't want to do this.

I didn't want to bring her back to hell with me, but I didn't exactly have a choice, and, whether he realized it or not, I was doing him a huge fucking favor by taking my sister away.

I was protecting them both.

Because if our parents got wind of her being here, it would bring the world of trouble to his door.

Leaving her here would open a can of worms that I didn't plan on sticking around to clean up.

I *couldn't* do it.

Not tonight.

Not anymore.

My entire fucking world was caving in around me, and fighting another person's battles was something I was incapable of doing in my current frame of mind.

Too much had gone down in the past forty-eight hours for me to comprehend or even think rationally.

My mother had given birth prematurely and the baby was dead.

My father had tried to rape my girlfriend.

And now, my girlfriend couldn't stand the sight of me.

She wanted space, and I couldn't blame her for it.

It was understandable; it fucking hurt like hell, but I got it.

I was the direct source to her pain, the link that had put her in danger to begin with.

It was entirely on me.

Uneasy and reckless, with notions whizzing around in my mind, I could feel the shift, the slip happening before it had, and I hated myself for it.

Still, I knew exactly where I was going the second that I had dropped my sister home.

Even though I accepted it, made peace with it, I still found myself despising myself for it.

"Is that what happened?" Shannon asked, dragging me from my thoughts, as I tried to keep my eyes on the road and focus on the conversation I was attempting to hold with my sister. "Was she in the hospital all weekend and we didn't know?"

I nodded.

"Oh, Joey." She covered her mouth with her hand. "She was all alone."

"She had *him*," I bit out, hands tightening on the wheel. "He was with her, and he's home now."

"What are we going to do, Joe?"

"I don't know." I shook my head. "I don't know what to do anymore, Shannon."

"It's okay," she was quick to soothe, reaching across to rub my shoulder. "You don't have to know. You're only eighteen."

Yeah, I was eighteen, but that was all my sister was right about.

Because *none* of this was okay.

It had *never* been okay, and it never would be.

Of *course* I needed to know what to do.

Deep down inside, I'd always *known* what to do.

It was a matter of overcoming the brainwashing fear that had paralysed me into silence.

And seeing what he did to Molloy tonight?

Yeah, that was my breaking pointing.

Never again would I cover for them.

Fucking never.

"I can't be there, Shan," I admitted, unwilling to go into the details of tonight's events, thinking of Molloy's wishes. "I *can't* live like this anymore."

"I know," she replied, but it was a generic response that didn't mean shit.

Stiffening with tension, I opened my mouth and uttered the words that I knew would cause a shitstorm, but needing to say it regardless. "I think we should consider what Aoife said."

"What *about* what Aoife said?" she was quick to ask, turning to watch me.

She knew exactly what I meant.

"Calling this in," I admitted anyway and then braced myself for the bomb I was sure would erupt.

"You *must* be joking."

I couldn't answer her.

I could hardly look her in the eye.

The betrayal blazing from her blue eyes, directed at me, was too fucking much.

"I am *not* going into care," Shannon screamed. "You're fine. You're over eighteen. You'll get to live your own life and walk away. I will be put in a home!"

"Shannon," I tried to placate, needing her to hear me out on this.

I knew she was scared, so was I, but this had to stop.

We couldn't live like this anymore.

If something didn't give, someone was going to die in that house.

It would either be him or me.

"Aoife was talking to me last night about my future, and it made a lot of sense—"

"*Your* future," she spat, like it was the most disgusting thing I could possibly say to her.

"No, not just my future – that didn't come out right." My shoulders slumped in shame. "Not just me, Shannon. All of us."

"I can't believe you would even *think* about doing this to us after what happened to Darren," she cried, shaking her head. "How could you think about doing that to us, Joey?"

Tears stung my eyes and I had never felt so fucking lost and hopeless.

Mam feared me.

Shannon felt betrayed by me.

Molloy couldn't stand the sight of me.

The only three women I had ever loved in my whole life, and I was letting them down left, right, and center.

I couldn't seem to do the right thing by anyone.

You are such a fuck up, lad.

"If you want to go then go!" Shannon screamed accusingly. "Go off and leave us! Go be with *Aoife* and have a wonderful life together! I'll protect the boys—"

"You can't even protect yourself!" I roared, losing my cool, as my pain hemorrhaged out of my body in words. "*I'm* doing that, Shannon. *Me! I'm* the one trying to soften the blows and they just keep coming!"

"Then maybe you and Dad will both get lucky and he'll finish me off the next time," she sobbed, dropping her head in her hands. "It'll save you the worry, and him the energy."

"Don't fucking say that, Shannon," I strangled out, flinching from both the impact of her words and the thought of it happening.

She couldn't have hurt me more if she stabbed me through the heart.

"Why not?" Gasping for air, she clutched her throat, panic overtaking her. "It's the truth."

"Shannon, breathe." I reached over and rubbed her back. "Take a breath."

Sagging forward in her seat, she clutched her skinny knees and wrestled to get her breathing back on track.

"Good girl." Pulling up to the footpath outside our house, I parked the car, but left the engine running. "Nice and slow."

She remained in the car long after her breathing had steadied, and the longer she lingered, the heavier my conscience became.

"Shannon?"

Silence.

"Are you listening to me?"

She nodded once, but kept her eyes trained straight ahead.

"If he touches you again, Shannon, I want you to grab the sharpest knife you can find, and I want you to plunge it into his heart."

Finally, she turned to look at me; eyes full of despondence. "You're not coming back, are you?"

"I *can't*," I strangled out, willing her to understand that my sanity was at stake. "If I go back inside that house, I'll kill them both."

The look on her face assured me that she didn't understand.

The look on her face assured me that I had broken her heart.

Bitterly disappointed in me, my sister unfastened her seatbelt, and climbed out of the car.

"Goodbye, Joey," was all she said, before slamming the door shut, and walking away.

I'm fine!

AOIFE

"Aoife?" My father stood in the doorway of my room, eyes full of concern. "Are you alright, pet?"

"Fine," I choked out, pacing my bedroom floor like a maniac, as I tried and failed to process that last few hours of my life. "Why wouldn't I be?"

"You don't seem fine."

That's because I'm not.

"What do you want me to do; take a fucking lie detector test?" I snapped, running my hands through my hair, only to shudder violently at the sensation. "I said I'm *fine*."

"It's just that I can hear you banging around up here from the sitting room, and I can't hear my film with all of the stomping."

"What do you want me to do?" I demanded, throwing my hands up. "Cut my legs off and crawl instead?"

"Jesus," Dad muttered, rubbing his jaw. "Right. I'm off out for a pint with your mother. Stamp away to your heart's content."

The minute he closed my bedroom door behind him, a full body shudder rolled through me and I shook my hands out, desperate to rid myself of this horrible anxiety.

Stripping down to my underwear, I quickly balled up my clothes and walked over to my window, not hesitating to throw them out of it.

It wasn't enough.

I could feel his hot breath on my neck.

It repulsed me.

It made my skin crawl.

Tears streamed from my eyes as I reached behind my back and

quickly unhooked my bra, letting it fall from my shoulders, before pushing my knickers down my legs and stepping out of them.

Grabbing my dressing gown off the back of my wardrobe door, I slipped it on and bolted for the bathroom, determined to wash the feel of that man off my skin.

The eleventh hour

JOEY

All the way back to Molloy's house, I fought an internal war inside of my body; where two parts of my mind battled it out for dominion over me.

On one side there was the demon that lived just beneath the surface; that horrible fucking voice that controlled every impulse, urge, and reaction I'd ever had.

It was the one that assured me that my life had indeed gone to shit, without any chance of recourse, and if the only relief I found came in the form of narcotics, then so be it. Because I'd done enough, fought enough, tried hard enough for everyone else.

I'd paid my goddamn dues, taken enough shit to earn my rite of passage. I wasn't hurting anyone, not really, and if I was careful this time, I could control my urges instead of letting my urges control me.

On the other side, all by its lonesome, and looking less appealing by the second, was my conscience. Crippling me with flashes of memories and images of the past, it urged me to step back and think about what I was doing.

No good will come of this, my conscience urged, *you'll break her heart all over again. Remember last time? Remember her face?*

Your father already broke her, and you gave him the access, the demon hissed, *do you want to sit with the visual of him spreading her legs open like a brood fucking mare, or do you want to forget everything bad you've ever seen, felt, and experienced? Because your conscience won't do that for you. You know what will work, though. You can make it all go away. You don't have to suffer like this.*

"I want to forget," I strangled out, chest heaving, as I pulled up outside Molloy's house, and killed the engine. "I *need* to forget."

Locking her car, I let myself into her garden and walked over to the front door to push the keys through the letter box.

I turned around to walk away, but stalled, unable to get my feet to cooperate.

Don't do this, my conscience reared its unwelcome head, *all you have to do is just keep trying – one hour at time, remember? You've got this.*

Exhaling a frustrated breath I took two steps towards the gate, before muttering out a string of curses and veering off in the direction of their garden shed.

Bad idea.

Bad idea.

Bad idea.

Hoisting myself onto the roof of the shed, I took a running jump at the side of the house, catching a hold of the ledge with a familiarity that should have concerned me.

Using all of my upper body strength, and ignoring the burn in my torn knuckles, I quickly pulled myself up onto Molloy's windowsill, and climbed inside her open window.

Her bedroom was empty when I stepped inside, so I walked over to her bed and sat down, needing to stay very much inside of this room and out of trouble.

This room, and the girl who it belonged to, had become my safety net.

My safe place.

Several minutes ticked by before her bedroom door finally opened inwards and she appeared, bundled up in a fluffy white towel.

The minute her eyes landed on mine, I saw the temporary fear, the momentary flash of horror, because it was like she said; I reminded her of *him.*

"I know that you want space." Standing slowly, I held my palms up and backed over to the window, giving her as much space as I could to put her at ease. "I heard you."

Her cheeks were flushed, and her eyes were bloodshot and swollen from the sheer height of crying, and her cute little button nose was red from sniffling.

Tightening her hold on the front of her towel, she walked over to her bed and sat down, keeping her eyes trained on mine.

The fear was gone now, replaced with the usual affectionate familiarity I saw when she looked at me, but the fact that it had existed in the first place troubled me deeper than I could ever explain.

"But?" she whispered, crossing one long leg over the other.

I shrugged helplessly. "How could I not come back?"

"Joe." Her voice cracked and she bowed her head, shoulders shaking violently, as she burst into tears. "I was so scared."

"I'm sorry," I strangled out, closing the space between us. "I'm sorry. I'm sorry, I'm so fucking sorry, baby." Sinking down on my knees beside her, I placed my hands on her hips, and then recoiled in horror when she flinched from my touch.

Mine.

"Jesus, I'm sorry," I told her again, beyond torn apart by it all. "Tell me what to do. Tell me how to fix this for you and I'll do it."

I leaned back on my heels to give her space, but she scrambled closer and gripped ahold of my arm.

Taking that as my green light to come closer, I placed my hands on her hips.

This time, she didn't flinch.

"I never should have left you there," I said hoarsely. "I didn't protect you, and I'm so fucking sorry for that."

"You're not supposed to *have* to protect me like that," she cried. "You're not supposed to have to worry about that happening. Fathers aren't supposed to do the things your father does, Joe."

I knew that.

Of course I fucking knew that.

"I'm not him," I choked out, needing her to hear me, to fucking believe me. "I'm not, Aoife, I swear." Reaching up to cup her face between my hands, I pulled her head close to mine and whispered, "I am *nothing* like that man."

"I know you're nothing like him," she cried, leaning close to rest her brow to mine. "But *I'm* nothing like you, Joe."

"What does that mean?"

"It means that I can't brush something like this under the table the way you can."

"I'm not asking you to," I hurried to say. "I'm not. I'll take you to the station myself, Aoif. I won't cover for him anymore, I swear to you, and I will *never* ask you to do that."

"That's not what I mean," she whispered. "I meant it when I said that I didn't want to report it." Sniffling, she added, "It's not like he actually did anything. I mean, what did he really do aside from push my pants down and pull my hair—"

"Only because I walked in on time! Don't play it down. Don't give that prick an out for what he did to you," I snarled, trembling with anger, as my mind tormented me with flashing images of what I'd walked in on. "He did enough, Aoife. Looking in your direction was too fucking much."

"That's still not what I meant, though."

"Then what?" I shrugged, at a loss. "What did you mean?"

"How you live? What you live with? I thought I knew about it. I thought I understood, but I don't, Joe. I never had a clue," she admitted hoarsely. "I don't come from a home like yours. I've never had to be afraid like that." Sniffling, she cupped my face between her hands and exhaled a broken sob. "Tonight, I felt a kind of fear that I *never* want to experience again."

"I don't know what to say." I couldn't change where I came from or how it had morphed me into who I was. "What do you want me to say here?"

"I'm just . . . " Shaking her head, she expelled another ragged breath before saying, "I'm seeing a lot of red flags shooting up around us now. Ones I never used to see before tonight, but can't get out of my head ever since."

Struck fucking dumb, I just stared at her, unable to read the signs, or hear the meaning of whatever the fuck she was trying to tell me. "What are you saying?"

"I'm saying that your life scares me and maybe you were right when you told me that you were a bad idea for me."

Her words hit me like a slap across the face and I physically recoiled, feeling like she had cut me open and left me to hemorrhage at her feet. "Do you really mean that?"

"No? Maybe?" Sniffling, she shrugged her shoulders. "I don't know what I mean anymore."

"Okay." Cold to the bone, I stared at her for the longest moment before shaking my head. "Okay, I should leave."

"What – no, no, don't go!" Sinking onto my lap, she threw her arms around me and buried her face in my neck. "Don't leave me!"

"I don't know what you want from me," I admitted hoarsely, as wave upon wave of devastation continued to crash over me, fucking drowning me. "I don't know what to do here, Aoife, because you're telling me to go with your words and to stay with your actions."

"I know," she cried, shaking her head, as she wrapped her arms around my neck and her legs around my waist. "I know, I know, I'm sorry, okay?"

"Are you breaking up with me?" I forced myself to ask. "Is that what you're trying to say?"

"I don't know what I'm doing, or how I'm feeling right now." Clutching the front of my hoodie, she choked out the most heart-breaking fucking sound I'd ever heard. "But I know that it hurts and I don't want to feel it." Her lips were on my neck when she cried out, "This feeling is killing me. I feel like I'm dying here, and I don't want it."

Well, that wasn't one bit comforting, and her words caused the tightening sensation around my windpipe to significantly worsen.

"What do you need from me?" I asked her – I practically begged her to show me how to make this right. "Whatever you want me to do, whatever you need, say the word and I'll do it."

With tear-filled eyes, she stared at me for the longest time, before exhaling a ragged breath and fusing her lips to mine.

I froze, hands still on her cheeks, uncertain and fucking terrified of doing something wrong.

"Kiss me back," she cried out against my lips. "Show me how to forget it."

Jesus.

Trembling, I did exactly what she asked. Kissing her with everything I had in me, our tongues and teeth and lips clashed in a frantic kiss that was nothing like how we usually kissed.

This kiss was one of desperation, I realized.

It was a matter of necessity, needing to have her mouth on mine as much as she needed mine on hers.

Technique or suavity didn't matter one bit right now, because the need to comfort the other was too fucking strong to think about anything other than touching, feeling, kissing, being . . .

When she reached a hand between our bodies and loosened the front of her towel, I felt my shoulders bunch up with tension.

"I don't want this if you don't want this," I warned, needing her to be very sure of what she was doing here.

She was all messed up in the head right now, and Christ, I didn't blame her, but I was *not* the man people thought I was.

I was *not* my father.

I would never take something that wasn't offered to me with a free heart.

"I mean it," I pushed. "Don't fuck me if you're going to regret me afterwards."

"Don't you want me?" she breathed, reaching for the hem of my hoodie and roughly dragging it over my head along with my t-shirt.

"You know I want you," I replied, as my dick strained against her. "But I don't want you to do *this* if you're not in the right frame of mind."

Tracing my bottom lip with the tip of her tongue, she leaned closer and teased my tongue with hers.

"What I want . . . " Pushing hard on my shoulders so that I fell onto my back, Molloy quicky rid herself of the towel and straddled my hips. "Is for you to make me forget." Her fingers traced the tattoo on my chest and she leaned in close to trail her tongue over the ink. "Can you do that for me, Joe?" Raising up on her knees, she pulled at the waistband of my sweatpants. Tilting my hips up, I allowed her to roughly pull the fabric down my legs, right along with my jocks. "Hm?" The moment it was freed, my dick shot to attention, visibly fucking straining to get to her. "Can you make me block it out just like you block everything out?"

She was saying all the right things, making all the right moves, but her eyes were all wrong, her voice was strained, and the bruising on her neck assured me that this was not okay.

"I don't think this is a good idea—" My words broke off in a hiss of pained-pleasure when her hand came around my shaft, fisting me roughly. "Fuck."

"You like it, don't you?" she breathed, reaching her free hand between my legs to cup my balls, while she fisted me and pulled on my shaft at a furious pace. "You like it when I touch you like this."

"Yeah," I strangled out, hands moving to my head, as I battled down the urge to cum right here and now.

"You like my tits, Joe?" Releasing me, she leaned in close and pressed my shaft between her bare breasts. "You wanna cum on my tits, Joe?"

Jesus Christ.

"Aoif, slow down," I tried to reason, while my traitorous bastard hips rocked into her touch. "You've been through some major shit tonight. You don't have to do this—"

Her lips came around my dick, tongue snaking out to trace the head before she took me in deep, pushing down until I hit the back of her throat and she gagged.

"Fuck," I groaned, eyelids fluttering shut when she sucked me in deeper, gagging harder, squeezing tighter, making me feel too fucking much.

"Mm," she purred, as she fisted to base of my shaft and pulled. "Mm."

"Aoife." Hips bucking against my will, I reached down and attempted to cup her cheek, but she snatched up my hand and pressed it to her throat instead.

"No." Shaking my head, I tried to pull free, but she held my hand there, trying to make me squeeze. "Aoife, stop."

"Mm."

"Aoife, I said stop," I ordered, yanking my hand away, panicked and disgusted and aroused all in one breath. "What the fuck are you doing?"

"I told you," she purred when she finally came up for air, leaving my dick glistening from her saliva. "I want you to make me just like you."

"I think we should stop for a bit," I said, feeling uneasy, as she straddled my hips and positioned the head of my dick against the wet folds of her pussy. "Aoif, please, baby, just—"

"This is what I want," she strangled out, impaling herself down hard my dick. "Just you in me." A pained sob escaped her. "Just you." A tear slid down her cheek. "Only you."

Fuck.

"Come here," I coaxed, dragging myself into a sitting position, and then pulling her to my chest, with my dick still fully inside her. "I'm here."

"I want it gone," she cried, clinging to my chest, as she wrapped her arms and legs around me. "Make it go away."

I didn't know how to do that for her.

If I could go back in time and change anything in my whole entire life, then it would be leaving her in my house.

I would gladly trade everything else, and forfeit all I had, to take this away for her.

To erase that bastard from her mind.

"Don't pull out," she begged, when I moved to do just that.

"Aoif . . . "

"No, no, no." Shivering violently, she croaked out, "Just stay *in* me."

"Okay, but you're freezing. So, let me just get you off the floor—"

"No." She shook her head. "Stay in me."

Jesus Christ.

Somehow, and I wasn't too fucking sure how, I managed to climb to my feet, taking her body with me, and walked us both back to her bed.

"It's okay," I tried to soothe her by saying, sinking down on the edge of the bed, with her body still wrapped around mine, still *joined* with mine. "I've got ya, Molloy."

In slow, stiff movements, I moved our bodies until we were in the middle of her bed, with me on my back, and her on top. "I love you, Joe."

"I know." Exhaling a shaky breath, I reached for the duvet and draped it over her trembling shoulders. "I love you, too."

"I *hate* him."

"I know." My chest constricted to the point I couldn't breathe. "Me, too."

"Joe," she croaked out, nuzzling my neck with her damp cheek. "You're still hard. I can feel you pulsing inside me."

"Yeah," I muttered, somehow managing to keep my hips in check and *not* flex. "My heart's in bits, but my dick's delighted."

She seemed to think about that for a moment, and then she gingerly rocked her hips in the sweetest fucking circular motion.

A pained groan escaped me and her breath hitched.

Moments later, she repeated the move.

And she did it again.

And again.

Over and over until her hips were gyrating against mine in a movement that had every muscle in my body coiling tight.

"What are you doing?"

"I don't know," she breathed, rocking her body against mine.

She was so wet; I could feel myself slipping deeper inside her with every rock of her hips.

"Aoif."

"Hm."

"Aoife."

"Hm?"

"I'm going to cum," I croaked out, hands squeezing her hips in warning, as my balls tightened in anticipation. "Aoif, you need to stop or I'm going to cum in you, and I don't think you want this right now—"

Covering my mouth with her hand, she leaned back, arching her spine, as she rocked and moaned above me, hips bucking wild and reckless now, as she chased that familiar wave of heat, the same one I was desperately trying to stall.

"I'm going to cum," she cried out, pussy tightening around the shaft of my dick to the point of pain, as she grabbed my hands and pressed them against her tits. "Joe, I'm coming, I'm—"

"Fuck!" I hissed, losing all control as the wave of heat threatening to consume me spilled over.

My calves burned, my thigh muscles locked tight, and I grabbed her hips and dragged her down on me, as my hips bucked restlessly.

I could feel her coming on my dick, clenching and tightening and sucking me in deeper, and the sensation was too much to handle.

Releasing a guttural groan, my hips jerked and twitched as I found my release, coming deep inside of her.

"God," she said, and then her entire expression caved. "Oh god."

Face distorting in pain, she roughly pushed her hair over her shoulder and scrambled off my lap.

I knew I'd made a mistake as she slid as far away from me as her bed permitted and choked out a pained sob.

"What the fuck is wrong with me?"

"Nothing." Breathing hard and labored, I turned to look at her, but she had her back to me. "There's nothing wrong with you, Molloy, it's okay."

"Your father tried to fuck me!" she cried, grabbing a pillow and clutching it to her chest. "And then I let you fuck me."

Mind-fucked from her mood swings and conflicted with more emotions than I knew how to handle, I sat straight up, and reached a hand over to rub her shoulder.

"No," she strangled out, shaking my hand off. "I need space."

Here we go again.

Shaking my head, I hooked my arms around my knees and just stared at her back. "Are you serious?"

I watched as she nodded slowly. "I need to be alone right now."

"Two minutes ago, you said you needed my dick inside you," I snapped, running a hand through my hair in frustration. "You tell me to go, and then you ask me to stay. You say you want me and then you don't. I try to leave and you stop me. You want to fuck me, and then you don't, and then you do again, until we do and then, when it's done, you decide that you don't. Jesus Christ. Make your goddamn mind up, Molloy, because I can't keep up."

"I'm sorry, okay?" she strangled out. "I guess I just don't cope as well with trauma as you do. I'm sorry that I'm not a robot without a heart, and possess an actual functioning set of feelings. Not everyone is as fucking perfect at turning off their emotions as you are."

"Does it sound like my emotions are turned off?" I demanded, tone thick with the very thing she accused me of not possessing. "Because from where I'm standing, I'm being pretty fucking transparent with my emotions here, Molloy. You're the one blowing hot and cold like a goddamn tap."

"And now you're shouting at me."

"I'm not fucking *shouting* at you," I shouted. "I'm trying to *be here* for you!"

"Well, I told you that I needed space."

"Jesus, Aoife, I don't know whether I'm coming or going with you." I pushed my hands through my hair. "If you have something you need to say to me, then you might as well get it over with."

Silence.

"You're mad at me."

More silence.

"You blame me."

She didn't respond, choosing to cover her ears with her hands instead.

"Admit it," I demanded, feeling helpless and frustrated, as my chest heaved. "Whatever you need to say to me, just fucking admit it, Molloy."

"Fine, Joey, fine! You want to know how I'm feeling? I'm hurt!" she screamed, scrambling onto her knees and throwing her pillow at me. "Because I was nearly raped tonight – by a man that looks just like you! And I was put in that position because of *you*! Because you didn't care enough to pick up the phone and tell me what was happening. Because you didn't spare a thought for me when you left and didn't come back!"

And there it was.

It was out there now.

She blamed me as much as *I* blamed me.

"I had my back to him when he grabbed me," she cried out hoarsely. "I thought it was you . . . I thought he was *you*, Joey! But it wasn't you. Those weren't your hands on my body, or your tongue on my skin, or your fingers in my hair, and now I don't know what to feel."

I flinched. "Jesus Christ."

Just when I thought I couldn't hate myself any more than I did, she opened her mouth and gave me her truth.

Choking out a huge sob, she cried, "So, yes, I'm mad at you, and maybe it's irrational to feel it, and my emotions are all misplaced, but I'm mad, and hurt, and I'm so fucking *angry* with you." Her voice cracked, and she choked out another pained sob before admitting, "Because I was there tonight for *you*. Looking after your brothers for *you*. And because every horrible situation that I've found myself in this past year and a half has been for *you*. I keep getting hurt because I love *you*!"

I could smell her perfume on my skin, could feel her devastation all around me, as she looked into my eyes and ripped my heart out of my chest.

This was exactly what I had tried to stop from happening.

I didn't want to fall in love with her and I did. I didn't want to let her in and I did. Everything I never wanted to do, I did with her, *for* her, because I loved her. Because she refused to accept nothing less.

I didn't know what to say to make it right.

I didn't have the words to comfort her in this moment.

I couldn't deny or rebuff what she was saying.

As hard as it was to hear, it was the truth.

I hurt her and she hurt me, it was what we seemed to do, but she couldn't look at me now without seeing my father, and all I could see in this moment when I looked at her was my mother.

My body bowed in pain.

I couldn't breathe.

Deciding it was safer to keep my mouth shut in this moment, I quicky climbed out of her bed and moved for my clothes.

"What are you doing?"

I didn't answer her.

"Joey?"

I couldn't.

Ignoring the pain impaling my chest, crushing down on my windpipe, I focused on what my brain was telling me.

Turn it off.

Just stop feeling.

Had I listened to my head from the start, I wouldn't be here.

My heart had fucked me over and opened me up to all of this unnecessary suffering.

With my brain in the driving seat and my mangled heart splattered all over her bedroom walls, I focused on putting my clothes back on.

My movements were rigid, automatic even, as I finished dressing, and walked over to her bedroom window, drowning in the sound of her pained cries.

"No, no, no, don't go," she begged, scrambling off the bed and closing the space between us. "I'm sorry, Joe. I'm sorry! I didn't mean it – I just . . . I need you to *stay.*"

"I meant what I said," I replied, straining my neck away from her lips when she tried to hold and kiss me. "If you change your mind about going to the Gards, I'll support you every step of the way."

"*Don't* go."

"I'm sorry." Gently peeling her hands away from my body, I placed them at her sides and moved for the window, needing to get as far from this girl as I could before I did any further damage. "I love you."

"Joey!"

"I'll be seeing ya, Molloy."

And then I climbed out of her window and slipped into the night.

A little while later, I found myself standing in front of a familiar house, with my hands in the front pocket of my hoodie, my heart in shreds, and my head bowed in resignation.

Expelling a frustrated breath, I reached up and rapped my knuckles against the graffiti-sprayed board that covered the broken pane of glass in the door.

When the door swung inwards, the only judgement I felt came directly from my conscience as it roared *scumbag* in my head.

"Lynchy," Shane acknowledged, cigarette balancing from his lips, as he waited for me to explain my sudden reappearance.

"I need somewhere to crash for a few days," I heard myself say, forcing myself to meet his gaze.

"Old man up to his tricks again?"

I knew he was searching my face for the usual bruises – the ones that had led me to take solace on his couch more times than I could count down through the years.

Remaining silent, I nodded stiffly.

"Why aren't ya crashing with that doll of yours?"

"That's done with."

"No shit?" His brows shot up, and he reached for the cigarette balancing between his lips. "Done with how?"

I shrugged, resisting the urge to fucking scream. "Meaning she's done with my bullshit. Can I crash here or not?"

Exhaling a cloud of smoke, Shane stepped aside and gestured for me to come in.

Just turn around and walk away.

Just fucking leave.

And go where?

Home?

Molloy's?

You have nowhere else to go.

You have nothing, asshole.

You are nothing.

With my head bowed in resignation, I walked inside.

PART 4

Mother knows best

AOIFE

I skipped the following few days of school and called in sick for all of my shifts; too miserable and frazzled to concentrate on anything other than the shitstorm that had become my life.

Everything felt like it was slipping away from me, and, in the middle of the madness, the only good decision I seemed to have made was confiding in my mother.

Since telling her about the pregnancy, Mam had been *amazing*.

When I felt like I was at my most vulnerable, and truly free-falling off the edge, she waded in and caught ahold of my hand. She gave me someone to lean on, and someone to show me the way. I knew she was disappointed in me – *for* me, as she had so delicately put it – but having her by my side made the thought of my unknown future almost bearable.

Enabling my temporary withdrawal from life by screening calls from my principal and boss, not to mention intercepting unprompted house visits from Katie and Casey. Mam had stuck her neck out for me and held out a hand to warn the world off while I tried to come to terms with the path my life had taken. Including accompanying me to that dreaded appointment with our family GP, where I had to sit in front of a doctor who'd known me since childhood and tell him that I'd made the age-old mistake of getting knocked up in secondary school.

He confirmed what I already knew, did my bloodwork, and gave me an estimated due date of September 20th. He then sent me on my way with a handful of pamphlets on teenage pregnancy and young mothers, and the knowledge that I would soon receive an appointment in the post for a dating scan at the public maternity hospital.

I had been so shaken up afterwards, that my mother had whipped out the emergency credit card that Dad thought she didn't know about and had taken me shopping. Blowing an inordinate amount of money in our regular hair salon and beauty bar, not to mention refurbishing my entire wardrobe with clothes that I wouldn't be able to wear for much longer, Mam had somehow managed to make light and normal of a situation that felt anything but.

Buttering me up with mugs of hot chocolate and plates of freshly baked pastries, she traipsed us around Cork City until I couldn't bear to look at another sale rail or rummage around in another bargain bin. Physically wearing me out from doing what I loved most was an impressive feat, and one I quickly learned was my mother's way of luring me into a state of exhausted pliancy.

Sitting across from me in matching leather armchairs, in a coffee shop on Patrick's Street, with a small round table and a dozen or so shopping bags separating us, Mam raised her foamy latte to her lips and took a small sip. Looking like such a lady, with her legs crossed at the ankles, and her beautiful blonde hair twisted back in a loose bun up-style, I felt that familiar swell of annoyance. My mother was beautiful, inside and out. She was clever and witty, and loyal. She kept herself well, had a lovely shape about her, and worked hard for her family. But none of that seemed to matter to my father when he continued to repeat the same mistakes over and over. It wasn't a matter of Mam having let herself go and Dad shifting his attention to someone better, because there was no one better.

"So, about Joey." Mam finally broached the topic that I had been carefully dodging all day. "What's going on?"

"Nothing," I replied, reaching for my mug of hot chocolate.

I hadn't seen or heard from Joey since the night he climbed out of my bedroom window. He hadn't come back, and I didn't know if he had tried to call or text, because I had unintentionally left my phone at his place that night. I had been so desperate to get out of that house and away from his father, that I had left it along with my charger, make-up, overnight bag, and most important of all, my necklace; the one he'd given me for my eighteenth birthday.

I'd taken my jewelry off before using his shower, and had forgotten to put them back on. It was still on his nightstand, along with my Claddagh ring, and earrings. I could survive without everything else that I left behind, but not having my phone was a disaster, and my neck felt so bare without that necklace. I found myself constantly reaching up to rub the locket, something that had become almost like a comfort blanket, only to feel a swell of unease when I remembered it was gone.

I was desperate to see him, to speak to him, to make up, but it had been radio silence on the Lynch front.

"Nothing?" Mam cocked a brow. "I haven't seen him in a few days."

Neither have I. "He's got a lot going on."

According to Kev, who had heard it from Mack, who heard it from Alec, Joey was on the missing list.

No one had seen or heard from him since the weekend.

Not at school, or training, the GAA grounds, or the pub.

I knew that wasn't entirely true, because, while nobody at school had heard from my boyfriend, he *had* reached out to my father.

Dad had mentioned to Mam that Joey had called him to ask for time off, something that Mam had later relayed to me.

Apparently, his mother had a late second-trimester miscarriage and he was needed at home to help out with the kids for a week or two until she was back on her feet.

I'd thrown up violently when I heard the news, quickly putting two and two together, and realizing that when he told me that something had come up that day, he wasn't feeding me a line.

He meant it.

And I had hurt him that night.

Badly.

My words had devastated him, and I had regretted them the minute they came out of my mouth. I hadn't meant any of it, but at the time I had been in such a state that I couldn't think clearly. Never in my life had I felt the level of fear and degradation as I had in that kitchen.

The assault, at the hands of Joey's father, had lasted no longer than ninety seconds at the most, but those ninety seconds had been the most terrifying of my life. Teddy Lynch was the scariest man I had ever encountered, and the desperate need I had to protect myself from ever encountering him again, had resulted in me pushing away the *one* person who knew what it felt like to fear that man. It gave me a glimpse into the fear that Joey and his siblings had been carrying around for their entire lives, and my heart broke for them.

"You need to have that conversation with him soon," Mam told me. "And your father and I will need to sit down with his parents and have a conversation of our own."

"No, you don't," I argued, heart fluttering wildly at the thought of my mother going anywhere near that house. She didn't know what happened to me. If she had, there would be a very different conversation occurring. One between her and the officer that arrested her for murder. "I know that me and Joey have to talk, and we will. But you and Dad don't need to have a conversation about anything with his parents, Mam. His mother is a wreck, and his father is a complete—"

"Asshole?"

Nodding, I exhaled a shaky breath. "A huge one."

"You don't need to tell me about Teddy Lynch, pet," she replied. "I spent six years of secondary school tolerating the insufferable bastard."

"Bastard?" My brows shot up in surprise. "You hardly ever curse, Mam."

"Yes, well, sometimes there's just no other word to fit the description," she replied, giving me a small smile. "And when it comes to describing that man, bastard is putting it mildly."

"He's going to take it badly," I heard myself admit, chewing on my lip, as a wave of anxiety came over me.

"Teddy?" she snorted. "Don't you worry about him, pet. Your father and I are more than able to handle him."

I shook my head.

Mam's eyes softened. "Joey."

I nodded anxiously. "He hates his father, Mam. I mean he really,

really despises the man. I mean it, Mam. He's so paranoid about turning into him, that it has really screwed with his mind growing up."

"That's so sad," Mam replied. "Joey is nothing like his father."

"I know. But once I tell him that I'm pregnant – that *we're* having a baby when we're still in school – he's going to take one look at our situation and compare it with his parents." I shrugged helplessly before adding, "I'm really scared that it'll push him off the deep end."

While we had never openly spoken about Joey's issues, my mother wasn't a stupid woman. For years, before we became a couple, Joey had worked with my father, and been to our home on countless occasions. If I could tell he was strung out back then, then so could my parents. Still, Dad never fired him, and Mam never turned him away from the door. Instead, they continued to hold the door open for a boy who had never been given a fighting chance.

"I love him, Mam," I declared, voice thick with emotion, as I locked eyes on my mother from across the coffee table. "I do. I love him so much that it blinds me."

"That is what tends to happen when you fall in love for the first time," she replied gently. "It happens to the best of us, pet."

"I mean, obviously, I know we don't have a perfect relationship. Far from it." Shoulders sagging, I waved a hand in front of me as I continued, "Being with him feels messy, and raw, and complicated as hell, but it also feels exciting, and addictive, and so incredibly *right*." I blew out a breath and shrugged helplessly. "There's no one else for me, Mam. I know it. I can feel it in my bones."

"I believe you," she replied, nursing her mug between her hands. "You've always been a drama queen—"

"Hey!"

"Let me *finish*."

"Fine," I huffed out a breath.

Laughing, Mam tried again. "What I'm trying to say is that even though you've always had a flair for the dramatics, and can be recklessly impulsive with your actions, you have never been reckless with your *heart*."

"Wow," I mused. "What a backhanded compliment."

"Oh stop," Mam chuckled. "Where is the lie in that?"

There wasn't one.

"Fine, I'm *dramatic*," I conceded, waving her off. "But Kev is the one starved for your attention."

"Aoife," Mam chuckled.

"It's true," I argued light-heartedly. "He's insanely jealous of all the time we've been spending together lately. Haven't you noticed the big cranky head on him? I wouldn't be surprised if there was a tiny doll version of me in his room with pins sticking out of it."

"Poor Kev," she laughed.

"Poor Kev my ass," I challenged with a roll of my eyes. "You've babied him, Mam, and he can't handle anyone else having your attention."

"If I've babied Kev, it's because he needed me to."

"Ugh." I fake gagged. "Sure."

"It's true. You've never needed me the way he has. You've always been my wild child," she continued to tell me. "More challenging than your brother – and more rebellious, too. While Kev has always hidden himself away in the safety of the shade, uncertain and unsure of himself, you, my dear girl, have basked in the sunshine. You refuse to shy away from the world, choosing instead to embrace all that life has to offer."

"I'm not sure if you're saying that's a good thing or not," I admitted, eyeing her warily.

"It's a good thing," Mam chuckled. "Sure, you've given me a few grey hairs down through the years, and I've had to rein that reckless streak in at times, but you've done a wonderful job of managing to find the balance between enjoying your teens and losing yourself in the process. And I'm so proud of you for that, my little darling."

"Uh, hello? I'm *with child*, Mam," I shot back dramatically, gesturing to the tiny swell of my stomach – the swell that looked more like I'd eaten a heavy meal than anything else. "I'm about to make you a *grandmother* before your forty-fifth birthday. I think it's safe to say that I haven't done such a great job of finding the balance in anything – unless you're referring to my ability to balance on Joey's *dick*, then in that case, the evidence is all in and it turns out that I'm a pro."

"Why would you say that to me?" Mam groaned, covering her face with her hand. "I'm your mother, Aoife. Jesus."

I shrugged. "I guess that's my reckless streak roaring its ugly head again, huh, Mam?"

"Yes, well, I'm all for an open and honest discussion with my daughter," she said with a grimace. "But please consider the fact that I birthed *you and* have known Joey since he was a boy of twelve. I don't need the mental image of you balancing on his willy, nor do I need you to delve into any sort of intimate details. Save that kind of talk for Casey."

"Willy," I snickered. "Say dick, Mam."

"I will not," she replied, flushed. "It's a horrible word."

"For a wonderful body part."

"Aoife!"

"Okay, okay." I held my hands up. "Shutting up now." Chuckling softly, I looked to Mam and said, "Remember a few years ago, when I told you that I would never allow myself to catch crazy deep feelings for a boy?"

"Ah yes." Mam smiled knowingly. "I seem to remember you insisting that you would never fall in love with Paul, or let any boy, for that matter, cloud your judgement."

I grimaced. "God, I was such a sanctimonious fool."

"You believed it at the time."

"Yeah, I really did."

"Ah, but Paul Rice was never Joey Lynch, was he?"

That's for damn sure.

"No." I exhaled a shaky breath and shook my head. "He wasn't."

"It used to make me sad, you know." Mam took another sip of her latte before adding, "Seeing you with Paul, forcing yourself to feel things I knew you didn't, while you carried such a strong torch for someone else."

I winced. "Was it that obvious?"

"Oh yes." Mam nodded. "You spent four years of your youth settling for *comfortable* with a boy you had nothing in common with, while your heart never once wandered from a boy who made your whole face light up when he walked in the room." A melancholy sigh escaped her. "I never saw you have that kind of reaction when you were with Paul. Your eyes didn't widen when he looked at you, and your cheeks never blushed when he winked. You used to look almost despondent when he called over to see you."

"Three and a half years," I reeled off with a wince. "I know that Paul was steady, Mam, and he comes from money and has a big future ahead of him, but I was never happy with him."

"If you want money, you can make that for yourself," Mam replied. "You don't need a man to do that for you."

"I know and I completely agree," I was quick to say. "But Casey thought I was crazy for letting him go. I mean, she's team Joey now, but for a while there, she was seriously questioning my judgement."

"You know as well as I do what kind of a home Casey comes from," Mam replied gently. "You know what her mother is like, Aoife. You've seen what that woman has exposed her daughter to down through the years. The kind of men she's traipsed through their front door."

"Yeah," I mumbled, shuddering at the memory.

"And you also know how strapped for cash they are in that little flat over in Elk's Terrace," Mam continued. "I can only presume that when Casey saw you throw away a boy with a solid future, for a boy with an unwritten one, she panicked on your behalf."

"Paul was no catch of the day," I muttered. "And we're not exactly flush with cash ourselves, Mam."

"We might not have money, Aoife, but we've always had each other," Mam explained. "We've always had our family unit, and that's a form of stability and comfort that we both know young Casey has never had."

Or Joey.

"I'm lucky to have you, Mam."

She arched a brow.

"What?" I laughed. "I was being sincere."

"Yes, well, I'm sure you'll mean that even more in six months' time," she chuckled. "When there's a baby crying the house down and you're up to your elbows in poo and vomit, screaming for your mother to come get her grandchild." Clearly amused with herself, she added, "At least your partner in crime has experience with newborns, because you've never held a baby in your life."

"I've held Sean."

"Sean's three."

"He was only two when I first held him."

"There's a big difference between a two-year-old that you can hand back, and a defenseless newborn baby, depending entirely on you to meet every one of his needs."

"Mam."

"He or she will need you to feed them, wind them, change them, clothe them, comfort them, love them, soothe them ... all of it and more. He or she will even depend on you to clear their airways with a tiny nasal aspirator, when they get a cold, because he or she won't be able to do that for themselves. This little baby will be completely reliant on his or her mother for survival. And that's just the newborn stage, which believe it or not, my darling girl, is the easiest stage of motherhood."

"Please stop," I begged, feeling dizzy at the thought. "I'm so unbelievably terrified of what's coming, that I'm surprised I can function."

"You *can* do this," she assured me. "You are going to be a good mother."

"I'm going to be a disaster," I mumbled glumly. "I can barely cook French toast."

"Because you're a spoilt princess who's used to having everything done for her," Mam laughed. "But we'll soon get you up to speed, pet. By the time my grandchild arrives, you'll be cooking up a storm and ready to take on the world."

"Don't ever leave me, okay," I strangled out. "I might be on the verge of becoming a mam, but that doesn't mean that I'll stop needing mine."

"You're stuck with me, I'm afraid," Mam laughed with a wink. "Whether you like it or not."

"I'm not moving out," I warned her, holding up a shaky finger. "I'm never leaving home, Mam. I'm staying put, where there's a veteran of motherhood in residence – and a veteran of the ironing board."

Mam laughed again. "That's another thing I'll have to teach you."

"I will *never* iron."

"You won't have a choice."

"Yes, I will," I shot back. "I'll buy all non-iron clothes for the baby to wear."

"And who, may I ask, will iron your clothes?"

I rolled my eyes. "My mother, obviously."

"Oh, Aoife, you do make me smile," Mam chuckled. "You're going to be okay, love. You truly are."

"I hope you're right, Mam," I replied. "I really do."

"Joey is going to be okay, too," she added. "You both are." Mam gave me another one of those perceptive smiles. "Do you want to know how I know this?"

"Pray tell, sensei."

"Because your baby's father might be as pigheaded and stubborn as you are when it comes to admitting his feelings, but his heart has never once wandered from you, either."

"No." I shook my head. "You don't know that, Mam."

"I *do* know that," she corrected in a soft tone. "Aside from the fact that I've watched you both grow up, and have firsthand experience of the kinds of qualities you both possess, I also happen to possess a pair of eyes – and ears – of my own that are in perfect working order."

"Meaning?"

"Meaning that when you peel back all the layers of yours and Joey's relationship, taking the flirting, raging hormones, and the physical aspect out of the equation, there's a rock-solid foundation underneath," she told me. "One that's based on *friendship*, and *respect*, and *trust*." Smiling fondly, she recrossed her ankles, switching them up, and leaned forward in her seat. "He's your *friend*, Aoife, and you're his. Never mind loving one another, that's the easy part, you and Joey *like* each other. You *enjoy* one another's company, and I can promise you that all of those wonderful aspects of your relationship, all of those effortless conversations you find yourself having with him, or all of the content spells of silence you spend in one another's company, will only strengthen your ability to stand the test of time. And more crucially; the test of parenthood."

"You really think that?"

"I do," she replied, giving me a reassuring smile. "And remember; mother knows best."

Think about your future

JOEY

"Joey."

Thump. Thump. Thump.

"Joey."

Thump. Thump. Thump.

"Joey."

Thump. Thump. Thump.

"Joey!"

Releasing a pained groan, I slowly blinked awake, feeling an abnormal amount of weight pushing down on the middle of my back, as I faceplanted my mattress.

The weight continued to bounce up and down on my back, and I slowly registered the weight as my baby brother. "O-ee. O-ee."

"Fuck, Seany-boo," I groaned, snaking a hand out from under my head and grab a pillow. "Stop jumping on my back, kid. I'm dying here."

Covering the back of my head with the pillow, I tried and failed to drown out the noise attacking my senses from all angles.

"Sean, go downstairs and play with Ollie." Mam's familiar voice drilled through my mind and I stiffened, body coiling tight with tension. "I need to talk to your brother."

Sean had another three good bounces on my back before obliging our mother and toddling away.

"Don't start," I grumbled, rolling onto my back. "Whatever it is, just leave it out."

"I wasn't going to start anything." Closing my bedroom door, Mam walked over to my bed and sat down beside me. "I just wanted to see if you are okay?"

Sighing heavily, she reached a hand out to brush my hair off my face, and that small act of affection had me scrambling to the far end of the bed and as far away from her as possible.

"You wanted to see if I was okay," I repeated flatly, as I leaned my back against the wall and glared at her. "Since when did you give a fuck about how I am?"

"Since the day you were born."

"Huh?" Confusion furrowed my brows. "Is there a social worker lurking downstairs or something that I'm not aware of?"

"No, Joey," Mam sighed, blue eyes full of sadness, as she watched me watch her with wary mistrust. "It was a genuine question."

"That I'm genuinely confused about," I deadpanned. "What do you want?"

"What makes you think that I want something?"

"Because you're in my room, asking how I'm feeling," I replied, shoulders tense. "So, come on, out with it."

"I don't want anything from you, Joey."

I remained silent and waited for her to get to the point.

This was not a spontaneous check-up on my emotional welfare.

"You haven't been to school this week," she finally said. "Mr. Nyhan phoned twice."

"So? Neither has Shannon."

"Yes," Mam agreed. "But Shannon has stayed home from school this week to help me."

"As opposed to me, the prick who's never helped you a day in his life?"

"No, that's not what I'm saying at all."

"Then what are you saying?" I shot back. "What do you want?"

"I'm worried about you."

Bullshit.

I folded my arms across my chest. "Since when?"

"Since what happened the other weekend," she replied, tone weary.

"Oh, you mean when my father tried to rape my girlfriend?" I bit out, trembling with anger again. "No, no, I'm grand, Mam. That didn't fuck with my head one bit."

"Oh, Joey." Mam choked out a shaky breath. "I'm so sorry."

"Why?" I deadpanned. "I wasn't aware that you tried to fuck my girlfriend, too?"

"Joey."

"Oh, wait, that's right, you didn't try to fuck Aoife. No, you just took her would-be rapist into your bed instead."

Mam flinched. "How is Aoife? Is she alright?"

"I have no idea," I replied tightly. "I haven't seen her."

"Why not?"

"Because she can't stand the sight of me," I told her. "I remind her too much of my father, the rapist bastard himself."

"He didn't rape her."

"He raped *you*."

Another flinch. "That's different."

"Because he put a ring on your finger when you were still young enough to play with dolls, and that gives him automatic dominion over your body?"

"Joey." She blew out a pained breath. "I wish you could understand."

"If you're referring to the perverted fixation you have with that man, then you can forget about it," I told her. "Because I will never understand."

"I don't want to fight with you."

"Who's fighting?"

"*You* are, Joey," she said with a sigh. "Every time I try to reach out to you, every time I try to pay you any sort of attention, you immediately go on the attack."

"Maybe I wouldn't if the experience wasn't so fucking foreign to me."

She shook her head sadly. "There you go again."

"Jesus Christ, I can't do right in your eyes, can I?"

"Do you want to know something I don't understand?"

"Not really." I shrugged. "That list is so long we'd be here for weeks."

"I don't understand how a boy, who despises his father as much as you despise yours, can follow him right down the garden path to addiction."

"I'm *not* an alcoholic."

"Worse, you're a drug addict!" she cried out hoarsely.

"No," I bit out, shaking my head. "I'm not."

"Yes, you *are*," she cried, reaching for my hand. "You have a *problem*, baby." Exhaling a shuddering breath, she added, "Yes, I know you're back to your old tricks. I found the empty bags in your jeans."

I narrowed my eyes. "You are way off the mark."

"Bullshit, Joey," she snapped. "I can smell the weed on your clothes."

"So, I had a smoke. Big fucking deal."

"And?"

"And nothing," I snapped. "So, get off my back, Mam."

"Then what's this?" she demanded, reaching inside her pocket to retrieve the cracked plastic casing of a pen.

My stomach sank, but I schooled my features, too fucking ashamed of myself to admit anything, and *never* to this woman. "Looks like a broken pen to me."

"Really? Because it looks like a makeshift straw to me!" She threw it down on the bed. "And I might not be the world's smartest person, but I know damn well that you don't need one of those for weed."

I shrugged noncommittally. "I don't know what to tell ya, Mam."

"How about you start by explaining where my medication has been going?" she urged, tears filling her eyes. "You have been so good for so long. Months, Joey, *months*! And now we're what? Back to square one? Why would you do this to yourself, Joey, *why*?"

"When have I *ever* laid a finger on you?" I demanded, heart gunning in my chest, as I snatched my hand back. "Or Shannon? Or the boys, for that matter?"

"I'm not talking about whether or not you would harm other people, Joey," Mam replied. "I'm talking about the harm you're doing to yourself. I don't understand how you can throw your life away on a habit that you know ruins lives."

"What do you want from me, huh?" I demanded, at my wits' end. "You let that bastard stay, *knowing* what he tried to do to my girlfriend, so I leave. Then you text me, three days later, begging me to come back and save you from him, so I come back and do exactly that. Now, you're in my room, grilling me on being absent from school, accusing me of being cold to you, and calling me a fucking addict?" I shook my head. "I'm here when I don't want to be, when I would rather be anywhere else on this planet – and that includes a coffin – but I'm *here* because *you* called. Because *you* need me. Because *they* need me. Even though being inside this house makes me want to peel my skin off. I'm fucking *here*. If that doesn't tell you everything you need to know, then I don't know what to say, I really don't."

"I want you to love yourself enough to stop destroying yourself."

"How do you ever expect that to happen when the very person who gave birth to me can't love me?"

Mam reared back like I had struck her – and maybe I had, but it was with the truth.

"That is not true," she cried, pushing her hair back. "You can't possibly believe that."

"Whatever." Shaking my head, I dragged myself off the bed, and moved for my clothes. "I'm not doing this with you right now. I have somewhere to be."

"Somewhere like Shane Holland's house?"

Remaining silent, I kept my back to her, and slipped on my sweats before pulling a hoodie on.

"Don't do it," she begged, following after me, as I pocketed my phone and wallet, and moved for the door. "Think about your future."

"I don't have one of those anymore."

"Yes, you do."

"No." I shook my head and yanked the door open. "He took her away from me."

With a cigarette balancing between my lips, I spent an inordinate amount of time slumped on the steps outside of the Garda Station, willing myself to just stand up and walk inside.

Just walk my legs in there and give the Gards my statement.

Give them my truth.

My father should be behind bars for putting his hands on Molloy, and the resentment I felt at having my hands, once again, tied behind my back by a woman I loved and was desperate to protect, was fucking with my head like nothing else.

I'd hit my limit that night and screwed up, but I didn't feel half the regret for using as I felt for keeping quiet.

For letting him get away with what he did.

He abused and raped my mother.

I was coerced into keeping my mouth shut.

He battered my sister.

Again, I was emotionally blackmailed into keeping quiet.

But Molloy?

Molloy, I had quickly realized, was my Achilles heel.

When he put his hands on her that night, he aimed an arrow right at my weak spot, and when she rejected me, when she compared me to *him*, that arrow had flown, striking me straight through the heel.

Bleeding out and wounded, I'd given up on any more bullshit pretenses about turning pages, and fresh starts, and gone straight back to the only thing I knew would help me drown out the noise.

Drown out the fucking agony of it all.

Because the truth was, I didn't want to lie anymore.

I didn't want to cover up.

I was completely done with the bullshit, and if that made me a shitty son and a horrible brother then so be it.

Because the old man exposed something inside of me that night.

A truth I hadn't realized myself until he forced me to face it.

It shook the foundations of my very being to acknowledge it, but the truth was that something had shifted inside of me this past year, my priorities had *switched*. I had come to the realization that Aoife Molloy had become the single most important person in my world.

Unnerving as it was to admit, there wasn't anything I wouldn't do protect her. Even if that meant going against my entire family to do right by her. Because, regardless of the consequences incurred by the rest of my family, I was willing to go against everything I had been programed to protect in order to protect *her*. Even if that meant going against every fiber of my being and remaining quiet about my father because that's what she needed from me.

Conflicted and furious, I remained right there on the steps of the Garda Station until the sky darkened, and my anger waned, making way for my depression.

And fuck if the depression wasn't worse.

Dying on the inside and burning on the outside, I stared down at the scars on my knuckles, and forced myself to pretend that I was fine.

That none of this hurt.

That I didn't care.

Finally, when I had the pain under control, I stood up, dusted myself off, and walked away, feeling the weight of the world on my shoulders with every step that I took away from doing the right thing.

What did you take?

AOIFE

When I finally returned to school the following Monday morning, and took my seat in tutorial, it was to an empty chair beside mine at a desk I had been assigned to share with Joey since the start of the school year.

"Arrrgggghhh!" Casey screamed, as she stood in the doorway of our classroom and stared at me in horror. "Where the hell have you been, and what the fuck have you done to your hair?" she demanded, pointing an accusing finger at me. "Oh my god." Her eyes widened in horror as she let her bag fall off her shoulder and ran behind my chair to get a better look. "It's *gone*."

"It's good to see you, too, Case," I chuckled, smoothing a hand over my shoulder length hair. "To answer your first question; I was home. I needed a few days to sort my head out. As for the latter; I needed a change."

No, what I had *needed* was to remove the memory of that man's hands from my hair, and it had cost me eighty euro for the pleasure, but she didn't need to know the finer details.

I still had enough length to tie it back in a small ponytail, but not long enough to put me in the vulnerable position of having a man restrain me with it.

"Do you like it?"

"No!" she spluttered, horrified, as she retrieved her bag.

"Wow." I rolled my eyes. "Thanks a bunch."

"Oh, shut up, you're still a complete ride," she shot back, eyeing my hair and pulling at a loose tendril. "I've just never seen you with hair shorter than the middle of your back, Aoif. You've had Rapunzel hair since we were in playschool." Giving me the side-eye, she added, "I tried calling you a hundred times, by the way."

"My phone is at Joey's," I told her. "And people change."

"Yeah, I suppose impending motherhood can change a girl."

"Say it louder, why don't you?" I hissed, twisting around to glare at her when she slid into the desk behind mine. "Jesus."

"Sorry." She winced and held her hands up. "Any updates on that front, by the way?"

"I told my mam."

Her blue eyes widened. "How'd she take it?"

"Better than I did, I think," I admitted with a pained sigh. "She went with me to the doctor last week."

Her eyes widened. "And?"

I nodded. "September twentieth."

"Your due date?" Her eyes widened. "That's two days after your nineteenth birthday."

"Shh," I warned, and then reluctantly nodded. "But yeah, that's my due date. I got my hospital appointment in the post – for my first scan."

"For when?"

"This Friday."

"What time? Because we finish school at twelve for the Easter holidays, and I can come with you if—"

"I appreciate the offer, but no," I replied, shaking my head. "Mam already offered, but I don't want her there, either."

"Why?"

Because I only want Joey.

"Because." I expelled a frustrated breath. "Because I just don't."

"So, how did he take it?" she asked then, eyes laced with sympathy. "Not well, I'm guessing, considering he hasn't been at school for the past week, either."

"I haven't told him."

"Still?" Her eyes widened. "*Aoife.*"

"I know, I know," I grumbled, feeling my windpipe constrict at the thought of him not knowing almost as much as having to tell him. "Ugh."

"When you both didn't show up to school, I convinced myself that you'd told him," Casey offered, brows furrowed. "I figured you wouldn't be coming back until after the Easter holidays."

The bell rang loudly then, interrupting our conversation, and I watched as the classroom began to slowly fill, rolling my eyes when Danielle and Paul swaggered into class, with their arms wrapped around each other.

"Ugh," Casey interjected, pretending to stick her finger down her throat. "What does she think will happen if she doesn't weld herself to his side for an entire class?"

"That he'll be stolen away, by the looks of it," I offered, turning around in my seat to lean against her desk. "Whatever. She's welcome to him."

"Yeah, you certainly made an impressive upgrade," Casey mused and then grinned, eyes shifting to behind me. "Speaking of which ... "

She pointed towards the classroom door and I turned around just in time to see Joey walk into class.

The minute my eyes landed on him, my heart bucked wildly in my chest, instantly recognizing its mate.

His hair was styled in the usual way he wore it, shaved tight at the back and sides, with a mop on top.

Minus his school jumper, the grey shirt he was wearing was untucked and hanging untidily over his belt buckle, while his school tie had been haphazardly thrown on. He had his sleeves rolled up to the elbow, revealing the impressive scrawl of black ink that he had been steadily adding to since fourth year, which now covered both of his forearms.

With his usual *fuck the world* expression etched on his face, he approached the teacher's desk, handing over what I knew was a behavioral chart book – otherwise known as the dreaded *red book*.

It was a report card type booklet assigned to the most disruptive students with the worst attitude problems and needed to be signed off by each teacher upon arrival to class and at the end. At the end of each day, the principal himself would have every student with a red book come to the office to have any or all comments received in their books checked over by him in person. As you can imagine, Joey had received more than his fair share of red books down through the years.

Usually, a student, no matter how badly behaved, only had to carry around a red book for a week at the most at any given time. But I specifically remember Joey having one for the *whole* of second and third year without a break.

Looking entirely unimpressed with whatever Miss Lane was saying to him as she pointed at the red book on her desk, Joey simply handed her a pen, and folded his arms across his chest, waiting for the signature.

And then he chose that exact moment in time to sweep his gaze around the room. I felt the weight of his stare the second it landed on me.

The air thinned around me, making it genuinely hard to drag breath into my lungs. Trembling beneath the intensity of it all, I forced a small smile and a small limp wave.

What other way was there to greet the boy you'd spent years loving?

The boy whose father had tried to *molest* you.

The boy who you ripped the heart out of the last time you saw him.

Jesus.

I watched Joey stiffen, his eyes heated and focused entirely on me.

He didn't smile.

He didn't wave.

He just stared at me.

This was too much.

It was way too fucking much.

There were so many unspoken words, so many unanswered questions hanging in the air between us both.

I knew that he felt it, too.

His expression wasn't hiding anything from me.

He was showing it all right now, every ounce of confusion, pain and annoyance.

Eventually, the teacher returned the red book to Joey, and I watched as he strode towards our desk, still staring at me, still unsmiling.

Dropping his bag on the ground at the side of our desk, he pulled his chair and sank down in his usual spot beside me.

The minute he sat down, the fresh and achingly familiar scent of Lynx and soap flooded my senses, causing me to shiver.

"Joey," I croaked out, watching him warily, unsure of how to react because of how we had left things the last time we spoke.

"Molloy," he acknowledged, shoulder brushing against mine as he adjusted his chair, pushing it back to give himself more leg room.

"Nice shirt," I whispered, nudging my shoulder with his, as I held my breath and waited for his age-old response.

Say it.

Please say it.

Two words.

That's all I need.

The breath he released was so deep, that it caused his shoulders to visibly rise and fall, before he shook his head in what seemed like reluctant surrender. "Nice legs."

Thank you, Jesus.

"I was hoping you'd be here today."

"Where else would I be?"

"You weren't at school last week."

"I had a lot on."

Yeah, with his mother. "How is your mam?"

He shrugged noncommittally and reached into the pocket of his school trousers, withdrawing my phone and setting it down on my side of the desk. "You left this."

"Yeah, I, uh, I know." Swallowing deeply, I quickly snatched up the phone and pocketed it. "Thanks for bringing it back."

He offered me a clipped nod in response. "No problem."

"I left my necklace there, too," I whispered. "In your room. The one you got me for my birthday last year."

"I'll get that back to you."

"Thanks," I breathed, hating the ridge between us. "So, are you okay?"

Nodding stiffly, he kept his eyes trained on the door in front of us. "Are you?"

"Yeah." I shrugged weakly. "I mean, I think so."

"That's good." His jaw ticked and I watched as he swallowed deeply. "I'm glad. I was worried about you."

"I was worried about you." Shivering, I reached under our desk and placed my hand on his hard, muscular thigh. "God, Joe, I've missed you so much."

A deep shudder rolled through him, but he made no move to respond or return any physical affection.

Instead, he leaned forward, rested his elbows on our desk, dropped his head in his hands, and muttered something unintelligible under his breath.

"You never came back," I heard myself say, eyes trained on his back.

"You wanted space," came his flat response.

"I *wanted* you to come back."

"How was I supposed to know that?"

"You weren't," I sighed. "I just ... never mind."

A horrible silence settled between us then; one I was desperate to get rid of.

"Joe?"

"Hm?"

"Can we talk?"

"We are talking." His response was automatic, almost robotic, as he slumped over our desk, head in hands.

"Properly," I urged, cracking my knuckles nervously. "Privately."

Shrugging lifelessly, he released a pained breath, but didn't respond.

"Can we hang out this evening?"

"I have to work. I've already missed a week. I can't skip anymore."

"What about tomorrow?"

He didn't respond.

"I wanted to know if you had plans at lunchtime on Friday?" I heard myself croak out, palms sweating, as panic filled me. "Because there's some place I need to be and I was, uh, well, I was really hoping that you could come with me."

More silence.

"Joe?"

Jerking upwards, he looked around himself, seemingly startled, before slumping back down on his elbows. "Hm?"

"Do you have plans on Friday?"

"I, ah, I don't know," he mumbled, sounding beyond exhausted. "I'm not sure."

"Well, are you busy at lunch today?" I tried instead. "I mean, do you have training or anything like that happening? Because I really need to talk to you in private about something."

"I don't want to talk in private," he replied quietly. "Not today, Molloy."

"But you don't even know what I want to talk to you about," I squeezed out. "It's important."

"Whatever it is, I don't want to talk about it right now."

"Why?"

"Because I'm too fucking tired, Molloy."

"You have to know I didn't mean it," I blurted, addressing the elephant in the room. "All of that shit I spurted out the last time we were together? It wasn't me, Joe."

He stiffened.

"I didn't mean it, okay?" Reaching up, I placed a hand on his back, frowning when I felt the heat emanating from his body. *Jesus, he was burning up.* "I swear, Joe. Not one word of it."

"Yeah, you did." The muscles in his back coiled tight under my touch. "And it's okay. I don't blame you."

"I don't blame you for what happened, Joe," I told him, feeling achingly vulnerable in this moment. "And I don't want space. I *never* want space from you."

"Neither do I," he replied quietly. "But just because we don't want something doesn't mean that we don't need it."

Anxiety churned inside of me. "What does that mean?"

"It means what it means, Molloy."

"Look at me."

He didn't.

"Joe."

"Just let it go, Molloy."

"Joey Lynch, you better look at me."

Blowing out a pained breath, he leaned back in his chair, rested his hands on his lap, and reluctantly looked at me.

All of sudden it made perfect sense.

The drowsiness.

The lethargy.

The scorching hot skin.

Eyes as black as coal.

"Oh my god." I sucked in a sharp breath. "What did you take?"

"Nothing."

He moved to turn his face away, but I caught his chin between my fingers and forced him to look at me. "What did you *take*?"

"Nothing," he argued before releasing a pained breath. "Today."

"Yesterday?"

He nodded slowly.

"And the day before?"

Another nod.

My heart broke further.

"When did it start?"

Silence.

"When did it *start*?"

"After I left your place."

Oh god, no . . .

"So, we're talking a week?"

"About that."

"What was it?" I forced myself to ask. "What did you take?"

"Not what you think."

"*What* did you *take*, Joey?"

"Not that."

"I didn't ask you what you didn't take," I hissed, heartbroken and furious. "Tell me what you took, dammit."

His eyes locked on mine, and stayed there, focusing on me as best as he could, given that he was clearly under the influence. "Just some pills and shit."

"And *shit*?" I glared at him. "What does *and shit* consist of? Because I've been with you long enough to know that when you say the words *pills and shit*, your meaning can vary wildly."

"Molloy."

"So, what are we talking about here? A joint, a line, or a fucking needle." It felt like I had been transported back in time to a place I never wanted to revisit. "Oh my god." My breath hitched in my throat. "Why, Joe, *why?*"

"Why do you think?" he whispered brokenly, still obediently keeping eye contact with me, as I held his chin in my hand. "I broke you."

"No, Joe, you didn't break me." I shook my head and blinked back the tears stinging my eyes. "You broke *you*."

"It's my fault." He looked away then, pulling his face free. "What happened to you is on me."

"You didn't do anything wrong."

"I brought you into that house," he hissed, swinging back to glare at me. "I put you in harm's way and harm *got* you."

"I'm okay," I choked out, reaching up to touch his cheek only to feel the sting of rejection when he leaned away from my touch. "Don't do this. Don't throw away everything you've worked so hard for."

"I don't have anything, Molloy," was his lifeless response. "I never did."

"You have me," I breathed, chest rising and falling quicky, as I fought to maintain my composure in a classroom surrounded by peers. "You still have me, Joe. I don't blame you, okay? I don't."

"I'm him."

"No, you're not."

"Yeah, I am." He shrugged. "You said it yourself."

"That was my hurt talking," I choked. "I didn't mean it."

"It was your brain talking," he corrected. "It was your truth."

"Joey, come on."

"I can't." I watched as another shiver rolled through him. "I can't do this right now, Aoife."

"Can't do what?" I strangled out, cheeks flooding with heat, as my pulse skyrocketed. "Can't talk to me? Can't look at me? Can't be with me? *What*?"

"I can't do *this*." I watched as he dragged his hands through his hair in frustration. "Yeah, I definitely can't do this," he muttered, shoving his chair back, and grabbing his bag off the floor, as he rose to his feet. "I'm out."

"Sit down, Joseph," Miss Lane ordered from her desk. "Class is just about to start."

"Yeah, without me," he shot back, moving for the classroom door.

"Don't even think about walking out of this classroom," she commanded, holding a hand up in warning. "You're already on a red book. Don't make it worse for yourself."

"Kind of like how me telling you to get fucked would make it worse?" he sneered, slamming his palm against the door, causing it to swing open in a whoosh. "Well, it looks like I just did, huh?"

"Joseph!"

"Get fucked, *miss*," he called over his shoulder, and then he was gone, storming away.

"Oh god." Dropping my head in my hands, I resisted the urge to chase after him. I managed to last a whole three minutes until I caved, bolting out of my chair and moving for the door like my life depended on it.

"Where do you think you're going, Aoife?"

"I think she's going to *get fucked*, miss," Alec offered up with a chuckle. "In the literal sense, this time."

"Language," Miss Lane warned Alec, before turning her attention back to me. "This isn't drama class, Aoife. No need for the Bonnie and Clyde re-enactment. Return to your seat."

"But—"

"Now, Aoife."

"Ah, miss, don't be a cock block," Alec chimed in, encouraged by the class full of boys egging him on. "Did ya see the big bull head on Lynchy? You only have one class with him; the rest of us will be in the firing line all day. Let her go and sort him out. He'll be in much better form for the rest of the day."

"You can get out of my classroom," Miss Lane ordered, glowering at Alec. "Straight to the office to collect a red book of your own."

Deciding this was my perfect opportunity to escape, I made a dash for the door.

Ignoring the laughter coming from behind me, not to mention our year head's voice as she shouted after me, or Alec subsequently calling out 'You're welcome,' I hurried out of the classroom, leaving my bag behind, and trusting that Casey would pack up for me at the end of class.

My original plan was to head for the back of the PE hall, knowing that was one of Joey's chosen spots to frequent, and if that failed, then I would try the school sheds, but my plan quickly flew out the window when I reached the front entrance of the school and my eyes locked on none other than Marie Lynch coming out of the principal's office.

"Aoife." The minute she noticed me, she moved in my direction, making a beeline for the exit that I was desperately trying to get to. "Please, can I speak to you?"

My feet reluctantly faltered before coming to an abrupt stop, while my head told me to *keep going*. "What are you doing here?"

"I had a meeting with the principal," she said, when she closed the space between us, meeting me at the door. "I know that I'm the last person you want to speak to right now."

"The second last."

"Excuse me?"

"You're the second last person I want to speak to."

She had the good grace to wince. "Yes, well, would you mind walking with me for a moment so I can talk to you?" she asked, gesturing to the entryway double doors. "Please. It's important."

Deciding that Joey's mother was someone that I couldn't avoid forever, I nodded stiffly and followed her outside, falling stonily into step beside her.

"How have you been?"

"Fine," I replied, tone stiff.

"Are you sure?"

"What did you want to talk about, Marie?"

When she realized that she wasn't getting anywhere with that line of questioning, she released a heavy sigh and rubbed her forehead with her small hand. "I'm worried about Joey."

Yeah, me too. "Why?"

"I think he's falling into bad patterns again."

"Yeah." Sighing heavily, I wrapped my arms around myself as we walked, ignoring the torrential March downpour. "I've noticed."

"So, he *is* here?" Relief flooded her eyes. "He came to school?"

"He *was* here," I corrected flatly. "He left class pretty much as soon as he arrived."

"Oh god, that's what I was afraid of," she choked out. "I don't know what to do with him, Aoife. I really don't." She shook her head. "I don't know how to help."

"No offense, but it's kind of impossible for you to help him when you're the source of his pain."

She flinched from my words, but didn't argue.

Because she knew just as well as I did that she had a huge role to play in her son derailing.

Again.

"I deserve that."

"It's not about what you deserve, Marie," I bit out. "It's about the truth."

"He told me that you asked him for space," she hedged nervously. "That you didn't want to see him anymore."

Devastation flooded me. "I said a lot of things that I didn't mean to him."

"Then we have something in common," she replied sadly. "We're both guilty of directing our anger and pain at the wrong person."

"Why are you telling me this?" I asked, coming to an abrupt stop when we reached the edge of the carpark and my eyes landed on her husband's car.

With said husband sitting in the driver's seat.

Oh god.

The mere sight of the man made me physically shudder, and I found myself taking a step backwards. "What do you want from me?"

"What I said to you when we first met," she blurted out, stepping in front of me, in what I presumed was her pathetic attempt at shielding me from his view. "About how I thought that you needed to stay away from my son? Well, I was wrong."

My brows furrowed. "You were wrong?"

"Joey needs you," she continued to say, blue eyes full of lonesome sincerity, as the urgency in her tone grew. "More than he needs me, or anyone else, for that matter. For most of his life, my son has been so hellbent on escaping his mind, that he's never given a second thought to destroying himself in the process. But with you, since my son has been with *you*, he's different. It's not only that he's present, but it's that he *wants* to be. You soothe something inside of him, something that his father and I are responsible for breaking, and I don't want to see him have that snatched away from him again."

"Why are you saying this?" I asked, gaze flicking from her face to the car I could see over her shoulder. Anxiety gnawed at my gut, and it took everything I had in me to stand my ground and not run away.

"Because I made a mistake, Aoife," she replied in a shaky tone. "I've made a lot of mistakes when it comes to my son, but this is one that I hope I can make right." She looked me in the eyes then, imploring me to hear her, when she said, "Don't give up on him, Aoife. Please don't give up on my boy."

The sincerity in her voice threw me and it took me a few moments to gather my thoughts before I could respond.

"Nothing you said about Joey changed anything for me," I heard myself say. "I know your son is worth loving – worth *saving* – even if the rest of the world can't see it." *Even if he can't see it himself.* "I know who he is, Marie – the kind of man he is – and I know his worth, so you can rest assured that nothing you," I paused to cast a look a disgust in the direction of their car before continuing, "your husband, or anyone else, for that matter, have ever said or done has come close to making a dent in my feelings for him."

Even though I was being catty towards her, and my tone was undisguisably bitchy, I watched as his mother visibly sagged in relief.

"Thank you," she whispered. "For loving my son. I know that it's not easy at times."

"Loving your son is effortless," I cut her off by saying, pushing my damp hair out of my eyes. "It's getting him to love himself that's the hard part."

Of course, her husband decided this was the perfect time to roll down the car window and shout, "Marie, wrap it the fuck up, will ya? I've places to be."

Fear flooded the woman, and I watched as she visibly recoiled before resigning with a slumped shrug.

"I'm sorry for what he tried to do to you," she whispered. "So sorry."

"Did ya hear me, woman?" he barked. "I said get your hole over here, or you'll be walking back to the house."

His attention flicked to me then and recognition pinged in his eyes.

Feeling like my skin was crawling from just having his gaze on me, but refusing to back down, I narrowed my eyes and returned his glowering stare with one of my own, along with a perfectly polished middle finger.

It was at that exact moment that Joey decided to appear from behind the PE hall, with what I could only assume was the end of a joint pursed between his lips.

Taking one final drag of his smoke, he tossed the butt on the ground and exhaled an impressive cloud of smoke from his lungs as his bleary-eyed gaze landed on us.

Blinking in confusion, Joey looked from his mother, to me, and then to his father parked nearby.

The confusion in his eyes quickly morphed into fury.

"What the actual *fuck*!"

"Oh god, no," his mother strangled out, sensing the potential danger of the situation. "No, Joey, no!"

"What did I tell ya about looking at her?"

"Joe, hold up. It's okay."

"What did I tell you about coming anywhere near her?"

"Joey, please."

"Get out of the fucking car, old man!"

Moving entirely on instinct, I stepped around Marie, and ran straight at her son as he stormed towards their car.

"No." Intercepting Joey before he reached his father, I placed my hands on his chest. "*No.*"

"Move." His entire body was vibrating with tension, as he strained against my hands, attention locked on his father. "Get out of my way."

"No," I snapped, and then, before he had a chance to respond, I slid my hands up his chest, not stopping until I had a firm grip on his neck. "I said *no*," I repeated, roughly dragging his face down to mine. "Put your eyes on me and your mouth on mine."

"*What?*" He shook his head in frustration as rain pelted down on us. "No, Molloy, we can't just fucking—"

Whatever he was about to say was swallowed up when my lips crashed against his.

With my mouth on his, and with one of my hands fisted in the front of his school shirt, I reached up with the other and guided one of his hands to my hip, before placing the other on my ass.

The tension emanating from him was slightly terrifying, but I knew that I was in no danger with this boy.

After a few unnerving moments of stoic rigidity, I felt the shift in him, as he reluctantly relinquished his tight-fisted hold on his anger, and reciprocated my affection.

The sound of an engine roaring to life and then tires squealing filled my ears, and I sagged in relief.

He was gone.

Falling into our kiss, his mouth moved against mine, as our lips parted, and our tongues dueled viciously.

Joey was hurt and he was letting me know just how much in a bruising, punishing kiss that catapulted my hormones into complete disarray.

Flexing his hand on my ass, he tightened his grip on my hip, dragging my body roughly against his, as he took from my body whatever he needed in this moment to stabilize and ground himself.

Needing him with an equal desperation, I pressed up on the tips of my toes, hooked my arms around his neck, and returned with my lips everything that he was offering me.

One moment, he was there, and the next, he was gone; jerking away from me like my kiss caused him some sort of physical pain.

"Don't do that to me," Joey warned, breathing hard, as he wiped residue lip-gloss from his mouth with his thumb, and glared at me. "Don't fuck with my head like that."

"What are you *talking* about?" I panted, completely thrown off-kilter by his reaction. "I wasn't trying to fuck with your head."

"Kissing me," he snapped, backing up a few steps. "Manipulating me with my feelings, Molloy. I've had enough of that to last a goddamn lifetime."

"Are you serious?" I narrowed my eyes in response. "How is me kissing you a form of manipulation?"

"It's manipulation when you use my feelings for you against me," he shot back, unyielding. "You did it that night and you're doing it again."

"Are you blaming *me* for what happened?"

"No, I'm blaming me for that!" he roared, livid, dragging a hand through his hair. "I'm blaming me for caring too fucking much about what you want, and letting my feelings for you blindside me into *not* doing the right thing!"

"I *told* you that I want to forget about it."

"And I *told* you that I'd do whatever you wanted me to do." A vein ticked in his neck as he watched me watch him. "But that doesn't mean that my silence isn't eating me alive."

"Joey, don't let him do this to us." I took a step towards him and reached for his hand. "Don't let him win."

"Don't you get it, Molloy?" Joey pulled his hand free from mine and backed away. "He always wins."

As I watched Joey retreat and withdraw from me, I realized that some pivotal piece of him had been snuffed out that night, and if I let him go now, I might not be able to reach him again.

"I love you," I heard myself call out, and I watched as Joey's shoulders tensed and his step faltered.

Moving on instinct, I closed the space between us, and snatched his hand up, unwilling to let him leave me twice. "I'm in love with you, and that's something he can never take away from you."

A shiver rolled through him. "Molloy."

"He didn't win, Joe." Not stopping until I was flush against his chest, with my hands fisted in the front of his school shirt, I tugged hard on the fabric, reveling when he relented and lowered his face to mine. "You did."

Releasing a pained groan when my lips crashed against his, he didn't push me away this time; choosing to wrap his arms around me and pull me closer instead.

With our lips fused together, we step-stumbled to the side of the PE hall before slipping around back of the building.

My back hit the wall a moment later, followed by his big body crashing against me.

"I don't know where I stand with you anymore," he admitted against my lips, as he thrust his hips against me and let his arms fall to his sides. "Your mood swings drive me fucking crazy."

"I know, stud," I breathed, reaching between us to quickly undo his belt and pop the button on his grey school trousers. "I'm a mess."

"Me too," he croaked out, voice thick with need, as he watched me free his dick from the confinements of his black boxers. "I'm a fuck-up, queen. I let you down again."

"It's okay," I breathed, reaching under my skirt to quickly push my knickers down my legs and step out of them. "We'll figure it out."

"Your hair," he said instead of answering me, studying me with eyes so dilated they were almost black. "It's gone."

A pang of sadness hit me and I quickly crashed my lips against his, desperate to avoid the ins and outs of that particular decision.

"Fuck." Releasing a pained groan, he grabbed the backs of my thighs, and hoisted me up in one swift move.

Wrapping my legs around his waist I slid my hand between us and guided the thick head of his dick inside of my body.

"Are you going to send me away again?" he asked in an achingly vulnerable tone, sinking deep inside of me. "Tell me now so I can be ready for it."

My heart skipped.

"No, Joe." Cupping his stubbly cheek, I leaned in close and brushed my lips against his. "I won't ever send you away again."

All fucked up again

JOEY

"What the hell are you talking about?" Alec demanded at big break, as he gaped across the lunch table at Casey. "Staind's 'It's Been Awhile' is a mint song."

"I didn't say it wasn't a good song," she countered, handing him the MP3 player they had been passing back and forth during lunch. "I said it wasn't a love song. It's too depressing."

"So? Life's depressing," he argued. "That's the point."

"Well, love's not depressing."

"Love is massively fucking depressing."

"We're never going to be on the same page with this, Al."

"Then by all means inflict upon my ears your version of a love song."

Casey tilted her head to one side, clearly thinking hard about her answer before swiping the MP3 player and pressing a few buttons. "'World of Our Own'." Casey smiled sweetly up at him. "Westlife."

Looking wary, Alec put the ear pod to his ear and balked. "You are such a girl."

"Don't pretend you don't know every word of the song."

He grinned wolfishly at her before bursting into chorus.

"I knew it," she laughed.

"You eating that, Lynchy?" Mack asked, gesturing to the untouched ham sandwich on the table in front of me.

I shook my head. "Have at it, lad."

"Cheers."

Leaning back in my seat, I stared aimlessly at the people sitting around me, with my mind reeling, and my stomach in knots.

"Are you okay?" Molloy asked, shifting her chair closer to mine as she spoke. "You haven't eaten anything all day." She placed her hand on my bouncing knee to steady the tremor running through my body. "You're really pale, Joe."

"I'm grand," I replied, turning sideways and forcing myself to give her my attention – and *stop* shaking. "It's all good, Molloy."

The look she gave me assured me that she didn't believe a word of it, but she didn't push. Probably because she already knew how very *un-good* life was for me right now.

Everything felt like it was derailing again, and instead of keeping her safely at arm's length, I had, once again, dragged her back into my bullshit.

This morning, when I fucked her against the PE hall of all places, only proved that I was just as reckless with my heart as I was with my body when it came to this girl.

I was a fool for her, and we both knew it.

The power she had over me was unsettling.

Knowing that a girl could bend my will to suit her agenda was a troubling fucking concept.

When I saw my father in the carpark this morning, with his beady eyes locked on her, I had made my peace with the man upstairs.

I had intended on killing him.

I truly had.

Until *she* waded into the middle of my personal breakdown, and reined me back in. Using her body to manipulate me into submitting was a sneaky fucking girl-move, and one that my girlfriend had honed to perfection.

Even now, as we sat in the school canteen, eating lunch, and surrounded by our friends, I could feel my anxiety eating me from the inside out.

Molloy soothed the pain, but she couldn't take it away.

Last night for example, I knew my old man put hands on Shannon. I fucking knew it. The way my sister had rushed into her room and barricaded the door told me all I needed to know about went down between them.

He hurt her.

And I wasn't downstairs to protect her.

I was in my room getting high.

I knocked on her door to check on her when I heard it slam, but she fobbed me off with some bullshit excuse.

I needed to get her out of that house.

I needed to get all of them out.

I just . . . I was so fucking *tired*.

I felt hollow.

Like I didn't have anything left inside of me.

Every time I closed my eyes at night, I was haunted by the sound of my mother and sister's screams. And if it wasn't their screaming, it was the image of him pinning my girlfriend to that table.

I wanted to destroy that table.

I wanted to take a sledgehammer to it and break it into a million pieces.

"Could we go for a spin somewhere after school?" Molloy asked, dragging my attention back to her. "Or you could come over to my place." Reaching up, she brushed her thumb over the bruise on my cheek and offered me a small smile. "I'm not fussy, but I just . . . we really need to talk."

My phone vibrated in my pocket, and I stiffened, not daring to take it out while she was watching me so closely.

"I'm actually fairly busy this evening with work," I heard myself say, and then felt like a piece of shit when her expression caved in disappointment.

"It's kind of important, Joe."

I knew it was.

I knew she had shit to say to me, to get off her chest. Nothing had been cleared up between us, we had just fallen into the same fucked-up pattern of physical affection, but I didn't have the energy to go another round with her.

With anyone.

I was too fucking worn out to do anything more than barely function right now.

Getting out of bed this morning felt like climbing Everest.

I was exhausted from just getting myself to school.

The monumental effort it took me to just walk from class to class all day was almost overwhelming.

I couldn't do deep conversations.

I just didn't have it in me.

"We really need to talk," she pushed, eyes full of uncertainty. "Please, Joe. It can't exactly wait."

"I can come over tomorrow night after work," I offered weakly, knowing that it was the very last thing I needed, but giving her what she wanted anyway. "If you're free."

"I'll be free."

Nodding, I leaned in and brushed a kiss to her cheek before rising to my feet. "I'll see ya later, okay?"

"Wh-what? Why?" Her eyes were laced with anxiety. "Where are you going?"

"Nyhan wants to see me."

Liar.

Liar.

Fucking liar.

"You never said."

"Forgot."

"Oh." She didn't look convinced.

"I'll see ya later," I muttered, brushing her chin affectionately with my knuckles and then sharply turning on my heels and walking away.

Needing to get away from the person who ignited my conscience like no one else.

Needing a fucking breather from this life.

Waiting until I was out of sight, I slid my phone out of my pocket and checked the unanswered text.

HOLLAND: I'M OUTSIDE. LET'S GO.

Sighing despondently, I tapped out a reply and slid my phone back into my pocket.

LYNCHY: ON MY WAY.

God loves a trier, but Aoife loves Joey

AOIFE

"Okay, it's been three weeks," Casey declared on Tuesday morning during French, when our teacher, Mr. Brady, left the room. Snapping her book shut, she twisted in her seat to face me. "Tell me that today's the day."

"Yeah," I whispered, knees bopping restlessly under the table, as I kept my eyes glued to my boyfriend's back. "Today's the day."

He was sitting two rows ahead of me with Neasa Murphy, slumped in his chair, looking mildly amused at whatever she was saying to him.

"Would you stop glaring at her like she pissed in your cornflakes?" Casey whisper-hissed, dragging my attention back to her, as she peeled my fingers off the pencil I was squeezing. "He has to sit with her. It's assigned seating, babe."

"He was with her before."

"So? That was a million years ago."

"I hate her."

"No, you don't," she scoffed. "That's your hormones talking."

"No, I really do." I turned to look at my best friend. "I hate everyone he's been with."

"Then you hate a lot of females in this classroom," Casey laughed.

"Funny."

"So, you're really going to tell him?"

Ignoring the anxiety clawing at my throat, I nodded. "Tonight. When he comes over after work."

"Oh, my Jesus, talk about a squeaky bum moment," she strangled out. "Do you have a speech planned?"

"It's more of a *'My birth control failed, you're going to be a daddy, please don't leave me'* rambling plea than a speech."

"Aoif." She placed her hand on my arm. "He's not going to leave you."

"Yeah?" I blew out an anxious breath. "I really hope you're right, Case."

We were interrupted then by Charlie, who leaned over his desk behind us and tapped Casey's shoulder. "Mack wants to know what's happening with Alec."

"Huh?"

"Alec," he repeated. "Are you with him or something?"

Casey and I looked at each other in confusion before turning back to Charlie. "I'm not—"

"Why does Mack want to know?" I quickly clamped a hand over my best friend's mouth and asked, "What's it to him who Casey's seeing?"

"Why do ya think?" Charlie winked. "He's clearly still bananas about her."

"Is that so?" I eyeballed her. "Did you hear that, Case? Cha says that old Mackie boy is still bananas about you."

"Yeah, well, you can tell Mack that I'm seeing someone," Casey replied, peeling my fingers off her face. "So, he can take his banana back to his side of town."

"Alec?"

"Nope."

"Then who are you seeing?" Charlie asked, leaning in close.

"That's for me to know and you to find out," she replied, tapping her nose.

"No, seriously." I frowned. "Who are you seeing?"

She gave me a look that said *get with the program* before rolling her eyes. "Now, off you go." Waving him away from us, she turned back in her seat, taking me with her. "I'm not seeing anyone, but he doesn't need to know that."

"But you like Mack."

"Meh."

"And Alec?"

She shrugged. "So many boys, so little of sixth year left."

"You're terrible," I laughed.

Another tap came, but this time it was on my shoulder.

"You rang," I said, mimicking Lurch's voice, as I turned in my seat to find Charlie looking at me expectantly. "What's up, Cha?"

"I have a friend who heard a rumor that you and Lynchy were on the outs." Smirking, he added, "And my friend wants to know if there was any truth to it."

"Oh, really." I grinned. "And why would your friend want to know that?"

"Because my friend thinks you are hands down the best-looking girl at school."

"Does your friend have a death wish?" Casey laughed. "Because my friend's boyfriend will kill you dead, Cha. Dead, I tell you."

"So, he's still your—"

"You can tell your friend that I'm flattered, but I'm still very much taken."

"And you can also tell your friend that *his* friend has an impressive set of balls on him to attempt a steal on Joey's Lynch's girlfriend," Casey snickered. "I mean, seriously."

Charlie shrugged sheepishly. "It was worth a shot."

"God loves a trier," Casey agreed, eyes dancing with mischief. "But Aoife loves Joey."

Taking my sweet time returning to my last class of the day, after being excused to use the toilet, I dawdled outside the girls' bathroom, admiring the latest aesthetic offering of art on display in the main hall, courtesy of the leaving cert art class.

Reluctant to return to my business class, because I had a handle on ABQs like I had a handle on my life, I dragged my heels, pausing every couple of moments to inspect a picture hanging on the walls, or pretending to read the latest newsletter.

When I passed the boys' bathroom, and heard the sound of coughing, I felt myself halt in my tracks again, but this time, I wasn't lingering without purpose.

No, because I recognized that cough.

Filled with mischief, I slipped inside the bathroom, tiptoeing past the row of empty cubicles. Ignoring the stench of urine coming from the disgustingly yellow-stained urinals, I reached the cubicle at the end, the one with access to the window. The door was slightly ajar, and I ever so gently pushed it inwards until I had just enough of a view to see Joey. However, any notions I had of mischief quickly died when my eyes took in the sight before me.

With one knee resting on the closed toilet lid, Joey leaned in close to the windowsill, and, with the rolled-up fiver in his hands, snorted a line of white powder up his nose.

Frozen in horror, and unable to make a single sound, I watched as he rested his elbows on the window, and dropped his head in his heads, sniffing and twitching his nose, as he exhaled a sigh of what sounded an awful lot like relief.

Minutes ticked by where I just stood there, watching as the tension in his shoulders slowly loosened and his body began to sway.

A small groan escaped his lips then, and he heaved himself closer to the window, resting his weight heavily against it now.

As his high took over and his body grew limp, I felt my heart shrivel up and die in my chest.

I couldn't go through this with him again.

Not now there was a baby involved.

My hand moved to the slight swell of my stomach, and, for the first time since realizing the mess I was in, I felt a surge of something peculiar rise up inside of me.

Something that felt an awful lot like protectiveness for the baby growing inside of me.

Something that felt an awful lot like *love*.

Something that grew hotter and fiercer with every breath I took.

The protective feeling was so strong, so dominant and potent, that it felt almost carnal in nature, as it eclipsed the fear that had kept me burying my head in the sand these past few weeks.

I'm *pregnant*, I suddenly realized, as if it genuinely only registered in my brain at this very moment that I *was*, in fact, having a baby.

His baby, my mind chorused, as my eyes looked on in horror at the boy bombed out in the cubicle, *you're having* his *baby*.

Look at him.

Look at what you've attached yourself to.

Taking a minute to regain my composure, to absorb the multitude of feelings rushing through me, I cleared my throat and pushed the door in enough to let him know that I was there.

Swaying against the windowsill, Joey turned his head to look at me.

"Molloy," Joey slurred, mashing his lips together, as he squinted and strained to focus on my face.

"I'm not doing this with you again."

His brows slowly furrowed and he tilted his head to one side, clearly trying to make sense of my words in the fog of his mind. It took him longer than usual to register what I had said before he slowly shook his head. "It's not what it looks like."

"Oh yeah, because I've clearly read the room all wrong," I choked out, gesturing wildly to where he was slumped. "I *can't*." I shook my head, feeling the threat of my emotions brimming to the surface, desperate to explode out of me. "I *can't* go through this with you again."

"Then keep walking," he mumbled, still swaying unsteadily, as he tried to straighten himself up, only to fail miserably and land on the closed toilet. "Because I am what I am."

His words were like a slap across the face and I flinched. "You are what you are?"

"Yeah." Shaking his head, he tried to climb to his feet again, and this time, he was successful. "So just walk the fuck away, Molloy."

Ouch.

"You're telling me to walk away when you can't even walk a straight line." I narrowed my eyes in disgust. "Look at the state of you."

"You said that you can't do this with me again," he slurred, as he half-walked, half-staggered out of the cubicle, reaching for the wall to steady himself when his balance went. "But it's the same for me." Brows furrowed, he shook his head again, looking completely spaced out, as he tried and failed to focus on my face. "I can't do this with you, either."

Forget being slapped by his words; I was being *stabbed* by them. "What are you saying?"

"I'm saying I should have stayed the fuck away when we ended it at Christmas," he slurred, aiming his words at my heart like bullets. "Instead of dragging this bullshit out for another three months."

"And I presume this bullshit you're referring to is me?" I swallowed down the lump in my throat before hissing, "Well, fuck you, Joey Lynch."

I turned around to leave then, only to halt in my tracks when his arm came around my waist, pulling me back against his chest.

"I'm sorry." He exhaled a heavy breath and tightened his arm around my body. "I fucked up."

"Yeah, you did," I squeezed out, trembling all over, as I resisted the urge to sag against him, because, let's face it, he could barely hold himself up in this moment. "You're a fucking asshole."

"I know." A pained groan escaped him and he dropped his head to rest on my shoulder. "I know, baby."

"You're hurting me."

He groaned in pain. "Shh, stop saying that."

"This *hurts* me, Joey."

Another pained groan escaped his lips. "No, no, no, I would never hurt *you*."

"You hurt yourself and that's the same thing," I choked out. "Because when you hurt, I hurt. When you burn, I go down in flames with you. We're entwined, Joe. We're mirrors. Don't you get that by now?"

"Ah fuck." Trembling violently, he pulled me closer. "I'm sorry for hurting ya, Molloy."

"Listen to me, Joe; I really need you to sort your shit out, okay?" Shivering when I felt his lips brush against my ear, I clenched my eyes shut and tried to steady my nerves. "Because remember when I said I didn't need you before?" I clenched my eyes shut and squeezed out, "Well, I definitely need you now, okay?"

"No, you don't," he mumbled, as his hand moved to splay over my stomach, causing everything inside of me to twist up in knots. "I'm the bullshit, Molloy. I'm the fucking bullshit in this relationship. You bring all the good, and I bring all the bad."

"That's not true."

"It is."

"Regardless," I croaked out. "I need you to draw a line under whatever the hell this is, and come back to me, okay? Because I'm, ah ..." Exhaling a ragged breath, I let my head fall back and stared up at the ceiling as I tried to find the words. "I'm having a – I mean *we're* having ..." *Ugh.* Shivering violently, I practically spat the words, "a baby," out of my mouth in a breathy rush.

"A baby," he repeated slowly, voice slurred. "Where's the baby?"

"In here," I croaked out, reaching down to cover the hand he had splayed over my belly.

"In you?"

With my entire body rigid with tension, I forced a small nod.

"What's it doing in there?"

"You put it there, Joe."

"I did?"

"Yeah." I blew out a shaky breath. "You did."

"Well shit," he slurred, nuzzling my neck with his nose. "I'm sorry, Molloy. I didn't mean to."

"Are you mad?"

"Hm?"

"Mad, Joe," I repeated, swallowing down a surge of hysteria. "Are you mad?"

"No, I'm not mad," he murmured drowsily.

"Are you hearing me?"

"Hm?"

"Joe?"

"Hm?"

"You'll remember this, right?" Turning around to face him, I cupped his face between my hands, and forced him to look at me. "This conversation." I reiterated when he didn't respond. When his black eyes stared straight through me. "Me?"

"Sure." Hooking an arm around my waist, he, once again, buried his face in my neck and released a sigh of contentment. "You smell like home."

This was pointless.

He wasn't here.

At least, his mind wasn't present.

"Come on," I cleared my throat and said, "I'll take you somewhere to sleep it off."

"I thought you were done with me," he replied, pressing the softest of kisses to my neck. "I thought he took you away from me." Exhaling a pained groan, he buried his face in my neck. "I've fucked it again, Molloy."

"I'm not done with you, Joe," I squeezed out, shivering. "And it's okay. You'll be okay."

"So will you, Molloy." His arms tightened around my body, and even in his altered state of mind, he somehow managed to say the right thing. "Because I'll look after the both of you."

My breath hitched. "You promise?"

He nodded. "I promise."

Moments later, Joey's legs gave out beneath him, and he went crashing to the floor.

I can't go in there

JOEY

Drifting in and out of consciousness, I could hear two familiar voices going back and forth around me.

"This car is a bucket of shit."

"I know."

"Seriously, your dad's a mechanic and this is the best he can come up with?"

"Just shut up and drive, Podge."

"Shutting up now."

"Molloy." Lips mashing together, I twisted my head to one side, and groaned in approval when my nose burrowed between her warm thighs. "Mm."

"Shh, Joe, it's all good," she soothed, stroking my cheek with her hand, as she cradled my head in her lap with the other. "Just sleep it off, okay?"

Obliging the wonderful fucking voice that belonged to the best face I'd ever seen, I let my eyelids flutter shut, and nuzzled into her warm lap, feeling safer than I had in years.

Maybe ever.

"You make me feel safe."

"Oh, Joe."

"I love you so fucking much it hurts."

"I know, baby. I love you, too."

"Don't send me away again, Molloy."

"I won't, Joe." Her hand was on my hair again. "Shh, now. Just sleep it off, baby."

"What did he take?"

"Some type of powder."

"Crushed oxy?"

"Don't think so. Something stronger."

"Coke?"

"He'd be bouncing off the walls."

"True."

"I think it might be heroin."

"No way. He's not that reckless."

"Can you snort heroin?"

"Shit, Aoif, I don't know."

"Neither do I."

"Fuck."

"Listen, I need you to do something for me. I need you to search his room. Go through every pocket of every pair of jeans you can find. Search his wardrobe. His chest of drawers. His nightstand. Every drawer. Every fucking inch of his bedroom. His school bag. His gear bag. There's a hole in the side of his mattress. Check that, too. He's using again, which mean he has a stash. Whatever you find, flush it. Can you do that for me?"

"You're not coming inside?"

"I *can't* go into his house, and I can't bring him back to my place like this. Not with my mam at home."

"It's grand, Aoife. I'll look after him. You know the drill. He needs to sleep it off. He'll be grand after a few hours' kip."

"Don't leave him, okay? Please, Podge. Not when he's like this."

"I won't."

"I mean it. Because he could get sick in his sleep and choke on his—"

"I won't leave him, I promise."

From bad to worse

AOIFE

Mam was waiting for me at the front door when I got home from school on Tuesday evening.

"Well?" she asked, tone hopeful, as she stepped sideways to let me inside. "Did you tell him? Is he coming over?"

Yes, I told him, but he was on another planet and didn't hear a word of it.

Shaking my head, I dropped my bag in the hallway, and hung my coat on the banister, feeling thoroughly deflated.

"Aoife." Her expression fell. "You need to tell the boy."

"I know," I quickly cut her off, moving for the kitchen, as my body thrummed with anxiety. "I tried. He was busy."

Busy losing his mind.

"We're all busy, Aoife," Mam offered, closing the front door and trailing after me. "There's never going to be a right time to have this conversation, but it has to be done."

"I know," I repeated, shoulders knotted with tension, as I rummaged in the fridge. "I tried."

"Do you want me to talk to him for you?"

"What?" Slamming the fridge door shut, I swung around to gape at her. "No, Mam. Jesus!"

"If you don't tell him soon, it's only going to make matters a million times worse."

My eyes narrowed. "I'm *trying*, Mam, but it's not something that spills off the tongue easily, okay. What am I supposed to do, huh? Just blurt it out in class?"

"You should call him," Mam said, moving to place a reassuring hand on my shoulder. "If you can't tell him face to face, then do it over the phone."

"Mam, I already *tried*." Swallowing down the lump in my throat, I implored her with my eyes to understand. I felt broken enough from this afternoon's shitstorm without my mother pouring on the pressure. "Just let it go, okay?"

"You *need* to do this, Aoife," she pushed. "You have the hospital on Friday and Joey needs to be there. He needs to know that he's about to become a father. He has rights, you know."

"A father?" Kev deadpanned, and I swung around to find him standing in the kitchen doorway.

"Kev, you really shouldn't eavesdrop on people," Mam admonished, pressing her hand to her chest, as she scolded my brother. "It's not nice."

"Joey Lynch is going to be a father," he repeated, eyes locked on mine. "Which clearly means you're going to be a mother."

"No, I'm not," I lied, red-faced and flustered, as I stepped around Mam and moved for the kettle. "Don't be thick."

"I'm not thick," my brother was quick to shoot back, stalking into the kitchen. "I happen to be your twin, you know? I could sense something was off with you for a while now." He shook his head. "And now it all makes sense." He turned and glared at Mam. "The two of you have been joined at the hip for days now. Whispering and sneaking off together," he sneered. "Because she's pregnant."

"Stop saying that," I strangled out, feeling weak. "It's not true."

"Bullshit," he argued, tone vehement. "You've been a nightmare to live with for weeks. It's like mood swing central in this place – not to mention all of the school Mam just let you skip." He looked me up and down, eyes narrowing in disgust. "It's because you let that waster get you pregnant?"

"That's enough, Kev," Mam warned, speaking up for me when I couldn't. "You need to back off right now, young man. This has nothing to do with you, so just drop it."

"Nothing to do with me?" he spat, looking furious. "Are you joking? I live here, too, you know. If she's bringing a baby into this house, then I have a right to know, and so does Dad."

"Stop it," I begged, feeling the blood drain from my face. "Just stop talking, Kev."

"At first, I thought you were just getting fat, but now it makes sense. All the weird food you've been eating is because of pregnancy cravings."

"Kevin!"

"You can't even deny it, can you?" he argued, ignoring our mother's protests, and keeping his furious eyes on me. "Because there's no denying that belly you've been trying to hide."

"Kevin!" Mam snapped. "I told you that's enough!"

"Yeah, I see it. I'm not blind, and I'm far from stupid," my brother sneered, glowering at me. "Unlike you. The fucking idiot who laid on her back and let a loose cannon like Lynchy get her pregnant."

"Fuck you," I choked out, feeling the tears spill from my eyes, as my brother hit me with a cold hard dose of reality. "You have no idea, Kev. No goddamn clue."

"Congratulations, sister," he continued to sneer. "You just let that asshole turn you into another teenage pregnancy statistic. Well done. You can kiss your future goodbye now that you've joined the long list of hopeless girls from our school that were thick enough to open their legs to fellas like that."

"I said that's enough, Kevin," Mam shouted, coming to stand between us. "I don't care how surprised or upset you are, don't you ever speak to your sister – or any woman, for that matter, like that again. You were *raised*, not dragged up."

"Yeah, and so was she," he countered, defensively. "But apparently, only one of us got the memo."

"That's not fair," Mam replied, tone thick with emotion. "You don't understand what your sister is going through."

"No, because I actually happen to possess a brain between my ears," he agreed, furious. "Unlike this idiot."

"Kevin!"

"Jesus, I always knew you weren't the brightest crayon in the box, but *this*?" my brother accused, eyes narrowed in challenge. "Getting pregnant while you're still in school? Off a fucking scumbag like Joey Lynch? Wow, talk about scraping the barrel by mixing your genes with his. That poor fucking kid's going to come out with a cocaine habit and the IQ of a gummy bear!"

"I said that's enough!" Mam screamed, opening the cupboard door just to slam it shut. She did it three more times until she had my brother's attention. "You," she hissed, pointing a finger in my brother's face. "Not another word."

"But—"

Mam slammed the cupboard door again. "Not another fucking word, Kevin, or the next thing I'll slam will be my hand across your face."

"So, she gets pregnant, and I get threatened with a slap?" my brother huffed, folding his arms across his chest. "Talk about favoritism."

"This has nothing to do with favoritism and everything to do with human decency," Mam growled, poking his chest with her finger. "And I'm telling you now, young man, you better not breathe a word of this to anyone. Do you hear me, Kevin? Not a soul."

"I'm obviously going to tell Dad."

"If you know what's good for you, you'll keep that mouth shut," Mam warned in a rare, threatening tone. "This is *not* your news to tell, Kevin. This is *not* about you. This is about your sister, and Aoife has the right to tell your father, and everyone else, when she's ready."

"Are you crazy? This is Aoife we're talking about. She's never going to be *ready* to have a baby," my brother said, pointing out one of my biggest fears. "She can't even clean up after Spud, and she's the one who begged you guys for him. How do you suppose she's going to look after an actual living, breathing human?" He looked to me and said, "You should do yourself a favor and get an abortion. Fix this mess while you still can."

"Fuck you!" With tears streaming down my cheeks, I shoved my brother out of my way, and ran for the stairs.

"You know I'm right," Kev called after me. "You won't last a day of motherhood until you're pawning the kid off on *our* mother to do it for you."

*

A soft knock on my bedroom door drew my attention away from the pillow I was attempting to drown out the sound of my banshee pitched wailing with.

"Aoife, love, it's Mam. Can I come in and talk to you?"

Why the hell not?

I was a pregnant teenager in secondary school. My twin brother, upon hearing the news, had labeled me a mindless slut, before berating me for my chosen mate, and threatening to out me to our father. All this while said chosen mate was passed out cold somewhere, blissfully sleeping off any memory he had of the lifechanging news I'd given him.

In all honesty, nothing my mother wanted to talk about could make this situation any worse.

"Door's unlocked," I croaked out, pulling myself into a sitting position on my bed, with my pillow tucked against my stomach.

My bedroom door opened inwards and my mother appeared, eyes laced with concern. "Are you okay?"

I shrugged. "Not really."

"Well, I've spoken to your brother, and he gave me his word that he'll keep quiet until you're ready to tell people."

"You believe him?"

"You don't?"

"I don't know." I exhaled a weary sigh. "He was pretty savage down there."

"Your brother was a being a little shit." Walking over to my bed, Mam sat down on the edge and reached for my hand. "Don't you mind a word of what he said, Aoife. Not one word of it should be taken to heart."

"I didn't know he hated me so much, Mam," I confessed, feeling teary again, as my brain rehashed every horrible word my brother had uttered. "I get that he's upset about the baby, but what he said to me? There was serious hatred in his voice."

"That wasn't hatred you heard, Aoife, that was jealousy," Mam corrected with a sad sigh. "And trust me, that has much more to do with your father than it has to do with you."

My brows furrowed in confusion. "Dad?"

"Your father and brother don't have a connection. They never have. There's love between them, sure, but there's no common ground."

"How does that have anything to do with me having a baby?"

"Because, in your brother's mind, the boy you're having a baby with is the same boy that bears the biggest threat to his relationship with your father."

"*Joey?*"

"Joey." She offered me a sad smile before continuing, "Can you imagine what it must have felt like these past six years for Kev? Watching your father develop and nurture a bond with a boy from his class, while barely acknowledging his own son's achievements?"

"Okay, but how is that Joey's fault?"

"It's not Joey's fault," Mam replied gently. "And it's not your fault, either. It's Dad's fault for not making a better effort with your brother over the years."

"Mam, I know that Kev's your pet, but you can't blame his outburst on *daddy issues*," I argued. *I've seen daddy issues in the flesh and that's not what's happening with my brother.* "Trust me, we have a good father."

"You're right, he *is* a good father," Mam agreed. "But you have to acknowledge the lack of harmony in their relationship."

"So, Dad likes cars and Kev likes computers. Dad's an easy-going man's man, and Kev's an introverted millennial," I forced myself to concede. "They're not compatible. Big deal. Neither are we, but you don't see me acting like that, because I know that you still love me, just like Dad still loves Kev."

Her eyes widened in surprise. "You don't think we're compatible?"

"Honestly?"

She nodded.

"No, Mam, I don't." I picked a piece of fluff on my pajama bottoms and shrugged. "Kev's always been your golden child, while I've always been too much of, well, *me* for you to handle."

"That's not true."

"Yeah, it is." I smiled ruefully. "To be honest, I think we've spoken more in the last week than we have in the last three years, and that's probably only because we finally have something in common now."

Pain encompassed my mother's face and I felt like crap for putting it there.

"That's not to say that I don't feel loved," I hurried to add, reaching for her hand and giving it a reassuring squeeze. "Just that I know what it's like to feel out of sync with a parent, but still feel supported and cared for. I mean, I don't resent you or anything like that. I don't harbor any ill will or have any mommy issues."

"I'm so sorry," Mam whispered, looking truly horrified. "I never realized that you felt this way."

"Mam." I rolled my eyes. "Get a handle on yourself, will ya? It's not that deep."

"I don't favor your brother," she blurted out. "I don't. I swear. I love you both the same."

"I know that," I told her, and I did. "And I also know that it's okay that you get along better with Kev. That's got nothing to do with love, Mam. That's just a matter of Kev's personality suiting yours better than mine, and that's cool with me. I'm good with it, Mam. Honestly."

"You really mean that, don't you?"

I nodded honestly. "I really do."

She stared at me for a long time before blowing out a breath. "You're going to make a wonderful little mammy, do you know that, my girl?"

"Yeah," I mumbled. "*Sure* I am."

"You are," Mam pushed. "I can see it now – I can see everything so much clearer now."

"See what?"

"You," Mam replied. "The woman you're becoming. That backbone of steel behind you. The reason why he's so drawn to you."

"Who?"

"Joey."

My face heated. "Oh?"

"Obviously, you're a beautiful looking girl."

I snorted and waved a hand in front of myself. "Obviously."

"And modest," Mam jibed before continuing, "But you're so much more than a pretty face. You are *warm*, Aoife. That poor boy never stood a chance with you, did he? Not when everything he's never been given flows from you like a waterfall."

"No, I'm drama, remember?" I joked, feeling embarrassed.

"You're that, too," she agreed with a smirk. "But my god does warmth shine out from beneath that mischievous exterior of yours. It's infectious."

"Ah, that would be the pregnancy glow shining, Mam."

"Would you stop deflecting and take the compliment."

"Yeah, well, I can't help it." I grimaced in protest. "It's weird."

"You don't have any problem taking a compliment when it comes to your face."

"Yeah, well, I can look in a mirror whenever I want validation for the physical," I shot back, unapologetically. "I can't exactly cut myself open and see all this fuzzy, infectious warmth now, can I?"

"Well, trust me, it's there," she replied, smiling. "And don't you dare ever lose it."

How did I get here?

JOEY

With the mother of all headaches, I slowly blinked awake. I felt fucking horrified as I slowly registered the fact that I was face-down in a stranger's floral-patterned bedsheets, with no recollection of how I'd gotten there.

Panic stricken, I quickly sprung up on my elbows and looked down, relieved to find myself fully clothed in my school uniform. I even had my shoes on.

Cracking my head off a familiar bunkbed bar above me, I slowly realized that I was in my own bed, but the sheets had been changed – by Shannon, no doubt.

"So, you live to tell another tale," Podge said flatly, as he sat on the edge of the mattress, with an empty water bottle in hand. "What the fuck, Joey? I thought you got a handle on this?"

"Why are you here?" I muttered, gingerly pulling myself into a sitting position, as the room felt like it was floating around me. Pushing my damp hair out of my eyes, I asked, "Why am I here?"

"I brought you here," he replied. "You passed out in the toilets at school this afternoon, asshole. Aoife found you and came and got me. You're damn lucky that Nyhan didn't catch you, or you'd be out on your ass."

"This afternoon?" Confusion echoed through my mind, and my heart gunned in my chest. "What time is it?" I shook my head. "Where's Aoife?"

"It's after two."

"In the afternoon?"

"No, lad, in the middle of the night." Podge sighed heavily. "You've been out for ten hours, Joey. So again, and I can't stress this enough; what the *fuck*?"

Jesus Christ.

"I don't know." Climbing unsteadily to my feet, I pushed my damp hair back from my face once more. "Why's my hair wet?"

"I had to wake you somehow," he defended, throwing the empty water bottle at my head. I didn't bother to duck, choosing to let the plastic smack me upside the head. "You've been out for so long; I was starting to think that you might be dead."

"Yeah, well, I'm clearly not dead."

"This time," he shot back, running a hand through his hair. "Jesus Christ, how long has it been going on again?"

"It was just a one-off."

"Bullshit."

"Leave it out, Podge," I muttered. "I fucked up. I get it. I don't need a goddamn lecture."

"Going by the look on Aoife's face, and the sheer volume of tears she spilled, you did more than just fuck up this time."

I tensed, on edge. "What does that mean?"

"Like you give a shit about anything other than what goes up your goddamn nose."

"What does that *mean*, Podge?"

"It means you completely fucked it with your girlfriend," he whisper-hissed, rising to his feet. "I don't know what you did to her, or what the fuck you said, but I have never seen devastation like that."

"What do you mean?" Panicked, I grabbed my phone, only to find zero notifications from Molloy. I quickly dialed her number but was sent straight to voicemail. "Jesus Christ, what did I do?"

He folded his arms across his chest and gave me a hard look. "You tell me."

"I wouldn't be asking you if I fucking *knew*," I snarled, losing my cool now, as I paced the room. "You said she was crying?" I looked to him, panicked. "Did I *hurt* her?"

He stared at me for a long time before shaking his head in resignation. "No, Joe, you didn't hurt her like that. You never laid a finger on her, lad, and you never would, so relax."

Heaving out a shuddering breath, I sagged against my bedroom wall and took a minute to regather my composure. "Fuck."

"You care about her," Podge stated, watching me carefully. "More than anything or anyone you have ever allowed yourself to care about. I've seen it – the shift in you, and so has Alec. The change. The *hopefulness* she brings out in you. Hell, the whole fucking world can see how good that girl is for you, man. But you're so determined to self-destruct that you're not looking at what you're doing to her." He shook his head before adding, "If you don't care about yourself, and it's pretty clear that you don't, then you need to think about what your actions are doing to *her*. Because guess what, fucker? Aoife Molloy loves you. Do you hear me, you lucky son of a bitch? Hands down the best-looking girl in our school – possibly in the whole town – with the best, top-quality banter loves *you*."

"Sound more surprised, why don't ya?"

"I'm not surprised," he shot back, without hesitation. "I've seen plenty of the dolls you've pulled over the years. I'm not insecure enough to deny that you're a good-looking son of a bitch." He shrugged. "You're both beautiful. It makes sense for her to be with you."

"You know, I'm not sure I like where this conversation is heading," I warned. "Because if this is the part where you tell me that you're attracted to my girlfriend, I'm going to be really fucking pissed, and if you tell me that you're attracted to me, then I'm going to be really fucking traumatized."

"Of *course*, I'm attracted to your girl," Podge shot back. "As is every other lad in our school."

"Yeah." I nodded to myself. "I'm pissed."

"Good looks aside, you're a fucking trainwreck to deal with," he argued. "And I should know. I've spent the last fourteen years watching you derail, but I've stuck around for the same reason she has. Because she sees the same thing I do; a good fucking person underneath all of the bullshit. But you're blurring those lines, Joe. You crossed a line today and you need to make it right," he said, holding a finger up. "I love you like a brother, I always have, but one of these days you're going to slip so far off the tracks that none of us will be able to reach you."

His words cut me deep, and I found myself reacting on instinct. "I don't need anyone to reach me." Rattled, I hissed, "I don't need you, or her, or anyone else to help me with shit."

He narrowed his eyes. "Keep on behaving like this and no one will want to."

I narrowed my eyes right back. "Suits me just fine."

"Go on, Joe; keep pushing the people that actually love you away," he argued, tone heated and eyes laced with disappointment. "Keep driving us out of your life and you're going to end up with only Shane Holland and his leeches sucking the life out of you."

"Are you done lecturing me?" Stalking over to my bedroom door, I swung it open and glared at him. "Because you can leave now."

"Lad, you're still off your rocker if you think my country ass is walking through your thug-infested terrace at two o'clock in the morning." Flopping down on my bed, Podge readjusted my pillow behind his head and made himself comfortable. "Nah, you're stuck with me for the night, so you might as well get yourself reacquainted with the doghouse on the floor," he offered, yawning. "Because I have a feeling that's where you'll be spending most of your time for the foreseeable."

"I should go see her—"

"No, you should lie your ass down before you get yourself in any more trouble," my friend commanded, throwing a pillow at me. "Leave the poor girl to get a night's sleep. You can go over there first thing in the morning."

Relenting, I dropped down on the floor and covered my face with my arm. "Fuck."

"Do you want to know something?"

"If it's anything to do with how much of a shitty person I am, then no, lad," I muttered. "I'm already fully aware."

"Charlie Monaghan tried it on with Aoife at school today."

"The fuck?" I lifted my arm off my face to gape up at him. "And you know this how?"

"Heard it from Rambo who heard it from Becca."

"What did he say?"

"What am I, a mind reader? I told you that I heard it from Rambo who heard it from Rebecca. I'm not tele-fucking-pathic, lad."

"That little shit-bag."

"Stuck it to her, apparently," Podge chuckled. "So, it sounds to me like you need to get your head out of your hole and up your game if you want to hold onto that girl."

"Sounds to me like I need to break Charlie Monaghan's fucking nose."

"Yeah," my best friend chuckled. "That, too."

Lay it on me

AOIFE

With my school shirt hanging open, and only my bra and knickers covering my dignity, I stood in front of the full-length mirror in my bedroom on Wednesday morning, and studied every inch of my skin, paying extra close attention to the parts of my body where there were obvious changes.

My breasts were enormous, and that was saying something because I had never been lacking in that department.

Seriously, they were so full and heavy, that it felt like I was carrying around bowling balls in my bra.

My nipples had decided to turn about ten shades darker in color, and I had very noticeable, very blue, *veins* appearing on both breasts.

Gross.

And that slight swell in my lower abdomen, the one I had managed to play off as bloating up until now, wasn't so slight anymore. The area of my stomach beneath my belly button had distended into a small but firm pooch.

The sight of it alone caused my pulse to skyrocket.

I called it a pooch because I refused to use the B-word that rhymed with pump.

Yeah, I was nowhere near ready for the B-word.

I wasn't going to be able to hide my situation for too much longer. The changes to my body had already been drastic, and I predicted that I had another month left tops before the whole world knew.

We were getting our Easter holidays from school on Friday. We would have two weeks off and a huge part of me was worried that I would somehow blow up in that space of time and end up returning to school looking like a beached whale.

It was a terrifying concept.

Turning from side to side, I studied my appearance, gently poking and prodding at the foreign entity that had hitched a ride inside of my womb.

Ugh.

Womb was definitely another word I hated, right along with placenta, milk ducts, labor, membrane sweeps, and, worst of all, *crowning*.

Struggling with the concept of a baby growing inside of my body, let alone burrowing its big, bald head and Joey-Lynch-sized shoulders out of my vagina, I shuddered violently, doing a little heebie-jeebies dance on the spot, while I battled down a surge of nausea.

Empty your mind.

Deep breaths.

Blank it out.

You're still beautiful.

Nothing has stretched your vagina.

Your body is still free from stretch marks.

It's all good.

Wrestling my anxiety into a manageable portion, I set to work on applying a full face of make-up and running the curling tongs through my hair, deciding on loose beach-wave curls for school today.

I was rummaging around in my crappy back-up make-up bag, the one that housed all of the reject items from unwanted beauty sets from birthdays and Christmas, looking for a bronzing palette, and mentally cursing myself for not buying two of every product that I used, when a pair of familiar tattooed forearms came around my waist, dragging me back against an even more familiar chest.

"On a scale of one to ten, how pissed are you with me?"

"Holy shit, Joe," I choked out, coming close to calling bullshit on the whole not being able to jump out of one's skin, because I had come pretty damn close. "You couldn't use the front door?"

"Why break the habit of a lifetime?" His lips brushed against my ear as he spoke, eyes locked on mine in the mirror in front of us. "And

I would say nice legs, but that would be doing the rest of you a serious disservice."

Smooth as sin, he let his hands wander from my waist to my hips, fingers dipping under the lace fabric of my knickers for the briefest of moments before letting the elastic waistband snap back into place, and returning his hands to my hips. "Nice everything, Molloy."

The move caused every muscle south of my navel to coil tight in lustful anticipation. "Thanks."

"So? On a scale of one to ten?"

My eyelids fluttered shut of their own accord; an inevitable reaction to this boy's touch, and I let out a shaky breath. "Eleven."

"Yeah." His lips brushed my neck and he inhaled deeply before releasing a heavy sigh. "I figured."

Like a lamb to the slaughter, I leaned heavily against him, as my body reveled in the feel of his hands on my skin. "That's all you have to say for yourself?"

"I'm an asshole," he offered, pressing a kiss to my cheek. "I'm undeserving." He switched sides and kissed my other cheek. "I'm sorry." Another kiss to the curve of my jaw. "I love you."

"You don't remember any of it, do you?" I asked, turning around just in time to receive the soft kiss he pressed to the corner of my mouth. "What we talked about yesterday?"

"I remember that I fucked up."

I rolled my eyes. "You always fuck up."

"Hey." Taking my face between his hands, he leaned in close, clear green eyes locked on mine. "I mean it." Nuzzling my nose with his, he pressed a kiss to the tip and sighed. "I'm sorry for yesterday."

"Which part?"

"The part where your asshole boyfriend made you cry."

"Yeah?" Hating how much I loved his attention and feeling lightheaded from how desperately my body craved his touch, I leaned into his hands, feeling helplessly hooked. "Well, if you see the prick around, make sure you tell him that I don't forgive him."

"You shouldn't." He stroked my nose with his again. "I hear he's a fuck-up."

"*Such* a fuck-up," I agreed, reciprocating his kiss when his lips lightly brushed against mine. "If it wasn't for that big damn dick of his, I'd drop his ass."

"Is that so?"

"Uh-huh." I nodded. "It's all about the dick for me."

"Then it's lucky for him that he knows how to use his dick, huh?" he teased, lips hovering close to mine, as he dragged my body flush against his. "And his fingers." My breath hitched when his hand slipped beneath the waistband of my knickers. "And his tongue."

And just like that, I melted like a goddamn fool against him, lips moving against his in a kiss that sent my already frazzled hormones into overdrive.

Fully aware that he was as dangerous to my mind as the drugs were to his, I broke the kiss before I fell any deeper into my feelings.

Into him.

Pulling back before I lost myself entirely in him, I placed my hands on his chest to steady myself and said, "You're not getting away with it that easily."

"Never thought I was."

"Why are you even here? I thought we were meeting at school, like usual?"

"Because I needed to apologize," he explained, once again using his thumb to wipe my second-hand lip-gloss from his mouth, before strolling over to my window and climbing back out through it.

A few seconds ticked by before his school bag came flying through my window, followed by his hurley, helmet, and the overnight bag I'd left at his house.

"Did you bring my necklace?" I asked, watching as he deftly climbed back through my window. "I feel like I've been walking around naked without it."

"Got it," he replied, retrieving the silver chain from his pocket, as he closed the space between us. "Turn around."

Obliging, I lifted my hair away from my neck, while he fastened the clasp. "Thanks, stud."

"Anytime, queen."

"You're still in trouble."

"Aren't I always?" he muttered, pressing a soft kiss to the curve of my neck before walking over to my bed and sinking down. "Okay. I'm all ears."

"Huh?"

"You wanted to talk." He leaned back on his elbows, looking way too familiar with my bed – and way too fucking sexy. "Let's talk."

"True," I replied, anxiety fluttering to life inside of me, as I quickly closed the buttons of my shirt. "But you were supposed to come over last night to talk." I paused to frown. "Which is clearly something else you forgot about."

"Well, I'm here now, so we might as well get it over it."

"Get it . . . over with?" I heard myself pant out breathlessly, unable to hide the near-hysteria threatening to overtake me.

"Talk, Molloy," he said. "Let's go."

I wasn't ready.

Unlike yesterday, when he was out of his mind on God knows what, my boyfriend was sitting on my bed, clear-headed, and looking at me expectantly.

Oh shit.

"It can wait," I tried to buy myself more time by saying. "Until lunch, or after school, maybe?" I rambled nervously, hands flapping aimlessly. "After work is fine, too. Or tomorrow. Hell, tomorrow's good for me, too. It doesn't have to be right this second."

"Listen, I already know how this conversation is going to go," Joey interrupted me by saying. "You've got shit to say to me, shit I deserve to hear, so just lay it on me."

"Lay it on you?" Confusion swept through me. "Joe, I don't think we're on the same page here."

"Yesterday," he blurted out, expelling a heavy sigh and rubbing his jaw. "The way I was? What you saw? I know that I let you down, okay? I fucked up and I get that, but you don't need to worry. It's not like it was before, Molloy. I am *not* the same person that I was before Christmas, and I have no intention to going back to that place. I've got a handle on it this time, okay?"

Drugs.

He was talking about drugs.

And while his behavior yesterday certainly needed to be addressed, it wasn't on the top of today's fucked-up agenda.

Because, as ridiculous as it sounded, we had an even bigger problem.

"When you say that you've got a handle on it," I said warily. "What you actually mean to say is that you had a momentary slip in sanity for a few weeks, but you've come to your senses, and will never do it again, right?"

Say it.

Please just say it.

Tell me that you're trying again.

All I need you to do is keep trying.

"I'm good, Molloy," he insisted, tone light. "It's all good. You don't have anything to worry about. I'm in control here."

I'm in control here.

Devastation flooded me.

My heart cracked in my chest. "That's not what I asked you, Joey."

"Everything's fine."

Pain.

It threatened to swallow me whole.

"Say it," I demanded hoarsely. "Tell me that you're trying again."

He didn't respond.

"Tell me that you're stopping, Joe. Better yet; tell me that you've already stopped."

"I just told you that I'm good," he replied, tone sharp, as he stood up, walked to the other side of my room, and made a half-assed attempt at inspecting one of the doors he'd hung on my wardrobe. "Stop worrying, okay? It's all good."

"Good?" I hissed, reaching for my school skirt and pulling it on. "I've been here before with you, remember? I've walked this path with you a thousand times, and if you're using again, then you're *not* good, and if yesterday's anything to go by, then you sure as hell aren't in control."

"You're wrong," he bit out, still inspecting the door. "You're overreacting here."

"And you're delusional," I hissed, pulling my school jumper over my head. "And a goddamn liar."

"Molloy."

"No." I shook my head. "Don't *Molloy* me, asshole. You can't sweet talk yourself out of this one. I am *not* okay with this, I have *never* been okay with this, and I *never* will be."

Shrugging, he closed my wardrobe door and turned to face me. "Then I don't know what to tell you."

"How about you start by explaining to me what possessed you to go back down this road?" I threw out there, bitterly hurt by his actions. "And don't even think about blaming it on what your father tried to do to me, because I found your stash the day before that even happened, Joey."

He tensed. "What are you talking about?"

"I found a bag of prescription tablets in the pocket of your sweatpants."

He narrowed his eyes. "Why were you searching my clothes, Aoife?"

I narrowed mine right back at him. "I wasn't searching your clothes. I was looking for something to wear. But more importantly, why were they there in the first place, *Joseph*?"

"Those pills weren't mine."

"No? Then why were they in *your* pocket?"

"I'm telling you, Molloy, I didn't buy those."

"I don't believe you."

"Fine." He shook his head and exhaled a frustrated growl. "Believe what you want."

"It wouldn't be the first time you've lied to me."

"Well, I'm not fucking lying about this," he spat, and then threw his hands up in frustration. "I messed up, okay? I get it. I fucked up. I thought you were done, and I threw in the towel. I gave the fuck up, because, in case you haven't noticed, Molloy, aside from you, I don't have a whole fucking lot else going for me. In my mind, you were done and I couldn't see a reason to keep this bullshit façade up."

"What bullshit façade?" I demanded.

"The one where I pretend to be someone I'm not," he snapped. "Everything I did, all of the changes that I made, I made for *you*. And then you were gone, so I just ... " He threw his hands up in defeat. "Stopped fighting my nature."

"Your nature?" I gave him a hard look. "That's not your nature."

He shrugged, but didn't respond.

"So, because we're going through a rough patch, you took it as a green light to throw the last three months away?"

"My father tried to fuck you, Molloy," he growled, tone hoarse. "And in your eyes, I look just like him, remember? I'd say that's more than just a rough patch."

And there it was.

The reasoning behind every bad decision my boyfriend had ever made came back to his father.

"I was hurt." I tried to reason with the part of him that was hellbent on self-annihilation. "I was *afraid*. I was in shock. I was fucking reeling, Joey. I didn't mean a word of what I said to you that night, and you know it, so stop trying to make me feel bad for it."

He flinched like I had struck him. "If you know me at all, and you're probably the only one that does, then you'd know that I would *never* do that to you," he bit out, looking hurt. "I deserved your pain that night. I fucking deserved everything you said to me and more."

"I know you wouldn't," I sighed, pressing a hand to my brow, as my emotions continued to flatten me. "I know, Joe."

"I'm not trying to make you feel bad about anything," he continued to say. "But you asked me for an explanation and I'm trying to give it to you."

"Well, I'm clearly not done with you," I said, urging him to *hear* me. "Your father did a terrible thing, that's true, but it isn't on you. Nothing has changed for us, okay?"

"I didn't know that." His words were barely audible as he swallowed deeply. "I didn't know."

"Well, now you do," I urged. "So, you need to knock this on the head again. Do you hear me? I need you to dust yourself off and keep *trying*."

"I already told you that I have it under control this time."

"See, that's not good enough for me, Joe," I heard myself reply. "I don't want your assurances. I want your sobriety."

"And you'll have it."

"I want it right now."

"I don't know if I can give you that."

Panic seared me. "Why not?"

"Because I don't want to lie to you," he bit out. "I promise it won't be like before."

"No." I shook my head, feeling my heart crack. "No, Joe."

"Molloy." Shoulders sagging in defeat, Joey released a resigned sigh. "I am what I am."

There it was again.

That horrible fucking sentence.

I am what I am.

I hated those five words when they came from his mouth.

"Yes, and who you are is a hell a lot better than the person standing in front of me, reeling off excuses for doing something that he knows almost destroyed him before," I snapped, hands planted on my hips, as I glared up at him. "You are a better man than this, Joey Lynch."

"Maybe I thought I was."

"You *still* are," I strangled, wrestling with my panic and pain. "You are *better* than the lifestyle you're determined to fall back into, and you sure as hell are a better man than Shane Holland, and you know it."

"This has nothing to do with Holland."

"This has *everything* to do with him."

"It's not your fucking problem!" Voice breaking off, I watched as Joey inhaled a deep breath, clearly trying to rein in his temper, and ran his hand through his hair, before trying again, this time in a relatively calmer voice. "Listen, I don't want to fight with you." Closing the space between us, Joey placed his hands on my shoulders, and stared down at me. "I don't want to hurt you, Molloy."

"Well, you did," I countered thickly. "You *are* hurting me, Joe."

Pain encompassed his features. "I'm sorry."

"But?" I managed to squeeze out.

"I'm just ... " Shaking his head, he rubbed his jaw and blew out a harsh breath. "I'm having a hard fucking time inside my head right now, and I need you to just let me deal with it my own way."

"By taking drugs?" I deadpanned. "By destroying yourself?"

"No." He shook his head. "That's not what I'm doing."

"Yes, Joey, it *is*." Tears filled my eyes. "And you're asking me to turn a blind eye to it *again*." My voice broke and I dragged in a quivering breath. "I did that before and it almost *killed* you and *broke* me. Now, you're asking me to do that again, and I *can't*. I can't watch you lose yourself again. *I* can't lose you again, Joe."

"No, Molloy, that's not what I'm saying at all. You're not losing me, okay? I fucking love you. I'm yours to keep for as long as you'll have me." He stroked my shoulders with his thumbs, breaking my heart with the gentleness of his touch, which was a stark contrast to the slicing sting of his words. "I just ... I need you to *not* hate me for getting through my shit in the only way I know how."

"You know other ways," I reminded him, tone laced with bitterness. "Better ways." *Ways that don't risk your life and break my heart.*

"Fine." Joey expelled a pained breath, unwilling to look me in the eyes. "In the only way that works for me."

"So, you're not even going to try?" I choked out, feeling shredded by the sudden change in him. In his unwillingness to at least *try*. "You're not even going to lie to me and *pretend* to try?"

"I *am* trying," he argued, voice strained. "I *will* try. I will sort this, okay? I will, Molloy. I just . . . I need some time."

"Some time to get *high* with your druggie buddies first?"

"No." His tone was hard when he said, "I'm not going back there, I swear."

"*Back* there?" Sniffling, I reached up and batted a tear from my cheek. "If you're using again, then you're already there, Joe."

"Molloy."

"Do you love me?"

"You know I love you."

"Then *stop*," I pleaded, reaching up to cup his neck. "Stop, Joe. Please."

"I will."

"No." I shook my head and stepped away from him. "Don't say you will. Say you are."

"Molloy . . ."

"You're putting me in an impossible position," I choked out. "You're forcing my hand."

"That's not what I'm trying to do."

"Well, whether that's what you're trying to do or not, that's what's happening," I argued, hating how pitiful I sounded. "Yesterday, you accused me of manipulating you by using your feelings for me against you, and now, you're doing the exact same thing to me."

His brows furrowed. "No, I'm not."

"Yes, you *are*," I strangled out. "Because what am I going to do, Joe? Leave?" I threw my hands up in utter resignation. "I don't have a bargaining chip here. I'm just the fool who's supposed to sit back and watch you wreck yourself again, and that's *exactly* what's going to end up happening, because we both know that I love you too fucking much to ever contemplate walking away."

"I promise, this time it'll be different," Joey tried to coax, ignoring every truthful word I had spoken in his bid to convince me of the same lies he had used to wallpaper over his common sense. "I only need a few more weeks. That's it, Aoif. Just a couple of weeks to get me through, and I'll be done."

"Whatever, Joe. I'm done talking about this." Weary to the bone, I stepped around him and grabbed my school bag off the floor, unable and unwilling to go another round with him, not when my heart had just taken such a beating. "Let's just go to school."

The birds, the bees, and the Dub

JOEY

"What are you doing in my room?" Shannon asked when she walked into her bedroom at lunchtime on Wednesday afternoon, breaking the rare silence I was soaking in, with everyone else out of the house.

"Sean pissed on my bed," I explained, exhaling a cloud of smoke, as I stared up at her bedroom ceiling, coming down from my high. "My sheets are in the wash."

"Oh." Dropping her school bag on her bedroom floor, she kicked off her shoes and walked over to her bed. "Push over."

Obliging, I shifted closer to the wall and rested an arm behind my head as she flopped down on her small single bed beside me. "It's lunchtime, Shan. What are ya doing home from school?"

"Like you can talk." Digging me in the side with her skinny elbow, she mimicked, "It's lunchtime, Joey. What are you doing home?"

"I'm in the doghouse."

"With Aoife?"

"Yep."

"Is that weed?"

"Nope."

"Are you lying?"

Inhaling another deep drag of my smoke, I held it there for a long moment before exhaling slowly. "Yep."

"Stoner."

"Slacker."

"So, what did you do?" she asked, batting a cloud of smoke away. "To get sent to the doghouse?" She sucked in a sharp breath before I could answer and hissed, "Please tell me you didn't cheat on her? Because that girl is amazing and you need to marry her."

"The fuck?" I narrowed my eyes and exhaled a cloud of smoke. "No, Jesus, I didn't cheat on her. I don't cheat, Shan."

"Sorry." She shrugged sheepishly. "It's just ... well, when I was at BCS, I used to hear a lot of the girls in the bathroom talking about you and you're, uh, well, your bedroom skills."

"My bedroom skills," I snorted. "Jesus Christ. Girls are fucked up."

"Girls *are* fucked up," my little sister wholeheartedly agreed. "I don't understand them at all."

"You know, they say fellas talk, but it's the other way around," I complained. "Girls talk." I twisted my head to find her staring wide-eyed back at me. "Girls do a lot of fucking talking, Shan."

"Yeah, I know," she sighed.

"You know, most of what they say is pure bullshit," I decided to add, feeling salty. "I've only been in one girl's bedroom."

Her eyes widened. "So, you've only been with one girl?"

"I've only been in one girl's bedroom," I doubled down and repeated.

"*Joey.*" My sister narrowed her eyes. "That's not the same thing."

"Like you can talk," I shot back, giving her back her earlier words. "How'd you get on in Mister Rugby's bedroom the other week? I'm guessing this little day trip home from school has something to do with him?"

"Wh-what?"

"Don't pull that shy card on me," I chuckled. "I can read ya like a book."

She nestled under my arm and sighed heavily. "I didn't come home early because of Johnny."

I stiffened. "Then who?"

"Bella Wilkinson."

"What did she do?"

"It doesn't matter," Shannon replied, shaking her head. "Forget it."

Frowning, I turned to look at her. "Did she hurt you?"

"No."

"Call you names or something?"

She stiffened.

"So, she called you names?"

She nodded.

"What did she call you?"

"The usual," she admitted quietly. "And then she made fun of me for coming from Elk's Terrace."

"Fucking bitch," I growled, taking another deep drag before sitting up, feeling my temper rise. "You get why these girls target you, don't ya?"

"Because they hate me."

"Because they're threatened by you," I corrected. "Because goodness shines out of you, and they're throwing shit to take that shine away. Don't let them win, Shan."

"How's BCS going for you?" she asked, clearly trying to take the limelight off herself by steering the conversation towards me.

"School is school, Shan," I replied, staring out the window. "Same shit, different day."

"You know the real reason I'm home in the middle of the day," she replied. "What's your real reason, Joe?"

"Already told ya." I shrugged and took another drag of my smoke. "I'm in the doghouse."

"Why do I feel like that's not true?"

I shrugged. "I just couldn't be bothered sticking around."

"Why don't you talk to me, Joe?" she asked then, tone laced with sadness. "I'm always confiding in you, but you never do the same."

Because I can't. Because you'd crumble. Because I need to protect you. "You know me, kid," I replied, climbing off her bed, and moving for the window. I turned back and offered her a smile. "I'm bulletproof."

She stared back at me, uncertain, for a long moment before whispering, "If I tell you something, do you promise not to get mad?"

Pushing her window open, I took another drag of my smoke before flicking the butt away. "Depends."

"Promise me, Joe."

"Okay, I promise."

Chewing on her bottom lip, my baby sister squirmed in discomfort before throwing her hands up and blurting out, "I kissed Johnny Kavanagh."

Well, shit.

I wasn't expecting that.

My brows shot up in surprise. "You kissed . . . "

"Johnny Kavanagh," she filled in with a nod, cheeks reddening.

"Okay," I replied slowly, as I tried to navigate this new fucking territory that my baby sister had unceremoniously thrown me into. This wasn't a conversation she needed to be having with her older brother. This was an older sister conversation. Or a mother and daughter conversation. Instead, she was stuck with me. *Fuck. My. Life.* I could feel my buzz deserting me at a rapid rate. "Was that all you did with him?"

Please say yes.

Please Jesus, don't tell me anything else.

"Yes," she strangled out, nodding eagerly.

"When?"

"Monday night. At his house."

"At his house?" I arched a brow. "Where in his house, exactly?"

"His bedroom."

Now both my brows rose along with my blood pressure. "His bedroom?"

"But he didn't kiss me back," she blurted, wringing her hands together. "And I feel so embarrassed about the whole thing, Joe."

"Why didn't he kiss you back?"

"He said that it wouldn't be fair to start anything up with me when he's leaving soon." She chewed on her lip, looking very young and uncertain. "But then he came over after school yesterday."

"He came over." My eyes widened. "Here. To this house."

She nodded. "He helped me with my homework."

"Did anything happen?"

"We hugged."

I fought back the laugh that was threatening to escape me. "You hugged."

"Uh-huh."

Desperately trying to keep a straight face, I asked, "Was it a good hug?"

She sighed wistfully and clutched her chest. "It was the *best* hug I've ever had."

Now, I did laugh.

"Joey!"

"I'm sorry. I'm sorry." Clearing my throat, I scrubbed my face with my hand and tried again. "So, the Dub gives good hugs, yeah?"

"Yes." She gave another uncertain nod and shrugged helplessly. "But I wanted it to be more than just a hug because I just . . . I really like him, Joe. And then, today at lunch, he literally punched Bella's boyfriend in the face because she was saying those mean things about me. But that scares me because you know how I feel about violence, but I'm not scared of him like that, you know? He's a good person. I mean he's a really, *really* good person. Excellent, in fact. I can tell. And I like him, Joe. I *like* him so much it's hard to breathe when he's near me. But I just . . . and he won't . . . and I don't . . . oh god, *help* me!"

Jesus, I needed another smoke for this.

"You couldn't have taken a shine to a lad from around here?" Shaking my head, I sank back down on her bed and sighed. "You had to pick the Irish international?"

She squirmed in discomfort. "I'm sorry?"

"Don't be sorry, Shan," I chuckled, rubbing my jaw. "You can't help who you like. And for what it's worth, I reckon he likes you too, kid."

"What do I do, Joe?"

"You're asking *me*?"

"Who else can I ask?"

"Fuck." Pressing my fingers to my temples, I tried to think up the appropriate answer to give her in this moment. "Give me a second to think about this."

"What would you do if you were me?"

Yeah, I wasn't going to tell her what I'd do.

"Or Aoife? What would she do in this position?"

And I *definitely* wasn't going to tell her what Molloy would do.

"Just take your time. Be his friend and just let whatever happens come naturally," I finally settled on, knowing it was lame as fuck, but unwilling to give my baby sister tips on how to seduce a fella. "If it happens, it happens, and if it doesn't, then that's okay, too. And please, for the love of Christ, don't ask Aoife for advice," I added, shuddering at the thought of the pointers Molloy would be only too happy to give her. "You're only sixteen, Shan. This is all new to you. You need to navigate this thing with Kavanagh at your own pace and nobody else's."

"I can do that," she whispered, looking up at me like I was giving her some sacred advice. "Thanks, Joe."

"Anytime."

"Can I ask you something else?"

"What?"

"How old were you?" She grimaced before adding, "When you first . . . you know?"

I eyed her warily. "Do we need to have the talk?"

Her eyes widened. "The talk?"

"The talk," I confirmed grimly. "You've had the talk, right?"

"I, ah . . . "

"Mam's had the talk with you, hasn't she?" I pressed, palms sweating.

"No, did she have the talk with you?"

"Fuck no, I learned along the way," I strangled out.

"Oh." Her cheeks flamed. "Okay."

"Don't do that, though," I added after a beat. "Don't learn on the job."

"The job?"

"You know what I mean."

"Uh." Her face flamed. "I really don't."

Jesus Christ. "Well, you know how it all works, don't you?" I asked and then shifted in discomfort. "Sex and intimacy, and birth control and all that shit?"

"Uh, yeah?" Exhaling a shaky breath, she nodded uncertainly. "I know enough."

"You do?"

"I mean, I think I do?"

That meant she definitely didn't.

Aw fuck.

"Do you, ah . . . " I let my voice trail off, and scratched my jaw, buying myself a few extra seconds before forcing out the words. "Do you need to ask me anything about it?"

"Like what?"

"I don't fucking know, Shan," I choked out. "Advice? You have three minutes to ask whatever the fuck you want and then I'm out of here and this conversation will never again be repeated."

"Is it like the movies?" She squirmed in discomfort. "Sex? Does it hurt?"

"Yeah, the first time can hurt for a girl," I replied, resisting the urge to crawl into the corner of her room and rock. "But it shouldn't hurt after that, and if it does, he's doing it wrong."

"Do we really bleed?"

"Uh, yeah, girls can bleed the first time, but it doesn't happen to every girl."

"Why not?"

Fuck if I knew. "Because it's different for everyone."

"What about guys? Does it hurt for guys their first time?"

"No, it's more of matter of trying to keep the head."

"The *head*?"

"Calm," I corrected with a grimace. "It's a matter of keeping calm and in control."

"What happens if you can't stay calm?"

"Then it's over before it starts."

"Over?"

"Over," I confirmed grimly. "As in the show's over."

"Oh." Her cheeks reddened. "What if his, you know, is too big? What if it doesn't fit in, um, well, you know?"

"It fits." I dropped my head in my hands and groaned. "It's always fits."

"But how?"

"Magic."

"*Joey.*"

"It just fucking fits, Shan," I replied. "Once the girl is relaxed and not feeling anxious or pressured . . . " I paused to give her a hard look. "Nobody's pressuring you, right?"

"Oh god, no," she hurried to say. "I'm just . . . curious."

"Okay then. Good. That's good to hear." Repressing a shudder, I quickly continued. "Jesus, I can't believe these words are coming out of my mouth, but foreplay helps a lot."

"Foreplay?"

"Yeah, Shan."

"What kind of foreplay?"

"Well, not hugging that's for fucking sure."

"Oh." She blushed. "So, you mean like kissing and stuff?"

"And stuff," I replied, feeling like I was seconds away from throwing myself out of her bedroom window.

"Like touching?"

"Yeah, like touching and tasting and . . . ugh, you know what?" Slapping my hands on my knees, I stood up and paced the floor. "You should stick to the hugging. Hugging is perfect. Hugging is plenty close enough until you're twenty."

"How old were you, Joe? When you first . . . "

"Too young."

"How young?"

"Younger than you."

Her eyes widened and she choked out a surprised cough. "*Joe.*"

I grimaced. "Yeah, I know."

"So . . . how was your first time?"

"Terrible," I admitted quietly. "I wasn't ready."

My baby sister's eyes widened. "Then why'd you go through with it?"

"I . . . " I opened my mouth to respond, but words failed me. "I . . . " Shaking my head, I racked my brain for the words I needed to answer her but came up empty.

Concern filled her blue eyes. "Joe?"

"I don't know, Shan." Shoulders slumping, I sank down on the bed beside my sister and rested my elbows on my thighs. "I think I . . . "

"You think you what, Joe?"

"I think I was . . . " Blowing out a strained breath, I wrestled with my hazed memories, trying to make sense of a night that had never made sense to me. "I think I wasn't in my own body, if that makes sense?"

"In what way?"

"I was high as a kite that night, and I mean, I can sort of remember it happening," I admitted, cracking my knuckles together. "But I don't remember how or why it happened."

"I don't understand," she whispered, turning her body to face me. "Are you saying you . . . " Swallowing deeply, my baby sister reached for my hand and squeezed. "Did you not want it to happen, Joe?"

"I don't know, Shan," I forced myself to admit out loud for the first time. "I mean, I know that I liked the girl it happened with, and I know that I wasn't upset about it afterwards, but I just *don't* remember *how* it happened."

"Joe." Her hand tightened around mine. "That kind of sounds like you didn't consent."

"Maybe," I muttered, scratching my head. "But I must have enjoyed it because I went back there with her multiple times over the years. She was actually a *friend* type person of mine back in the day."

"It doesn't matter if you did it a thousand times with a thousand different girls," Shannon croaked out. "You both need to consent every time, Joe."

"Jesus," I muttered, shaking my head. "How did this conversation get so deep?"

"Does Aoife know?"

"Does Aoife know what?"

"About what happened to you on your first time . . . "

"No, because nothing happened to me, Shannon," I was quick to point out, quickly shutting down the conversation before it went to a place that my mind had no intention of visiting. "I got high, I got fucked, I got over it, and then, when I got high again, I got fucked some more. Rinse and repeat. That was my mantra. So yeah, I was way too young and way too fucking reckless with my body," I admitted, giving her a hard look. "Don't make my mistakes, Shan. Don't give yourself away to the first person who shows you an ounce of affection. Just take your time. I promise the right person is worth holding out for, okay?"

"Joe, I really feel like you weren't . . . "

"Don't, okay?" Annoyed, I stood up and moved for her door. "Don't make me a victim, Shan. It's not the narrative of my story."

"Do you wish Aoife was your first?" she thankfully changed the subject by asking.

"Every day," I admitted with a shrug. "It's fucking miserable knowing that I threw something around that means so much with the right person. It's even worse knowing that she knows it."

"So, she waited for you?"

"I'm not talking about Aoife, Shan," I replied. "A lad has limits, ya know. Ask what you want about my sex life, but not my girlfriend's, okay?"

"You really love her, don't you?"

"It's not just about love. It's about respect."

"And compatibility."

"And friendship."

"And loyalty."

"Exactly."

"Wow," Shannon breathed. "You're very sweet under that prickly exterior, aren't you?"

"I'm hungry under this prickly exterior," I muttered, desperate to get away from the topic of the birds and the bees. "Want to make your favorite brother something to eat before he has to go to work?"

"Okay." Sighing heavily, she climbed off her bed and walked right up to me, wrapping her skinny arms around my waist. "But only because you *are* my favorite brother."

You don't get to let me

AOIFE

JOEY: ARE YOU GOING TO SPEAK TO ME?

AOIFE: NOPE.

JOEY: COME ON, MOLLOY. DON'T BE CRANKY.

AOIFE: SHUT UP AND WATCH THE MOVIE.

JOEY: I'M NOT TALKING. I'M TEXTING.

AOIFE: YEAH, WELL, I CAN HEAR YOUR STUPID VOICE IN MY HEAD.

JOEY: WITCH.

AOIFE: ASSHOLE.

JOEY: I'M NOT STAYING OVER IF YOU'RE NOT GOING TO TALK TO ME.

AOIFE: HA! TRY AND LEAVE. I DARE YOU.

JOEY: FINE, BUT I'M NOT SNUGGLING YOU.

AOIFE: GOOD. I DON'T WANT YOU TO SNUGGLE ME. YOU STINK OF WEED.

JOEY: PITY IT'S NOT MELLOWING YOU OUT.

AOIFE: SHH. I'M TRYING TO WATCH THE FILM!!!

JOEY: FINE.

AOIFE: STOP PLAYING SNAKE ON YOUR PHONE.

JOEY: STOP BEING A BITCH.

AOIFE: I WILL, AS SOON AS YOU STOP BEING AN ASSHOLE!

"For fuck's sake." Tossing his phone down on the mattress between us, Joey folded his arms across his chest and glared at my bedroom ceiling. "This cold shoulder crap is bullshit."

No, it wasn't bullshit.

It was a direct consequence of *his* bullshit.

With only the screen of my portable television lighting the room, I watched from the corner of my eye as Joey huffed and puffed like a frustrated bull.

My boyfriend was being an asshole, and I had every intention of letting him know it.

Surprisingly, my silence was irking him a hell of a lot more than my words had.

"Molloy." Shirtless, he sat straight up on my bed and ran a hand through his hair. "Come on. I haven't done anything wrong today."

"The fact that you have to add the word *today* to the statement 'I haven't done anything wrong' speaks volumes, Joe."

"I said I'm sorry."

"I know you did."

"Then what do you want from me?"

"I want you healthy."

"I *am* healthy," he growled, flopping back down on the mattress. "Fuck."

I knew that he was teetering on the edge of trouble again, and I refused to let him topple over that cliff twice.

The fact that he couldn't remember a word of the conversation we had yesterday when I spilled my damn guts to him was horrible.

I couldn't explain how difficult it was for me to get those words out, and he just didn't *hear* me.

Knowing that I was carrying his unborn child, while he was dallying with his health was even more terrifying.

"I'm not doing this again, Joe," I told him. "I'm not letting *you* do this again."

"Letting me," he spat the words like they were offensive. "You don't get to *let me* do shit, Aoif. I do my own thing."

"Uh-huh, sure thing, asshole," I mocked, increasing the volume on the television remote. "I flushed your stash, by the way."

He narrowed his eyes at me. "I don't have a stash."

"You don't?" I narrowed my eyes right back at him. "Then whose prescription pills were those in the front pocket of your school bag?"

"You searched my bag?"

"Yep." I smiled sweetly. "Sure did."

"For fuck's sake," he muttered, rubbing his face with his hand. "Where's the baggie, Molloy?"

"The baggie is in my rubbish bin. The *contents* of the baggie are on the way out to sea."

"You didn't seriously flush my pills?"

"I seriously did, stud."

"Jesus Christ. Do you know how much those cost me?" Sitting straight up once again, my boyfriend dropped his head in his hands and bit back a roar. "Fuck, Aoif, I told you I have it under control."

"And I told you that I'm not letting you do this again."

"I'm *fine*."

"And I'm making sure that you *stay* fine."

"This is ridiculous," he grumbled, twisting around to face me. "You do realize that no other lad would take this shit from his girlfriend."

"What shit exactly?" Tossing the remote down, I sat straight up and faced him. "The part where I try to keep you *alive*?"

"I'm not dying."

"You could die—" My voice cracked, and I sucked in a sharp breath, desperately trying to school my features, as I met his stare head on. "I love you."

"I know." Emotion flickered in his eyes, and he bowed his head. "I love you back."

"No. You don't get it. You are the love of my life," I bit out, catching his chin and forcing him to look at me. "What I feel for you? How deeply I love you? It's fucking insane, Joe. So, yeah, I'm going to do the right thing for you every time, whether that pisses you off or not, because I want you *here* with me. On planet earth. For a long time."

"I'm not going anywhere," he whispered, snatching my hand up in his. "I'm never leaving you, Molloy."

"See, I know you *believe* that," I replied, tone thick with emotion. "But every time you snort a line or pop a pill, you're playing Russian roulette with your life and *my* heart."

Hurricane Molloy

JOEY

The anger emanating from the girl in the driver's seat assured me that not only had I been given permanent residency in her doghouse, but I'd earned the title of king of *fuck-ups*.

By the time we reached school on Thursday morning, the silent tension building up between us was unbearable.

Both unwilling to budge an inch, I let her sit in her anger, while she let me stew in my guilt.

After her fourth piss-poor attempt at reversing into a narrow parking space, and this time almost taking the bumper off a neighboring car, Molloy released a furious growl. She jacked the handbrake, put the gearstick in neutral, and climbed out, leaving the car in the middle of the line of traffic.

Wordlessly, I climbed out and rounded the driver's side, while Molloy folded her arms across her chest, tapped her foot expectantly, and gave me a stormy-eyed glare.

Reversing the car into her intended parking spot, I killed the engine, climbed back out, and rounded the boot.

Yanking it open, I grabbed both of our bags and tossed them over my shoulders, before reaching for my hurley and helmet.

Slamming the boot shut, I locked the car back up and tossed her the keys.

Catching them mid-air, she pocketed them, and then, with her nose cocked in the air, she walked over and yanked her bag off my shoulder.

Fine.

Suit yourself.

Arching a brow, I watched as Molloy slid her bag onto her shoulder and strutted off in the direction of the main entrance, keeping at least ten feet between us, and giving me a glorious view of her peachy ass, as her hips swayed with temper.

"Lynchy?" I heard Rambo call out, dragging my attention from my girlfriend's fantastic rear end.

I turned to see him waving me over to the side of the PE hall, with smoke drifting up from beneath the sleeve of his school jumper.

"You coming, lad?"

Offering him a clipped nod, I veered off path, feet moving in the direction of my buddy, when a hand wrapped around mine and pulled me to a stop.

I swung back to find Molloy standing there, with my hand in both of hers, as she glared up at me and shook her head.

Still refusing to speak to me, but unwilling to walk away, she stood there, glowering up at me, giving me an ultimatum with her eyes.

Do it, she mentally dared me, *see what happens.*

Beyond fucking irritated, I glared down at her, equally unwilling to be the first one to give in and speak.

Releasing my hand, she gave me one final hard look before backing up a few steps, and then, with that sexy fucking nose cocked in the air, she turned on her heels and walked off.

Fine.

Blowing out a frustrated growl, I turned on my heels and walked towards the PE hall, but only managed to make it about five steps before swinging back around.

Goddammit to hell!

I could hear Rambo and the lads cracking up with laughter, and making the mandatory whipped sound as I trailed after my girlfriend like a fucking puppy.

Jesus Christ.

When I caught up with her at the door, she didn't look behind her when she slid her bag off her shoulder and held it out.

Jaw ticking, I begrudgingly took her bag and slung it over my shoulder.

Clearing her throat, she folded her arms across her chest, and inclined her chin to the door.

Biting back a growl, I stepped around her and held the door open.

"Hm," she huffed prissily before sauntering inside.

Resisting the urge to swing the door shut on her ass, I ground my teeth together and followed after the girl who had a firm hold on my heart – and my nuts.

"What's ailing ya?" Alec asked, tossing a cigarette towards me when I joined him at the back of the PE hall for a smoke. "Sexy-legs still giving you the cold shoulder?"

"Let's just say that the women in my life have my head in a fucking spin, lad," I muttered, hopping up on the wall next to him. "Cheers, Al," I mumbled, cigarette balanced between my lips, as I took the lighter he held out for me and sparked up. "Sound as a pound, lad."

"Girls are a mindfuck, Lynchy."

"Oh, believe me. I'm only too aware."

"How's your sister getting on with the elites of Tommen?"

"Good," I told him, exhaling a cloud of smoke. "Really fucking good, Al."

"I'm glad," he replied, nudging his shoulder with mine. "She was always too pure for this place."

Nodding my agreement, I inhaled another deep drag before saying, "Got herself a fella."

"One of those preppy rugbyheads?"

"Yep."

"Well shit," he chuckled. "Do we need to give him a warning?"

"Nah, he seems like a decent enough lad."

"Must be if you're not stringing him up by the bollocks."

"Ah, it sounds fairly innocent," I mused, taking another drag of my smoke, and ignoring the bell signaling that small break was over. "Once he's good to her, he won't have any hassle from me."

"Well, if he isn't good to her, there'll be a queue waiting to take his place." He slapped a hand on my shoulder. "Because I hate to break it to ya, Lynchy, but that sister of yours is a ride."

"Jesus Christ," I groaned, unable to stop the shudder rolling through me. "Why do you have to ruin my life by saying shit like that?"

"What?" he laughed. "It's true. We all think it. None of us ever went there out of respect for you."

"She's my baby sister, you fucking pervert."

"She's no baby, lad," he said with a chuckle. "Shannon Lynch is sweet sixteen and looks like a wet dream."

"I *will* kill you."

"I'm only saying."

"Well, don't say it." I shuddered again. "Don't even think it. Jesus."

"She has epic blue eyes."

"I have an epic right hook."

"Then save it for the fella actually banging your sister, not the fella admiring her from a distance," he laughed.

"He's not *banging* her."

"Not yet."

"Stop it."

Weathering the storm that was Hurricane Molloy, I managed to keep off her radar and out of trouble for the first four classes. Until double Maths before big break, where not only did I have to face her wrath, but I had to do it in the seat next to hers.

With a face like thunder, Molloy strolled into class five minutes late, which was abnormal for her, while spinning some yarn to our teacher about needing to use the bathroom.

With all eyes on her, and her long legs on full view to every eager-eyed prick watching her, which, let's face it was most of the class, my girlfriend strutted down the aisle to our desk, with her tits pushed out and her hips swaying.

See that was the thing about Molloy – and one of the earliest things I'd learned about her – when she got pissed, she got sexy.

That wasn't to say that she wasn't ridiculously sexy every day. It was more that she was never more aware of her feminine supremacy than when she had a point to prove.

Like right now, for example, she was letting me know that I was topping her shit-list, and she had plenty of options if I didn't get with the program and up my game.

"Molloy," I decided to breach the silence by saying when she took her seat next to me. "Nice legs."

Her lips reluctantly tipped upwards, but she quickly steeled her features, keeping her scowl in check, as she set her books and pencil case on our desk.

"Can we just . . . " She shook her head, letting me know in no uncertain terms that she wasn't ready to wave a white flag of her own.

She had a lot of nerve.

If anyone had the right to be pissed off it was me, the misfortunate bastard whose stash she flushed down the damn toilet the night before.

Shrugging at her prissiness, I leaned back in my seat, pencil in hand, and stared out the window, watching as the March rain pelted against the pane of glass outside.

Deep in my thoughts, I let myself delve into the mess that was my life, all the while wondering how the fuck the girl sitting beside me was still, well, *beside me.*

Yeah, stash flushing aside, I knew I was punching.

And in the wrong.

I'd made a hash of everything.

Again.

I'd gone back on my word.

Again.

I'd let her down.

Again.

Nothing about our relationship was balancing in my favor anymore, and honestly, aside from my ability to put my dick to good use, I couldn't see the appeal of being with me.

I thought she was done with me that night.

I *expected* her to be done with me.

My father assaulted her, for Christ's sake.

No relationship, no matter how much love or loyalty there was, came back from a blow like the one ours had taken.

But here she was, mad as hell, and pulling on her boxing gloves to go another round with me.

I didn't know how Molloy could love me after what he did to her, much less want to be with me. I sure as hell couldn't stand the sight of myself.

"Joseph, do you need a hand with something?" our teacher asked, dragging my attention away from the window and to the front of the class.

I stared blankly up at her. "Huh?"

"Page 457," she said with a weary sigh. "Eyes on the book please."

Rolling my eyes, I turned my attention back to Molloy's textbook laying open on our desk, the one I'd been using since the start of the year, and frowned when my gaze settled on one lone earphone.

The cord attached to it led back to the MP3 player balancing on Molloy's lap under the desk, while the other earphone dangled from her right ear.

Picking it up, I discreetly popped it in my left ear, and listened as Puddle of Mudd's 'She Hates Me' drifted into my ear.

Lovely.

What a sweet way to serenade your boyfriend.

Fuck. My. Life.

Turning the page in her copybook, I watched as Molloy hovered over the page, and scribbled something down before pushing the copybook towards me.

You're an asshole.

Sighing heavily, I grabbed my pencil from behind my ear and quickly jotted down a response.

You're only figuring that out now?

Reading over my words, she quickly put pen to paper and responded.

I was blinded by your big dick.

Shaking my head, I snatched the page up and wrote my reply.

So, you're writing me notes and playing me love songs.
Does this mean I'm out of the doghouse?

Her brows furrowed as she read my question and scribbled a furious response.

No, dickhead, you're not out of the doghouse. Consider this note my version of throwing you a bone. As for love songs? Ha! You should be so lucky.

I smirked and wrote down a reply.

Yeah, well, this dickhead loves you.

You can't write things like that.

Why not?

Because I'm trying to be pissed at you.

So? You're always pissed at me, and I'm always loving you.

Okay, now you're just being smooth.

Smooth like a Rolo?

Oh god, I'd love a packet of Rolos right now.

Check the front pocket of my bag.

"Aoife! Joseph!" A hand reached between us and snatched up the cord of the earphones, yanking the MP3 player away. Miss Murphy stood in front of our desk, MP3 player in hand. "What have I told the two of you about distracting each other in my classroom?"

"Do it quietly?" Molloy offered with one of her award-winning smiles etched on her face – the kind of smile that got her out of trouble on the regular. "Which we were."

"Don't do it at all," Miss Murphy corrected, glowering. "Honestly, you two are old enough to know that bringing music into my class is not okay. This is your leaving cert year," she urged with a weary sigh. "Your last few months to revise as much as you can to get you both through your exams."

"Apparently, those two don't need any practice with maths, miss," Ricey piped up from the front of the class. "From what I hear, they're both pros at multiplying."

"Paul, back to your work please," Miss Murphy admonished.

I watched as Molloy's mouth fell open, and my back was up in an instant.

Molloy's gaze flicked to Casey in the desk in front of us, who shrugged in confusion and mouthed the words '*I swear it wasn't me*' to my girlfriend.

"The fuck are you talking about, asshole?" I demanded, glaring across the room at the smarmy bastard leering at us.

"Your brother has a big mouth," Paul continued.

"Kev?" she strangled out, and the look of hurt in her eyes was sobering. "*Kev* told you?"

"He's been telling anyone who will listen to him."

"No," she choked out, shaking her head. "No, no, no, no." She dropped her head in her hands. "This isn't happening."

"I dodged a bullet with you, didn't I? What a fucking cliché you turned out to be," he sneered. "Good fucking job on ruining your life, Aoife."

A cliché?

Good at multiplying?

I felt the air leave my lungs in a rush. "What. The. Fuck."

"I don't . . . I, uh . . . " Exhaling a ragged breath, Molloy choked out a sob. "Oh Jesus."

My heart slammed wildly against my chest, as I turned my attention to the girl sitting beside me.

"Molloy."

I wasn't fucking stupid.

"Molloy."

I could hear the penny dropping.

"Molloy."

Shit, I could hear the sound of my pulse ringing in my ears.

"Aoife!"

"Joe," Molloy whispered, turning her panicked eyes on me. "I . . . "

"Looks like he's having trouble doing the maths," Danielle laughed, joining in. "Let me help you out with that, Joe," she added, looking only too happy to throw her two cents into the equation. "Your penis, plus her vagina, equals a baby."

Everyone in class went deathly silent.

Aside from a few sharp intakes of breath, you could have heard a pin drop.

Meanwhile, my heart thundered in my chest, as my entire fucking world came crashing down around me.

"I told you that you wouldn't reach graduation without a baby in your belly," Danielle sneered. "Looks like I was right."

"Oh god." Choking out a pained sob, Molloy shoved her chair back and bolted out of our desk, moving for the classroom door quicker than I could process what the fuck was happening.

"Aoife!" Miss Murphy called after her, before turning her wide-eyed, horrified gaze on me. "I didn't know."

"Neither did he, by the looks of it."

"Shut up, Paul!" Miss Murphy barked, red-faced, as she continued to stare at me expectantly. "Joseph, I'm so sorry. I didn't know."

Unable to comprehend a word of what was coming out of her mouth, I rose to my feet, stunned that they could still hold my weight, and walked out of the classroom, ignoring the sound of whispers as the rumor mill kicked into high gear, no doubt.

My entire body was on fire, rattled further by an anxious tremor, when I reached the corridor and my eyes landed on Molloy.

My feet faltered when I took in the sight of her leaning against the wall opposite our classroom door in the empty corridor, clearly waiting for me. "Joe."

"What's going on?"

"I'm so . . . " Swallowing back a sob, she looked up at me with tear-filled eyes. "Sorry."

"For what?" I didn't recognize my own voice, as I watched her watch me, feeling unsettled and on edge. "What the fuck is happening here? What are they talking about?"

"I've been trying to tell you," she strangled out, as she reached up and tucked her hair behind her ears. "I *did* tell you, but you for— " Her voice cracked, "got." She dragged in several shaky breaths before trying again, "I'm so sorry, Joe." Clutching her face between her hands, she shook her head and choked out a sob. "Please don't hate me."

"Stop saying sorry, Molloy," I snapped, holding a shaky hand up, as I resisted the urge to fucking scream. "I don't hate you, but you need to just . . . just *tell* me what's going on here."

I watched with my heart in my mouth, and a horrible sinking feeling in the pit of my stomach, as my girlfriend pressed the heel of her hand to her forehead and strangled out the words that would forever turn my world on its axis.

"I'm pregnant."

"Pregnant." How I got the word out, I would never know, but I said it, and I managed to keep my tone level in the process. "You're pregnant."

Trembling, she kept her hand pressed to her forehead like a shield and nodded weakly.

"Pregnant."

A pained sob escaped her. "Yes."

"*You're* pregnant."

"Yes."

"You're saying you're pregnant," I heard myself repeat like an idiot, as my heart jackknifed in my chest. "Pregnant with a baby, pregnant."

"Yes, Joey, I'm saying I'm pregnant with a baby," she snapped, and then choked out another sob. "So just *stop* saying the word pregnant. Jesus!"

"I'm sorry, I'm just . . . " I tilted my head to one side, feeling a mixture of disbelief and confusion, as I waited for her to break out of character and yell *got you*. "Are you fucking with me?"

"I *did* fuck you," she ground out, looking flustered. "Many times. That's precisely the problem."

"You're not messing, are you?" I choked out, thoroughly fucking rattled, as I felt myself sag against the wall at my back. "You're seriously . . . " I shook my head and gaped at her. "Pregnant?"

The tears in her eyes assured me that this was no joke.

Jesus Christ.

My brows furrowed as a surge of raw, undiluted terror coursed through my veins. "How?"

She gave me a look that said *how do you think?*

"But you're on the pill."

"I know, and I've never skipped or missed a day, I swear," Molloy urged, hand still shielding her face. "But it was that house party. The one those Tommen boys threw." She shivered violently before adding, "I spent the whole night puking. And that following evening, too, remember? After we ordered that Chinese when we were babysitting Sean? Remember I was sick for hours afterwards? It must have messed with my birth control."

"The Tommen party?" My heart slammed wildly against my ribcage. "Jesus Christ, Aoif. That was months ago."

She flinched. "I know, Joe."

Blowing out a shaky breath, I ran my hand through my hair, completely fucking reeling. "Exactly how pregnant are you?"

"Joe."

"Tell me."

"About three and a half months."

"Three and a half months!" My eyes widened and the panic I was feeling multiplied by about three and a half months' worth. "Three and a half fucking months and I'm only hearing about it now?"

"I was scared, okay," she cried out defensively. "And I didn't know myself until a few weeks ago. I tried to tell you a million times, I swear, but I was just so fucking scared, Joe. I was *terrified* of sending you off the deep end again. You were doing so well, and I just . . . I didn't want to risk that. But then everything with your father happened and you went off the deep end anyway—"

"Oh, my fucking god." My stomach heaved and I had to press a hand to my chest to steady myself. "He did that to you while you were pregnant with *my* baby?"

"Joe, it's—"

"He did that to you." Heart hammering wildly in my chest, I squeezed out, "He hurt you when you were . . . are. Jesus Christ, you *are*."

"When I finally did work up the courage to tell you, you weren't even present."

"What?" I demanded, hoarse. "When?"

"The other day," she admitted brokenly. "But you were strung out."

Heart gunning in my chest, I tried to wrangle in my raging fucking panic, as words from a conversation I *couldn't* fucking remember flashed through my mind.

*

"We're having a baby."

"Where's the baby?"

"In here."
"In you? What's it doing in there?"
"You put it there, Joe."

"And you're sure there's no mistake?" I asked, out of sheer desperation. "You're definitely pregnant?"

"I've taken a ton of tests and they've all come back positive," she replied, eyes wide and full of uncertainty. "And Mam took me to the GP last week to confirm it."

"Your mam?" Her words were like a slap across the face. "Hold the fuck up." Shaking my head in my desperate attempt to make sense of the madness, I held a hand up and said, "You told your mam before you told me?"

Grimacing, she offered me a small nod. "I'm sorry."

"Who else?"

"Joe."

"Who else did you tell before me, Aoife?"

"Casey knows," she admitted quietly. "But only because she guessed. I swear, I wouldn't have told her if she hadn't figured it out."

"Whoa, whoa, whoa, so, let me get this straight." Pressing my fingers to my temples, I strived for calm while my entire fucking world shattered around me. "You, Casey, and Trish have been walking around for the past few weeks, knowing that we're going to have a baby when I *didn't*?"

"It wasn't like that, Joe."

"Does your old man know?"

"No." She shook her head. "I swear."

"What about Ricey and Danielle?" I demanded, voice torn. "I'm guessing those two are also in the loop, considering the shade they were throwing in class. Did you tell your ex before me, too?"

"No," she snapped. "Of course I didn't. Don't be so ridiculous."

"I just found out that you're pregnant during double fucking Maths, Molloy. How else am I supposed to react?"

"I don't know how Paul found out," she cried, shaking her head. "Kev must have told him."

"Kev?" My eyes bulged. "*Kev*. Fucking *Kev*?"

Her eyes widened in horror. "Joe."

"Your *brother* knows?" I shook my head. "I don't believe this."

"Stop shouting at me, asshole."

"I'm not shouting at you," I shouted, throwing my hands up. "I'm having a panic attack."

"Then calm down, Joey."

"I *am* calm. This is about the calmest a fella can get when he discovers that he's the last to find out that his girlfriend is having his *baby*," I practically roared.

"I'm sorry, okay. I was trying to *protect* you," she shouted back hoarsely. "That's all I was trying to do."

"That wasn't your call to make," I shot back, trembling. "I had a right to know what was going on."

"Yeah, well, I thought that I was doing the right thing," she bit out stubbornly. "Besides, it's my body this is happening to."

"It's my baby," I countered doggedly, and then reeled when I registered what I'd just said. "Oh Jesus," I wheezed, feeling my heart constrict so tight, I thought I might be having a heart attack. "It's my *baby*." Pressing a hand to my chest, I heaved out a breath, and tried to get the gasps under control. "Oh fuck."

"I'm so sorry, Joe." Throwing her hands up, Molloy spun on her heels and bolted away from me. "Please don't hate me."

I knew that I needed to go after her, but I couldn't get my feet to cooperate.

Managing to make it two steps in the direction she went, I collapsed in a heap on my ass, completely fucking reeling.

Pregnant.

She was pregnant.

With a baby.

With *my* baby.

Get the fuck up and take care of her.

Stop thinking about yourself, you fucking pussy.

Don't even think about pretending that you don't care.
It's yours and you care.
She's yours and you care.
It does *matter and you* do *care.*

PART 5

The black sheep of the family

AOIFE

"Mam!" I screamed, throwing the front door open, and barreling into my house on Thursday afternoon. How I had managed to drive home from school without crashing, I could only put down to my desperation to get to safety. *To get to my mother.* "Mam!"

"Aoife?" With a tea towel in her hands, and a startled look on her face, my mother appeared in the kitchen doorway. "What's wrong?"

"Mam!" I cried, moving straight for her. "He lied."

"Who lied?" she demanded, sweeping me up in her arms, as I collapsed against her. "What happened, Aoife? Who lied, pet?"

"Kev." Crying hard and ugly, I wrapped my arms around my mother's neck and clung to her for all I was worth. "He told *Paul*, Mam. He told *everyone* at school."

"He did *what*?"

"Joey knows – he found out in class," I cried, tightening my hold on her, as my entire body racked and heaved with sobs. "I didn't even get a chance to tell him myself."

"Oh Jesus. How did he take it?"

"How do you think?" I cried. "Horribly. He's furious with me for keeping it from him."

"Oh, Aoife."

"He didn't deserve that, Mam," I sobbed. "To be told like that in front of everyone." I shivered violently at the memory. "It was so *wrong*."

"I can only imagine."

A few moments later, the front door swung inwards, and my brother appeared, looking red-faced and flustered.

"Aoif." Holding his hands up, Kev approached with caution. "Before you say anything else, just know that I didn't know that Paul was going to—"

"You bastard!" Not giving him a chance to finish speaking, I swung around and lunged for my brother, scratching and clawing at his face, as I stooped to a level of despair I had never felt before in my life. "How could you do this to me?"

"You did this to yourself," Kev roared back, snatching my wrists up and pinning my arms to my sides. "Keep your goddamn hands to yourself, Aoife."

"I hate you," I screamed, ripping my hands free only to shove him in the chest. "Do you hear me? I fucking hate you, Kevin."

"Yeah, well, I'm not too crazy about you, either."

"Stop it, you two," Mam snapped, coming to stand between us. "That's enough."

"She's the one throwing slaps."

"Because he told our entire school that I'm pregnant."

"I didn't tell the entire school. I told a few close friends."

"Since when is my ex your close friend?"

"Since always," my brother roared back.

"Bullshit," I strangled out. "Paul was only ever nice to you because he was with me."

"You really believe that, don't you?"

"Because it's *true*."

"You don't have authority over who I'm friends with, Aoife," Kev sneered. "And if you took your head out of your ass long enough to see what's happening around you, then you'd know that I've been friends with Ricey since first year. We actually got a lot closer this past year."

"I wonder why?" I rolled my eyes. "You are such an *idiot*."

"Not everything is about you, Aoife," Kev snapped. "He actually gives me the time of day – unlike that asshole you've attached yourself to who can barely muster up the energy to acknowledge my existence."

"Why should Joey acknowledge you?" I demanded. "It's not like you're even remotely friendly towards him to begin with. You never have been. Every time he comes over you act all superior around him, all the time, and it's disgusting. Seriously, you talk about me having my head in my ass, when you're the one with your nose cocked in the air, walking around thinking you're better than everyone else."

"I *am* better than him."

"Because you're school smart, and he's not? Because you're going to *university*, and he isn't? Because you've been given the luxury of concentrating on your studies, while he's had to work since he was twelve? You think that makes you better than him?"

"See, you're trying to insult me, when all you're really doing is listing off positive characteristic traits."

Ugh.

"Kevin, Aoife," Mam tried to interject. "Let's just back up a second and breathe."

"Newsflash, asshole, there's a whole big world out there that won't give a crap about how many points you get in the leaving cert, or how high you rank in your class," I shouted, ignoring our mother's request. "And if you keep this *holier than thou* attitude up, I guarantee you won't last a week in the real world. So, you can go on thinking that you're better than my boyfriend, but the truth is you couldn't hold a candle to him," I spat. "You're a spoilt, pampered, little boy and Joey is a real man. You could try your whole life and never come close to being on his level!"

"If not being on his level means not having to slog it out under the bonnet of a car for the rest of my life, with permanently oil-stained hands, for a shitty wage at the end of the week, that won't secure a decent mortgage, then you won't hear me complaining."

"Oh my god, you are such a *snob*," I screamed, throwing my hands up.

"Why?" Kev demanded. "Because I'm a realist? Because I'm stating facts? Because I'm pissed that my sister has thrown her future away for an asshole from Elk's Terrace, with no decent prospects?"

"Because you're ungrateful," Mam interjected, looking beyond hurt. "All of those fancy computer games lining the shelves in your bedroom were paid for with oil-stained hands. Every stitch of clothes on your body, and every morsel of food you've put in your mouth since the day you were born came from those same hands. Your *father's* hands. Your father the *mechanic*, who has spent most of his life busting his bollocks to give his children a better life than the one he had."

"Which is exactly why you should be praising *me* for appreciating the sacrifices that you and Dad have made for us, and berating *her* for throwing them back in your face."

"How have I thrown anything back in their faces?"

"By being thick enough to let that scumbag drug-addict between your legs," Kev snarled. "You do realize that the father of your grandchild is a fucking junkie, don't ya, Mam?"

"Shut the hell up, Kevin," I hissed, lunging for him once more.

"Stop," Mam warned, separating us again. "Calm down, Aoife. This isn't good for you."

"*He* isn't good for her."

"You don't know what the fuck you're talking about!"

"Look at you," my brother roared. "Look at the state of you. Picking fights in your condition. You know why, don't you? It's because he's after rubbing off on you. You had everything going for you, and you threw it away." He shook his head in disgust. "For *him*."

"What's going on in here?" Dad asked then, strolling into the kitchen, lunchbox in hand – and yes, his hands were stained with engine oil. He looked from me to Kev, and his brows furrowed in confusion. "What are you all shouting about?" He looked to Mam. "It's lunchtime, Trish. Why are the twins not at school?"

"Nothing," Mam was quick to interject, moving to our father. "It's nothing, Tony."

"Enjoy becoming his mother, Aoife," Kev continued, ignoring our parents, as he glowered at me. "Because the entire town knows what kind of a doormat she is. You should take some tips from her sometime, because that's all you'll amount to now."

"Shut up, Kevin," Mam hissed. "Not another goddamn word."

"Mother?" Dad blinked in confusion. "Whose mother?"

"This is *your* fault," Kev snapped, turning his accusing glare on our father. "You brought him into our lives."

"Please, Mam," I groaned, dropping my head in my hands, while Mam tried and failed to silence my furious brother. "Just make him stop *talking*."

"Who?" Dad demanded, looking wholly confused. "What are you talking about?"

"Aoife's pregnant!" Kev roared, jabbing a finger in my direction, and with those words, he blew my world to smithereens. *Again*. "Off that piece of shit that you're so hellbent on seeing the best of."

My father reeled back like the words my brother spoke had physically struck him.

"Kevin," Mam strangled out and then quickly placed her hands on my father's chest. "Tony, breathe. It's alright, love, just take a breath."

"Yeah, golden boy doesn't seem so perfect now, does he?" Kev taunted, looking angrier than I'd ever seen. "Not when he's knocked up your daughter, huh, Dad?"

"What are you . . . ?" My father's panicked eyes flicked to me. "Aoife?"

"Dad, I didn't mean . . . I'm so sorry," I sobbed, hands hanging limply at my sides. I looked at my brother and shook my head. "I *hate* you."

"I tried to tell you about him," Kev continued to shout, aiming his pain at our father now. "But you wouldn't be told. I *warned* you about what kind of person he was, but you insisted on hiring him – on treating him like the son you always wanted but never got with me!"

"*Kevin*."

"Well, congrats, Dad," Kev croaked out, voice breaking. "You finally got your wish. You'll have a grandchild off him soon enough that will cement him deeper into the family. You'll finally have the son you always wanted."

Unable to handle another second of watching my world fall around me, I bolted from the kitchen, ignoring my mother's pleading and father's shouting, as I made a beeline for the front door, desperate to escape.

"Aoife," Kev called out, hurrying after me. "Wait up."

"Don't touch me," I spat, yanking my arm free from his hold, and I glared up at him. "And don't *ever* speak to me again."

"I didn't . . . " my brother began to say, but then jutted his chin out defiantly and hissed, "He had to know."

"It wasn't your place to tell him," I countered shakily, feeling the ultimate form of betrayal at the hands of the person who'd shared a womb with me. "It wasn't your place to tell anyone. It was mine, and you took that choice away from me."

Regret flickered in his eyes.

"You're so jealous of Joey's relationship with Dad that you threw your own twin under the bus to get one up on him."

"Aoife."

"You literally destroyed my entire world, Kevin." I shook my head, not bothering to wipe the tears from my cheeks. Fresh ones would just take their place. "*Why?*"

"I didn't . . . " He ran a hand through his hair and sighed. "Look, at least it's out in the open now. If anything, I did you a favor."

"You told my *father* before I could," I choked out, chest heaving. "You told Paul who told my *baby's* father before I could."

Confusion filled his eyes. "Joey didn't know?"

I shook my head.

"I didn't know that." Sighing heavily, he reached for my hand. "Shit, Aoif, I didn't—"

"No." I held a hand up and warned him off. "Stay back."

"Aoife."

"I mean it," I snapped. "I'm ashamed to call you my brother."

"And you think I'm *proud* to call you my sister?" he shouted back, cheeks reddening. "Proud to have a slut in the family? You're the embarrassment here, Aoife. You're the one bringing down the tone. You're the screw-up, not me," he tossed out defensively. "It's not my fault that you didn't tell the guy. He's the first one you should've told."

"Not your *fault*?" I gaped at him. "This is *all* your fault. You might have the brains when it comes to school, but you're a cruel, spoilt, jealous bastard, without a shred of heart, and I will never forgive you for this. Do you hear me, Kevin? I will *never* forgive you!"

"Fine," he shot back defensively, tone thick with emotion. "See if I care."

"Oh, you'll care, you spiteful little shit," I growled, backing up the garden path towards our gate. "And you'll be sorry."

"What are you going to do?" he called after me. "Set your guard dog on me? *Again*?"

"I pulled him off you the last time," came my heated reply. "Don't think I'll make that mistake twice."

"And I let him off the hook the last time," my brother reminded me. "Don't think I'll make that mistake twice."

"No, Kev, I won't set my boyfriend on you," I hissed, shoving the gate open. "Because, unlike you, I don't need anyone to fight my battles for me."

"What's that supposed to mean?"

"It means that you've never fought your own battles a day in your damn life," I practically screamed. "You're too busy hiding behind Mam's skirt."

"Bullshit."

"Oh, you think you've just sailed through secondary school based on your stellar personality alone?" I demanded. "No, asshole, you've been wrapped in bubble wrap for six years, because *I've* had your back the entire time."

"I never asked you to do that for me."

"You didn't have to ask me," I bit out. "That's what *family* does. They look out for each other. They protect each other. They have each other's backs." I shrugged my shoulders. "Or at least, that's what I thought we were, but clearly, I was wrong."

"You're overreacting here," he muttered, rubbing his jaw.

"No, *you're* underestimating the damage you've done to our relationship," I corrected, pointing a finger at him. "I'm done having your back, Kev. I'm done being your sister. It ends today. And good luck getting Mam back on side now that she's finally seen you for what you truly are – a fucking brat!"

"I was upset," he tried to defend himself, throwing his hands up. "You and Mam were keeping secrets, and spending so much time together—"

"And poor little Kev spat the dummy because he wasn't getting his mammy's undivided attention like he's used to getting every second of the day since we were born," I filled in, tone laced with sarcasm. "Well, boo-fucking-hoo, you sap. So, Mam gave me a sliver of attention for once after you've spent eighteen years monopolizing her time. Get the hell over yourself!"

"Like your boyfriend has done with *our* father?"

"If you have a problem with Dad's relationship with Joey, then take it up with Dad," I shot back, wholly enraged. "Don't ruin *my* life because you want to put a wedge between them."

"That's not what I was trying to do."

"That's *exactly* what you were trying to do," I snapped. "And yeah, you might have achieved it, but you also lost yourself a sister in the process."

"Aoife, come on," he called after me. "I'm sorry, okay?"

"Don't come too close, Kev," I called over my shoulder, as I stormed down the footpath away from my brother. "You wouldn't want the neighbors seeing you associating with the family *slut*."

"What did you say to her, ya little bollox?" Rushing into the garden, with Mam hot on his heels, Dad called after me, "Aoife, get back here in your condition."

"Don't go running off like this," Mam added. "Come back inside, love. Your father's not going to shout at you."

"Leave me alone!" I screamed, breaking into a run, as I raced down the footpath, needing to get as far away from my family as possible.

Because I couldn't do this.

It was too much.

I couldn't handle the emotions rushing through me.

I was too close to my breaking point to take another hit.

However, when I rounded the corner at the end of my street, and smacked into a hard chest, that's exactly what happened.

"Holy shit." A familiar pair of hands came around me, moving to grip my shoulders and steady me. "Molloy." Joey was breathing hard and fast, clearly having sprinted all the way over here from school. "The fuck are you running off to?"

I couldn't answer him because I had no idea where I had intended to go.

I only knew that he was *exactly* where I needed him to be.

"Joe." Unable to shoulder this crippling weight by myself for a second longer, I slumped against him, needing to feel his arms around me in this moment more than I needed my next breath. "Joe."

"It's okay." His arms came around me, tight and full of comfort, as he pulled me into his embrace. "Shh. It's okay."

Burying my face in the front of his school jumper, I clutched the fabric at his back, and let him take my weight, taking every ounce of support he was offering me. Because I needed his support. I needed *him*.

"I've got you, Molloy."

"Please don't hate me."

"I don't."

"I'm so sorry for not telling you sooner," I cried. "For you having to find out like you did."

"Listen to me." With his hands on my cheeks, and his fingers tangled in my hair, he forced me to look up at him. "Don't apologize. I get it, okay?"

"You get it?"

"I get it." He nodded slowly. "Why you didn't tell me. What you were trying to do. I don't like it, but I get it." He exhaled a shaky breath. "I'm just so fucking sorry for being the kind of person that you felt you needed to protect, when it should have been the other way around."

Unable to tear my eyes away, I watched as Joey absorbed the brunt of the metaphorical axe that I had just swung down on his neck – on his entire world.

I could see it all in his eyes.

Everything he wanted to say, everything *I* wanted to say, but never would.

All of the fear.

The regret.

The hurt.

The guilt.

Expelling a pained breath, Joey lowered his face to mine and gently rested his brow against mine. "I'm so sorry, Molloy."

Tears spilled down my cheeks, and my breath came in short puffs, as I reached up and covered his hands with mine. "I'm sorry, too, Joe."

"I don't know what to say here," he admitted in a hoarse tone. "I'm scared to fucking death right now, so I can only imagine how you've been feeling. But I'm here, okay?" He shrugged his shoulders helplessly. "I'm here and I'm going nowhere."

"Yeah?"

"Yeah." He nodded slowly, eyes locked on mine. "I won't run."

"You swear?"

"I swear," Joey replied, tone laced with sincerity. "I won't leave you alone in this."

"Then that's all you need to say," I sobbed, nuzzling his cheek with mine. "Because that's all I need to know."

I'll be there

JOEY

Having had a grand total of seventy-three minutes to get my head around the fact that my girlfriend was housing an atomic fucking bomb inside her belly, with fifty percent of my genes, I held her in my arms, and tried to comfort her, while my brain freewheeled into overdrive.

The fuck were we going to do?

We were still in school.

She had her whole future in front of her.

She was supposed to go out in the world and leave her neon-colored mark on it.

Instead, I had saddled her with a baby.

A baby!

Jesus Christ.

It was like I was watching my worst nightmare unfold around me, and I was too paralysed to stop it.

The knowledge that I was, singlehandedly, responsible for ruining her future was *crippling*.

Well, you finally did it, asshole, a voice in my head taunted, *you finally came full circle and turned into your father.*

Feeling too much in this moment, feeling too goddamn exposed and vulnerable, I tried and failed to steady myself.

It was pointless.

The panic and uncertainty thrashing around inside of me was unlike anything I had experienced before.

I could feel Molloy's anxiety.

It was palpable.

It mirrored mine.

"I'm scared, Joe," she continued to whisper, over and over, as she buried her face in my chest and leaned against me. "I'm so scared."

I couldn't reassure her of shit.

Not when I had no clue of this would play out.

All I could do in that moment was hold her.

Because I didn't have the words to fix this, to make it right for her.

All I had was my body.

My presence.

My ability to *stay*.

Sniffling, she looked up at me, eyes puffy and red. "Thank you."

"For what?"

"For proving me right."

Confused, I frowned. "How have I proved you right, exactly?"

"Well, you're here for a start," she said, offering me a small smile. "And you haven't hit the roof."

"Molloy, you didn't climb on top of yourself and get pregnant," I bit out. "I'm the asshole who did that. I'm not going to hit any damn roof. This is on me a hell of a lot more than it's on you, okay?" I shook my head, feeling lost and frustrated. "I didn't realize your birth control mightn't work. I didn't even think about it when you were throwing up that weekend. I should've put a condom on. I should've taken better care of you."

"I shouldn't have kept it from you."

No, she shouldn't have, but I got it.

"I have an appointment at the hospital tomorrow," she blew my world by saying. "It's for an ultrasound – a dating scan, they called it." Shivering, she added, "I really don't want to go on my own."

"You won't be on your own. I'll be there."

"You will?"

"Of course," I ground out, feeling too much in this moment. "I would've been there for the doctor's appointment, too, you know. If I had known. I'm a lot of things, Aoif, but I'm not a coward, and I don't run."

"I've been trying to ask you for days," she whispered. "Trying to work up the courage to tell you."

"It's okay." I pulled her close. "It's going to be okay."

"I'm going to be the talk of the town, Joe," she admitted in a small voice, looking achingly vulnerable. "Everyone at school probably knows by now. Paul and Danielle will make sure of it. How am I supposed to walk back through the doors of BCS?"

"*We* are going to walk back into school with our heads held high, and if anyone has something to say, then they'll have me to deal with," I replied, hackles rising. "Because fuck them, Molloy."

"Fuck them?"

"Fuck them," I confirmed.

She sniffled. "Kev told Dad."

My heart dropped into my ass. "Kev has a big fucking mouth."

"I don't want to go home yet." She worried on her lip. "I'm not ready to face my father, and if I see my brother, I'll kill him."

That made two of us.

"Then don't go home yet," I replied. "Stay with me."

"What are we going to do, Joe?"

I have no fucking idea. "We'll figure it out."

Sharing a bag of chips at the GAA grounds probably wasn't what Molloy had in mind when she told me that she didn't want to go home, but in all fairness, what the hell else was I supposed to do?

I didn't have a car to bundle her into.

I didn't have a home to take her to, not one where she would be safe.

I had no big-time future ahead of me like her ex, or no family to prop me up like him, either.

I had a grand total of thirteen euro in my pocket, and the prospects of a gutter rat.

Fucked didn't even come close to defining how much trouble we were in.

The only thing that I had going for me, that most of the lads I knew who were in similar positions didn't have, was the fact that the girl carrying my kid happened to be my best friend.

In a way, that made her being pregnant significantly worse, because the guilt was so staggering.

My conscience was weighing on me in a way that Dricko or any of the lads I knew with kids had never experienced.

Because, for me, it wasn't my future I was mourning.

It was hers.

Because I loved her.

I loved her so fucking much that I let myself get reckless and ruin her.

I didn't meet her on a whim, stick my dick in her after two or three weeks of messing around, and become a makeshift family overnight.

I had six years of friendship racked up with Molloy.

I knew the girl inside and out, and she knew me.

We'd grown up together.

Our lives were tangled up and entwined.

She had never been someone to pass away the time with until something better came along.

She *was* the time, the better, the goal, the whole nine yards.

Any future I had ever dared to imagine for myself never veered from having her slap bang in the center of it.

I never wanted to be a parent, babies were never part of *my* plan, but if it had been a dealbreaker for Molloy, far, *far* into our future, then I maybe could have been persuaded.

Now, it was being thrust upon us both.

"Don't even think about it, Houdini," I heard myself warn an hour later, as I watched my girlfriend eye the towering wall surrounding the GAA pavilion. It was a wall I'd watched her effortlessly scale a thousand times before.

Not anymore.

"I mean it, Aoif," I warned. "Keep those feet on the ground."

"You're being a tad dramatic."

"It's called being sensible."

She rolled her eyes. "Since when do the words *Joey Lynch* and *sensible* go hand in hand?"

"Since the words *Aoife Molloy* and *pregnant* joined forces," I shot back, holding my school jumper out for her. "Sit your ass on the footpath."

Begrudgingly complying, she took my jumper, folded it in half, and then placed it on the concrete before lowering herself down.

"Thanks for the food, Joe." With legs for days stretched out in front of her, she placed the warm brown bag of steamy chips on her lap and sighed. "I'm flat broke right now, and I missed all of my shifts at work last week, so I don't have any money coming in for a few weeks."

We were both flat broke, but if I couldn't buy my pregnant girlfriend a measly bag of chips, then I needed to be taken out into a field and shot.

"Don't worry about money," I replied, doing more than enough worrying for the both of us, as I sank down beside her. "I'll figure it out."

"What do you mean?"

"I mean if your father can't take me on full-time at the garage, I'll find something else to tide us over." I shrugged. "I told you that I would look after you, and I will, okay? Money is the last thing you need to worry about right now. Let me do that for us."

"What about school?"

"What about it?" Sighing heavily, I hooked my arms around my knees. "Babies aren't cheap, Molloy."

"No." She shook her head. "No way, Joe. You *need* to finish school."

"No, *you* need to finish school," I corrected. "I don't need a piece of paper to bring in money. I can do that now."

"You heard my dad," she argued. "He'll agree to your apprenticeship, but only *after* you finish school and sit your leaving cert exams."

"Aoife, what am I going to do with a piece of paper? Wipe my ass with it?" I shook my head. "It's an exam that doesn't mean shit for me. For you, *yes*, absolutely, but me? Not so much, baby."

"I'm not due until September," she hurried to add. "We can both finish school before we even have to think about anything else. We only have two months left, Joe. Two months and we're finished with BCS."

"September?" Jesus Christ. "You're due in September."

She nodded. "The twentieth."

"Right after your birthday?"

She nodded.

I blew out a breath. "How many weeks does that make you now?"

"Um, fourteen weeks and two days, I think?"

"Jesus, you're already in the second trimester, Aoif."

"I know," she squeezed out. "I'm terrified."

"Don't be," I tried to soothe, while I mentally went into panic mode as I struggled to rack my brain around the constant stream of life-changing information that just seemed to keep coming at me.

"If you're due late September, and it's April next week, then we have five and a half months to get a handle on this."

"A handle?"

"Yeah." I nodded. "Save up some cash, Molloy."

Her eyes narrowed. "You're not quitting school."

"Listen, there's no point in wasting two months in a classroom, working for something both of us know I will never need. Not when I could be *actually* working for the money that we *are* definitely going to need," I tried to reason. "Come on, Molloy, think about this. You know I'm right."

"I *have* thought about it," she argued back. "I've done little else these past few weeks, and it's not happening, Joe. We started BCS together and we're going to see it out together."

"You *still* can," I shot back. "I want that for you. All I'm trying to do is get a head-start on this, Molloy. We're going to need a lot of stuff, and it all costs money. Money neither of us has. The baby's going to need a cot, and clothes, and nappies, and formula. There's a long list of shit we're going to need, and I can't provide that on a part-time wage from the garage."

"You already work yourself to the bone."

"It's not enough."

"Mam said I can stay at home," she offered, like it was something I wanted to hear. "We don't have to worry about where to go when the baby's born."

I balked. "I'm not living apart from you and my baby."

Her eyes widened. "You're not?"

"Fuck no." I shook my head. "I'll get us a flat, Aoif."

"Joe, if it's at the expense of your education, then I don't want it."

"You just need to let me worry about the money side of things," I argued. "I'll take care of everything."

"Are we together, Joe?"

I rolled my eyes. "Obviously."

"Are we going to do this together?"

I gave her a hard look. "Where are you going with this?"

"Are we a team or not?" she demanded.

"Yeah, fuck, we're a team," I conceded.

"Then we're both finishing school," she ground out. "Together."

"Listen, I don't want to fight with you about this."

"Then don't," she cut me off. "Because as far as I'm concerned, it's a done deal. You're finishing school and that's that. Apartments and houses can come afterwards."

"You're not thinking clearly here."

"You're not thinking at all."

"Molloy."

"Lynch."

Frustrated, I reached into the brown paper bag on her lap, grabbed a soggy chip, and grimaced the moment it touched my tongue.

It tasted like shit.

With a mouthful of chips, Molloy offered me a sheepish smile. "Too much vinegar?"

I gave her a look that said *always*, before asking, "How are you feeling?"

"About the vinegar?"

"No, genius, about being pregnant."

Anxiety flashed in her eyes and I watched as a small shiver rolled through her. "Oh, I think it's safe to say that I'm sufficiently terrified to my core, you?"

Oh, I'm right there with you. "I'm fine."

"Fine." She arched a disbelieving brow. "Bullshit."

Of course I was bullshitting, but I had the wherewithal to not reveal just how panicked I was to the girl who'd clearly gotten the shorter end of the straw in this deal.

"Are you mad?" she asked again, but this time, she chewed on her lip nervously before adding, "That I'm having it?"

"Having it?" I frowned. "That's generally how this kind of thing goes."

"Not always."

"Don't go there."

"You know what I mean."

Yeah, I did, and I didn't like where this was heading one bit. "I would never ask you to do that."

"But if you could choose?" she swallowed deeply. "Would you?"

"No, Molloy." I shook my head. "I wouldn't want you to do that."

There was a hopeful note in her voice when she said, "You wouldn't?"

"Never."

Relief flickered in her eyes. "Really?"

"Really," I confirmed. "If you didn't want to have my baby, I'd understand – hell, I'd hold your hand the whole way over and back, but I know that's not what you really want."

"Maybe it should be, Joe."

I leveled her with a hard stare. "Is it?"

She stared back at me for the longest time, before blowing out a breath and shaking her head. "I want to keep it."

"Exactly," I replied, nudging her shoulder with mine. "Looks like we're doing this."

"Yeah." Sighing heavily, she slipped her arm through mine, and leaned her cheek on my shoulder. "Looks like we are."

"We've got this, Molloy," I tried to reassure her. "We'll figure it out."

"Just ... just stay with me, Joe," she squeezed out in a small voice. "Like you are right now. This version of you? I need this guy to *stay*."

"I'm going nowhere."

"That's not what I mean."

Yeah, I knew what she meant.

"There's too much at stake now, and I can't do this without you," she admitted, nuzzling my shoulder affectionately. "Don't lose yourself again, Joe."

Shoulders weighing heavily with shame, I dropped my head to rest against hers. "I won't."

"I need you to be done with it," she pushed. "Like the way you were after Christmas. That determination and willpower? I need you to find it again, Joe. I need that guy."

"I know," I ground out, feeling like a piece of shit for putting her in a position where she needed to have this kind of conversation with me. "I'll sort that, too, Molloy."

"By stopping," she added. "Sort it by stopping right now, Joe. Not tomorrow or next week. Right now."

"You know I love you, right?" I heard myself say, knowing that it would never be enough, but knowing that it was all I had. "There's nothing I wouldn't do for you in this life, Molloy. Nothing."

"Then be done with the drugs and the bullshit," she pleaded. "Do *that* for me."

"I will."

"You're not supposed to say you will," she whispered sadly. "You're supposed to say that you already are."

"I'll fix it," I heard myself offer up weakly, trying to give this girl everything that she needed from me, but it felt like I was a pouring from an empty cup. I could taste the lie on my tongue, and, apparently, so could she. "I'll sort it."

"I want to believe you," Molloy replied, shifting closer. "I want to believe you so bad."

Me too.

Feeling too fucking exposed, I untangled myself from her and stood up.

"Listen." Reaching into the pocket of my school trousers, I withdrew a packet of cigarettes and quickly sparked one up. "I don't know how this is going to go." Backing up a few feet to keep the smoke away from her, I inhaled a deep drag before letting it out. "I don't have a crystal ball to look into the future with. I wish that I could tell you that everything will be perfect from here on out, but we both know that'd be me spurting bullshit."

"Feel free to spurt all the bullshit you can think up," she grumbled, dropping a chip back in the bag, and wiping her hand on her thigh. "I could use a little fabrication right now."

Couldn't we both?

"The truth is that I'm half scared to death here, Molloy."

"Not helping."

"I'm not scared of stepping up, Molloy. I'm scared of it not being enough," I forced myself to continue – to admit. "I'm scared of letting you down."

Emotion flickered in her eyes. "Joe."

I shook my head and turned away, staring out at the empty pitch, needing a minute to gather my thoughts before I could continue.

"Being there for you isn't the problem." *It's being good enough for you that I'm struggling with.* "I just . . . I wish I wasn't who I am." Letting my head fall back, I took another drag and stared up at the darkening sky. "I wish I was someone else for you." I exhaled a cloud of smoke. "Someone better."

"I don't." Footsteps closed in on me, and I felt her arms wrap around my waist. "I wouldn't want you to be anyone other than who you are right now," she said, pressing her cheek to my back. "I just want you healthy."

"I *am* trying, Aoif," I told her, dropping a hand to cover hers. "I've *been* trying."

"I know, Joe," she soothed, nuzzling my back with her cheek. "And I love you for it."

"I love you, too." Heart gunning in my chest, I took one final drag of my smoke before tossing the butt away and turning to face her. "I do, Aoif." I blew out a shaky breath, hands moving to settle on her hips. "I fucking *love* the bones of ya."

Sighing heavily, she draped her arms around my neck and smiled sadly. "But?"

"Sometimes I can't control it," I admitted brokenly. "It's like something goes off in my head, and I check out. I stop thinking. I stop feeling. I stop fucking remembering all of the reasons I have to keep going and start thinking about all of the reasons why I should give up."

"Joe."

"I'm *scared* to be in my own head, Molloy," I croaked out, feeling a shiver rack through my body. "I'm fucking terrified of my inability to control my own actions, and what's worse is knowing that, at any point, I could end up going too far and driving you away. I could push away the one person, the *only* fucking person, who has even given a shit about me." I exhaled a ragged breath, feeling torn and exposed to this girl. "I don't want to go back to how it was – to how *I* was. I know what's at stake. I see you; I fucking see you standing right here in front of me, and my heart is screaming at me to cop the hell on and get my shit together. And I want to. I want to so fucking bad, but it's like this . . . " Frustrated, I reached up and pressed my fingers to my temples, trying to get the words out, to make it all make sense to her, which was impossible considering I didn't understand it myself. Still, I tried, knowing that she deserved nothing less. "It's like I have this whole other person in my head, a whole other voice, even though I *know* it's me. It's my voice, but it's a destructive fucking voice that rears its head every time I'm stressed."

"Which is constantly," she filled in knowingly.

I heaved out a breath and nodded. "The worse shit gets in my life, the louder the voice gets, louder and louder and louder, until it's literally screaming in my head, and I can't focus on anything other than doing the one thing that I *know* that will quieten it down."

"Self-medicating." She swallowed deeply. "Losing yourself."

"You asked me why I fucked up and caved after three months? It's because I couldn't *take* it anymore." I shrugged helplessly. "And now there's a baby coming, and I have so much to lose that I'm fucking terrified of blowing it again. I know that I need to get my shit together, and I will. But that's the problem right there, because I can tell you that I'm going to be good, and I'll mean it when I say it, but I don't trust myself, Aoif." My shoulders slumped and I exhaled a pained breath. "I just don't."

She didn't shout or berate me.

She didn't slap my face and run away, either.

Instead, she stood there, eyes locked on mine, as she absorbed my painful truth.

"Right now," she finally said. "What are your thoughts right now?"

"My thoughts?"

"Your thoughts."

"You," I admitted. "You and the baby."

Shivering, she nodded and tightened her arms around my neck. "And your head? Where's your head at, Joe?"

"Same place as it's always been," I replied. "With you."

"I believe in you."

The words hurt to hear and I flinched. "Molloy."

"I. Believe. In. You," she repeated slowly. "I'm not expecting perfection from you, Joe. Hell, I don't want it, because I'm definitely not perfect. So, all I need you to do is be honest, be faithful, and keep *trying*."

"And if I'm not worth it?" I dared to ask. "If I'm not worth believing in? If this all goes to shit and I end up letting you down again? What happens then?"

"You see, you're not taking into account my feelings for you," she said, stroking my cheeks with her thumbs. "And I know being loved is a foreign concept to you, but it doesn't come with strings or conditions. It's unconditional, Joe."

I looked at her, feeling at a total loss. "I don't get it."

"I know you don't." Nodding, she leaned up on her tiptoes and pressed a kiss to the corner of my mouth. "That's okay."

"Everyone has their limit, Molloy," I said. "One of these days, you're going to reach yours with me."

"Do you love me, Joe?"

I pulled back to frown at her. "You know I do."

"Do you plan on lying to me?"

I shrugged. "No more than the usual amount."

She cocked a brow before asking, "Do you plan on fucking around behind my back with other girls?"

I rolled my eyes. "Be serious."

"Do you?"

"No, Molloy," I grumbled. "I value my dick."

"Nuh-uh." She slapped my chest. "Wrong answer."

"How about I don't plan on fucking around on you because it takes up all of my time and energy just trying to navigate your many sparkling personalities."

"Try again, asshole."

"Fine. I don't plan on fucking around on you because I don't want anyone else. Because I don't *see* anyone else."

"And?"

I stared at her. "And?"

"And," she pushed, giving me an expectant look.

Blowing out a frustrated breath, I relented and said, "And because there's no other girl on the planet as sexy – or as *vain* – as you."

"Perfect." Nodding her approval, she asked, "And finally, do you plan on dropping off the face of the earth when the time comes? Do you plan on checking out on me?"

I gave her a look that told her everything she needed to know.

"Then you just answered your own question," she replied. "You're worth believing in, Joe. You are so incredibly worth it all."

Sound the alarm

AOIFE

When the sky grew dark, and the cold started to seep into our bones, Joey and I trudged back to my estate.

With a whole heap of uncertainty still hanging over my head, and my father's interrogation looming, I was glad to have him by my side. The familiar way he had his arm slung over my shoulder somehow meant more tonight than any of the thousand other times he held me like this in the past. Because we were in trouble, and he was still here, still backing me up like a loyal teammate.

We both knew that whatever my father planned to say about our situation, the blame would inevitably fall at my boyfriend's feet, and still, his step never faltered. I was incredibly grateful to him for being the kind of person who followed through on what he said.

Joey said that he would be here, and he *was*.

I knew that he was afraid of the unknown.

Of his ability to get clean and stay clean.

He'd opened up more this afternoon than he had in a long time, and even though the demons that plagued him scared me half to death, I was grateful that he was willing to let me in. I was grateful that he had found a way to trust me, even when he didn't trust himself.

"What the actual fuck," Joey bit out, when we rounded the corner of my street, and locked eyes on a familiar, ancient Honda Accord parked outside my house.

My heart slammed in my chest at the sight and my eyes widened in horror. "Is that—"

"My old man's car?" Furious, he nodded. "I'm going to kill him."

"No, you're not," I choked out, twisting around so that I was facing him. "Hey, hey, Joe." Reaching up, I grabbed his face and forced him to look at me. "Shh, just calm down a sec, okay?"

"He's in your *house*, Molloy!" Beyond livid, Joey, stalked towards my garden gate, hooking an arm around me and taking me with him when I didn't step out of his way. "What the fuck is he playing at?"

"It doesn't matter, Joe – do you hear me?" Digging my heels into the footpath, I pressed my hands to his chest. "It's okay. I'm not afraid of that bastard."

"Well, I don't want him anywhere near you!"

I didn't want him anywhere near either of us, but I had a feeling his father being here had more to do with my father than anything else. "Just breathe, okay? Take a breath."

His eyes bulged in outrage. "Are you fucking crazy?"

"Don't take that tone with me, you big bastard!" I snapped, slapping at his chest to regather his attention. "So, stop walking and just *breathe*."

Releasing a frustrated growl, Joey reluctantly came to a stop and made a pitiful attempt at reining in his temper. "See?" he barked, inhaling an exaggerated breath. "I *am* breathing."

Yeah, he was breathing *flames*.

"If your parents are here, it's because they were invited by mine," I tried to wrangle him in by saying. "I need you to be calm, okay? I mean it, Joe. Don't react to him. *Please*."

"Why?" he demanded hoarsely, throwing his hands up. "*Why* in the name of god would your parents invite *my* parents over?"

"To talk, most likely."

"About *what*?"

I rolled my eyes. "Uh, gee, I don't know, Joe; maybe about the fact that their children are having a baby?"

Joey stared at me like he didn't understand a word of my logic, and it made my heart ache for him.

He truly didn't understand how parents should behave.

He had never experienced a remotely loving act from either one of his.

"Listen to me," I coaxed, hands drifting to his neck. "This isn't an ambush, okay? You're not under attack here. My parents don't know any of it, okay? All they know about your dad is that he's a shitty person, and they're about to share a grandchild. That's all this is, Joe, a sit down."

"He *is* a shitty person," my boyfriend agreed, voice laced with pain. "A *very* shitty person."

"Which is why you need to keep the head in there, okay?"

"I can't."

"Please, Joe," I begged. "Just stay *calm*, okay?" When my words failed to reach him, I grabbed his hand and pressed it to my stomach. "Feel this?" I demanded; eyes locked on his. "This is ours."

"Molloy."

"This baby is *yours*," I urged, shivering when I felt his fingers splay across my belly. "But this baby is *not* you, the same way that you are *not* him. So, we're going to in there, and we're going to take all of the shit our parents throw at us on the chin, because we both know that nothing they say or do could ever change a damn thing for us. Because I've got your back and you've got mine." Leaning up on my tiptoes, I caught hold of his chin and kissed him hard. "We're a team, Joey Lynch, and that bastard doesn't stand a chance against us."

His breath hitched in his throat. "Fuck."

"Are you with me?"

He nodded slowly. "I'm with you, Molloy."

Knowing exactly who I would find at the kitchen table made the walk from my front door to the kitchen so much harder. The concept of facing my own father was already sending me into a silent panic attack, without throwing Joey's parents into the mix. Finding immense strength from the boy who had my hand wrapped safely in his, I found myself plucking up enough nerve to walk my ass into the kitchen and face them all.

My parents.

His parents.

My brother.

Even Spud was sprawled out, belly up, in a food-coma, on the mat at the back door.

"Oh, thank god," my father broke the silence by saying, as he set his mug down on the table and blew out a relieved breath. "You're back."

With my heart bucking wildly in my chest, and tension oozing from my boyfriend, we stood in the doorway of the kitchen, hand in hand, and absorbed the five pairs of eyes that landed on us.

"Trish," Joey acknowledged quietly. "Tony."

"Joey," both my parents said in unison.

"Aoife," Marie offered in a small voice, gaze flicking from me to her son. "Joey."

I nodded in return. "Marie."

Joey stiffened beside me, but didn't acknowledge his mother, because all of his attention was on the man glaring back at him.

His father.

"Well, aren't you every bit the fuck -up that I warned your mother you were," Teddy Lynch sneered, getting right down to business, attention locked on my boyfriend. "Just when I thought you couldn't disappoint us any further, you take it to a new level."

Joey sucked in a sharp breath, but thankfully made no move to respond. Instead, he remained rigid beside me, locked in a heated stare down with a man, who, as far as I was concerned, was the devil incarnate.

"That's hardly necessary, Teddy," my mother chimed in, looking uncomfortable. "There's no need to berate the boy."

"You bring us over here to tell us that our young fella is after catching your young one and you don't think I need to discipline him? I'd say that there's every need," the bigger man snapped. Turning back to his son, he hissed, "Are you happy with yourself, ya little bollox? Stupid little cunt, letting your cock do the thinking for ya!" He shook his head in disgust. "You can kiss goodbye to the hurling. You won't have time for it with all the nappies you'll be working to pay for!"

"Teddy," Marie whispered, placing her small hand on her husband's. "Please."

"Don't you fucking start with me, woman," he warned, roughly shaking her hand off. "It's your fault the young fella is so—"

"Enough," my father barked, glowering across the table at Joey's father. "I don't know how things work in your house, Lynch, but you're in my house now, and you will keep your tone in check."

Whoa.

Go Dad.

Teddy glowered at my father, but he didn't respond, which proved my point all along, which was that this man was only good for beating on women and children. When faced with someone his own size, he quickly climbed back in his box.

"Dick," I muttered under my breath at the same time as Joey did.

We flicked our gazes to each other.

I squeezed his hand.

He squeezed mine back.

"Okay, you two," Dad said then, addressing us both. "Take a seat. We have a lot to discuss."

"I want him out," I stated, ignoring everyone except my dad. "Put him out." I pointed to where my brother was perched at the table, next to Joey's mam, looking like he had every right to be involved in this conversation. "This has nothing to do with him."

Kev opened his mouth to protest, but Mam quickly cut him off. "Go upstairs, Kevin."

"That's not fair."

"You either go upstairs, or you go out," Dad snapped, turning to glare at my brother. "Either way, you're not staying in this kitchen."

"This is bullshit," my brother grumbled, and then turned to me for help. "Aoife, come on, you know I didn't mean for any of this to come out the way it has."

Yes, he did.

The only remorse Kev felt was for the fact that he now found himself on the sour end of our parents' good graces.

Bristling like a caged tiger beside me, I watched as Joey's gaze flicked to my brother, and I could feel his temper rising. Joey never said a word, but the look he gave my brother had Kev quickly rising from the table, with none of his earlier bravery.

Refusing to step aside for my brother to pass easily, Joey remained in the doorway, forcing Kev to turn sideways to pass him. With his face crimson, and his shoulders bunched tight, my brother squeezed past my boyfriend, keeping his gaze trained down at the floor to avoid the death glower he was receiving.

Ha-fucking-ha, I mentally cheered, *go upstairs and change your boxers, you little shit.*

Only when my brother was gone, and the kitchen door was closed, did I move for the table, stopping mid-stride when the boy who had a firm hold of my hand refused to move.

I knew why of course.

He didn't want me anywhere near his father.

Neither did I, but I wasn't going to cower from a creep like him.

I would *never* back down to this man.

Because he didn't beat me that night and he never would.

This was a battle of wills and he would *never* win.

Never.

Call it pluckiness, or just plain pig-headedness, but I refused to give that man a second more of air-time in my thoughts. Teddy Lynch was *irrelevant* to me, and by standing there facing him, I was letting him know that.

Fighting with him would give him exactly what he wanted.

He was a bully, and bullies fattened on fear, tears, and pain.

Rising above him was a form of defiance that was alien to him, and, whether Joey realized it or not, we could hurt his father a lot more by showing a united front.

Giving his hand a hard tug, I tried again, and this time, Joey relented. He followed me over to the table, where we sat opposite his parents, with my mother and father heading and footing both ends of the table.

"I'm not happy about this," my father came right out and said, breaking the horrible strained silence. "I'm devastated, if truth be told, but the horse has left the barn, so shouting and roaring about it won't change anything."

His words hit hard and I flinched. "Dad."

"I'm sorry, Tony," Joey interrupted me and said, addressing my father. "I fucked up."

"Understatement of the century," Teddy sneered. "Bright spark."

I could feel Joey's knee bopping restlessly against mine, as he thrummed with barely restrained anger. Reaching under the table, I hooked my foot around his and pulled his big, knuckle-torn hand onto my lap, holding onto it with both of mine. Jaw-ticking, my boyfriend did exactly what I asked him to do and ignored his father, focusing on mine instead.

"I fucked up," Joey repeated, tone thick with emotion, eyes locked on my father, while ignoring the muttered rantings coming from his own. "I let you down, and I let your wife down, but I won't let your daughter down." Knees bopping restlessly, he swallowed deeply and said, "I won't let your grandchild down."

"Joey, lad." My father's eyes flashed with emotion. "I'm not—"

"The road to hell is paved with good intentions," Teddy interjected, sounding entirely unaffected by the sincerity in his son's voice. "Talk is cheap. It's grand saying you'll be there now, but you haven't a notion of what's coming down the line, boy."

"I won't leave her," Joey continued, ignoring his father. "I'll be here. For all of it. I won't run, Tony."

"I didn't run either," his father reminded him. "I stayed for all of it, too, boy, and look where it got me."

"I'm not *him*," Joey strangled out, as a vein bulged in his neck from the force it was taking him to not respond to his father's goading. Turning to my mother, he shrugged his shoulders almost helplessly, clearly willing her to believe him, "I'm not him, Trish."

"I know, pet," I heard my mother whisper.

"This isn't a wham-bam relationship," I decided to interject, desperate to take the heat off Joey, and shoulder some of this pressure. "Joey's my best friend." I looked around the table, imploring our parents to hear me. "We've known each other since we were twelve. So, when he says that he'll there for me, I believe him and all of you should too. Because his word is good."

Surprised by my words, my boyfriend turned to look at me, green eyes burning with unspoken emotion. It was almost like it hurt him to hear someone speak kindly of him. It was foreign to him, and it broke my heart.

"He's the best person I know," I added, keeping my eyes locked on his as I spoke. "And I trust him with my life."

"Then you're even thicker than my wife," Teddy dismissed with a shake of his head. "Because that young fella of mine is a walking disaster." Looking to my father he said, "You know he's off his trolley most of the time, don't ya, Molloy?"

"Teddy," his wife croaked out, pressing her small hand to her brow. "Please."

"Shut up, Marie," Teddy warned. "The man has a right to know what kind of serpent got his young one pregnant." He turned his attention back to my father. "It's no secret that I've battled with the drink for most of my life, but this fucker." He leaned back and whistled. "This fucker takes it to another level."

"The boy is grand with alcohol," I heard my father defend. "And if you're referring to the bit of grass he smokes, then I'll be talking to him about that."

"Grass?" Teddy threw his head back and laughed. "Don't be so fucking naïve, Tony. The lad's a full-blown drug addict."

Both of our mother's gasped, while Joey's shoulders slumped and he bowed his head, still remaining silent, even when his character was being shredded to pieces around us.

"No, he's not," I heard myself defend – I heard myself *lie* – tightening my hold on the hand balled into a fist on my lap. "He made a few mistakes in the past, but that's over and done with."

"I've been in your shoes," his mother said, looking directly across the table at me, with so many unspoken words glistening in her forlorn blue eyes. "I know where this is going, and I think . . . " Pausing, she sucked in a shallow breath and tentatively tucked her dark hair behind her ears before continuing, "I think you should consider a termination."

"So, you're saying if you could go back in time, you would choose the same?" I demanded, furious and unwilling to back down. "You would have aborted Darren?"

"Maybe not Darren, but definitely him," Teddy spat, and if any other father said that to his son, I was sure there would be eruptions, but Joey didn't bat an eyelid at his cruelness.

He was used to it.

He'd heard it a thousand times before.

"Kind of like what your mother should have done to you, Teddy?" I heard myself hiss.

"Aoife!" Mam gasped, tone shocked. "We don't speak to people like that."

"People, no," I agreed. "But he's not people, Mam." I glowered around the table at each one of our parents and said, "It doesn't matter what any of you think. I don't care if you agree with my decision or not. I'm sorry, Dad, but that includes you. Joey and I talked about it, and we're *keeping* our baby."

"Are you sure?" Marie choked out, looking devastated.

"Yes," I narrowed my eyes and growled. "The only thing I've ever been surer of is your son."

"You're making a mistake," Marie sobbed, dropping her head in her hands. "This is a mistake."

"We've all made mistakes," Mam offered, trying to be the voice of reason. "Not one person sitting at this table is perfect, and I, for one, think it's very admirable of our children to stand over—"

"Oh, for Christ's sake, woman, get a grip, will ya?" Teddy snapped, slamming his fist down on the table in annoyance. "There's nothing admirable about two teenagers shacking up to play house. You want a preview of how it goes, take a good fucking look at us."

"Don't raise your voice to my wife," my father warned in a deathly cold tone of voice. "And her name is Trish, not *woman*."

"Well, knock some damn sense into her," Teddy argued, looking at my father like he couldn't understand why he was letting my mother lead the conversation. "Because her head is in the clouds if she thinks this can work."

"Knock some sense into her?" Dad's face reddened. "A bit like—"

"Steady up, Tony, love," Mam interrupted, offering my father a knowing wink from across the table. "We're here for our daughter, remember?"

With a pained sigh, my father offered her a loving nod and unclenched his hands from the rim of the table. "So, you're keeping the baby." He looked to me and Joey for confirmation.

We nodded in unison.

I presumed to my father that we looked like a duo of nodding seals.

Or a couple of deer caught in headlights.

"Fine, I accept this as your decision, and I respect your willingness to go ahead with your plan," he replied after a long pause of silence. "But you both need to be aware that at the end of this pregnancy, there will be a child to care for, and this child will bind you together." Blowing out a heavy breath, he added, "A child is not a relationship that you can walk away from, or a marriage that can be dissolved. This is a lifetime commitment. You'll forever be entwined in one another's lives. That baby will need the both of you for the rest of your lives. Together or apart. The baby will need its mother and father in equal measures."

"Right now, you're both eighteen and in love," Mam offered up. "But you won't always be young, and you might not always be in love either."

"If you are, then fantastic, you have nothing to worry about," Dad chimed in, giving my mother a knowing smile. "But if you fall out of love with each other, if you grow apart, are you sure you're both ready to deal with the consequences?"

"I've loved your daughter for six years," Joey finally broke his silence by saying. "I can easily love her for another eighteen."

Goddamn . . .

My heart skipped in my chest.

He wasn't trying to sound sweet.

He was trying to sound convincing.

Still, I was ready to jump his bones.

"*Love?*" Teddy sneered. "You think *loving* each other is all you need to make this work?"

"It's half the battle," my mother replied in a curt tone.

"It's bullshit," Teddy argued, dismissing her, making it clearer every time he opened his mouth that he did not care for a woman's opinion on anything. "I'll tell ya something, Tony," he continued, looking to Dad instead. "Your wife might have rose-tinted glasses on, but I know deep down you can see this for what it is. A fucking shitstorm. That boy of mine is in no position to raise a baby. He's on a fast-track to nowhere, and if you don't want that young one of yours following after him, then you'll put her on a boat to England and have her cut ties with him."

"She's not going to fucking England!" Joey spat, as he erupted on his father. "And you've got a lot of fucking nerve to sit across this table from me, offering up fatherly advice, and accusing me of not being able to raise a child."

"Joey, son—"

"No, Tony, let me finish, because this needs to be said," Joey argued, holding a hand up to my father, while focusing on Teddy Lynch. "You might have fathered six kids, but you sure as shit didn't raise them."

"Joey," Marie choked out, looking anxious. "Please don't go there."

"And you sure as shit didn't mother us," he snapped, tone laced with accusation, as he glared at his mother. "Darren raised me and Shannon. Not you, and not him. *Darren* raised us – until your husband literally drove him out of the fucking country. And then, all of the raising was left to me. So, don't fucking sit there and pretend that I'm incapable of being a good father to *my* kid when that's *exactly* what I've been doing for *yours* since I was twelve!"

I didn't open my mouth to stop him because these assholes deserved to hear his pain.

They deserved to hear the *truth*.

"I'm not him, and Aoife's not you," Joey continued to tell his mother. "And you can say what you want about me, old man," he added, addressing his father now. "But you don't know a goddamn thing about the kind of person I am."

"I know exactly who you are," his father shot back, unyielding. "You're me twenty-four years ago."

Nothing else he could have said could have hurt Joey more than that comparison, and I felt his hand grow limp in mine, as he leaned back in his chair, looking winded.

"It's not true," I hurried to soothe. "You're *nothing* like him."

And this time, when I said the words, I meant it physically as well as every other way. For a long time, I thought Joey bore an uncanny resemblance to his father, and to anyone not looking closely enough, it was certainly true. But sitting here, looking at both father and son in the clear light of our kitchen, the differences were obvious.

Beefy and paunch-bellied from years of alcohol abuse, even though he wasn't a fat man, he weighed substantially more than his son.

There was a softness to Joey's eyes that his father's eyes were void of. He had his mother's nose, I noted, and her high cheekbones, too. Similar to his sister, he had swollen, puffy lips that they had also clearly inherited from her. And sure, while they were both tall, broad, tanned, and blond, Teddy Lynch had cold, dead, emotionless, brown eyes, while emerald-colored embers of fire burned in his son's eyes.

Joey might have shared his father's height, hair color, golden-rich complexion, and stature, but the two were like fire and ice. He had a lot more of his mother in him than anyone realized.

"Everyone just calm down," my mother interjected, holding her hands up. "We're not here to talk about the past. All of that can be hashed over another day. Right now, we need to talk about this pregnancy, because in a little over five months, our children are going to have a baby, a baby that the four of us will be grandparents to."

"If anyone at this table thinks that I'm going to let him anywhere near my kid, then you're all fucking crazy," Joey bit out, glowering at his parents. "Over my dead body."

"Joey," his mother sobbed, voice cracking. "Please."

"Yeah," I decided to pipe up, for no other reason than to let him know that I had his back in this fight. "What Joe said."

"Aoife," Mam sighed, with a shake of her head. "You're not helping."

I gave her a look that said *so?*

"You think I give a shit?" Teddy laughed cruelly. "I never wanted to see your face, boy. I still don't, so what makes you think that I would want to see anything that came off ya?"

"My heart's bleeding," Joey drawled sarcastically.

"You'll be bleeding alright, when I get my hands on ya."

"Jesus Christ, Teddy," Dad snapped, running his hand through his hair. "That's your boy, you're talking to."

"Everybody needs to calm down," Mam commanded, addressing the whole table. "This doesn't have to get personal."

"You know what, I think it already has," Joey declared, as he shoved his chair back and stood. "I'm sorry, Trish, I am, but I won't sit here and talk about a baby that I have no intention of ever letting these two fuckers taint."

"Who the fuck do you think you're talking to?" Furious, his father stood up, rounded the table and roughly clamped his beefy hand around the back of his neck. "Sit your hole down, boy," he commanded, forcing Joey to sit back down.

Jaw ticking, I watched as my boyfriend kept his hands at his sides, refusing to spill blood in my family home, as he let his father man-handle him.

It was degrading.

It was disgusting.

"Hey!" Unable to stop myself, the urge I had to protect the boy I loved so fiercely, I clawed at the hand he was using to grip his neck. "Get your filthy hands off him."

"Aoife!"

"Don't even look at her," Joey snarled, rising to his feet to block me from his father's view when he opened his mouth to respond.

"Joey," his mother sobbed. "Please . . ."

"I'm done talking to you," Joey told her in a shaky tone. "I'm done *with* you." He turned back to my father and said, "This isn't me walking away from my responsibilities. This is me walking away from a murder charge." Blowing out a frustrated breath, he tenderly tipped my chin up with his knuckles and said, "Are you with me?"

Out of my chair and up on my feet in seconds, I was moving for the door, with my hand firmly entwined with his. "Oh, I am *so* with you."

"Wait right there," Mam called after us. "Don't even think about wandering around town in the dark of night, in your condition. Take Joey up to your room, while we finish up here."

"Upstairs?" Dad muttered. "Really, Trish?"

"What are they going to do, Tony?" Mam sighed. "Get pregnant again? They have to get this one out to put another one in."

"Jesus, don't give them any notions."

"He has some goddamn nerve coming here," Joey bit out, as he paced my bedroom floor. "Sanctimonious bastard thinking he has any right to lecture me on parenthood. Fucker never changed a nappy in his life, and he sure as hell never paid for one, either!"

Over an hour had passed since we came up to my room, leaving our parents downstairs to hash it out, and he was still pacing around like a madman.

"His entire side of the family is the same," he continued to rant, as his hair stood up in forty different directions from the sheer height of pulling on it in frustration. "Assholes, the lot of them."

Clad in his school uniform, and looking entirely too comfortable in my sleeping quarters, Joey stomped around my room like a powerhouse, stopping every few minutes to re-align a crooked poster on my wall, or to fold one of the many items of clothing I had strewn on the floor.

"If you ever met his asshole father and scumbag brothers, you'd know what I'm talking about," he grumbled, folding another pair of my discarded jeans. "And his mother?" He shook his head and shuddered. "Don't even get me started on that fucking demon of a woman."

"Your nanny?" I asked, from my perch on my bed, as I gave my toes a dodgy French pedicure. "I thought she was nice."

"No, no, that's Nanny Murphy," he corrected, bundling a stack of neatly folded clothes into my wardrobe. "She's from my mother's side. Nanny *is* nice. You've met Nanny."

"With the cute perm?"

"Yeah, she's the one who gave me that miraculous medal from Knock to give you for your eighteenth."

"Oh yeah, I *love* Nanny."

"Yeah, we should go see her," he muttered, rubbing his jaw. "Tell her the news ourselves."

"About the baby?"

"Yeah." He nodded. "Nanny's a saint. The witch is my father's mother," he fell back into explaining. "She's a tyrant, Aoif. You've never met anyone as cold as— Hold up. Should you even be using that stuff?" He stopped his rant-induced pacing to swipe up my bottle of nail polish and eye it warily. "Doesn't this shit have chemicals that might be bad for my baby?"

"It will be bad for you if you don't back up from my top coat," I grumbled, reaching up to swipe the bottle back. "Don't get all anal on me, Joe."

"Hey." He held up his hands. "I'm only asking out of concern for the kid."

"Such a law-abider."

He rolled his eyes. "Back to the witch."

"The witch," I mimicked with a snort. "That's a conversation I look forward to listening to you have with our child." Cackling to myself, I feigned his deep voice and said, "Hey, kid, so this is your great-grandmother, the witch, and these are your great-uncles, the scumbags."

"And this is your grandfather, the rapist, alcoholic bastard himself."

Groaning, Joey stopped pacing to bang his forehead against the wardrobe door. "Poor kid is fucked and she isn't even here yet."

"It might be a boy."

"Christ, I hope not."

My heart flipped. "You want a girl?"

"I just don't want anything remotely like me," he replied, and his honesty broke me. "Let it be all you, and I'll be happy."

"I do," I replied. "Want it to be like you, that is."

He paused to glare at me. "Be serious, Molloy."

"What?" I argued back. "You're loyal, you're strong, you're athletic, you're talented, you're beautiful." I shrugged. "Why wouldn't I want our baby to be like you?"

"Because I'm a fuck-up."

I smirked. "Only some of the time."

"Oh, that's alright then," he shot back, tone laced with sarcasm. "If it's just *some* of the time.

"Not to mention the fact that you're *way* smarter than me."

He snorted. "You're crazy."

"You're probably the smartest guy in our year, and if you had been born into any other family, you'd be in the brainiac class with Kev and the other swots."

"I'm barely hanging on in school, Aoif," he ground out, looking flustered. "I'm passing my classes by the skin of my teeth."

"But you're *passing*, which is exactly my point," I reiterated. "Because if Kev, or Paul, or anyone else in our year had to deal with what you do on the daily, then I guarantee you that they would crumble," I replied. "Deny it all you want, but there's one hell of a sharp mind inside that thick skull of yours," I mused, as I coated my baby toe with one final layer of nail varnish before resealing the bottle. "Now." Smiling sweetly up at him, I leaned back on my elbows and wiggled my toes. "Blow."

Joey looked at me like I had grown an extra head. "You are fucking crazy if you think I'm blowing on your toes."

"Come on, Joe," I whined, toes still wiggling. "I'm pregnant."

"So?" he shot back, looking personally insulted.

"I don't want the polish to smudge."

"Then don't smudge it."

"Blow."

"No."

"Blow on my toes."

"Absolutely fucking not."

"Joey Lynch."

"Aoife Molloy."

"You said you'd be there for me."

"As your boyfriend and the father of your baby," he spluttered, throwing his hands up. "Not as your personal fucking groomer."

"There were no stipulations spoken when you made your promises," I argued. "Now come here and blow me."

"That's my line."

"It won't ever be again if you don't do this for me."

"Jesus fucking Christ." Rolling his eyes, Joey sank down on the edge of my bed and pulled my feet onto his lap. "You have an eejit made out of me."

"You're the best," I crooned victoriously. "I lucked out in the baby-daddy stakes."

"Hm," Joey grunted, entirely unimpressed with me, as he blew each one of my toenails dry before unceremoniously dropping my feet back on the bed, and stalking over to my window.

"Wow, good job, Joe," I crooned admiring my toes. "Next time, you can help me paint—"

"Don't push it," he grumbled, shoving the window open and pulling a packet of cigarettes out of his pocket. "I need a smoke." Throwing one leg over the ledge to dangle outside, while keeping the other on my bedroom floor, he sank down on the sill, and sparked up.

"And you had the gall to lecture me on painting my toenails?" I cocked a brow. "You should think about quitting."

"I'm quitting an awful lot of stuff lately. Give me something to cling to, will ya?" came his smart-ass response, as he leaned out my window. "Do you think they're still downstairs with your folks?"

Yes. I shrugged. "I haven't heard the front door slam."

"The hell are they talking about?" he muttered, looking stressed and on edge. "I don't like this, Molloy."

Neither do I. "It'll be okay, Joe."

"You're right." Inhaling a deep drag, he leaned out the window to expel the smoke from his lungs before adding, "It'll be grand. If the kid is as persuasive as his mother and can throw a punch like his father, then we're golden."

I arched a brow. "He?"

"He. She." He waved a hand around aimlessly. "Whatever."

"Do you want to find out?"

"Find out what?"

"The gender."

"Tomorrow?" He turned to frown at me, lips pursed around his cigarette. "Because they can't tell this early, Molloy." He leaned back out the window to exhale another cloud of smoke before adding, "You'll need to wait for the anomaly scan."

"Anomaly scan?" I gaped at him. "What the *hell* is that and why does it sound like it's going to be painful?"

"Jesus, you're all drama," he chuckled, rubbing his jaw. "It's not painful, it's a detailed ultrasound they give you around the twenty-week mark."

"Where?" My eyes widened in fear. "Because I saw this really horrible documentary where this doctor guy put a condom on this giant dildo-shaped camera and literally rammed it up this poor girl's fanny—"

"They scan your *stomach*," he laughed, cutting me off. "Come on, Molloy. You're a girl. How do you not know this stuff?"

"Well, I'm sorry, baby whisperer," I shot back huffily. "We don't all come from families that rival the size of a football team. We're not all acquainted with the harrowing throes of pregnancy."

"Well, you better get acquainted and fast," Joey replied, exhaling another cloud of smoke. "Because it's coming."

"Jesus." A full body shudder rolled through me. "Hey, Joe?"

"Hm?"

"Are you going to still want me when I'm the size of a whale?"

"Molloy." He chuckled under his breath. "For fuck's sake."

"I'm serious."

"I know you are." With a shake of his head, he tossed the cigarette butt away and climbed back inside. "You're not going to be the size of a whale."

"But if I am?"

"You won't be."

"I might be."

"You're having a baby, Molloy, not inhaling a town."

"But say it happens."

"Jesus Christ." He rolled his eyes to the heavens. "Yes, I'm still going to want you."

"How?"

"How?" His brows furrowed in confusion as he closed the space between us. "What do you mean *how*?"

"How are you going to still find me sexy when I'm big and round and swollen?" I gestured to my body and sighed. "Look at me, Joe. Won't you miss this body?"

He threw his head back and laughed.

"Hey – don't laugh at me, asshole." I narrowed my eyes. "I'm feeling vulnerable here."

"You are the vainest girl I've ever met."

"It's not vanity when it's *true*," I sniped. "Then it's just plain honesty."

Still chuckling, he shook his head, clearly amused. "Christ, I love you." Grinning, he flopped down on the mattress beside me and stretched his arm out for me to join him. As soon as I snuggled into the crook of his arm, he pulled me close and released a contented sigh. "Don't ever lose it, Molloy."

"Lose what?"

"That spark of fire that makes you so incredibly *you*," he replied, tightening his arm around me. "It doesn't matter how your body changes, because I'm always going to keep coming back to *you*. Because I might enjoy touching all of this," he explained, fingers trailing over my body until he reached my face and gently tapped my temple. "But I'm hooked on *this*."

"My mind?" I asked, tone incredulous. "Bullshit."

"It's true," he coaxed. "Nobody else can fuck with my head quite like you can, and that has nothing to do with your body, Molloy."

"Okay," I conceded with a lopsided grin. Twisting onto my side, I slid my hand under his shirt to rest on the bare skin of his stomach. "That was ridiculously smooth."

"I'm known to have my moments," he laughed, rolling onto his side, mirroring me. "When I'm not fucking up."

"We're going to be okay, aren't we, Joe?" I heard myself ask.

"Aren't we always?"

"I'm serious." I reached up to stroke his cheek. "Everything is moving way too fast."

"Yeah." He grimaced. "Shit has a habit of going that way when I'm around."

"Seriously, Joe, my head is spinning from all of the twists and turns."

"I have no idea how all of this is going to pan out," he admitted truthfully. "But whatever way it goes, I've got your back."

"And I've got yours."

"Then we'll be okay," he replied with a small nod.

"Yeah?" I breathed, watching him closely.

His green eyes burned with sincerity when he whispered, "Yeah."

A knock on my bedroom door sounded then, and I watched as Joey's entire frame stiffened before he reluctantly slid his arm out from beneath me and sat on the edge of my bed.

"Come in," I croaked out, really not wanting anything or anyone from the outside world to come into this room and burst our bubble.

I only wanted to be with him.

All alone.

Just us.

"Joey's parents are gone," Mam announced when she walked into my room, gaze sweeping over us both, no doubt to see if we were *behaving* ourselves. "Are you alright?"

"You shouldn't have done that, Mam," I heard myself say, sitting upright now. "Brought them over here? Ambushing us like that?"

"I didn't," Mam was quick to correct, gaze flicking between us. "Your father wanted to talk to Joey's father."

"Yeah, well, I'm sure you've realized by now that there's no talking to him," Joey replied with a sigh. "He only hears what he wants, Trish."

"Yes," Mam agreed sadly. "Listen, Joey, if we've made it worse for you at home . . ."

"It's grand," my boyfriend was quick to dismiss. "I understand why ye had to talk to my parents. I get it." Standing up, he moved to where his bag was resting against my wardrobe and quickly bundled his uniform inside. "I meant what I said," he added, zipping it closed and hoisting it onto his back. "I'm not him, Trish."

"I know you're not, pet," Mam was quick to soothe.

Nodding stiffly, Joey flicked his gaze to me. "I better go."

My heart sank.

"You could stay?" I looked to my mother hopefully. "He could stay the night, couldn't he, Mam?"

Mam worried her lip. "Well, yes . . ."

"No, I need to go home," Joey cut in, slipping his arms through the straps of his school bag. "What time is the scan tomorrow?"

"Half past one."

"We finish school at twelve, so we can go straight to the appointment from there." Retracing the steps back to my bed, he leaned down and brushed a kiss to my cheek. "I'll see ya in the morning."

"You can stay," I pleaded, reaching up to grab his hand.

Giving my hand a small squeeze, he winked down at me before letting go. "I'll see you tomorrow, okay?" he called over his shoulder, as he moved for my door.

"I don't know the ins and outs of what happens in your home," my mother blurted out, causing my boyfriend to freeze in my bedroom doorway. "But I've heard enough stories and seen enough bruises on your body to know that it has to stop."

"Mam!"

"You should know that I've phoned the Gards and reported your father."

"Mam," I strangled out, dropping my head in my hands. "What the hell?"

"And you should probably know that this isn't the first time that I've reported him, either, but I've never had enough proof."

"Oh my god, Mam."

"But tonight, he threatened to harm you in front of me," she continued to say, eyes locked on my boyfriend. "And while it might not be my business, I refuse to sit back and do nothing."

"Jesus, Mam," I croaked out, feeling my heart hammer violently, as I waited for him to erupt.

"I presume they'll pay a visit to your house before the night's out," Mam added, looking red-faced. "I'm sorry, love, I really am, but I couldn't have it on my conscience."

"It's grand, Trish," was all Joey replied, not turning back to look at either one of us. "I understand."

"You can stay," she repeated, tone thick with emotion. "There's always room for you in this house."

"Thanks." With a heavy sigh, he shook his head in resignation and said, "But I have to go home," before walking away.

Light footsteps sounded on the staircase then, followed a few moments later by the sound of the front door opening and closing shut.

I shook my head and glared at my mother. "What have you done, Mam?"

"What's right, Aoife," my mother replied. "I've done what's right."

Just this once

JOEY

By the time I reached the end of my road, the squad car was pulling away from my house. Knowing that the Gards in this town didn't need much of a reason to throw me in the cells these days, I slipped into a side alley until they drove past.

When they were gone, I flicked the butt of my cigarette behind me, and jogged up the footpath to my house, needing another arrest under my belt like I needed a hole in the head.

Because that's what would happen.

It didn't matter what Trish Molloy told the Gards.

My father wouldn't be punished for a damn thing.

He never was.

The blame would fall at my feet.

Same as always.

When I walked through the front door a few minutes later, I was greeted by my father's fist as it connected with my jaw.

"Jesus." Unprepared and taken aback by the unsuspected assault, I stumbled backwards and landed on my ass in the hallway, feeling a lightning bolt of pain ripple through my face. "Christ."

"You dumb cunt," he sneered, towering above me. "Running your mouth to those people. Telling them our private business. Running to your girlfriend's mammy with sob stories. What did ya think was going to happen?"

I wanted to get up and fight back, I really fucking did, but the pain shooting out of my cheekbone was so severe, it made my stomach heave.

Twisting onto my hands and knees, I hurled my guts up on the floor, unable to mask my agony, as fire burned through my face. "Fuck ... you."

His boot connected with my stomach next, taking the wind clean out of my lungs. "If you don't want to be under my roof, boy, you know where the door is. Nobody's stopping ya from leaving if ya don't want to be here."

"Teddy, no." That was Mam. I could hear her pleading with him to stop kicking me. He didn't stop. Not until he had a good half a dozen more kicks in. "Please, stop. He's only a boy."

"Pack his fucking bags, Marie," my father commanded, while I lay in a heap on the floor, trying to breathe through the pain. "I want this little prick out!"

I knew that I needed to get back up, but I just didn't have anything left in the tank.

Still, that fire of prideful self-sabotage continued to burn bright inside of me, demanding that I get back up on my feet and not lie down to this man until my heart gave out.

"You think you're ready to be a father?" he roared, and I could hear him unbuckling his belt. It was a sound that I was all too familiar with. "Right you are, ya little bollox. Lesson number one on being a father? Knowing when to put your little bastards back in line."

A pained grunt escaped me when the whip of leather came down on my back.

"Teddy, no!"

The belt came down on my back again.

Harder this time.

"Please, Teddy, don't!"

Shuddering violently, I bit down so hard on my lip that I could taste blood, but I refused to cry out or beg this man for anything.

"Joey!" That was Tadhg.

I could hear him crying somewhere nearby.

Another crack of the belt sliced through my skin and a mouthful of vomit spluttered out through my teeth.

"Get up those stairs to bed or you'll be next!"

The metal buckle sank into to my flesh and I choked back a cry.

Shaking violently, I twisted onto my side, and covered my head with my hands.

"Daddy, no, don't hurt him!" Ollie's voice infiltrated my ears.

"I'm . . . f-f-fine," I tried to tell them, nostrils flaring, as I forced myself to breathe through the pain. "Go t-to b-bed."

I couldn't tell you how many times he swung that belt down on my body, but I must have passed out from the pain, because when I finally came to, everything was quiet, and my father was gone.

Numb to the bone, I remained exactly where I was, too fucking broken to lift a finger, while I took stock of the night's events.

Finally, when I couldn't take the cold creeping into my bones a second longer, I forced myself to sit up, hissing out a sharp breath when my back burned in protest.

"Joey." Falling off the bottom step of the stairs where she had been sitting, Mam crawled towards me. "Oh, Joey."

Too weary to fend her off, I let her cup my face in her small hands and pepper kisses to my cheek, while using her sleeve to clean my face. "I'm sorry, baby. I'm so sorry. He's gone out. He left."

"Can I have a cigarette?"

Her brows furrowed as her eyes continued to spill giant teardrops. "A cigarette?"

I nodded slowly. "I'm out."

Pain filled her eyes and she shook her head before choking out a sob and nodding. "I'll get you a cigarette."

"Thanks."

Scrambling to her feet, she hurried into the kitchen, returning a moment later with a packet of twenty Rothmans and a lighter.

Trembling, she slowly withdrew a cigarette from the packet and put it to my lips before igniting a small flame on her lighter.

I leaned towards the flame and sparked up before sucking in a deep drag.

"Are you okay?"

I shook my head.

"Is anything broken?"

Probably. I inhaled another deep drag before asking, "Where are the boys?"

"In bed." Her hands were on my shoulders now, moving over my skin, as she checked the damage.

"Where's Shan?"

"Bed. She has headphones on."

"Thank fuck."

When she raised the hem of my school shirt, she choked out a pained sob. "We need to get you cleaned up. Can you stand up for me?"

With slow, calculated, rigid movements, I forced myself to get back on my feet and follow her into the kitchen.

"Take your shirt off," she instructed, moving for the kettle. "I need to wash those cuts before they get infected."

Jesus.

I didn't even want to see what my back looked like.

Balancing my cigarette between my lips, I fumbled with the buttons of my shirt before gingerly sliding it off my shoulders, grimacing when my eyes took in the streaks of blood splattered on the fabric. "Is it bad?"

Mam sucked in another sharp breath.

Yeah, it's bad.

"Here," she said, handing me a bag of frozen veg wrapped in a tea-towel. "Press that to your cheek. It'll help with the swelling."

"I'm going to need a new shirt for school," I muttered, reaching for my smoke. "Fucker ruined this one."

"There's a spare shirt in the hot-press." Her hands were on my back then, pressing a wet cloth over my burning flesh. "Just stay still and let me clean this."

"Am I still bleeding?"

"A bit."

"Do I need stiches?"

"I don't think so. Not this time."

Shaking my head, I took another drag of my cigarette, while my mother cleaned me up. "If he wants me out, I'll go."

"I don't want you out."

"But I'm not leaving Shan or the boys here," I continued, ignoring her words. "If I go, they go with me."

"Joey."

"I mean it."

"Nobody's going anywhere."

That was the problem. "I know you agree with him."

"Agree with him about what?"

"About Aoife."

Her hands stilled on my back. "I don't want this life for you."

"Yeah, and I don't want this life for *you*."

Mam sighed wearily. "Joey."

"I'm going to stand by her, Mam. She's my girlfriend, and believe it or not, I happen to love her a lot." Repressing a shudder when her fingers probed a particularly tender part of my back, I bit out, "I'll stand by her and I'll do a hell of a lot better job than he did with you."

"Aren't you frightened?"

I'm terrified.

"I'm frightened for you," she said when I didn't answer. "I wish it wasn't happening."

"Well, it is."

"I wish you both would reconsider getting a—"

"Stop," I cut her off and warned. "That's not what Aoife wants."

"And what about what you want, Joey?"

"I want her to be okay."

"That's not an answer."

"Yeah, well." I shrugged and tossed the bag of frozen veg on the counter, before turning to face her, grimacing when my eyes landed on the blood-stained towel in her hands. "It's all I have."

"I need you to keep your head down for a few days," she whispered then, eyes full of guilt. "Just stay out of his way until he calms down. Don't tell the boys about Aoife. Don't tell Shannon. Just . . . just give me some time to work on your father, okay?"

"Are you serious?"

"Joey, it's complicated."

This time when she reached for me, I took a step backwards. "It's always going to be him. You're always going to choose *him*."

"I'm not choosing him. I'm trying to keep my family together." She took another step towards me and I took three more away from her. "Joey, please."

"Got anything for the pain?" I asked, unwilling to continue a conversation that would end with me being blamed for everything. "My face is killing me."

"There's paracetamol in the cupboard."

"Mam."

"No, Joey."

"I'm asking ya to help me," I bit out, feeling the desperate hunger for relief steadily clawing its way up my throat. "Please, Mam."

"Joey."

"*Please*," I ground out. "I'm in pain."

"I told you that I have paracetamol in the cupboard."

"*Please*," I choked out, resisting the urge to scream *fuck your paracetamol*. "Just this once and I'll never ask again."

"Joey."

"I'll beg if I have to."

"Don't beg."

"Please, Mam. Fucking *please*."

"Fine." Tears filled her eyes. "Just this once."

"What do you have?"

She sniffled before whispering, "Clonazepam."

Thank fuck. I sagged in relief. "Where?"

Her face contorted in pain and she whimpered, "My handbag," before walking over to the table and retrieving her bag that was hanging off the back of her chair. "You can have one and that's it."

"I need more than one, Mam," I replied, trailing after her. "Please. One won't do shit for me."

"These are very strong." Sniffling, she unscrewed the cap on her prescription bottle and tipped two C2s into my outstretched hand. "Don't ever ask me to do this again."

"I won't," I replied, even though we both knew it was a lie.

My heart is inside her

AOIFE

"Well, you sure know how to make a splash," Podge said on Friday morning, when he joined me at our usual lunch table in the canteen for small break. "The whole place is talking about you, Aoif."

Yes, the entire student body at BCS *was* talking about me.

Some of the bolder ones were even talking *to* me, asking me for answers to questions that were nobody's business.

Hell, even one of the substitute teachers asked me if it was true.

Worst of all, Joey wasn't here.

He hadn't shown up.

"Is he here yet?" I croaked out, not bothering to acknowledge the obvious. "Was he outside when you went for a smoke at the start of break?"

Grimacing, Podge shook his head. "Not yet. But he'll be here."

I glanced at the clock on the wall, feeling my anxiety swell. "It's ten past eleven, Podge. He's already after missing the first three classes. School ends at twelve. We only have one class left after lunch."

"Something must have come up at home." My boyfriend's best friend offered me another uncomfortable shrug. "Listen, I know it looks bad, but there's no way Lynchy would leave ya to deal with the mob on your own unless it wasn't important."

"Yeah." Feeling sick to my stomach, I drummed my fingers on the desk, and fought back the urge to scream. "That's what I'm worried about."

Because I had enough faith in my boyfriend to know that he wouldn't skip out on me. Joey was a lot of things but he was no coward. Never in his life had he backed down from responsibility, which only caused the anxiety festering inside of me to swell.

Mam had called the Gards last night and reported Teddy. It didn't take a genius to know that his absence at school was linked to it.

"That's her," a group of baby first years whispered, as they hurried past our table, huddled close together. "The pregnant sixth year."

"Is the guy she's sitting with the father?"

"I heard she doesn't know who the father is."

Damn Miss Lane for giving Casey lunchtime detention. It wasn't so bad when she was with me during class. She had a mouth like a sailor and an answer for every eejit stupid enough to approach me in the hallway. That mouth had landed her in detention, though, which meant that I was alone and bleeding in the shark tank.

I was grateful to Podge for coming to sit with me. Every other one of my so-called friends were treating me like pregnancy was contagious. Aside from Casey, it was the boys in my class who were being kind.

The girls were *awful*.

I hadn't been summoned to the office for the dreaded talk yet, but I knew there was only time in it before the rumors of my wayward ways reached our principal's ears.

"How'd Lynchy take the news?" Podge asked, dragging me back to the present. "I tried to call him a few times, but he didn't answer."

"Better than could be expected." I blew out a shaky breath. "Especially after how he found out."

"Shitty behavior out of your brother," he offered. "Telling Ricey before Lynchy knew. Jesus, that's low."

"Don't," I groaned, still feeling sick at the thought. "I'm so done with Kev."

"So, what's the plan?"

I blinked. "The plan?"

"Yeah." Podge nodded. "Are you going to have it?"

"Yes," I bit out, feeling oddly defensive. "Obviously."

"Good for you." Nodding to himself, Podge scooped up a spoonful of yoghurt and popped it into his mouth. "He'll do right by ya."

"Yeah," I whispered. "I know he will. It's just . . . It's just a huge mess, you know?"

"I don't want to even think about it."

"I don't blame you."

"Listen." Reaching across the lunch table, he pressed a hand on my shoulder and gave me a supportive squeeze. "You're not the first to have a baby off a lad in school, Aoif," he offered. "And you sure as shit won't be the last. Just ignore them. You'll be old news soon enough."

"Yeah, Podge, thanks and all," I mumbled, feeling my cheeks burn from the intense stares I was receiving. "But somehow I doubt this is going away any time soon."

"Hey, sexy-legs, I slapped the shit out of your brother just now," Alec declared, sinking down on the table in front of us. "Hope ya don't mind."

My eyes widened. "You did?"

"Of course." He winked. "Lynchy's on his last warning, so he couldn't do it. And I couldn't have Brains doing my favorite girl dirty like that."

"Where is he now?"

"Who? Brains?" Alec shrugged. "On the phone to your mammy, I suspect."

"Aw, Al . . . " I couldn't stop the smile from spreading across my face, thrilled that little shit got put in his place. "Thanks, buddy."

"Anytime," he replied with a grin. "And just so you know, even with a big belly on ya, you'll still be completely rideable."

"Smooth, Al," Podge chuckled. "What every girl wants to hear."

"I call dibs on godfather," Alec chimed in.

"You can't call dibs on godfather, asshole."

"I just did."

"Well, it doesn't count," Podge huffed. "If anyone's going to be god-father, it's going to be me."

"Nope, see, sexy-legs is going to give devil-tits the nod as godmother, which gives Lynchy free rein over who his spawn's godfather will be."

"Yeah, because referencing our best friend's unborn child as spawn is something a godfather would say."

"Listen, ginger-pubes, it's happening, so back the fuck off and don't even think about trying to steal my thunder on this."

Podge shrugged. "Yeah, well, I'd rather have ginger pubes than a crab infested cock."

Alec gasped. "I don't have crabs."

"Anymore."

"I *never* had crabs." He narrowed his eyes. "I was scratching because I shaved my balls and the itch was fucking horrendous!"

I laughed. "You shaved your balls, Al?"

"Oh yeah, Al here is big on the man-scaping," Podge chimed in, as the bell sounded around us, signaling the end of small break.

"What can I say?" Alec jumped up and offered me a lopsided grin. "I'm a gentleman."

"Do you want to walk with us, Aoif?" Podge asked, rising to his feet. "We're all in Irish with Dineen next."

"I'll catch up with you guys," I said, waving them both off. "I need to pee."

"Keep that head up, sexy-legs," Alec called over his shoulder as he sauntered out of the canteen with Podge. "And keep those legs closed until my god-child is fully cooked."

"Thanks, Al." I sighed heavily, ignoring the gawks and stares I was receiving. "Thanks a lot, buddy."

I was in coming out of the bathroom, on my way to Irish, when my brother stopped me in the hallway. "We need to talk."

Dutifully ignoring him, I sidestepped him and kept walking.

"Aoife, stop." He caught ahold of my arm and pulled me back to him. "Please. We need to talk about this."

"What's wrong, Kev?" I snapped, begrudgingly falling into step alongside him as we walked down the corridor towards my classroom. "Are you blaming me for your busted lip, too?"

"Your boyfriend's henchman hit me."

"Yeah, well, snitches get stiches, asshole."

"I'm sorry, okay?" Holding his hands up in front of me, my brother tried to reason with a part of my heart that wasn't there anymore. Not for him, at least. "I know what I did was shitty, okay? It was a really bad thing to do, Aoif. I get that now."

"Too little, too late."

"Aoife, please?" He sighed heavily. "Come on."

"No. You've heard what people are saying about me," I replied flatly, stopping outside of my classroom door. "You've seen how they've been treating me. You cultivated that, Kev. You orchestrated this whole damn thing. So, shove your apology up your ass, because it doesn't fix anything for me."

"What you said yesterday about Joey? You were right," he admitted, scrubbing his jaw with his hand. "I *don't* like him. He *does* threaten me. I *did* do it to hurt him."

He wasn't telling me anything I didn't already know.

"But I didn't take into account what my actions would do to you," he added, sounding genuinely remorseful. "I didn't *think*, period."

"What you did can't be fixed with an apology," I replied, unwilling to bend. "You can't detonate a bomb on someone's life and then say oops when everything is blown to hell."

"How's the uncle-to-be?" Paul said, when he stepped out of our classroom. Slinging an arm around my brother's shoulder, he smiled cruelly at me, while addressing my brother. "Alright, Kev?"

Looking embarrassed, my brother shrugged awkwardly before muttering, "Alright, Ricey?"

"Oh, bog off, Paul," I growled, just about done with his bullshit. "I'm trying to have a private conversation with my brother."

"Private?" He sneered at me like I was a piece of shit on his shoe. "There's not a whole pile private about you, now is there, Aoife?"

Glaring up at him, I gave him the finger. "Screw you."

"I told you that he'd ruin you," he pushed cruelly. "And now look at the state you're in." His gaze trailed over me, lingering on my stomach before he shook his head. "You're already getting fat."

"Ricey," my brother tried to defend. "Leave her alone." It was a pitiful attempt, and once put under the pressure of Paul's stare, he crumbled, shoulders slumping.

"What do you care, lad?" Paul laughed. "You said it yourself; your sister's a fucking slut."

I cast a glare to my brother, who had the good grace to bow his head in shame.

"You think I care about your opinion, Paul?" I shot back, determined to defend myself against this asshole's taunting. "The best thing I ever did was get away from you."

"No, that was the best thing you ever did for *me*," he sneered. "It was the worst thing you ever did for yourself, because now all you'll ever be is the mother of that junkie scumbag's little bastard."

"Say it again."

The breath left my body in a dizzy rush when a familiar menacing voice filled my ears.

My shoulders sagged and I honestly felt like I was about to collapse from the surge of relief that rocketed through my body.

"Say it again, asshole," Joey repeated, coming up to stand behind me.

Tossing his hurley and helmet on the floor, he let his schoolbag fall off his shoulder, and hooked one strong arm around my waist before backing me up against his hard chest. "I dare ya."

Shivering when his hand smoothed over the small swell of my stomach, I felt like crying when his thumb gently moved up and down.

"This is the part where you run," I told my asshole ex. "Fast."

My brother opened his mouth to speak, but Joey got there first. "You should listen to your sister."

It was almost comical how quickly both boys took off, bolting off in opposite directions.

"Yeah, you *should* run," I called after my brother, thoroughly enjoying his discomfort, as I leaned against my boyfriend's chest. "You little bitch."

"I'm so fucking sorry I'm late," Joey muttered when they were out of earshot. "I overslept."

"I'm just glad you're here," I replied, turning in his arms. "I didn't think you were going to show – what the *hell* happened to your face?"

My mouth fell open and I gaped at the horrific bruising and swelling on the left side of his face.

"Jesus Christ, Joe." I reached up to touch him. "Your cheek."

"Yeah, I think it's broken," he muttered, gently batting my hand away, as he reached for his bag and hurley. "Don't touch it, okay? It's tender as fuck."

"Broken?" I swallowed the lump in my throat as my heart cracked clean open.

He took another beating from his father.

Another broken bone.

Another chip of his heart that would never be pieced back together.

"He did this to you." My voice cracked. "Because of me? Because of the baby?"

"No, not because of the baby," he replied in a soft tone. "Because he's a prick." He opened the classroom door and gestured to me to go first. "This isn't on you."

"And what time do you call this?" Mr. Dineen demanded when we walked into class.

"Sorry we're late, sir," I declared before the teacher could go in on my boyfriend like he usually would. "We're having a bit of a crisis."

"A crisis?"

"Morning sickness," some asshole fake-coughed from the back of the class, evoking a chorus of wolf-whistles and ooohs.

"Right, well, I'll let you off just this once," our teacher replied, cheeks reddening, as he gestured for us to take our seats.

Hurrying to the back of the class, I took my seat in the back row and watched as Joey waited at Mr. Dineen's desk for him to sign his red book.

On his way back to our desk, his movements were stiff and rigid and I knew all too well that the marks on his face weren't the only ones his father put on his body.

My heart cracked at the thought.

"Joe," I whispered, when he carefully lowered himself onto the seat beside mine.

"It's all good, Molloy." He tossed his hurley and helmet on floor at his feet, before turning to give me his full attention. "I'm fine." His green eyes were warm and full of affection when he leaned in close and whispered, "How are you feeling?"

"I'm fine."

"Yeah?" He slipped his hand under the desk and squeezed my thigh. "Well, you look good, baby."

How he could be so good to me, so considerate and caring of my feelings, when he was going through hell, was beyond me.

"I love you," I whispered, covering his hand with mine. "So much."

"I know." Blowing out a pained breath, he entwined his fingers with mine. "I know, Molloy."

"It's bad enough that you're both late to my class, but you have the nerve to have a full-blown conversation," Mr. Dineen barked, glowering at us. "Joseph, would you care to tell the class what you two are whispering about? In your native tongue, if you will, since I have spent the past six years attempting to teach you the language."

"Ceart go leor, a mhúinteoir," my boyfriend replied with a nonchalant shrug as he replied in As Gaeilge. "Bhí mé ag rá le mo leannán go bhfuil grá agam di."

My heart slammed wildly in my chest as I mentally translated his words.

Fair enough, teacher. I was telling my sweetheart that I love her.

"Dúirt mé léi freisin go bhfuil cuma álainn uirthi," Joey continued to say, not missing a beat. *I also told her that she looks beautiful.* Shrugging, he added, "Agus go bhfuil mo chroí istigh inti." *And that my heart is inside her.*

"Go hiontach," Mr. Dineen replied, arching a brow. *Impressive.* "Le haghaidh buachaill nach n-éisteann sa rang." *For a boy who doesn't listen in class.*

"Sea." Joey smirked. "Tá a fhios agam." *Yeah, I know.*

Plead the fifth

JOEY

We had barely warmed our seats in Irish when the bell of the intercom sounded. The school secretary's voice pierced through every speaker in the school saying, "Could Joseph Lynch and Aoife Molloy please report to the principal's office immediately."

"Can they expel him for knocking her up?" Alec asked from the desk beside ours, and if it wasn't for the fact that he was genuinely serious, I would have decked him. "Because we have a match coming up and we're bolloxed without him."

"Don't think so, Al," Podge chuckled beside him. "But you never know."

Gathering my books, I tossed them into my bag and stood up, ignoring the *ooohs* and *oh shits* coming from our fellow classmates.

Walking over to the classroom door, I yanked it open and waited for my partner in crime to hurry her ass up and join me.

"Good luck," Alec called out, giving me two enthusiastic thumbs up, when Molloy joined me in the doorway. "Plead the fifth."

"What do you think Mr. Nyhan's going to say?" Molloy asked, reaching for my hand, as she fell into step beside me. "Is he even allowed to bring it up to us?"

"How the fuck am I supposed to know?"

"Well, you're the one who spends most of his time in the office."

"Only because you're too sneaky to get caught."

"Well, I've clearly been caught this time."

"Funny."

"What if he shouts at me, Joe?"

"If he shouts at you, I'll break his nose."

"Don't break his nose," she hurried to say. "I need you to not get expelled, okay? Or arrested. Yeah, I'm going to need you to *not* do both of those things."

"Fine. I'll try my best."

"Oh god, I feel sick," she groaned when we reached the familiar frosted glass door of the office. "Can we just sneak out and leave early?"

"No." Shaking my head, I pushed the door open and had to physically lift her inside. "Come on, Molloy. Let's just get it over with."

"Your mothers are in the office with Mr. Nyhan. You can go straight in," Betty announced, not looking up from her computer, as she tapped furiously on the keyboard in front of her. "Good luck."

"Whose mother?"

"Both of your mothers."

"My mam's in there?" I glared at the secretary, who I was on a first name basis with. "Why?"

"Why don't you go on in there and find out, Joseph," old Betty shot back, not missing a beat. "You know which door it is."

Yeah, I did.

Third on the right.

"Good luck, Joe," Molloy whispered, giving my hand a small squeeze. "Love you."

"Yeah." I blew out a breath and held the office door open for her. "Right back at ya, Molloy."

Beyond uncomfortable, I sat at one side of the meeting table next to my mother, while Molloy and Trish sat opposite us.

On either end of the table sat Miss Lane, our year head, and Mr. Nyhan, our principal, who were doing a fantastic job of talking *at* us rather than *to* us.

It wasn't like Molloy and I were the ones immediately impacted by the pregnancy or anything. Oh no, it was far more pertinent to address our mothers when making decisions on our futures.

Dicks.

Unable to put any amount of pressure on my back, I leaned forward instead, resting one elbow on the table, while dropping my free hand on my lap.

When our principal asked Mam a question, and she turned to give him her full attention. I took the opportunity to discreetly drop the hand I was resting on my lap into her handbag that was sitting on the floor between our chairs. Barely breathing, I rummaged around inside until my fingers probed the familiar circular pill bottle.

Closing my hand around it, I quickly slipped it into my pocket, feeling a rush of relief fill my body at the prospect of not having to face into another night of hell at home.

Zoning their voices out, and the unsettling urge I had to escape to the bathroom and pop a few C2s, I concentrated all of my attention on my girlfriend, who was nervously chewing on the nail on her baby finger, while her wide-eyed gaze flicked between the four adults in the room.

"By which time you'll be how far along in your pregnancy, Aoife?"

Molloy's guilt-ridden eyes snapped to Mr. Nyhan. "Hm?"

Immediately my back was up.

She didn't need to feel guilty about a damn thing.

This was on me.

"How far along in your pregnancy will you be when you sit the leaving cert in June?"

"Oh." Her cheeks flamed and she roughly cleared her throat before casting a nervous glance in my direction. "What date in June?"

"The seventh."

"Oh." Another deep swallow. "I think I'll be twenty-five weeks by then?"

"You think?"

"Yeah, uh, well, you see, I don't know for sure."

"You don't know for sure?"

"Well, I haven't had my dating scan yet," she hurried to explain. "It's today, actually."

"Why are you pushing her on this?" I snapped, irritated that he was interrogating her. "She already answered you. Give it a fucking rest, will ya? Jesus."

"Joey," Mam snapped, nudging me with her elbow while Molloy gave me a grateful smile.

Choosing to ignore my outburst, which, to be honest, I was mildly disappointed about, Mr. Nyhan turned his attention to Mam. "I know you and Teddy have your hands full with this one, Marie, and I hate to bring it up during such testing times, but I have to ask about Shannon. I sincerely hope that she is settling in well at Tommen."

"She's doing very well there, thank you," Mam replied quietly. "And as for my son, he's doing a lot better at school since Christmas."

"Yes, well." Not bothering to finish his sentence, he turned back to Trish. "Please know that while here at Ballylaggin Community School, we strongly discourage student relationships, we will not turn your daughter away in her hour of need."

"Turn me away?" Molloy choked out, brows furrowing. "What does that mean?"

"Her hour of need?" I chimed in, shaking my head. "What in the hell kind of statement is that to make?"

"Joey," Mam snapped again. "Enough."

"She's not riding into school on a donkey, looking for shelter," I growled. "She's looking for an education, not gold, frankincense, and myrrh."

Mam dropped her head in her hands and sighed wearily. "Oh, Joey."

"There's a lot to be taken into account here, Joseph," Miss Lane interjected in a haughty tone. "First and foremost, there's the matter of whether or not the school's insurance covers having a pregnant student on school grounds."

"What are you saying?" Aoife croaked out, paling. "Insurance not covering me?" She looked to her mother. "Am I being expelled?"

"You are *not* kicking her out of school," I snarled, sitting straight up. "This isn't the nineteen fucking fifties. There's no goddamn way that I'm going to allow you to shun her like she's some sort of scarlet woman. If anything, I'm the scarlet fucking man."

"Joey."

"Seriously. I'm as pregnant as she is."

"Joseph, please."

"What?" I demanded. "It's true. I'm the father. I put that baby in her. If you want to lay blame, lay it at my door, not hers. She has just over two months of school left, and she's finishing it out. Over my dead body are you taking that away from her."

"Joey, calm down. Aoife, just breathe. Nobody is kicking anyone out," Trish tried to soothe, eyes locked on Mr. Nyhan. "It's discrimination, not to mention completely against the law, to exclude a student from attending school on the sole basis of her being pregnant. Isn't that right, Eddie?"

"Well, yes, of course it is," the prick tried to back pedal. "Nobody is suggesting that your daughter be removed from school."

"Just like nobody suggested that Samantha McGuiness be removed from school, or Amy O'Donovan, or Denise Scully. All girls from my terrace," I sneered, giving him a look that said *yeah, asshole, I know how it works*. "If that's the case, then explain to me what her angle is when she says the school's insurance won't cover Aoife being here?"

"I didn't say it wouldn't. I was just saying—"

"You were just trying to intimidate my girlfriend into going quietly, without making a splash for the school," I corrected, cutting her off. "Yeah, I know your game. I didn't come down in the last shower. I know how much easier it is for the school board when pregnant girls disappear from the roll book. Difference is, those girls had to do it alone," I paused to point at Molloy before adding, "Aoife has me, and I have no intention of going quietly."

If I could do nothing else for her, then I could stand in front of her and take the pressure, the disappointment, the pain. I could take the blows for her, and I would.

I sat there, back poker straight, muscles locked tight with tension, and took their disappointment on the chin, knowing that she was in no fit state to take another blow.

"Joey." Mam placed a hand on my bopping knee and squeezed. "Please settle down, will you?"

"Yes," Mr. Nyhan added, giving me a glaring look. "There's no one fighting you on this."

"Only because I made a preemptive strike," I muttered under my breath. "What are we even doing here?" I looked around at their faces. "Aoife's pregnant. I'm the father. She's due *after* we finish school, so I really don't understand the need for this bullshit meeting."

Go to war for you

AOIFE

If I had any doubts about Joey Lynch's willingness to stand by me before this meeting, they were long gone now.

Because, as I sat in the office, listening to my boyfriend go to war for me against our year head and principal, all I could think was '*thank god he's mine*'.

Having my name added to the dreaded list of girls-who-got-pregnant-in-secondary-school was, by far, one of my most shameful moments, but I could feel nothing but pride when it came to *who* I was having this baby with.

Haunted and beautiful, Joey sat across the table from me with his mother by his side, looking like he was seconds away from flipping the table.

Yes, he was brash, and yes, he was cursing like a sailor, but his words meant more to me than any well-rehearsed speech ever could.

Because he was speaking from the heart.

Every word he uttered, he *meant*, and that sentiment soothed something deep inside of me.

Maybe we *were* going to be okay.

Maybe I *could* actually do this.

With him.

The situation I found myself in was beyond terrifying, but unlike the other girls from school that had fallen victim to the same hormone-ridden, nine-month-long affliction, *my* partner is crime was standing by me.

In a weird way, I felt like Rose from *Titanic*, when all of the other girls were drowning, but Jack kept her afloat. While Joey was no angel, he was loyal and accountable, and a better man than anyone in this room gave him credit for.

I felt better just being in his presence.

That's the kind of person he was.

I listened to our mothers talk back and forth with Mr. Nyhan and Miss Lane for another few minutes, talking about restrictions around me taking part in PE and so on, but to be honest, Joey had been dead on the money.

This meeting *was* pointless.

All I had taken away from it was high blood pressure and a dodgy stomach.

"Do you want to go for coffee?" I heard Mam ask Joey's mother when we reached the school carpark afterwards. "There's a lovely little café at the corner of main street. We could have a little sit-down together. Mother to mother."

Both Joey and I, who were walking a few feet behind them, hand in hand, turned to gape at each other.

"Coffee?" he mouthed. "What the fuck?"

"No clue." I rolled my eyes. "Maybe it's an olive branch?"

"Or we could go back to my house? I've a lovely, fresh madeira cake in the bread bin," Mam suggested, unlocking the driver's door of Dad's transit van. "What do you say, Marie? Coffee and cake, while we dissect the prospect of grand-motherhood?"

Joey's mam looked like she had just been asked to explain Fermat's Last Theorem. "Coffee?" Her mouth opened and closed several times before she whispered, "I, uh, I don't know?"

"Did you drive here?"

"No." With wide, uncertain blue eyes, she looked up at my mam and shook her head, and the move made her look a lot like her daughter. "I, uh, I walked over here from work."

"Well, hop in," Mam instructed, climbing into the driver's seat of the van. "You can come over to mine for a cuppa and I'll drive you home afterwards."

She looked to Joey and shrugged helplessly, almost as if she was looking for permission.

"What do you want to do, Mam?"

"I, ah . . ." Voice trailing off, she glanced around nervously before taking a step towards the van. "I . . ." She straightened her frail shoulders then and reached for the passenger door. "Thank you."

"You two," Mam called out, as she rolled down the window. "Straight home after the hospital, ya hear? You're not out of the woods by any stretch of the imagination. I haven't even started on the lectures."

"I don't know how I feel about that," Joey noted, watching as our mothers drove off in my dad's van. "That makes me feel really fucking uncomfortable, Molloy."

"Yeah, I know," I agreed with a sigh, as I slid my arm around his waist. "But do you want to know something that made *me* feel *really* comfortable?"

"Hm?"

"You, Joe." I smiled up at him. "What you did back there in the office with Mr. Nyhan? What you said? It meant a lot to me."

He looked down at me, brows furrowed. "I didn't do anything, Molloy."

"Yes, you did," I replied, leaning into his side, as we walked over to my car. "And it meant everything."

"I don't know what to say," he replied, still looking confused. "You driving, baby?"

"Nah." I shook my head and tossed him the keys. "Can you do something for me?"

"Name it."

"Stay with me tonight."

He sighed heavily. "Molloy."

"Don't say no." Sinking into the passenger seat, I tossed my school bag over my shoulder into the back seat before turning my attention to Joey, who was cranking the engine. "Say yes."

"What about the kids?"

"What about you?" I shot back, flicking on the car stereo and nodding my approval when No Doubt's 'Underneath It All' drifted from the speakers. "This one's you, Joe."

"Give it a rest with the songs," he muttered. "And I'm grand."

"Your face tells a different story."

"Aoife."

"Joey." I reached across the console and covered the hand he was resting on the gearstick with mine. "Please."

He didn't answer me until he had pulled away from the school and was on the main road. Only then did he release a sigh and turn his hand over.

"You win, Molloy." He entwined his fingers with mine. "Again."

"Yay."

"So, are you ready for this?" he asked, attention flicking between my face and the road ahead of us. "To see the baby?"

"No," I admitted quietly. "Are you?"

"No." He squeezed my hand. "But we've got this, Molloy."

Maybe we should have changed our clothes?

JOEY

"Joe, it's me, Shannon. I'm on the way to Dublin with the school. I won't be back until late tonight. Can you tell Mam? He has my phone so don't call it, okay? You won't be able to get ahold of me, but I'm okay, Joe. Don't worry about—"

I replayed the voicemail my sister left me for the third time and contemplated how the hell I was going to smooth this over at home.

Deleting the message from my phone, I slid my phone back into my pocket and ran a hand through my hair in frustration.

Mam was going to hit the roof.

The old man would blow a fuse if he found out.

"Maybe we should have changed our clothes," Molloy whisper-hissed, drawing my attention back to the present.

We were sitting in an overcrowded waiting room at the maternity hospital, surrounded by heavily pregnant women and their husbands – any number of which could have been mistaken for *our* parents.

"It's grand," I replied, resting my hand on her bouncing knee. "I've got you, Molloy."

"Yeah, Joe, that's the point," she mumbled. "Everyone here knows just how well you *got* me."

I laughed because in all honesty what else could I do in this moment? She wasn't wrong.

We were sitting in our BCS uniforms and attracting an array of different looks from the people around us.

Pity. Disgust. Sympathy. Surprise.

The list went on.

"Fuck them," I told her, casting a warning glare to a particularly pervy father-to-be who was eyeing my girlfriend's legs. "They don't know us."

"Joe, we're the only teenagers here," she continued to ramble, tone panicked. "That girl over there looks like she's in her early twenties, but that's it. All these women are way older than me."

"It doesn't matter, Molloy," I tried to soothe. "Age is just a number."

"You're right," she agreed, smoothing down the hem of her pleated skirt. "You're absolutely right, Joe." Reaching for my hand, she shifted closer, welding her side to mine. "God, I need to pee so bad."

"Just hold it," I replied. "You read the form. It said you need a full bladder."

"Yeah, but it's so uncomfortable." She squirmed in discomfort. "Distract me."

"How?"

"Tell me who was on the phone?"

"Shannon," I replied, sighing heavily. "She's gone to Dublin with the school."

"Really? You never mentioned it."

"Because I didn't know," I admitted. "Yeah, that'll be fun to explain to the old man when he gets wind of it."

"No." Her hand tightened around mine. "No, no, no, you don't need to explain anything, okay? You need to just stay away from that asshole. Let your mother handle it."

"Molloy."

"I'm serious, Joe," she choked out, pulling my hand onto her lap. "I can't cope with knowing he's hurting you—"

"Aoife Molloy?" a frazzled looking nurse called out, thankfully putting an end to the conversation. "You're up, sweetheart."

"Oh Jesus." Looking like a deer caught in headlights, Molloy sprang to her feet, dragging me with her. "Don't leave me, Joe," she whispered, with a death grip on my hand, as we followed the nurse. "Don't leave my side."

"I won't," I promised, letting her pull me into the dimly lit room with her. "I'm not going anywhere."

"My name is Margaret, and I'm the ultrasound technician," the woman introduced herself, closing the door behind us. "You're here for your dating scan, is that right?"

"Uh, yeah?" Molloy croaked out, and then reluctantly let go of my hand when the woman led her over to the examination table. "Uh, he's the father, so can he stay with me?"

"Sure, Dad can sit on the chair next to you."

Dad.

Holy fuck.

"Joe?" Molloy squeezed out, eyeing me meaningfully from her perch on the table, as she laid on her back and held out her hand.

"Shit, yeah." Shaking my head to clear the panic, I closed the space between us, and sank down on the chair next to the table and grabbed her hand.

"According to your notes, this is your first pregnancy," the technician stated, as she lubed my girlfriend's belly with a bottle of clear gel. "The first day of your last menstrual cycle was December fourteenth, is that correct?"

"Uh, yeah," Molloy croaked out. "That's right. I had some spotting at the end of January, but my friend was saying that might be—"

"Implantation bleeding," the technician filled in with a knowing nod. "Uh-huh. And you're a half twin, is that right?" Stuffing a wad of tissues under the waistband of my girlfriend's skirt, she fiddled with the ultrasound machine next to the table, tapping buttons and typing on the little keyboard. "Fraternal? Dizygotic?"

"Uh . . . " Molloy looked to me and I shrugged, having no fucking clue what any of it meant. "Yeah, sure?"

"Okay, well, let's just have a look." Retrieving the wand from the machine, the woman rolled it over my girlfriend's stomach. "You'll feel lots of pressure on your lower abdomen and pelvic area, but it shouldn't be painful."

Attention riveted to the screen in front of us, I watched as it transformed from darkness to a weird pale orb, with a strong pulsing movement coming from the middle of it.

"Lovely," the technician said, gaze flicking between the wand and the screen as she tapped on the keypad and changed angles. "Yes, you're definitely pregnant."

"Oh fuck," Molloy and I choked out at the same time, as we both shifted closer to get a better look at the screen.

"That's it?" Molloy asked, squeezing my hand, as we both eyed the tiny alien shaped creature floating around on the screen. "That's the baby?"

"Yeah, and listen to this." Pausing, the technician pressed a few buttons on the screen, causing a galloping noise to fill the room. "That's a beautiful, strong heartbeat."

"That sounds like a racehorse," Molloy breathed. "That's really the heartbeat?"

"Uh-huh, and judging by the size of this little bean, you have your dates spot on. You're fourteen weeks and three days gestation, giving you an EDD of 20-09-2005. Congratulations, Mom and Dad."

"Oh Jesus, Joe," Molloy choked out, swinging back to look at me. "It *was* the Tommen party."

"Yeah," I managed to get out, though I was sure my heart was thundering ten times faster than the kid housed in my girlfriend's womb. "Fucking Gibsie and his spliffs of Moher."

"And the *champagne*."

"Fucking champagne."

"I beg your pardon?"

"Nothing," we both chorused in unison.

Shaking my head, I asked, "So, ah, what happens next?"

"Well, Mom here will be given an appointment with a midwife to go over medical history, family history and what not, and we'll go from there." She continued to scan Molloy's stomach as she spoke. "As you can tell from the crowded hallways and waiting room, we're pretty swamped this afternoon, so an appointment will be sent out in the post for the next week or so."

"What are you checking for?" Molloy asked, tone wary, as she watched the technician move the wand over her stomach.

"You're a twin, so I'm just making sure we don't have any little surprises hidden away from view."

"What the fuck?" I demanded, heart gunning in my chest. "There's more?" I glared at my girlfriend. "There's *more*?"

"No, no, no," Molloy chuckled nervously, pushing the technician's hand away. "One surprise was quite enough, thanks. Don't go looking for problems, dammit."

"Don't worry. I can only see one fetal membrane sac."

"Thank Jesus for that," I strangled out, sinking back on the chair and pressing my hand to my chest. "Don't do that to me."

Sold on you

AOIFE

"Are you okay?" Joey asked, when we parked up at the footpath outside of my house later that afternoon.

The drive back from the hospital had been spent mostly in silence, while we both mentally reeled. He had his eyes locked on the road ahead of us the entire time, while I had been unable to tear my gaze away from the strip ultrasound images the technician had printed off for us.

It was real.

I heard the heartbeat.

There really was a little baby growing inside of my body.

"Molloy?" Killing the engine of the car, Joey unfastened his seatbelt and turned in his seat to face me. "Are you okay?"

I wasn't sure.

It all felt so surreal.

I didn't know what to do or how I felt.

"Are you?"

He shrugged almost helplessly. "She called me *Dad*, Molloy."

"I *know*." Relieved that he seemed to be reeling too, I nodded eagerly and turned in my seat and mirrored his actions. "She called me *Mom*, Joe."

"It sort of just hit me when we were in there, you know?" he mused, rubbing his jaw. "We're going to be parents."

"To a *person*," I agreed, chewing on my nail nervously. "A literal human being."

"This time next year, there's going to be a kid back there," he added, gesturing to the back seat of my car. "One *we* made."

"Never mind next year," I choked out. "We're going to have a baby *this* Halloween." My eyes widened. "*Halloween*, Joe. We're going to have a trick-or-treater."

"And Santa at Christmas."

"And the Easter bunny in spring."

"And I don't have a house, or a car, or a fucking qualification." He scrubbed his face with his hand. "We are so out of our depth here, baby."

"You're fine," I accused. "You're amazing with babies. I'm the one in trouble here. The only infant I've ever held was my cousin's pet baby gerbil and guess what happened to it, Joe? I dropped it. Uh-huh. That's right. The poor thing nose-planted its cage when I was left in charge."

"Okay, comparing your ability to mother our child to caring for your cousin's pet rodent is not the same thing, Molloy."

"Maybe not, but I'm not exactly the responsible mother-type, am I?"

"And I am?"

"Oh please." I rolled me eyes. "You've been a dad for your entire life. You even have that 'don't make me come up those stairs' dad threat down to a fine art."

"Wow. Thanks."

"I'm serious, Joe. You've got this. *I'm* screwed."

"Give me another look at that," he muttered, snatching the baby scan out of my hand and holding it up to his face. "Oh Jesus, I think I see a dick."

"What? No, you don't." Gaping, I snatched the picture back and studied where he was pointing to. "That's not a dick, that's a leg."

"No, that's a leg," he corrected, tapping the picture. "That's another leg. And *that* is a dick."

"That's the baby's cord."

"That's a dick, Molloy." Dropping his head on the steering wheel, he muttered something incoherent under his breath and groaned loudly. "It's a boy."

"But you said it's too early to tell."

"Yeah, well, I don't know what to tell ya, because *that's* a dick."

"But how can you tell?"

"Trust me, I have seen too many of those fucking sonograms down through the years. I know a dick when I see one."

"What if you're wrong?"

"I hope I am."

"Joey." I slapped his arm. "Don't say that."

"Don't give him my name," he whispered, head still resting on the steering wheel. "Please, Aoif, just give him yours and break the cycle."

His parents.

It always came back to his parents.

"There's nothing to break, Joe," I replied, stroking his hair. "You are *not* him, and I am *not* her."

"Please listen to me. I don't want you to give him my name," he admitted quietly. "Not my first name and definitely not my last name. I don't want that kid to have a single thing passed down to him that came from me."

"Joey, come on, we don't even know if it's a boy."

"It's a boy," he mumbled, pulling back to look at me. "Regardless, you need to make that baby a Molloy. Don't give him my name."

"Joey." My heart sped up. "You're this baby's father, and I'm proud of that." I reached up to stroke his bruised cheek. "I'm proud of *you*. I have never been ashamed of who you are or where you come from, and neither will our baby."

Emotion flickered in his green eyes. "What if I turn into him?"

"You won't."

"But what if I do? What if I already am?"

"That's impossible."

"How can you be so sure?"

"Because I know him and I know you." I stroked his cheek. "He's a bully and you're a man. There's no comparison. You are polar opposites. You and Teddy are *not* the same person, Joe," I whispered. "You're not even close."

"I'll never hurt you."

"I know."

"I mean it." He snatched my hand up and held it to his bruised cheek. "I will *never* put a finger on you, Aoife Molloy. Never. Not on you, or our kid."

"I *know*," I repeated, leaning in close to press my forehead to his.

"I'll do right by you," he vowed gruffly. "I swear I will."

"You don't need to convince me, Joe." I leaned in and pressed my lips to his before whispering, "I've been sold on you since I was twelve years old."

He looked at me for the longest time before blowing out a pained breath. "I love you, Aoif."

"Love you, too, Joe."

"Can I keep one of these?" he asked, holding up the long strip of sonogram images.

"Of course," I replied, heart-bucking wildly in my chest, as I watched him carefully tear one off the strip and place it in his wallet. "It's your baby, Joe."

"Yeah." Nodding to himself, he placed the sonogram in the picture slot in his wallet and smiled. "He is."

Put your hand in my hand

JOEY

"Give me a song, Joe."

"Hm?"

"A song."

It was a little after ten o clock, we were holed up in her room keeping a low profile from Tony, who was banging around downstairs like a bear with a sore head, and Molloy had somehow managed to rope me into watching another horror movie from her collection. Tonight's chosen number was *Final Destination 2*.

Completely fucking reeling from the events of the last twenty-four hours, I was doing everything I could to take the pressure off my girlfriend.

To make her feel like she wasn't in this alone.

Because she might be the one currently housing our baby, but the responsibility of parenthood was coming for both of us.

Just thinking about it caused my heart to catapult around in my chest.

The fuck was I going to do?

I had a girl and a baby to look after.

But I still had Shannon and the boys.

And Mam.

Jesus Christ.

"What do you mean give you a song?" I asked, slotting another pillow behind me to take the pressure off my back and ease the pain coursing through my flesh. "I don't sing, baby."

"You know that's not what I mean," she replied, nestling between my legs, with her back to my chest. "Give me a song for us."

"For us," I repeated, mulling it over, as I hooked an arm around her middle and drew her body closer to mine.

"Yeah, for us."

"I don't have a song."

"Well, find one because I need a song."

"Fine." Dropping my hand to rest on her stomach, I said, "Madonna."

"'Like a virgin'?"

"'Papa don't preach'."

She snorted. "Nice."

I smirked. "Thanks."

"For real, though." Breaking free from my hold, she twisted around until she was straddling my lap. "Give me something real."

"You're putting me on the spot here."

"So?" Leaning in close, she nuzzled my nose with hers. "You're excellent under pressure."

Sighing heavily, I loosely clasped her waist. "Molloy."

"Please . . . "

"Fine." Shaking my head, I racked my brain for something – anything – to appease the girl, before finally coming up with, "Divine Inspiration's 'The Way'."

"From the rave in Kerry?" Recognition flashed in her green eyes, and she beamed at me. "You remember that?"

"That surprises you?"

"No, I just . . . " Shaking her head, she scrunched her nose up before admitting, "It's just that you were pretty buzzed that night."

I was worse than buzzed that night.

I was out of my fucking mind.

"I can still remember the way you looked when you were dancing in that field, with your yellow wellies and tiny denim shorts," I heard myself say, remembering the moment clearly. The clearest of my memories involved nights with her. The only nights I ever wanted to remember were the ones I spent with her. "You had that little bra top thingy on, your tits were spilling out," I continued to tell her, needing her to know that she was forever on my mind. "The cheeks of your ass were on full display, and I swear to Christ, I was driven half mental from watching you."

"Really?"

"Really, really," I confirmed, mirroring her smile.

"And you *danced*," she teased, snaking a hand out to playfully pinched my good cheek. "The boy who refuses to dance was throwing shapes like a raver."

"I didn't have much of a choice, did I?" I shot back. "It was safer to join the madness. You had that neon body paint all over you—"

"Oh my god, the body paint!" she squealed out a laugh. "So had you."

Yeah, because she caked me in it. "And every time the strobe lights flashed around us, you lit up like a firework."

"I did?"

"Yeah, Molloy." Releasing a contented breath, I reached a hand up and tucked her hair behind her ear. "I was high that night, but you sent me soaring."

"Smooth."

"Not smooth, just honest."

"That was an epic summer, Joe. Wrapped up in you." Her eyes lingered on mine for a long moment before she released a wistful sigh. "I guess all that's behind me now, huh?"

"No, Molloy." My heart gunned in my chest, twisting and morphing between sorrow and guilt. "We'll do it again."

"Yeah," she replied, but it was a half-hearted mumble. "With a baby on my hip."

"We'll do it again," I repeated, catching her chin with my hand and forcing her to look at me.

"Yeah?" she whispered, tone hopeful.

"Yeah," I confirmed gruffly. "And you'll be just as reckless." Leaning in, I brushed a kiss to her lips. "And I'll be slightly less high."

Easter break

AOIFE

"Where are you going?" I asked my father on Saturday morning, watching from my bedroom doorway as he thundered down the stairs with a furious scowl etched on his face. "Dad?"

"Work," my father roared over his shoulder. "So, you better tell that boyfriend of yours to get his hole out of your bed!"

Oh crap.

"Joey's not here."

"I know he stayed over."

True. "He left a while ago."

"Well, then, let's hope he's at the garage, because if he's not then he better start looking for somewhere else to work because I'm done with the bullshit."

"Dad, wait!" Hurrying down the stairs after him, I chased him all the way outside to where he had parked his van. "Don't hit him, okay?"

"I'm not going to hit him."

"You swear?"

"If I was going to hit the lad, I would have done it the other night," my father grumbled as he climbed into his van. "Go inside out of the cold before you get sick on top of everything else."

"Don't fire him either," I pleaded, holding onto the door of his van so he couldn't close it. "Please, Dad. He needs his job."

"Of course he fucking needs his job," my father snapped. "He has a child on the way to pay for, doesn't he?"

Clearly sleeping on the news had done my father no favors.

He seemed angrier now than when he found out.

"But you were supportive the other day when the Lynch—"

"Because you're my daughter, dammit. Of course, I support ya. I'll always show a united front for your benefit. But I'm not happy about it, Aoife," he growled, cranking the engine. "My child is having a child while she's still a child with another fucking child! I am not okay with any of this, but I don't exactly have much of a say in the matter now, do I? Not when the horse has already bolted. No point in wringing the lad's neck after the fact, now is there? Can't exactly go back in time and put a condom on the little prick's dick now, can I?"

I didn't have an answer for him, so I let go of the door and watched as he slammed it shut before tearing off. Hurrying back inside, I raced up the stairs to grab my phone and warn my boyfriend that my father was on the warpath.

AOIFE: CODE RED. CODE RED. AVOID THE GARAGE AT ALL COSTS. DAD'S OUT FOR BLOOD.

JOEY: SORRY, I BOUNCED WITHOUT WAKING YA. HAD TO CHECK ON THE KIDS BEFORE WORK. HOW ARE YOU FEELING? X

AOIFE: ME? I'M FINE. IT'S YOU I'M WORRIED ABOUT. ARE THE BOYS OKAY?

AOIFE: JOE?

JOEY: ALL GOOD.

AOIFE: AND SHAN?

JOEY: STILL NOT BACK FROM DUBLIN. X

AOIFE: AW CRAP.

JOEY: YEAH, I KNOW. X

Aoife: Just steer clear of your house, Joe. You can crash at mine for a few days. I don't want you in harm's way.

Aoife: Joe?

Aoife: Joey!

Joey: It's all good. Don't worry. I'm at work now, so I'll talk to you later. x

Aoife: Seriously, Joe, about my dad. I saw a pair of rusty pliers on the passenger seat of his van. I think he might be considering castrating you.

Joey: I can handle Tony. Just mind yourself, okay? Don't go climbing any walls or any wild shit like that. I'll see you tonight. x

Aoife: I love you. x

Joey: I love you back. x

"Well, I have to hand it to him," Mam said when she walked into the kitchen after dropping off my father's lunch at the garage. "Your baby's father is brave."

I sprang off my chair. "Joe?"

"Mm-hm." Mam nodded. "He actually showed up to work."

"In one piece?"

Mam grimaced. "Relatively."

"Oh my god, Mam. Please tell me that Dad didn't hit him."

"According to your father, he threw a wrench at Joey's head, but had no hand in the black eye he's sporting."

"Oh my god," I cried, sinking back down, and dropping my head in my hands. "Kill me now."

"Your father will calm down," she replied, tone assuring. "They'll be okay, love. They'll patch it up in time. They've been working together for a very long time now. They're practically an old married couple."

"You should have heard him this morning, Mam," I groaned, watching my mother as she whizzed around the kitchen. "He was so hostile."

"Your father's not hostile, love, he's heartbroken."

"Well, that's even worse," I strangled out. "I broke his heart. That's why he avoided me like the plague when he came home from work last night. He hates me."

"Can we talk?" Kev asked, walking into the kitchen, hands in the air. "Civilly."

"Kev," Mam sighed wearily. "I don't think now's the time for that."

"We need to sort this out, Aoife," he pushed, ignoring our mother. "Come on. Let's just sit down and hash it out. We can't go around ignoring each other."

"You can talk to him all you want," I told Mam, as I jerked to my feet and grabbed my car keys off the table. "I'm going to Casey's."

"Aoife," Kev groaned when I brushed past him. "Please."

"Fuck off, Kevin."

Fathers and grandfathers

JOEY

Aching in places I never knew could hurt, I took Tony's bad mood on the chin at work and navigated the extremely dangerous waters I found myself in, while trying not to collapse in a heap from the pain coursing through my body.

The pain in my back had worsened to the point where I was half afraid to take off my t-shirt and look in the mirror. I didn't want to see what kind of damage that belt had done the other night.

Knowing that stripping off would only stress my pregnant girl-friend out further had been the reason I slept in a t-shirt and sweats the night before, much to her suspicion. Sleep had come easy, with the help of a couple of my mother's prescription benzos that I'd popped in the bathroom after Molloy dozed off, but by morning I was feeling everything again.

Still, I scraped my ass out of bed, and made it to the garage on time, knowing that I had to prove myself to Tony Molloy now more than ever. Because for the first time in my life, I was on the outs with my boss, and it was not a good feeling.

Not one word had he spoken to me since the night we sat around his kitchen table with my parents, and the pressure was mounting.

When he pulled up at the garage this morning, and found me waiting at the door, I wasn't entirely sure of how it would go down. When he didn't outright tell me to go fuck myself, I stuck around and dodged every spanner, wrench, and ratchet he threw my way. And when I said threw my way, I meant *at* my head.

The man was beyond livid with me, and I didn't blame him.

Worse than disappointing him, I'd taken his daughter down with me. Enduring his silent treatment and flying missiles, I kept my head down, ignored my phone, and worked through lunch, unwilling to give him another reason to toss my ass to the curb.

Whatever way he wanted to handle it was fine by me. It wasn't like I had a leg to stand on.

I'd fucked his daughter's life up.

If the baby Molloy was growing turned out to be a girl, and she fell in with a scumbag like me, I would take leave of my senses just like Tony.

It was a little after five o clock in the evening when he finally breached the stand-off by slamming a mug of coffee down on the trolley next to me. Not daring to say anything to piss him off further, I raised the mug to my lips only to halt in my tracks and eye the rim warily.

"Relax, I didn't poison ya," he grumbled, taking a sip from his own mug and then swapping it with mine to prove it. "Can't be leaving my grandchild without a father."

He was saying the words, but the look on his face assured me that he had thought about it.

"Thanks," I muttered before taking a sip.

"What happened to your face?"

"Walked into a door."

He shook his head but didn't push, choosing to take another sip of his coffee instead.

Thankful for his small act of mercy, I swallowed down another mouthful of coffee. "So, are we going to do this?"

"You want to do this now?"

"No time like the present."

"Fine," he said, giving me a hard look.

"Fine," I replied, giving him the respect that he deserved by keeping eye contact with him, while my conscience screamed, *It's showtime. Get ready for the pain.*

"You let me down, Joey."

Christ, hearing him say it out loud hurt worse than I thought it would. "I know, Tony."

"But worse than that, you let my daughter down."

"Yeah." Jaw ticking, I nodded stiffly. "I know that, too."

"What are you going to do about this mess?"

"I'm going to step up."

"Step up."

I nodded stiffly. "Do whatever Aoife wants me to do."

"What about what Trish and I want you to do?"

"That too." I shrugged. "As long as it aligns with what your daughter wants."

"You're going to stick by her?"

"I am."

"Are you going to marry her?"

"If that's what she wants."

"What do you want?"

"Her."

He stared hard at me for a long moment before blowing out a frustrated breath. "Goddammit, Joey, this would be so much easier if I didn't like you."

Yeah, I know.

"She might be having your baby, but she's still *my* baby," he snapped. "She will always be my baby. I would die for her. I would kill for her. I know you're a good lad, but I'm telling you now, man to man, if you ever consider laying so much as a finger on my daughter or that child—"

"You wouldn't have to kill me, Tony," I cut him off and said. "I'd do it myself."

"I'm not saying that I think you would, but you know why I have to say this to you, don't ya? I have time for ya, boyo, you know that, and I know you love her, but the home you come from, and the man you were raised by . . . " His words broke off and he dragged in a sharp breath before leveling me with a warning look. "Do we understand each other?"

Sick to my stomach, and feeling like I'd taken a knife to the back, I forced myself to swallow down the bitter taste of betrayal and nod stiffly. "Yeah, Tony, we understand each other."

"I'm not saying that I think you'd do it," he offered. "But you're—"

"I'm my father's son," I filled in flatly. "I get it."

"Well?" Molloy demanded down the line as I walked home from work that evening. "How did it go? Was he horrible? Are you okay? Did he hit you? Tell me that he didn't hit you—"

"Molloy, take a breath. I'm grand," I cut her off by saying before she could launch a full-blown interrogation. "I'm almost home. I'm going to grab a shower and check on the kids, and I'll swing by your place afterwards."

"So, you're really okay?"

Not even close. "Yeah, Molloy, it's all good."

"What did he say?"

"He asked me if I planned on marrying you."

"Oh my god," she groaned dramatically. "What did you say?"

"I told him that we already got married in secret, and that you got my name tattooed on your ass instead of a wedding ring."

"You did *not* say that to my dad."

"No, I didn't," I chuckled. "How are you feeling?"

"The same as I was when you last asked," she mused. "Chill, Joe, I'm still me."

Thank fuck for that.

"Well, I'm literally down the street from your house," she added. "I have the car, so just call me when you're ready and I'll come get you."

"You at Casey's flat?"

"Yep. I'm putting highlights in her hair. I had to get out of my house or I was going to stab my brother with a spoon."

"If you're going to stab him, use something sharper."

"Like a knife?"

"Maybe just a fork. We don't need you having that kid in prison."

She laughed down the line. "I'd look hot in stripes."

"You definitely would," I agreed. "Listen, hang up, and I'll call you later."

"Love you."

"Love you back."

Ending the call, I slid my phone into my pocket only to retrieve it once more when it started ringing.

Not bothering to read the display screen, I clicked accept and put the phone to my ear. "No, Molloy, stripes don't make you look fat, and no, you haven't put on weight, either, and yes, even if you do put on weight, I'll still want you just as much as I want you now—"

"Joey, come home. Come home quick!" Ollie screamed down the line. "Please, come home. Daddy's going to kill her!"

"Who, Ollie?" I demanded, as my legs broke into a run in the direction of my house. "Is it Mam?" My heart jackknifed in my chest. "Is he hurting Mam?"

"Shannon!" Ollie screamed down the line. "He's killing Shannon!"

Him or us 2.0

JOEY

Running faster than I ever had in my entire life, I sprinted the rest of the way home, with my heart gunning in my chest, and my mind free-wheeling into overdrive.

It's okay.

It won't be that bad.

Just breathe.

I could see Ollie at the front door when I rounded the garden, waving wildly at me to hurry.

I knew he was screaming and tears were spilling down his cheeks, but I couldn't make out a word of it.

The only sound in my head was the thundering roar of my pulse in my ears, as I staggered through the front door and followed a trail of blood into the kitchen.

It took me a moment for my brain to absorb what my eyes were seeing.

Blood smeared on the kitchen tiles.

Shannon limp of the floor.

Tadhg covering her body with his.

Blood on his face.

Mam standing in the kitchen screaming.

And him.

Him.

Standing in the middle of the carnage was *our father*.

My gear bag slipped off my shoulder, and the noise it made when it clattered to the floor seemed to awaken me from the trance-like daze I was suffocating in.

My throat felt like it had closed up.

My heart shriveled up and died in my chest.

My gaze flicked to Shannon once more, and the pain I felt when I took in the sight of her mangled body was too much to take.

It was all too fucking much.

"You fucking bastard!" The words tore from my lips like a battle cry, and I felt myself moving, barreling straight for him, my heart demanding vengeance. "You dirty fucking animal."

"Joey, wait!"

I didn't wait.

I couldn't.

"Hit *me*." Taking him to the ground with more force than I knew I was capable of I slammed his head against the hard tiles before quickly climbing back up and dragging the worthless piece of shit with me. "Come on, asshole. Hit someone your own fucking size."

"Joey, please don't—"

"Shut the fuck up," I roared, losing my fucking mind when *she* tried to speak to me. My sister was lying in a heap on the floor and instead of going to her, she was trying to protect *him*. "You are the most pathetic excuse for a mother that ever walked the earth."

Spitting piss and fire, he reared back and socked me in the jaw with his beefy fist. "You little shit."

"Did you see that?" I demanded, not even feeling the pain now, as I glared at our mother. I knew it should hurt, his fist was like a goddamn bulldozer, but adrenalin was flooding my system, giving me strength, I had no right to possess. "Did you see him hit me?"

"I'll put manners on you yet, boy," Dad slurred, throwing another punch, but this time he missed, giving me giving me ample opportunity to return the gesture.

"Can't you see what he's doing to your children?" My fist connected with the bridge of his nose causing blood to spray all over the both of us, as he collapsed in a heap on his ass. *"Are you fucking blind?"*

"Joey, stop," I heard my sister strangle out, but it was too late for words. "He's not worth going to prison over."

Because I couldn't stop.

Not until I made him stop.

Forever.

He needed to be stopped.

I needed to make it all fucking *stop*.

"Joey, stop," Mam begged. "You're going to kill him."

"Good!" My fists kept swinging of their own accord, in a frenzied blur of reckoning, as my knuckles ripped open and bled all over the both of us. As I let my heart do the thinking for once and finished him off.

If I did time for it, so be it.

Someone had to end this.

It had to be *me*.

"Joey, you . . . promised . . . " A small hand pulled at my arm, breaking my concentration. "You promised you'd . . . never . . . leave . . . me . . . "

Shannon's voice broke through the red haze in my mind and I jerked backwards, letting my hands falls to my sides, as my sister's voice continued to seep into my fucked-up brain.

Shannon.

Thump, thump, thump.

Shannon.

Thump, thump, thump.

Shannon.

Thump, thump, thump.

Numb to the bone, and with my mind reeling, I abruptly climbed off my father and stepped away.

"Teddy, oh god, Teddy," Mam cried, rushing to his side. "What have you done?"

And there it was.

There *she* was.

Running straight *to* him.

It broke me.

Whatever held me together these past eighteen years splintered and spliced.

Eyes wild, I looked around me, trying to make sense of the warzone we had been raised in. The warzone I was standing in.

Blood and tears.

Pain and pressure.

It was too much.

"Ollie." Turning my attention to where he was cowering beside Shannon, I crooked my finger and beckoned him. "Go upstairs and get Sean."

Because I had no doubt that the baby was hiding under my bed.

I didn't blame him.

I wanted to be under that bed with him.

"Why?"

"Because we're leaving." Trembling from head to toe, I said, "We are not staying in a house with that piece of shit a day longer."

Thankfully, Ollie did as I asked, making a beeline for the stairs without the hint of hesitation.

"Tadhg. Go with Ollie."

"But I—"

"Please," I strangled out, chest heaving at the sight of the blood smeared all over his face. "Go upstairs and pack your bags, kid."

After a ten second stare down, he relented and hurried for the stairs.

Only when the smaller children were out of sight could I focus on my sister.

I didn't want to.

I wanted to run away and hide, but I forced myself to take in the sight of her mangled body.

"You're okay," I lied, dropping to my knees beside her, feeling more broken in this moment than any other in my living memory. "I'm here." I gently lifted her into my arms. "I'm here, Shan."

She slumped against me like a rag doll and panic seared me because I just knew that this time was worse.

This time, he'd damaged her worse than ever.

"You're bleeding." Mam was wailing. "Oh god, Teddy."

That was all it took.

Those words were all it took for me to lose ahold of the small shrivel of self-restraint I had managed to garner. "Are you fucking blind? *She* is bleeding. Shannon. Your daughter!"

"Shannon." Blinking rapidly like she was coming out of some sort of haze, Mam's expression caved. "Oh baby, your face—"

"Don't you dare oh baby her," I snapped, carefully lifting my sister to her feet.

She wobbled and slumped against me like a newborn baby foal, and her lack of balance and coordination only increased my panic.

Because this was bad.

This was so fucking bad.

"You're okay," I continued to coax, as I carried her over to the table and set her down on a chair. "You're okay. I'm here." Snatching up a tea-towel, I pressed it to the side of her face where most of the blood seemed to be coming from. "I'm right here, Shan."

"Shannon, I didn't mean to—"

"Don't fucking speak to her, creep!" I roared, taking a protective stance in front of the chair my sister was slumped on when that bastard tried to speak to her. "I will kill you. Do ya hear me? I will slit your fucking throat if you so much as look at my sister again!"

How dare he look at her?

How *dare* he fucking say he didn't mean to hurt her?

Everything that man had ever done had been orchestrated with intentional malice and cruelty.

He was only sorry now because he knew as well as I did that he had gone too far this time.

He did something in this kitchen that couldn't be hidden or buried.

It was over for him, and the bastard knew it.

Instead of feeling glad about that, I felt on edge.

Because Teddy Lynch was never more dangerous and unpredictable than when he was cornered, and right now, the bastard was backed in deep.

The boys returned to the kitchen a few moments later with their backpacks laden down with clothes and toys and I sagged in relief to see Sean's unmarked face.

He was okay.

The baby is okay.

"Now, here's how this is going to go," I said when all three of my brothers rushed to stand behind me. "Either you find some maternal instinct deep inside that cold fucking heart of yours and put that bastard out for good," I said, addressing our mother. "Or I'm taking these kids out of this house and they are never coming back."

"Joey, I'm so sorry—"

"Don't apologize," I cut her off and snapped. "Protect your children and put him out."

"Joey, I—"

"Make a choice, Mam." I mentally willed her to do the right thing for once in her life. I knew she was scared. So was I. But these kids deserved better. She needed to be better, dammit, because this version of a mother wasn't good enough to keep a litter of kittens safe. "Him or us!"

"Joey, if you just calm down for a moment—"

"Don't you fucking dare try to talk your way out of this," I seethed, feeling my heart crack with every second that ticked by that she didn't choose us. "Just do the right thing for once in your fucking life and put him out!"

"Joey, can we just—"

"Him or us," I bit out, teeth chattering from the pain clawing its way up my body that I was desperately trying to ignore. "Him or us, Mam."

Silence.

Blank stares.

Nothing.

She just continued to sit by his side, staring vacantly up at me.

"I want you to know something," I managed to say, fighting back the tears that were trying to fill my eyes. "I want you to know that I hate you right now more than I have *ever* hated him. I want you to know that you are no longer my mother – not that I ever had one of those to begin with."

"Please . . . "

"No." Sniffling back a sob, I shook my head and said, "From this moment on, you are dead to me. All of your shit, handle it yourself. The next time he hits you, I won't be there to shield you. The next time he drinks all the money, and you can't feed the kids or get the electricity switched back on, find some other asshole to get cash from. The next time he throws you down the staircase or breaks your fucking arm in one of his whiskey tantrums, I'll turn a blind eye just like you did right here in this kitchen."

"Joey."

"From this day on, I won't be there to protect you from him, just like you weren't there to protect *us*."

"Don't talk to your mother like that." Climbing unsteadily to his feet, the prick attempted to threaten me. "You ungrateful little—"

"Don't even think about speaking to me, you scummy piece of shit," I roared, unwilling to dance a tango with him another second. "I might share your blood, but that's as far as it goes. You and me are done, old man. You can burn in hell for all I care. In fact, I sincerely hope you do."

"You think you can talk to me like that?" he seethed, wiping the blood from his face. "You need to settle the fuck down, boy."

"You're calling me boy?" I threw my head back and laughed humorlessly. "Me? The one who's been raising your fucking kids for most of my life." I gestured to the four children hiding behind me. "The one who's been cleaning up both of your messes. Taking care of both of your responsibilities, picking up the slack for two worthless, piece of shit parents." These were the very people who decided that I wouldn't make a good father. Fucking hypocrites. "I might be only eighteen, but I'm more of a man than you'll ever be."

"Don't push your luck, Joey. I'm warning ya."

"Or fucking what?" I sneered, glaring back at him. "You'll knock me around? Hit me? Kick me? Get your belt out? Take a hurley to my legs? Bust a bottle over my head? Terrorize me? Guess what? I'm not a scared little boy anymore, old man." I shook my head in utter fucking contempt for the man. "I'm not a defenseless child, I'm not a scared teenage girl, and I'm not your battered wife. So, whatever you do to me, I can promise you that I'll return tenfold."

He knew this.

He knew that the only way to keep me down was to kill me.

Because I would never back down from him.

As long as there was air in my lungs, I would continue to stand my ground.

I would *always* fight back.

"Get out of my house," he demanded, letting me know that he heard me loud and clear. "Now, boy!"

"Teddy, stop." Mam hurried to intercept him. "You can't—"

"Shut the fuck up, woman! I'll break your face for ya. Do ya hear me?"

"You can't throw him out," she whimpered, cowering from him. "Please. He's my son."

"Oh, so *now* I'm your son?" I shook my head in disgust. It was too little too late. "Don't do me any favors."

"This is your fault, girl," Dad accused then, turning his whiskey tantrum back on my sister. "Whoring around the fucking town. Making trouble for this family. You're the problem in this—"

"Don't even go there," I seethed, blocking her from his view. "Keep your goddamn eyes off her."

"It's the truth," he continued to goad, focusing on Shannon when he wasn't getting anywhere with me.

You see, the blood I shed was the physical kind, but our father wanted more than that. He was starved for evidence of the mental anguish he inflicted upon us. It was something he would never drain from me, so he took it from my sister.

"You're a waste of space and you always have been. I told your mother about ya, but she wouldn't hear it. I knew, though. Even when you were small, I knew what kind you were. A fucking runt. Don't know where ya came from."

"That's a lie, Teddy," was my mother's pathetic attempt to protect her. "Shannon, baby that's not—"

"We never wanted you. Did ya know that? Your mother left you for a week in the hospital, debating whether or not to give ya up. Until the guilt got the better of her. But I never changed my mind. I couldn't even stand the sight of ya, let alone love ya!"

"Shannon, don't listen to him," I warned, feeling her wilt at my side. He was getting into her head, just like he intended, and it was crippling me. See, he mightn't be able to hurt me, but when he hurt her, it fucking shredded me. "It's not true. The bastard's unhinged. Just block it out. Do ya hear me, Shan? Block him out."

"I didn't want you either," he tried again with me.

"My heart's bleeding," I spat, words dripping with sarcasm. He couldn't hurt me with his words. Only the woman standing beside him could do that.

"Well, we feel the same about you," Tadhg tossed out. "None of us want you!"

"Tadhg, be quiet," I warned, feeling my panic rise when my little brother put himself directly in the line of fire. "I've got this."

"No, I won't be quiet, Joe," he argued. "He's the fucking problem in this family and he needs to hear it."

I wholeheartedly agreed with him, but he needed to keep quiet and let me do the talking. I could take the shit our father threw. I could take the blows. Tadhg was just a little kid. He needed to stay in his lane and more importantly, stay unharmed.

"Get him out of my sight," our father roared, gesturing to my brother. "Now, Marie. Get him out before I do away with the little bastard."

"I'd like to see you fucking try," I snarled, roughly shoving the mouthy little fucker behind me before he got himself in deeper. "Try it, old man."

"No." Mam stepped between us. "You need to go."

"What did you say to me?" he snarled. "What the fuck did you say to me?"

"Leave," Mam whispered breathlessly, looking like she was seconds away from faceplanting the floor. "It's over, Teddy. I'm done. We're done. I can't. I need you to go away."

"You're done? You think you're leaving me? You're mine, Marie. Do ya hear me? You're fucking mine. Think you can throw me out? Walk away from me?"

"Just go! I want you gone, Teddy. Get out of our lives."

You need to go.

I want you gone.

Get out of our lives.

She was directing the words at my father, but I didn't feel a thing.

Because her words didn't mean shit.

They were meaningless.

It was too little, too late.

The damage was done.

The time to stand up to him had long since passed.

Whatever move she made now was out of fear for herself, not fear for her kids.

"You think you have a life without me?" he continued to taunt her. "You are nothing without me, bitch. The only way you're leaving me is in a box. I'll kill ya before I let you leave me. Do ya hear me? I'll burn this fucking house to the ground with you and your cunts in it before I let ya go!"

"Stop," Ollie sobbed, clinging to my leg. "Make him stop. Please."

"Are ya a girl now?" Dad sneered, glowering at his second youngest son. "Toughen up, Ollie, ya little bollox."

"That's enough, Teddy," Mam tried again. "Get out."

"This is my fucking house," he doubled down and roared. "I'm going nowhere."

"That's fine," I said in a strangely calm tone of voice, considering I felt anything but calm in this moment. "Ollie, go outside and take Sean with you." Reaching into my pocket, I grabbed my phone and handed it to him. "Take this and phone Aoife, okay? Call her up and she'll come get us."

I hated dragging Molloy into this.

Fucking despised myself for dragging her back to this house.

But I didn't have a choice.

I didn't have anyone else.

She was it.

My entire lifeline.

She was my ride or die, and whether it was right or wrong, I knew she would come.

"No, no, no. Please, Joey. Don't take them away from me." Panic-stricken, my mother rushed for me. "I told him to go. I told him, Joey." Eyes wild with fear, she pulled on my hoodie, pleading with me to do something we both knew I couldn't. "Of course, of course I choose you. Please don't do this, please, Joey. Don't take my children."

"What good are you to them when you can't keep them safe?" Every inch of my body shook and trembled as I fought against the desperate urge that I had to comfort her. I couldn't do it again. Not this time. "You're a fucking ghost in this house. You're wallpaper, Mam. A mouse. You are *not* good for us."

"Joey, wait, wait, please don't do this." Grabbing onto my hands, my mother dropped to her knees in front of me, and the move made me want to die. "Don't take them from me."

"I can't leave them here," I choked out, feeling too much for her, as my heart gunned in my chest. "And you've made your choice."

She had.

Whether she denied it or not, she chose him.

She would *always* choose him.

But this time, I was choosing my siblings over her.

"You don't understand," she wailed. "You don't see."

"Then get up, Mam." Tears filled my eyes, and it honestly felt like she stuck her hand through my chest and wrapped it around my heart. "Get up off your knees and walk out of this house with me."

"I can't." She shook her head, eyes pleading. "He'll kill me."

He'll kill them, too, I wanted to scream.

What part of that didn't she get?

How the fuck could she justify keeping them in this house?

This wasn't love.

This was sick.

She was as sick as him and I wanted no other part in this.

"Then die," was all I replied.

"Let him go, Marie," my old man commanded. "He'll be back with this tail between his legs. Cunt is useless. Won't survive a day on his own."

"Shut up!" Throwing her hands up, my mother screamed at the top of her lungs. "Just shut up! This is all your fault. You've ruined my life. You've destroyed my children. You're a fucking madman—"

He struck her so fast that I didn't have time to react.

His fist connected with her face, and I watched as my mother hit the ground like a sack of spuds.

Crumbling onto her hands and knees just like a million other times in a million other arguments in the same damn kitchen.

"Think you can talk to me like that?" he sneered, towering over her. "You're the worst of the lot, you fucking whore!"

Don't do it.

Don't do it.

Don't do it.

"Keep your fucking hands off my mother," I heard myself roar, reacting on a lifetime of instinct as I shoved him away from my mother's broken body and moved straight for her. "Mam."

I could feel myself breaking, my voice, my self-control, my heart.

All of it was just shattering into a million pieces.

I knelt down beside her, hating that she feared my touch almost as much as his when all I ever tried to do was shield her.

"Just walk away from him." Pushing her hair out of her eyes, she looked so much like Shannon as she looked up at me. So frightened and child-like. "We'll figure something out, okay? We'll sort this, but we can't stay here. I'll take care of you ."

"Who the fuck do you think you are?" he snarled, clamping a beefy hand on the back of my neck. "Think you know it all, boy? Think you're better than me?" His touch brought with it a lifetime's worth of horrendous memories and flashbacks. "Think you can take her away from me?" Overpowering me with strength, he forced me to my knees. "She's going nowhere." Increasing the pressure on the back of my neck, he pushed me onto my stomach. "I told you I'd put manners on you, ya ungrateful little bastard." The weight he was pushing down on me was unsurmountable and rendered me completely fucking helpless against his assault. "Think you're a man now, boy?" His knee dug into my back, and I had to bite back a scream when pain scorched through my already mangled back. "Show your mother what kind of man you are, crying on your knees like a little bitch!"

"Stop it," Mam begged and pleaded. "Get off him, Teddy."

"I'm more of a man than you," I forced out, desperately trying to keep my face off the tiled floor he was intent on crushing me into.

"Oh, you think so?" Laughing cruelly, he knotted his hand in my hair and snapped my head back before roughly slamming my face into the tiles. "You're a piece of shit, boy."

Everything inside of me was eerily calm for the briefest of moments before the sudden rush of heat and pain coursed through my face, bringing with it the familiar metallic taste of blood in my mouth.

Forcing myself to fight back against his hold, I spat out a clump of blood and heaved against the tiles, desperately trying to buck him off my back.

Relentless, he reared my head back and smashed it back down again.

Again and again.

Over and over.

"Get off him. Teddy, you're going to kill him."

Dizziness engulfed me.

"Good. And you're next, you turncoat whore."

Pain ricocheted through me.

I could feel the bone in my nose twisting sideways from the brunt of his blows.

In a way, I was relieved because I thought this might finally be it.

It's finally over.

"That all you got?" I snarled, still fighting against his unbreakable hold, because I would never give in to this man. He would have to stop my heart from pumping first. "You're losing your touch, old man."

It was only ever going to go one of two ways.

Either he was going to kill me, or I was going to kill him.

At least, if he finished it, I could rest.

I could just have *peace.*

Don't you dare stop.

You've got a girl and a baby depending on you.

Get the fuck back up on your feet.

Don't you dare leave her alone in this.

Furious, I kept fighting, kept goading, kept fucking going, until I somehow managed to twist my body sideways and drag him onto the floor with me.

But I was too weakened, my body too worn to fight him off.

Desperately fighting for my life, I tried to inflict as much pain as I could on him, but my hands felt like concrete blocks.

It was so hard to lift them, let alone throw a punch.

Getting the better of me once more, my father straddled my chest, and clamped his big hand around my throat, sealing my airways, and restricting my lungs.

I could hear the kids crying, I could hear Mam wailing, I knew Shannon needed help, but all I could think of in this moment was my girlfriend.

All of the bad shit I'd done, all of the horrible fucking situations I'd put her in down through the years.

I could feel the tears trickling down my cheeks as my body weakened.

I love you, I mentally told her. *I'm sorry.*

I gave it a fucking shot.

I wanted to close my eyes.

To just stop.

But something caught my eye in the haze.

Shannon caught my eye.

I could see *her*.

At the other side of the kitchen.

Slumped over and bleeding from her mouth.

Panic clawed at my gut.

She's dying.

She's dying.

Get up.

Get the fuck up and help her.

"Help . . . her," I tried to scream, but my words were barely more than a whisper. "Fucking . . . help . . . her!"

"Get off my brother!" Tadhg's scream infiltrated my mind moments before the pressure on my throat eased.

Gasping for air, I pulled and tore at the hand still wrapped around my throat. He wasn't choking me anymore, but he hadn't released me, either.

"Tadhg, put down the knife," I heard my mother strangled out. Please, baby."

"Fuck you," he screamed back. "Get. Off. My. Brother."

"Don't be stupid, boy."

"I'm not stupid, and I'm not Joey. I won't stop just because Shannon says so."

Light headed and exhausted from the exertion it was taking to keep my heart beating, I swung my bleary-eyed gaze to where my little brother had a knife pressed to our father's throat, with the sharp tip pressed precariously close to his jugular.

"Tadhg," I choked out through splutters, when the old man's grip loosened further. "It's okay. Just take it easy."

"It's not okay, Joe." With tears streaming down his cheeks, he shook his head. "None of this is okay."

"What are you going to do, boy?" the stupid prick taunted. "Stab me?"

"Yes."

The old man moved for the knife, but my baby brother doubled down and stepped closer, still wielding the knife.

"Jesus Christ, Tadhg," Dad yelped, hands moving from my throat to his, as blood trickled from the nick the knife had given him. "You cut me."

"This ends now," Tadhg growled, holding the knife a lot steadier than any boy of eleven should. "Get off my brother, and get out of this house for good, or I'll slit your fucking throat."

Highlights and heartache

AOIFE

"You are the queen of all things hair and make-up," Casey declared, doing a 360 twirl to get a good look at herself. "Insane, Aoife. Your skills with make-up are un-freaking-real, girl!"

With her bedroom stereo turned up full blast, my best friend bopped around to KC & The Sunshine Band's 'Give It Up', while striking different poses in the full-length mirror glued to the back of her bedroom door.

After spending most of the day at her mam's flat, I felt better.

Casey had this innate ability of making me feel like my life wasn't going to shit. It wasn't that she was overly optimistic, she just happened to possess enough crazy to complement mine.

We just fit together like bacon and cabbage.

Or vodka and Coke.

"I'd like to thank the academy." I took a dramatic bow before tossing my make-up brushes back into my bag. "And myself, because, you know, I'm so amazing and all that jazz."

"You could make some serious side cash doing make-up and up-styles."

"Yeah." I flopped down on her bed and sighed heavily. "That's the plan, Case."

"I hope we have a girl," she said. "So, we can instill on her a lifetime of contouring wisdom and fashion knowledge."

"Joey wants a girl."

"He does?"

"Yep, and that's the one," I declared, watching as she readjusted the skimpy black dress that she was modeling for her date tonight. "Seriously, Case. You look fierce."

"Hm." Sounding unconvinced, she studied her appearance in the mirror for a long beat before shaking her head and whipping the fabric over her head. "I'm going with the pink dress."

"You're making a mistake," I chimed in. "The black one makes you look like you have legs for days."

"But the pink one makes my boobs look epic."

"So?" I snorted. "Alec's seen your boobs a dozen times. He already knows how epic they are."

"I'm not going out with Alec tonight."

My eyes lit up. "Mack?"

"Nope."

"Rambo?"

"Nope."

"Charlie?"

"No one from our year, Aoif."

"Who then?"

"Patrick."

"Patrick?" My brows furrowed in confusion. "Who the hell is – oh my *god*." My eyes widened to saucers. "That lad from the Tommen party?"

Grinning, she bit down on her lip and nodded. "Not too shabby for a girl from Elks, huh?"

"Wait." I choked out a surprised laugh. "Isn't he like a fourth year?"

"He's seventeen and in fifth year. And like you can talk," she laughed back. "Isn't your baby daddy younger than you?"

"Oh yeah, by three whole months." I rolled my eyes. "I'm the ultimate cougar."

"Yeah, well, enjoy sitting your ass on the couch tonight growing your cub, because I am going on the prowl."

"Hey, don't diss the couch life," I grumbled. "Where's he taking you?"

"The back seat of his car, if he's lucky."

"Wow. Make him work for it, why don't you?"

"Stem the bitchy pregnancy hormones, unvirginal Mary."

"I'm more virginal than you," I huffed. "At least I've only had one dick inside of me."

"Yeah." She snorted. "One un-protected, over-productive dick."

I grinned. "I'd take his dick any day over Sticky-Dicky."

"Hey now, don't knock Sticky-Dicky." She waggled her brows. "It's not all about the size of the boat, Aoif, it's the motion in the ocean."

"Whore."

"Blasphemy." She feigned a gasp. "Who's the one living in sin here? For shame, Molloy. What would Sister Alphonsus say if she saw you now? Tut-tut."

"There's something seriously wrong with us, isn't there?'

"Probably," she agreed with a laugh. "I blame you."

"And I blame you."

"So, Joey was really okay about the baby, huh?" she asked, sobering her features, as she toed on a pair of six-inch heels. "He was supportive?"

"He took it so well, Case." I blew out a breath. "I was so scared about how he would react."

"Nah, I knew he'd stick by you." She waved a hand around aimlessly. "Say what you want about that boy, but he's good with kids."

"He *is* good with kids," I agreed with a sigh. "He practically raised his youngest brother."

"Well then. At least one of you guys will know what you're doing," she replied, flopping down on the bed next to me. "So, any idea about what you're going to do about *your* brother?"

"Don't, Case," I grumbled, feeling a swell of anger rise up inside of me at the mere mention of Kev. "I'm so done with him."

"You can't be done with him, Aoif," she replied with a weary sigh. "Not only is he your brother, but he's your twin. You guys shared a womb."

"I know, and that's what makes it worse," I bit out, scowling. "He really screwed me over, Case."

My phone rang then, and I was glad of the reprieve.

Unwilling to talk about Kevin, much less consider forgiving him, I reached into my jeans pocket and smiled when Joey's name flashed on the screen.

"It's Joe." Springing to my feet, I grabbed my bag and threw it over my shoulder. "He's ready to get picked up."

"Fine." Casey rolled her eyes and waved me off. "Abandon me for your baby daddy."

"Enjoy your date," I called over my shoulder as I swung her bedroom door open and hurried through her tiny sitting room/kitchen to the flat door. "Text me all the details tomorrow."

"Will do."

"And use a condom."

"I always do," she sang out. "I'm not you."

Laughing to myself, I closed the flat door behind me before clicking accept and putting my phone to my ear. "Hey, stud."

"Aoife," a young voice came down the line, followed by the sound of sniffling. "Aoife, can you come get us?"

"Ols? Is that you?" Frowning, I readjusted my bag on my shoulder and hurried down the communal stairwell to the ground floor of the building. "Are you okay? You sound like you're crying? Where's Joey?"

"You gots to come get us," he cried down the line. "Please, Aoife, please. You gots to come quick."

"Okay, okay, I'm on the way right now," I tried to coax, panic setting in, as I hurried outside to my parked car. "I'm getting into my car right now, Ols. I'll be at your house in two minutes."

When I pulled up outside Joey's house a couple of minutes later, and climbed out of my car, I honestly felt like my heart was trying to beat its way out of my chest.

I didn't want to go into his house, but the terror in Ollie's voice had me doing just that. With sweaty palms and a racing pulse, I moved for the front door, feeling my panic climb with every step I took.

"E-fa." Trip-tumbling off the front doorstep, Sean came barreling towards me with tears streaming down his cheeks. "E-fa."

Oh God.

This was bad.

This was so fucking bad.

"Hey, Seany-boo," I strangled out, hoisting him into my arms, as I kept moving for the door. "Are you okay?"

"E-fa." Sniffling, he burrowed his face in my neck and the feel of his small body trembling caused my heart to seize with dread. "O-ee."

"I called an ambulance," Tadhg choked out, greeting me at the front door. "I think she's dead."

"He killed her," Ollie was screaming from the hallway. "Daddy killed Shannon."

Feeling faint with panic, I stumbled through the front door with Sean in my arms, only to be greeted with a scene right out of the *Texas Chainsaw Massacre*.

There was blood *everywhere*.

"Joey," I called out, feeling lightheaded, stopping in the kitchen doorway with my eyes clenched shut, almost afraid to see what was beyond the doorway.

If anything had happened to him, I wouldn't cope.

I couldn't *think* about it.

"Joey!" My voice cracked and I clung tighter to his baby brother. "Joey, please tell me you're okay!"

"Molloy," I heard him call back, and the sound of his voice gave me the courage I needed to cross the threshold of the doorway and step into the kitchen.

I knew what I was about to witness would be bad, but nothing could have prepared me for the sight of my boyfriend, bloodied to a pulp, slumped on the kitchen floor, cradling the lifeless body of his sister in his arms.

The fact that Teddy was nowhere to be seen gave me little comfort in this moment.

Because I knew that he had been here.

This *brutality* had his name written all over it.

"What's wrong with her?" I demanded, almost dropping Sean from the fright I got when my eyes absorbed the carnage in front of me. "Oh god, why is she bleeding out of her mouth?"

"She's dying," Tadhg screamed, shaking his mother's shoulders. His mother who was sitting on the kitchen floor, holding a bag of peas to her daughter's chest like it was the solution to everything. "He killed my sister and you're doing nothing."

"Shannon, breathe," Marie sobbed. "Breathe, Shannon. Breathe, baby. The ambulance is on the way."

"It's okay, it's okay. Shh, I've got you." Ignoring his mother, my boyfriend continued to whisper in his baby sister's ear. "I love you. I love you, Shan. Just hold on for me, okay?"

"Shannon!"

"Jesus Christ, Shannon!"

"I'm here. I'm right here, Shan," Joey continued to cry as he rocked her back and forth in his arms like a mother would a small child.

I couldn't tell which one of them was bleeding more.

I suspected Joey.

But Shannon?

Shannon was just *limp*.

"Is she breathing?" I jumped into action and asked, setting Sean down, as I hurried over to them.

"I don't know, I don't know," Joey choked out a cry, and it was the worst sound I had ever heard come from his mouth.

He sounded so young.

So frightened.

So utterly broken.

"Can you hear me?" he sobbed, holding her bloodied face between his hands. "I'm going to get you out of here, okay? Shannon, can you hear me? Shan? Come on, talk to me."

"Get that away from her," I warned Marie, roughly tossing the bag of peas away from her daughter's small frame as I felt for a pulse. "You'll send her body into shock!"

"I'm sorry, I'm sorry," their mother cried. "I'm trying to help."

"Okay." I sagged in relief when I felt the faint thrum of her pulse against my fingertips. "She has a heartbeat, but it's faint."

"I don't know where the ambulance is," Marie cried, dropping her head in her hands. "It should be here by now."

"Stop crying and do something useful," I ordered, battling down a surge of fury directed entirely towards her. Because this woman. Yeah, I couldn't even go there with this woman. I would snap. "Just get out of the way, Marie. Go and hold Sean or get a blanket or something."

Waiting until she had moved aside, I shifted closer to my boyfriend, who was still cradling his sister's limp body in his arms.

"I'm going to get you help, okay?" Joey was whispering in Shannon's ear, as he pressed a kiss to her bloody forehead, smearing and mixing the blood on his face with hers. "Don't leave me."

She stared back at him with a blank, glazed over looked in her eyes, and the horrific gurgling noise that came from her throat, along with clumps of blood when she tried to answer him, was something that would haunt my nightmares for the rest of my life.

"Aoife." Sniffling, he pressed his cheek to his sister's face, and mumbled something incoherent to her, before exhaling a ragged breath and kissing her cheek. "Give me your keys." Sucking in a labored breath, he grunted out a pained snarl before hissing, "Fuck waiting for the ambulance. I'll take her myself."

"Joey, don't move her," I tried to instruct, knowing that neither one of them was in any position to be moved right now. Shannon looked like she was dying, and Joey didn't look like he was far behind her. "She could have internal—"

"Give me the fucking keys, baby," he cut me off and roared, voice breaking, as he stumbled unsteadily to his feet with his sister in his arms. His face was beaten so badly he was barely recognizable in this moment. "*Help* me."

He was moving for the front door before I had a chance to answer him. Before I could beg him to sit down before he passed out.

Panic swirled inside of my stomach, spiraling my heart into a frenzied flush of fear and dread. As I hurried after him, I knew that it was a bad idea, but went with him anyway because he needed me.

Because for the first time in his life, he had asked for help.

Two words.

Help me.

I'd never heard them come from his mouth before and knew there was a chance I'd never hear them again, but I had to help him.

I couldn't not.

Rushing around to the driver's side door, I swung it open and pulled the seat forward for him to climb inside.

He didn't.

"I'll drive."

"Joe, no." I shook my head. "That's not a good idea. I'll—"

"I'll drive," he choked out. "I'm faster, and I can't—" His voice broke, and he sucked in a quivering breath. "Please just *hold* her for me. I need to not, ah, I need to just . . . " Staggering, he leaned against the side of my car and clung to Shannon's small body. "Molloy, I'm really scared."

My heart cracked clean open in my chest.

"It's okay, Joe, baby. You drive." Scrambling into the back seat of my car, I held my hands out and gestured for him to pass her to me. "I've got Shan. I'll keep her safe. I promise."

PART 6

Breathe, baby. Just breathe

JOEY

"Joe?"

I could feel her hands on my face.

"Joey, baby?"

Her smell was all around me.

"Breathe, baby."

Her hands were on my face.

"Just breathe."

I couldn't feel my body.

I couldn't feel anything.

I knew I was trying to sit up. I could feel my legs kicking the blankets away from my waist, but my head wasn't complying.

My brain wasn't working.

Everything was fucking broken.

"Molloy." My voice was slurred. My lips brushed her neck as I spoke. "Where is she?"

"She's okay." She pulled me in tighter, wrapping me up in a tight cocoon of heat and warmth. "Shannon's okay, Joe. She's out of surgery and everything went great. The boys are fine, too. It's all good, baby."

Slumping forward, I let myself lean against my girlfriend, knowing that I needed to not put my weight on her, but unable to stop myself.

"The baby ..."

"The baby's fine." Her lips were on my forehead. "We're both fine."

She was the only thing that felt real in this moment.

She was here and she was real.

I could smell her, touch her, feel her.

Just her.

"What time is it?"

"It's about half past six."

"What day is it?"

"It's Sunday morning, Joe."

"My head," I groaned, burying my face in her neck when pain spliced through me. "My eyes."

"Shh, it's okay. Don't try to stand up." I felt her lips on my temple and then her hand was on the back of my head, fingers gently stroking my scalp. "Just stay on the trolley. I've got you, Joe."

The trolley?

I couldn't remember getting onto a trolley to begin with.

"Where am I?"

"You're in your own private cubicle in the A&E." Another kiss found my temple. "You've been in and out for a while now."

"I have?"

"Uh-huh. You've had a lot of tests done. A CT scan, some X-rays, and an MRI." Her breath hitched and I could hear the cry she was trying to bury. "But you're going to be fine, okay? I won't let anything else happen to you."

"Don't cry, Molloy." Nuzzling her neck, I tried to raise my hands to her face to comfort her, but they felt so fucking heavy that I only managed to hook them loosely around her waist. "You know it kills me when you cry."

"I'm not crying." Sniffling, she pressed another kiss to my head before cradling my face to her chest. "It's all good, Joe."

"Shannon?"

"She's fine," Molloy was quick to soothe. "I already told you, remember?"

Nah.

I didn't remember shit.

"I love you," I slurred. "That's all I remember."

"I love you, too," she replied, voice thick with emotion. "More than you'll ever know."

"Fuck, my eyes," I groaned, wincing when the brightness around me became too much. "Where's Seany?"

"He's at home with Nanny Murphy." Another kiss. "So are Ollie and Tadhg. They are all *fine*."

"Tadhg was, ah . . . " Shaking my head, I gripped at her waist, needing to hold onto her in this moment because my body felt like it was falling apart. "He had a knife."

"He's not hurt, Joe," she whispered. "Shh, baby. Don't say anything else, okay? Just wait until you feel better. We'll talk about it then, okay?"

Nodding weakly, I groaned when the pressure in my head grew to epic proportions. "Am I wearing pants?"

"No, baby, you're not. You're wearing your boxers and a hospital gown. They had to take off your clothes for the MRI."

"Aw fuck."

"Why?"

"I've a nodge of hash in my jeans," I mumbled drowsily. "I could really use a smoke."

"Oh, Joe." A broken laugh escaped her. "Trust you to think about getting high in your condition."

"Can I come in?" a strange voice asked and suddenly we were bathed in an abnormal amount of light as the sound of a curtain moving filled my ears. "Are you next of kin?"

"Yeah, I am."

"Is his mother or a guardian around?"

"No. It's just me."

"I can come back when his mother—"

"He's over eighteen," I heard her say. "I'm down on his paperwork as next of kin. He's my baby's father. We're a family." Cupping my face between her hands, she lifted my face to hers. "Can you see me, Joe?"

Wincing from the pain the bright lights were causing me, I forced myself to focus on the only face I'd been able to see since I was twelve. "Molloy?"

"The doctor's here, Joe." She smiled and my vision blurred in and out before settling on her green eyes. "We're going to talk to the doctor, okay?"

"Okay." I forced myself to nod and then winced in pain. "Whatever you say, queen."

"His MRI results show three separate linear fractures to the skull," the voice was telling her. "He has a nasal fracture, an orbital fracture, and hairline fracture to his left zygomatic bone."

"Zig-o-what-ic?" I heard Molloy croak out. "In plain English please, doctor."

"Aside from three hairline fractures on Joseph's skull, he also has a broken cheekbone, a broken nose, a broken eye socket, and a grade three concussion," I heard the man say. "His MRI also showed up several old contusions, extensive damage to his humerus not to mention signs of multiple metaphyseal-epiphyseal fractures that seem to have healed remarkably well without causing any major deformation or debilitation to his skeletal frame."

"I don't know what any of that means," I heard my girlfriend strangle out. "What do you mean they've healed remarkably well?"

"May I be frank?"

"Yeah, yeah, be frank."

"Joseph, may I be frank?"

"Be whoever the fuck you want, doc. I'm not your keeper," I mumbled, enjoying the feel of Molloy's fingers in my hair so much, I leaned in closer and rested my chin on her shoulder. "You be Frank and I'll be Joey."

"No, Joe, he meant . . . Never mind. Go ahead, doctor."

"In cases like Joseph's —"

"Joey," I grumbled. "It's Joey, Frank."

"In cases like Joey's, when patients present under these kinds of circumstances, there's generally a long history of domestic violence, and to break it down for you, your partner's test results reveal a pattern of child abuse that clearly stretches back to infancy."

A pained sob escaped my girlfriend. "Infancy?"

"No, no, no," I tried to coax, nuzzling her. "Don't be crying, Molloy."

"I'm okay, Joe," she whispered, stroking me. "How can you tell, doctor?"

"The results of his scans clearly show evidence of malunion fractures that went untreated and healed improperly. There's very clear evidence of a poorly healed mid-shaft fracture to his right humerus. Unfortunately, this is something commonly seen in infants under the age of eighteen months who have been exposed to physical abuse. In your partner's case, while his bones may have healed over time, many of the injuries his body sustained left residual shadows. Or blemishes, if you will."

"You're saying this has been happening since he was a baby?"

"I'm saying there's evidence that leads me to believe that your partner has sustained a tremendous level of physical abuse over an extended period of time."

"That leads back to when he was a *baby*?"

"It's possible."

"Oh my god." Molloy heaved out a sob and pulled me closer. "Oh my *god*!"

"Quite frankly, it's a miracle he's sitting here."

For better or worse

AOIFE

Twenty-four hours had passed since we had barreled into the A&E with Joey carrying his sister in his arms, while I screamed the place down for help.

To be fair, help had come instantly, but once Shannon was rushed away on a gurney, surrounded by a flurry of nurses and doctors, Joey had unceremoniously collapsed in a heap on the waiting room floor.

Reeling didn't come close to describing how I felt as I sat at my boyfriend's bedside, behind a pale blue curtain, in the middle of a jam-packed accident and emergency, as we continued to wait for a bed on a ward to become available. Whatever they had given him for pain relief a few hours ago had knocked him out cold and I was relieved.

The longer he slept, the longer I knew he was safe.

The longer he was protected from the pain that I knew would swallow him up.

Because I knew in my heart once the meds wore off and his poor knocked around brain came back to its full senses that he would be up and out of here. It wouldn't matter to him that he needed to rest, or that his body had taken an unmerciful battering. Joey would go straight to his sister's bedside without thought for the consequences – or himself.

And after he visited his sister, I didn't want to think about what would follow.

Resting my elbows on his bed, I continued to watch him sleep, and I continued to cry.

His face was barely recognizable beneath the gauze, tape, and bandages. His left eye was hidden behind a white bandage, while the bridge of his nose was taped up. The bruising and swelling around his right eye so extensive that even when he was awake, it was hard to tell.

Biting down on my lip, I smothered a sob and reached over to brush his hair off his forehead, only to expose more bruising.

It was everywhere.

Every inch of his skin told a story of vicious abuse at the hands of a monster.

The raw welts on his back that I discovered when helping him undress last night had caused everything in my stomach to come back up.

There was no hiding what had happened to him.

His father's belt had left welts deeply imbedded into his flesh.

Forcing myself to be strong for him, I remained right by his side, unwilling to leave him for longer than it took me to grab a cup of tea from the vending machine. Mam had called countless times, begging me to come home for a shower and to have something decent to eat, but I couldn't do it.

I couldn't leave him.

I never would.

The Garda Siochana had come and gone, looking for statements from my boyfriend that he was in no fit state to make. Social workers, a Garda victim service officer, not to mention many other authority figures had made an appearance, too.

Nanny Murphy had somehow managed to get ahold of my phone number and had called several times to check on her great-grandson and to relay messages to Joey, but that was it.

She was the only one.

Not once since he was wheeled into triage had I caught a glimpse of Marie Lynch.

I understood that Shannon was in a bad way, Nanny had told me that she had a collapsed lung, but Joey was hurt, too, dammit.

He had a fractured skull for fuck's sake!

It was a wonder that his brain wasn't complete mush.

The doctor said it himself; it was a *miracle* that he was still here.

"Molloy." Releasing a pained groan, Joey covered my hand with his and blinked his one good eye open. "What did I tell ya about crying?"

Sniffling, I forced a smile and whispered, "Hey, stud."

"Hey, queen." His voice was raspy and torn. "Nice legs."

I choked out a sob. "Nice everything."

"Don't cry for me."

"I'm not." I forced a brighter smile. "Your nose is pancaked again."

"Hm." He grunted out a breath. "What's new."

"I think it's sexy." Sniffling, I lifted his hand to my mouth and kissed all of his torn knuckles. "You've got the roughed-up bad boy look down to a tee."

"How's my baby?"

"Still cooking?"

"How's my other baby?"

"I'm okay, Joe," I breathed. "We're both fine."

"Good." His eyelid fluttered shut. "I need you to be okay."

"I *am* okay, Joe."

"Both of you."

"Both of us are fine."

"I need it to stay that way," he whispered, giving my hand a squeeze. "It's important to me."

Desperately fighting down the urge I had to climb onto the bed and hold him, I stood up and hovered close instead. "You're important to us." Leaning down, I pressed a lingering kiss to his clammy forehead. "You're everything to us."

"I want the baby, queen."

Sniffling, I nodded. "I know, stud."

"I heard the heartbeat."

"Yeah, you did."

"It's really in there."

"Uh-huh."

"We made a baby."

"Yeah, Joe, we did."

"I'm scared."

"I know you are. It's okay."

"When can I get out of here, Aoif?"

"The doctors want to keep you in for a few days for observation," I explained, fingers trailing over his swollen face. "We're just waiting on a bed upstairs to become available."

"No," he groaned, shaking his head. "No, no, fuck that. I'm going home."

"You're going to stay here," I warned, snatching up the hand he was attempting to use to pull his IV line out. "You have one hell of a concussion, Joe. The doctor explained it to me. You *need* to be here, okay?"

"I need to see Shannon."

There it is.

"Shannon is fine," I tried to soothe, sinking down on the edge of his bed, as I gently pinned his hands to his chest to stop him from hurting himself. "She's being well looked after upstairs, okay?"

"Yeah, but she needs to see me," he tried to argue, voice croaky and raw. "You don't get it. I need to be there when she wakes up. She'll be scared. She won't know what to say. I need to check on her."

"Joe." Cupping his face between my hands, I leaned in close and forced him to look at me. "I promise you that Shannon is *fine*." Pressing a soft kiss to the corner of his mouth, I avoided stitches on his swollen bottom lip, and mentally willed him to stop thinking about everyone else. "You trust me, don't you?"

He nodded slowly.

"Good." I smoothed his hair back and kissed him again. "Then trust me when I tell you that the best thing you can do for Shan is to rest up and heal."

"Joey?" Marie's sorrowful voice came from behind the curtain, causing us both to stiffen. "Can I speak to you?"

"No, no, no," he croaked out, snatching my hand up in his. "I can't deal with her."

"It's okay," I whispered, nuzzling his good cheek with mine. "I'm here, Joe. I've got your back."

"Fuck." Blowing out a pained breath, he relented with a stiff nod. "Okay."

"Come in, Marie."

The curtain was drawn back, and his mother appeared, looking every bit as small and frail as the last time I'd laid eyes on her.

"Joey." Her eyes were sunken in her head, clearly swollen from crying, as she took an uncertain step towards us. "Aoife."

"Marie," I acknowledged coolly. My gaze flicked to the tall, dark-haired man standing behind her. The suit he was wearing looked too flashy to belong to a social worker, so I pegged him for a solicitor.

God knew she needed one.

"Oh, Joey, baby." Sniffling, his mother moved for his bed, but stopped when she realized that I had no intention of getting out of her way.

I couldn't if I wanted to.

Joey had a death grip on my hand.

"How are you feeling?" Marie asked him. "Your poor face."

My boyfriend didn't respond.

He didn't move a muscle.

His face was void of all emotion as he continued to stare at the man standing behind his mother.

"Hey kid," the man said, tone thick with emotion, as he stared straight past me, attention riveted on my boyfriend. "It's been a while."

It's been a while?

Brows furrowing, I swung my gaze on the man and studied his familiar face.

High cheekbones.

Dark brown hair.

Puffy swollen lips.

Eyes the color of midnight blue.

"Crap," I strangled out, quickly putting two and two together and coming up with a big fat Darren. "It's you."

His attention flicked to me and I watched as a flicker of recognition flashed in his blue eyes. "And it's you."

I frowned, knowing full well that I had never met this man before in my life. "What?"

"So, you went there anyway and threw your hat in the ring, Joe?" he mused, this time addressing my boyfriend. "Well, no one could accuse you of being fleeting."

"Seriously." I blinked in confusion. "*What?*"

"Never mind," Darren replied with a shake of his head. "How are you feeling, Joey?"

"What are you doing here?" Joey replied, tone cold and hard. "What do you want?"

"Mam called me."

"What do you mean she *called* you?"

"Listen, Joe, I know there's a lot of—"

"What do you mean she *called* you, Darren?" he repeated, tone laced with venom. "What the fuck?"

"Back up," I warned, taking a protective stance in front of my boyfriend when his brother moved to come closer. "Just back right up, buddy."

"Aoife, you need to stay out of this."

"How do you know her name?" Releasing my hand, Joey dragged himself into a sitting position, chest rising and falling quickly, as he glowered at his mother and brother like they were the enemy. "How the fuck does he know my girlfriend's name?"

"I called him," his mother strangled out, pressing a hand to her chest.

"You *called* him," Joey deadpanned. "You just called him up? So, you had his number all along?" he choked out, trembling. "For the past five and a half years? You were in contact with him and never told me."

"Joey, listen to me—"

"Don't fucking speak to me!" my boyfriend roared, pointing a finger at his long-lost brother. "Don't fucking look at me." Turning back to his mother, he hissed, "I understand why you couldn't tell Dad, and I get why you didn't tell the boys and Shannon. But me?" His lip wobbled and I felt my heart crack when he asked, "Why couldn't you tell *me*?"

"I'm sorry I didn't tell you," Marie tried to explain, but Joe was having none of it.

"Shut the fuck up!" Hooking an arm around my waist, he pulled me closer, and I could feel just how badly his body was shaking. "Just get the fuck out. Both of you."

"Joey, please—"

"You heard him," I snapped, holding a hand out to warn his mother off. "Leave now."

"You need to stay in your own lane here, Aoife," Darren said, giving me a cool look. "I know you mean well, but this is a family matter."

"Don't fucking speak to her like that, asshole," Joey was quick to jump to my defense. "She *is* my family."

"Joey," Marie sobbed. "I'm your mother."

"And she's the mother of my kid. So, don't even think about pulling that card," he sneered. "Because she wins. Every damn time."

"Yeah." Nodding vigorously, I folded my arms across my chest and gave his mam a *ha* look.

"This isn't a pissing contest, ladies," Darren drawled. "Can you please step out for a moment, while our mother has a word with her son?"

"Hell no I won't step out," I spat, feeling my hackles rise. "I'm the one who's been sitting by his bedside since he was admitted. I'm the one down as his next of kin because not one of you assholes decided to show up. Where the hell were either one of you?"

"That's not fair," Marie wailed. "Shannon was . . ."

"Don't talk to me about what's fair," I came close to screaming. "Look at his face."

"Aoife, please."

"Look at his face," I repeated, voice rising right along with my temper. "Take a good fucking look, Marie. Because that's your son." Furious, I pointed to my boyfriend. "He's just as much your child as Shannon or the boys or *him*."

"I know he's my child."

"Then fucking act like it!" I hissed, narrowing my eyes in disgust. "Stop treating him like an afterthought. He's not a fucking afterthought, okay? You can't just show up here and lay down the law after not checking in on him once! It doesn't work like that, and I won't stand by and let you sink your twisted claws any deeper into him than you already have—"

"Molloy."

"No, Joe, she needs to hear this." Swallowing down a scream, I blinked away my temper tears and pointed a finger at his mother. "He's the best damn thing that came out of your marriage and you're too stupid to see it. He's not your bodyguard. He's not your bank account. He's not your babysitter. He's not your fucking husband. He's your *child*. He's your *son*!" Furious, I turned my glare on his brother. "And as for you? Well, I don't really know you that well yet, but I'm feeling like this is a *fuck you* kind of moment. So, fuck you."

"Are you quite finished your outburst?" the oldest Lynch asked calmly, arching a brow. "Because I'm not leaving until I speak to my brother in private."

"Then I guess we're all staying," I shot back, unyielding.

"Molloy." I felt Joey's hand on my waist. "It's okay."

Feeling panicked, I swung around to look at him. "You don't have to talk to them, Joe. Do you hear me? You don't need to listen to another word she says."

"It's okay," he whispered, giving my hip a reassuring squeeze. "Go home and get something to eat. I'll be fine here."

"I'm not leaving you."

"I'll be fine."

"I'm not going, Joe."

"I'm going to have to talk to them at some stage."

"But I—"

"It's all good, baby. Just give me a few hours, okay? I'll be fine."

No, this wasn't good at all.

This was all *bad*.

I didn't want these people anywhere near him.

"Joe." Chewing on my lip, I implored him with my eyes to not do this. "Are you sure?"

He didn't look sure.

He didn't look like he was in any fit state to handle these people.

Still, he nodded stiffly and released me.

"Fine. It's three o clock now," I squeezed out, briefly glancing at the screen of my phone before shoving it back in my pocket. "I'll go home and have a shower and I'll be back at six, okay?"

"Take your time," he replied. "It's all good."

No, it wasn't.

Everything inside of me screamed *wrong, wrong, wrong.*

But what could I do?

I couldn't exactly force his mother and brother out of the hospital, and if Joey wanted to speak to them, then I couldn't stop him.

Even if I really, really didn't want him anywhere near these people.

"I love you," I said, ignoring his family, as I leaned in close and pressed a kiss to his lips. "I'll be back."

I'm your brother

JOEY

"Where is he?" I asked the moment my girlfriend was gone, as a million thoughts were rushing around in my mind. While my heart was demanding answers to even more questions, only one question stood out in my hazy thoughts. "Where's Dad?"

"The Gards haven't been able to find him."

Of course they hadn't.

The old man wouldn't resurface until the time was right.

He was as sharp as a tack.

He knew how to play the system better than anyone.

I didn't want Molloy to have to hear any of this. I didn't want that man tainting her life any more than he already had.

"They'll find him, Joey," Darren continued to say. *To fucking lie.* "The Gards are scouring the countryside looking for him. He won't get away with it. Not this time."

"Not this time," I repeated his words slowly, gaze flicking from Darren to Mam. "What makes you think this time is different?"

All along they had been in contact with each other.

Never once in the past five and a half years had he attempted to reach out to me.

When I thought about Shannon and how my disappearing for five years would affect her, I physically recoiled.

I could never do it.

I could never leave them like that.

Knowing that he could and did made me so fucking resentful that I was practically choking on my hatred.

I knew he had to get out, we all did, but it didn't change how it all rolled out.

Now he was here, acting like the fucking savior of all things Lynch, and I despised him for it.

"Because Mam is ready to leave him." Darren's tone was laced with sincerity, which assured me that he truly believed the shit he was spurting. "This time she's really ready, Joe."

"She's not ready," I replied flatly, ignoring the way my mother nodded eagerly like a loyal dog. "She won't leave him until she's in a box and you're a fool if you believe otherwise."

"That's not true, Joey," she tried to coax, closing the space between us and taking the spot my girlfriend had vacated. "I've been to the court. There was an emergency hearing. I've been granted a safety order."

Words.

They were just words.

I'd heard them all a million times before.

They meant as little now as any other time.

Promises made, promises broken.

It was bullshit.

"And you?" I turned my attention to the turncoat bastard I hadn't laid eyes on since puberty hit me. "What's your angle?"

Darren's brows furrowed. "My angle?"

"What do you want?" I asked, tone void of all emotion. "What are you doing here?"

"I'm back to help," he said, roughly clearing his throat. "I came home for my family, Joe."

"Your family."

"Yeah, my family." Tears filled his eyes. "I missed you so much, kid."

There was so much resentment built up inside of me that I was honestly afraid to open my mouth out of fear of what might slip out.

It was a good thing that I was heavily medicated in this moment or I might have lunged for the prick.

"Have you spoken to the Gards?" Mam asked, pulling a tissue from the sleeve of her cardigan and wiping her nose.

"Why?"

"Because I think we need to get our stories aligned," Darren answered for her. Another man answering for her. Another fucking boss. "We need to figure out how we swing this to the Gards."

"There's no story to align," I deadpanned. "I won't lie for either one of them. Never again. As far as I'm concerned, she's as responsible for what happened to Shannon as our old man is. So you two can swing whatever the fuck you want, but leave me out of any bullshit fabrications."

"Come on, Joey, I know you're hurting right now, but you're not the only victim here. Mam is a victim, too."

"Did I say *I* was a victim?"

"No, *I'm* saying that you're a victim—"

"You don't know the first thing about me," I spat, cutting him off. "You don't know what the fuck I've been through, so don't swan in here trying to feed me a line and slap a label on my forehead. I'm done with it." I turned to my mother and doubled down. "I am done with *you*."

I was.

I meant it.

I fucking meant it.

Never again would I give her the opportunity to let me down.

"I know you've been going down a bad path for a long time now," Darren had the gall to say. "I also know that you've got yourself a little Joey on the way."

"Good news travels fast," I replied coolly. "Get all that from one of your mommy and son phone calls?"

"She's the girl from the wall, right? The one you had your eye on back in first year?"

"The fuck would you know about it?" I seethed, jaw clenching. "You weren't around when I was in first year. You bailed, asshole."

"I remember your reaction to her that day."

"Good for you."

"You got the girl pregnant while you're still in school, Joe? Really?" His tone was dripping with condescension when he said, "Talk about following in the old man's footsteps and repeating the goddamn cycle!"

"Don't even think about lecturing me, asshole," I snapped, refusing to show him how deeply he cut me with his words. "I am *not* our old man, and *she* is none of your fucking business!"

"And Shane Holland?" he continued to challenge, giving me a hard look. "Is he none of my business either? Goddammit, Joey, what did I tell you about messing around with that guy?"

"Shit, Dar, I can't remember." I shrugged. "How long's it been since we spoke? Five, six years?"

"Joey." He sighed wearily. "You know why I had to leave."

"Don't Joey me," I sneered. "You don't get to stroll back in here and call the shots. You're not the patriarch of the family, asshole."

"And you are?"

"I did the best I could with the hand I was given," I shot back. "So, don't look down your goddamn nose at my choices. At least I stuck around."

"Please don't fight with each other," Mam pleaded, placing her hand on Darren's shoulder. "We're all family here."

"No. You two are family," I bit out, tone hoarse. "My family just left."

"Wh-what do you mean?"

"That girl isn't your family, Joe. We are."

Not bothering answering either one of them, I pulled at the wires and leads attached to my body and climbed unsteadily to my feet.

"Joey, what are you doing?"

"Shannon," I bit out, searching the small area for my clothes. "Aoife said she's upstairs. Which ward is she on?"

"Joey, stop," Mam cried, when I ripped the needle out of my arm and moved for my jeans that were hanging on the back of the chair next to my bed. "Lie down and rest. You're not supposed to be out of bed."

Ripping off the hospital gown, I stood shivering in my jocks, feeling like my head was about to explode, but needing to move because the prospect of staying here was unthinkable.

"Jesus Christ," I heard Darren choke out when I turned my back to them. "What did Dad do to him, Mam?"

Darren.

Fucking Darren.

"Shannon," was all I managed to get out, as my head spun and my mind struggled to focus. It wasn't too bad when I was lying down, but standing up made my head swim. "I need to see my sister."

"Joey, you can't leave."

"Fuck you."

"You have to be discharged by a doctor and you're in no fit state to go anywhere."

"I said fuck you."

"Joey, please!"

"Where is my *sister*?" Mind reeling, I clumsily stepped into the legs of my jeans, and dragged them up my hips before snatching up the blood-stained hoodie. "Where's Shannon?"

Fuck if I knew where my t-shirt was, and in this moment, I didn't care.

The only thing I cared about was getting out of this place and far away from these people.

"You're not leaving." Two hands came down on my shoulders and I all but took leave of my senses. "Just lie down and rest, okay?"

"Get your fucking hands off me," I snarled, stumbling away from the ghost of my past. "Don't you ever put your hands on me again!"

"It's me." Holding his hands up in retreat, Darren watched me warily. "I would never hurt you, Joe. You know that."

"I don't know you," I spat, ripping off the bandage from my eye that was preventing me from seeing clearly. From protecting myself. "I don't know who the fuck you are anymore!"

"Joe." Emotion filled his eyes. "I'm your brother."

"You're no brother of mine," I sneered and then winced when pain rocketed through my eyes. Fuck, the lights hurt so damn bad. "So, keep your goddamn hands to yourself. Because I don't care whose body you came out of, I will . . . " Staggering sideways, I gripped the wall for balance. "Just leave me the fuck alone!"

"What's going on here?" the nurse who'd been looking after me all day asked, pushing the curtain open. "Joseph, sweetheart, you need to get back into bed."

"No, you need to get whatever paperwork I need to sign, because I'm out of here," I replied, leaning heavily against the wall, as I toed on my runners. "Fuck, where are my socks?"

"Joey, you can't just leave!"

"I told you to fuck off!" Wincing in pain, I clutched my head and tried to stop my head from spinning. "I need to see my sister. Make sure she's okay."

"That's not a good idea," the nurse said in a coaxing tone, moving to my side. "Why don't we send your family home and sit down for a little chat? Just the two of us?"

"I'm leaving," I bit out, shuddering in revulsion when her small hand cupped my elbow. "Do I need to sign a discharge form or something?"

"Why don't we give your girlfriend a call?" she suggested, trying to steer me back to the bed. "Hm? What's her name again?"

"Aoife."

"That's right. How about you get back into bed and I'll go and call Aoife? She left her phone number back at the nurses station. You just rest up here and I'll go and call her for you. Hm?"

"No, no, no," I groaned, shaking my head when a wave of confusion hit me. "Don't call her. She needs to rest. Just help me get out of here."

"Joey, please just lie back down and rest."

"How about we all give Joey some space," I heard the nurse instruct. "Good lad yourself. Just hold onto my hand and you're nice and safe."

"Joey, baby, are you okay?"

"My eyes," I groaned, blinking rapidly when my vision blurred in and out of focus. "There's something wrong with my eyes."

"You're going to feel disorientated for a few days," the nurse coaxed as she walked me back to my prison. "Which is why you need to rest up and let us take care of you, okay?"

"Is he going to be okay?"

"Out," I heard the nurse command. "Now please."

"Tell him that we'll come back later."

"Leave now, please. Or I will call security."

"Fuck," I groaned, feeling faint. "I don't want to see them."

"You don't have to," I heard the nurse say. "Now, I've spoken to the ward manager on floor 3, and there's a bed after coming available upstairs for you. The porter will be around shortly to take you up."

"I don't want to go upstairs," I croaked out, feeling myself sink down on the bed. "I want to go home."

"Good lad," she coaxed, fluffing the pillows at my back. "What have you done to your poor arm, hm?"

Groaning, I slapped a hand over my eyes and winced. "Fuck knows."

"I'll put a fresh line in for you."

"I don't want a line," I mumbled, clenching my eyes shut when the room started spinning. "I just . . . I want something for the pain."

"Okay, I'll get you something for pain, Joseph," I heard her reply. "Where is the pain worse? In your head?"

"No, it's here," I whispered, rubbing my chest. "Here's the worst."

"Your heart?"

I nodded stiffly.

"Okay, sweetheart," the nurse replied softly. "Just close your eyes and get some rest. I'll go and fetch you something for the pain."

Back to him

AOIFE

"How are you feeling, love?" Mam asked when I stepped into the kitchen later that evening, fresh from a shower and feeling like something Spud shat out.

"Don't ask," I muttered, moving for the washing machine to deposit my towel. "I don't think you're going to be able to get the stains out of these," I added, holding up my blood-stained jeans and hoodie. "Should I just chuck them?"

"Oh Jesus." Setting the iron down, Mam covered her mouth with her hand, eyes filling with tears. "Yes, chuck them, love. I'll take you shopping for some new ones next week."

"I don't want to go shopping, Mam," I replied with a weary sigh as I dropped onto a chair at the kitchen table. "I just want the Gards to find that bastard, lock him up, and throw away the goddamn key."

"How is young Joey?"

"Destroyed." I couldn't hide the pain in my voice. "He's broken physically and mentally."

"Oh, Aoife, love."

"I will never get the image of them on that kitchen floor out of my head."

"I can imagine."

"No, Mam," I said, shaking my head. "You can't and be glad of it."

"How are you feeling, Aoife?"

"Like my heart was beaten to a pulp and is lying on a trolley in A&E."

"Oh, love."

"I hate his parents, Mam." Feeling my eyes burn with tears, I dropped my head in my hands and bit back a roar. "I hate those fucking *monsters*."

"Oh, love, I know you're upset." She closed the space between us and placed a hand on my shoulder. "But you need to stay calm and look after yourself. You've a little baby growing in your belly. You can't be getting worked up."

"Worked up?" I choked out, voice cracking. "Mam, I'm fucking *devastated*."

"I know." She wrapped her arms around me and pulled me to her chest. "I know, Aoife, love."

"He's my best friend," I cried, twisting sideways in my seat to clutch her. "Forget the romantic side of things and all of the bullshit. He's my closest friend on the entire planet and this is *killing* me." Sniffling, I gripped her jumper and sagged against her. "You don't understand how much it hurts. Watching him go through everything he goes through and feeling utterly useless."

"You're not useless, love," Mam soothed, wrapping me up in her arms. "You're a lifeline to that boy. A life-jacket, if you will."

"No, I'm not."

"Yes, you are," she coaxed. "You've been keeping him afloat for years now."

"But it's not enough, Mam," I cried hoarsely. "I can't keep watching him *suffer*. I'm so afraid for him. You don't understand. It's paralysing. I am so fucking scared for him that I can barely *breathe*. One of these days, he's going to go under, and I won't be able to pull him back."

My phone rang loudly in my pocket. With a gasp I sprang away from my mother, snatched it out and quickly clicked accept as I put it to my ear. "Hello?"

"Hello, am I speaking to Aoife?"

"Yeah, that's me."

"Hi, Aoife, my name is Stephie Hubbard. I'm the nurse looking after Joey this evening."

"Is he okay?" I demanded, feeling faint. "Did something happen?"

"He's fine," she was quick to assure me. "He was a little disorientated after his mother and brother visited, so I told him that I would call you. We have a bed for him on the main ward, but he's insisting on discharging himself."

"Are they still there? His mam and brother?"

"No, he was growing increasingly distressed, so I asked them to leave."

"Good." My heart thudded painfully in my chest. "Tell him that I'm on my way, okay? I'm leaving right now. I'll be there in half an hour."

"Oh, Aoife," Mam sobbed when I ended the call. "I know you're worried about Joey, we all are, but I'm worried about you, too. Can you go for a lie down before you go back to the hospital? For the baby's sake. I can pop up to the hospital to see him instead."

"No." Shaking my head, I stood up and schooled my features. "I'm going back to him."

"Then I'll have your father drive you," Mam replied, sounding deflated. "You're in no fit state to be driving into the city."

"Do you have credit in your phone to call me for a spin home later?" Dad asked, a little while later, when he pulled into a parking space in the carpark of the hospital. "Do you have a few bob in your purse in case you get hungry or want a cup of tea?"

"I have credit, Dad." I unfasted my seatbelt and reached for the door. "And I don't need money. I'm not hungry."

"Aoife, wait." Leaning across the seats, my father closed my car door. "Just sit and talk to me for a minute."

"What's to say, Dad?" I replied, numb.

"Are you alright?"

"No. I'm not alright," I choked out. "How could I be alright when he's . . ." A sob tore from my chest. "He could have died, Dad."

"Jesus."

"His face," I squeezed out, feeling the familiar sting of hot tears. "He's barely recognizable."

"Poor young fella."

"You don't know the half of it."

"He's a troubled lad."

"He's a *good* man."

"I never said he wasn't."

"No more, Dad." Sniffling, I looked to my father. "I know you're upset about the baby, but you can't be hard on him. It's too much. He has too much shit in his life. Just . . . just be kind to him."

"Aoife." My father's eyes were filled with emotion when he whispered, "I'm afraid for you."

"And I'm afraid for him," I replied, pushing the car door open and climbing out. "Thanks for the spin, Dad."

"Aoife, wait!"

I didn't wait.

I couldn't.

Instead, I closed the passenger door of my father's van and strode off in the direction of the entrance to the A&E department.

Blinking away any residue tears, I slapped on my brightest smile when I walked through the triage area and headed down the jam-packed corridor in the direction of the admissions cubicles, not stopping until I had reached Joey's.

"I hear you've been causing trouble," I teased, pulling back the curtain. "Plotting a jailbreak, stud?"

My smile remained in place, but my heart plummeted into my ass when my gaze landed on the empty trolley.

His blanket was strewn over the bed, while his clothes and shoes had disappeared from the chair at his bedside.

His IV pole held a full bag of clear fluid, while the line that was supposed to be attached to my boyfriend's arm was on the floor, dripping clear fluid into a little puddle.

Panicked, I looked around wildly, frantically searching for his face in the crowded corridor, even though I knew in my heart it would be a fruitless search.

Because my boyfriend was gone.

The ledge I had been desperately trying to pull him back from?

There was no doubt in my mind that he had gone trip-tumbling over it.

PART 7

The Missing List

AOIFE

After searching the hospital for Joey, and coming up empty, I had called up our friends to come get me, needing bodies on the ground to help sniff him out before he came to any harm.

> **AOIFE: TELL ME THAT YOU'RE OKAY. PLEASE. I'M GOING OUT OF MY MIND HERE.**

> **AOIFE: ANSWER YOUR PHONE, ASSHOLE!!!**

> **AOIFE: HOW COULD YOU JUST VANISH ON ME? WTF JOE! CALL ME, DAMMIT!**

> **AOIFE: WHERE ARE YOU? COME ON, JOEY, PLEASE.**

"We'll find him," Podge tried to appease me, as I sat in the passenger seat of his Ford Fiesta, with my entire body racking with shivers, on the way back to Ballylaggin. "It's only been a couple of hours since he left the hospital, Aoif."

"Exactly," Alec and Casey agreed from the back seat. "He won't have gone far."

"You guys don't get it," I strangled out, knees bopping restlessly as I tried his phone for the millionth time, only to be sent to voicemail again. "He's not in his right frame of mind."

His sister was lying in a hospital bed with a collapsed lung. He was too injured to be out on the streets, but that was exactly what was happening. I knew in my heart of hearts that there was a ninety-nine percent chance that he had gone off the deep end. I hoped with everything I had inside of me that he hadn't, but the fear still festered away inside of me.

"So? Lynchy's never in his right mind," Alec piped up. "He spends a solid eighty percent of his time off his trolley and it's never stopped him from looking after himself."

"Not helping, Al," Casey grumbled.

"He has a concussion," I hissed, brushing my hair off my face. "A really bad one, and his head is all smashed up. He shouldn't be out of bed, let alone wandering around by himself."

"Don't do that in here," Casey snapped, and I twisted around to see her smack an unlit cigarette out of Alec's hand. "She's pregnant, asshole."

"Oh shit, yeah." He rummaged around the floor of the car for his cigarette. "My bad, sexy-legs."

"Can you drop me off at Elk's Terrace?" I asked Podge. "I'll check his house and ask around his neighbors."

"No problem," Podge replied. "I'll take a spin over to the GAA grounds and search there."

"Yeah, and I'll check Biddies," Casey offered.

"I'll go with you," Alec chimed in.

"No, Al, you need to go to Shane Holland's gaff," Podge interrupted. "See if he's been there."

"What? No fucking way," Alec vehemently protested. "That prick's a psycho. He's as likely to stab me as he is to speak to me."

"Come on, Al."

"Why me?"

"Because you're ... well, you're you," Podge settled on. "Come on. You know Lynchy would do it for you."

"Fine," he huffed. "But if anything happens to me, it's on you, ginger-pubes!"

CASEY: HE'S NOT AT BIDDIES, BABE.

PODGE: NO SIGN OF HIM AT THE PAVILION.

ALEC: NOBODY HOME @ PYSCHO'S HOUSE.

Anxious, I tapped out a two-word response and clicked send before sliding my phone back into my pocket.

AOIFE: KEEP LOOKING.

The night air whipped at my face, as I stood at the Lynchs' front door, with my fist banging incessantly on the frosted panel of the door.

"What did you do?" I demanded when Darren finally swung the door inwards. "What did you say to him?"

"Maybe you should calm down—"

"Don't bullshit me, Darren."

Furious, I pushed past him and stalked into their house, unwilling to pander to anyone's bullshit, not when he was teetering on the edge like I knew he was.

"You," I spat when I stormed into the kitchen and was confronted by the woman who bore him. "It's always you."

"Aoife?" Marie's eyes widened. "What are you talking about?"

"Your son is gone!"

"What do you mean he's gone?" Darren demanded, joining us in the kitchen. "Gone from the hospital?"

"Yes, he's gone from the hospital," I snapped. "He discharged himself and I want to know what you fuckers said to him."

"He wasn't supposed to do that," Marie sobbed, sinking down on her smoking chair at the table. "Oh, Darren."

"What did you say to him this time, huh?" I sneered, hands on my hips, turning my attention on her. "And don't even think about feeding me a line, because I *know* you've caused this. Your 'poor me' act might work on your sons, but I see through you, Marie."

"Listen, he showed up at Shannon's hospital room earlier." Eyeing me warily, Darren added, "There was a conversation, we had words, and he stormed off. I presumed he went back to his bed."

"You had *words*?" I seethed, feeling my temperature spike right along with my anxiety. "What kind of words?"

"He has a really bad attitude problem."

"Of course he does!" I sneered, throwing my hands up. "How else is he supposed to be? You don't know what he's had to deal with these past six years."

"You're overstepping, Aoife."

"What did you say to him?" I pressed. "Something pushed him over the edge and I want to know what that something was!"

"I know you mean well, but I don't need to explain myself to you."

"Yeah, well, explain yourself to your conscience," I shot back, trembling. "Because if anything happens to him then it's on you!"

"Let's cut the bullshit here. If Joey signed himself out of hospital it's for one reason and one reason only," Darren was quick to counter. "He's out chasing his next fix."

"Shut up," I warned, holding a hand up. "Shut your goddamn mouth."

"He's an addict, Aoife, and that's not on me."

"It's not that cut and dry, Darren," I heard myself choke out. "He wasn't born an addict. That's not who he is. His issues with addiction are a direct result of spending eighteen years in this hellhole house, with those godawful people you both have the misfortune of calling your parents."

"Aoife, stop it!"

"Don't get even get me started on you, Marie. You don't deserve to call him your son," I snarled, swinging around to glare at his mother. "You have *never* deserved his love and you never will!" Blinking back my tears, I spat my pain out at the woman who had created so much turmoil in my boyfriend. "Everyone thinks your husband is the abusive parent, but I see what you do to your son." I tapped my temple, beyond livid. "I know what you are, Marie. I see right fucking through you."

"Don't speak to my mother like that," Darren warned, taking a defensive stance in front of her. "You can speak civilly or you can leave."

"You're a fucking joke," I continued, pointing my finger at her.

"You've spent years getting into Joey's mind, twisting his thought process and fucking with his confidence. Convincing him that he's the second coming of his father. That he's dangerous, and a liability, and a disappointment!"

"How dare you!"

"Yeah, I know what you've done to him," I sneered unapologetically. "And you can bury your head in the sand all you want, but you're the mental abuser in this instance. You broke him, Marie. You have damaged Joey deeper with your words than his father ever has with his fists. You're a gaslighting bitch!"

"Like you can talk."

"All I have *ever* done is love your son."

"A little too much," she erupted on me, hands clutching her head as she screamed, "You want to throw blame on who fucked up my son's life then you need look no further than the person staring back at you in the mirror! Because you're the one destroying his future, Aoife. You're the one saddling him with a baby he doesn't even want!"

"You don't know what you're talking about," I choked out, feeling like she rammed a red-hot poker through my chest with her words. "He wants the baby."

"He wants to make you happy," she roared in my face. "That's not the same thing as him wanting to be a father."

"Tell me something," Darren decided to interject. "If you knew my brother was in such a bad way, why didn't you do something to protect him?"

"Fuck you, Darren," I spat. "You don't know a damn thing about either one of us."

"I know my brother isn't well," he countered evenly. "And so do you. So, why the hell would you trap him into fatherhood?"

"I didn't trap him." I stiffened, feeling my hackles rise and my heart crack all in one breath. "I hardly got pregnant on purpose, did I?"

"Didn't you?"

My blood ran cold. "What's that supposed to mean?"

"Oh, come off it, Aoife." He gave me a hard look when he asked, "He's a handsome lad. How many times was he off his head when you let him inside your body?"

"*Excuse* me?"

"Hey." He held his hands up. "If you want to storm into this house, all guns blazing, laying blame at our feet for Joey's downfall, then I'm more than happy to hold the mirror up to you."

"I would *never* hurt Joey," I heard myself defend, refusing to back down to this emotional manipulation. This shit might float on his siblings, but not me. "I love your brother."

"No, *I* love my brother, Aoife," he argued hotly. "So, make no mistake about it when I tell you that I'm willing to do whatever it takes to protect him."

"What are you saying?"

"I'm saying that if you love my brother as much as you say you do, then you'll do the right thing for him and make this go away."

"*This* being your niece or nephew?"

"Let's not be overly dramatic here and start labeling a fetus," he replied evenly. "Listen, my mother already told me that you don't come from money. If it's a matter of not being able to afford the trip to England, then I am more than willing to take care of the financial side of things."

"Think about it, Aoife," Marie joined the fray, tone desperate, as she pleaded with me. "If you won't put your own future first, then think of my son's."

"I can't fucking believe this." Choking out a humorless laugh, I roughly batted away a tear. "Every time I think you can't stoop any lower, you just keep on hitting it out of the park."

"Aoife, be rational here."

"I am being rational," I snapped, glaring at Darren. "You do realize if Joey knew what you just offered me, it would kill him? You do get that, don't you? This is just another in a long list of betrayals."

"I'm not betraying my brother," he argued. "I'm trying to protect him.

And the way I see it, the only way he gets hurt is if you go running your mouth off, which in that instance, then you would be the one crushing him, Aoife, not me."

He had me over a barrel and he knew it.

Bastard.

"Yeah, well, we're keeping the baby," I spat, feeling my hand drop to the small swell of my stomach, as a wave of maternal instinct washed over me. "It's a done deal, asshole. We've already decided."

"You mean you've decided."

"No, I mean we *both* decided," I countered, unwilling to back down or be bribed by this asshole. "And there's absolutely nothing either of you can say to change that. You can't pay me off or bribe me because I'm not going away."

"Then you're going to ruin his life."

"Then at least he'll be ruined with love and not pain."

Blurred days and wasted nights

JOEY

My body was floating.

Slipping in and out of consciousness.

I couldn't feel a thing.

And it was fucking glorious.

Weirdly enough, the only part of reality that my brain insisted on clinging to was the lyrics of that song.

That Mazzy Star song Molloy played on a loop.

With my eyes rolling back in my head, and my legs twitching sporadically, I lay on my side, trying to focus on the needle in my arm.

Slow.

Slow ...

Not too fast.

Nice and slow.

Numbness filled my body at a rapid rate, sending me freewheeling into oblivion.

Euphoria flooded my veins, taking with it every one of my problems, until there was nothing but darkness.

Emptiness.

No pain.

Void.

I still love you

AOIFE

AOIFE: JOEY, PLEASE. IT'S BEEN TWO DAYS. JUST TEXT ME AND LET ME KNOW THAT YOU'RE OKAY.

AOIFE: CAN YOU JUST LET ME KNOW THAT YOU'RE OKAY!

JOEY: I'M SORRY.

AOIFE: JOE? OH, THANK GOD! ARE YOU OKAY? WHERE ARE YOU? TEXT ME WHERE YOU'RE AT AND I'LL COME GET YOU.

JOEY: I FUCKED IT, BABY.

AOIFE: THAT DOESN'T MATTER. JUST TELL ME WHERE YOU ARE, AND I'LL COME GET YOU.

AOIFE: I'M NOT MAD, JOE. I JUST WANT TO SEE YOU.

AOIFE: JOEY, PLEASE!

JOEY: I DON'T KNOW, MOLLOY. MY HEAD IS . . . I, AH, MY PHONE'S NEARLY DEAD.

JOEY: I'M SORRY. I LOVE YOU.

AOIFE: IT'S OKAY, JOE. EVERYTHING'S OKAY. I LOVE YOU, TOO. JUST TELL ME WHERE YOU'RE AT, BABY, AND I'LL COME GET YOU.

AOIFE: ARE YOU OKAY?

AOIFE: IF YOUR PHONE IS DEAD, CAN YOU BORROW SOMEONE ELSE'S AND JUST LET ME KNOW?

AOIFE: JOEY!

AOIFE: FOUR DAYS, JOE. FOUR FUCKING DAYS.

AOIFE: THE HOSPITAL CALLED. I GOT THAT APPOINTMENT.

AOIFE: I NEED YOU TO COME HOME, JOEY!

AOIFE: IT'S BEEN FIVE DAYS.

AOIFE: HOW COULD YOU DO THIS TO ME?

AOIFE: I HAVE A HOSPITAL APPOINTMENT ON MONDAY. DO YOU PLAN ON COMING?

AOIFE: EVERYONE IS ASKING ABOUT YOU, AND I'M COVERING FOR YOUR ASS, WHEN I DON'T EVEN KNOW IF YOU'RE ALIVE!!! PLEASE, JOEY. IT'S BEEN 6 DAYS! JUST CALL ME. PLEASE!

AOIFE: SEVEN DAYS. YOUR HANDS BETTER BE BROKEN, ASSHOLE, BECAUSE THERE IS NO EXCUSE FOR NOT CONTACTING ME.

AOIFE: PLEASE COME BACK TO ME, JOE.

AOIFE: Day eight and I'm going to the hospital. I have that appointment with the midwife. You're supposed to be there too, you know.

AOIFE: I'm scared.

AOIFE: I still love you.

Do you feel safe?

AOIFE

Feeling extremely self-conscious, I stood on the physician scales in examination room 3B in the maternity hospital and watched as the midwife fiddled with the reading rod.

My heart was racing violently in my chest, and every ounce of blood I seemed to possess had decided to rush to my cheeks.

I loathed being weighed.

I loathed being here even more.

But the worst part of the whole ordeal was that I had to do it alone.

Today was day eight of Joey being AWOL and I was at my breaking point.

"You're a fine tall girl, aren't you? Just under 5'9," the midwife mused, distracting me from my internal meltdown. "Is the baby's father tall?"

"Um, yeah, he is," I replied, stepping off the scales, and toeing my pumps back on. "He's about 6'1."

"You'll have a fine tall baby on your hands so," she chuckled, scribbling in the red folder that I had been given at reception. "Now, you've had your urine sample taken and your bloodwork done, so why don't we take a seat and go through some medical history."

"Okay."

"Is baby's father joining us?"

"Uh, no, he's, ah . . . " Voice trailing off, I slumped in the chair before adding, "He really wanted to be here, but he couldn't get time off work."

The lie slipped off my tongue to join a whole host of other lies I had told this past week to explain my boyfriend's absence to the people in my life. Because telling the truth was out of the question.

The only one I had been able to confide in was Casey.

"No problem," the midwife replied, taking the seat opposite me. "You can answer any of the questions you know about your partner's family history, and if he has any concerns, he can have additional information added at any time."

"Okay." Clasping my hands on my lap, I nodded and forced a smile. "Ask away."

"First day of your last menstrual cycle?"

"December fourteenth."

"And how long does your cycle last?"

"Anything between 28 and 35 days usually."

"Do you or your partner, or any family members have any history of diabetes, hypertension, heart disease, autoimmune disease, epilepsy, or any other serious medical illness not mentioned?"

"Uh, no . . . " I roughly cleared my throat. "Not that I'm aware of."

"Are there any genetic conditions in your family or your partner's family of Down's syndrome, muscular dystrophy, spina bifida or any other serious genetic condition not mentioned?"

"No," I breathed, heart fluttering nervously. "Nothing."

"What about a history of twins?"

"I'm a twin," I replied. "I've a twin brother. My mother's aunt has two sets of twins. That's all as far as I know."

"Are there any allergies in your family or your partner's family?"

"I have an intolerance to bullshit if that counts?"

She smiled. "No, that's okay."

I shrugged, face flaming with heat. "Okay."

"Any recurrent miscarriage or stillbirth in the family?"

"Uh no, not on my side."

"Your partner's?"

"Uh, his mam lost a baby late into her last pregnancy."

The midwife's eyes flickered with sympathy. "I'm sorry to hear that. Do you happen to know what the cause of that loss was?"

"I think she had a placental abruption?" I squeezed out, flustered. "I'm not entirely sure. She's had a lot of children. I think that one was her seventh?"

The midwife's brows rose in surprise. "And your partner? He's number . . ."

"Two," I filled in. "He's her second son."

"Big family."

Big mess. "Yeah."

"Sexual partners—"

"I've only been with him," I blurted out, cutting her off. "We've been together since fifth year, but we've been friends since first year."

She smiled warmly at me. "And your partner?"

"Uh, he's had other sexual partners, but since we've been together, it's only been us."

"Uh-huh, and are you a smoker?"

"No."

"Is your partner a smoker?"

"Uh, yeah."

"And your alcohol intake?"

"I'm eighteen," I replied with a shrug. "When I went out, it was a matter of go hard or go home."

"And during this pregnancy?"

"God no," I spluttered. "I would never knowingly drink while I'm pregnant."

"And baby's father?"

"No." My palms began to sweat. "He's not a big drinker."

"What about birth control?"

"I was on the pill," I explained. "Obviously, I stopped taking it once I found out."

"Do you use condoms?"

"No."

"Any vitamins and supplements?"

"I've been taking folic acid and these multivitamins for pregnancy that my mam bought in the chemist."

"What about recreational drug use?"

Oh Jesus, here we go.

"I've never taken anything stronger than a paracetamol in my life."

"Uh-huh," she replied, scribbling down everything I told her in my folder. "And your partner?"

I hesitated.

"I'm not here to judge, Aoife," she said, noticing my reluctance. "Everything I'm asking is for the benefit of your baby." Her eyes were warm and full of kindness when she said, "It's all in confidence."

"He's fine," I squeezed out, heart hammering wildly in my chest. "I mean . . . yeah, he dabbled a little in the past, but he's fine now."

"And when you say he dabbled?"

I shrugged, unable to get my voice to comply because talking meant betraying him, and my heart strings refused point blank to do that.

"Aoife, if there's a pattern of drug abuse in," she paused to glance at her notes before adding, "Joey's history, then that's necessary information for your unborn baby."

"A little weed," I finally came out with, deciding that weed was the lesser of evils in this instance. "But like I said, he's fine now."

"Okay." Setting my folder down on the chair beside her, she leaned forward and rested her elbows on her knees. "I'm going to ask you some questions and I want you to be completely transparent with me."

"Okay."

"Does your partner have a history of alcohol or substance abuse?"

"No, I already told you that he's not a big drinker."

"Aside from marijuana, does your partner consume other illegal substances?" she pushed. "Substances that could put you at risk?"

"Like what?"

"Is he an intravenous drug user, for example?"

"No," I choked out, flustered. "I mean, not really."

"Not really?"

"He has in the past."

"Okay." Concern flooded her eyes. "And has your partner ever been violent with you?"

"What?" I balked. "No."

"Has your partner ever caused harm or pain to your body?"

"That's the same question," I snapped. "And the answer's still no. He has never laid a finger on me, and he never would."

"Do you feel like you're in danger?"

"Oh my god, no," I snapped, knees bopping restlessly. "He wouldn't harm a hair on my head."

"Okay." Reaching over, she gave my knee a supportive squeeze. "I don't want you to panic, and it's purely hospital protocol, but we're going to have to have more extensive bloodwork sent off."

"For what?"

"To eliminate any sexually transmitted diseases not screened in your previous bloodwork."

"Why?" I demanded. "Joey and I are only with each other."

"More often than not intravenous drug users have a tendency of using contaminated needles. Not to mention the lack of inhibition when under the influence. It's not uncommon for pregnant women in similar circumstances to present with STDs, even when they have only been with their partner, therefore I can't stress to you enough the importance of protecting yourself during intercourse."

"He's not *dirty*," I strangled out, mind completely reeling from the information she was throwing at me. "He's a great guy. He's smart and responsible, and in school, and has a job. He's a Cork hurler for God's sake."

"We have a service available at the hospital for young mothers that I think might be of great benefit to you—"

"No thank you." I shook my head. "I don't need any of that."

"I'm going to refer you anyway and have a member from their team contact you in due course." Ignoring my wishes, the midwife reached for my notes and resumed her scribbling before standing up and moving for the door. "I'm going to need you to wait here, Aoife. I'll be back shortly."

Oh god.

This was not good.

This was not good at all.

Sliding my phone out of my pocket, I quickly dialed the one number I knew would always answer me and held the phone to my ear.

"Aoife, love, are you alright?"

"Mam. Can you come up to the hospital?" Clenching my eyes shut, I blew out a ragged breath before whispering, "I really need you."

Leave me out with the waste

JOEY

The sound of my pulse thundering in my ears was the first telltale sign that I wasn't dead.

My sister's voice was the second.

"Shan?"

I could hear her.

I could feel her hands on my face.

Her breath on my cheek.

But I just . . . I couldn't fucking focus.

"What did you take?" Her voice was in my ear again. "I know you're drunk, and I can smell the weed off you, but there's more, isn't there? What was it? What did they give you?"

I couldn't answer her.

Because I couldn't remember what I'd taken.

I didn't even know where I was.

Hell, my lips didn't feel like they were working.

I was coming down from a high, crashing hard and fast.

Shivering violently, I tried to curl up and die.

Maybe if I held my breath, the pain would stop.

My heart would just *give up*.

"Sorry," I mumbled, wincing when her disappointment rained down on me like verbal bullets. "Please don't hate me."

Hemorrhaging vomit and bile, I battled with the nausea attacking my senses, while desperately trying to survive the agonizing burning sensation flushing through my system.

Don't hate me.

I hate me.

I hate me.
I hate me.

As the fog in my mind lifted, and I slowly registered my surroundings, I realized that I was bollocks naked in Johnny Kavanagh's bathroom, with his creepy bastard of a flanker lifting me out of the shower.

"Don't fucking touch me!" I snarled, staggering away from him, only to collapse on my ass in a heap.

They were talking to me, fucking shouting at me, but I couldn't make out a word of it. I knew that I was responding because my lips were moving, but I had no fucking clue of what was coming out of my mouth. It was a vulnerable position to be in, to be so unhinged that I was unable to control the words coming out of my mouth.

Everything was so intense.

Everything *hurt.*

Body racked with tremors, I tried to control my breathing, as flashbacks of the past two weeks slowly came back to me.

Dad.
Shannon.
Molloy.
Mam.
Darren!
Shane.
Pain.
Pain.
Fucking pain.

Repressing the urge to scream, I clutched my head in my hands and tried to stop the room from spinning.

The pain between my eyes was so severe it made me feel faint.

I could hear the Dub giving me shit, talking down to me like I was a piece of shit, and he was right.

I absolutely was.

He loves your sister my brain told me through the fog and the withdrawals. *She's not on her own anymore.*

Mind reeling, I tried to piece together everything he was saying with the events that had happened, but my fucked-up mind wasn't complying.

My tongue was spewing poison, giving away too many family secrets to this lad, but I wasn't in control anymore. I'd lost myself somewhere along the way.

All I could remember was Shannon slumped on that kitchen floor and the blood coming out of her mouth.

I'd been helpless.

Fucking useless.

I hadn't done shit to protect her.

I'd let her down.

Again.

And then Molloy's face flashed like a neon sign in the forefront of my mind.

The guilt and pain I felt when I thought about her swamped everything else. The darkness I always felt on the inside was nothing compared to the eternal pit of night I found myself in.

I wanted out.

I needed out.

I couldn't *take* this anymore.

"Can I help?" Kavanagh's voice broke through my panicked thoughts. "Can I do something for you?"

"Yeah, you can loan me some clothes." I needed to get the fuck out of this place. Holding onto the nearby sink, I forced myself to get back on my feet.

Without another word, Kavanagh walked out of the bathroom, returning a few moments later to toss a bundle of clothes through the door. Feeling lightheaded, I scrambled for them, and quickly dragged on a pair of grey sweatpants and a white t-shirt over my head.

His clothes swamped me, but I didn't give a damn.

I was so fucking cold.

It was in my bones.

Shivering, I stepped out of the bathroom and into a bedroom that could have housed the entire first floor of my house.

"Thanks for the clothes," I managed to get the words out coherently before asking, "Do you have a phone I could use?"

I could hear the hesitance in his voice when he asked, "Why?"

"Because I need to call my girlfriend."

Disbelief flickered in his eyes. "Your girlfriend?"

"Yeah, my girlfriend," I bit out, resisting the urge to lose my shit on him when he had done me a solid. "Can I use your phone or not?"

"You don't have to leave," Kavanagh said, placing a sleek phone in my hands. "You can stay, lad. For as long as you need."

No, I couldn't.

I had to get out of here.

My father was still out there.

And Molloy?

Jesus Christ, I'd checked out on her.

"Come the fuck on," I hissed when my hands wouldn't cooperate. My fingers wouldn't push the damn buttons.

"What's her number?" he asked, snatching the phone back. "Call it out and I'll dial it for you."

Blowing out a pained breath, I forced myself to take a good hard look at the towering lad standing in front of me. I didn't trust him, but Shannon clearly did, which made me curious. It made me second guess my instincts.

Johnny Kavanagh was standing here, in the middle of all of my family's bullshit, and he wasn't running.

Something about him reminded me of Molloy and I frowned.

"I warned her off you, ya know," I heard myself say, brows furrowed as my vision blurred in and out. "Told her you'd be leaving." Wincing from the pain attacking my skull, I shook my head and refocused my attention on him. "Told her not to get her hopes up on you."

He didn't react.

Didn't seem surprised by my statement, either.

Instead, he asked, "What's her number?"

Pressing the heel of my hand to my forehead, I reeled off the phone number I had memorized since first year, the only number I had stored away in my mind, before saying, "Don't let her down." Steadying my body from swaying, I looked him in the eyes and said, "Whatever you're doing here, Kavanagh, don't fuck my sister over."

He tapped on the keypad of his phone before handing it back to me. With eyes full of unrestrained emotion, and his tone thick with gritty sincerity, he looked me dead in the eyes and vowed, "I won't."

Lost boy

AOIFE

"Aoife, I promise you faithfully that nobody is going to take your baby," my mother said for the millionth time when we walked into the house after spending most of the day at the hospital being poked, prodded, swabbed, and grilled. "They already explained this to us. Nobody is questioning you. They're only looking out for your welfare, sweetheart."

"Well, I didn't ask them to," I strangled out, mentally reeling from the twists and turns the day had taken. "I'm clearly fine, Mam. I'm healthy, I look after myself, I come from a warm safe home, so I don't understand why my life needs to be put under the microscope like that."

"It's not your lifestyle they're concerned about," she replied, setting her handbag down on the table. "Jesus Christ, Aoife, you should have come to me."

"About what?"

"About Joey."

My heart sank. "Joey's fine," I heard myself defend. "He's dealing with a lot with his family right now, but he'll be fine, Mam."

"Aoife." She turned to look at me. "Can you not?"

"Not what?"

"Not lie to me."

"I'm not lying." I threw my hands up. "He's fine!"

My mother sighed wearily. "Why didn't you tell me that he's missing?"

"He's not missing," I argued weakly. "He's just clearing his head."

"Aoife!"

"Maybe because I didn't want you to think badly about him," I admitted, voice torn. "Which is exactly what you're doing now."

"I don't think badly of the boy," she argued. "I'm worried about him. I'm worried for *you*."

"Joey would *never* hurt me."

"That's not what I'm saying."

"Then what?" I demanded. "What's there to worry about?"

"My daughter was just put through rigorous testing for diseases I've never heard about before today," she snapped, moving for the kettle. "Of course I'm worried!"

"Well, you weren't the one prodded with needles, and you didn't have multiple swabs rammed up your fa—"

"Don't use that word," she warned, shuddering. "That's a terrible word."

"Vagina," I changed course and said. "Or your asshole, Mam, which, FYI, is not a pleasant experience."

"Well, we'll know more when you're results come back."

"We already know," I growled, stalking out of the kitchen. "I'm clean because Joey is *clean*!"

"Aoife, wait, we need to talk about this."

"No, we don't," I called over my shoulder as I stomped up the staircase. "I need to shower."

"This conversation isn't over, young lady."

"Want a bet?" I grumbled, storming into my bedroom and slamming the door behind me.

Kicking off my runners, I moved straight for my bed, wanting nothing more in this moment than to curl up in a ball under the covers and hibernate.

Because it was too much.

It was all too fucking *much*.

Depressed and angry, I stalked over to my wardrobe and kicked the door in frustration. "Assholes."

Furious when my phone vibrated in my pocket, I pulled it out and glared at the screen, fully prepared to see my mother's name on the screen.

The number calling wasn't one I had stored in my contacts.

Instantly, I was racked with panic as I clicked accept and put the phone to my ear. "Hello?"

"Aoife, it's me."

Three words.

Three words that took the air clean out of my lungs and my legs from beneath me.

Staggering over to my bed, I sank down and allowed myself to absorb the tsunami of relief flooding my body.

Eight days of silence had brought me close to the brink of a nervous breakdown.

Hearing his voice melted the ice around my poor battered heart.

"You bastard," I choked out when my voice found me.

"I know."

Trembling violently, I switched my phone to my left hand and pressed it to my ear, as tears streamed down my cheeks. "You fucking asshole!"

"I know, okay?" His voice was torn, his words slurred, and I didn't need to be standing in front of him to know that his eyes were black as coal.

"Goddammit, Joey." I bowed my head, feeling too much in this moment to have the strength to hold my head up. "You promised."

"I know I promised," came his torn response. "I fucked up."

"You think?" I sneered, resisting the urge to throw my phone at my bedroom wall. "I'm pregnant with your baby and you just fall off the goddamn map! *Anything* could have happened to you, Joey. *Anything.* Don't you get that? Don't you understand how scared I've been?"

"I'm so fucking sorry, baby."

Pain.

Relief.

Fury.

Devastation.

I was feeling *everything* in this moment.

"Are you okay?" I forced myself to ask, voice trembling. "Are you hurt?"

"I, ah, I don't know," he mumbled, voice strained and slurred. "Everything's hazy and my eyes hurt."

"Because you should still be in hospital!"

"Don't hate me, Molloy."

"I don't hate you, Joey, I'm—" Voice cracking, I sucked in a sharp breath and changed angles. "Where are you?" I demanded, shaking violently. "Whose phone are you calling me from?"

"I'm at, ah . . . " his words trailed off and I heard him bite back a pained groan before saying, "Kavanagh's place."

"Johnny Kavanagh?" My brows shot up. "How? Why? Who took you there?"

"I don't know, Aoif," he admitted quietly. "I'm feeling really fucked in the head here, baby. I don't have my phone, and my ah, my wallet's gone, too."

"Dammit, Joe." My heart sank. "Who were you with?"

"I don't know," he whispered. "My head's in pieces. I can't remember shit. I'm just so tired."

"Because you're not well," I strangled out, blinking back my tears. "You're sick, Joe."

"I don't know what I am," I heard him say. "I don't feel human anymore."

Fear catapulted me into springing off my bed and pacing my bedroom floor. "Joey, you need to come home, okay? You need to come to my house right now."

"No, no, no, I don't want you to see me like this," he croaked out. "I don't want to hurt you anymore than I already have."

"The only way you can hurt me is by avoiding me," I urged, clutching my phone. "Ride or die, remember? It still stands, Joe. I love you."

"I love you so fucking much." His voice cracked. "I can't even tell you how much because I don't have enough words in my head to say it."

"I know you do." I clenched my eyes shut and gripped the phone tighter. "I know, Joe."

"I'm so sorry." His voice was slurred and held the hint of sleepiness. "I want you to be okay. You and the baby."

"We are okay," I tried to reassure him. "But we need you."

"Nobody needs me."

"That's not true," I argued, heart disintegrating in my chest. "Come back to me."

"I just need to sleep," he whispered brokenly. "I'm so fucking tired all the time and my eyes just hurt so fucking bad. It's hard to stay awake."

"Is Shannon with you?" I pressed my hand to my forehead and fought back my anxiety. "At Johnny's place? Did she bring you there?"

"I think so," he replied uncertainly. "I'm so fucking sorry."

"Joey, listen." Sniffling, I cleared my throat and tried to be the voice of reason for him. "Yeah, you fucked up, okay? You screwed the hell up. You can't go back, but you *can* go forward. You don't have to stay in this headspace, baby. I can help you. We can get you some help."

There was a long pause before his sleep-deprived voice slurred, "What kind of help?"

"The professional kind," I offered. "They have rehabs for teens in your position. They have to. I'll find one for you, okay? We'll get you the help you need to beat this thing, but you need to come back to me. Just come back to me, baby, and I'll help you . . . "

"No one can help me, Molloy."

"That's not true," I argued vehemently. "You've got a beautiful mind, Joey Lynch, and a wonderful heart. You *can* beat this. You just have to want to. It's half the battle. You can still fix this. You have time. You can get better. Just try, Joe. That's all you have to do. Just try, baby. I love you so much. Watching you self-destruct like this is killing me."

"I only want you."

"And I only want you," I choked out. "But I need you healthy. I won't let you destroy yourself. We have a baby on the way, Joey. I won't let you throw in the towel now."

"It's too fucking late for me, Molloy."

"No." I shook my head. "Don't say that."

"I'm fucked in the head."

"I'm coming to get you," I declared, searching my room for my car keys. "Just wait there and I'll be over."

"No, fuck, don't come here," he groaned. "I don't want you to see me like this."

"Joey, I'm coming."

"If you come here, I'm out."

"Joey!"

"No, don't come here, okay?" He groaned down the line before adding, "Just let me get straightened out and I'll come to you."

Dragging my hands through my hair, I resisted the urge to pull on the ends and exhaled a strangled breath.

I couldn't just leave him there.

Not when I finally knew where he was.

He had put me through hell the past eight days.

I knew he was high.

I knew he was self-destructing.

I knew I couldn't do a damn thing to stop him, but I still wanted to.

I still wanted to dive headfirst into the world he was drowning in and pull him to safety – or at the very least, keep his head above water.

"Stay on the line," he whispered, voice drifting in and out. "I love you."

"Promise me you'll stay at Johnny's house."

"I promise."

"And you'll come see me first thing tomorrow."

"First thing."

"Joe, I mean it. Promise me."

"I promise, I promise. I'm just ... so tired."

"Where are you now?"

"His room. Big bed."

"Okay." Exhaling a ragged breath, I tried to wrangle my emotions into check, while I listened to the sound of him breathing down the line. Taking comfort in the knowledge that his heart was still beating. "I want you to curl up on that big old bed and get some sleep. Can you do that for me, Joe?"

"Mm."

"Hey, Joe?"

"Hm?"

"Can you roll on your side for me, so that I know you won't choke if you get sick?"

"Mm-mm."

"Good job, stud."

"Don't go, queen."

"I won't."

"Stay with me."

"Always."

With my heart thundering in my chest, I walked up the private driveway towards a familiar front door.

Knowing that I was clutching at straws by coming here, but having little else to cling to, I pressed my finger against the fancy doorbell and held my breath.

A few moments ticked by before the door swung inwards, and I was greeted by a middle-aged woman in hospital scrubs. "Can I help you?"

"Hi, yeah." Blowing out a breath, I offered her a small smile. "So, I know he doesn't live here, but I'm looking for, ah, for Gibsie?"

Recognition immediately flickered in the woman's brown eyes, and she smiled warmly at me. "Usually, you would find Gerard here, but for once, he's raiding his own fridge." With her hand outstretched, she pointed to yet another impressive looking three-story house on the opposite side of the street. "He lives at number nine, sweetheart."

"Thanks so much," I replied, feeling myself sag with relief, as I quickly spun on my heels and moved to cross the quiet, cul-de-sac road.

"If you happen to see his curly-haired sidekick in your travels, please tell her that her mother said she's grounded," Mrs. Biggs called after me.

"Yeah, sure, no problem." Too frazzled to take in a word of what she was saying, I hurried up to the front door and knocked repeatedly until the hall light came on.

This time, when the door opened, I was greeted by a surprised looking Gibsie. "Well, hey there, Mrs. Joey the hurler."

"I need your help."

"Okay . . ." Brows furrowing, he stepped aside for me, but I stayed where I was. "But if it's advice you need help with, then I must warn you that I am a *terrible* choice of candidate."

"I don't want your advice, Gibsie."

"That's a relief," he chuckled. "Because I'm bad at it. And when I say bad, I mean *terrible*. Ask anyone on this road. I am the very last person you should come to in a crisis—"

"Oh my god, stop talking and start listening."

"Shutting up now."

"I need directions to your friend Johnny Kavanagh's house," I stated, feeling my anxiety rise with every minute that passed. "I've been there before, but I can't remember the way, and I need to get there."

"Shit." Concern flicked in his grey eyes. "You're looking for Joey."

My heart skipped a beat. "You've seen him?"

He nodded.

"When?"

"Today."

"How was he?"

He winced but didn't reply.

That was enough to tell me what I already knew.

"Oh Jesus." Feeling like my lungs had been severed, I pressed a hand to my chest and choked out a labored breath. "I need you to help me."

"I think you should come inside," he replied, still holding the door open for me.

"*Please.*" Tears burned my eyes, and I quickly blinked them away. "I need you to take me to him."

"I don't know." Scratching his broad chest, Gibsie looked around aimlessly. "I, ah, I don't think it's a good idea."

"A good idea?" I glared at him. "I don't give a shit what you think, Gibbers, I need to get to my boyfriend, and I'm asking you to *help* me."

"I hear you," he tried to coax, holding his hands up. "And I want to help you. I swear, I do. But—"

"Eight days," I choked out, not bothering to lie or hide my emotions. If Gibsie saw Joey today, then he knew what I was dealing with. "I haven't seen him in eight damn days."

"He's safe," he replied, his voice taking on a sincere tone. "I promise, okay? Kav's got this. Your boy is sleeping it off at his gaff. Shannon's there with him. You don't have anything to worry about."

"You don't get it," I bit out, repressing the urge to scream. "I *need* to see him."

"I'm not going to lie to you. Your lad is in a real bad fucking way," Gibsie came right out and told me. "But he's *safe.* If you go over there and wake him up, fuck knows what he'll do or where he'll go." He shook his head and gave me a sympathetic look. "I'm not trying to get in your business here, but I really *really* think you should let him sleep it—"

"Hi," a familiar voice interrupted, moments before a blonde head of curls peeked out from under Gibsie's arm. "It's Aoife, right? From our 90s party?" Clad in an oversized rugby jersey and a pair of fluffy pink pajamas bottoms and matching bunny slippers, she beamed at me. "You remember me, don't you? I'm Claire Biggs."

"Yeah, hi, I remem—" Before I had a chance to finish, she snaked her hand out and caught ahold of mine.

"Come on inside before you freeze to death on the doorstep." She slapped her pal's chest. "Honestly, Gerard," she scolded as she pulled me inside and led me down the hallway, through a dimly lit kitchen, and into a spacious conservatory. "Where are your manners? You don't leave girls on the doorstep at night."

"I didn't," Gibsie was quick to protest as he ambled along behind us. "I was holding the door for her like a gentleman."

"Are you hungry?" Claire continued, leading me over to a cardboard box on the glass coffee table in the center of the room. "Thirsty?"

"No, I'm fine," I replied, prying my hand free. "I just really need to . . . what the hell is that?" My mouth fell open and I watched as she dropped to her knees in front of the table, awing and cooing at the contents of the box. "Is that a *rat*?"

"What? No," Claire replied, retrieving the gardening glove next to the box and pulling it on before reaching inside and retrieving the prickly creature. "We found him in the middle of the road on the way back from Johnny's place. He was all alone in the dark, and we couldn't leave him there in case he got driven over, so we brought him home." Smiling dotingly at the 'thing' in her hand, she cooed, "Isn't he the most adorable ball of cuteness you've ever seen?"

"I, ah . . . " Shaking my head, I tried to come up with something logical to say when it felt like I had entered the twilight zone. "Guys, that's a hedgehog."

"His name is Reginald Gibson-Biggs," Gibsie corrected, sitting cross-legged on the plush rug next to his gal-pal. "Come on, Claire-Bear. Don't be greedy. It's my turn." Setting a pillow on his lap, he patted it and cooed, "Come to Daddy, Reggie."

"Careful, Gerard, he's really skinny."

"I know what I'm doing, Claire-Bear."

"I know you do, but he's just so itty-bitty."

"That's because he's just come out of hibernation. Poor baby is starving."

"Should we get him some worms?"

"Do hedgehogs eat worms?" His brows furrowed. "I thought they ate grass."

"I think I remember learning about a hedgehog's diet in nature class."

"Shit, I didn't take nature class."

"Everyone in Ireland takes nature class in primary school, Gerard."

"Well, I didn't."

"Yes, you did."

"When?"

"Remember being taken out on long walks with your teacher and class?"

"Yeah?"

"Those were nature walks," she explained. "For nature *class*."

"Well shit," he chuckled. "I thought they were movement breaks."

Morbidly curious, I tilted my head to one side, watching as they took turns mothering a wild animal. "Should you be touching that thing?"

"Reggie."

"Reggie," I corrected, shuddering when Gibsie tickled its little underbelly. "Animals in the wild can carry diseases, you know."

"Look at him," Claire cooed, holding the prickly creature up for me to pet. "How can you even think that about something so precious?"

"Yeah, so ... precious." Achingly aware that I, too, was mothering something equally as precious to me in my womb, I took a safe step back and shrugged. "Listen, all I need is directions to Johnny's house and I'll be on my way." Grimacing, I added, "And you guys can have all of the quality time you want with, uh, little Reggie."

Flying high, falling low

JOEY

Blood on the walls.

Blood on the floor.

Vacant blue eyes.

Terrified brown eyes.

Disappointed green eyes.

Faces of loved ones I continued to let down flashed in front of my eyes in the darkness, sending my anxiety to levels I couldn't cope with me.

Trembling from head to toe, I stared at the unfamiliar ceiling, feeling the cold seep so deep into my bones that I briefly pondered if I was on the brink of death. I could hear my heart still thundering in my chest, but I was numb, and my limbs felt lifeless.

Cloaked in darkness, I scratched and tore at my arms, desperate to rid myself of the unbearable itching sensation just beneath the surface of my skin. Knowing that the hunger threatening to eat me from the inside out had little to do with food, I twisted onto my side and swallowed down a mouthful of bile.

Get the fuck up.

No, just lie down.

Don't you dare stay down.

Go into the bathroom, find a razor, slit your goddamn wrists, and be done with this nightmare.

Don't worry, Peter Pan. I'll be your Wendy.

Think of the baby.

"Molloy." Licking my cracked lips, I forced myself to twist onto my side, and then, when the movement didn't cause me to spew my guts up, I pressed on and slowly pulled myself into a sitting position at the edge of the bed.

Pain.

It was everywhere.

In my arms.

In my eyes.

In my ribs.

In my heart.

There wasn't an inch of me that didn't ache anymore.

In the midst of the madness and the pain, I was drowning in my shame, knowing that this time I had pushed the boat out too far.

There was no coming back from the hell I had landed in.

The hill I needed to climb back up was too steep.

Her face.

It was all I could see in this moment.

Like a beacon of light in the darkness, guiding me home.

She doesn't want you.

Who the fuck would want you?

Just come back to me, Joe . . .

On unsteady legs, I stood up and blindly felt my way around the room until my fingers landed on a light switch. The minute the room was bathed in light, I felt like passing out. The pain in my head was too fucking much to handle. Clutching onto a wooden dresser, I tried to steady my breathing and not pass out from the pain, while I squinted and slowly brought my vision into focus.

I was still here.

Still in the manor.

Mister Rugby.

"Fuck." Blowing out a pained breath, I forced myself to look at my reflection staring back at me in the mirror over the dresser.

With my face distorted from bruising and swelling, and a couple of weeks' worth of stubble to contend with, I struggled to recognize myself.

I didn't look like me anymore.

I didn't look like anyone I'd ever known.

With one hand still clutching the dresser for balance, I reached up and trailed my fingers over the yellowish bruising swelling on my face. Leaning in closer to get a better look at the damage, I squinted to focus and studied my bloodshot eyes.

I couldn't see the white of my eyes anymore.

It had been replaced with burst blood vessels.

Confused and panicked, I jerked away from the mirror, unable to look at myself a second longer.

Because I despised the person staring back at me.

I fucking hated that piece of shit.

It took me a ridiculous amount of time to locate my runners, and even longer to get them on my feet and tie my laces.

But I did it.

Grabbing a random hoodie off the back of a chair, I gingerly shrugged it on, and pulled the hood up, before moving for the door. Somehow, I managed to put one foot in front of the other and navigate my way out of the bedroom I'd unintentionally taken refuge in and find my way to the staircase. Trip-tumbling down the steps, I clung to the banister for balance, barely making it to the bottom without breaking my fucking neck.

Shivering from the cold, I made my way to the front door and let myself out. Feeling off center and confused, I tried to get my bearings, tried to figure out where the fuck I was and where I needed to go to find my way back to her, but it wasn't coming easy to me. My thoughts were all jumbled up and my sense of direction had deserted me.

He's out there.

He's coming back for you.

You're all going to die.

Find her.

Come back to me, Joe.

Joey, don't leave me on my own.

Shaking my head, I wobbled unsteadily on my feet as I followed the tree line down a long lane, letting my legs lead me when my brain wouldn't comply.

Keep going.

Just get back to her.

One foot in front of the other.

After what felt like forever, a set of headlights came into view and I clumsily raised my arm, trying to flag down a spin.

The lights weren't coming closer, though.

They were still and unmoving.

Trapped behind a set of cast-iron gates.

Stumbling along, I continued to wave my arms around, needing to get to that car.

To find my way back to her.

"Joe!"

Fuck, I was even hearing her voice now.

"Joe!"

There was something seriously wrong with me.

"Joe, it's me."

Blinking in confusion, I looked around. "Molloy?"

"Yeah, baby, I'm over here. The gate's locked and I can't get in. I've been here for hours."

"You have?"

"Yeah, just keep walking towards the gate."

It took me a moment to process her voice, and a little while longer to register the meaning behind the words coming out of her mouth, before I managed to switch my attention to the gate.

And there she was.

Standing on the other side of what looked like a fifteen feet cast-iron gate.

"Molloy." Staggering forwards, I closed the space between us, not stopping until I reached the gate. "Molloy."

"I'm here, Joe." Snaking a hand between the metal bars, she reached up and cupped the back of my head and leaned in close. "I'm right here, baby."

"I'm sorry, queen," I croaked out, resting my forehead against the bars she was resting hers against. "I'm so fucking sorry."

"Shh." Both of her hands were on my face then, fingers tracing my cheeks and brushing back my hair, as she peppered kisses to the parts of my face she could reach. "I've been so fucking scared for you."

"I'm a prick."

"You're a huge prick," she wholeheartedly agreed, still kissing and petting and nuzzling me. "I'm so mad at you."

"Me too." Trembling I reached a hand through the bars to touch her, to just feel her and assure myself that she was in fact real. "I think I'm broken."

"You're going to be okay," she cried, and the tears landing on her cheeks dampened mine. "I'm not going to let anything else happen to you."

"Get me the fuck out of here, baby."

"I can't, Joe," she strangled out. "I don't know the code to open the gates and they're too high to climb."

"I do," I mumbled. "I know the code."

"What is it?"

"I, ah . . . " Blinking rapidly, I scoured my brain for the information that I knew I once possessed before coming up empty. "I swear I have it in my head somewhere."

"It's okay," she replied, sniffling. "Don't worry about it. You can stay here tonight with Shannon and Johnny."

"No, no, no, I don't want to stay here," I groaned, clutching onto her with everything I had in me. "I want to come home with you."

"I know you do," she coaxed, sounding pained. "But I can't get you out, Joe."

"I can climb—"

"No, baby, you can't," she cut me off and said, "You're too hurt."

"*You're* hurt. I hurt *you*." I groaned, flinching when a surge of pain hit me square in the chest. "Fuck, I think my brain has stopped working."

"Where have you *been*?"

"I don't remember," I mumbled, feeling drained of any hope. "I'm just so fucking sorry. I love you so much, Molloy. I swear I do."

"I know you do, Joe. God, I know . . . " Her voice trailed off and a sob escaped her. "Listen, I need you to show me your arms, okay?"

"My arms?"

"Yeah." Sniffling, she took a step back and snatched one of my hands up in hers. "It's okay," she coaxed, slowly peeling the sleeve of my hoodie up, only to burst into tears when she reached my elbow.

"I'm sorry."

"The other one," she squeezed out, taking my other hand and doing the same.

"So sorry."

"You've been with Shane Holland, haven't you?"

"I don't remember."

"You could *die*, Joe!"

"I don't know if I want to live, Aoif."

"Don't say that!" she warned, reaching her arm back through the bar to hook it around my neck. "Don't you ever say that again, do you hear me?"

"I'm only here *for* you," I confessed, reveling in the warmth of her hands on my skin. I was so fucking cold. She was the only thing that could warm me. "I want it gone, Aoif. I want it to be done with—"

"No, baby no." Sniffling, she pulled me close and sealed her mouth to mine. "I won't let you go."

Shivering when the heat from her lips and tongue melted the ice inside of me, I tried to get closer, needing to be with her. "Don't run, Molloy. I know I don't deserve you, but please just . . . don't *run*."

"Never."

"Please just . . . please keep loving me."

"Always, Joe," she breathed against my lips. "Always."

"Because I feel like I'm all alone here, baby."

"No." Shaking her head, she pulled back to wipe the tears that were trickling down my cheeks and then leaned back in to gently stroke my nose with hers. "You have us."

Trembling, I reached my hand between the bars and reached for her.

"I want to be good enough for you." Sniffling, I cradled the small swell of her stomach as the wind whipped at my face. "For both of you."

"I believe in you," I heard her say through her tears. "Do you hear me, Joey Lynch?" Clutching my face between her hands, she looked me right in the eyes and whispered, "I *still* believe in you."

You're the only one.

You're not taking him

AOIFE

I had problems.

Many of them.

My biggest, aside from impending motherhood and my boyfriend's drug dependency, was my inability to back the hell down from a fight.

Many would label my ability to love unwaveringly a positive personality trait, but when it led me back to the lion's den, I knew it was a reckless fucking habit. Still, I parked my car outside the shitty, graffiti-ridden house and climbed out, poised for battle.

Gripping my car keys in one fist for protection, I stalked up to the house and hammered on the door with the other. When the door opened inwards, and Shane's grotesque fucking face greeted me, I felt the fire of a thousand volcanos build up inside of me.

"Back for round two?"

"Before you start, I know he's been here with you. So, I want his phone, his wallet, and everything else you stole from him," I stated coldly, looking him dead in his eyes. "Fight with me on this, and I will rain *hell* down on you."

His lips tipped upwards. "Is that so?"

"Try me, asshole." I folded my arms across my chest. "I dare you."

Looking more amused than annoyed with me tonight, Shane shook his head and chuckled. "You want your boyfriend's shit? Come in and find it yourself. I'm not his housekeeper."

My heart sank, but I schooled my features and stepped around the drugged-up gangster.

"You know the room he stays in," Shane called over his shoulder, as he disappeared into the sitting room, sounding thoroughly amused by my boyfriend's downfall. "Have at it, princess."

Swallowing down my fury, I moved for the staircase, not stopping until I was standing outside the door of the room that I found him in last year.

Deep breaths.

You can do this.

Pushing the door inwards, I held my breath and stepped inside.

Repressing the urge to shudder when my eyes landed on the blood-stained mattress that I knew Joe had slept on, I stepped over several discarded syringes and random pieces of tinfoil, feeling myself die a little more with every step I took. Filthy didn't come close to describing the decrepit conditions of this room, and knowing this was where he came to for sanctuary sickened me.

Careful not to touch anything for fear of disease or infection, because who the fuck knew who else stayed in this hellhole, I reached for a familiar discarded hoodie.

Joey's hoodie.

I'd bought it for him last year.

Trembling violently, I reached into the front pocket and sagged in relief when my fingers brushed over both his phone and wallet. Silently pocketing both, I bundled his hoodie under my arm and took another quick glance around the carnage before heading back downstairs.

"You can tell your boyfriend that he owes me money," Shane called out from the sitting room when I was halfway down the staircase. "He has a week to come up with the cash or he can work it off for me."

Unable to contain my emotions a second longer, I thundered down the staircase and stormed into the sitting room.

"Stay the fuck away from him, Shane," I snarled, not caring about the four other men lounging around on couches in the shithole he called his home. "I mean it, asshole. Keep your filthy fucking habits away from my boyfriend!"

"My filthy habits?" he laughed from his perch on the couch. "Don't you mean Lynchy's filthy habits?"

"People like you make me sick," I hissed, glaring down at him.

"Sinking your claws in vulnerable people. You're disgusting!"

"Words," he chuckled, mocking me with hand movements. "Get the fuck out of here, princess, and tell lover boy that I've a job lined up for him." His gaze trailed over my body and when he reached my middle, his brows shot up. "Or should I call him baby-daddy?"

"You're not having him," I seethed, standing my ground. "I won't let you take him from us."

"He's already gone, kid," another man said. "Clear off before he takes you down with him."

I couldn't.

That was the problem.

I *couldn't* leave him.

"How much does he owe you?" I heard myself ask, keeping my eyes glued to Shane. "Joey. What does he owe?"

"Six hundred," he mused, arching a brow. "You got that kind of cash on you, princess?"

No, I didn't.

I didn't make that kind of money in a month at work.

My parents were barely breaking even, so they didn't have cash to spare.

Neither had any of my friends.

Fuck.

Smiling knowingly, Shane inclined his head to the door. "Don't worry. I have plenty of work for him."

"He's not dealing for you."

"You get a say in this, princess."

"I don't need one," I shot back, shaking. "I know Joey. He will *never* deal."

"Then he'll pay with his arms," one of the men joked.

"And his legs," laughed another.

Panic-stricken, I racked my brain for a solution to the mess my boyfriend had gotten himself into. "I can get you the money."

"Now you're speaking my language."

"But that's it," I warned. "I get the money, and you leave him alone."

The men around me all laughed again like it was the funniest thing they'd ever heard.

"I'm not fucking joking," I snapped. "I'll pay what he owes, but you have to back off, do you hear me?"

"You get me what he owes, and we'll talk," Shane replied, eyes dancing with amusement.

I knew I was being played.

I knew these men had no intention of following my wishes, but what could I do? Walk away knowing what they had planned for my boyfriend?

Never.

Trembling when I reached my car, I sank into the driver's seat and locked all the doors, while I waited for my recently acquired pal to pick up.

"You rang, Mrs. Joey the hurler?"

"Gibsie?" Pressing the heel of my hand to my forehead, I exhaled a ragged breath. "I need a favor."

A little while later, a silver Ford Focus parked up behind my car. With bated breath, I watched from the rearview mirror as Gibsie climbed out of his car and walked to the passenger side of mine.

"I know I have no right to ask you for anything," I blurted out the minute he climbed into the passenger seat beside me. "We barely know each other, and you're probably thinking that I'm some sort of crazy person for showing up on your doorstep earlier, and for phoning you, but I'm so damn desperate and he's—"

"You said six hundred?" Gibsie cut me off by asking, as he retrieved a wad of cash from his coat pocket and placed it on my lap. "It's all there."

"Thank you." Shoulders slumping in both guilt and relief, I nodded wearily. "Seriously, thank you so damn much, Gibsie. I know it was a lot to ask of you, and I promise you that I will pay you back every cent. It might take me a while, but I will get it all back to you with interest—"

"Relax, I don't care about the money," he cut me off and said, turning in his seat to face me. "It's yours. No strings attached."

"No, I can't," I hurried to protest. "I'll pay you back, I swear."

"You can try, but I won't take it," he replied calmly. "The fact that you needed it badly enough to come to me in the first place is the scary part." He stared at me for a long moment before saying, "Lynchy's in deep, isn't he?"

I debated lying to him, but how the hell could I?

Whether he realized it or not, this boy had unintentionally spared my boyfriend another hospitalization.

Or worse, an early grave.

"So deep, Gibs," I squeezed out, heart racing wildly. "And I'm trying . . . " I swallowed the lump in my throat. "I'm trying so hard to save him, but it's just getting harder and harder."

"How bad are we talking?"

"It's heroin," I choked out, quickly batting a rogue tear from my cheek. "And oxy, and coke, and pretty much anything he can snort up his nose or inject in his veins."

"And the money?"

"For his dealer," I admitted, pressing my temples. "If I don't pay up, he'll make Joe work it off or worse."

Gibsie blew out a harsh breath. "Shit."

"Yeah," I agreed, demoralized and weary. "He's also really unwell. Like, physically unwell. Everyone is looking at Shannon and I get it, I do, but what about Joe?" Shaking my head, I bit back a sob. "He could have died in the kitchen that day, too."

"I didn't know that," Gibsie replied quietly.

"Because his entire family treats him like an afterthought," I choked out. "And no, I don't mean Shan and the little ones. I mean his mother and his brother and his . . . " Breaking off before I had a nervous breakdown, I sucked in several calming breaths before trying again. "I just need him to be okay, Gibs. I just . . . I need that boy."

"Because you've got a bun in the oven?"

"What?" I stilled, frowning. "How did you—"

"Don't worry, I can keep secrets, too," he surprised me by saying. "Word of advice, though. I would start doubling up on those oversized hoodies if you don't want people catching on, because, and I mean this in the kindest of ways, you're blooming."

"Oh fuck."

"I'm guessing Shannon doesn't know?" he mused. "Which means Johnny doesn't know, because if Johnny knew, I would know."

"No, and you can't tell them yet because—"

"Like I said, I can keep a secret," he offered with a wink. "I've got your back, Mrs. Joey the hurler."

Mrs. Kavanagh

JOEY

I wasn't sure how I made it back to Johnny's house in the dark, but I must have, because when I woke up the following morning, it was to the sight of the rim of a porcelain toilet bowl. There was also the sound of a woman losing her shit on the other side of the door.

Feeling a small bit more together than I had the day before, I climbed to my feet and quickly checked the bathroom for damage. Relieved to find none, I decided to bite the bullet and step outside, needing to get my ass out of Mister Rugby's manor and back to the mother of my child without delay.

Disgust didn't come close to explain how I was feeling about myself.

Hatred wasn't a strong enough word, either.

What I'd done.

My behavior.

How I'd left her.

I couldn't allow myself to think about it, because thinking about it made me want to die.

Wincing when pain ricocheted through my temple, a direct reaction to the sunlight pouring through the window, I opened the bathroom door and stepped into the hallway. I had a perfect view of who I presumed was Kavanagh's mother, giving her son a piece of his mind. With her hands on her hips, and her back to me, the low-size blonde stood in the doorway of yet another room in their fortress of fortune.

The sound of my sister chiming in, "I'll go. Right now, I promise," instantly had my back up.

Fucked in the head or not, I knew that voice.

Her panic beckoned me like a siren.

Falling back into the habit of a lifetime and taking the heat off

590 • REDEEMING 6

my sister, I called out, "Thanks for the bed, Kavanagh, can I borrow a hoodie?"

Because I could take whatever this lady might throw at us for intruding on her home.

Her disdain.

Her outrage.

Her accusations.

She couldn't hurt me because none of it mattered to me like it did to Shannon.

Kavanagh's mother cast a brief glance in my direction before turning back to her son and resuming her ranting.

Fair enough.

I couldn't exactly blame the woman for her reaction.

When she was finished giving her son a piece of her mind and turned her attention back to me, I braced myself for battle, but it wasn't anger I saw in her eyes.

It wasn't fear, either.

It was sadness.

And fuck, somehow that made it worse.

"Hello."

"Hello."

"What's your name, love?"

"Joey." Eyeing her warily as she walked towards me, I stepped out of her way, backing up against the bathroom door. "Lynch."

"Joey Lynch," she repeated, not stopping until she was standing directly in front of me. "I'm Edel." She held her hand out to me. "Edel Kavanagh."

"Okay," I replied, eyeing her outstretched hand.

I didn't move.

Instead, I watched and waited.

This was her turf.

I was the intruder.

The next move was on her.

"Shake my hand, love," she instructed. "It's good manners."

Brows furrowed, I forced myself to accept her handshake.

"Now." Giving my hand a small squeeze, she smiled up at me. "Are you hungry, Joey Lynch?"

"Uh." Confused, I stared down at her and slowly shook my head. "No."

"No?" Warm brown eyes shone up at me and her lips tipped upwards. "Are you lying to me, love?"

Completely fucking thrown, I shook my head again. "No, I just . . ."

"You just what, love?"

"I need to leave," I heard myself tell her, still confused as fuck at this tiny woman. "I, ah, wouldn't have stayed at all, but I couldn't climb the gate to get out."

"It's a tall gate," she replied with a knowing smile. "I've climbed it a time or two back in the day."

Well shit. "Sounds like there's a story there."

"Like you wouldn't believe." She offered me a devilish grin and headed off down the hallway. "Follow me, Joey, love. No child leaves my house without a full belly."

"I'm not a child," I replied, reluctantly trailing after her.

"How about no friend of my son leaves on an empty stomach then," she called over her shoulder, leading me into the kitchen. "Man, woman, or child. Does that suit you better?"

Hovering in the kitchen doorway, I watched as she busied herself with setting the island with cutlery. "I'm not his friend, either."

"Well, your sister certainly is."

"Yeah, well, when it comes to my sister and your son, labeling them as *friends* is a fairly naïve, not to mention an outdated notion."

"Intuitive," she mused. "You know what, Joey love, I think you might be right."

"Your son could do a lot worse," I heard myself say, immediately shifting into defense mode, as I watched her plate a heap of scones onto a serving dish. Scones. She was making scones and tea in an actual fucking teapot. "But he couldn't do better than my sister."

Her lips tipped upwards. "Is that so?"

"Just putting it out there." Shrugging, I folded my arms across my chest. "Don't judge a book by its cover."

"I could say the same thing to you."

"How'd you figure?"

"Well, aren't you doing the same to me?" She smiled over her shoulder before moving for the kettle.

"With all due respect, lady—"

"Edel."

"Edel," I reluctantly corrected. "No offence, but you're the one with the mansion. I think it's fair to say that your story is self-explanatory."

"You'd be surprised, Joey love."

"Yeah, well, listen, I know you already know about our family." There was no point in denying our circumstances to this woman. Her son knew all about us. Besides, she had eyes in her head. She could see the marks on my sister. Either way, I was done with the pretenses. I was done with the bullshit. "Your son's been sniffing around long enough to figure out we've got shit to deal with at home, which means you do, too. I just don't want you to judge my sister based on bullshit that she can't control. She couldn't be more different from the rest of our family."

"You sound like you're including yourself in that statement."

"Because I am." With my skin itching and my body cold to the bone, I forced a nod. "Shannon's the best person I know."

"Oh, Joey, love." Sympathetic brown eyes locked on mine. "Why do I get the feeling that Shannon would say the exact same thing about you?"

Unsettled by the way she looked at me, and with the mother of all headaches attacking my senses, I pinched the bridge of my nose and leaned against the door frame.

"Are you alright, love?" Concern flashed across her features. "Do you need to sit down?"

"No, no, I'm grand," I muttered, feeling like I needed to be anywhere but here. The woman was throwing me off-kilter, which was an impressive feat considering my life was already on its axis. "Listen, I appreciate the offer of breakfast, but I need to get going."

"Why don't you sit down, love, and have a cup of tea first?" she coaxed, as she walked over to the marble island and pulled out a stool for me to sit on. "I'll drop you back into town myself afterwards."

I didn't move.

I couldn't.

I felt wary and on edge.

This woman?

I didn't know this woman.

Couldn't figure out her angle.

"I have places to be."

"Not on an empty stomach."

"My girlfriend's waiting for me."

"I'm sure she wouldn't mind you having a bite to eat first."

"I'm not hungry."

"Humor me, love."

Uncomfortable and on edge, I pulled at the sleeves of her son's hoodie that I was wearing and mentally tried to take her measure. "Fine, I'll, ah, have a cup of tea . . . please."

Her eyes lit up. "Good lad, yourself."

"And if it's not too much trouble, could I, ah . . . well, do you maybe . . . " Blowing out a breath, I reached up and scratched my jaw before forcing out the words that made me hate myself worse than I already did. "Have anything for pain?"

"For your face, love?"

No, for my heart. "Yeah." I nodded. "I, ah, I left my meds at home."

"I'll poke something out for you from the medicine cupboard," she replied, moving for a cupboard in the far corner of the kitchen. "Are you allergic to anything?"

"No," I replied, forcing myself to not move an inch. "I can take anything."

"Let's see . . . there's some ibuprofen here?"

Fuck.

"Yeah." Shivering, I released a despondent sigh and nodded wearily. "That'll be grand, thanks."

"Oh, hold the phone ..." Still rummaging around, she retrieved a white plastic pill tray. "There's few Solpadol left over from Johnny's surgery in December."

Bingo.

A sudden rush of relief washed over me, and I couldn't stop my feet from moving towards her. "That's great. That's what I'm on from the hospital."

"Here you are, love. I'll get you a drink."

"Thanks," I replied, gratefully accepting the pills she dropped into the palm of my hand before taking the glass of water she offered me.

It wouldn't do much, but it would take the edge off until I could get sorted.

Get sorted.

What a fucking joke.

You are a joke, asshole.

You're no better than him.

"So, tell me about this girlfriend of yours."

"Hm?"

"Your girlfriend."

I narrowed my eyes, suspicious. "Why?"

"Would you prefer if we talked about how you got those bruises?" came her clipped response. "Because we can go there if you prefer?"

"Her name's Aoife." Draining the contents of my glass, I rinsed it out in the sink before placing the glass on the draining board and returning to my perch of hovering awkwardly near what I presumed the back door. "I, ah, work for her father."

"Oh?"

"Yeah." I nodded. "He, ah, runs a small mechanics garage in town."

"Which garage?"

"The Free-Wheeler one at the end of Plunkett's Road, across the street from Market Place."

"Is that how you met?"

"No, we're in the same class at school."

"High school sweethearts." She smiled knowingly. "Oh, to be young again."

"You could say that."

"Have you been together long?"

"Yeah," I muttered, feeling completely off balance around this woman. "We have."

"You don't give much away, do you, Joey, love?"

"Why would I?" I replied. "I don't know you."

She stared at me for a long moment before shaking her head and offering me another warm smile. "You know, love, I'm sure I've heard about that garage. I'll bring the car down the next time it needs a service."

"Really?" My brows furrowed and the pain in my head slowly dulled. "You don't have to."

"I'd like to." She smiled again. "How long have you worked there?"

"Since I was twelve or thirteen." Another shrug. "Been on the books since third year."

"That young?"

"Needed the money."

"And you like it?" she pressed, still busying herself with prepping food and making tea. "Mechanics? That's something you might be interested in pursuing after you're done with school?"

Jesus, what was with this woman and all the questions?

I hadn't endured this level of interrogation since my last trip in the back of the paddy wagon.

Or maybe since the last time I'd come under fire from Molloy.

Come to think of it, this little woman gave off a similar air of confidence to the one that wafted from my girlfriend in waves.

It was confusing and I didn't know if I liked it.

"Money's decent."

"Well, I think you are a credit to yourself, Joey Lynch." Somehow, I earned myself another megawatt smile from Mister Rugby's mother.

"Working all those hours after school. And in your leaving cert year. You should be so proud of yourself."

If she knew me, really knew me, she would quickly change her opinion.

I pinched my temple, fucking aching from head to toe, as I tried to clear my thoughts and focus on this woman. "Why?"

"Why what, love?"

"Nothing." Fuck, I needed to stop letting her lure me into conversation and get out of there. "Doesn't even matter."

"I think it does." Turning to face me, she gave me her full attention. It was a worrying fucking concept considering I didn't know her. "Say what you were going to say, love. I'm listening."

She *was*.

That was the unsettling part.

She was *listening* to me.

Fuck.

"I, uh . . ."

The kitchen door swung inwards then, and my eyes landed on my sister and Kavanagh.

The minute my eyes landed on her face I wanted to die.

I wanted to drown.

I wanted fucking out.

Jesus, the guilt was crippling me.

Feeling useless and unimportant, I willed myself to be a man and stand my ground, to not cower in shame because I'd let this happen to her.

I'd let her down again.

Again.

"Alright, Shan?" My voice was raw and thick with emotion I couldn't seem to conceal. "How's it going?" I forced myself to take it all in. Every bruise. Every broken fucking promise on my behalf to protect her. "You okay?"

"Hey, Joe." Her blue eyes locked on mine, and I could feel the pain emanating from her. With a small smile, she nodded once and tightened her hold on the hand of the boy she was clinging to. And with that small, subtle move, she let me know that this was okay, and that we could trust these people.

She might, but I didn't.

"Are you?"

"All good," I managed to croak out, quickly breaking eye contact, feeling too much for the little girl I'd spent my life trying and failing to protect. "Kavanagh," I acknowledged then, turning my attention to the lad she was welded to. "Thanks again."

For holding onto her.

For looking after her when I couldn't.

"Joey." Steel blue eyes landed on my face. "Anytime."

I hoped he meant it.

Because as much as I hated myself for thinking it, I knew in my heart that I didn't have anything left to give her.

I was empty.

I was done.

Don't give up on my brother

AOIFE

"Julie, I swear to God, if you even think about bailing on me during the lunch rush, I will rain hell down on you," I growled, eyeing the redheaded barmaid who was reaching for her cigarettes under the bar. "Hell, I tell you."

"Oh, simmer down, princess," she grumbled, as she snatched up the packet and moved for the opening at the other end of the bar. "I haven't had a smoke all morning. I'll be five minutes."

"Bitch," I growled – and not quietly – as once again I picked up the slack for my co-worker.

Once I had taken and fulfilled all the drink orders on my section of the bar, I reluctantly moved to Julie's section and started pulling pints and quenching thirsts. It wasn't until I reached the end of the bar that I recognized a pair of familiar brown eyes staring back at me.

"Tadhg." My heart leapt in my chest. "What are you doing here?"

"I need to talk to you," he replied, tone hard, as he sat on a towering bar stool and stared back at me, unyielding. "It's important."

Yeah, I figured it had to be if he had traipsed across town to track me down.

"Tadhg, you know you're not allowed in the bar without an adult here with you."

"I have you, don't I?"

"Yeah." Emotion racked through me, and I nodded. "I guess you do."

"He's back."

My heart jackknifed in my chest. "Joe?"

The younger Lynch offered me a stiff nod and I choked out a huge sigh of relief.

Leaving Joey at those gates last night was about the hardest thing I'd ever done in my life, but I did it with the knowledge that if I couldn't get to him, then neither could Shane Holland. Temporarily appeased with the wad of cash I had borrowed from a boy I barely knew I wasn't foolish enough to believe that Shane was gone forever. But right now, temporary was all I could hope for. "Is he okay?"

"No."

My heart cracked in my chest. "No?"

"There was a big fight between Mam and that blonde lady with the posh car who brought Joey and Shannon home," little alpha came right out and told me, blunt as always. "Shannon was crying over the posh lady's son, Mam was going mental, and Darren stormed off."

"What about Joe?"

"After he put Mam to bed and fed the boys, he locked himself in his room."

Jesus.

With my heart bucking wildly in my chest, I looked around the bar, desperate to drop everything I was doing and go to him, even though I had another four hours of my shift left. But then I thought about the lack of funds in my bank account and the growing intruder in my womb and I paused. I couldn't afford to lose this job. If I walked off, they would fire me, and nobody was going to hire me in my condition.

I needed the money, dammit.

"By the way, I know about the baby," Tadhg blew my mind by saying. "My brother got you pregnant."

My blood ran cold. "Who told you?"

"Nobody," he replied flatly. "I overheard Mam and Darren talking about it."

"Okay." Clearing my throat, I quickly popped the cap on a bottle of Coke and set it down in front of him, along with a couple of bags of cheese and onion flavored crisps. "Listen, I'm due a break in twenty minutes. Can you wait here for me until then?"

"Don't worry." Nodding stiffly, he tore open the crisp packet and tucked in. "I'm not going anywhere."

*

"So, does your mam know you're here?" I asked, sitting down on an old barrel in the smoking area. "Because I have to say, Tadhg, your mother isn't exactly my number one fan. I don't think she'd be too happy to know that you're here with me."

"Do I look like I give a shit about what she thinks? Besides, I already told ya she took to the bed again," he responded harshly as he sat on the empty beer barrel opposite me and polished off his fourth bag of crisps. "I'm here for my brother."

I sighed heavily. "Come on, Tadhg, we both know Joe didn't send you here."

"Never said he did," he replied, scrunching the empty crisp bag up and stuffing it into the pocket of his navy tracksuit. "Listen, I'm not thick. Everyone treats me like I'm the same as Ollie and Sean when I'm not. I'm not a baby, Aoif. I know things too, ya know."

Yeah, he knew things alright. Things no boy of his age should know or be subjected to.

"I'm here for Joe because I know he's fucked in the head right now," Tadhg continued, taking another swig from his bottle of Coke. "I saw it in his eyes that day in the kitchen. I saw him check out. I know he's not here anymore. Dad broke Shannon's lungs, but he broke Joey's mind and Mam helped him do it."

"He's still here, Tadhg," I croaked out, repressing a shiver from how accurate this boy had taken his brother's measure.

"No, he's not," the little guy challenged. "He's gone and you know it, too." He gave me a hard stare when he said, "But my brother *can* get better. I know he can, and you need to not give up on him."

"Tadhg . . . " My breath caught in my throat, and I sucked in a shaky breath, wondering just how much he knew. He was turning twelve in a couple of days and knowing that he had this level of intuition and awareness about his family was heartbreaking. "I'm not giving up on your brother." Swallowing deeply, I offered him what I hoped was a reassuring smile. "I never will."

"He's going to make it hard."

"Nothing worth having comes easy."

"And it's going to get worse before it gets better."

"I'm well aware."

He watched me for a long beat, clearly taking my measure, before nodding his blond head. "Good. Because you won't get better than him."

"I know."

"I mean it," he pushed, tone defensive. "Joe's the only parent I remember having, so, trust me when I tell you that your kid . . ." He paused to gesture to my stomach before adding, "Is going to have one hell of a father."

I absorbed his words like an addict would crack cocaine because in this moment, whether he meant it or not, Tadhg Lynch was giving me everything I needed. He believed in his brother in the same way I did. It didn't matter that he wasn't yet a boy of twelve, the fact of the matter was that he got it. He saw the same person I did and was prepared to fight for him. It gave me hope. It gave me comfort.

"I'm going to come over as soon as my shift is over," I told him, unable to disguise the emotion in my voice.

"They're going to try to force you out," Tadhg said, standing up, seemingly done with our conversation. "Mam and Darren." He gave me another hard look before saying, "Don't let them. Don't give up on my brother."

"Don't worry," I replied. "I won't."

"Good."

"Do you want to hang out here until I'm finished work?" I asked, watching as he moved for the wall of the smoking area. "I'll drive you home."

"That's what I've got legs for."

"But your dad's still out there."

"My dad can go fuck himself," little alpha called over his shoulder as he climbed onto a wheely bin and vaulted effortlessly onto the stone wall enclosing the smoking area. "If anything, he needs to hope he doesn't run into me."

"Tadhg, hold up—"

"I'll be seeing ya," he called out, offering me a half-assed sailor salute before disappearing over the wall.

The family line

JOEY

Our life was a trainwreck.

Standing in the kitchen doorway, after persuading the younger boys to go for a kick about on the green across the road, I watched as the older members of my family ranted and roared at each other. Reminding me of a scene straight out of one of those soap dramas that Molloy roped me into watching with her, I was glad that, for once, I wasn't the instigator of the drama. No, that title had undisputedly fallen to our mother, who had made the fatal error of accusing some rich lady's son of statutory rape.

I mean, really?

It was fucking embarrassing.

There was only one rapist in our midst, statutory and otherwise, and it was the man she'd nestled down in bed with every night for the past twenty-four plus years.

Fucking hypocrite.

Watching Kavanagh's mother go for mine in my front garden earlier was a foreign sight to me.

I'd never seen a mother throw down like that for her kid. But Edel Kavanagh had and somewhere, in the back of mind, I got the distinct feeling that Molloy would do the exact same for our kid.

Jesus.

Wishing I was anywhere but back in this house, I looked on as Shannon and Mam battled it out for the title of Ballylaggin's loudest screamer. While Darren the dildo tried to wave a white flag between them.

Fucking eejit.

Having Mam's back in it was not going to win him any favors. He was going to bat for the wrong female. Christ, even Seany-boo, who was only three, knew that Darren was flogging a dead horse with our mother.

I might be fucked in the head, but I'd meant it when I'd said that I was done with her. I didn't have it in me to forgive her again, not after that evening in the kitchen. Not with the memory of my sister's almost lifeless body still haunting me.

Him or us, Mam?

"Joey was right." Shannon cried out, dragging my scattered attention back to the argument ensuing a few feet away from me. "You're not good for us."

I felt like slow-clapping, grateful that someone else could see what I did.

"Come on, Shannon," Darren, the expert at running out on his family, threw his two cents into the mix. "Screaming and name-calling isn't helping anyone."

"Then stop sitting there and *do* something," my baby sister spat back. Fighting and willing our oldest brother to do something he would never be capable of doing for her. *Helping her.* "You know this is wrong. You know what she did was *awful*, and you're just letting her get away with it."

Shannon was spot on.

The shit Mam had spurted to the Kavanaghs was horrendous and he was feeding into her bullshit by pandering to her mental breakdown.

I might need locking up, but she sure as shit needed to reserve the padded cell next to mine.

"No, I'm not," Darren tried to placate. "She knows she was wrong, don't you, Mam?"

If he was expecting a coherent answer from the woman that birthed us, then he was about to be sorely disappointed. She didn't have it in her. She was incapable of thinking beyond the fourteen-year-old version of herself that had been thrust into motherhood. Her brain had stopped growing at that age.

The woman was broken in the head.

Same as me.

"Mam, tell Shannon that you know you were wrong." If I was a better person, I would have felt sympathy for the man. He still thought the mother he left behind more than half a decade ago was still inside the shell sitting at the kitchen table. "*Mam.* Answer us."

Looking weary, Shannon shook her head and turned away from Mam. Darren, though, he continued to watch our mother like he was waiting for some divine intervention.

"Don't bother," I heard myself tell her golden boy. "Because she's broken. You'll figure that out soon enough."

"Joe." Bolting towards me like a wobbly foal, our sister threw her arms around my neck and clung to me. "Make this stop."

I wanted to.

There was a still a part of me alive inside that wanted to fix this for my sister.

For the boys.

But I was so fucking worn out.

My head didn't seem to be working right anymore. Whatever the old man had done to me in the kitchen that evening had broken me. The cord that attached my heart to my head had been severed.

It had been beaten out of me.

"This is what you wanted, Darren. You wanted her home with us," I told our brother. "One big happy family." Hooking an arm around the trembling girl in my arms, I glared at the man who considered himself to be wiser than us. "I hope we've met your expectations."

He didn't respond. Instead, he pushed his chair back and stood. Taking one final look at our mother, he turned on his heels and walked away.

"I don't know why I'm surprised anymore," Shannon mumbled.

The sound of the front door closing behind him was the only confirmation I needed to that I was right.

His return was temporary.

He wouldn't stick this out.

He couldn't the first time.

This time would be no different.

With the mother of all headaches, and my body in withdrawal, I stepped around Shannon and moved for the cooker. Mam could check out and Darren could run, but there were still four mouths to feed in the house.

Battling the tremors in my hands, I prepped a saucepan of pasta and set it on the hob to boil, before turning my attention to the woman in the corner. "Get up and take a shower. I need to feed the boys and they don't need to see you like this."

She didn't budge.

It didn't surprise me.

It didn't do anything to me.

I felt completely dead inside as I walked over to where she was sitting and snatched the cigarette out of her lips and stubbed it out in the already overflowing ashtray. "Get up. You stink of smoke and booze."

Nothing.

Setting the ashtray and her stained coffee cup on the draining board, I returned to her side. "Get up."

I didn't need this shit.

I had enough on my plate.

I had Molloy, dammit.

"Joey." It was the first sign of life in her, and it caused something to die inside of me. "Joey." Reaching up, she snatched up my hand in both of hers and sobbed. "Joey."

I could smell the drink wafting off her in waves.

Whiskey.

I would know that smell anywhere.

Repressing a shudder, I reached for my mother and helped her to stand. I needed to get her out of sight before the boys came back in from playing and she fucked up their heads even more.

"Keep an eye on the dinner, Shan," I called over my shoulder, as I helped Mam up out of the kitchen and up the staircase to her bedroom.

The more she sobbed and leaned against me, the more I felt suffocated.

The urge to break through the walls of this house and escape was so strong, I could practically taste it.

I would never have it, though.

I couldn't physically break the chains that shackled me to this house.

To these children.

To this woman.

The only reprieve would get was the one I took for myself.

"Come on, Mam," I mumbled, feeling the weight of her body against me, as I tried to get her upstairs. "You need to help me out here."

She didn't.

She couldn't.

Because my mother was as dead on the inside as I was.

Beyond exhausted, when we reached the top of the landing, I swooped her into my arms and carried her the rest of the way to her bedroom.

Their bedroom.

It's his room, too, remember?

Dick.

Ignoring every muscle in my body as it screamed in protest, I managed to make it to her bed without collapsing in a heap. Setting her down on the mattress, I knelt at her bedside and pulled off her slippers before rolling her onto her side to face the window.

"I'm sorry, Joey," she sobbed, resting her small hands under her cheek. "So sorry."

I heard the word, had a feeling she might mean it this time, but I felt nothing.

"You need to keep your shit together," I replied in a flat tone, as I sank down on the edge of the bed beside her and rummaged around in her nightstand drawer. "You might be all fucked up in the head, but those boys don't need to see it."

"Darren," she wailed softly, clutching my forearm. "I want Darren."

"Yeah, well, Darren bailed," I muttered, focusing on the countless blister packs of pills, while tossing empty pill bottles out of the way.

"Fuck, Mam, what have you been taking?"

"Like you can judge me," she sobbed, burying her head in her pillow. "I'm in pain."

Me too. "Here," I said, finally settling on a pill bottle containing a few valiums. "Take a couple of these. It'll take the edge off."

"What if he comes back?"

"Who?" I asked, only half-listening to her, as I continued to search for what I wanted. I knew they were in here. *I fucking knew it.* "Darren?"

"No," she mumbled, choking back the tablets I'd given her. "Your father."

"You know what'll happen, Mam," I muttered, mentally sagging in relief when I found a full bottle of Clonazepam. "You'll take him back," I added, slipping the bottle into my pocket. "And all will be well in the world of Marie Lynch again."

"I'm your mother," she sobbed, voice slurring. "Why do you hate me so much?"

"I'm your son," I replied, giving her back her words. "Why do *you* hate *me* so much?"

"Because you're him," she slurred, twisting away from me.

"Yeah," I deadpanned, standing up, feeling nothing. "I'm him, and you're worse."

"Joey, wait," she cried out as I moved for the door. "I'm sorry. I'm sorry, baby . . . Please don't leave me."

"Sleep it off, Mam," I deadpanned, unwilling to stick around to be her personal punching bag until she passed out. "I've got shit to clean up and your kids to feed."

We found love in a hopeless place

AOIFE

With Keane's 'Somewhere Only We Know' blasting from the car stereo, and my good nerves in tatters, I pulled up outside 95 Elk's Terrace and killed the engine. Taking a few moments to compose my emotions, I pulled the visor down and checked my appearance in the tiny mirror.

Reapplying my lips with a fresh coat of Black Cherry, I pressed my lips together and practiced my best smile before blowing out a shaky breath and popping the lid of my lipstick back into place.

You can do this.

He's still your Joey.

He's still in there.

Bring him back.

Pulling my hair out of its ponytail, I fluffed it over my shoulders and tossed my hair-tie on the passenger seat, and then climbed out of the car.

Braced for trouble, I rounded the graffiti-stained wall surrounding their front garden, ignoring the usual overgrowth of grass and weeds, as I moved for the front door with my fist raised to knock. However, the door opened before I had a chance to knock, and I was greeted by Shannon.

"Oh my god." Relief flashed in her eyes, and she quickly snatched my hand up and pulled me inside. "Aoif."

"Hi, chickie," I replied, voice thick with emotion, as I pulled her skinny little frame into my arms and hugged her a little tighter than I should. I couldn't help it. The last time I'd laid eyes on her, I'd been afraid that it would be the actual last. Seeing her back on her feet, battered and bruised but with a smile on her face was sending my pregnancy hormones into overdrive. "I was so bloody worried about you."

"Thank you so much for what you did for me," she squeezed out, hugging me back. "Getting me to the hospital so fast? The doctors told me that you guys saved my life. I wouldn't have made it if I had gotten there any later."

"That was all your brother," I was quick to explain. "Joe was the one who made the call."

"He's always saving me," she whispered, releasing her hold on me. "I wish I could do the same for him."

Yeah, me, too.

"Where are the boys?"

"In their room playing," she was quick to explain. "Mam's in bed."

"And Darren?"

Her expression turned stormy. "Don't know. Don't care."

"And Joe?"

"He's upstairs." Offering me a sad smile, she gestured to the staircase behind her. "After he put Mam to bed and sorted the boys out, he went into his room and hasn't come out since."

Thank God.

He's still here.

He's still safe.

"So, how was he?" I asked, following her into the thankfully empty kitchen. "When you brought him to Johnny's place?"

She chewed on her lip nervously, clearing unwilling to betray her brother's trust.

"Shan, come on," I said in a weary tone. We were way past the pretenses. "It's me."

"I think he's back on the . . . well, the uh, you know."

Drugs.

She meant drugs.

"When I found him, he had stumbled out of Shane Holland's car and was sprawled out on the road," she added, moving for the kettle. "He wasn't uh, he wasn't himself."

No shit.

Because that bastard sunk his claws into a vulnerable lad with a grade 3 concussion, three cracks in his skull, and a lifetime of abuse under his belt.

"How bad was he?" I forced myself to ask her.

"Tea?"

"No thanks. Back to Joe. How bad was he?"

"Not that—"

"Don't lie to me, Shan. Not about him."

After a long pause, Shannon tossed her soggy teabag in the sink and blew out a strained breath. "He was the worst I've ever seen him."

I already knew it, but somehow, hearing her admit it made it all a million times worse. Because Joey was the master of concealment. He buried everything from his siblings, the fear, ache, and pain, desperate to protect them. If Shannon and Tadhg were both seeing the cracks in Joey's meticulously masked world, though, then they were as wide as the Grand Canyon.

Fuck.

"Okay." As a tsunami of concern and fear crashed over me, I abruptly turned on my heels and moved for the door. "I'm going up there."

"Wait." Hurrying towards me with what looked like a ham sandwich on a small plate, Shannon thrust it into my hands. "Can you give this to him?" With her eyes full of unrestrained panic, she shrugged helplessly. "He had a little dinner earlier, but he just looks so . . . gaunt."

I didn't have the words to make her feel better, Joe was the only one I'd ever seen manage his sister's anxiety, so I offered her a half-hearted smile and moved for the staircase. Ignoring my pulse thundering in my ears I climbed the stairs and walked to his door.

"Joe?" I knocked lightly before pushing the door inwards and stepping inside.

His room was in darkness, with his curtains closed, and clothes strewn everywhere, which wasn't like him. The boy kept his room remarkably spotless given the circumstances, but right now, it looked like a pigsty.

"Joe?" I croaked out, feeling my heartrate spike when my gaze landed on him face down on the bottom bunk of his bed. Wearing only a pair of black boxer shorts, every bruise, scar, and blemish on his body was on full display. "Joe?"

I wasn't naïve enough to believe that it was exhaustion that had plummeted him into a deep slumber. With my heart in tatters and my hope hanging by a thread, I closed the door behind me, set the plate down on the dresser, and removed his phone and wallet from my handbag. Setting it and his wallet on the dresser, I attached his phone to its charger before moving for the bed. Kicking off my heels, I removed my coat and apron, letting them fall to the floor, before clambering onto the bed. Repressing a shiver when the distinct stench of vinegar and weed filled my senses, I settled down on my side, facing him.

"Come back to me, Joe," I whispered, reaching out to stroke his bruised cheek. "I know you're still in there."

Stiffening when my hand made contact with his skin, I watched as a full body shudder rolled through him.

A god-awful pained cry escaped his parted swollen lips and he moaned drowsily into the mattress, as his body stiffened and flinched with every gentle stroke of my thumb on his cheek.

Fucking monsters.

The both of them.

We were so far away from each other even though we were laying side by side, with a baby we'd made together growing in my belly. He had never felt more detached from me.

I knew he was still in there, though.

My Joey was still inside the person strung out next to me.

And I loved him enough to keep fighting for him.

Even when he'd given up on himself.

"It's okay." Sniffling, I didn't bother to fight the tears that were trickling down my cheeks, as my eyes took in the carnage. Knowing in my heart that the damage to his face paled in comparison to the damage to his heart. "Nothing's going to hurt you, baby."

"Mol . . ." With a great deal of effort, he shifted onto his side to face me and blinked an eye open. " . . . loy."

I smiled sadly. "Hey, stud."

"I'm . . . sorry." His words were slurred, his eyes bloodshot, his pupils dilated. "So . . . sorry."

"I know, Joe." Moving closer, I cupped his damaged cheek with the palm of my hand and leaned in close. "I know."

"The . . . baby."

"Still cooking." I pressed a featherlight kiss to the tip of his nose. "What have you done to yourself, huh?"

He groaned in response. "I was coming . . . to find you, I swear. I just got . . . "

"Sidetracked," I answered for him, breaking my own heart in the process. "Yeah, I can see that, Joe."

And this is it, I thought to myself, *this is your future.*

This is the boy your heart is set on.

"I need you to get back up, Joe." Crying quietly, I pushed his hair off his face and pressed a kiss to his forehead. "I'm hanging in here, baby, doing the fighting for both of us, but I needed to climb back on your feet."

"I'm just so . . . tired."

"I know you are," I agreed, feeling my soul crack. "But I need you to keep fighting."

"I'm no . . . good for . . . you."

"That's not true."

"I don't have feelings anymore."

"Yes, you do, Joe," I whispered, clinging to his trembling body with mine. "You just need to remember who you are."

"I tried to warn you," he slurred. "You didn't hear me and now we're both fucked."

PART 8

Our new reality

AOIFE

The next several weeks passed by in a horrendous blur of deception, heartbreak, and broken promises.

Joey's descent into addiction had come on as rapidly as the weight he continued to lose.

He was barely recognizable now.

With track marks on his arms and bruising on his veins, I watched on helplessly as he continued to numb his pain.

My boyfriend was back in the flesh, but the boy I'd fallen in love with all those years ago, seldom made an appearance anymore.

As the child in my belly continued to grow, so did the gaping ridge between us.

I couldn't seem to reach him anymore.

It didn't matter what I said or did, he wasn't listening.

Joey had well and truly checked out on life.

He was my closest friend, and I felt his absence everywhere I went and in everything I did. I felt his withdrawal in the deepest corners of my heart.

He had fallen headfirst into old patterns and, right there with him, I was repeating past mistakes.

Giving him a pass and turning a blind eye to things that I knew were wrong. Things that I knew could destroy him. Because the fear I had of losing him was too great.

Falling in love had exposed the biggest weakness in me because my heart refused to allow me to walk away from him, no matter how hopeless it seemed. Weakened and demoralized, I watched on daily as he continued to splinter both his world and mine, because I knew he was still my Joey underneath the ghost he had become.

Every now and then, rare as they had become, I saw glimpses of that boy who stole my heart all those years ago. I saw the person he used to be, and I reveled in it. It gave me hope, seeing him, knowing he was still in there somewhere.

With his father hiding from the law in rehab, his mother falling apart at home, and his brother's sudden reappearance, I knew the pressure my boyfriend was under was insurmountable. It didn't take away the fact, though, that time was ticking, and we had a baby on the way.

It didn't take away the fact that in a few short months, I would have a choice to make.

If Joey didn't get a handle on things, he was going to end up forcing my hand. The thought of what might happen when that day came caused my heart to shrivel up and die.

Because I couldn't do this without him, but I refused to repeat past mistakes.

I refused to subject our baby to the same ordeal their father had been exposed to.

I wouldn't be Marie Lynch.

My baby would come first.

Remember my face

JOEY

"Molloy, wait up!" Pushing off the wall outside the GP surgery, the one I'd been waiting against for the past twenty minutes, I hurried after her. "Wait up, will ya?"

"Can't," she called over her shoulder – her rigid shoulder – as she pulled up the hood of her raincoat, gave a quick glance left and right and crossed the road. "I'm late for school."

Yeah, we were both late for school, but I was the asshole late for her appointment.

Swallowing down my self-loathing, I clenched my jaw and jogged after her. "How did it go?" I asked, falling into step beside her when I reached the footpath. "Is everything okay with the, uh . . . " Shoving my hands into the front pocket of my hoodie, I concentrated on the footpath as I spoke. "Are you okay?"

"Am I okay?" She stopped dead in her tracks and let out a humorless laugh. *"Am I okay?"* she repeated, swinging around to glare at me. "Hmm, let's see, I've just spent the last hour being lectured by a doctor who's known me since childhood about the dangers I've been exposed to, because unlike the pregnant women waiting with their husbands and partners for good news, I'm the fool at risk."

"Risk?" Panic roared to life inside of me. "For what?"

"I'm at risk," she hissed, "because I was the fucking eejit who laid on her back for an intravenous drug user who can't remember his own bloody name half the time! A little fucking humiliating, don't you think, Joe?" she demanded, tears filling her eyes. "To be *that* girl." She narrowed her eyes. "To be the girlfriend of *that* guy."

It took me a while to register her words.

The fog in my head made it so fucking hard to focus.

But once I did, my heart cracked in my chest. "Jesus Christ," I strangled out. "I didn't give you anything, did I?" Panicked, I choked out, "I've never cheated on you."

"I know, Joe." Sniffling, she shook her head. "My test results are all clean."

Relief flooded my body. "I'm so fucking sorry."

"Yeah, well, I guess I should say thanks for showing up," she deadpanned, turning on her heels. "Better late than never, huh?"

"I overslept."

"Uh-huh. I bet whatever you took knocked you out hard."

"Aoife, I'm sorry!" I called after when she stormed off. "I can do this. I can take care of you and the baby—"

"You can't even take care of yourself!" She pulled her hood back up when the wind knocked it down. "You're sick, Joe. You're so sick and you can't even see it."

"I'm not sick," I argued, hurrying after her. "I'm just going through some shit right now."

"You are a *drug addict*," she cried out hoarsely, as she swung around to glare at me. "You are killing yourself and you are killing me!"

"No." I shook my head, desperately refuting her words. "It's going to be okay."

"Look at what's happening to your life!" she all but screamed. "You've been kicked off the hurling team. You're failing at school. You're constantly off your head. You've lost yourself, Joe. You promised me that you'd stay, but you're not *here* anymore. I bet you don't even know what day it is."

"It's Thursday," I choked out, trembling. "And I don't give a fuck about school or the hurling team."

"What about me?" she sobbed. "What about our baby? Do you care about us?"

"You're all I care about," I snapped, pushing my hair back. "Fuck, you're all I've ever cared about, Molloy. You know that."

"Then *fight*, Joey Lynch," she begged, fisting her hand in the front of my school jumper. "Fight this."

"I am."

"Liar." She accused, tears spilling down her cheeks. "You've thrown in the towel. You've given the hell up and we both know it."

"What do you want me to do?" I shot back, struggling to rein in my temper. "Jesus fucking Christ, Molloy, I am doing everything that's been asked of me. Fucking everything!"

"The only thing I'm asking you to do is the one thing you point blank refuse to do," she argued hotly. "Get clean."

"Aoife—"

"You don't get it," she screamed. "You can't see how far you've fallen, Joey. I've had to beg and borrow to get you out of trouble with Shane Holland and those monsters, and you *keep* going back to them! I owe Gibsie money. I owe Podge money. I owe Casey money and she doesn't even have it to spare. I am doing everything I can to keep you alive, but you just won't help yourself!"

"I'm *fine*," I bit out. "It's all good." When she didn't respond, I gently tipped her chin upwards, forcing her to look at me. "I love you."

"I used to think that was true," she breathed, tears flowing freely down her cheeks. "But I'm beginning to think that you don't know what love means."

"Molloy—"

"Look at my face, Joe," she told me, and I did. *Fuck, I did.* "This is what hurting the person who loves you most in the world looks like." She sniffled, tears dripping down her face, mirroring mine. "Remember this moment," she added quietly. "Remember what I looked like the day you broke my heart."

One song at a time

JOEY

My mind was playing tricks on me.

Or maybe my body was the one playing tricks on my mind.

Either way, I couldn't figure anything out anymore.

Confusion had settled deep in my bloodstream, and I was lost.

I knew that I was physically present, back in the house I hated, surrounded by people I couldn't look in the eye. Yet, it felt like I was looking down on myself from above. Like I was a spectator, seeing all the bullshit unfold around me, while I was powerless to stop it.

I'd gone too far, I realized.

The hunger eating away at me, the aching in my veins, it was too necessary now.

Too fucking deeply imbedded in me to try and fight it.

I didn't want to fight.

I was tired.

When the chips were down and the cards had folded, Molloy was the only reprieve from the pain.

I wanted to reach for her.

I wanted so fucking badly to grab the hand she was holding out for me, but catching hold of her hand meant that she could be dragged down with me, and I couldn't fucking risk it.

Ignoring the noise around me, focusing on putting one foot in front of the other, I walked into class. Which class, I had no fucking clue, but I could see *her* face, standing out to me like a beacon of light in the darkness.

Hating myself with every fiber of my being, I let the beating heart in my chest lead me back to her.

Back home.

I could hear my name being spoken around me, but I just ... I couldn't get my brain to focus on anything but her.

Slumping down in the chair beside her, I let the familiar scent of her perfume fill my senses and shivered.

"Molloy."

"Joe."

She needs you, something deep down inside of me screamed, *wake the fuck up!*

I could see the swell of her stomach.

The baby I'd put inside of her body.

It couldn't be hidden anymore.

Knees bopping restlessly, I tried to grapple with the tremors racking through my frame, but it wasn't coming easy. Only when she reached under the desk and took my hand in hers did I find the ability to steady myself.

"Nice legs."

Tears filled her eyes and she quickly looked away, but she didn't stop holding my hand. Instead, she squeezed it tighter, warming my coldness with her warmth. Wordlessly, she shifted her chair closer to mine and gently popped one earphone in my ear. It was something she had done every day since Easter break. We had settled into a strange routine, where every morning at school, Molloy would hand me an earphone, giving me a glimpse into how she felt that morning.

One song at a time.

One day at a time.

That's all she gave me, and it became the song I got up for in the morning.

It became the best part of my day.

The part before everything got too heavy and the urge to shoot up got the better of me.

For weeks, it continued.

Keane's 'Somewhere Only We Know'.

Mazzy Star's 'Fade Into You'.

Matchbox Twenty's 'Unwell'.

Sheryl Crow and Kid Rock's 'Picture'.

Dido's 'White Flag'.

Shakira's 'Underneath Your Clothes'.

Avril Lavigne's 'I'm With You'.

The Beatles' 'Don't Let Me Down'.

The Verve's 'The Drugs Don't Work'.

The Calling's 'Wherever You Will Go'.

Every day I walked into class, right before my will buckled and I freewheeled into hell, I sought her out.

Still chasing after the girl from the wall.

Still wanting her more than I wanted to live.

It was the small things she did, like continuing to wear the necklace I bought her. Or some days, she would be eating in class and then place her last Rolo on the desk in front of me.

It took me a while to recognize this morning's song as LIVE's 'Lightning Crashes' and even longer to register the importance of that song for us. I turned my head to look straight ahead, feeling too much in the moment, too exposed and guilty.

This hurt.

It fucking burned and scorched me.

I knew what she was trying to accomplish by playing me this song, but I couldn't get back there. Still, unable to stop myself, I allowed her to hold my hand under the desk, I allowed myself to absorb the feeling of her skin on mine, of her light temporarily chasing the dark away.

It wasn't right, I was only hurting her further, but I needed this small scrap of affection. I needed her for just a little bit longer.

Frozen to the spot, I allowed her to do whatever she wanted to me.

God knows she owned me.

She entwined her fingers with mine and squeezed, and while I didn't squeeze back, I couldn't stop my thumb from tracing over her small knuckles.

I knew my actions were hurting her in a way that could send her away permanently, but I couldn't stop myself anymore.

I couldn't pull myself back out of the hole I'd fallen into.

Worse, a huge part of me didn't want to.

He's waiting for me

AOIFE

The father of my unborn child was a heroin addict.

That was a painful admission. It hurt so hard I could hardly breathe.

For years, I had hung on every word that came from his mouth, too in love to see the warning signs and red flags dancing in front of my eyes. Unknowingly wearing my trust around my neck like a noose until it strangled me.

Even now, as I watched him crawl through my bedroom window and stumble towards my bed in the darkness, I couldn't find it in my heart to send him away.

Because I was in love with him.

The boy he used to be.

The man he had become.

All of his versions.

I loved them all.

The mattress dipped and then he was there, shivering and trembling beside me. "Molloy."

Clenching my eyes shut, I willed myself to hold on, to remember the boy still inside the ghost in my bed. "Joe."

"I'm so c-cold."

"Come here," I whispered, moving on instinct, as I rolled onto my side to face him and draped an arm over his chest.

"So f-fucking c-cold," he slurred, teeth chattering violently, as he clutched my forearm with both hands. "So f-fucking s-sorry."

I knew he was.

He said it daily.

Showed it, too.

Problem was, afterwards he continued to repeat the cycle.

He continued to drown his pain in the worst possible way.

He would always go back to Shane.

"Do you s-still love m-me?" he asked, still trembling violently, and I could tell that he was coming down from an unmerciful high. I could also tell that when he crashed and burned, it would be horrendous. "Because I w-wouldn't blame you if you d-didn't."

"I still love you, Joe," I assured him, feeling my heart hemorrhage from the pain of it all. "I can't stop."

"I can't sleep," he confessed, rolling onto his side to face me. "And I'm so f-fucking tired, queen."

"Why not?"

"Because when I close my eyes, he's w-waiting for me."

"Who, Joe?" I squeezed out, reaching up to wipe a tear from his cheek. "Who's waiting for you?"

"My father."

"No, baby, he's not waiting for you," I whispered, closing the space between us and fusing my lips to his. I couldn't help it. I had to be close to him. "He can't hurt you anymore, Joe."

"He's coming for me," he whispered against my lips, and I felt his tears mix with mine. "He's coming for a-all of us."

"We're going to die in that house, Molloy."

"No, you're not. Don't say that, Joe."

"He won't let her go. He'll n-never let her go."

"Your mam?"

He nodded sadly. "He'll kill her before he lets her leave h-him." Sniffing, he added, "I know him, Aoif. I know the b-bastard better than anyone. He's waiting for his chance."

"Joe, you're scaring me," I admitted, feeling panicked by his words. "Nothing's going to happen, okay? It's just the drugs, baby. They're messing with your mind."

"It's true. I can feel it," he choked out. "But I don't want to go out that way," he argued weakly, shifting closer to nuzzle me. "If I'm going to die, I want it to be on my terms, not his."

"You're not dying, Joe," I warned, tightening my hold on him. "Because you promised that you wouldn't leave me alone in this."

"No one sees me," he whispered. "No one hears me. No one listens, but I'm r-right. It's coming. I can feel it in my b-bones."

"Joey, please, you're scaring me!"

"If anything happens to me, I want you to m-move on," he mumbled, pressing a kiss to the curve of my neck. "I want you to be s-strong for our s-son."

"Joe, nothing's going to happen to you." I took a breath, hating every second of this morbid conversation. "And we don't know if we're having a boy."

"We are." He reached a hand between us and cradled the swell of my stomach in his trembling hand. "You're growing my son."

"You know, if you're right about this baby's gender, then I'm taking you to a circus," I tried to joke, desperate to lighten the atmosphere, as I pushed him onto his back and straddled his lap. "Because you are freakishly intuitive, and we could make a killing off your predictions."

"I want the baby, Molloy," he slurred, hands moving to my hips as he looked up at me through hooded eyes. "I know I'm all fucked up in the head, but I swear it's true. I want this baby with you."

And there he was.

My Joey.

He was still in there.

His heart was still beating inside that shell.

"We're going to make it, Joe," I whispered, leaning down to press my lips to his. "You're going to get better and we're going to have a long and happy life together. I refuse to accept anything less."

"I hope you're right," he replied sadly. "Because I've got this awful feeling that it's too late for me."

You're late – again

JOEY

Late.

I was late again, and it wasn't fucking good enough.

I was a disgrace.

I knew it when I woke up this morning on the mattress in a pool of my own vomit, and I knew it now as I tried to find my way through the maze of corridors at the maternity hospital.

Going through the horrors of a particularly rough comedown, I used my sleeve to wipe the cold sweat beading my brow, as I waited my turn at the receptionist's desk.

"Yes?"

"I'm looking for the ultrasound department," I mumbled, trying my hardest to keep my shit in order and look somewhat presentable. "I'm, ah, my girlfriend has an appointment."

"Name?"

"Joey Lynch."

"No, love. I need your partner's name."

"Oh, shit, yeah." Swallowing deeply, I shook my head and said, "Aoife Molloy."

The woman behind the desk clicked a few buttons on her computer before saying, "She already had her anomaly scan. She's waiting for the consultant now. Straight down the corridor. Last door on the left."

"Thanks." Repressing a full body shudder when a wave of nausea attacked me, I pushed it down and hurried off in the direction the lady had sent me.

After fumbling with a few doors, I finally located the right room and slipped inside. And there she was, sitting all alone in the consultant's waiting room. The moment the door closed behind me Molloy's attention snapped my way.

"You're late," she accused, tears filling her blazing eyes.

"I know." Guilt churned inside of me. "Can I come in?"

"What's the point?" she tossed back bitterly. "It's not like you'll remember any of this."

Fuck.

Shoving my hands through my hair, I closed the space between us and leaned in to kiss her.

"Don't!" She turned away and my heart cracked clean open in my chest. "You're high and you stink."

"I'm not high," I tried to persuade her. "I'm not, I swear, Aoi—"

"Don't, Joe," she choked out, holding a hand up to warn me off. "Just don't."

"How was the scan?" I asked, sinking down on the chair next to hers. "Is the baby okay?" I swallowed down another surge of bile and forced myself to look her in the eyes. "Are you?"

"The baby's fine," she replied, voice thick with emotion. "Where *were* you? This was an important scan, Joey."

"I know," I groaned, feeling like a piece of shit, as I pressed the heel of my hand against my forehead. "I overslept."

"You mean you got high with Shane and your boys last night and forgot about us," she snapped back, resting a hand on her bump.

My heart cracked in my chest.

"When the doctor comes in, I don't want you to say a word," she instructed in a strained voice. "Just . . . just stay quiet and let me handle everything, okay? I don't need another report going in against me."

"Aoife, I'm so fucking sorry."

"No," she warned when I reached for her hand. "Not here, Joe," she bit out, blinking her tears away. "I can't do this here."

Swallowing deeply, I shoved my hands into the front pocket of my hoodie and attempted to sit straight and not sway.

"Look at you," she said, as tears trickled freely down her cheeks. "Wake the hell up and look at yourself, will you!"

Stiffening in my chair, I tried not to let her words wholeheartedly consume me. "I love you." Panicking when she didn't respond, I reached for her again. "Aoife – did ya hear me?"

"Yeah, and you love that shit you inject into your veins more." She batted my hand away. "I don't want anything to do with that kind of love. Keep your love for the drugs."

"What do you want me to say?" I demanded, feeling lost and fucking broken. "You asked me to come and I'm here."

"I don't want your words, Joey," she cried. "I want action."

"I'm here, aren't I?"

She shook her head. "I'm not the rest of them, you know. I'm not ever going to give up on you." Sniffling she added, "Remember that, Joe."

"Why tell me that?" I asked, thoroughly fucking rattled by her words.

She looked me dead in the eyes when she said, "So you can stop disappointing me."

Teardrops and text messages

AOIFE

"Are you feeling okay?" Casey asked on the first Saturday in May. We were sitting on the footpath outside my house, watching as Podge, Alec, and several other lads kicked a ball around on the green across the road from my house.

"No," I replied, not bothering to lie. The blasé façade I used for the rest of the world was exhausting and after a long week of bullshit smiling at school, I was running on empty. "I'm tired, I'm fat, and I'm going out of my mind with worry."

Casey didn't ask me why. She was all too aware of Joey's behavior these past few months.

"Where is he now?"

"At work, supposedly."

"You don't believe him?"

"I don't believe anything he says anymore, Case."

I can't afford to.

That was the sad truth.

Keeping my eyes trained on the football match unfolding on the green, I shook my head and shrugged. "Dad says he's been showing up for his shifts, but I just . . . I don't know."

"Oh, babe."

"Don't say *oh, babe* like that," I begged, repressing a shudder. "I'll cry and I really need to *not* cry anymore, okay?"

"He'll come right, Aoif," she said. "He will."

"Maybe," I whispered, chewing on my lip, as my gaze flicked to my stomach. "But I need him to do it now."

"When's your next scan?" she asked, reaching a hand over to rub my bump that was discreetly hidden beneath an oversized hoodie. "The anomaly one is coming up soon, isn't it?"

"No, that's the one I had last week."

"When's the next one?"

"My twenty-eight week one."

"Shit, Aoif, I can't believe you're already halfway there."

"Yeah." I sighed heavily. "Me either."

"Listen." Twisting sideways, to face me, my best friend took my hand in hers and squeezed. "I know you don't want to talk about Joe, but I just need to make sure you know that none of his behavior has a thing to do with his feelings for you and the baby." She gave me a sad smile. "He's messed up in the head, babe. He's dealing with a lot of unresolved trauma. I mean, the shit with his father is enough to give me PTSD, let alone Joey. But none of that means that he doesn't love you and baby bear."

"I know he loves us," I whispered, gaze flicking to my lap, as a tear threatened to spill. "But he just loves that poison he injects in his veins more."

"We both know that's not true," she was quick to soothe. "But we also both know that he's not getting better without professional help. It's gone too far, Aoif, and lying and covering for him isn't going to help him in the long run."

"What am I supposed to do, Case?" I choked out, swinging my attention back to her. "I can't force him into a rehab program, and even if I could, how am I supposed to pay for it? His mother doesn't give a damn, and every penny I'm earning at the pub, I'm either using to pay off his debts, or trying to save up for the baby. Because that's another thing I have to worry about. What if he's not there when the time comes?"

"Don't think like that," she argued, flinching. "He'll be there, Aoif."

"But if he's not?" I pushed, forcing myself to admit my greatest fear aloud. "What if he slips so far off the map that I can't reach him? What if he overdoses? If he dies? Or gets killed? What then, Case?" The tears I'd been trying to fight escaped me and I sniffled back a sob. "What am I supposed to do? Mam and Dad can't finance this baby. They're barely making ends meet as it stands. I know what Joey needs, but I just ... " Feeling helpless, I shrugged. "I just *don't* have the money to fix him."

"Doesn't his older brother have a good job?"

"Fuck Darren," I spat, narrowing my eyes. "He would rather pay me to have an abortion than pay to fix his brother's mental health. Besides, he's been spending more and more time in Belfast lately. Mark my words, Case, he'll be gone before the baby's born."

"You could ask him to help you."

"I did."

"Ask him again."

"Please don't start," I warned, holding a hand up. "I already have Mam on my back twenty-four-seven, lecturing me on everything that I *should* be doing. Please, Case, I don't need it from you, too."

"Never," she soothed, slinging an arm over my shoulder. "In my humble opinion, I think you're a bomb-ass bitch for handling all of this so well."

"Funny."

"It's true," she pushed. "You are incredible, Aoif. The definition of a strong woman. All the crap you've been taking from assholes at school? How you handle yourself? How you get up and hold your head high each morning? Babe, you are amazing."

"Except that I've never felt less like a woman, Case," I admitted hoarsely. "And more like a lost child."

Distracted when the sound of a car engine revving filled my ears, we both turned to see a fancy Lexus pull up at the footbath in front of Katie's house next-door.

"Well, if it isn't Miss Slick, riding shotgun with the rich boys," Alec called out from the green, whistling loudly. "Fuck me, Podge, we're in the wrong damn school. The best I've ever been dropped home from school in was the back seat of Aoife's banger."

"Hey, you leave Rattles and Squeaks alone, ya hear," Casey called back with a laugh. "It beats the hell out of the shitty saddler you gave me on the back of your mountain bike."

"Stolen mountain bike," Podge chimed in, as both boys crossed the road to meet us.

"Don't pretend like I didn't give you the ride of your life," Al teased, winking at my bestie.

"Did you?" Casey pretended to think hard about it. "Must not have been that memorable if I can't recall."

"Cheeky fucker," he chuckled, tossing his sweat-soaked t-shirt on his lap. "When you're ready for the sequel just say the word, devil-tits."

My laughter quickly died in my throat when the passenger seat of the Lexus flew open and a teary-eyed Katie emerged, followed by a boy I knew *wasn't* her boyfriend. "Katie?"

"Patrick?" Casey called out, sounding confused, as we both scrambled to our feet.

"Okay," I growled, as I both moved straight for my friend, with my bestie and my boyfriend's besties flanking me. "Who the hell hurt you and where do we find them?"

"Honestly, I'm fine," Katie replied, eyes bloodshot, as she quickly slipped around us and hurried into her front garden. "I just n-need to go h-home."

"Hey!" Closing the space between herself and Patrick Feely, Casey poked him in the chest and glowered up at him. "What the hell happened to her?"

Silently and stoic, Patrick looked from my one of my besties to the other and shook his head. "Ask her," was all he finally said.

"I'm asking you," Casey growled, not giving an inch. "If you hurt her . . . "

"I don't go around hurting girls," he said, blue eyes darkening. "I don't go around breaking hearts, either."

"Katie, hold up," I called out, moving to go after her only to halt in my tracks when I heard a familiar voice behind me.

"Molloy."

Repressing a shiver, I swung around to see Joey crossing the road towards me, still clad in his work overalls, with the sleeves tied around his waist, and the white t-shirt he had on underneath smeared in engine oil. He had a baseball cap slung on backwards, and his lunchbox dangling between his hands.

I found myself looking at him – really looking at him – and I sucked in a sharp breath at the sight.

He looked haunted.

Hollowed cheeks.

Dark circles beneath his bloodshot eyes.

Several weeks' worth of stubble on his face.

He looked lost in his world, not even seeing me, as he stared off into nothing.

I'd often heard the term functioning alcoholic thrown around in conversation, but my boyfriend was the definition of a functioning drug addict. It didn't seem to matter what Joey took or how high he got, he continued to present himself and function at a level that kept everything ticking over. If it wasn't so soul-crushingly depressing, it would be impressive.

"Go," Casey whispered in my ear. "I'll deal with Katie."

"What are you doing here?" I asked, meeting him halfway, so that our friends were out of earshot. "It's only four o clock." I folded my arms across my chest, desperately trying to soothe the ache beneath my ribcage. "You don't finish work until six."

My question seemed to take him aback, and his brows furrowed for a moment before the guilt kicked in, clouding his surprisingly clear eyes. "How are you feeling?"

"Fine."

His eyes searched my face. "Yeah?"

I didn't respond.

I couldn't.

It hurt too damn much.

"What's up, Joe?" My gaze flicked to the track marks on his arms, and I flinched. "Why aren't you at work?"

Wordlessly, he pulled out his phone and held it out for me.

Frowning, I took his phone and unlocked the screen, opening a string of messages between Joey and none other than Johnny Kavanagh.

KAVANAGH: YEAH, SO STRANGE THING HAPPENED TODAY . . .

LYNCHY: WHY ARE YOU TEXTING ME?

KAVANAGH: BECAUSE I TOOK YOUR BROTHERS AND THEY'RE AT MY HOUSE.

LYNCHY: WHY?

KAVANAGH: I DON'T KNOW.

LYNCHY: DO YOU PLAN ON GIVING THEM BACK?

KAVANAGH: I GUESS.

LYNCHY: YOU'RE REALLY FUCKED UP, KAVANAGH.

KAVANAGH: I KNOW.

LYNCHY: I'M ON MY WAY.

"Johnny Kavanagh took your brothers?" I gaped at my boyfriend. "Where? When? *Why*?"

"I don't know."

"Where's your mam?"

Joey shrugged but didn't respond.

"Darren?"

Another shrug.

"So, it's left to you to clean up the mess and pick up the pieces." It wasn't a question. More of a resigned statement. "Again."

"I know I've been letting you down," he explained, tearing at his forearms with his nails, as his attention flicked from me to the commotion behind us. "And you're pissed with me, but I was sort of hoping you might give me a spin over there to collect them." Shrugging helplessly, he added, "I don't have anyone else to ask."

My heart cracked in my chest.

"Yeah, I'll take you," I replied, repressing the very strong urge I had to close the space between us and take him in my arms.

Because I loved this boy so fucking much that it almost killed me to stand here and not throw my arms around him.

But I couldn't.

Because it wouldn't change anything.

Because in the end, I would end up as the injured party.

That wasn't to say that I had given up on him.

It simply meant that I had boundaries now.

I believe in you

JOEY

Molloy turned the heater on full blast in her car on the way to the Kavanagh's house and I was glad.

I was so fucking cold; I couldn't get warm.

It was in my bones.

When she retrieved a hoodie from the back seat and instructed me to put it on, I did as she asked without argument.

Molloy's favorite band, The Cranberries' song 'When You're Gone' was drifting from the car stereo, but I couldn't focus on the lyrics.

Because I wanted to talk to her.

Wanted to find the words she needed from me, but they didn't exist in my brain anymore.

I felt very little these days, but every single I emotion I did feel was evoked from, directed at, and aimed towards her.

I loved her and no number of drugs could change that. Neither could the depression that was eating me from the inside out. Because it had to be depression, right? Wanting to die wasn't something an eighteen-year-old fantasized about.

"You're thinking about it, aren't you?" Molloy asked, breaking the silence that had built up between us.

My brain was too hazy, my heart too checked out, to understand or interpret her words. Instead, I reached into the pocket of my overalls and extracted my wallet. "I have your money," I told her, splitting my wage packet in half. "Here."

"That's not my money, Joe," she replied sadly, refusing to take the cash just like last week. "That's your money."

"No," I muttered, tossing the cash into the glove compartment of her car before I could do something reckless with it. "It's the baby's money."

Because we both knew that I would.

If I didn't get it away from me, I wouldn't have it to give her.

I couldn't trust myself anymore.

I wasn't safe or reliable.

"I'm not your mother," she told me, keeping her attention trained on the road ahead of us, as she drove down a narrow country lane. "I don't want you for your money."

"I'm sorry about the missing the scan," I heard myself tell her for what had to be the hundredth time. "I'm sorry for all of it."

"I know, Joe," she replied with a small sniffle, still avoiding looking at me. "I know."

"I love you," I added, knees bopping restlessly, as I chewed on my nails. "More than life."

"Yeah," she replied, voice thick with emotion. "I love you, too."

How she could say that and mean it was something I'd never understand.

How she could continue to love me?

I wasn't worthy.

"I'm going to get myself sorted out," I strangled out, reaching across the console to place my trembling hand on her jean-clad thigh. "I'll fix this, Molloy. Soon. I promise."

"Okay, Joe," she replied, tone laced with sorrow, as she covered my hand with hers. "Whatever you say."

Anxiety and panic gnawed at my gut. "You believe me, don't ya?"

Molloy was quiet for a long time before she glanced sideways at me and said, "I believe *in* you."

When we parked up outside Kavanagh's house and climbed out of the car, we were ambushed by an army of dogs and children and one guilty-as-fuck looking rugby player.

"Joe!" Ollie and Tadhg both called out before running off in the opposite direction with two demented looking golden retrievers.

"Hi," Kavanagh said, rounding the car with my brothers hot on his heels. "I'm ah . . . " Words trailing off, he reached up and scratched the back of his head, expression sheepish. "Sorry about this."

"Sorry for snatching his siblings?" Molloy teased, leaning a hip against the bonnet of her car, as she reached down and patted the head of an ancient looking Labrador. "Strange behavior, rugby boy. Very strange indeed."

"O-ee," Sean squealed in delight when he rounded the corner of the house and noticed me. "O-ee," he cried out, arms outstretched, as he ran straight for me. "O-ee."

"How's my baby?" I coaxed, lifting him into my arms. "Hm? Did ya go for a spin with Johnny?"

Nodding solemnly, Sean pressed his slobbery hand to my cheek and then buried his face in my neck. "Me loves O-ee."

"Good job, kid," I whispered in his ear, as he wrapped his tiny arms around my neck and squeezed. "I love you, too."

"O-ee."

Turning my attention to where my girlfriend was having an animated conversation with my sister's boyfriend, I asked, "What happened?"

"They were alone," he replied, gaze flicking from Sean to me. "*He* was alone."

"She wasn't there?" Molloy asked him before I could.

"In bed, apparently," Kavanagh told her, and I watched as something passed between them. An understanding of sorts.

"Fuck," I muttered, feeling my anxiety rise, right along with the aching in my stomach. "Jesus fucking Christ!"

"It's all good, Joe," my girlfriend was quick to soothe, coming to stand beside me. "Looks like the boys had a ball at the manor."

"Joey Lynch," a woman called out and it took me a minute to register the voice as Kavanagh's mother. Moments later, she appeared at the front door with a towering man flanking her. "We meet again."

"So, we do," I replied, eyeing her warily as she approached.

"You have three little reincarnations of you," she mused, not stopping until she was once again all up in my personal space. "What a beautiful family."

I didn't know what to say to that, so I remained silent, eyes trained on the man by her side. I could smell the law a mile away and this fucker, while too well dressed to be a garda, reeked of authority.

And money.

And power.

"John Kavanagh," he said, introducing himself with a warm smile and an outstretched hand. "Johnny's dad."

I didn't take the bait.

But my girlfriend did.

"Aoife Molloy," she chimed in, taking his hand in hers when it became clear that I wasn't going to. Flashing one of her infamous smiles, she flicked her hair back and beamed up at both Kavanaghs. "Joey's girlfriend."

MILFs, DILFs, and drug addicts

AOIFE

Johnny Kavanagh's mother looked like she had fallen from heaven, while his father looked like he had been carved from gold. Seriously, the boy had some damn fine genes flushing through his veins. He was almost as blessed in the looks department as the little bruiser growing in my belly was going to be.

Almost.

"So, this is the famous Joey Lynch," John Kavanagh said, giving my boyfriend a polite smile. I had to give the man props for not adding the 'in' to the 'famous' statement. "I've heard a lot about you."

Unmoving, Joey studied him, looking a little cornered and a lot defensive. Interjecting on his behalf, I took what I hoped was an inconspicuous step in front of him, knowing that he needed a minute to take a breath and *not* react on instinct.

"Looks like this little guy had a ball at your house," I offered, reaching behind me to ruffle Sean's curls. "You have a lovely home."

"Your brothers were alone," Edel Kavanagh cut the bullshit and stated, never once taking her eyes off Joey. "Johnny couldn't leave them on their own."

I could read Joey like a book, and it broke my heart knowing that every instinct inside of his body was screaming danger. Knowing that he wasn't in his right frame of mind right now made him even more unpredictable. My gaze flicked to Johnny, who seemed to be thinking the same thing, and had taken a step towards his mother.

I narrowed my eyes and gave him a look that said *as if.*

He shrugged unapologetically.

"I'm sorry," Joey surprised me by responding, giving the woman his full attention. "I was at work."

The lack of bite or fire in his response gutted me because it just clarified what I already knew to be true: he had checked out.

Pain flickered in her brown eyes, and she cast a worried glance to her husband before shaking her head. "No, Joey, love, I wasn't implying that you had done anything wrong."

"Either way," Joey replied with a shrug, as he rounded the passenger side of my car with his youngest brother in his arms and opened the door. "It won't happen again."

"You don't have to leave right away, love," Edel was quick to protest as she watched my boyfriend settle Sean in the back seat and fasten his seatbelt. "Stay for dinner. All of you. It would be our pleasure."

"No, we've stayed long enough," was all Joey replied, straightening back up and searching the grounds for the others. "Boys," he called out, followed by a piercing whistle. "Let's bounce."

As loyal to their brother as these dogs were to Johnny's mother, Ollie and Tadhg came thundering towards Joey, not stopping until they were standing beside him.

"Thank Johnny and his parents for holding on to ye today," Joey instructed quietly.

"Thanks," Tadhg parroted, more interested in saying goodbye to the dogs than the humans before climbing into the back seat with Sean.

"Thanks, Dellie," Ollie chimed in, bolting back to the blonde woman and throwing his arms around her waist. "I had the bestest time."

Clearly taken aback, she hugged him back tightly. "You come back to see me soon, love."

"I will," Ollie replied, taking a little too long to release her. When he finally did, he took a safe step back and eyed her husband warily before holding his small hand out. "Bye, John."

"Bye, Ollie," the big man replied in a soft voice, accepting his handshake. "Remember what I told you."

"Uh-huh." Ollie nodded brightly up at him and smiled. "I gots it, John. I won't forget."

"It's got not *gots*," little alpha piped up from the back seat. "Learn to speak, asshole."

"Pack it in," Joey warned, steering Ollie into the car to join his brothers. Only when they were all sitting down with their seatbelts fastened did Joey turn back to the Kavanaghs. "Thanks for everything. It won't happen again."

"And your mother?"

"She doesn't need to know about it."

Looking defeated, Joey climbed into the passenger seat and closed the door, leaving me standing alone with all three members of the Kavanagh family looking at me expectantly.

"It'll be fine," I mumbled. "They'll be fine."

"Are you sure?" Edel asked, looking as convinced as I felt.

No.

Forcing myself not to cry, I offered her the brightest smile I could muster and nodded. "Uh-huh."

There was a storm brewing in my boyfriend's heart.

Silent and brooding the entire drive back to Elk's terrace, Joey drummed his fingers on his knee. He glared out the passenger window, while the boys laughed and joked in the back seat, blissfully unaware of their older brother's inner turmoil. The minute I parked up outside his house, though, Joey was out of the car and stalking into the house.

"Fuck, he's raging," Tadhg surmised, making eye contact with me in the rearview mirror.

"You're not 'posed to curse," Ollie scolded as he worked on unfastening both his and Sean's seatbelts. "It's not good manners."

Tadhg rolled his eyes. "Hey, Ollie, I don't give a flying fu—"

"Okay," I interjected before Tadhg schooled the minors on the more colorful side of the English language. "Let's just go inside, lads."

With Sean's sticky little hand in mine, I followed the boys into the house, only to wince as the sound of shouting coming from somewhere upstairs filled my ears.

"Wow, you guys got a new television."

"Darren gots it for us," Ollie explained with a huff.

"Why don't you put some cartoons on," I suggested, ushering all three into the sitting room before moving for the stairs. "I'll be back in a sec."

"Fine, but I'm not watching shitty cartoons," Tadhg called over his shoulder. "There's a match on RTE."

Leaving the boys to battle it out over the remote, I followed the sound of shouting and raced up the staircase, not stopping until I was standing in the doorway of their parents' bedroom.

"How many fucking times do we have to do this?" Joey was demanding, as he ripped at the curtains to flood the once dark room in evening sunshine. "You can't leave Sean on his on like that!"

With my heart racing wildly, I flicked my gaze to the woman curled up in a ball on the bed.

Marie.

"Just go away, Teddy," she slurred, clutching her pillow, as sob after gut-wrenching sob escapade her. "I'm tired."

"It's *Joey*," he choked out. "Christ, what have you taken?"

"Like you can judge me."

"I'm not judging you. I'm telling you to get the fuck up and be a mother to your children!"

"I'm so tired."

"And I'm not?" my boyfriend demanded, running his hands through his hair in obvious frustration. "You don't get to do this, Mam. You don't get to check the fuck out on them," he spat. "You wanted to keep them. You wanted your family together. That was yours and Darren's number one goal, right? To keep the boys here? To pull the wool over Patricia and every other social workers' eyes. Well, you did it. Congratulations. Because those boys are downstairs. But they're on their own, Mam. Without a mother or father to look out for them. So, stop feeling sorry for yourself and take some goddamn responsibility!"

"I said go away," she screamed, throwing her pillow at him. "I don't want you here."

"You don't want me here," Joey roared, throwing his hands up. "Well, we have something in common because I don't want to be here, either!"

"Joe." Moving on instinct, I went to him. *Like the habit of a lifetime.* "It's okay."

"You see this?" he strangled out, trembling violently, as he pointed at his mother. "What the fuck am I supposed to do about this?"

Nothing.

Because he'd done enough for her and had it thrown back in his face.

All he needed to do now was look after himself, but he couldn't hear me.

He was too far gone.

Just like his mam.

"Look at me ... hey, hey, look at me." Catching hold of his face between my hands, I forced him to make eye contact with me. "Just leave her, okay?"

"But I—"

"Shh, shh." Pulling his face down to mine, I pressed a kiss to his brow and focused on his eyes once more. "It's okay."

It wasn't.

None of this was okay.

But this boy needed something to cling to.

"I just ... " Breathing hard and fast, he reached for my hand and let his shoulders slump in defeat. "I can't do this anymore."

"I know." Taking his hands in mine, I led him out of her room and closed the door behind us. "Listen to me," I coaxed, moving for the bathroom. "I'm going to go downstairs and sort the boys, and you're going to take a shower."

Pain and confusion flashed in his eyes. "But I—"

"Just breathe, Joe," I instructed, ushering him into the bathroom. "Take a minute, okay? Shower and change out of your work clothes. I'll hang with the boys for a bit."

"I can't do this, Molloy," he repeated, sounding as broken as he looked. "I can't."

My heart seized with a horrible concoction of fear and dread.

"You've got one more night in you," I replied, reaching up to stroke his cheek. "I promise."

"I don't want to let it go."

"What?" was all I managed to croak out.

"Us," he replied. "I'm not letting it go. I can't do this without you."

The words escaped his lips like a torn admission.

Like it pained him to say this.

Like he was only registering the impact of his words as they spilled from his lips.

"And I don't want to," he whispered, dropping his head. "I don't want a life without you in it."

Broken in half from his admission, I could do nothing but wrap my arms around his lean frame and pull him close. "I'm still here, Joe."

"Don't go downstairs," he mumbled, snaking an arm around my back and pulling me flush against him. "Be with me."

"Joe . . ."

"Just be with me," he begged, dropping his head on my shoulder. "You don't have do anything with me, I promise. I just . . ." He exhaled a ragged breath and said, "Just hold onto me, Molloy."

"Okay," was all I could say in response, while my heart well and truly split down the center. "I'll be with you, Joe."

Always.

After coaxing Joey into the shower, I popped downstairs to check on the boys to find them still arguing over the remote. Settling grudges and doling out snacks, I then returned to Joey's room to find him fresh from a shower. With a towel wrapped around his narrow hips, he sat on the edge of his bed, with his shoulders slumped, and his head in his hands.

"What's wrong?" I asked, closing his bedroom door behind me. "You look sad, Joe," I noted, moving to stand in front of him. "You look devastated, if truth be told."

"It just ah . . . " Shaking his head, he forced himself to look at me when he said, "I thought you left."

My poor heart slammed violently against my ribcage. "Nope. I'm afraid you're stuck with me for the evening."

He blew out another shaky breath, and then his hands were on my hips, tugging me closer until my belly was touching his nose. "Good."

"Joe."

Without a word, he reached for the hem of my hoodie and pulled it up to reveal my bump. "I love ya." He pressed a lingering kiss to my belly. "Both of ye."

My breath hitched in my throat, and I couldn't stop my hands from knotting in his hair. "We love you too, Joe."

"I'll sort this," he continued to whisper, as he peppered kisses over my stomach. "I promise, I'll fix everything."

And that was all it took.

Just a glimpse of the boy I'd fallen in love with was all it took to rid me of my clothes and have me on my back beneath him.

Trembling when his lips moved over my skin, as he buried his face between my thighs, I clutched at the bedsheets, and blinked my tears away, feeling too much for this boy than was good for me.

"Joe," I whispered hoarsely when he moved between my legs. "I need you to wear a condom, remember?"

He stilled for a moment, and I could see the devastation washing over him in waves before he nodded in shame and reached for the drawer of his nightstand to retrieve a foil wrapper.

Ironically, it was during pregnancy that we had finally decided to use protection. I could count on one hand the number of times we'd been intimate since his father's attack, and I had been careful to protect myself each time.

"I know you haven't been with anyone else," I hurried to soothe, watching as he clumsily rolled a condom on his shaft with trembling hands. "I'm just . . . you remember the doctor said that I need to protect myself and the baby in case."

"It's okay," he replied, voice cracking, hands resting on his thighs. "I understand."

"Joe." Pulling myself up on one elbow, I hooked an arm around his neck and drew him down to me. "It's okay. Just be with me."

"I'm sorry," he strangled out, pushing himself deep inside of me. "You'll never know how much."

PART 9

You call and I come running

JOEY

Allergic.

It was the only word to describe how I was feeling when I walked through the front doors of BCS on Monday morning.

An epic showdown between Mam and Shannon over Kavanagh picking her up for school, followed by a shitshow of a shouting match between myself and Darren was the reason I was late. When I walked into class, ten minutes after the bell, and my eyes landed on Molloy sitting at our desk, I felt every muscle in my body coil tight in dreaded anticipation.

Would today be the day she had enough?

Would today be the day she finally told me to go fuck myself?

Because, let's face it, we both knew I was on borrowed time with her. Being with her on Saturday night had done something to me, though. It had sparked a fire inside of me that resulted in my holding out yesterday. Somehow, and I wasn't too fucking sure how, I had managed to steer clear of Shane and survive on a couple of joints.

My head was in bits and my body was in worse shape, but I could see clearly, and I was thinking a little more rationally.

It was nothing to sing home about, but it was a start.

I had to start somewhere.

And that girl was my everywhere.

"Time management, Joseph," Miss Lane snapped, giving me the evil-eyed glare that she reserved especially for me, as I waited for her to fill in my red book. "Last warning."

Like I gave a fuck.

I was here for two reasons.

The blonde at my desk and the baby in her belly.

Ignoring Podge and Alec who were trying to grab my attention, I moved straight for my desk, not stopping until I was in the seat next to hers with our knees brushing. "Molloy."

"Joe," she replied, keeping her gaze trained on the copybook laying open on the desk in front of her.

Without a word, I retrieved the earphone waiting for me and popped it in.

Tracy Chapman's 'Fast Car' filled my ears and fuck if it didn't pour salt in my already gaping wounds. Like always, she reached under the desk and took my hand in hers, but when I entwined our fingers and squeezed back, she turned in surprise to look at me. "Hey, stud."

"Hey, queen."

"Nice shirt."

"Nice legs."

Her eyes widened in surprise.

I winked.

"You're . . . " she whispered, studying me with wary eyes, "you?"

"No." Resisting the urge to bow my head in shame, I held my ground and forced myself to keep eye contact. "But I'm . . . trying."

To give this girl what she needed.

What she deserved.

It was too much – her, the moment, my feelings, the way my heart beat for her– it was all too fucking much. And still, I remained completely motionless, letting her take her fill.

"Joe." Her fingers tightened around mine. "*Joe.*"

"Just have to get through one hour at a time, right?"

With tear-filled eyes, she nodded rapidly and choked out a pained smile. "Right."

Struggling to concentrate on a word of what was being said around me at lunch, I shivered in my seat as the most horrendous cold sweat bled through my skin.

The lads were talking about hurling, the girls were chatting about babies, and I was fucking drowning in the horrors of withdrawal.

"I need something," I admitted, turning in my seat to face the only reason I had to not throw the towel in and be done with the pain. "I need something, Molloy."

"Jesus, Joe, you're burning the hell up," Molloy replied, reaching up to wipe a bead of sweat from my brow. "Are you—"

"No, I'm freezing," I assured her, snatching her small hand up in both of mine. "But I need something or I'm going to be sick."

Panic filled her eyes. "You can't."

"I have to."

"No." She shook her head. "One hour at a time, remember? You've got another hour in you, Joe."

"I'm dying here," I admitted, shifting closer so that only she could hear me. "Help me."

"I *can't*," she choked out, tightening her hold on my hand. "You can do this, Joe. I know you can. You've done it before. Just let the poison seep out of your system, baby, and you'll feel so much better."

"I'm telling you that I'm going to fucking die if I don't get something," I strangled out. "I can feel it." I blew out a strained breath. "My heart's going to burst in my chest."

"Then we'll leave," she tried to soothe. "We'll go home."

"If I get off this chair, it's not home I'm heading to," I forced myself to be honest and tell her. "I'm so fucking sorry."

"No, no, no," she replied. "Don't be sorry because you're still hanging in there."

I wasn't.

I was seconds away from peeling the skin off my bones.

The urge was too fierce.

The need was too strong.

The hunger was too consuming.

"I can't do this, Molloy."

"Yes, you can."

"No, I really can't."

"A smoke will take the edge off, lad," Alec interjected in a rarely tender tone of voice, as he placed a hand on my shoulder. "Say the word and I'll get you sorted."

Molloy's eyes flicked to me and after a moment of hesitation, she reluctantly nodded. "Help him."

I was out of my chair and moving in an instant, unraveling faster than I ever had before, as the cravings tormenting my body caused my stomach to roll and protest.

"That's it, lad," Al coaxed when we reached the back of the PE hall, and I unceremoniously puked my guts up. "You get that shit up and I'll spark us up some grade A weed, my friend."

"Fuck my life," I groaned between wretches, as I hemorrhaged bile and poison.

It physically hurt to breathe.

Every time my heart pumped, the blood rushing through my veins burned and scalded me.

"I'm dying."

"You're not dying. You just can't go cold turkey on this," my friend coaxed, placing a neatly rolled joint between my fingers. "Take a hit, lad. It'll help with the sickness."

Shaking violently, I took a deep drag, filling my lungs to the point of pain, and then I held it there until dizziness engulfed me.

"That's it," Alec said, giving my shoulder a supportive squeeze. "Sit your ass down, lad, and just soak it in."

Trembling, I managed to sink down on the footpath at the back of the hall and take another hit. "Fuck," I said, slowly exhaling a cloud of smoke.

"You know I'm the last person to judge you, because God knows I'm a fair bit of a fuck-up in my own right," he said, lowering himself down to sit beside me. "But you need help, Joe."

"Al, please, lad, I can't hear this right now."

"You're going to have to, Joe. You've got a girl in there and a baby on the way, and I would be a piss-poor friend if I didn't step in and at least try to talk some sense into you," he continued. "The shit you've been messing around with. Heroin? People don't just stop cold turkey. If they could, then there wouldn't be any need for methadone clinics and rehabilitation facilities. It's serious, lad. And you don't just walk away from people like Holland, either. You know this."

"I don't know what to do," I admitted, feeling broken. "I know she needs me."

"She's still here, man," he offered, nudging my shoulder with his. "She's still holding out for you, which means there's still hope. You've got a little family waiting on you to get better. You *can* get better, Joe, but you need to want it, lad. You need to fight."

"I just … I don't know if I have another fight in me," I admitted quietly. "I'm so tired, Al. In the head. My mind is fucking weary."

"Hey, stud." Molloy's familiar voice drifted through the air, causing everything inside of me to spring to attention. Appearing from the side of the PE hall, she sat on the wall opposite me, keeping her distance from the smoke. "Feeling better?"

Disgusted with myself for becoming this decrepit creature, I forced a small nod, while buckling under the weight of my shame.

"He'll be grand," Al was quick to interject in his usual jokester tone. "Lynchy here just needs to get back to basics."

My phone decided to torment me in this moment by ringing loudly in my pocket.

Taking another deep drag of my smoke, I passed it to Alec and reached for my phone.

Concern roared to life inside of me when I saw my sister's name flashing on the screen.

Her calls had come less frequent since the arrival of Mister Rugby, and she never called during school hours anymore.

The fact that she was calling me now assured me that something was very wrong.

"Shan?" I demanded, putting the phone to my ear. "What's going on?"

"Joey," she cried down the line. I could hardly make out her voice from the sheer height of crying. Instantly, my back was up and the blood in my veins had turned to lava. "I n-need you to come g-get me."

Boyfriends, brothers, and battle-axe bitches

AOIFE

One minute Joey was thrown down on the footpath, looking like death warmed up and the next, he was on his feet.

Whatever his sister had said on the other line of the phone had caused a switch to flip in his brain. With his inner turmoil momentarily forgotten, and fury coming off him in waves, he threw his head back and roared, sounding genuinely feral, as he stormed off in the direction of the carpark, demanding my car keys.

"Joe, just hold up a second, will you?" I called out, struggling to keep up with his feet *and* his mood swings. "Talk to me, will you?"

"She was attacked," he roared over his shoulder. "My sister was mother-fucking attacked, Molloy." His voice louder with every word that tore from his lips. "Again!"

My heart plummeted into my ass. "No."

"Keys," he demanded when we reached my car, holding his hand out. "She needs me to come get her."

"You're not driving to Tommen in your condition," I flat out told him. "Put that notion out of your head."

"Fine, then you drive," he conceded, stalking around to the passenger side of the car. "I don't care how I get there as long as I get there."

"Okay, but—"

"Please, Molloy," he choked out. "We can talk on the way. Just drive, baby. Drive!"

Knowing this was a terrible idea but unwilling to leave Shannon at Tommen after being attacked, I unlocked the car and climbed into the driver's seat. "Promise me, Joe." Cranking the engine, I chugged out of my parking spot, slipping gears before finding my groove. "Promise me that you'll ask questions first."

"What's to ask?" he spat, knees bopping restlessly, as he gnawed on his knuckles anxiously. "My sister was attacked. I'm going to make it right."

Jesus.

"Just keep the head," I instructed, pulling onto the main road in the direction of Tommen College. "No fighting, Joe."

"Yeah, fuck that."

"No," I argued, "No, not fuck that. You need to not go in there all guns blazing, baby."

"My sister phones me up hysterical, saying someone attacked her at school, after all the shit she's been through this year, and you expect me not to *retaliate*?" he demanded and then shook his head in blatant frustration. "It's not happening, Molloy. It's not fucking happening, ya hear? I'm done with this shit. I'm through with letting people stomp all over my siblings."

Meaning his father.

He wasn't thinking logically.

This was more about his father than anything else.

He was looking for redemption for something he didn't need to feel guilt for.

"Joey, this isn't the same thing," I tried to placate. "What happened to Shannon in the kitchen that day—"

"I couldn't stop it," he filled in for me. "But I can stop this, Molloy, and I will."

"I don't want to go," I blurted out, slowing the car when the gates of Tommen College came into view. "This is a bad idea."

"Molloy! Drive the car."

"No." Shaking my head, I flicked on my indicator and pulled onto the side of the road before killing the engine. "I'm not taking you. Not while you're this worked up. You need to calm down and breathe, Joe."

"Fine." Releasing a furious growl, he unfastened his seatbelt and flung the door open. "I'll walk the rest of the way."

"No, wait!" I tried to call after him, but it was too late. He was already sprinting at full speed in the direction of his sister's prestigious private school.

"Shit," I hissed, slamming my hand on the steering wheel. "Goddammit to hell, Joey Lynch!"

Cranking the engine of my old faithful, I attempted to pull back onto the road, but of course I ended up tailing a tractor and slurry tank moving along with all the speed of a sedated turtle.

Fuck my life.

By the time I reached the school, there was a huge crowd forming in the nearby carpark. It didn't take a genius to know why the crowd had formed, or why they were chanting *fight, fight, fight* like a bunch of deranged lunatics.

To spare Joey a conversation he wasn't ready for with his sister, I pulled on one of his hoodies from the back seat, before shoving the door open and springing out – not an easy feat with a belly that was growing rounder by the day.

"Joey!" I called out, pushing through the large crowd that had built up around . . . yep, around my boyfriend.

He was lunging for *Johnny Kavanagh*.

But being held back by *Gibsie Gibberson*?

Fuck my life.

"What are you doing, Joe?" Pushing past a particularly boisterous bunch of teenage boys, I moved straight for him. "I thought we said no fighting?"

Slaps had clearly been thrown. The blood trickling from Johnny's busted lip was proof of that pudding.

Breathless, I hurried to reach him before all hell broke loose again. Stepping between two testosterone fueled alpha males clearly wasn't my brightest idea, but I couldn't leave him alone in the lion's den.

We were ride or die.

"Joe!" Pushing Shannon's boyfriend aside, I stepped in front of mine and grabbed his face, forcing him to focus on me. "Ask questions first, remember?"

Wild, fevered eyes glared back at me for the briefest of moments before recognition flickered in him and he stopped thrashing against Gibsie's hold. Gibsie, to his credit, wasn't trying to hurt Joey or hold him down while his buddy gave him a beating, he was truly trying to diffuse the situation.

A lot like I was.

"I forgot," Joey replied as his wild eyes flicked from me to Johnny before returning and settling on my face.

That's it, I mentally coaxed, not taking my eyes off his, *just breathe, baby.*

Clearly noting Joey's withdrawal, Gibsie released him and took a few steps backwards, offering me a knowing wink as he went.

If he only knew.

If Joe only knew how much that boy had helped us.

"What the hell is happening?" Johnny demanded, dragging my attention back to present, as he wiped a trickle of blood from his lip.

"You tell me," Gibsie muttered under his breath. "I've a headache coming on from the sheer height of confusion."

"Shannon called me," Joey was quick to answer, as anger emanated from him in waves. "Someone in this stuck-up school did something to her!"

"Did something to her? *What?*" Johnny stared blankly. "I was just with her at lunch." He looked around, clearly confused. "What did they do to her?" He looked around wildly, clearly willing any of his friends to give him the answer. "What the fuck is going on?"

Gibsie opened his mouth to reply, but Hughie quickly covered his mouth with his hand. "This is the part where you shush, lad."

"When I find out which one of you privileged pricks hurt my sister, I'll do time for ye!" That was Joey, who was literally thrumming with tension.

"What's going on here?" a man I presumed was a teacher at Tommen demanded. However, the speed in which the crowd around us quickly scattered led me to believe that this man was higher up the rank than a regular teacher.

"Fuck," I heard tell his friend as they ran off. "It's the principal."

Lovely.

Just lovely.

Alone with three Tommen rugby players, their patriarch, and a BCS hurler suffering a horrendous case of delirium tremors, I watched on helplessly as their principal gave Johnny a resigned look before turning his attention to us. "Are you two aware that you are not permitted on school property if you are not enrolled here."

"Fuck you!" *Of course* that was Joey.

"Joe," I groaned, trying to rein in his reckless temper "He's their principal."

"So? He's not mine," he shot back, well and truly on the edge now. "I'm here to pick up my sister since your piece of shit school can't control its students and keep her safe."

"And your sister is?"

"Shannon Lynch."

The man visibly paled.

"Yeah, that's right," Joey sneered, focusing every ounce of his fury on the older man. "You know who I'm talking about. You made all sorts of promises to her, didn't ya? About keeping your students safe? What a fucking joke you are!"

"I beg your pardon." The older man looked genuinely affronted. "I have no idea what you're talking—"

"Hi, Joe."

Every head turned in the direction Shannon was coming from, soaked to the skin, and looking like she went ten rounds with Rocky.

"Oh, sweet mother of mercy," I mumbled to myself, forcing back the urge to hurl when the smell of sour milk wafted towards me, wreaking havoc on my poor pregnancy-enhanced sense of smell.

Clearly, whoever had dunked her in sour milk had rubbed salt in the wound by scribbling something derogatory about blow jobs on her face. Even though she'd clearly tried to wash it off, it was still there for the world to see.

Sniffling, she looked to her giant of a boyfriend and only then did the tears she'd clearly been holding back spill over. "Hi, Johnny."

"What the actual fuck!" Johnny roared, first to react, as he closed the space between them and caught ahold of his girlfriend before she hit the ground. "What happened to your face, Shannon?"

"I want to go home." I watched with my heart in my mouth as she fell against his big frame and clutched him tightly. "I just want to go."

"It's okay." Inspecting every inch of her like she was the greatest of importance to him, I watched as the big lad was overcome with emotion. "Shh, baby, shh." Seeing her hurt affected him. No, it was more than that. It *crushed* him. "Just calm down."

"Who did this to you?" Joey demanded, jumping into action, as he moved straight for his sister. "Shan, what the fuck happened?"

"Was it her?" Johnny asked, joining my boyfriend in the interrogation. "What am I saying – of course it was her!"

"Who?" their principal asked. "Who did this to you, Shannon?"

"Bella fucking Wilkinson," Gibsie chimed in, tone laced with disgust. "Who else?"

My brows furrowed as a wave of recognition washed over me. "Bella Wilkinson?"

"Oh *yeah*." Nodding eagerly, Gibsie's eyes widened to saucers as he said, "Cap's crazy obsessed, super stalker ex bitch."

"I want her out of this school," Johnny ordered, tucking Shannon under his arm. "She can't get away with this. You know what she's been going through. She's supposed to be safe at school!"

"Shannon, are you saying that Miss Wilkinson did this to you?"

"Back the fuck up," Joey warned when the older man moved towards his sister. "Don't come near my sister. I'm warning you."

"Fucking Bella Wilkinson," Hughie grumbled, coming to stand beside Gibsie. "It's always something with her."

"Because she is *Lucifer* with tits," Gibsie confirmed grimly. "The living, breathing devil in carnage."

"It's incarnate, Gibs, not in carnage."

"Whatever, lad. I tried to warn you all, but oh *no*, nobody listens to the beautiful one." His tone was laced with a heavy dollop of sarcastic outrage. "I'm just a pretty face to you assholes. Some eye candy for the ladies. Well, I know things, too, you know. It's not all about books. I'm an excellent judge of character."

Bella Wilkinson.

Why the hell was that name so familiar?

"I slept with someone."
"You lost your virginity? To who?"
"A girl from Tommen."
"What's her name?"
"Bella Wilkinson."

"No," I gasped, wide-eyed when awareness finally dawned on me. The girl Paul slept with behind my back. It was the same person. "What the—"

"You!" Johnny roared, startling me from my thoughts, as he took off like a thundering bull in the direction two students were coming from. "I want a fucking word with you!"

"Johnny, don't," Shannon sobbed, covering her face with her small hands.

"Cap, you're in contract."

"Think about Saturday."

"Take the high road."

"Fuck your high road," Johnny roared back, ignoring his friends, as he moved straight for who I presumed was Bella and her beau. "What did I tell you, huh?" the big lad demanded, closing the space between them. "What the fuck did I tell you about that bitch?"

"Joe, he's in contract," I said, attention flicking between Johnny's worried-looking circle of buddies to his sobbing girlfriend. I had no clue what that meant, but clearly it was a pretty big deal. "Stop him, baby. Don't let him fight."

"Aw shit," Joey muttered under his breath and then he was darting off in the same direction.

"Whoa, Johnny," the older lad tried to appease, holding his hands up. "I have no idea what you're—"

Bam!

A well-trained fist clocked him straight in the face before he could finish his sentence, and the boy hit the deck with a thud.

However, the right hook that pancaked the lad on the ground hadn't been the result of Johnny Kavanagh's fist, but Joey's.

Always the protector.

"What the . . . fuck?"

"I owed you one," my boyfriend explained, shaking out his hand, before gesturing to the busted lip of his nemesis-turned-ally. "Besides, I'm already getting arrested."

Johnny gaped at him. "For what?"

"For this," Joey explained, seconds before lunging for the lad on the ground.

Oh Jesus.

"Get off him, you dirty, little scumbag " Bella screamed, and then she did the unspeakable; she put her hands on *my* man.

Oh hell to the no.

As I witnessed the bitch slap Joey, I couldn't see beyond the haze of red blinding me.

"Hey! Don't call my boyfriend a scumbag." I roared, taking leave of my senses, as I hauled ass towards the whore putting hands on him. "Is this her, Shan? Did she do this to you?"

"No, Aoife, please just leave it."

Nope.

Nu-uh.

Wasn't going to happen.

Because she had the nerve to put hands on *my* man.

"Who the hell are you?" Bella demanded, casting a menacing glare in my direction.

Oh, you poor, sweet summer child.

"Oh, I'm your worst nightmare, bitch," I snarled, knocking her off Joey's back and onto the flat of her own. "You like terrorizing little girls? Try someone your own size." Losing my ever-loving shit right there and then, I straddled her chest. "Think you can call my boyfriend a scumbag? Think you can bully his sister, huh? Think you're safe because you're a girl and he can't hit you back?" Narrowly avoiding a nail to the eye, I reared my fist back and socked her in the nose. "Well, I can!"

"You're a psycho," she screamed, as she tried to tear and scratch at my face.

Bitch *please*. She was about to get schooled real fast.

"Nails?" I spat, deftly pinning her arms to her sides with my knees – a skill I'd honed to perfection after countless battles with my asshole twin. "You think nails are going to do it?" I reared my fist back and hit her again. "Rule number one, you boundary-absent, morally-lacking, conniving bitch: if you put hands on another girl's fella, make damn sure you know how to throw a punch!"

"How's your money fairing out for ya now, rich boy?" I heard Joey taunt from nearby, as he got the better of Bella's beau and pinned him to the ground. "Being a scumbag has its benefits, doesn't it?"

"I'm calling the Gards," I heard their principal command. "Stop it this instant or I'll have every last one of you arrested!"

I couldn't stop. People were shouting and arguing around me, but I couldn't hear a word of it. All logic had flown out the window and I was running solely on temper fumes.

Six years.

Six long ass years I had watched Joey Lynch take beating after beating.

Seeing Bella put hands on that boy had been the straw that broke the camel's back in my mind.

Besides, she had this coming.

Fucking around with other girl's boyfriends when their backs were turned.

Bullying and tormenting girls younger and weaker than her.

She deserved everything she got and more.

"Molloy – come on, baby." A pair of strong arms came around my waist then, lifting me off my target and away from the fight. "She's not worth it." With his hand wrapped protectively around my middle, and his chest heaving against my back, Joey continued to pull me away from trouble. "You can't be fighting in your—"

"She called you a scumbag," I choked out, struggling to rein in my fury now that it had finally been unleashed. "I'm not having it, Joe." My voice broke and I sucked in a shaky breath, feeling like I needed to scream at the top of my lungs to project the anger raging inside of me.

"I know, baby." Breathless and panting, he turned me in his arms to face him and cupped my face between his hands. "But I need you to be careful."

My heart jackknifed in my chest as reality smacked me square in the chest.

The baby.

"Oh shit." My hand automatically moved to my bump hidden beneath his oversized hoodie and I sagged against him. "Oh god, Joe what did I do?" Disgust filled every pore in my body. "I didn't think." I shook my head, feeling helpless and filled with self-loathing. "I'm so stupid! What if I hurt the baby?"

"No, you didn't. It's all good, Molloy," he was quick to soothe, tightening an arm around me. "You're grand, and the baby's grand, okay?"

"But what if—"

"Everyone, follow me to the office. I'm calling your parents," the principal yelled, commanding everyone's attention, as he ordered Bella and her bloodied beau in the direction of the school. "*All* of your parents."

"You do that," Joey sneered, still keeping ahold of me. "Be useful for something!"

Parents meant Gards.

Gards meant handcuffs.

Reality hit me like a wrecking ball, and I stiffened.

He was over eighteen now.

The Gards in this town weren't going to give him any more chances.

"Joe." I couldn't hide the fear in my voice. "You're on a warning."

"Listen, I need you to get out of here." Catching ahold of my hand, Joey led me towards where I had haphazardly parked my car, sounding more composed than he had in months. "You weren't here, and you didn't see shit." Stopping when we reached the driver's side door, he turned to face me. "You got that?"

"What?" I gaped at him and shook my head. "No, no, I'm not leaving you—"

"Get in the car and go home, baby," he cut me off and ordered. "Now."

"Joey, no, I can't leave you!"

Reaching up, he cupped my face between his hands and gave me a meaningful look. "Nobody's going to mention you."

"No, Joe," I strangled out, chest heaving. "No, I can't."

"Aoife."

"But you're going to be . . . "

Fisting my hair, he leaned in and pressed his lips to my ear. "You listen to me," he said, low enough that only I could hear him. "You get your ass in that car and straight to the hospital. Don't worry about me, okay? I'm grand. You tell those doctors whatever the fuck you need to tell them to make them scan you to check our kid is okay."

"Joe."

"When they give you the all-clear, because they *will* give you the all-clear, Molloy, I want you to go home and stay there. Don't come looking for me, and don't go fighting my battles, baby. I can do the fighting for the both of us."

"But—"

"I'll look after everything else, okay?" He exhaled a harsh breath and momentarily sagged against me before straightening back up. "All I need you to do is look after yourself and my kid."

"Let's get out of here," I blurted. "Come with me."

"I can't."

"You have to." My heart bucked wildly in my chest, as it cracked down the center. "They'll arrest you if you stay."

"It doesn't matter."

"It does matter," I cried, clinging to him. "*You* matter. You—"

"I'll be grand. Just go and I'll call you when I can," he cut in, pressing a hard kiss to my forehead. "I'll be seeing ya, Molloy," he called over his shoulder, as he walked away.

And then he was gone.

Jailhouse rock

JOEY

It was no big revelation when the only handcuffs the Gards withdrew at Tommen were the ones they used to cuff me with.

Nor did it come as a surprise when I was read the usual '*I'm arresting you under section 4 of the criminal justice act*' spiel, because, quite frankly, I'd heard it a dozen times before.

Thrown into the back of the squad car, I'd been taken straight to the station, where I had been searched, stripped and slapped around by none other than Paul the prick's daddy. All that before being tossed in the cells for a time-out, while I waited on legal aid to show up and escort me to the courthouse.

Unapologetic for my actions, I took my punishment on the chin, unwilling to show emotion or feel bad for defending my sister.

Because fuck those pricks at Tommen.

Fuck the whole damn world.

My only regret about the day's events was that I had dragged my girl-friend into it. Because Molloy wouldn't have been there if it wasn't for me, and she sure as shit wouldn't have been fighting if it wasn't to defend me.

Her face continued to haunt me long into the evening as I sat on a concrete slab that doubled up as a bed in the holding cell which I was being retained in. I battled with both my conscience and my body as it reeled from withdrawal.

The stainless-steel piss-hole in the corner of my cell had seen more vomit than I cared to admit, as I continued to eject the contents of my stomach.

Black gunk.

Green bile.

Clumps of blood.

Jesus Christ, I was hemorrhaging poison.

The phone call I'd been awarded, I had naïvely used on a woman who wouldn't even pick up the phone.

My mother didn't care.

She had never cared.

Christ, I had a better chance of the old man showing up to get me.

You already know this, asshole, so stop *caring about her!*

Disgusted with myself for being so damn weak, I refused the chance to make another call, because in all honesty, I didn't have anyone *to* call.

The beef I had with Darren meant that I would gladly serve an eighteen-month sentence for assault and battery before crawling on my knees to him for help.

Because fuck Darren.

The only person I could call, the only person who hadn't completely given up on me was the one person I needed to protect.

The person I cared about most in the world.

I knew Molloy would answer.

I knew she would come for me.

She would fight my corner, regardless of what it cost her.

That was the whole fucking problem.

I had to stop this.

I had to *stop* putting her at risk.

"On your feet, Lynch," a male Garda ordered, as he unbolted and opened the metal door containing me. "You have court in twenty minutes."

Peachy.

Just fucking peachy.

Not bothering to argue, I complied with his orders and remained still as a statue as I was re-cuffed.

Yeah, this wasn't going to end well for me.

Maybe this is a good thing, I thought to myself, as I was led out back to an awaiting prison van. *Maybe the judge will decide to remand me, and I'll be transferred to Cork prison. At least then, Molloy and the baby will be safe from me.*

Going stir crazy

AOIFE

Tears.

I couldn't stop them from falling.

It was ridiculous because I'd always thought of myself as a strong girl, but lately, all I seemed to do was cry.

And lie.

Oh yeah, I seemed to be doing a whole heap of lying these days.

When I arrived at the maternity hospital earlier, I'd lied through my teeth and told the admissions nurse in the A&E that a car had backed into mine and I needed to get checked out.

I mean, seriously?

Too worked up to think straight, I'd sat in the waiting room all alone bawling my eyes out while I waited to be called in for an ultrasound. The one that assured me what Joey had; everything was fine with the baby.

Knowing that I couldn't go home in my current state, I somehow made it to Casey's flat feeling overwhelmed with regret and disappointment in myself. The minute she opened the flat door, I barreled into my best friend's arms, crying hard and ugly. "They arrested him."

The text message I'd received from Shannon had confirmed it.

"Oh shit, what did he do this time?" Casey spluttered in surprise, wrapping her arms around me and pulling me inside. "Wait – we are talking about Joey here, aren't we?"

"Yeah, Case," I choked out, chest heaving. "Obviously."

"Obviously," she agreed, walking us over to the couch. "Okay, you sit and start explaining, and I'll boil the kettle."

"I don't want you to make tea," I cried, dropping my head in my hands. "I want you to help me get him out."

"Of jail?" Her brows shot up. "How?"

"I don't know, but I can't just leave him there."

"How about you explain why he's there in the first place and then we can make a plan."

Sucking in a shuddering breath, word for word I delved right into the day's events at Tommen, leaving no stone unturned.

"Come on, Aoif, this is Joey we're talking about," Casey tried to coax once I was finished regaling her with my tale of woe. "He's like a cat with nine lives. He'll get a slap on the wrist and be out in no time."

"No." Sniffling, I shook my head. "You don't get it. He's over eighteen now."

"Shit, you're right," my best friend agreed, flopping down on the couch beside me. "The Gards in this town have been dreaming about this day. They're going to throw the book at him."

"Not helping."

"Yeah, sorry, I just heard myself out loud." Slapping her forehead, she twisted sideways on the couch and offered me a supportive hug. "Listen, I know it's really fucking scary, but you need to listen to what Joe said." She squeezed me tighter. "You need to look after that baby."

"And who's going to look after *Joey*?"

Unanswered calls and unexpected lifelines

JOEY

Clad in my BCS school uniform and rocking handcuffs, I was escorted by the Gards into a private waiting room at the back of the courthouse to meet my legal aid and await my turn before the judge.

The most shocking part of the whole ordeal was the well-dressed man waiting for me in said waiting room.

"Joey Lynch." John Kavanagh looked up from the table he was sitting at and smiled. "We meet again."

The fuck?

"What are you doing here?" I asked, sinking down on the chair opposite him. "You're not my solicitor."

"I am today," he mused, combing through a stack of paperwork that I assumed contained my file. Shit, knowing my luck, the whole damn stack was dedicated to me. "If you'll have me."

"I'm broke," I decided to throw out there. "And no offense, it's pretty clear from the mansion you live in and the designer suit you're wearing that you don't work for free."

"And I'm actually a barrister."

"Even more expensive." I shrugged, feeling at a loss. "Listen, John, I appreciate this, but I could work for a year and never be able to afford your services, so I'll just take my chances with the free legal aid rep."

"I'll be requiring an urgent meeting with your superintendent to explain to me in grave detail why my client is displaying very clear physical evidence of excessive force at the hands of your colleagues," he surprised me by saying, turning his steel blue eyes on the Garda lingering near the door. "Which, before you try to excuse away, I am more than willing to have a medical professional attest to."

"Your client was arrested for fighting. He got those bruises from—"

"My client is an eighteen-year-old boy with a horrendous, detailed history of domestic violence. There are decades of reports of him being the victim of atrocious child abuse at the hands of his caregivers. That's not to mention his even more troubling history of being let down by both the state and the Garda Siochana in this town," John interjected coolly. "Quite frankly, I'm astounded your superiors had the nerve to take this boy before the judge. Once I'm finished making a spectacle of them, I'll be turning my attention to the long list of Gards, social workers, and authority figures that failed my client and his family." Leaning back in his chair, John rolled a pen between his fingers absentmindedly, while giving the officer a cool appraisal. "Now, when you're ready, my client and I will have the room."

Red-faced and fuming, the Gard turned on his heels and stalked out, leaving us alone in the room.

"Well shit," I mused, begrudgingly impressed. "Flexing your muscles there, John?"

"It's always good to practice."

"I bet."

He smirked. "So, am I representing you?"

"Do I have a choice?"

"Not if you want to stay out of prison."

"Fuck." Reaching up with my still-cuffed hands to scratch my nose, I pointed to the stack of paperwork in front of him. "Is that all about me?"

"Every page," he replied, pushing the stack towards me. "Front and back."

Shoulders slumping in defeat, I leaned back in my chair and studied him. "Why are you helping me?"

"Why did you hit the Ryan boy?"

I shrugged. "He had it coming."

"Try again."

I met his unyielding stare, before blowing out a breath and mumbling, "You clearly already know why."

"Indulge me."

"Because if I didn't, your son would have, and he has a hell of a lot more to lose than I have," I came right out and told him. "Is that indulging enough for ya?"

He didn't look one bit surprised by my admission.

Because this man was smart.

Hell, he was sharp as a razor.

"You protected my son's future, and now I'm here to protect yours," he finally said, folding his arms across his chest. "Sounds like a fair trade if you ask me."

"Except that I don't have one of those."

"I'm sure my wife would argue that statement." He smiled ruefully before adding, "You've won yourself a fan, Joey Lynch."

"Your wife," I deadpanned, repressing the urge to groan when a sudden pang of intense pain and hunger attacked my senses. Fuck, it was never going away. "Can't see how when your wife doesn't know shit about me."

"And you clearly don't know shit about her – excuse the term of phrase," he replied with a smirk. "She has a feeling about you."

I narrowed my eyes, instantly suspicious. "A feeling."

He nodded. "She wants to help you."

I stiffened. "I don't want her help."

"Ah, but do you need it?"

"Can you just get to the point?" I flat out asked him, feeling confused as fuck. "I don't do beating around the bush. Just tell me what you want."

"First, I'm going to get you out of this mess," he said, rising to his feet. "And then we'll talk."

Too good to be true – or safe

JOEY

After spending a grand total of seven minutes in front of the judge, John Kavanagh not only had my case thrown out, but had somehow managed to coerce a judge – a fucking judge – to take pity on me enough to apologize to me.

If I wasn't drowning in the unbearable pain of my latest comedown, I would have been seriously impressed with the man's powers of persuasion.

Completely fucking reeling, I sat in the passenger seat of his high-end Mercedes after court, too overwhelmed to argue when he took me back to the manor.

I needed something.

Anything to take the edge off.

The adrenalin that had been pumping through my veins earlier had long since deserted me, leaving my body cold to the bone and every muscle attached to me aching. It didn't seem to matter how fiercely my mind protested or my heart resisted; the physical pain from withdrawals was too goddamn much for me to handle.

I hated myself for not being strong enough to push it down anymore, but it was too big for me.

It was too big of a fight.

I couldn't win.

"Sit down, Joey love," Edel instructed when I walked into her kitchen a little while later. Feeling like an intruder I wanted to be just about anywhere else. "How are you feeling? How's your face? How did court go? Oh, you poor love, you're all battered and bruised."

"Give the boy some breathing space, sweetheart," John said, following me over to the island. "Sit down, Joey. We can talk."

I didn't want to sit down.

I wanted to talk even less.

But I owed the man my freedom.

If a conversation was all he wanted as payment for keeping my ass out of prison, then I would gladly give it to him.

Slumping down on a stool at the island, I had to resist the urge to lash out and react when his wife literally put her hands on my *head*.

"Jesus, Mary, Joseph, and the donkey," she strangled out, investigating my scalp like a mother would check their child's hair for lice. "What happened to your skull?" she demanded, pushing clumps of my hair aside, as she trailed her fingers over my head.

My father happened.

"Edel," John said in a slightly sterner tone. "He's not Johnny, sweetheart. You can't touch the boy like that."

"But he's—"

"Sweetheart."

"Right, right." Thankfully, she removed her hands and took a step back, giving me some personal space. "Sorry, Joey love."

"It's grand," I said trying to appease her and wanting them to know that I was grateful for their weird intrusion on my life. Even if I couldn't stop the full body shudder that rolled through me. "I'm ah, I just ... I'm not a hugger."

"Not a hugger," she repeated, sounding like she was storing that piece of information safely away. "Got it, love. No hugs."

"Relax," John coaxed, giving his wife a wink. "Just be yourself, sweetheart."

"I'm trying," she replied, as she buzzed around the kitchen like a tiny blonde whirlwind, fetching cups and saucers. "I'm just nervous."

"Why?" I asked, instantly on edge. My gaze flicked to John. "What's going on?"

"Remember earlier, when I said that we would talk after court?" John answered, tone eerily calming.

I nodded stiffly, hackles rising.

"Well," he continued to coax. "My wife and I have been doing a lot of talking lately, and we wanted to speak to you about the possibility of—"

"We want to keep you!" his wife blurted out, causing John to drop his head in his hands and groan. "All five of you," she continued, hurrying over to the island and catching ahold of my hand. "Especially you." She smiled down at me. "I think I want you the most."

"The fuck?" I choked out, yanking my hand out from under hers. "What are you . . . " Shaking my head, I practically fell off the stool in my bid to get away from this strange woman and her hands-on nature. "You want to *keep me*?"

"Tact, sweetheart," John groaned, biting down on his fist. "Where's the tact we talked about?"

"I forgot," she argued before turning her attention back to me. "That didn't come out right, Joey love."

"Listen." I held a hand up to warn her off. "I appreciate everything you've done for me." Keeping my back to the kitchen cupboards, I stepped sideways in my bid to escape the second coming of Mother Teresa. "And how good you've been to my sister, but I'm not interested in anything else, okay? I don't need anyone . . . *keeping* me. So, I'm going to go home now."

"She means fostering," John explained with a sigh. "Edel, would you back up, sweetheart, and give the boy space. You can't crowd him, remember? Baby steps."

"Oh Jesus, yes," she mumbled, hurrying to her husband's side. "Of course, I'm sorry, Joey love."

"Fostering." I stared blankly at them. "The fuck?"

"We're already approved," Edel blurted out. "We've been foster parents before. It's not our first time, love. And we can offer you stability and safety and—"

"No!" I choked out, practically climbing the wall backwards in my bid to escape. "Jesus Christ, no." Panic-stricken, I looked around uncertainly before locking eyes on John. "I want to leave."

"You can leave any time," he assured me, keeping a firm hand on his wife's shoulder, who looked like she was seconds away from springing towards me. "Right now, if you wish."

"Good." Blowing out a shaky breath, I cagily walked to the utility room door that led to the back door, only to hesitate when I reached for the door handle.

No, wait.

Hear them out.

Think of the kids.

Jesus Christ, what was I doing?

Run, lad.

Get the fuck out of this place.

"When you say you want to foster us." Turning around, I eyed them warily. "Are you offering my siblings a home?" I looked around. "Here?"

"We're offering all of you a home," John replied. "Sean, Ollie, Tadhg, Shannon, and you, Joey."

"I don't ... " Swallowing down the lump in my throat, I quickly shook my head. "No."

I could see the devastation flash across his wife's face, and I felt like a prick.

"I don't want to be fostered," I said slowly, trying to find the words I needed to make sense of this madness. "But I think ... " Jesus Christ, why was this so fucking hard? Why couldn't I just think clearly? "My brothers and sister might ... would ... need ... fuck, I can't get it out!"

"Take your time, love," Edel said in a soothing tone. "Take all the time in the world."

"I don't know you," I bit out, pinching the bridge of my nose, as I forced down a wave of nausea. "And you don't know me."

"We'd like to get to know you, Joey," John said calmly.

"No." I shook my head. "Not me. I'm off the table."

Edel shook her head. "But—"

"Let the boy speak," John cut in, giving her hand a supportive squeeze. "I'm listening, Joey."

"I'm fucked up," I admitted, shrugging helplessly. "And I mean I'm really fucked up in the head."

"No, you're not."

"Yeah, I am."

"That's okay, love."

"No, it's not," I protested with a shake of my head. "You don't want me in your family. Trust me. But Shannon and the boys?" I shrugged again, filled with desperation. The prospect of getting my siblings out of the shitstorm of a life we'd been born into was dangling in front of me like a gold nugget. God knows I didn't know these people, and I wasn't even sure if I trusted them, but right then, in the state we were in, they could offer the kids a hell of a lot more than Mam could. "They deserve a better life than the one they've been dealt." Swallowing deeply, I forced myself to say, "They deserve to have *parents*."

"From what I can tell, they've always had one," John said, giving me a meaningful look. "You've been one hell of a father, Joey Lynch."

"Except that I'm not," I croaked out. "I'm not their father, and I'm fucking tired of having to be." There it was. Admitted out loud. For what I thought might be the first time ever. "I can't do it anymore," I continued to spill my confessions, too weary and broken in the head to cover it up. "I can't keep raising them in that environment. If someone doesn't get them out of that house, they're going to die or worse, turn into me."

"When you say die?"

"I mean die," I confirmed, feeling weirdly liberated having adults finally listen to my worries and take me seriously. "Our father's not done with us and our mother's not stable enough to protect us. If they stay in that house, they're fucked, and I don't want that for them. So, if ... fuck, I can't believe I'm even saying this, but if you're serious about fostering Shannon and the boys, then I won't stand in your way." I paused for a moment, trying to clear my thoughts, before warning, "But Darren will."

"Ah yes," John sighed, drumming his fingers against the marble island. "Darren."

"He's not in this for the long haul," I decided to throw them a bone by saying. "He couldn't stick it out before, so he's even less likely to do it now that he's had the taste of freedom. But he's our mother's blue-eyed prince, and his word is golden. Those two are thick as thieves, so he'll take you on to retain his spot as mammy's righthand man." Folding my arms across my chest, I gave them a hard look, trying to take their measure before throwing my two cents into the mix. "The way I see it, the younger kids are crying out for change. They don't want to be in that house with our mother any more than I do. Problem is they've never been offered a safer alternative." *Until now.* "All four of them will fold like a deck of cards," I added. "If they're told they *can.*"

"By someone they look up to," John filled in knowingly. "By someone they trust. By someone like you."

"You want me to go out on a limb for you and your wife. You're asking me to do something I've never been able to do before. Something I've been programed to *never* do." Returning to the stool I'd abandoned, I sank back down and dropped my head in my hands, elbows resting on the marble countertop, as I fought my fears and tried to do the right thing. The *real* right thing. Not the fabricated version that had been drilled into my mind since childhood. "I want to help."

"You do?"

With my brother's voice inside of my head screaming *no, no, no,* I forced myself to nod stiffly and bit down on my fist.

Do this for them.

You can save them.

Get them out.

Trust these people.

"I'll support your case. I'll back you up with the social workers. I'll give an honest statement to the authorities. I'll lay all of my parents shit bare, and expose them for the neglectful pieces of shit that they are, if it means those kids don't end up like me, but if you fuck me over? If you hurt them . . . " Exhaling a shaky breath, I turned my glare on John Kavanagh. "If you even *think* about putting your hands on my siblings, it won't matter how much money you have, or what fancy law degrees line the walls of your office, I will come for you, and Jesus Christ himself won't be able to save you."

"I wouldn't expect anything less," John replied calmly, not taking my threat to heart. "I'm not going to promise you with words, because it's clear to me that you're a man of action."

I nodded, appreciating the fact that he didn't try to bullshit me or fob me off with empty promises.

The shrill sound of a mobile phone piercing filled the air and John quickly stood. "That'll be the school," he said, moving for the hallway. "Please excuse me."

"When did it happen?" Edel asked once her husband had left the room.

"When did what happen?"

"When did you lose yourself?"

"The day I was born."

Sadness filled her eyes. "And the drugs?"

I stiffened.

"I'm not blind, love," she said in a gentle tone, inclining her head to where I had my sleeve rolled up to my elbows. "I'm don't come from a sheltered home, either, which means that I know track marks when I see them."

Ashamed, I pushed my sleeves down and stared at the counter.

"How long has it been since you last shot up?"

I remained silent, knowing there was no right answer to this question.

"A day? Two at the most?" Her voice was gentle and full of understanding when she asked, "Does your skin itch so bad you want to tear yourself open? Has the cold gotten into your bones so deep you feel like you'll never be warm again? What about the cold sweats and the nausea? Have you reached the stage where you would rather die than go without?"

"I have it under control."

"Do you?" she sighed heavily. "Or does it have control of you?"

"You don't know me."

"What did it start with, love? Cannabis? Prescription medication? Benzos? Uppers? Hmm? How long did those keep you sated until you moved onto something stronger like coke or fentanyl? When did you take the plunge?"

"What fucking difference does it make to you?" I spat, feeling my hackles rise, as I tried to defend the inexcusable. "I'm not hurting anyone."

"Joey love, you deserve a good life, too," she pushed. "Everything I want for your Shannon and your brothers, I want for you as well."

"I'm eighteen."

"Love, it wouldn't matter to me if you were eighty," she said. "We would still want that for you."

"Well, I don't want that for me," I argued. "I don't want to be mothered, and I don't need a father figure. I'm too old for that shit."

"You're never too old to be loved, Joey."

"My childhood ended a long time ago."

"It doesn't have to be like that."

"It's too late for me."

"It's never too late, Joey."

"Aoife's pregnant," I decided to throw out there, deciding I had nothing to lose. "I'm about three and half months away from becoming a father myself, so I appreciate the offer, but the only family I'm interested in being a part of is the one I've made with her."

"Pregnant?" Edel's eyes widened. "You don't do things by halves, do you, Joey love?"

I shrugged in response because, in all fairness, what the fuck else could I do?

"And where does this little habit of yours fit in with your girlfriend and baby?"

"It clearly doesn't," I bit out, hating that she hit the nail on the head. "I'll fix it."

"Look at you," she said, with tears filling her eyes. "Look at how articulate you are. How smart. How brave." She smiled sadly. "You know that this is too big for you, love." She reached across the counter and covered my hand with hers. "Let me help you."

"No." Jaw clenched, I shook my head. "I don't need your help."

"Joey, love—"

"No," I repeated, yanking my hand away. "Don't talk about this, okay? It's a hard fucking limit for me."

"Because you know you're in trouble, love."

"Because it doesn't matter to you," I snapped. "It doesn't matter, okay? So just drop it."

"I think is does matter, Joey, and I think you matter, too."

"You're wrong," I bit out, needing this woman to just back off. "So, just give up."

"You've been traveling down a very long road, love. Maybe it's time to rest those feet and let someone else carry the load for you?" She implored me with her eyes to listen. "Let me help you. Let me save you, Joey."

"You *can't*." What part of that didn't she get? "There's nothing left to save, Mrs. Kavanagh, so please just *stop*."

When her son strode into the kitchen a moment later, I could have kissed the fucking ground at his feet.

"Oh, love, you're home." Springing to her feet, Edel rushed for her son, thankfully taking her hugs and cuddles with her. "How was training?"

"Grand," Kavanagh replied, accepting his mother's kiss on the cheek. "What's going on?"

"Are you hungry, Johnny? I've made roast beef with pepper sauce."

"Jesus." Sinking down on the stool his father had vacated, he let out a whistle and pointed to my face. "Cormac got you good."

No, my girlfriend's ex-boyfriend's father got me good.

"Yeah, and I got you good," I said instead, feeling like a piece of shit for clocking him earlier. "Sorry about that," I offered with a shrug. "Poor communication skills." *Understatement of the century.*

"So, what's happening now?"

"I'm in a fair bit of shit," I deadpanned. "That's what's happening now."

"Yeah, I gathered that much," he replied evenly, sounding eerily similar to his father in this moment. "Are you being charged?"

"He's not going to be charged with anything," his mother answered for me as she fussed at him and ruffled his hair. "Your father has made sure of that."

Kavanagh's brows shot up. "You're off the hook?"

"Apparently." I shrugged again. "According to your parents."

"Where's your ma?" Jesus Christ, he was as nosey as his mother. "Did she go down to the station for you?"

Did she fuck.

"She's working," I deadpanned, knowing that a fella with parents like his could never in a million years understand my situation. He could try. He could sympathize. He could listen to all of my sister's tales of woe. But he could never truly get it. No one could. Not unless they lived through it. "Couldn't get through to her phone."

"That was principal Twomey," John announced, returning to the kitchen, phone in hand. "The school board held an emergency meeting tonight."

"And?"

"And Bella will not be returning to Tommen to finish out the school year."

"Thank Christ for that," I muttered, thankful that at least something good had come from a very unproductive day. One of my sister's bullies was gone. Permanently. I considered that to be worth the hassle. Knowing that Shannon would have one less tormentor made the whole ordeal worthwhile.

"She will be allowed to sit her leaving cert in one of the local schools, but she will not be welcome back at Tommen. Her locker has been cleared out, her phone has been confiscated, and all images she took of Shannon have been erased," John continued to reel off in that no-nonsense lawyer voice of his. "Natasha O'Sullivan and Kelly Dunne have both been given a week's suspension for their roles in the incident. Due to Shannon's statements, though, and following a lot of discussion, it has been decided by the board that both girls will return to Tommen after their suspension and will be permitted to sit their exams there."

"That's bullshit," we both chorused in unison.

"Pick your battles, boys. This is a good result." Accepting the cup of coffee his wife held out for him, John kissed her before turning his attention back to us. "Take emotion out of the equation and look at the result for what it is: a win."

"And Cormac?" Johnny pressed. "How'd you manage to pull that one off? He was hellbent on pressing charges earlier."

"With a great deal of persuasion."

"Well shite." Leaning back in his chair, he let out another whistle. "Remind me to never go against you."

"It's not all good news. You've been expelled from Ballylaggin Community," John added, turning his attention back to me. "Apparently, you were on your final warning, following seven suspensions this year alone and countless others tracing all the way back to your first week of first year." A flicker of guilt flashed in his blue eyes when he said, "I did what I could, Joey, but they're not budging. Committing an act of violence against another school while wearing your BCS uniform is against their policy and punishable by immediate expulsion."

"It's okay," I replied, too numb to give a damn. Nyhan and Lane had been chomping at the bit for years to get me out of BCS. They finally had their excuse. I wanted to care about it, but I just . . . couldn't.

"*Okay?*" Kavanagh looked at me like I'd grown an extra head. "But you're supposed to sit your leaving cert next month."

"Doesn't matter."

"Yeah, it does," he argued, tone passionate for a fella whose future this didn't affect. "It does fucking matter."

"I wasn't going anywhere anyway, so it's all the same to me," I replied, which was mostly true. I never planned on college. I never planned on leaving Ballylaggin. I couldn't, so why worry about it?

"What the hell, Joey? This is important," my sister's boyfriend argued. Turning back to his father, he asked, "Is there anything you can do for him?"

"My hands are tied, son. Joey here has a record for violence that makes Gibsie look like a saint." John sighed heavily. "They're unwilling to negotiate having him return to school – not even to sit his exams."

Of course they weren't.

Those fuckers had wanted me out since first year.

"What about Tommen, love?" Edel asked, worrying her lip.

"Tommen is private, sweetheart."

"Another public school then?" their son suggested, running a hand through his dark hair in obvious frustration, which puzzled me because why the fuck did he care?

"Not in the area," John explained evenly. "Nothing public, at least."

Meaning the only way that I was stepping foot inside of a school to sit my leaving cert was if I had the cash to bribe my way through the door.

"The city then?" Kavanagh, ever the optimist, suggested.

"No school will touch me with a ten-foot barge pole," I interrupted, just about done with the whole conversation. I wasn't his pet project. He didn't need to find solutions to my problems. All he needed to do was treat my sister well and we were golden. "Your dad's right, Kavanagh. My record is shocking. No one's going to want me, and it doesn't matter anyway, because I don't care. So, don't waste your breath talking about it."

"Jaysus." Sounding thoroughly deflated, he sighed heavily, shoulders slumping. "What a disaster."

Yeah, this was all getting a bit too fucking chummy for me.

A little too family-meeting-ish for my liking.

"Can I use your bathroom?" I asked, standing up. "Please."

"Of course you can, Joey," Edel replied, waving me off. "You don't have to ask, love."

"Thank you." Feeling like a dick for doing what I was about to do but knowing that I honestly couldn't handle another minute, I stopped in the kitchen doorway and added, "For everything."

"No problem, Joey," John called after me. "Remember what we said," he added in a meaningful tone. "The offer's on the table and it has no expiration date."

"Yeah." I nodded stiffly. "I'll think about it."

And then I got the hell out of dodge.

I won't be long

AOIFE

"Oh, thank god," I strangled out when Joey's name flashed across the screen of my phone a little after nine that night. "Joe?" Trembling, I pressed my phone to my ear and bit back a sob. "Are you okay?"

"Molloy," his voice came down the line and I collapsed in a heap on my bed, body flooding with gratitude. "Are you good? Did you get checked out at the hospital? Did they scan you? Is the baby okay?"

"Yeah, they did and everything's fine," I told him, heart thumping hard in my chest. "It's all good, Joe. Our baby's healthy as a horse."

"Oh Jesus." I heard him release a huge sigh of relief. "Thank fuck for that."

"Joe, where the hell are you?"

"I'm on my way to your place," he replied. "It might take me a while." The sound of traffic whizzing past filled my ears. "I'm walking back into town from the Kavanagh's place."

"Johnny Kavanagh?" I frowned in confusion. "What were you doing there? What happened with the Gards?"

"It's a really long story, queen," he replied. "I'll explain everything when I get to you."

"I'll come and get you," I hurried to say, searching my room for my keys. "Just wait there, and I'll drive—"

"No, baby, stay where you are," he instructed. "I'm like twenty minutes away tops. Just relax and rest up, okay? I won't be long."

"Joe." Instantly suspicious, I demanded, "Tell me you haven't?"

"I haven't."

"Promise me."

"I haven't, I swear."

I sagged in relief, wary, but needing to believe him. "Come straight here, okay? Don't get sidetracked." *Don't fuck up.* "I'll be waiting for you, okay?"

"I love you, Molloy."

"I love you, too."

"See you in twenty."

The apple doesn't fall far from the tree

JOEY

After bumming a lift halfway there, and then running the rest of the way into town, I was rounding the corner of my girlfriend's street in Rosewood Estate, when a dark figure stepped out from a side alley.

Startled, because what the fuck, I staggered sideways, knocking up against a row of wheelie bins and dropping my phone in the process.

"What the hell, lad?" I growled, pissed off and agitated, as I hunched down to retrieve my phone, only to reach for it a second too late. "You owe me a fucking phone, asshole," I snarled, watching in dismay as mine fell through the metal slats of a road drain.

"I figured I'd find ya sniffing around her neck of the woods." The familiar sound of *his* voice had every muscle in my body locking tight in fearful anticipation. "Relax, boy, I only want to talk to ya."

Panicked and off-kilter, I quickly straightened up to my full height, poised for trouble. *And pain.* "What the fuck do you want?"

"To talk," my father slurred, holding one hand up, while the other fisted a bottle of his poison of choice. *Whiskey.* "Just talk, boy. That's all."

"We have nothing to talk about," I sneered, taking a safe step back from him, and then hating myself for doing it.

Jesus, this man made my skin crawl. The familiar smell of that particular top shelf spirit twisted my stomach up in knots. It had been so long since I'd laid eyes on him that I'd almost forgotten about the feeling of terror he could evoke from me.

Almost.

"I'm not talking to you," I warned, holding a hand up when he stepped closer.

"Did you read my letter?"

"Fuck your letter," I spat, vaguely remembering the bullshit spiel he'd put down on paper to make us feel sorry for him. But then again, a lot of the past few months was a jaded blur to me. "And fuck you."

"I need you to do something for me," he said, somehow angling our bodies so that I was the one cornered in the alleyway entrance, with him blocking my escape. "I need you to talk to your mother for me. She listens to you. She'll take me back if you tell her to."

"Take you back?" I laughed humorlessly. "Are you completely off your head? There's no back for you, old man. You almost killed your own *daughter*. You're going to prison, asshole, not home to your wife."

"I'm not going to prison, boy," he replied, sounding so sure of himself that it didn't settle well with me. "But you're going to hell if you don't sort this out for me."

"Then I'll see ya there," I spat, unwilling to bend to this asshole, no matter how badly he set my teeth on edge.

In a weird way, his abuse was familiar.

Unlike my mother, I knew where I stood with my father.

It gave me a sick sort of fearful comfort.

I knew that didn't make sense, but it was how I felt – on the rare occasion I slipped up and allowed myself to *feel*.

His cruelty was home to me.

It was all I knew.

I could handle his attacks because I knew they were coming.

I never knew what was coming with Mam.

Jesus, I was seriously messed up in the head.

With the hairs standing on the back of my neck, I watched him watch me.

His cold dead eyes were locked on mine, sending a cold shiver down my spine that resulted in my body shuddering.

"You think you know it all, boy," he said, taking a menacing step towards me. "Think you're better than me, but you'll see. As soon as that pretty girl of yours spits that kid out, you'll see. You'll understand what it's like to be trapped."

"Don't fucking talk about her," I warned, hackles rising. "I mean it."

"You'll know what it feels like," he continued to goad me – and step closer. "You'll finally learn what it feels like to be me."

"I'll never be you," I warned, backing up further. "I'd rather slit my fucking wrists than become you!"

"You're already me," he roared heatedly. "You've always *been* me, boy. Look at ya," he pushed, closing the space between us and clamping a beefy hand on my shoulder. "You can't leave her alone any more than I can leave your mother. Isn't that proof enough for ya?"

My blood ran cold.

His words rocked me to my core.

Because he was voicing my deepest fears aloud.

Worse, he was voicing the truth.

Because it *was* true.

I *couldn't* leave Molloy alone.

The resemblance was uncanny, and it caused my mind to spiral.

"It's not the same thing," I strangled out, feeling my body bow from the pressure as I jerked away from him, while drowning in the comparison. "I would never hurt her the way you hurt Mam."

"That's what I used to think," he replied. "I used to think I'd never hurt your mother the way my old man hurt mine. Believe it or not, I've loved her my whole life. I can remember how it felt at the beginning. How special she was. How much I adored her. I swore to myself that I wouldn't repeat my own father's mistakes." He choked out a humorless laugh. "And look where I am, boy?"

"My mother was a vulnerable teenage girl, and you took advantage," I choked out, trembling. "You're a fucking monster!"

"Do you think I was born this way, boy?" he demanded, taking another swig from his bottle. "I'm a product of my upbringing. Same as you."

"I'm not you," I ground out. "I refuse to be you."

"You can't stop it, Joey," he replied, using my name for impact. It worked. It rattled me. "You can't fight your nature, boy." He took another slug of whiskey. "Only way you're changing the ending of your story is if you walk away from that girl and her kid and we both know you'll never do it." He shook his head in defeat before adding, "God knows I couldn't."

Bated breath

AOIFE

When twenty minutes past by with no sign of Joey, I didn't panic too much, deciding to give him the benefit of the doubt. After all, he wasn't superman. The boy was a fast runner, but he couldn't fly here. However, when twenty minutes turned to thirty, and then forty, and fifty, I began to pace my bedroom floor, anxious and on edge.

When I phoned him, the call went straight to voicemail.

An hour passed by.

And then another one.

Something was wrong.

I could feel it in my bones.

Frantically trying and failing to get hold of my boyfriend, I bombarded his sister with text messages, desperate to know if he had been in touch with any of his family.

Because this felt all wrong.

I knew Joey, hell, I knew him like the back of my hand, and while he absolutely had a serious drug problem, he wouldn't call to say he was coming over if he didn't plan to. If Joe wanted to get high, he would do exactly that and then show up. He was an 'ask for forgiveness, not permission' type of guy. The only time in our entire relationship that he bailed on me like that was the night his father beat Tadhg, which led me to believe that something very bad must have happened to him.

With bated breath, I grabbed my phone and tapped out another frantic text message to his sister.

AOIFE: ANY SIGN OF HIM?

SHANNON: NOT YET. MAM'S DOWNSTAIRS WITH DARREN. I CAN HEAR THEM ARGUING ABOUT JOE.

AOIFE: NO OFFENSE, BUT DARREN IS A BIG DILDO.

SHANNON: AGREED. THEY'RE TALKING ABOUT JOE LIKE HE HASN'T KEPT THIS WHOLE FAMILY TOGETHER FOR THE PAST SIX YEARS. IT MAKES ME SICK.

AOIFE: PLEASE, SHAN. THE SECOND YOU SEE HIM, TEXT ME. I NEED TO KNOW HE'S SAFE.

SHANNON: I WILL.

AOIFE: I MEAN IT, OKAY? PLEASE JUST . . . JUST TEXT ME, OKAY?

SHANNON: I PROMISE. X

Quiet warnings

JOEY

My father got in my head again, but this time it was different.

Because this time his words meant sense to me. They had gotten through the walls I'd built up to keep everything out. Because this time I *finally* understood what he meant.

If he had walked away from Mam back in the beginning, everything would be so different.

Hell, not even in the beginning, if he'd just walked away after Darren's rape, when it was just the three of us and Mam, then we might have made it. We might have been able to pick up the pieces and build some semblance of a life for ourselves.

But he didn't leave and the repercussions of him staying had sent shockwaves through multiple lives. Worse than sending shockwaves, the repercussions had ruined us.

Would that happen with me?

Would the baby growing in Molloy's stomach turn around some day and resent me for not being a man enough to walk away and give him the chance of a decent life?

Would I have a son who hated me as much as I hated my old man?

Would he resent his mother like I resented mine?

Would he fall into the same pattern of addiction that I had?

Was I forever destined to repeat the cycle, and then produce more sons to carry on the fucked-up gene?

Jesus, I could barely breathe just thinking about it.

It was for those reasons that I couldn't do it.

I couldn't go to her.

Not tonight, at least.

Dejected and thoroughly demoralized, and with my father's words still fresh on my mind, I returned to the only place I felt some semblance of control over my life.

"Word on the street is the shades lifted your ass from that prissy private school today," Shane said when I walked into the sitting room of his shithole house and slumped down on the couch. "Fighting with the rich boys, Lynchy? Never a smart move."

"Yeah," I muttered, dropping my head back to rest against the couch. "Sounds about right."

"Heard you snagged yourself a fancy-assed barrister to get the charges dropped." Exhaling a cloud of smoke, he turned to give me a hard look. "Heard you were spilling your guts to that fancy-assed barrister. Had the judge weeping like a little bitch over your sad little life story."

I stiffened, noting the threatening lilt to his voice.

"Relax, I didn't say shit," I growled, giving him a *what do you take me for* look. "I'm no rat, Shane."

"You better not be, kid," he replied coolly. "Because you know what happens to rats." He narrowed his eyes. "They get poisoned. Right along with every member of their little rat family."

"I'm here, aren't I?" I spat, forcing down the urge to shudder, as I slipped my hand into the front pocket of my school trousers and pulled out what was left of my wages. "Just give me some oxy and a few benzos to get through the night."

He stared at the money in my hand for a long moment before blowing out a breath and reaching for it. "I don't know what's going on in that head of yours, kid, but if you're palling around with lawyers, then you're no friend of mine. If you're thinking about jumping ship, then forget it, because you're in as deep as I am. There's no walking away from this world, Lynch."

"I'm not palling around with anyone," I bit out, watching as he retrieved the familiar tin from under his couch. "I'm just trying to get by."

"So long as your version of getting by doesn't result in name-dropping or throwing your old friends under the bus, we're golden," he replied, handing me a baggie of pills. "But the minute you even *consider* crossing me, it'll be over for you, kid. I'll come down harder on you than your daddy ever did. You remember that."

By the time I managed to make it back to the house, every wall in my world felt like it was closing in on me and I was suffocating from the pressure.

Mam.

Dad.

Darren.

Molloy.

Shane.

The baby.

The Kavanaghs.

The kids.

Shannon's bullies.

I couldn't fucking *breathe.*

With my body in pieces and my mind reeling, I barely managed to get my key out of the front door when Shannon came barreling towards me. "You're back!" She threw her arms around me as her small body trembled. "Thank God."

I was tired.

I was so fucking weary, and my sister's arms felt like concrete boulders weighing down on me, pushing me deeper into the darkness.

"It's okay, Shan. It's all good," I tried to soothe, because I had a love in my heart for this little girl that no volume of drugs or depths of depression could kill.

Except that she wasn't a little girl anymore.

She was a young woman, and it gave me hope.

Hope that she'd survive what I couldn't.

What I failed to do.

There was a family waiting to take her in.

To take all of them in.

Because something deep inside of me, in the parts that still worked, assured me that I could trust the Kavanaghs. It was the same part of me that had locked on tight to Aoife Molloy.

If I did nothing else in this world, I would see this through.

I would get these kids the fuck out of this hellhole I would.

"Wait!" Catching ahold of my arm when I tried to step around her, Shannon pulled me back to face her. "Look at me."

Having nothing left to give or lose, I did as she asked.

"Joe." She sucked in a sharp breath. "*Why?*"

"Just get off my back, Shan," I replied, too damn weary to go another round with anyone, much less her. I knew what she was upset about, but I couldn't hide it anymore. "I'm fine."

"Joey," Mam cried out when I walked into the kitchen with my sister hot on my heels. "Oh, thank God."

Thank God?

Yeah fucking right.

"Mother. You're keeping well?"

"What's wrong with you?" Darren demanded, stalking towards me. "Why are you shaking?" When he put his hands on me, touching and probing my face, I had to use every ounce of self-control inside of my body to *not* react. "For fuck's sake, Joey," he boomed, coming to the same conclusion as Shannon, before roughly shoving me out of his sight. "What the hell is the matter with you?"

Everything, I felt like laughing. *Fucking everything, asshole.*

"What's wrong?" That was Mam.

Again, I felt like laughing manically.

Like she gave a fuck.

"What's wrong?" Darren exclaimed. "What's wrong is your son is back on drugs!"

"Is this true, Joey?"

Resisting the urge to laugh in their fucking faces, I made a sandwich and grabbed a drink from the fridge. "I'm not back on drugs."

"Yeah, because you were never off them to begin with, were you?"

Fuck you, golden boy. "You're all overreacting."

"You're high." Darren narrowed his eyes. "Again."

Whoop-de-fucking-doo. "And you're an asshole," I shot back. "Again."

"What are you doing, Joey?" Mam decided to throw her two cents into the mix. "Why would you put that stuff in your body again?"

Had I entered the fucking twilight zone?

At what point in time did she assume that I stopped?

She knew the score.

She goddamn knew it.

This whole damn fiasco was a show put on for Darren's benefit.

"You're one to talk," I laughed. "Drowning yourself in Prozac and Valium."

"Prescribed to me by a doctor. Not the thugs from the terrace."

"Okay, Mam." I rolled my eyes and took a bite of my sandwich. "Whatever you say."

"Is it Shane Holland?" she demanded. "Is he sniffing around again?"

"Jesus Christ, what do you care?" I snapped, having had just about enough of the bullshit interrogation. "Everyone get off my fucking back!"

"No, I won't get off your back," the golden boy himself interjected. "You're back on drugs, you've been expelled from school, you're off the hurling team, and you're—" He stopped just short of saying *about to become a father.* I knew that was on the tip of his tongue. "You are ruining your life!"

"I don't have a life!" I roared, losing my ever-loving shit with him. "I've never *had* a life!"

"Well, life or not, if you keep this up, you're going to turn into him. You're going to end up becoming the one thing you hate most in the world."

"Shut up, Darren!" Shannon was quick to defend, as she rushed towards me. "Joey, shh, shh, it's okay. Don't listen to him, okay? It's not true. You're going to be okay."

"Stop fucking saying that, Shannon. Nothing's okay. *Nothing*!" I strangled out, feeling myself slip. Feeling the mask that I wore to shield my emotions fall away. "You know, I sat in that cell for hours, thinking how did this happen to me. How did I end up the way I am. All fucked up in the head. But then I called *you*." My voice cracked and I forced myself to point at *her*. "I called you to come help me and you didn't pick up. And then I knew." Sniffling, I threw my hands up, feeling helpless and alone. "I said to myself *that's why*. That's how I turned out like this." Narrowing my eyes at the woman who gave me life, I spat, "Because you *broke* me!"

"That's not true," Mam cried out, shaking her head. "Take it back."

It *was* true.

It was the truest thing that had ever come out of my mouth, dammit.

"You fucked my head up worse than he ever did. He used his fists, but *you*? You got in my head," I admitted, on a roll now, as pain and poison spilled from my lips. "You broke my *mind*." I slammed the heel of my hand against my temple, desperately trying to emphasise to this woman just how badly she had damaged me. "I don't work right anymore and it's because your voice is stuck in my head! The sound of you crying and begging me to help you is *all* I can hear!"

"Joey—"

"Every time I close my eyes, you're there. In my head. Crying for me. Begging me. Screaming, Save me, Joey, save me!"

"Joey, stop—"

"But I couldn't ever save you, Mam," I cried, hating myself for my weakness, as tears trickled down my cheeks. Hating myself for *still* loving her. "I couldn't save you because you didn't want me to! You wanted him to be here! You wanted all of this to happen—"

My mother struck me so hard across the face that I momentarily lost my train of thought.

"Don't you dare blame me," she hissed, poking me in the chest. "I did everything I could for you and your brothers and sister!"

"You did everything you could for him," I retaliated. *For them.* "You can't lie to me, remember? I see right through you."

My mother hit me again.

Harder this time.

Hard enough to twist my head sideways.

"Mam." Darren was the first to react, stepping between us. "What are you doing? Don't hit him!"

And yeah, her slap hurt, but not nearly as much as the truth I'd given her.

"And I'm the one turning into him?" I said, glaring at the pair of them.

Fuck it.

What was the point?

"I'm not living like this anymore."

I'd had it.

I couldn't take another fucking second.

There and then the decision was made.

"I'm done!"

Moving for the stairs, I thundered up to my room, and started piling random items of clothing into my gear bag. Why? I had no fucking clue. It wasn't like I was going to need them. Not where I was going.

"Joey, stop . . . wait! Wait!"

Still, it felt sickeningly liberating to do it.

To pack my shit up for the last time.

To walk out of this house and know that I would never have to come back.

"What are you doing?" I heard Shannon ask from my bedroom doorway.

"I can't stay here anymore." Knowing that it would kill me to look at her, I kept my head down as I packed. "I'm sorry." *You're going to be okay. I'll make sure of it.* "But I'm going to explode if I stay in this house."

"You mean for the night? You'll go to Aoife's and come back tomorrow, right?"

No.

I wasn't going to Aoife's.

I wasn't coming back, either.

"Joey, please."

"I'm sorry!" Hating myself for knowing what my decision would do to her, but knowing that I had no other way out, I zipped up my bag and flung it over my shoulder. "I've tried, but I can't do this."

"Joey, please," she sobbed, clinging to me just the same as always. "What about me?"

What about her?

What about Tadhg?

What about Ollie?

What about Sean?

What about Darren?

"What about *me*?" I broke down and cried. "What about *me*, Shannon? What about *me*!"

"I love you," she wept, unwilling to let me go. "I do. I love you so much, Joe. I care about you. You're important to me. We can figure this out." Desperation filled her voice. "We can get through this together. You don't need to do—"

"Listen," I interrupted before she could cut me any deeper with her words. "I need you to take care of yourself, okay? I need you to do that for me." Trembling, I leaned in close and pressed a kiss to her forehead. "Don't depend on her, or Darren, or anyone else, because in the end, the world will let you down. They will *all* let you down." Anyone with the Lynch last name, at least.

"And you?" my baby sister asked, looking up at me like I could somehow fix her world when I couldn't even fix my own. "Does that include you?"

"Especially me," I forced myself to tell her, though it almost killed me to say it.

And then I did the best thing I could for her.

For all of them.

I walked away.

"Where's he going?"

"Is he leaving us?"

"Forever?"

"But he can't go!"

"Joey, don't go!"

"Joey, think about this!"

Forcing myself to block out their voices, I hurried down the staircase and moved for the front door, needing to get the fuck away from these children before I lost my nerve.

They would be okay.

I *had* to believe it.

"Do something, Mam. Say something. Please! Stop him!"

"Joey, don't go!"

"You swore. You fucking promised you wouldn't leave us!"

"Don't rush out," Darren tried to plead, blocking my exit. "Please. Just sleep on it and we can talk about it in the morning when you have a clear head."

"I can't do this," I replied lifelessly. "Get out of the way."

"Joey, no. Talk to me."

"Get out of the way, Darren," I repeated. "Now."

"O-ee. O-ee."

Sean's voice almost broke me, and I sucked in a shuddering breath, too afraid to turn around and look at the baby I'd given up so much of my life to raise. "I'm so sorry."

I could only hope in time that he would forgive me.

That he would be able to understand why I had to do it.

Why I had to go.

The Kavanaghs would give him a good home.

They could give him what I never could.

"Stay, Joey," Darren pleaded, voice breaking. "I can't do this without you."

"You're going to have to," I deadpanned, before stepping around him and opening the door. "Don't let them down."

Don't hold them back like you held me back.

Let them have the life we were both deprived of.

Stepping outside, I closed the front door behind me, pulled my hood up, and moved for the wall, only to stop dead in my tracks when my eyes landed on Molloy.

She was standing in the middle of the driveway, in a pair of yellow pajama bottoms and my hoodie, with her arms folded across her chest.

"You were going to leave without telling me?" Her tear-filled eyes flicked to the bag thrown over my shoulder and devastation and fury encompassed her features. "I'm not even worth a fucking goodbye!"

Of course she was worth a goodbye.

She deserved an explanation more than anyone else on this planet.

Problem was, I couldn't tell her any of that to her face.

The only way I could give her my truth was on paper.

On pages of paper that I had neatly folded in the ass pocket of my school trousers.

On pages of paper that I had planned to put through her letterbox.

"Look at me."

I couldn't.

She was my breaking point.

If I looked at her, I would do what he did and that might be the right thing for me, but it wasn't the right thing for her.

"Goddammit, Joey Lynch, you better look at me."

"Aoife, please." I could feel my tears soaking my cheeks, but I didn't look up. "Just let me *go*."

"I can't." Her perfume filled my senses when she closed the space between us. "I won't."

"I have *nothing* to give you," I said brokenly. "I'm not good for you. Why can't you get that into your head?"

"I don't care about stuff, Joey," she cried, throwing her arms around me. "I only want you."

"I'm done." I had to be. *For both of their sakes.* Trembling, I reached into my pocket and retrieved the folded-up letter I'd written her after leaving Shane's. "I'm done dragging you down with me," I whispered, slipping it into the front pocket of her hoodie without her noticing. "I'm sorry."

"Please!"

"I *can't*." I would not turn her into the woman in my kitchen. I loved her too much to allow that to happen. My father didn't do the right thing for the mother of his children, but I *would* do it for mine. "I'm so sorry."

"Don't go," she cried out, when I stepped around her and moved for the road. "Please. Please don't go, Joey. Joey! I love you!"

I love you too.

More than this life.

"I know," I forced myself to shout. "And it's not good for you to love me."

"Joey, I need you."

"No, you don't!" What she needed was for me to get the fuck away from our baby before I turned him into another version of me. Another version of his grandfather. "You need to let me go, Aoife. That's what you need to do!" It was the only thing I could do for her. It was the right thing to do *for* her.

"What about the—"

"Just go home, and don't come back here," I called over my shoulder, blinking the tears from my eyes, as I forced myself to walk away from her. *It'll all be over soon.* "Do yourself a favor and forget about me!"

Everything has changed

AOIFE

Hysterical, I sat on the cold concrete path, watching as Joey Lynch disappeared from sight, leaving me alone, with only his sister to comfort me.

Come back.

I wasn't sure if I was thinking the words or screaming them.

But I knew.

I *knew* this was different.

Something had changed in Joey.

I saw it in his eyes.

He was resigned.

He was finished.

For him, the fight was over.

The fire inside of him, the one that had kept his heart beating through all the hardship and pain, had been snuffed out.

His brother came bolting out of the house, shouting something about going to find Joe, but I couldn't take a word of it in.

The sound of my heart shattering in my chest was so loud and violent, it drowned everything else out.

We were having a baby.

And Joey was leaving.

Worse than leaving, he had *left*.

How could he *leave* me?

He promised.

I trusted him.

I *still* trusted him.

No, no, no, this was all wrong.

Something's wrong.

Don't give up on him.

He's not well.

Find him before it's too late.

With a horrible sense of dread settling in the pit of my stomach, and an even bigger urge to find my boyfriend before it was too late. I climbed to my feet and moved for my car, unable to form the words I needed to hold a coherent conversation with poor Shannon who looked almost as devastated as I felt.

Almost.

Mumbling something about needing to go home, I climbed into the driver's seat and cranked the engine before quickly tearing away.

It wasn't a lie.

I *was* going home.

I just needed to find him first.

Because that boy was my home.

It's not the way out

JOEY

For most of my life, I felt like I was running out of time.

Now, as I sat on the metal railing of the footbridge that separated Molloy's estate from mine, with the end in sight, it suddenly felt like I had all the time in the world.

The night air whipped and lashed at my face, but I felt nothing. Eyes locked on the raging current of water flowing through the river, crashing against the foot of the bridge, I felt a level of calmness that was staggering.

Several weeks of rainfall meant that the town's river was close to bursting its banks.

Good.

The current would take me quickly.

All I had to do was *let go*.

Just close my eyes and let myself fall.

Eerily at peace with my decision, I tossed my bag into the water and watched as the river swallowed it under and washed it away.

That could be me.

I could just disappear.

I will disappear.

It's the best thing for everyone.

Especially her.

Because she'll never stop fighting for me while my heart's still beating.

And I'll never stop dragging her down.

"Don't do it." A voice called out, and I stiffened, before reluctantly twisting around to find a familiar blonde watching me from the Rosewood side of the bridge.

"Don't, Joey." Clad in an oversized hoodie, I watched as Lizzie Young slowly walked towards me. "Don't."

"Just turn around and walk away," I replied, bone weary, as I turned my attention back to the river. "Just . . . leave me alone."

"Please," she whispered, as she slowly closed the space between us. "*Please*." Trembling, she reached out and gently covered my hand with hers. "Don't go over the edge." The wind blew her hair around her face, but she never faltered when she stepped closer, and circled my wrist tightly with her hand. "It's not the way out."

I sighed wearily; eyes locked on the hand she wrapped around mind. "Lizzie, please just—"

"No!" Momentarily releasing my wrist, my sister's friend wrapped both of her arms around my body and pressed her cheek against my back. "I won't let you do it to Shannon."

"Do what?"

"Turn her into me."

"I don't need this shit," I choked out, voice breaking mid-sentence, making me sound like my fucking sister. "Do ya hear me? I don't need anyone to save me!"

"I don't care what you want," she screamed back at me. "I care about what you need!"

"Let go."

"No!"

"*Lizzie*."

"It won't fix anything," she strangled out, burying her face in the back of my hoodie. "You think it's the answer to all your problems, and maybe it is, to *yours*." She sucked in a sharp breath. "But what about the people you leave behind? You think they'll be able to accept it?" I could feel her shaking her head. "They'll never accept it, Joey. It will haunt them forever. It haunts *me* forever."

"I'm not your sister."

"You know this is the same bridge, right?" she sobbed, holding onto my body for dear life. "The same fucking spot, Joey!"

No.

I didn't know that.

"Nobody was there to stop her," she continued, crying hard and ugly. "Nobody was there to stop my sister, but I'm here now. I'm here to stop my best friend's brother from following my sister!"

"I'm not your sister," I repeated on a croak, tears flowing freely down my face. "I'm not worth saving."

"Do you have any idea how fucking selfish that sounds?" she demanded. "When you mean so much to so many people!"

"You don't know what you're talking about."

"Your sister and brothers love you," she screamed at the top of her lungs. "They love you so fucking much it's *palpable*. And your girlfriend? Aoife? Holy shit, lad, I have *never* seen someone look so in love with another human being in my life."

"You don't get it." I shook my head, trembling. "I'm not good for her."

"Then *get* good for her, dammit," she snapped, as the sound of fire engine sirens filled the air. "Don't throw in the towel and ruin her life before it's even started. Because that's what you'll do. You jump and you're killing more than just yourself. You're killing everyone that loves you. You're sentencing them to a life in prison. Trust me. I should know."

"I'm trying to do the right thing." I pleaded, "Please just let me do the right fucking thing for once in my goddamn life!"

"You've always done the right thing!" she shouted back at me, as the wind howled, and the sirens grew louder. "That's never been your problem, Joey Lynch."

"You don't know me."

"You're a piece of shit for thinking about doing this," she argued. "But as a whole, you're a good fucking human, dammit, and I'm not going to stand back and watch another person I know erase themselves from this world because of another asshole's actions. Because that's what this is about, right?" she demanded. "Your father?"

"You don't know a fucking thing about my father!"

"Fine," she agreed, still shouting. "I don't know you. So, change that. Climb down from the railing and tell me about him!"

With my heart hammering in my chest, I stared down at her hands that were knotted together and resting on my stomach. "If you don't let go, we're both going under."

"Yeah?" She doubled down and tightened her hold on me. "Then I guess we're both going under. And please bear in mind that, going off rumors and the color of your eyes, you're clearly high as hell right now, therefore any decisions you make may be heavily influenced by the shit pooling around in your veins, and not how you would genuinely feel in your right frame of mind."

"Jesus," I bit out, frustrated. "You're so fucking stubborn."

"Says the pot to the kettle," Lizzie countered. "So, what's it going to be, Joey Lynch? Are we dying tonight, or are we living?

"You're living," I begrudgingly conceded, allowing her to pull me back over the railing and onto solid ground. "I'm being emotionally blackmailed."

"Hey, whatever keeps your heart ticking," she replied. "Sorry, not sorry."

Another loud scream of a fire engine siren filled the air, and we both turned towards Elk's side of the bridge, to see flashing lights whizzing by in the distance.

"Looks like you're not the only one being a menace to society tonight," she jibed, folding her arms across her chest, still watching me warily. "Sounds like it's coming from your neck of the woods."

"Yeah," I muttered, feeling a wave of unease creep over me, as I watched in the distance the stream of fire engines, ambulances, and squad cars speeding towards Elk's Terrace. "I think you might be right."

Queen of hearts

AOIFE

Queen,

There's so much I want to say to you. So much I want to apologize for. I know that writing this down looks like I'm taking the coward's way out, and you're absolutely right. I am a coward, but then again, I've always been weak when it came to you. But I'm not doing it anymore. I'm not taking you down another day. I refuse to. Besides, I've done enough of that shit to last a lifetime.

I spoke to my father tonight. Talked things through. He made a lot of sense, said a lot of shit that rang true with me. He told me the only way I can break the cycle is by leaving you and the baby before I destroy you. For the first time in my life, I feel like he gave me solid advice. Because if he'd left my mother then maybe everything would be different.

He didn't love her enough to do the right thing for her, but I do. I love you enough to do the right thing for you. And the right thing for you and our baby is to live a life without me in it. Because let's face it, baby, I'm not getting better.

I'm sorry, queen. For the lies I've told. For the names I've called you. For the times I've made you cry. For every ounce of shit I've put you through. For leaving you alone in this. I know what you're thinking: that I'm bailing, but I'm not, Molloy. I'm trying to make sure that kid doesn't end up like its father. I'm trying to make sure that you don't end up like my mother. Knowing that I'm sparing you and the baby a life like the one I've lived gives me so much peace. You deserve to live a good life and as long as I'm still here that'll never happen for you.

I love you, okay?

Please don't ever doubt that.

I love you so fucking much I don't even know how to put it into words.

But I just . . . I need to set you free.

Yours always,

Joey x

PS: On the other side of this letter is a full confession of the shit that went down at home in my words, dated and signed. I want you to give it to John Kavanagh. It will help him in court when he goes for custody of my siblings.

Tell them I was sorry.

Tell them I loved them.

Tell my son that I loved him.

Tell yourself that I loved you most.

I'll be seeing ya, Molloy. xx

Frantic, I shoved the letter I'd found in the front pocket of my hoodie down on the counter in the Garda station and cried, "You have to help me find him before he does something!"

"Aoife, pet, try to stay calm," Dad instructed, as he wrapped his coat over my shoulders. "The Gards are doing all they can. They've already sent a car out looking for him. Podge and Alec are out looking for him. Darren's out looking for him. Your mother and Kev, too—"

"It's not enough!" I screamed, clutching my stomach, as I leaned heavily against my father so as not to collapse in a heap on the floor. "You don't understand. He's not well right now. He's so vulnerable!"

"What did you say his home address was?" the female Gard behind the counter asked.

"Ninety-five Elk's Terrace," I strangled out, chest heaving. "Why? Is he there? Did they find him? Is he okay?"

Looking concerned, the Garda tapped on the keyboard attached to her computer before switching up to read something scribbled down on a notepad. She then picked up the ringing phone on her desk and paled as she listened to whatever was being said on the other line.

"No, no, no," I cried, sagging heavily against my father, as my legs gave out beneath me. "He's dead, isn't he?"

"There's been a fire," the Gard told us, wincing when she set the phone down. "At 95 Elk's Terrace. All fire department units have been dispatched."

"A fire?" My eyes widened in horror. "What do you mean a fire? At their house? Is anyone hurt?"

"I'm sorry, but that's the only information available to me at this time."

"Dad?" I spun around to face him. "We need to go."

"Aoife, love—"

"No, you either take me or I'll walk, but I'm going, Dad."

I had a dream about a burning house

JOEY

When I reached the end of my road and my eyes landed on the orange flames swelling from my house the heavy weight of disgust and self-loathing that had been pressing heavily on my shoulders was quickly replaced with sheer fucking terror

The fire engines.

The ambulances.

The squad cars.

The sirens.

It was for *my* house.

My *family.*

"Joey!" Fran, our next-door neighbor cried out, hurrying towards me as hordes of our neighbors began to gather on the road. "I don't know what happened. Your father showed up a couple of hours ago, and then all of a sudden, the entire house just went up in flames. I phoned the Gards as soon as I heard the bang, but they . . . I overheard them talking about accelerants."

"My father?" Trembling violently, I looked from her face to the house. "He was here?"

"He's still in there, love."

"Where's my mam?" I demanded, feeling my body grow limp, as a horrendous feeling of cold dread washed over me. "Where are the kids?"

"I don't know, love." She shook her head, eyes filled with tears. "I think they might be still inside. I didn't see anyone leave."

Jesus Christ!

With my heart gunning in my chest, I sprang into action, my body automatically shifting into fight mode, as I ran towards the flames.

"Joey, no!"

"You can't go in there, pet."

"It's not safe!"

Ignoring Fran and every other one of my neighbors trying to get in my way, I darted under the tape cordoning off my house from the rest of the street, narrowly avoiding two firemen in the process. However, the second I touched the door handle, a sudden blast of blistering heat shot through my flesh.

It was burning.

Fuck.

"Shannon!" I roared, voice rising with my panic, as I pulled my sleeve over my hand and persevered, needing to get inside that house more than I needed air. "Tadhg!"

Choking and spluttering when the sudden wave of black clouded smoke greeted me in the hallway where I'd witnessed both Sean and Ollie take their first steps, I covered my nose and mouth with my arm and staggered through the doorway, only to be swallowed up by the smoke. Momentarily taken aback by the unbearable heat that attacked my flesh, I felt around in the darkness, trying to familiarize myself with my surroundings and locate the staircase.

"Ols?" A fit of coughing enveloped me and I gasped and clutched at my throat in the darkness. "Seany-boo?"

Blinded and suffocating from smoke, I managed to find the staircase and made it about three steps up when I was roughly dragged backwards.

"Get the fuck off me," I spluttered and coughed, fighting against the fireman's hold, as he carted me outside. "I need to—"

"Stand back!" he commanded, pushing me roughly aside, as three of his coworkers rushed forward with a hose. "There's nothing left."

Nothing left?

Nothing fucking left?

I moved to run forwards but ended up staggering backwards and falling on my ass in a heap when someone tackled me.

"We have one."

"Move aside, move aside."

"Child or adult?"

"Adult female in the kitchen doorway."

"And?"

"I think we're too late."

"Paramedic! Now!"

"Oh fuck—" Everything inside of my stomach came rushing back up when I watched a fireman place my mother on a gurney.

Her face.

Her hair.

Her burned and blistered *hand.*

Heaving, I watched in horror as they started to cut her clothes.

"Mam!" I cried out, feeling my tears dampen my cheeks. "Save her!"

Oh, Jesus.

There wasn't an inch of her that wasn't burned and blistered.

The fire had *ravaged* her.

"Mam!" Twisting onto my hands and knees, I scrambled towards her, only to be pulled back. "Is she alive? Is my mother alive?!"

"Don't look, lad," someone was saying in my ear as they draped a blanket over my shoulders and hauled me away from the scene. "Just close your eyes."

I couldn't close my eyes.

I couldn't take the medics working on my mother.

My mother.

That was my mother.

With the flesh peeling from her hands.

I wanted to scream at them to look at her hand, but the words wouldn't come out.

"Mam," I whispered, body shaking violently. "Mam . . . "

"We have another one."

"Adult male."

"In the sitting room."

"He appears to have been trying to escape through the window."

"Deceased."

"The damage is contained," I heard someone shout out moments before another body was carried from the house. "The upstairs is clear."

No, no, no!

The upstairs was not clear.

I had kids up there.

I'd fucking left them up there, dammit!

"My brothers and sister!" I strangled out, scrambling to my feet as I fought against the hold the man with his arms around my shoulders had on me. "Let me the fuck in!"

"There's no one else inside."

"You're wrong!" I vehemently argued with the man I now realized was a Garda. "My brothers and sister are upstairs!" I knew they were. Worse, if they were aware that our father was in the house, then there was a huge change they had barricaded themselves into their rooms and were in hiding. "Fuck. They're inside that house. You have to let me get them." Wheezing out a pained cry, I fought against his unbreakable hold. "I left them! I left them in there with her!"

"The entire house was checked," he tried to placate. He fucking lied to my face. "There's nobody inside."

Bullshit.

Lunging away from him, I managed to break free and make it a couple of feet towards the house before he dragged me backwards once more. "Get your hands off me you dirty fucking pig!"

In the middle of my world falling down around me, Johnny Kavanagh's face came into view.

"Joe," he called out, slipping under the tape. "It's okay."

"Kav!" Breaking away from the asshole trying to hold me down, I moved for Shannon's boyfriend. "You have to help me get them out!" Feeling frantic, I rushed at him, knowing that if anyone in this world would want to save my sister, it would be this guy. "I walked out. I got pissed and left. But I couldn't do it! I couldn't leave them, so I came back, but the house was . . . my mother!" The image of my mother caused my stomach to heave, and I choked out a sob. "Fuck! Shannon. Tadhg . . . Nobody's listening to me—"

"I have them, Joey." Four words that shook the foundations I was standing on, followed swiftly by four more. "I got them out."

"You have them?" Dizziness engulfed me as I tried to comprehend what the fuck he was saying. He *had* them? *My* kids? *He* had them? "You got them *out*?"

He nodded vigorously as his arms came around my body. "Ollie, Tadhg, Sean, and Shannon."

Ollie.

Tadhg.

Sean.

Shannon.

Johnny Kavanagh had them?

What the fuck?

If this was a trick, it was the cruelest kind.

"Shit," I choked out, suddenly remembering, "Darren!" I dove for the burning house once more. "My brother's still in there."

"No, he's at my house, too," he said in my ear, as he heaved my back against his chest and dragged me away from the flames lapping at us. "They're all there. I swear to God, lad, all of your brothers and Shannon are at my place right now." He tightened his hold on me, and I was fairly sure he was taking the weight for both of us when he whispered in my ear, "They're safe."

They're safe.

They're safe.

They're safe.

"You both need to get out of here," someone commanded. "It's not safe."

"We're going," Kav replied, carting me away from the house. "Come on, lad."

His words broke off when two body bags were wheeled onto the back of an ambulance.

Mam.

She didn't make it.

Flinching, Kav spun us around, but it was too late for me.

I'd already seen it.

I'd seen *them*.

Him and her.

My parents.

Laying side by side.

Even in death.

"This is my fault."

"No." Hauling us both under the tape that was cordoning off my childhood home, Kav pulled me along towards a familiar Mercedes. "This is his fault, Joey. His."

"I was high," I confessed, feeling like my mind was slipping on me, as I struggled to take everything in. As I checked the fuck out. "I lost my head and walked out on them."

"And if you'd stayed, you'd have been passed out in your bed. Darren wouldn't have been out looking for you, Shannon wouldn't have been awake to call me, and you all would have burned to death in your sleep."

He was saying the words, but they weren't helping.

Nothing was helping.

"Jesus Christ." Another horrific visual of her hand flashed in my eyes. "My mother."

"This is *not* on you. So, don't you dare let that bastard get in your head," he commanded, as he pushed me into what I thought might be the back of a car.

I couldn't tell anymore.

"You didn't do this," I heard my sister's boyfriend say from somewhere nearby. "He did this."

Everything was slipping on me.

It was as if my mind had reached its limit and decided to shut down.

Was it self-preservation?

Was it a mental breakdown?

Had I jumped off the bridge?

Was I in hell now?

It felt like I was in hell.

I was trapped in a nightmare.

Wake up.

Wake up, Joey.

"Joey, you're going to come home with us now, okay?" a familiar voice was saying, but I didn't know where it was coming from. My heart was beating so hard that it was making my eyes blur. Or maybe that was the tears? "We're going to take care of you, and that's not me asking you, son. That's me telling you."

You jumped.

Don't worry, you jumped.

None of this is real.

It's not happening.

"I should have been here," I heard myself say – to who, I wasn't sure. But I said it. "It's my job to keep them safe."

"They *are* safe." Someone was holding me. There was an arm around my shoulder and a big hand covering mine. "And so are you."

Was it God?

Was it The Devil?

Where the fuck was I?

"No," I mumbled drowsily, as I felt the last strand of my sanity snap. "It was my job to keep *her* safe."

High time

AOIFE

The smell was the first thing that hit me when I jumped out of Dad's van at the bottom of the road and ran towards the crowds gathering on the street outside 95 Elk's Terrace.

Huge plumes of black smoke continued to rise into the sky as the fire brigade battled to extinguish the blaze that was devouring my boyfriend's house.

"Aoife!" Casey called out. "Oh my god, Aoif!" Slipping around a group of pajama clad women, she ran straight for me. "You have no idea how good it is to see you." Breathless and panting, she threw her arms around me when she reached me. "I heard the sirens, and then I saw all the flames, and everyone started coming out of their houses. Jesus, I tried to call you, but your phone's going straight to voicemail. I was terrified you might be in there. When I saw Joey losing his shit—"

"You saw him?" I demanded, chest heaving, as I struggled to make sense of what I was seeing. "When? Where? Is he okay? Was he—"

"Yeah, I saw him. He's okay – well, clearly, he wasn't okay. I mean, he was understandably losing his shit, trying to go back into the house, but Johnny Kavanagh showed up and hauled him away."

And that was all it took.

He's okay.

Two words.

"He's okay?" Sobbing uncontrollably as a tsunami of relief washed over me, I felt my legs give out beneath me. "Joe's okay?"

"You're okay, too," Dad soothed, catching me before I hit the ground. "You're okay, too, pet." Turning to Casey, he asked, "Did everyone get out?"

"All the kids got out," I heard her tell him. "From what I've been hearing from the neighbors, Joe and all the kids have been taken to Shannon's boyfriend's house. It's just his mother and father. They're the only ones who burned—"

"Right, that's enough," Dad interrupted, hooking an arm around me and pulling me to his chest. "You're coming home with me right now. Casey, pet, are you coming? I think Aoife could use her little sidekick tonight."

"For sure, Daddy-T, I'm coming."

"What? No, no, no!" Wide-eyed and horrified, I spun around to gape at me father. "Dad, no. I can't go home. I have to go to him. He's—"

"No." Cutting me off, my father wrapped a strong arm around my shoulders and led me back to the van. "You're not. You're coming home with me and Casey, and you're going to stay home. Tomorrow's another day. You can go and see him then. I promise you faithfully I will take you to the Kavanaghs' house myself, but right now, I need you to come home and rest."

"Dad, you don't understand—"

"No, *you* don't understand, Aoife," he snapped, helping me into the passenger side of the van, and then waiting for Casey to climb in beside me before slamming the door shut and rounding the driver's side. "You're pregnant, for Christ's sake," he continued, climbing in alongside us and starting the engine. "This isn't good for you. I know you love the boy, and my heart is breaking for him, too. I've indulged you all night. I've done everything I can to help and support you, but I'm putting my foot down now. This isn't good for the baby, and I think it's high time you start putting the *baby* first."

Wake me up when it's all over

JOEY

"How am I supposed to do this, John? How am I supposed to arrange my mother's funeral?"

"You're not on your own here, Darren. We'll support you in every way we can."

People were talking around me.

"It will be some time before they release the bodies."

Making plans.

"I presume they'll release his body to your family, too."

Making decisions.

"She's not being buried with him."

I couldn't take in a word of it.

"The Gards will take another round of statements, but it's safe to say it's looking like arson."

Slumped against the dining table of a room I'd never been inside, I rested my cheek against the solid oak, and held the back of my head with my hands.

"Of course it's arson, the bastard burned her alive! It's a murder-suicide."

Her hand.

"He tried to take the kids out with him."

Why the fuck could I not get the image of her hand dangling out of that body bag out of my head?

"The doctor is on the way again. He'll look after them both."

That's your mother, asshole.

She's cold on a slab now.

Because you couldn't stay.

"Jesus Christ, Nanny keeps calling. I can't deal with her right now."

Trembling violently, I focused on the sound of my heart hammering violently against my ribcage.

"Here. Give me the phone. I'll talk to her, love."

On the way my body wouldn't stop shaking.

"Alex. I need to get in contact with Alex. He's in Belfast. He doesn't know . . . "

As the memory of my brothers wailing continued to haunt me.

"I'll do all of that for you."

Her hand.

"And Mam's sister Alice in Beara."

Was it the one with her wedding ring?

Fuck, it was.

I'm sorry, Mam.

I'm so fucking sorry, Mam.

"Joey, love, how do you feel about this?"

It *was* her left hand.

Was she wearing it?

"Is this something you'd be interested in trying?"

I couldn't remember seeing it.

Fuck, she always wore that thing.

"He needs to go. He'll die if he doesn't get treatment and I can't lose another member of my family."

Where did her ring go?

Did it melt into her skin?

"Joey love, can you hear us?"

I wasn't entirely sure why she or any of the others were asking me questions.

I didn't have words left in my head to answer them.

"Joey, sweetheart. Do you have your phone? I can call your girlfriend for you."

"No," I mumbled, body stiffening, as her face broke through the darkness. The only face I'd been able to see since I was twelve.

Blonde hair.

Green eyes.

Smiling.

Loving.

Warmth.

Light.

That face.

Her face.

Queen.

"No." I managed to strangle out the words, as my heart gunned in my chest. "I don't want her to . . . see me like this."

"Joey love, I'm sure Aoife is very worried."

"No, Edel. I don't want her coming anywhere near him."

So, do you have a name, boy-who-can-think-for-himself?

"Darren love, that's not your call to make. It's your brother's."

You're my favorite friend, with my favorite everything.

"Yeah, well, my brother's not well. He doesn't need more pressure on his shoulders. Can't you see he's already reached his breaking point?"

If I had a packet of Rolos right now, I'd give you my last one.

"What do you think bringing his pregnant girlfriend over will do to him? He needs to focus on himself right now. He can't do that with her in his face."

Don't worry, Peter Pan. I'll be your Wendy.

"You can't shut her out, love. She's having his baby."

It's okay. Just concentrate on us.

"Listen, I'm just trying to keep my brother alive here. If that makes me the bad guy, then so be it. I'll take that title and all the shit that comes with it on the chin for him. Because he can't do this, Edel. He can't take another person sucking the life out of him."

I love you, Joey Lynch.

"Have you ever considered that she might be the one pouring life *into* him?"

Ride or die, Joe.

"I know what I'm talking about. He can't cope with her right now.

He just watched our mother's body being dragged from our childhood home! He needs to be in rehab, not playing house with a teenage girl!"

"Darren love, I know your heart is in the right place, but I have to tell you that I think you're going about this all wrong. Keeping them apart will only backfire on you in the long run."

"I don't care! He's going to rehab, he's *agreed* to go, and I'm not going to stand by and allow her to put notions in his head and make him change his mind."

"This is going to backfire on you."

"I don't care. Joe? It's me, Dar. Can you hear me? I need you to sign these forms for me, okay? I can't do it for you, buddy. You're over eighteen. You'll have to sign yourself in."

Whoever was sitting to my left reached over and wrapped their arm around my shoulder, and that's when knew I was broken.

Because I didn't flinch.

Because it didn't hurt.

Because I didn't care.

"Give me a pen," I managed to say, using every ounce of strength I had left inside of me to lift my head off the table. "I'll sign."

"Thank Jesus."

"You're doing the right thing, son."

"Promise me something," I mumbled.

"Anything, Joey love."

"I'm so proud of you, Joe."

Scrawling my name across the page, I released the pen and dropped my head in my hands, feeling like I didn't have an ounce of life left inside of me. "Promise me you'll keep her safe from me."

"Who, Joey love?"

"Molloy."

You can't stop me

AOIFE

"It's not right, Tony," Mam said, setting a fresh mug of hot chocolate down in front of me on Friday evening. "It's been four days. The girl has a right to see him."

"Listen, Trish, I'm not arguing with you here. I don't think it's right either," Dad replied, sinking down at the kitchen table beside me. "But he's their brother. He's the eldest. Their parents are dead. We have to respect his wishes. Darren's doing the best he can under the circumstances to keep the family together."

Four long days had passed since the fire that had taken the lives of Teddy and Marie Lynch.

Four days in which I had zero contact with Joey.

Four days since my world had fallen apart when I read the words on what could only be described as my boyfriend's suicide note.

My mind was still reeling.

My heart was in tattered shreds.

All of this I could have handled, if they would just let me *see* him.

But no, apparently, I wasn't what Joey needed right now.

According to Darren, I needed to keep my distance and give his brother time to grieve.

Like hell.

Joe wasn't just grieving.

If they had him holed up in a room somewhere, then he was going through withdrawals.

He was *suffering* and the fact that I couldn't get to him made me physically sick.

"Darren is not the patriarch of the Lynch family," I spat, feeling my stomach twist up in knots. "He's a piss poor substitute for the only parent those children ever had."

"Their mother—"

"I'm not talking about their mother, Dad," I snapped, pushing the mug away from me. "I'm talking about Joe."

"Well, when Darren phoned, he asked us to keep Aoife away from the funeral on Monday," Mam said. "Apparently, Joey is going straight to a rehab facility afterwards, and he doesn't feel that seeing Aoife will be good for him. In case he changes his mind."

"What the fuck am I?" I demanded, pushing my chair back and standing up. "The devil incarnate?"

Mam sighed heavily. "Aoife . . . "

"No, Mam, it's bullshit," I cried out, hating myself for sounding so weak in that moment. "It's not fair. I've been here the whole time. I didn't run away. I didn't check out on Joey. Six years, Mam. For six years, I've stayed, and I've helped him. I've pulled him out of drug dens. I've taken needles out of his arm. I've begged and borrowed to pay his dealers and keep him safe, and now, because I'm pregnant Darren's making it out like I've caused Joey's entire downfall."

"Jesus Christ," my father choked out, dropping his head in his hands. "Why didn't you tell us it had gotten that bad?"

"How could I?" I cried. "Look at how you're reacting now? You would have fired him from the garage and sent him away, and he doesn't have anyone else!"

"You're only eighteen," he bit back, tears filling his eyes. "I don't want this life for you."

"He's only eighteen," I shot back, trembling. "And he *is* my life, Dad. He's my life and I'm *his*. We're a family." My voice broke, and I sucked in a shuddering breath before squeezing out, "He's the father of my baby, and Darren's taking him *away* from me."

"Aoife, pet, I know you—" The sound of the doorbell ringing pierced through the kitchen, causing my father to pause and frown at the closed kitchen door. "Are you expecting anyone, Trish?"

"No, love," Mam replied, patting Dad's hand. "I expect it'll be young Casey. She usually comes over at work."

"Aoife?" Kev called from the hallway a few moments later. "I know you don't want me to speak to you, but there's a woman at the door for ya."

"If it's another fucking reporter looking for a statement, I'll lose my mind," Dad snapped, rising to his feet and stalking out of the kitchen.

All week, we had been bombarded with phone calls from local radio stations and reporters coming to the house, looking for a scoop.

We were a small country, which meant that fire was big news in Cork, it had even made the national news, and the media was disgustingly intrusive about it. Casey even heard a rumor that the national news broadcasters planned to attend the funeral. It was beyond insensitive to six children who had just lost both of their parents – shitty as they were.

Dad returned a few minutes later with a familiar blonde woman in tow. "Trish," he said, gesturing for the glamorous blonde to join us at the table. "This is Edel Kavanagh."

"Hello, Trish," Edel said, offering my mother a soft smile before turning her attention to me. Warm eyes full of sympathy greeted me. "Aoife love, how are you?"

My mouth fell open and I tried to answer, but I couldn't get the words out. Not when my entire attention was riveted to the small child whose hand she was holding.

"Oh my god," I cried, practically falling off my chair in my bid to get to him. "Seany!"

"E-fa," he mumbled around the fingers he was sucking, before releasing himself from Edel and toddling towards me. His little hand covered in its usual slobber. "E-fa."

"Oh, Seany-boo." Scooping him up in my arms, I broke down there and then, as a wave of relief washed through me at the sight of his little curly head. "You have no idea how good it is to see you, baby boy."

"O-ee sad," he told me, touching my cheek with his hand. "O-ee miss E-fa."

The fact that he was trying to speak and doing such a good job at articulating himself only made me cry harder. "Yeah, buddy," I sniffled, burying my face in his neck and soaking in his familiar smell. "Aoife misses Joey, too."

"That's actually what I'm here to talk to you about," Edel chimed in, taking the seat my mother was offering her. "Thank you."

"Coffee?"

"I'd love a cup, thanks, Trish."

"How are the others?" I asked, unable to keep the emotion out of my voice. "And Joe . . . " Blowing out a shaky breath, I climbed to my feet, taking Seany with me, and returned to my seat at the kitchen. "Is he . . . doing okay?"

"Thanks, Trish," Edel said, accepting the mug of steaming coffee my mother handed her, before turning her attention back to me. "Darren, Shannon, Ollie, and Tadhg are doing remarkably well under the circumstances." She smiled indulgingly at the little guy on my lap. "And Seany here is the sweetest little soul."

"And Joe?"

She shook her head sadly. "Not as well as the others."

My heart plummeted.

"He's in bad shape," she added, and I tightened my hold on the small boy on my lap, feeling like I had a connection to my boyfriend for the first time in days. "He hasn't spoken a word since the night of the fire."

"Jesus," my father muttered, scrubbing his face with his oil-stained hand. "Poor lad."

"He hasn't eaten a single bite either," she offered, concern evident in both her voice and her features. "To be honest with you, I'm not sure he's even slept. When he's not vomiting, he's staring lifelessly at the wall."

"I *need* to see him," I told her slowly, emphatically, fucking desperately, willing this woman to do the right thing for my boyfriend. "You don't get it. Darren thinks he knows everything, but he doesn't have a clue. He doesn't know a damn thing about his brother, but I do. I *know* Joey. I can *help* him. I can get *through* to him, if you just give me a chance."

"I agree," she surprised me by saying. "That's why I'm here, love."

My brows shot up in surprise. "You agree?"

Edel nodded. "I wanted to have you over that night. I thought it would be good for Joey to have you with him, but Darren had just lost his mother, too, and I didn't have the heart to fight with him. He genuinely believed that he was doing the right thing for his brother. He was so adamant that he knew what was best." She took a sip of coffee before setting the mug back down and saying, "But I have a feeling that the best thing for Joey is sitting in this kitchen."

Her words.

God, her words meant so much to me in this moment.

They curled around my heart like a warm hug.

"You'll take me to him?"

She offered me a sad smile and nodded. "You should have never been kept apart in the first place, love. It was an error of judgement on my part, and it will never happen again."

I was on my feet before she finished her sentence. "I'm ready now."

"No," Dad blurted out. "I don't want her to go."

"Tony," Mam sighed. "Please just—"

"I'm sorry, I know the lad's in a bad way," Dad argued, sounding genuinely torn. "And I would half my heart with him to make him better, I swear I would, but not at the expense of my daughter's welfare."

"Tony."

"Aoife's over five months pregnant. She needs to be here where she's safe and not stressed out."

"I'm going, Dad."

"Aoife, no, please. Would you just think of yourself for a minute?"

"I'm *going*, Dad," I repeated, setting Sean down on his feet. "And there's nothing you, Darren, or anyone else can say to stop me."

Back to me, back to you

AOIFE

Edel Kavanagh's house was packed to the rafters with people when I stepped over the threshold an hour later with her and Sean.

Armed with an overnight bag filled with prenatal vitamins, spare clothes, and snacks, I followed after the woman who had taken mercy on my poor frazzled emotions, smiling and nodding at anyone who stopped to greet me. It wasn't until we reached the sitting room and were greeted by Darren that I felt my hackles rise. He was sitting on the couch, tucked under the arm of who I presumed was his boyfriend Alex, as they spoke quietly to each other.

The minute his eyes landed on me; I felt the shift in the air.

The unwelcome feeling.

"Aoife."

"Darren."

"What did you do?" His attention flicked to Edel. "You know he doesn't want to see her."

Ouch.

I couldn't hide how badly hearing that hurt me.

My sharp intake of breath was proof of that.

"Shannon has Johnny, and you have Alex," Edel explained calmly, reaching out a hand to stroke my back reassuringly. "Joey has Aoife."

"She's not good for him right now."

"I'll show *you* something not good for you if you don't shut up," a little old lady ordered from her perch on an armchair by the fire. "The cheek of ya, laying down the law in this kind woman's house."

"But Nanny—"

"Don't you *but Nanny* me," she chastised, holding up a wrinkly finger. "You're not too big for a clip around the ear, young man."

I watched as she turned her attention to where I was standing and smiled. "Aoife." Looking withered and worn from the knocks she had taken, but with kindness still shone from her eyes, she held out a hand to me. "It's been too long."

We'd only met a handful of times down through the years, but this woman meant a great deal to Joey, which meant that I held her in the highest regards.

"Hi, Nanny," I replied, closing the space between us, attention flicking to her adorable, cloudy white perm. "I'm so sorry for your loss."

"Come here to me and let me see you," she instructed, catching hold of my hand in both of hers and squeezing. "One of my grandson's tell me that you're in the family way with another one of my grandsons."

Jesus Christ.

I cast a scathing look in Darren's direction before reluctantly nodding. "Listen, Joey really wanted to tell you about the baby himself, but his parents didn't want the younger children finding out, and then everything just sort of spiraled these past few months. I mean we've never openly announced it or anything—"

"You'll have a fine son," she cut be off by saying, as a strange wave of warmth flushed through me. "Strong like his mother." I could feel the tremor of old age running through her when she placed her hand on my stomach. "Loving like his father."

"We don't know what we're having," I heard myself whisper.

"You'll have a boy," she told me. "And he'll be just like his father."

"I hope so."

"You're a good girl." Her eyes burned with emotion. "With a heart of gold."

I shrugged in response because I didn't know what to say.

"You should bring her to him and watch her work her magic," Nanny said then, turning to Edel. "Return my grandson's heart to him, and he'll start living again."

*

"He's in here," Edel said, knocking lightly on a closed bedroom at the far end of the right wing of the house. "Just give me a second to coax Shannon out."

Nodding, I clasped my hands together, barely able to contain my emotions.

"Hello, Shannon, love," Edel said when she pushed the door inwards and stepped inside. "You have two visitors here to see you. Claire and Lizzie. They're downstairs in the sitting room, pet."

"Maybe I shouldn't leave him on his —"

"And I have a visitor for you, too, Joey," Edel interrupted, gesturing for me to follow her inside. "Go on in, love."

With my heart hammering violently in my chest, I stepped inside, immediately taking in the sight of my boyfriend curled up on his side in the fetal position. Clutching a pillow to his chest, he remained still as a statue on the plush bed, facing the window.

Oh baby.

He looked so young.

So utterly broken.

The memory of the words he'd written in that letter continued to haunt me so much that it was a struggle to contain my emotions. Finally seeing him and knowing that he was still *here* made me want to bawl like a baby in relief.

"You can't hide from me," I cleared the lump in my throat and declared. I felt bad for ignoring Shannon, but in that moment her brother was my number one priority. "And you can't give up, either."

His body jerked; a telling sign that even though he looked like a ghost, he *could* hear me.

Stepping around his sister, I sat on the edge of the mattress facing him and exhaled a shaky breath when my eyes took in the sight of him.

His gaunt features.

His haunted expression.

His vacant eyes.

"My Joey."

His body twitched.

"My baby."

His body shook harder.

That's it.

Follow my voice.

"Come back to me." With trembling hands, I stroked his cheek, and brushed his hair out of his eyes, before leaning in close to nuzzle him. "Because I'm not giving you up."

Jerking in what looked like genuine agony, a pained groan tore from his throat.

"I know," I coaxed, as I continued to trail my fingers through his hair. To touch him. To bring him back to me. "You're in there, aren't you?"

He twitched again, hands balling into fists.

That's it.

"I see you, Joey Lynch," I whispered, pressing a kiss to his cracked and peeling lips. "You can't hide from me."

His hand moved then, settling on the swell of my stomach, and I swear I could have cried in relief.

"That's it," I coaxed, gently lifting his head onto my lap. "Come back to me, baby."

Instinctively, he rested his cheek against my belly button, against the part of my body that separated him from his baby.

"It's okay," I whispered, cradling him when he shook and trembled and clawed at any part of me that he could catch ahold of. "You can't scare me away," I promised, holding him closer when his hands knotted in my hoodie. "You're mine, remember?"

It wasn't until Edel had taken Shannon from the room and closed the door behind them, that Joey finally spoke.

"Queen."

My heart soared to new heights.

There he is.

He's still here.

"Hey, stud," I replied, using my shoulder to wipe a rogue tear from my cheek, as I continued to cradle his face to my stomach. "I'm right here."

"Am I dead?"

"No, baby, you're not dead." I tilted his face up so that I could look at him. "You're safe, okay?"

Lonesome green eyes, so full of heartache and loss, stared up at me. "Is she dead?"

Sniffling back a sob, I cupped his tear-stained face between my hands and pressed a kiss to his forehead. "Yeah, baby, your mam didn't make it."

He didn't react.

He didn't stiffen or flinch or scream or cry.

Instead, he closed his eyes, settled his head back on my lap, and whispered, "I thought it was a nightmare."

Shredded.

I felt *shredded* to the bone.

"I know you're hurting, and I know you're tired, baby," I whispered, holding him as close to me as I physically could in this moment. "But I promise, if you just hold on a little while longer, it'll get better." I kissed him again. "You're going to make it, Joe. I swear it."

"Okay, Molloy." Another tear trickled down his cheek. "Whatever you say."

"I'm sorry." His words were barely more than a broken whisper in the darkness, as he lay on his side facing me.

His eyes, full of tears, were glazed over, and it felt like he was looking straight through me, but he was holding my hand.

I could feel him coming back with every timid stroke of his thumb. "I'm sorry."

"It's okay." Sniffling back my emotion, I cleared my throat and rested my hand on his damp cheek, feeling his tears as they slowly trickled onto my skin. "You're okay."

The same two words fell from his lips again. "I'm sorry."

"You've got this." Shifting closer in the semi-darkness, I placed my hand on his cheek and brushed my nose against his. "Ride or die."

"The letter . . . did you read it?"

"Yeah, Joe, I read it."

"I didn't want to leave you," he admitted and then a heart wrenching sob tore from his chest. "I only wanted to protect you."

"That's my job, remember?" I joked through my tears. "I'm the one saving 6."

"What if I can't get better, Aoif?" he choked out, holding onto my body for dear life "What if this is who I am?"

"Then you'll still be stuck with me," I told him. "Because I love you, stud. In all your shapes and forms."

"I let them down."

"Who?"

"The boys." He shuddered. "Shannon."

"No, baby, you didn't let anyone down."

"They hate me."

"Nobody who knows the real you could ever hate you," I whispered, wiping a tear from his cheek. "If you could only understand how much you mean to those children, how much they adore you, appreciate you. If you could only see yourself through their eyes . . . " I exhaled shakily. "You are *so* important to so many people."

"Well?" Edel demanded, when I stepped into the kitchen later that night. "Any luck?"

I waved the empty plate and glass in front of her. "It was a battle of wits there for a while, but he knows I always win."

"Oh, thank god," she replied, sagging in relief, as she pressed a hand to her chest. "That's the first bite he's eaten since Monday."

"Ham sandwiches and cans of Coke," I reeled off, setting the plate and glass in the sink. "That's the way to his heart."

"Good to know. Has he said anything else?"

"He wants a song played at the funeral," I told her, relaying one of his heartbreaking ramblings. "'Lightning Crashes' by LIVE. It's the only thing he wants," I explained. "Well, the song and the promise that Marie isn't buried with Teddy."

"Any other advice, Aoife, love?" she asked with a weary sigh.

"Yeah, don't give up on him," I told her, forcing my lip to stop wobbling, as I spun around to face her. "I know he's difficult and can be a right pain in the hole at times, but you need to *not* quit on him, Edel. No matter what. If you quit one time, one single time, then that's it." Leaning against the sink at my back, I snapped my fingers for emphasis. "He'll be done. That flicker of hope? That tiny semblance of a bridge he's offering you and John into his world. He'll burn it to the ground the minute you let him down and you'll never get back in."

I paused for a moment before reaching into pocket of my sweats and handing her the letter. "He left that for me, but I think you should read it."

You could hear a pin drop as I watched Edel read my boyfriend's suicide note. With every line she read, the harder her hands shook.

"Read the part at the end," I instructed when she gasped and clenched her eyes shut. "Read the part where he was trusting his babies with you and John."

"The poor boy."

"Because that's what Ollie, Shan, Tadhg, and Sean are," I forced myself to continue. "They're *his* babies, and something about you and your husband resonated with him. You don't realize how momentous that is. He planned on killing himself, and the saddest part about it is that he's been fighting his whole life. He's tired. He's so damn weary, and I know that despite everything he would never contemplate leaving those kids unless he had a plan for them. He did have a plan for them. He finally found a *home* for his babies with people he feels he can *trust*. If you knew Joe like I do, then you'd know that he doesn't trust. He's been through too much, so the fact that he wrote all of this down, and was prepared to go against his mother and brother to get his siblings to safety? Well, that's one hell of a compliment to you and John."

"Oh, Aoife love."

"But he'll push it," I warned her, wiping a tear from my cheek. "Joey will do everything in his power to prove himself right and prove you wrong." Shivering, I rested my hands on my swollen belly and sighed. "He'll take you on like a soldier at war because all he's used to doing is being in battle with grownups. He's going to question everything you do, from the television shows you let them watch, to the food you feed them. He'll watch you like a hawk and make you feel like a paranoid wreck. It's nothing personal. You need to understand that these kids are cubs. He's a glorified mama bear. Giving up power to you will be his biggest sacrifice because you're a woman, and women have always let him down. He's not fixable like Tadhg, Ollie, and Sean. You can't slap a plaster on him and heal the scars they put in him. He's not forgiving like Shannon or diplomatic like Darren. Joey's not open to change. He's a closed book. He's been traumatized far deeper than you, his siblings, or anyone else could comprehend. But you?" I looked her dead in the eyes. "There's something about *you* that calls to him. He's trusting you with his babies. That's a breakthrough."

"I am all in with these children," she vowed, voice thick with emotion. "I am all in with *him*."

"I hope so," I replied, tone mirroring hers. "Because he's going to get better, I can promise you that, and then your family is going to meet the real Joey. And I promise, you guys are going to fall head over heels in love with him."

She smiled softly. "We already do, love, we already do."

Like a noose around my heart

AOIFE

The mid-morning heat, emanating from the relentless sun, was stifling, causing what little make-up I had managed to apply that morning to sweat down my face. Summer had well and truly arrived in Ballylaggin, bringing with it green trees, freshly cut silage, and bittersweet goodbyes.

Unperturbed by everything but the blond in the suit, I kept my eyes trained on his back, as he stood at his mother's graveside. I felt an unbearable urge to protect the boy that had been thrust into manhood several years before today. It was a yearning so strong it almost rivaled the one I felt for the child growing inside of my womb.

His child.

The only time I had left his side was that morning, when I reluctantly went home to change for the service. I'd even showered at the Kavanaghs' house, in the en suite bathroom attached to Joey's room. It was the only way I could get him in there. To hold him and wash him and stay with him the entire time.

That designer suit he was rocking. Yeah, I'd dressed him in it before I left this morning.

Entirely alone in his thoughts, in his pain, my boyfriend remained rigid at the graveside. Long after his mother was lowered into the ground, and the other Lynch children had dispersed, Joey continued to stand vigil, still trying to protect her, even in death.

It broke my heart because I knew she had put more holes in Joey than his bastard of a father ever had. There was a Marie-Lynch-sized hole in my boyfriend's heart that no amount of loving could heal.

God knows I'd tried.

She didn't deserve Joey's unconditional love, not when she had never loved him the way he deserved. Yet she had always received it anyway.

Maybe it was the pregnancy hormones elevating my frazzled emotions and causing me to think more irrationally than usual, but I was so fucking angry with her. Her death, as horrible and unspeakable as it had been, didn't absolve her of the sins she had committed against her children when she was alive.

Those sins which had left her second-born son's heart almost unsalvageable.

All he ever wanted was her love.

And she never gave that to him.

Bitterly sad for all they had lost, I looked around, knowing that the other Lynch children would be okay in the long term. Darren would return to the life he had built for himself in Belfast, while Shannon and the three younger boys had the Kavanaghs to care for them. It wouldn't be easy, with plenty of teething pains along the way, but they would adapt.

They sure as hell had a better chance now.

That left my Joe.

The one shipping himself out of his family.

Shipping himself out of Ballylaggin.

Out of my life.

He had checked himself into a rehabilitation center up the country. The Kavanaghs, once realizing how severe his addiction was, had offered to finance it, and in a rare moment of clarity, Joey had signed the papers.

When his mother's funeral service ended, he was leaving.

For the whole summer.

Maybe forever.

Fuck.

Don't think like that, Aoif.

Last night, when he questioned whether he was doing the right thing by going, I had fiercely supported and encouraged his decision, even though it broke my heart to do it.

He needed to go.

And I needed to let him.

Exhaling a pained breath, I tightened my hold on the red rose I was fisting, and closed the space between us, ignoring all the curious stares and gawks I received in the process.

Some people knew.

More people didn't.

Truth be told, I didn't give a damn about what anyone thought. They could speculate all they wanted about the drastic weight gain I was attempting to conceal behind my black dress.

Fuck them all.

Not stopping until I was shoulder to shoulder with the only boy I had ever loved, I kept my eyes trained on his mother's freshly dug grave and tossed the single rose inside before finally finding the courage to face him.

Keep it together, Aoif.

Don't scare him off.

Don't try anything stupid.

Sucking in a sharp breath when my eyes landed on his gaunt, beautiful face, I masked my devastation with a steely look of determination.

That was the thing about Joey Lynch; he couldn't handle weakness.

It wrecked him.

He spent so much of his life caring for his family, fending for those weaker than him, that he didn't have any room left for vulnerability.

He needed a strong partner.

Someone who could look after themselves.

Someone who didn't need to be treated with kid gloves.

Enter Aoife.

"I told you not to come."

No *hello, Aoife*, or *anything*.

Just blunt honesty.

He wanted to say goodbye this morning.

But I couldn't do it.

I needed another minute.

Steeling my nerves, I arched a brow, burying down my insecurity and replacing it with feigned bravery. "And I told you to save your breath."

"Aoif." Pain encompassed his features and a shiver racked through his lean frame. "You shouldn't be here. It's not good for the—"

Baby.

Yeah, I knew all about the old piseog, another old wives' tale.

Stare at the face of death, never feel your baby's breath.

Thing was, I was more in love than I was superstitious.

"I don't care," I shot back defiantly. "As if I wasn't going to come, Joe."

We had been through hell and highwater together.

I wasn't about to let him bury his mother alone.

"Still." His eyes continued to search mine, for what, I had no idea, but he seemed to find whatever it was, because he exhaled a sigh of what sounded like relief.

"So, are you ready?" I clasped my hands together to stop myself from reaching for him.

In truth, I wanted to snatch him up and lock him away in my bedroom.

So I could keep him safe.

So I wouldn't be alone in this.

I forced a small smile before adding, "For what comes next?"

Lonesome green eyes seared something deep inside of my soul. "No."

More blunt honesty.

"Good. Because neither am I." Breath hitching in my throat, I wrapped my arms around my body, willing myself to be a stronger woman and not breakdown.

You can do this, Aoife.

You can let him go.

No, you can't.

You can't.

Don't let him go!

"Molloy."

"Just put your arms around me and hold me like you're not going to see me for another three months," I ordered hoarsely, needing him to not say anything that would shatter my barely held together resolve, as I walked into his arms.

Inhaling deeply, I noted the clean scent of him. Lynx, fresh air, and nothing else.

No alcohol or smoke.

God, he must be in so much pain right now . . .

"Jesus." His lips moved to my hair, and like the habit of a lifetime, my trembling hands moved to hook the waistband of his trousers. "You don't wait, do you hear me?"

His words infuriated me, but I didn't respond.

How could I?

It was taking everything in me to hold it together.

I wouldn't fall apart now.

Not here.

"You live your life, okay, Molloy?"

As if that was even an option.

I was pregnant with his baby, for Christ's sake.

His comments only went to show how unattached from the real world he had become.

How badly his mind had slipped.

How utterly broken and irrational his thought process had become.

Another could mistake his words for selfishness, but it wasn't true.

He was the least selfish person I knew.

He just wasn't *here* mentally.

He had detached from reality.

"Just shut up, Joey Lynch." My voice cracked, and I clung to him, not daring to give into any notions of doubt I had that this wouldn't work.

I couldn't afford to think like that.

He *was* going to get better.

And then he was going to come home to me.

"I love you," I squeezed out, clenching my eyes shut tightly.

"You shut up, Molloy," came his broken reply, pressing a hard kiss to my forehead. I wanted to tattoo the feel of his lips on my skin, terrified that I would never feel it again. His hands moved from my shoulders to my neck, before settling on my cheeks. "I love you, too."

"I'll be here when you get out." I knew I sounded pathetic, like another stupid woman putting her future on the line for a man, but I needed to give him hope.

"Don't be here." He leaned in and kissed me hard. "Be somewhere better."

"I don't take orders from you," I breathed, lips moving against his. "You should know that by now."

"Because you're crazy stupid." His lips, all swollen and busted up, brushed against mine as he spoke. "You're wasting your life on me. You know this. Everyone keeps telling you, but you won't listen—"

"Because it's my life to waste," I snapped, reaching up to grab the lapels of his suit jacket. Keeping my eyes clenched shut to keep the tears at bay, and trying for humor, I added, "Now, you get your sexy ass better and come home to me. Because I'm going to need you healthy, okay?"

That was the truth.

I needed him healthy.

Hell, I just needed him, period.

"Aoife." Pain washed over his features. "I'm a bad bet."

"*Okay*," I repeated, not finding any comfort in his lack of confidence. *Oh god.*

He doesn't think that he could do it either.

"Yeah." Nodding slowly, he stroked my nose with his, "Okay."

"Now, give me a kiss and tell me you love me," I instructed, cupping the back of his head. "And make it a good one."

"You should have told me to fuck off," he whispered, leaning in close. "All those years back when we were in first year." His lips brushed mine once, twice. "I've loved you since then." Another kiss. "From the first time I laid eyes on you, sitting on the wall with your blonde hair blowing around your face." His tongue snaked out, teasing mine. "I just didn't know it then."

"Joe."

"I know I've done you wrong, Molloy," he quickly continued, seeming to stumble over his words as he tried to piece reality back together in the haze of withdrawal and grief. "But you're the only one," he continued to tell me, voice low, pained and urgent. "You were *always* the only one. My one. In the good times and the bad. I swear to Christ ... " He cleared his throat and tipped his head towards the freshly dug grave beside us. "On her grave. I swear it. No matter how fucked up I ever got, I never touched another girl." He shook his head again, blew out a pained breath, and said, "All of the crazy shit I did? Fucking around with Shane and the lads? The drugs? The fighting. All of it. It was never about me replacing you. It was about me replacing *me*."

"You were sick, Joe," I squeezed out, feeling my heart hammer violently against my ribcage, his words taking aim at my heart in a deliciously devastating new way. "I know that you never intended to hurt me with any of it."

"But we both know that I did," he answered gruffly. "Hurt you."

I had no answer to that.

He *had* hurt me.

Worse than hurt me, I think he ruined me.

"I love you," was the only thing I could say to justify my staying, as illogical as that sounded. It was all I had. And somehow, it had been enough to weather the storm with him. "I love you, Joe."

"Joey," Mrs. Kavanagh called out, causing us both to swing our gazes to where she was standing with who I knew were two rehab porters. "It's time to go, love."

No!

Don't go.

Stay with me.

"Yeah, I know, I'm coming," Joey replied, turning his attention back to me.

Don't go! I wanted to scream, physically had to clasp a hand over my mouth to keep from blurting. *Don't leave me alone in this. I'm so fucking scared ...*

"I love you, queen. Always have and always will," he continued to break me down by whispering. "There was only ever you for me. Stone cold sober or off my trolly, my head knows that." Taking my hand in his, he pressed it to his chest before adding, "My heart knows that, too."

"Joe."

"I've done you wrong in so many ways, I couldn't even begin to list them, but I would never do ya wrong like *that*. I have *never* done you wrong like that, okay? If I've given you nothing else these past few years, trust that I've given you fidelity. I never broke that promise, Molloy. Fucking never."

"Joe, I just want you to get better," I pleaded, clutching him with a death grip. "I need you too. So badly."

"Joey, it's time to go," John Sr. called out, sending another sucker punch to my gut.

"Yeah, two secs," he called back in a frustrated tone. "Fuck, Aoif, this is it, baby. I have to go."

"Just a few more minutes," I heard myself beg and a pained groan tore from his chest. "I'm sorry. It's just hard."

"It's time to go, Joey, love."

"Crap," I strangled out, chest heaving from pressure. "Joe."

"You look after yourself, ya hear?" he said, tone gravelly and thick with emotion. "Don't be climbing any walls while I'm gone, Houdini." Roughly clearing his throat, he pressed a hard kiss to my brow and then stepped back. "I'll be seeing ya, Molloy."

And then he was walking away from me.

Walking out of my life.

Leaving me behind.

I stood at his mother's graveside and watched him go.

With my fingertips touching the locket around my neck, the one he'd given me for my eighteenth birthday, I watched them take him away.

I stood and watched, my heart cracking and splintering with every step he took.

And I had no control.

He was leaving me, and I didn't know if he would ever come back.

Trying to be strong for the both of us, because God knows he needed someone to be strong for him, I smacked on the smile I had spent my whole life perfecting, and kept my eyes trained on his back, feeling like I seconds away from dying.

I couldn't breathe.

The pain inside of me was stifling.

Several headstones separated us now, as death surrounded us in the most poignant way.

It was almost symbolic really.

We were in the place a person went to when their life ended as our relationship potentially ended.

Well, the cruel fucking irony of it all.

My world was falling down around me, and I was powerless to stop it.

No.

No.

No!

I couldn't save him, I accepted that now, but the scary part was that I wasn't sure anyone could. Underneath it all, he was the person I loved, and I still wanted to be with that person.

My flag was still stitched to his broken mast.

I had his baby growing inside of me, a baby I couldn't think about raising alone, even though I knew there was a very high probability that I would have to.

I just wanted to make him better.

"Promise me, Joe!" I broke down and called out, crying hard, as I watched him walk away from me for what could potentially be the last time. "Promise me that you'll come back for me!"

Weak girl.

Weak, weak, weak, fucking weak!

Shoulders stiffening, he stopped walking and turned back to me.

An expression of pain and frustration was etched on his face.

"Molloy."

"Come back for me, Joe," I cried out hoarsely, clutching my stomach. "Get better and come back for me ... For your family."

Looking shattered, he stared at me for the longest moment before nodding. "I'll come back for you. For both of you."

And then he was gone.

PART 10

Don't go there

JOEY

At the rehab facility, they told me that I had to remember.

That in order to get better, I had to go back to the start.

To my earliest childhood memories.

If I didn't, the holes my parents had left inside of me would never heal.

I knew that was bullshit.

They couldn't heal me.

No amount of remembering could fix what was broken inside of me.

All I needed from these people was to keep me locked up until I had detoxed.

Until I had sweated every one of my demons out of my body.

So that I couldn't hurt *her* anymore.

So that I didn't break her heart for the hundredth thousandth time.

I wanted to get clean, but most importantly, I wanted to *stay* clean.

That was the best I could possibly hope for.

I didn't need my mind patched up.

Just my addictive nature.

I wasn't sure how long I'd been here, or how many days it had been since my mother's funeral. I didn't know what day of the week I had, or when I'd last felt the sun on my skin, because I couldn't think – at least not about anything but the pain coursing through my veins as my body endured the withdrawal process.

It was beyond agonizing.

The shakes, the puking, the relentless fucking muscles spasms.

It was never-ending.

For the first time in years, I forced myself to stare at the reflection in the mirror, staring back at me.

I honestly didn't recognize my own reflection looking back at me.

Jesus, I looked like shit.

I was sick of myself.

That was a weird statement, but it was the god honest truth.

I was sick shit of every thought, notion, and idea that traveled through the fucked-up brain I had been given at birth.

I wasn't sure where it all went wrong, or if it had always been wrong and I was only noticing now.

Either way, my life had gone to noticeable ruins, and I was standing slap bang in the center, the master of my own destiny, the destroyer of all things good.

"You want to know how it feels to be me?"

"Yes."

"Hopeless. It feels hopeless."

"Are you still frightened, Joey?"

"I was never frightened."

"I think you've spent your whole life in a state of fear, and it's your reaction to that feeling that fear that made you so reckless."

"I was never frightened of him."

"Only of what he might turn you into?"

"Don't go there."

"Your father hurt you."

"You already know this."

"And you're still here."

"Yeah, I fucking am."

"You came about as close to death as a person does."

"I'm not a victim."

"He knew just how to get inside of your head."

"No."

"No, your father didn't know how to get inside of your head?"

"No, he didn't."

"But your mother did."

"I'm done talking now."

Unanswered messages

AOIFE

AOIFE: HEY, STUD. I KNOW YOU DON'T HAVE YOUR
PHONE WITH YOU, AND YOU'LL PROBABLY NEVER READ
THESE MESSAGES, BUT I'M HAVING A REALLY HARD
DAY, AND I NEED TO FEEL CLOSE TO YOU. TEXTING YOU
HELPS. READING YOUR OLD MESSAGES, TOO. IT HURTS
SO BAD, JOE. BEING APART FROM YOU. I REALLY HOPE
YOU'RE KICKING ASS RIGHT NOW. BECAUSE I NEED YOU
HOME, OKAY?

AOIFE: SO, REBECCA CALLED ME A WHALE AT SCHOOL
TODAY!!! LIKE SHE CAN TALK. BITCH MADE A WHALE
NOISE WHILE I WAS CHANGING FOR PE. CAN YOU BELIEVE
THE NERVE OF HER? ANYWAYS, IT WASN'T ALL BAD
BECAUSE CASEY TRIPPED HER UP ON THE BASKETBALL
COURT AFTERWARDS AS PENANCE AND THEN ALEC
RUBBED HIS SWEATY ARMPIT IN HER FACE. NOT GOING TO
LIE, THOUGH, THE WHALE JOKES ARE GETTING TO ME.

AOIFE: OKAY, IT'S OFFICIAL. I AM TURNING
INTO A WHALE.

AOIFE: I'M STILL A TEN IN YOUR EYES, RIGHT?

AOIFE: SO, I WAS IN SUPERVALU DOING THE BIG SHOP
AFTER SCHOOL WITH MAM, AND GUESS WHO WAS THERE?
SHANNON. WITH HER BOYFRIEND!!! HATE TO TELL YOU
JOE, BUT THEY WERE LINGERING IN THE CONDOM AISLE.

But I guess that's good, huh? At least they're being safe. She didn't see me, and I didn't approach her. I just ... couldn't, you know? It's too hard. But she's after changing a LOT. She was smiling like the cat that got the cream, and her cheeks were rosy, not that deathly pale color, and she had this calmness about her. Like she was content. It was pretty epic to see.

Aoife: So ... I'm fairly sure Casey had a three-way with AL and Mack. They're all denying it, but something definitely happened between the three of them in Podge's hayshed last weekend.

Aoife: I felt the baby kick for the first time today.

The girl from the wall

JOEY

With my heart frozen in my chest, I folded my arms behind my head and stared up at the ceiling, with nothing but my thoughts to keep me company.

From as far back as I could remember, I had a job.

At first, that job consisted of doing one thing: protecting my sister.

As the years passed by, my job became more complicated.

More babies arrived, the hits came harder, and my mother's presence in my life grew fainter.

The light in her eyes slowly dimmed into the darkness.

I watched it happen.

Powerless, I witnessed her turning into a ghost.

It seemed to happen over a spell of years and then all at once.

By the age of twelve, she was gone.

By the age of twelve, so was I.

My broken bones healed, my scars faded, and my body grew.

Puberty hit and I found comfort in girls.

Except, I never really did.

Sex was something I took when it was offered.

It was the same with drugs.

Whatever I was offered, regardless of the consequences, if it was bad for me, I welcomed it with open arms.

During therapy, they tried to tell me this was a version of self-harm.

I said nothing.

They told me I had PTSD.

Again, I remained silent.

They promised that I wasn't to blame for her death.

Nothing.

They assured me that I had a bright future ahead of me.

Empty.

At night, when the withdrawals still hit me deep, I curled up in the smallest ball I could and thought about her.

That was the only thing that kept me going.

Her face.

The only face.

Her picture in my pillowcase was the only thing I had from back home.

She was the only one I brought with me.

The only one I prayed would be there when I got out of here.

Even though I knew she would be better off far away from me.

I'd dragged her down to my toxic level.

And then I'd left her, alone, carrying a baby inside of her belly.

My baby.

I did that. I wrecked her future before her life had even started.

I was no better than *him*.

I'd done to Molloy what my father had done to my mother all those years ago.

And still, she remained by my side.

Through the storm, through the category five fucking hurricane that was my life, she stayed, never giving up on me even when I'd given up on myself.

Nobody ever got me like she did.

Nobody ever accepted me like she had.

For me.

I spent so long trying to push her away that when I stopped, it was so easy. Being with her was like breathing. I didn't know I needed the air, but I knew that I would die without it.

That's what she was to me now.

How important her presence in my life was.

Being without her now felt alien.

The thought of not having her in my life made me want to stay down.

Sometimes, I wondered if I stayed still enough, would the world just forget about me? Would I join my mother? Wherever the fuck she was.

In therapy, they told me to write about my feelings, but the truth was that I didn't know where to begin.

I wasn't sure what I felt anymore, didn't know and couldn't tell what was real and what was synthesized.

All I could see was her.

The girl from the wall.

Cramming and cracking

AOIFE

I'll be seeing ya, Molloy.
I'll come back for you.
For both of you.

"Aoife, come on, will you? You need to focus!" My brother's voice penetrated my thoughts. I looked up from the copybook I was doodling in to find Kev staring at me from across the kitchen table with an expectant look etched on his face. "Have you taken in a word of what I've been saying for the past two hours?"

I could have lied, but I didn't have the energy. "No?"

"Aoife." He sighed heavily. "This is your leaving cert. You can't go into the exams tomorrow and doodle all over your English paper."

"But my doodles are cute," I replied, adding a little smiley face to my latest creation. "Look at this cute little spider in its web."

"I'm sure the cute little spider drawing will be a fantastic addition to the baby's nursery," he shot back dryly. "But it won't help you pass your exams, and we need you to pass your exams, remember?"

"What's the use, Kev?" I showed my vulnerable underbelly by admitting aloud. While we had called a fragile truce, and my brother was attempting to make amends by taking on the role of my personal tutor, our relationship was far from back on track. "We both know I don't have a hope of passing the leaving cert. There's too much to do and too little time to do it in."

Honestly, I had read more in the past three days than I had in eighteen years.

Cramming for exams was a disaster, and while my brother was an exceptional teacher, nothing was going in because I couldn't concentrate on anything but my boyfriend.

Three weeks had passed since the funeral, since Joe had been admitted to a rehabilitation facility up the country, but I swear, I was still stuck in that day. Time was passing by, but my head was stuck in that moment.

I couldn't reach him, and it was killing me.

According to Edel Kavanagh, who *had* reached out to me every week since the funeral, Joe didn't have phone privileges in rehab. It was against their policy for patients to have access to mobile phones or have any contact with the outside world until they were further along in their recovery.

"All you need to do is scrape a pass," Kev told me, setting his pencil down and reaching for another textbook. "I know you've got a pass in you, Aoif. You can do this."

"What if I don't?"

"You think this year is hard, trying to get through sixth year while pregnant?" he tried to play tough cop by saying. "Imagine how hard it's going to be, having to go back to BCS and repeat next year with a baby on your hip." He narrowed his eyes. "Everyone in our year will have moved on to college and work. Hell, even your boyfriend's dopey sidekicks have snagged themselves a J-1 visa to the States for the summer. They won't be there to have your back if you flunk out and have to repeat sixth year."

That was true.

As soon as the exams were over, Podge and Alec, along with a whole heap of other people from our year, were heading to America for the summer, and I didn't blame them one bit.

It was the opportunity of a lifetime.

Aside from me, the only other person in my friendship circle with no plans to leave Ballylaggin for travel or college was Casey – well, aside from a two-week piss-up in Benidorm in late July.

"I'm not going back either way," I told my brother. "Even if I fail, I'm not going back to BCS to repeat sixth year. I'll apply for hairdressing at the PLC college in the city and hope for the best."

"And if you don't get into your course? What then? You're going to raise a kid off a barmaid's wage? You're not flaking out without an education, Aoif," he growled. "I won't let you."

"It's not up to you, Kev."

"Well, I know Mam and Dad won't let you either," he argued. "So, you need to pass these exams, and if you don't want to do it for yourself, then do it for the baby."

That stung.

Everything I was doing *was* for the baby.

I'm here, aren't I?

JOEY

"Joseph, you lost your mother in the most tragic of circumstances, and it's okay to grieve for her."

No shit, Sherlock.

"It's okay to miss your mother."

Keeping my back poker straight, I stared back at the doctor, or therapist, or counselor, or whatever the fuck she was, and waited for her to be done.

All I needed from this woman was to test my piss and stick a needle in my arm. To take all the samples she needed from my body but leave my head the hell alone.

"Joseph." A heavy sigh escaped her parted lips. "Part of your treatment plan is participating in therapy."

"I'm here, aren't I?" came my sharp reply, knowing what I had regrettably signed up for.

"Are you?" she countered, adjusting her glasses. "Are you here?"

"I don't know." Shrugging, I raised my hands and gestured to myself. "You tell me, doc."

"Seems to me like your mind is elsewhere. Back in Ballylaggin, perhaps? According to your file, your long-term girlfriend ... " she paused to read over her notes before struggling to sound out her name, "A-oi-eef ... "

"Aoife," I corrected, knees bopping anxiously now. "It's pronounced E-fa." Shrugging, I added, "It's basically Eva in Irish."

"Thank you," she replied with a rueful smile. "I'm from South Dakota, and while I find Gaelic names beautiful, they can be extremely hard to interpret on paper."

I shrugged. "It makes sense to me."

"According to your file, you and *Aoife* are expecting your first child —"

"Can we not?" I muttered, hardly able to sit still now, as a tsunami of guilt and self-loathing flooded my body. "I don't ... I can't ... I'm not talking about her."

"Why not, Joseph?"

"Because she has *nothing* to do with this." I gestured angrily to the room I had been holed up in for the past god knows how long, heart bucking wildly in my chest. "Aoife is nothing like me."

"Nothing like you?"

"She's not a fuck-up."

"So, you consider yourself to be a fuck-up?"

"Shit, I don't know, doctor." I narrowed my eyes, tone dripping with sarcasm. "What else would you call someone like me?"

"Traumatized?" she offered kindly. "A victim of extreme violence."

"I am *not* a victim."

"You're not?"

"No. I'm not." I glowered at her. "I'm the one who got expelled from school before I could do my leaving cert, I'm the one with fuck all in the line of qualifications. *He* didn't do that to me. *I* did that to me." Blowing out a ragged breath, I hissed, "And I'm the one who's taken the only person who's ever genuinely loved me down with me. Yeah, Aoife's pregnant, and not only does she have to deal with that alone, while I'm holed up here like the pathetic fuck-up I am, but she also has to do it with the label that comes with having *my* baby."

"You sound angry with her."

"I'm angry with myself," I spat, legs shaking restlessly, hands balled into fists on my thighs. "I'm pissed that I took her down with me ... " Words breaking off, I exhaled another shaky breath and glared at her. "I see what you did just there – bringing her up like that."

"Yes." The doctor smirked. "She certainly got you talking, didn't she?"

"When she told me that she was pregnant, I wasn't present," I heard myself admit. "I'd been gone a long time before the pregnancy. All the appointments and scans, I'd only been there in the flesh. She was scared and alone, depending on me to help her, and all I did was make it worse for her."

"But she didn't leave," the doctor surmised. "She didn't give up on you."

"No," I replied. "She didn't."

"Why do you think that is, Joseph?"

"Because she's the most stubborn person you'll ever meet," I muttered, rubbing my jaw. "Because Molloy doesn't quit on anything, even when it's not good for her."

"You include yourself in that statement?"

"Look at me," I deadpanned.

"I am," the doctor replied calmly. "I'm looking at a young man, who, despite all of the trauma and horror he's had to endure, has continued to focus solely on recovering and returning to her." She smiled. "I'd say that makes this Molloy an excellent judge of character."

"Hm."

"Maybe she needs you?"

"She needs to run a mile in the opposite direction of me."

"But that's not an option, is it?" she probed. "Your child deserves a father, and you of all people, know how influential that role can be in a child's life."

You're just like me, boy.

You'll do more harm than good.

"He's in your head again, isn't he?" the doctor noted. "Your father?"

Fuck, she was intuitive.

"I don't know if I can break the cycle, but I want to." Needing to move, I stood up and paced the small confines of my room. "I want to so fucking badly that it keeps me up at night. It's why I went back that night. Why I let Lizzie talk me off the edge. Why I didn't throw myself off that bridge. Why I'm here right now." Frustrated and anxious, I cracked my knuckles and walked to the window. "I know I'm not good enough, but I *want* to be."

"How are the withdrawals?" she changed the subject by asking.

The withdrawals were the worst.

For days, I felt numb, angry and lacking in energy.

I didn't want to speak to anyone, didn't want to lift a finger.

"Better," I told her, eyes locked on a group planting flowers in the gardens outside. "Manageable."

"That must be a relief for you."

"Will the memories fade?"

"Doubtful. But they *will* become manageable. Bearable. You'll find a middle ground on which to rebuild your foundations. You'll learn to cope. That's why you're here. To rebuild."

"I can still smell her." I released a shuddering breath. "I can still smell him."

Deciding it was too painful to breathe, I kept poker stiff, nostrils and airways on lockdown, waiting for the wave of sorrow to pass.

Praying it would do so quickly.

Finally, it did.

"When can I call her?" Turning back to face the doctor, I leaned against the windowsill at my back and asked, "I need to talk to her."

"Not yet."

"I've never not spoken to her in this long," I admitted, feeling pissed off, but knowing that this woman was relentless. She wouldn't bend. God knows, I'd tried enough times. "Please, doc. She's my best friend."

School's out for summer

AOIFE

"That was painful," I declared, following my friends out of school after finishing up the last exam of our secondary school academic career.

Six years of preparation.

Well, six years of prep work for Kev and the others.

It was more like six years of shits, giggles, and banter for us four.

And now it was all over.

"That was a total bust," Podge grumbled, scratching the back of his head. "My mam's going to go mental when the results come out in August."

"At least you guys will be away when the LC results come out. I'm going to have to deal with my mam in the flesh." With a dramatic sigh, Casey unzipped her school bag and emptied the contents into the huge communal wheely bin outside the school, while Podge did the same.

Meanwhile, Alec threw his entire schoolbag inside before stripping off his school uniform and tossing that in, too. "I've waited six bastard years to do that," he declared, standing shamelessly in his jocks, while he rummaged around in his gear bag for a t-shirt and shorts to throw on. "And I'm telling ya, lads, it felt just as good as I imagined it would."

"I can't believe you guys are going to miss the debs," Casey grumbled, giving Alec an accusing look. "What am I supposed to do, huh? By August, Aoife's going to be ready to pop. Joey's ... let's not even go there. And you guys? You'll be off whoring and touring across the United States, leaving me friendless, dateless, and dickless. It's bullshit."

"Ah, don't be cranky," Alec crooned, wrapping an arm around her shoulders and pressing a kiss to her hair. "You know I'll be coming back for my little devil-tits."

"He might be out by then," Podge said, giving me a sympathetic look. "Any word?"

I shook my head, feeling that familiar swell of devastation wash through me. I hated being asked that question. It was something my parents had asked me three times a day since he left for rehab. Every time I had to answer and say no, another little piece of my heart was chipped away.

I got it.

Joey couldn't call.

He didn't have access to technology, nor had he been granted visitor privileges.

But that didn't mean that his lack of contact didn't scald me.

"Lad, I can't wait to see him again," Alec said in a wistful tone. "It'll be weird as hell, though," he added with a chuckle. "Having a conversation with Lynchy when he's not off his tits." He frowned then and scratched his chin. "You know, I don't think that's ever happened before."

"Not helping, dopey," Casey grumbled, elbowing him in the ribs. "Joe's going to kick ass in treatment, and then he's going to come home, clean, sober, and ready to kick ass in fatherhood."

"Well, that's a given," Podge replied.

"Lynchy's got this, sexy legs," Al agreed, giving me a supportive smile. "You'll see."

"Yeah," I replied, offering them a bright smile.

I hope so.

Poking and prodding

JOEY

While the rest of my family and friends were enjoying their summer, I was spending mine inside a mental health facility, with doctors who tried to undo the damage already done to my fucked-up brain.

Every day it was something.

Every damn day, there was a new topic to broach.

If the doctors and therapists weren't probing my feelings towards my father, then they were forcing me to speak about the death of my mother or dissecting my relationship with my girlfriend.

Christ, even Granda Murphy had been dragged up in conversation. Nanny, too. Nothing was sacred to these people. Every inch of my life, from birth to present day, was as enticing to them as drugs were to me.

The worst was when they asked me how I felt about my mother's passing.

Passing.

Like she *passed off* somewhere.

I hated that world.

Mam didn't pass away.

She was taken.

Fucking stolen.

And I blamed her.

I spent my life hating on her, blaming her for things I couldn't understand at the time.

I didn't get it.

Still couldn't.

But she was my mother, and she died thinking I hated her. That would never sit well with me, and nothing these doctors could say would repair that hole in me.

Nothing.

Thinking clearly for the first time in several years, I faced my demons with a loaded conscience and a crushed heart.

The stupid fucking journal I'd been encouraged to keep in hospital felt unbearably heavy in my hands, filled with more darkness than I knew what to do with.

Trusting wasn't something that came easily to me, not even when it came to writing in a fucking journal.

Hating, on the other hand, did.

I excelled at hating the world.

Not just the world, but everyone in it.

Except for her.

Yeah, she was my only exception.

Long hot summer

AOIFE

I saw him again yesterday.

Coming out of the GAA pavilion when I was driving home from work.

Of course, I was wrong.

It wasn't Joey; just some tall lad with his hood up, and a hurley in hand.

But I pretended it was him. For a split second, I imagined he was still here, and I wasn't completely alone.

Depression had set in pretty quick after that, and I had eaten half my weight in cheese and onion crisps before passing out on my bed, with the scrap book I'd spent all summer making. I wasn't entirely sure if it was a healthy hobby to have undertaken, but it gave me unmeasurable comfort, so I was going with it.

When I woke this morning, that scrap book was the first thing I reached for. It was like my own personal comfort blanket, filled with six years of memories of Joey Lynch.

Every photograph, every perfect summer night, every horrible roaring screaming match, everything I was from the age of twelve to this exact moment involved Joey.

Revolved around our relationship and the way he made me feel.

My eyes landed on a picture taken the night of my eighteenth birthday.

I stared down at the two fresh-faced teenagers smiling back at me.

It felt like a million years ago, but I remembered the moment, the feelings I had in my heart at that exact time in space.

"This is Daddy," I said, stroking my ever-expanding belly, as I sat cross-legged on my bed and turned the page of my scrap book.

When I first started talking to my bump, it was right after Joey left for rehab, and I felt like a tool.

But now, it felt as natural as breathing.

All day every day, I chattered away to my little intruder.

Having Joey's baby inside of me felt like I still had a part of him with me.

Like I was talking to him.

"See?" I let my finger trail over the photograph. "That's your daddy holding the winner's cup in third year. He was the captain of the school hurling team that year, and he was the best on the pitch. And that's uncle Podge standing beside him, and right in the back with his shirt over his head is uncle Al. He's a little unstable, but we love him anyway." My gaze flicked to Paul who was also in the team photo, and I grimaced. "And that guy right there is Mammy's first boyfriend. Daddy likes to call him Paul the prick."

A weird little shiver rolled through me when the baby squirmed in response, causing my poor, overstretched stomach to ripple. "Take it handy, little hurler," I cooed, stroking the part of my stomach where I felt the most pressure. "Poor Mammy doesn't need any more stretchmarks, okay? So, you just hang tight in there."

Let's talk about intimacy

JOEY

"Let's talk about intimacy."

"Let's not."

"I want you to go back to the beginning," my psychiatrist said calmly. "Back to your earliest memories."

"Intimacy." I glared across the room at her, feeling beyond irritated. The shit this woman asked me. It was beyond the pale. "The fuck has intimacy got to do with anything?"

"A great deal," she replied, offering me a reassuring smile. "Let's start off with your earliest memory of being held."

"Sexually?"

"Let's start off with emotionally," she instructed. "Do you remember a time in your life when your parents held you?"

"My parents."

She nodded. "Your mother, for instance."

I stiffened. "This is fucked up."

"Just go with it," she coaxed. "Have I led you astray yet?"

"No," I reluctantly had to admit, while I tried to think back to when I was a kid. "I remember my *father* hugging me."

"Let's evaluate on that, shall we?"

"As in?"

"As in tell me about that memory."

"I think I was about five or six?" I offered, struggling to hold the memory in place. "It was before we went into care for those six months. And I'd scored the winning goal in a match."

"A hurling match?"

I nodded. "He was so fucking excited about it, that he picked me up and threw me in the air." I rubbed my jaw and blew out a pained breath at the memory. "Took me to the shop afterwards and bought me a pound's worth of penny jellies." Frowning, I said, "I remember thinking 'if I can keep winning, it'll keep him happy, and he'll stop hitting my mother'." Shrugging, I added, "So, I kept winning."

"Did it work?"

I gave her a hard look. "What do you think?"

"That's very interesting."

"How'd you figure?"

"Because your mind didn't automatically return to your mother."

"Because I don't remember her hugging me."

"That's a heartbreaking statement to make, Joey," she surmised, scribbling away on her clipboard."

"She was good to Shannon," I offered, feeling that familiar urge to defend her, even from beyond the grave. "The boys, too."

"But not you."

I shrugged. "We had a different kind of relationship."

"Meaning?"

"Meaning I don't think she looked on me like a son," I admitted gruffly. "More like a teammate."

"A teammate."

I nodded.

The doctor was quiet for a long moment before changing it up by saying, "Tell me about the first time you had sex."

"Why?" I glared at her. "Are you looking for tips?"

"How old were you?"

"I don't know. I was in third year at the time." Frowning, I scratched my jaw and thought back. "I think it was a couple of months before my fifteenth birthday."

"You think?"

I shrugged in response.

"That's very young."

Again, I shrugged.

"How did it make you feel?"

"Not good."

"Because you weren't ready?"

"Because I wasn't in control."

Her brows furrowed. "Tell me about the girl."

"She was just a girl from school." Leaning back in my chair, I pushed my hair off my face, and tried to focus on the memory. "We'd been scoring on and off—"

"Scoring?" she interjected. "I'm sorry, Joey, but I'm not familiar with the slang."

"Kissing," I explained. "It means kissing." I paused for a moment before adding, "Shifting means kissing, too."

"So, you and this girl were *shifting*."

I nodded. "If we were both at the same party or disco, then nine times out of ten, we'd end up scoring with each other."

"Did you have feelings for this girl?"

"No," I admitted truthfully. "I mean, I didn't dislike her or anything like that. She was a nice girl. We were friendly enough, but I didn't have any real feelings for her. Not like . . . " I shook my head again. "She was just . . . there."

"Aoife," she filled in knowingly. "Not like the feelings you had for Aoife?"

"*Have* for Aoife," I corrected, and then shifted in discomfort. "We were just friends back then. She had a fella. I told you this before."

"Ah, yes," she mused, flicking through her notes. "Paul the prick, if I recall correctly."

I snorted. "Yeah."

"Tell me about that night," she instructed. "About the lead up."

"You're asking me to remember something that happened a million years ago."

"Three and a half years ago, not a million," she replied calmly.

"Three and a half," I repeated with a chuckle.

"This is funny?"

"No, it's just . . . " Shaking my head, I smirked to myself as memories of past conversations flashed through my mind. "It's just something Aoife would say a lot."

"When?"

"When asked about how long she was with her ex."

Dr. B smiled before turning her attention back to her creepy quest. "The night you lost your virginity. Tell me about the lead up."

"Jesus, this is awkward."

"Humor me."

"It was Halloween night," I admitted. "The night Sean was born."

"2001?"

"Yeah."

"Please continue."

"There was this underage disco being held in town, and I went with a few of the lads," I told her, thinking back. "I had a run in with Paul the prick. He was getting handsy with Aoife at the time."

"And that triggered you?"

"It did more than trigger me."

"Keep going."

"I fucked off with a few of my friends, did a line of coke – actually, I did a lot of lines."

"All cocaine?"

"No." I shook my head. "I had a thing for oxy at the time."

"The pills."

"Yeah, but I preferred to crush and snort them."

"For a faster, more intense release."

I nodded, shifting around in my seat, as the familiar hunger roared to life inside of me. "Anyway, I was off my head, and I remember her taking me around the side of the building."

"Aoife?"

"No." I shook my head. "Danielle."

"And what happened next, Joey?"

"I was just . . . " I frowned, trying to piece it all together again. "I was kissing her, and then she was unzipping me, and had her hands on me."

"On your penis."

"I didn't mind," I replied with a nod. "I mean, it was nice. It *felt* nice. It was just . . . more of a surprise than anything."

"Because she was touching you intimately?"

"Because I was off my head at the time," I admitted before adding, "Because I wasn't even seeing her in my mind."

"Who were you seeing?"

"Aoife."

She jotted something down on paper before saying, "Keep going, Joey."

"She had me pinned to the wall, and I remember trying to lift my hands up to calm everything down, but I just . . . I couldn't move them. And then, she was, ah, then I was sitting on the ground, with a condom on my dick, and I was inside her."

"You were inside her." The doctor frowned. "Would it be more fitting to say that she was *on* you?"

I shrugged in response. "It was just . . . a very confusing fucking night."

"Because you didn't consent."

"I was *hard*."

"Having an erection is a perfectly human reaction to stimulation."

"Pretty sure I came, too."

"Again, ejaculation is the body's response to stimulation."

"Yeah, well." I threw my hands up and laughed. "I went back and willingly fucked her a least a dozen more times over the years, so it mustn't have been that bad."

The doctor didn't laugh. "But you weren't willing that night. And even if you were, you were intoxicated and incapable of giving consent."

"Can we not?" I said, tone warning. "I've already heard this spiel from Shannon, and I'm not buying in, okay? I'm not a victim. I wasn't fucking raped. I got high and I fucked around. It happens."

"Are you open to acknowledging the possibility that you were taken advantage of?"

"No."

"Why not?"

"Because I'm not a victim."

"Can I suggest something?"

"Go for it."

"If your sister came to you with the same scenario, some random boy from her class at school had taken her virginity in the same way yours was taken, how would you react?"

I stiffened. "Don't."

"How would you feel about that, Joey?"

"Murderous."

"Because?"

"Because it wouldn't be right, dammit!"

"But it's okay that it happened to you because you're a male?"

I opened my mouth to answer her, but nothing came out.

Fuck.

"I . . . " Shaking my head, I hissed out a growl. "I see what you're doing here, doc, and it won't work."

"You have been let down and taken advantage of in terrible ways," she continued. "I understand why you refuse to consider yourself a victim, and whether I agree or not, I respect your narrative, but I need you to accept that what happened to you was *not* acceptable and a serious breach of trust and consent."

Birth plans

AOIFE

"So, you've hit the twenty-eight-week mark," the doctor mused, wiping the gunk off my belly when she was finished scanning me. "How are you feeling?"

"On the way over here, we drove past a field with a pregnant pony in it," I told her, as she helped pull me off the examination table so that I could adjust my clothes. "I swear, that poor pony was wider horizontally than she was long vertically." I blew out a breath and padded back to the desk. "So, yeah, I feel like that pony."

"Aoife," Mam chastised from her chair.

"What?" I huffed, lowering myself down on the seat next to my mother. "She asked."

Smothering a laugh, I watched as the doctor flicked through my maternity folder, scribbling and jotting down notes as she went. "You'll come back to see us at 32 weeks, and again at 36 weeks. After that, you'll come bi-weekly until 38 weeks when you'll come weekly until you deliver."

Deliver.

Jesus, that was a scary word.

"Have you discussed your birth plan with a midwife?"

"Yeah." I squirmed in my chair, feeling a sudden spark of panic rise up in me. "I've been through the plan."

"And you've chosen your birth partner?"

"Me," Mam interjected. "I'll be going with her when she delivers."

"No." I rolled my eyes. "My boyfriend will be coming with me."

"Aoife." Mam's eyes filled with concern. "We don't know if he'll be back by then."

"He'll be back," I confirmed, turning my attention to the doctor. "Joey Lynch," I said, pointing at my file. "You can jot that down. He's my birth partner."

Breakthroughs and begging

JOEY

"Come on, Joey," the good doctor coaxed, as she sat opposite me in my own personal prison cell. Yeah, we had moved on from Joseph to Joey, and Dr. Bianca Rushton to Dr. B, or just plain doc. "We have another forty-five minutes of our daily session left. You've been doing so well at articulating your feelings. Don't clam up now."

Jesus, she was a demon of a woman.

Ruthless in her quest for whatever the hell she wanted.

I pitied her husband.

Poor bastard.

"I already told you," I said, leaning back in my seat and folding my arms across my chest. "You can have more out of me when I get a phone call."

Smiling, she leaned back in her chair, mirroring my actions. "To phone Aoife."

"*Obviously.*"

"And say what?"

"How about I'm really fucking sorry for skipping out on you, for a start," I snapped. "And maybe check on my baby, while I'm at it? You know, the usual."

"Could we step back for a moment and consider the possibility that Aoife is extremely proud of you completing your treatment program?"

"It would be a lot easier to believe if you let me speak to her."

"You know the rules, Joey. This program is for *you*. To focus on yourself for a change. Not on your siblings, or your girlfriend, or anyone else. I know it's a foreign feeling for you, to put yourself before others, but this time-out from the outside world is necessary for your recovery."

"Like you'd know a goddamn thing about it."

"Put the gun down, Joey," she replied with a sad smile. "The fight's over."

"Yeah, well, I've been fighting for so long, I don't know how to take my finger off the trigger," I muttered, cracking my knuckles. "Fuck it, maybe I *am* crazy. Maybe it is better that I can't talk to her. I've already dragged her through the ringer."

"What makes you think you're 'crazy'?"

"Gee, I don't know," I drawled out sarcastically. "How about the fact that I'm hearing my dead father's voice in my head, to go with my dead mother's one."

"Trauma reveals itself in many shapes and versions."

"Yeah, well, in my head, I'm still fighting a war that I *can't* win. Against people who *can't* hurt me anymore, but still *do*. So, I reckon that goes a little deeper than trauma, doc."

"Good, Joey," she surprised me by saying. "That's *really* good. Keep talking."

Deciding I had nothing left to lose, I let her have it.

Every fucked up thought and notion in my head.

I didn't know if any of it made sense, and I cared even less.

She wanted words.

Well, she could have them.

"I tried to get them out of there, so many fucking times, but I always caved," I blurted out. "There was always a part of me that held out hope for her. The same way she held out hope for him. In the end, look where it got the both of us. *He* killed her, and I stayed for as long as I did to prevent that. The night I walked out, it happened, how can I get over that? How can I ever move on from it? The guilt is drowning me on the daily." Blowing out a frustrated breath, I hissed, "It all feels so fucking needless. I could've stopped it all from happening. I could have saved her if I'd just stuck in there. But I lost it, my temper, my patience, whatever I had left inside of me, I lost it that night. And because I lost that, I ended up losing everything. Those kids don't have a mother and it's because I walked away."

"Those kids don't have a mother because their father – your father – killed her, not you. He was willing to kill *all* of you."

"I have a hard time with living," I admitted. "Being alive is a challenge for me because I don't work right. I don't seem to have the right tools for going through the motions. It's like I'm stuck on fight mode. I'm constantly watching for danger. Doesn't matter if it's there or not, I'm programed to sniff it out. Wasn't so bad when I self-medicated. The drugs took the edge off everything. Made being alive bearable. Until I couldn't go an hour without them. Then I wanted to live even less."

"That sounds miserable."

"No shit."

"Keep going."

"I can't trust anyone," I added. "Not you. Not my thoughts. Not the people around me. No one."

"Your siblings?"

"That's different." I narrowed my eyes in disgust. "They're babies."

"Your sister is going to be seventeen on her next birthday. That hardly makes her a baby, Joey."

"She's still a baby to me," I argued. "Anyone whose nappies I've changed or knees I've put plasters on will always be a baby in my eyes. Besides, they're not included in that statement."

"And Darren?"

"You really want to push the boat out today, don't ya?"

She laughed. "Let's go there, shall we?"

"I'd rather not," I replied flatly. "I wasn't entirely hating today's session. Bring him up and I've a feeling that'll change."

"Not entirely hating today's session." She grinned. "That's a compliment if ever I heard one. It only took, what eleven weeks?"

"Don't get too cocky."

"Would you like to know what I think?"

"No."

"Humor me."

"Again, no."

"I think your relationship with Darren is one of your biggest triggers."

"I don't do triggers, doc."

"Because he broke your heart," she pushed on. "Because he broke your trust."

"On the contrary, he taught me a valuable lesson," I replied coolly.

"Which was?"

"Everyone leaves, and nobody fucks you over like your own blood."

"But Darren came back."

"Too little, too late."

"I think you desperately miss your big brother."

I snorted. "Like fuck."

"He wants to visit you."

I stiffened. "And?"

"And I think it might help you heal."

"No." I was up and out of my seat within seconds. "You tell that prick to go back to Belfast and go back to forgetting about me. And if I'm suddenly being allowed visitors, then there's only one face I want to see."

"Do you think, at her late stage in pregnancy, it would be wise for Aoife to travel four hours to visit you? Do you think it would be good for her emotionally to have so little time with you, and then have to leave again?"

My heart gunned in my chest.

No, I didn't think that.

"Then just let me phone her."

"Joey—"

"Please," I bit out. "I will do whatever the fuck you want. I'll talk about all the shit. I'll deal with Darren. Just let me have one phone call with my girl. Please, doc. I don't do begging, but I'll do it for her."

Out of the blue

AOIFE

I was half-way through my shift at work, sweltering in the early August heat, and feeling like I had hooves for feet, when my boss stopped me dead in my tracks.

"Aoife," he said, taking the tray I was attempting to carry into the kitchen out of my hands. "How are ya, love?"

"Fine," I replied, instantly suspicious. "How are you, Garry?"

"To be honest, I'm a bit concerned about you, love."

"Why?"

"Well . . ." Red-faced, he gestured to my stomach and shrugged. "I'm just thinking that it might be time you consider taking it easy, pet. You look exhausted. Absolutely dead on your feet."

Ha.

No fucking way was he getting rid of me that easily. If I left early, it could mess with my maternity leave.

He might not take me back afterwards.

I had too much to lose.

I had a baby to raise, dammit.

"I'm not due for another eight weeks," I reminded him. "I don't plan on starting my maternity leave for another six weeks, Garry. You know this. We agreed on it."

"I know what we agreed, but aren't you tired, love?"

I'm beyond tired. "I'm happy to work."

"I don't want you carrying heavy trays back and forth to the kitchen anymore."

"Then put me behind the bar," I argued. "Or doing the pot wash in the kitchen. Whatever. I don't care. But I need to work, Gar. I need the money."

"And you're a great little worker," he tried to fob me off by saying. "We're lucky to have you."

"Then let me get back to work," I said, snatching my tray back, and stepping around him. "Because I have another six weeks of work left, and I plan on showing up for every shift."

"Look at the size of you," Paul whistled, when I came to take his order a little while later. He was sitting alone in a booth and that pissed me off no end, because he could have easily taken a spot at the bar and leave the space for larger groups. "Jesus, I've seen women having triplets with smaller bumps."

"Hello to you, too, Paul," I drawled, not taking one word of it to heart. Not when it was true. My bump *was* huge. I'd heard just about every joke, snide comment, and surprised gasp in the book.

The baby was measuring so big that I had been tested four times for gestational diabetes. The results came back negative every single time. Apparently, I was just growing a baby sumo-wrestler.

Even Mam had warned me off buying anything in the newborn size, advising that 0-3 months was a better choice for the little whopper.

Yeah, that wasn't terrifying at all.

"What can I get you?" I asked, flipping over to a blank page on my little notepad, and retrieving my pencil from behind my ear. "Today's specials are seafood chowder and roast lamb, with the chef's homemade mint sauce."

"I actually wanted a word," he said, reaching up to scratch the back of his neck, as he eyed my belly nervously. "With you."

"I'm sorry, but a conversation with me isn't on the menu for today," I replied. "Neither is forgiveness."

"Then I'll have the roast lamb," he said with an awkward shrug. "And a pint of Guinness."

"You've got it." Snapping my notepad shut, I turned on my heels and headed back to the kitchen with his order before moving for the bar to pull him a pint of the black stuff.

When I returned a few minutes later with his order and set it down in front of him, my ex did the unthinkable and curled his hand around my wrist. "Two minutes," he said, tone full of urgency. "Just two minutes of your time. That's all I'm asking for."

"Why should I give you one second of my time?" I demanded, yanking my hand away. "You're damn lucky I need this job, because in any other circumstances, you'd be wearing that pint."

"I know," he agreed, holding his hands up. "And I would one hundred percent deserve it. But I'm leaving for college in a couple of weeks, and I couldn't go without at least trying to make amends."

I arched a brow. "You want to make amends?"

"I want to apologize," he offered. "For what I did to you. Telling the whole class you were pregnant? It was fucking terrible of me."

"Yeah," I deadpanned. "It was."

"I've spent a lot of time thinking about my behavior," he added. "About the way I treated you when we were together."

"I don't see why any of this needs to be rehashed, Paul," I quickly said. "School's finished. We're finished. You're going off to college to start a brand-new life. I'm about to have a baby with your arch-nemesis. Let's just leave it at that, yeah?"

"That's precisely why we need to talk," he said. "Please, Aoif, just give me five minutes of your time."

"First you said two minutes," I grumbled, plopping down on the seat opposite his. "Now you're saying five. I'll give you three and a half."

"Thank you." Releasing a sigh of relief, he smiled at me. "Seriously, thank you."

Remaining stony-faced, I rested my hands on my bump and waited for him to get to the point.

"I was a shitty boyfriend to you," he started off by saying. "I didn't pay you enough attention. I never asked you what you wanted to do. I put my needs, my feelings, and my wants before yours. I fucked around behind your back constantly, and then blew a head gasket when you gave me a dose of my own medicine."

"Paul, it's in the past."

"Yeah, it is," he agreed with a nod. "But that doesn't change the fact that I feel horrible about how it ended. Especially about revealing your pregnancy. And afterwards," he continued. "When it all came out about what Lynchy was going through at home." He shook his head. "And then the fire?" He exhaled heavily. "I never felt shittier."

"Yeah."

"I tried to talk to you at school after the funeral," he reminded me. "To apologize. But you were completely closed off."

"I had a lot on my mind."

"I know," he agreed. "I just . . . I feel so bad about everything, Aoif."

"Listen, it's not like I was an angel," I offered. "You were paranoid about my friendship with Joey, and you had every right to be. It might not have been physical, but you were dead on the money when you said that I was having an emotional affair with him."

"But a lot of that had to do with the fact that he gave you everything I didn't. I gave you presents. He gave you his presence," he said calmly. "I didn't understand it at the time, why you were so insistent about being his friend. I thought having a girlfriend was all about material shit, but then I would see you hanging out with him, and he had *nothing* to offer you, and still managed to give you *everything* you wanted."

I shrugged helplessly. "Where's this change of heart coming from?"

"Because I don't want to go off to college and start a new life without making peace with my old one," he explained. "And whether you want to hear it or not, you were a huge part of my old life for a very long time."

"Okay." Slightly confused, I leaned back and said, "Quick question."
"Shoot."

"Bella Wilkinson." I shook my head. "Lad, what were you *thinking*?"
"Full disclosure?"

"Go for it."

"I was with her more than once." His cheeks reddened. "When we were a couple."

"Well, shit." I grumbled, patting my belly. "Now, I'm really glad I kicked her ass."

"I figured you were screwing Lynchy behind my back, and that was why you refused to sleep with me, so I went hell for leather with pretty much any girl who looked sideways at me."

"I wasn't screwing Joey," I told him. "Nothing physical happened with Joe until that kiss in fifth year." I narrowed my eyes. "When you and Billy double teamed him before getting him arrested."

He winced. "Yeah, I know that now."

"So, speaking about batshit girls." The baby jabbed me in the ribs, and I shifted around in discomfort. "How's Danielle?"

"Danielle?" He laughed humorlessly. "Danielle was a distraction from you. We parted ways shortly after the leaving cert exams in June. Last I heard she was seeing Bella's ex from Tommen."

"Yeah, well." I shrugged noncommittally. "I hate to say it, but you probably dodged a bullet with that one." Snorting, I added, "Which is rich coming from your knocked-up ex."

He laughed in response before saying. "Listen, I wanted to do something for you before I left. Help you in some way."

"You don't need to do anything for me, Paul."

"I know you're on your own right now, while Lynchy is at rehab—"

"Joe's coming home," I was quick to declare, hands moving protectively to my stomach. "He's getting better and then he's coming back for his family."

My ex shifted in discomfort.

"I'm sorry if that's still hard for you to hear," I added. "That I love him? But it's the truth, and I'm never going to give up on him."

"Yeah," he replied with a heavy sigh. "I know you're not, which is why I did it."

"What?" Sitting upright, I studied him warily. "What did you do, Paul?"

"I'm guessing you didn't read today's paper."

"No." I rested my elbows on the table and leaned forward. "Why?"

"There was a huge drug bust in Ballylaggin last night," he blew my mind by saying. "According to my father, they've had eyes on the Holland brothers for a long time now."

My eyes widened. "Are you serious?"

Paul nodded. "He's being remanded in Portlaoise until sentencing."

"Shane is?"

"And more with him," he confirmed. "According to my father, Shane's already up for sexual assault, GBH, and several other unanswered charges. Dad reckons the judge will throw the book at him. He'll be lucky if he doesn't celebrate his thirtieth in prison."

"That's six years." I felt my body sag in a rush of instant relief. "You're saying he's going away for six years?"

"Longer if the DPP have their way."

"Jesus Christ." I blew out a ragged breath and clutched my chest. "How did this happen?"

Paul shrugged. "Someone tipped the drug squad off about a shipment of coke, with a street value of six hundred grand."

"*What?*" My mouth fell open as awareness dawned on me. As I took in everything he *wasn't* saying. "How would someone know to tip them off?"

"Maybe someone has friends in the right places," he offered, reaching across the table to cover my hand with his. "Maybe before they moved on, someone wanted to make sure his first love had a fighting chance with her first love."

Hello, brother

JOEY

One of the earliest steps in my treatment plan was to make amends, which was how I knew I would never get off the ladder of recovery for three reasons.

First, I wasn't going to apologize to anyone for surviving.

Second, fuck that.

Third, I didn't know if I had it in me to fight the battle that I was told would last a lifetime.

Because I was an addict.

I would *always* be an addict.

I would never *stop* wanting to use.

The prospect of fighting my urges for the rest of myself was depressing.

Still, I woke up this morning and dragged my ass out of bed, completed all of my chores, and sat my ass in the visitors' room, with only one goal in my head.

Sit through a meeting with Darren and get that coveted phone call privilege.

Dr. B had convinced the whole treatment team that a reconciliation between me and Darren would be hugely beneficial to my recovery. In my humble opinion, I considered it to be the worst form of emotional blackmail, to dangle a call with my girlfriend in front of me like carrot. But hey, the fuck did I know?

I wasn't the one with the fancy degree.

I was the washed-up addict, depending on these people to patch me up and send me back into the world.

Dammit, though, I hated that it had to be Darren.

I would have preferred anyone else to walk through that visitors' room door and that was not an exaggeration.

Hell, I would have even preferred Gussie.

At least he would have smuggled me some cigarettes.

Pushing the sleeves of my grey jumper down to my wrists, I concealed the scars and marks on my veins. Jesus, it felt like a lifetime ago, but I knew I was only one slip away from returning to that world.

It couldn't happen.

Now that I had a clear head, I knew that I could never go back.

Not even weed.

It was too fucking risky.

The urge was still there, though, bubbling away just beneath the surface, and I was beginning to come to terms with the fact that it would never entirely leave me.

I would always crave opioids.

I would always crave heroin.

In a fucked-up way, I was starting to make *peace* with it.

When Dr. B finally walked into the room with my brother in tow, I felt the walls I'd been trying to lower shoot back up at a rapid rate.

"Joey," Darren acknowledged, eyes filling with tears, as he stood in the middle of the room with a bunch of flowers in his hands. "It's good to see you, brother."

"Darren." I stood up and offered him a curt nod. "Please tell me those aren't for me."

He glanced down at the flowers in his hand and choked out a laugh, as tears trickled down his cheeks. "I didn't want to show up empty-handed."

"I wish you had," I drawled sarcastically. "You're going to ruin my street cred in here."

"Nah," he chuckled, closing the space between us. "You're too notorious."

When he pulled me in for a hug, I forced myself to not shove him away. Instead, I offered him a small pat on the back.

It was the best I could do.

It was progress.

"Let's sit down and get started, shall we?" Dr. B suggested, leading my brother over to a large leather couch.

Instinctively, I walked over to the one opposite.

"You have no idea how happy I was to get the call," Darren got the ball rolling by saying. "When I got home from work and Alex told me that your doctor had called to say I could visit—"

"Hold up," I interrupted, leaning back on the couch and folding my arms across my chest. "You're back in Belfast."

He nodded.

"Since when?"

"What do you mean?"

"I mean how long did it take before you left the kids?" I arched a brow. "How long did it take before you went back to your real life?"

"Joey."

"Hey, I'm not judging you." I shrugged. "Look at where I'm sitting, Dar. I'm in no position to throw stones."

"They're in good hands with John and Edel."

Yeah, I didn't doubt it. But it still pissed me off that he left them. Especially when I wasn't there for them, either.

"Joey," Dr. B interjected. "Remember how we talked about relinquishing control. You are not your siblings' parent, and neither is Darren."

I didn't respond, because I wanted to get my damn phone call, and the explicit words on the tip of my tongue would assure that I didn't.

The good doctor and Darren delved into deep conversation then.

About my issues.

About my recovery.

About my sixty-day chip.

About what a good little recovering addict I was.

About bla-fucking-bla.

Entirely uninterested, I zoned in and out of the conversation, I nodded at all the right cues, not really giving two shits what he thought about me. My feelings towards him were too complicated to be worked through in a therapy session.

They had built up over the course of almost six years.

It would take at *least* that amount to time to resolve them.

It was only the mention of an extended stay in treatment that had my ears pricking up and my attention riveted to the conversation. "What the fuck?"

"Joey, calm down please, it's just a suggestion," the doctor began to say, but I was already on my feet.

"No." I shook my head and paced the room. "No, no, no. I'm out of here in three weeks. I've done my time."

"Joe, if the medical team feel that you'll benefit from an extra couple of months, then I think you need to listen to them," Darren tried to interject, but I wasn't having it.

"They didn't suggest it, asshole," I shot back. "You did."

"Because I think you need it," he argued. "I think it might be good for you."

"And I think you need to shut the fuck up," I sneered. "I've done everything I've been asked to do. I've done the detoxing. I've done the counselling. I've done the group fucking therapy. I've planted the fucking flowers and painted the pottery." Furious, I turned to glare at the doctor. "I agreed to do two weeks of detox and twelve weeks of treatment. Not a day over it."

"Actually, once you voluntarily signed yourself into our care, the length of your treatment is at our discretion."

"Bullshit."

"Sit down, Joe," Darren tried again. "Just hear us out, will you?"

"I'm not staying here another day longer than I agreed to," I warned, shaking my head at the both of them. "My girlfriend is due in September. Not that either one of you give a shit, but I've already missed most of her pregnancy, but if you think that I'm missing the birth, too, then you're fucking crazier than I am!"

"This is exactly what I was telling you on the phone," Darren told the doctor. "He can't see beyond her. He'll put her needs first, even if it's not what he needs."

"Excuse me?" I glared at my brother. "You two were talking about me?"

"It's protocol to have an informal weekly meeting with your next of kin to discuss your treatment," Dr. B explained calmly. "You already know this."

"Except that he's not my next of fucking anything," I snapped. "I thought you were giving the updates to Edel and John. They're the ones footing the bill for this place, aren't they?"

"We've been informing Mr. and Mrs. Kavanagh of your progress, but neither one is your next of kin, so the information we've been able to provide them with has been limited."

"Who put him down?"

"You did, Joe," Darren offered calmly.

"No." I shook my head. "No, I wouldn't."

"You signed the forms, Joe."

"The forms *you* filled in. The ones you had *me* sign," I shot back accusingly. "You shouldn't have done that, Dar. You know it should have been her," I continued to argue, voice rising. "I have three weeks left, and I'm out of here. I don't care what either one of you say."

"Listen," my brother tried to placate. "Nothing's set in stone, okay? All I'm saying is that I think it might be better for you to stay for another few months."

"And miss the birth of my child?"

"Please just consider what I'm saying," he tried to argue. "Think about the pressure that kind of an environment would be on you. You're just coming out the other side of this, Joe. What you've been through this year? I swear to you that Aoife will understand. And the baby? The baby wouldn't even know. I mean, fathers in Ireland didn't even attend the births until—"

"Okay, you need to leave."

"Joey, come on."

"No, you need to get the fuck away from me before I lose my mind," I warned, holding a hand up to warn him off when he moved towards me. "Now, Darren."

"I think that might be best," Dr. B said when he looked to her for help. "Joe, please . . . "

When he tried to speak to me again, I turned my back and walked over to the window, refusing point blank to engage with him.

It wasn't until my brother had left the room, that I released the death grip I had on the windowsill.

"How are you feeling after that, Joey?" Dr. B asked, returning to her perch on the couch.

"Like I want to put my fist through the wall," I bit out.

"And?"

"And through my brother's head."

"Tell me something," she pushed. "When your back was to the ropes just now, what was your first thought? Your immediate inclination?"

"My immediate inclination was to put my fist through my brother's head," I repeated in a flat tone. "And the wall. But his head more."

The doctor smiled. "Then you passed."

"*What?*"

Her smile widened. "You were thrust into confrontation with a person who triggers you like few can, and your immediate urge wasn't to use."

"I wanted to physically harm him," I said, brows furrowed in confusion. "How does that mean I passed anything?"

"Did you harm him?"

"In my head."

"In your head is acceptable," she laughed. "Congratulations, Joey. You've earned yourself a phone call."

Incoming calls

AOIFE

The call came on a Sunday night.

The one I'd spent the entire summer waiting for.

When the unknown number flashed across my screen, I debated answering, but something inside of me told me *not* to ignore it.

Sprawled out on the couch, looking like a beached walrus, and stuffing my face with grapes, I snagged my phone off the sitting room floor and clicked accept. "Hello?" I said with a yawn, using the remote to turn the volume down on the television, where *Scream*, my old creature comfort, was playing.

"Molloy."

My heart.

My poor, poor heart jackknifed in my chest at the sound of his familiar deep timbre. "Joe?"

"Yeah, baby, it's me."

"Joe?" I cried, face contorting with emotion, as I tried to roll myself off the couch, knocking my punnet of grapes all over the floor in the process. "Is that really you?"

"It's really me," his voice came down the line and I had to sit back down because my legs were shaking too badly to keep me upright.

"Oh my god." The floodgates opened and I cried loud and ugly down the line for a solid three minutes before I had the ability to compose myself. "Hey, stud."

"How's my queen?"

"Missing you," I choked out through tears. "How are you calling me right now? Are you home? Oh my god, please tell me that you're back in Ballylaggin and on the way over to my house."

"Soon," he told me. "I promise, baby. I'll be back to you soon."

"Then *how*?"

"Finally earned myself some phone call privileges," he explained. "So, expect a *lot* of phone calls."

"What are you calling off?"

"There's a communal phone in the day room."

"I'm surprised you remembered my number?"

"Are you kidding? I memorized your number when I was twelve."

"You have no idea how good it is to hear your voice," I told him through tearful laughter. "God, Joe, I'm shaking so hard I can hardly hold my phone to my ear."

"I know the feeling," I heard him say. "I'm sorry it took me so long to call you. I've been trying since the day I left, I promise. It's just . . . " He sighed heavily down the line. "They have all these rules and shit here, and there's no getting around any of them."

"So, you're doing okay?" I dared to ask, and then clammed up tight with tension. "You're staying clean?"

"Sixty-two days," he replied, sounding more even toned than he had in years. "They even gave me this weird little gold chip for hitting the two-month mark."

"They did?" Sniffling, I clenched my eyes shut and sagged against the couch. "I'm so proud of you."

"So, how's it going?"

"Uh, you know," I replied with a sigh, feet tapping with excitement, as I feigned playful boredom. "This asshole guy I used to go out with abandoned me, so I've been pretty pissed about that."

"What a prick."

"He is," I agreed with a nod. "Turns out I'm having his baby, too."

"No shit."

"I shit you not."

"And the prick still left you?"

"Yep." I feigned another sigh. "Turns out he's this huge drug addict."

"I hear drug addicts make the worst boyfriends."

"They really do."

"Does he at least have a big dick?"

"He definitely has big dick energy."

"Okay, I'm not even going to pretend to know what that means."

Sniffling, I choked out a pained laugh. "Keep talking. I need to hear your voice."

"Aoif." There was a pause and then his words came in a flurry. "Christ, Aoif, I'm so sorry, baby. For all of it. For leaving you. For the letter. Jesus, I can't into put into words how bad I feel for everything I put you through these past few months. When I came here, I wasn't myself. The truth is, I haven't been myself in a very long time. I'm not sure if you've ever met the real me or if you'll even like him, but I'm trying. I'm trying so fucking hard to get back to you—"

"I already love him," I blurted out. "All of your shapes and versions, remember?"

"You have no idea how much it means to hear you say that."

"What? I love you?"

I heard him sniff before saying, "Yeah."

"Well, I love you, Joey Lynch," I croaked out, wiping my cheeks with my free hand. "And apparently, I can't stop."

"Thank fuck for that," he replied. "Because, apparently, I can't stop loving you, either, Aoife Molloy."

"Joe, I'm so – ugh!" I sucked in a sharp breath.

"What's wrong?" he demanded, instantly on alert.

"Nothing. Baby's just kicking me really hard these days."

He was quiet for a long moment, clearly absorbing my words, before asking, "How's my baby?"

"Growing by the minute," I half-laughed/half-sobbed as I stroked my bump. "You should see me now, Joe. I'm like a beached whale."

"I wish I was there with you," he admitted quietly. "So fucking sorry for leaving you alone in this, Molloy. You'll never know how much."

"Just come home," I whispered, feeling a shiver roll through me. "Get better and come home to us."

"I am."

"Wow."

"Wow, what?"

"You said *I am*." I clenched my eyes shut as a wave of hopeful warmth washed over my heart. "Not *I will*." Sniffling, I added, "You don't know how long I've waited to hear you say the words *I am*."

"About time, huh?"

"Just a tad overdue."

"That's putting it mildly."

"Joe." I couldn't stop myself from smiling as I soaked in every second of having his voice on the other line. "I can't believe we're finally talking."

"I know," he agreed thickly. "So, come on, queen, talk to me. Tell me what's happening at home. Give me all your gossip."

"Oh, so *now* you want my gossip?"

"The heart wants what it wants, Molloy."

"Yeah, it does." I bit down on my lip and grinned. "So, gossip. Hm . . . Al and Podge are in America for the summer."

"No shit?"

"I shit you not." I choked out a laugh. "They managed to snag J-1 visas."

"Doing what?"

"Nannying."

"Are you shitting me?"

"I swear it's true."

"Jesus Christ," he chuckled, sounding half-amused, half-appalled. "Those two shouldn't be left in charge of a tray of eggs."

"Hey, you're preaching to the converted," I agreed with a snicker. "And Casey's gone to Benidorm for two weeks with some of our class from school, so you can only imagine the deviant adventures she's having over there."

"Actually, I'd rather not," he drawled. "So, you're alone, queen?"

"Yeah." I sighed in contentment. "But it's not so bad."

"No?"

"Not since you called."

"Aoif."

"Oh my god. I almost forgot to tell you!" I gasped and slapped a hand on my head. "Damn this baby brain."

"Tell me what?"

"I had a visit from Paul."

Silence.

"Chill, Joe." His silence spoke volumes and I rolled my eyes. "I'm eight months pregnant. He's not looking to steal me away."

"I wouldn't put anything past that prick."

"Well, that prick came bearing the most amazing news."

"Which is?"

I sucked in a deep breath before blurting, "Shane Holland is in prison."

Another long stretch of silence followed.

"Did you hear me, Joe?" I repeated when he didn't respond. "The drug squad caught him up in a massive drug bust. According to Paul's dad, he's looking at some serious time."

"Can you, ah . . ." I heard him exhale shakily before adding, "Can you say that again?"

Not leaving anything out, I told him word for word about the conversation I had with Paul at The Dinniman. "Of course, I wasn't entirely sure if he was being truthful," I added when I finished. "So, I did a little snooping of my own and it's all true, Joe. He's gone."

"Fuck."

"How do you feel about that?"

"How do I feel?"

"Yeah." I shrugged. "I mean, I know you had this weird bond with Shane."

"Aoife, I feel like the weight of the world has just been lifted off my shoulders," he interrupted me to say. "I was dreading having to deal with him."

"Yeah, I know what you mean," I agreed. "Every time I had to pass him on the street since you left, he would wink or leer, or make some snide comment about how he couldn't wait for his best customer to come back to town."

"He didn't threaten you, did he?"

"No, no, nothing like that," I replied honestly. "He was just being Shane. His usual asshole self."

"I can't believe he's actually in prison."

"Well, now you have one more thing to look forward to when you come home in three weeks," I told him with a smile. "A Shane-less Ballylaggin."

More silence.

It unsettled me.

"Joe?"

"Listen to me," he said, tone thick and gravelly. "I don't want you to worry about anything, okay, but there's talks of them keeping me here a little longer."

My heart sank into my ass. "How much longer?"

"I don't know."

"What?" My breath hitched in my throat. "But you're supposed to get out on the 22nd of August, right? Fourteen weeks, Joe. That's what they said. The first two weeks for detox and then the twelve-week treatment plan afterwards. I've been marking it off on the calendar. That's what they said."

"I know, baby," he groaned, sounding pained "But Darren went meddling in shit he has no business meddling in, and apparently, I can't sign myself out. I have to be discharged, and the doctor heading up my treatment thinks it's a good idea."

"But if you stay, that means you won't be home in time—"

"I'll be home before you have the baby," he cut me off and said. "I *will* be there for you."

"Joe," I squeezed out, clutching the phone with a death grip. "I can't do this on my own."

"You won't have to," he vowed. "I'm coming home to you, Molloy. I promise."

Foster mothers

JOEY

Ridiculously nervous, I dialed the number on the piece of paper in my hand and listened as it rang.

Ring.

Ring.

Ring.

Ring.

"Hello?" The sound of her thick Dublin accent was momentarily foreign to my ears. After all, it had been a while since I had heard her.

"Edel?" I cleared my throat. "It's ah, it's Joey Lynch."

"Joey!" she squealed – actually fucking squealed – down the line. "Oh love, it's so good to hear your voice. How are you? Are you well? Are you eating? Have they been treating you kindly? How's the detox going? Now, don't you worry about a thing down here. The boys and Shannon are in safe hands. How are you fixed for underpants, pet? Do you have enough of them? And socks? I sent up more tracksuits, but if you need more, I can—"

"I'm grand," I quickly said, preventing her from continuing her ramble. "I'm ah, I'm better than grand, actually."

"Ah, love, that's the best news I've heard all year." Her tone was laced with affection and emotion. "John and I never doubted you for a second."

Her response momentarily took me aback, and I had to compose myself before I could speak. "I just, ah, I finally earned phone privileges, and I, ah, I wanted to call to check in."

"Well, I'm delighted to hear your voice," she replied. "You sound so well in yourself, pet."

"Yeah." Feeling like a tool, I leaned against the phone attached to the wall of the day room and clenched my eyes shut, second guessing myself throughout the entire conversation. "I'm a lot more clear-headed these days."

"Well, John and I have a big surprise for you when you get home next week."

"That's actually what I wanted to talk to you about."

"Joey." Her voice was laced with concern now. "You're coming to live with us, and that's final. I don't want to hear a word of protest, and if you even think about going out on your own, I should warn you now that I have the nose of a bloodhound. You need only ask Johnny and Gerard. I *will* sniff you out and bring you home."

"No, that's not what I'm ... " Pausing, I pinched the bridge of my nose, as I strived to say the right thing. "I don't have any plans to go out on my own for a while." Couldn't afford to if I wanted to. "I'm grateful for the roof over my head you're offering," I added, chewing on my lip. "I don't want to be separated from them." *The kids.*

"You'll never have to be," she soothed down the line. "Once you're home, love, you'll stay home. With your family."

"That's the problem." I gnawed on my knuckle as a surge of anger rose inside of me. "Darren went talking to my team behind my back."

"Darren?" I could hear the surprise in her voice. "What did he say to them, love?"

"He was discussing my treatment plan with them. Apparently, he's down as my next of kin – by the way, can you get that changed for me? Because it's supposed to be Aoife."

"Of course, I can. That makes sense."

"Thanks. Anyway, they were talking, and they want me to stay on at rehab."

She was quiet for a long moment before asking, "And what do you think, Joey love?"

"Honestly?"

"Always."

"I'm ready to go home now, but the fact that the doctor is *agreeing* with Darren has me second guessing myself."

"In what way?"

"She hasn't put me wrong yet." I chewed on my nails, beyond anxious. "What if she's right? What if I'm wrong? What if I fuck this up?"

"How long are they wanting you to stay for?"

"I don't know, Edel," I forced myself to say. "But I can't do it. I can't stay any longer than I already have. I can't do it to Aoife. Not after everything I've put her through."

"Is there a way to negotiate?" she suggested. "How about another two weeks treatment? Although, if you feel you're ready to come home on the 22nd like originally planned, then you're ready. You have excellent instincts, love. Don't let anyone shake you."

"I think the doctors were expecting Darren to vouch for me when he came to visit, and when he didn't, it threw some red flags up for them."

"Can I do something to help?" she asked. "I mean, I would never force myself into your private life, Joey love. You're a brilliant, capable young man, and I respect that you aren't a child. That's not the kind of relationship I want us to have, but if you need me to step in at any time on your behalf, then I am willing and ready to go to bat for you."

"You could vouch for me?" I said and then exhaled a shaky breath before admitting, "Because I could really use your help."

Meet the parents . . . kind of

JOEY

Like a flurry of unrestrained blonde energy, Edel Kavanagh strutted into the room the morning after our phone call, reminding me of a glammed-up version of Sarah Connor from *The Terminator*.

Flanking her in his usual attire, which consisted of a top end, tailored suit, with an amused expression etched on his face, and a briefcase in hand, was John Sr.

"Joey," Edel exclaimed when she spotted me leaning over the win-dowsill, thoroughly enjoying the cigarette I'd managed to snag from one the security guards I'd become friendly with after giving him a hand to change a flat, while trying not to set off the smoke alarm.

As soon as her eyes landed on me, the hard expression she'd been wearing melted away. "Oh love, would you look at you." Shaking her head, she smiled widely, as she rushed towards me. "Look at him, John. Isn't he only handsome?"

"Sweetheart, we've talked about this," John tried to interject, but she was already up in my personal space with her arms wrapped tightly around me.

"I ah . . . " Feeling awkward, I quickly tossed the butt out the window patted her back, mentally counting down from five before escaping from her stranglehold. "When I said I could use your help, I didn't mean you had to drive halfway across the country to see me."

"Excuse me," one of the porters rushed into my room, all red-faced and flushed. "All visitors need to report to reception. And like I told you already, lady, patients are forbidden to have guests in their room."

"Ah, would you cool your jets, detective inspector," Edel drawled sarcastically, dismissing him with a flick of her wrist. "Do I look like I'm smuggling contraband up my backside?"

"Edel," John said wearily.

"Now." Turning her attention back to me, she reached up and pushed my hair off my face and smiled. "Let's go, love."

"Go where?"

"To sort this mess out."

"As you're well aware, my husband and I have been awarded guardianship of the Lynch children," Edel declared a little while later, as she paced the visitors' room, while John looked on from his perch on the leather couch with his usual amused expression. Sitting beside him was a stressed looking Darren. "If Joey was under eighteen, then he would be legally under our care, too." She turned to stare at Dr. B. "However, I consider age to be just a number, doctor. That boy belongs with us. He has a home with our family – *his* family – for the rest of his life. If you have concerns about his ability to cope after leaving treatment, then be rest assured that he will have the world of support at his fingertips."

"His brother has voiced some concerns about the pressures he feels Joey will be exposed to upon discharge."

"My brother's a dick," I sneered, glaring across the room at enemy number one.

Darren sighed heavily. "Joey."

"What?" I shrugged unapologetically. "You *are*."

"I'm not doing any of this to hurt you," my brother was quick to defend. "I'm trying to protect your sobriety, Joe."

"It's not yours to protect," I snapped. "It's mine, Darren. Staying clean is *my* responsibility. Looking after myself is my goddamn responsibility, not yours, and no offense, but I've been doing it for long enough without ya."

"Yeah," he muttered, rubbing his jaw. "And look where being left to your own devices got you."

I narrowed my eyes in disgust. "It's a good thing I'm *reformed*, because that snide comment deserves a smack in the mouth."

"Okay, everyone," Dr. B interjected. "Let's just take a breather, shall we?"

"If he wants to come home with us, then I really don't see why you would want to stop him – or how, for that matter," Edel interjected hotly.

Everyone started speaking over each other then.

The doctors.

The therapists.

The social workers.

The bulldozing blonde.

My brother.

"All I'm trying to do is protect him," Darren exclaimed, throwing his hands up in defeat. "That's it."

"Nobody is questioning your intentions, Darren."

"I am." I held a hand up and waved it around. "*I'm* questioning his intentions."

"Darren is concerned that without schooling or college to focus on, Joey will fall back into old patterns," another member of my team offered, turning to the Kavanaghs. "He's also worried that Aoife belongs to the same friendship circle where Joey was exposed to substance abuse in the first place."

"Well, I don't believe that for a second," Edel was quick to defend. "And if you met the girl, you'd wholeheartedly agree with me."

"She was never a part of the problem," I repeated for what felt like the millionth time. "She was never a part of the drug scene. I've *told* you this."

"Not to mention the pressure of a newborn baby," Greg, my turncoat counsellor chimed in. "It's a lot to put on his shoulders."

"And what about *her* shoulders?" I demanded, glaring at him. "Aoife's fucking *shoulders*? She's the one at home having to deal with all of this on her own. Have you thought about that?"

"Our job is to consider your welfare."

"And my job is to consider *hers*!"

"Aoife has her family to look after her, Joey," I heard Darren say. "Why can't you let yours look after you?"

"Because she *is* my family, Darren!" I roared, losing my cool. "How do you not *get* that? You're a smart fella. Christ, you have a fancy education and a shiny college degree under your belt, so how can you be so fucking dense?"

"Joe—"

"How can you not see that what you're doing here is wrong?"

"Joey, please calm down."

Like hell I was calming down.

"You know I'd be dead without her, right?" I declared hoarsely. "This entire conversation wouldn't be happening because I wouldn't be *here* to argue about if it wasn't for Aoife Molloy."

"Jesus." My brother winced like my words caused him physical pain. "Don't say that, Joe."

"It's the truth, Dar," I retorted hoarsely. "I wouldn't have made it to eighteen without her. Hell, I probably wouldn't have made it to fifteen without her. You weren't there. You didn't see. I was a piece of shit. Sincerely. I was fucking terrible. To myself. To her. My behavior towards her was horrendous. I was the worst possible version of myself. And still, she stuck it out with me. She saw something worth saving in me, and she decided to love me anyway, and I am so fucking thankful that she did." I shook my head. "You will never understand how much I owe that girl. How much I fucking worship the ground she walks on!"

"I know you love her," he groaned, sounding pained. "I can see it, but it scares the hell out of me."

"Why?"

"Because . . . " He stopped short and shook his head.

"Say it," I pushed, already knowing what was on the tip of his tongue. "Tell them all how much I remind you of *him*. Just like I reminded Mam of *him*. You know, if you had said that to me three months ago, I would have crumbled," I shot back. "But not anymore because I might not know who I am, Darren, but I sure as hell know who I'm not!"

"No, it's not that," he tried to coax. "It's not you individually. It's the two of you as a couple. When you get out of here, you don't have a job, or school, or hurling anything to focus on except her. To me, that reeks of toxicity. It scares the damn hell out of me, Joey, because we've both seen what happens when teenagers who are obsessed with each other shack up and play house. We've lived through it, Joey, and I don't want that for you. I don't want you and Aoife becoming a second-generation version of *them*."

"Jesus Christ."

"Look, maybe I'm projecting my own trauma on your relationship here, Joe, but I'm so fucking scared for you. I'm so afraid of sitting back and watching you follow in Mam and Dad's footsteps. It's the only reason Mam and I tried to put a stop to it."

"Put a stop to our relationship?"

When he didn't respond, my blood ran cold.

"The pregnancy."

"It was at the start." His face reddened. "Early on."

Of course they did.

"You tried to put a stop to my baby?" I bit out through clenched teeth. "Is that what you're saying? You and Mam tried to convince Aoife to get rid of *my* baby?"

"Okay, I think we should take a short break."

"I think he should answer the fucking question," I snapped, ignoring my social worker's attempts to diffuse the situation. "What did you and Mam do to my girlfriend, Darren?"

"We didn't do anything to your girlfriend," he explained with a weary sigh. "I offered her an alternative."

"Meaning you offered to foot the bill for an abortion?" When he didn't reply, I choked out a humorless laugh. "I don't fucking believe this."

"Joey, please calm down."

"And people wonder why I sank into addiction." I shook my head and looked around the room. "Take a good fucking look, people. This right here is what I've been dealing with. My own mother and brother tried to do that to me!"

"I was trying to help you," Darren tried to explain. "You're too young to be a father."

"I've always *been* a father!" I roared back, chest heaving. "And I've done a pretty fucking good job with the four I've raised. And yeah, I'm a mess, and yeah, I'm an addict, but I'm a good father! I'm a good fucking parent, Darren. I kept them alive. I kept them fed, and loved, and nurtured and goddamn educated. I did that. Not you. Not him. Not Mam. Me. So, call me a junkie and whatever the hell else you want to call me, but don't say that I'm too young to be a father!"

"I didn't mean it like that," he argued. "I meant that I didn't want you saddled down with—"

"I *want* my baby, Darren!"

You could have heard a pin drop in the room.

Everything went eerily quiet.

Finally, Darren broke the silence when he said, "You do?"

"Damn straight I do," I confirmed, furious. "How fucking dare you and Mam try to take that away from me."

"I realize now that it wasn't my place to get involved."

"No, it wasn't your place," I sneered, beyond furious. "And you're goddamn lucky Aoife didn't fold under the pressure I have no doubt you put her under." I shook my head in disgust. "Jesus Christ, Dar. I would *never* do that to you. Never. Every choice you've ever made, I've had your back. I've always *supported* you. *Defended* you."

"I know you have."

"Then why couldn't you do the same for me?"

"I thought that's what I *was* doing."

"By hating on my girlfriend?" I spat. "Jesus, Darren. After all the shit we've been through, *why* would you do that to me? Why would you try to scare off the one good thing in my life?"

"I don't hate Aoif, Joe. Christ, I don't even know the girl. Not really. I'm just . . . I wanted a *different* life for you."

"Well, it doesn't matter what you want, Dar, because this right here *is* my life," I shot back, shaking. "It's mine to live, and I plan on living it side by side with her. Because newsflash, asshole, that girl *is* my life. Her and our baby. And if she wants a ring, she'll get it. And a house, she'll get that, too. And if the time comes where she wants more kids, then I'll give them to her. Whatever she wants. Because we're mirrors. Her and I. We're aligned. *That's* my future, Darren, and if you keep meddling in it, then you won't be a part of it."

"You don't mean that."

"I have never been more serious in my life."

"This is a disaster," Darren mumbled, dropping his head in his hands.

"On the contrary," Dr. B said. "I think this conversation was long overdue."

"Damn straight," I agreed as six years of resentment and pain burst to the surface. "You left me, Darren. You fucking *left* me with them. I loved you most. I looked up to you. I worshipped the goddamn ground you walked on, and you just *disappeared* from my life."

"I know," he choked out. "Jesus, I know."

"I was twelve." My voice was strangled and my chest heaving, as I spilled my pain. "Twelve, Darren. When you were twelve, you had *me*. When I was twelve, I had *nobody*."

"I'm so sorry, Joe."

"Saying you're sorry doesn't fix it," I choked out. "It's a *word*. I know you mean it; I know you're sorry, but it's a fucking word, Darren. It doesn't fix the *hole* you left in me."

He flinched. "Joe."

"What hurts the most isn't the fact that you left," I admitted, wiping a tear from my cheek. "I know you had to go. You were dying in that house. I get it. I understand that. What hurts the most is the fact that I stayed, and she *still* loved you more! And I'm jealous of that. I'm jealous and I'm resentful and I'm so fucking hurt that nothing I ever did was enough for her! And then you came back," I quickly continued. "And it was as if everything I did for her, every sacrifice I made, every slap

I took, was irrelevant. *I* was irrelevant because you were all she could see. I mean, let's face it, Dar; you were all she ever saw, even when we were kids, but it never bothered me until you left. She put you on this pedestal, her precious, perfect firstborn, and nothing I did in the flesh could match her memory of you!"

"Yes," Dr. B exclaimed, almost punching the air with excitement. "Fantastic, Joey."

Darren and I both turned to gape at her. "Excuse me?"

"Verbalization," she quickly explained. "Fantastic verbalization of your feelings. We have been working on this for months." She smiled up at me like I was her favorite student and offered me a supportive thumbs up, while every other member of my medical team looked on in horror.

"Listen, if I could interrupt for a moment," John Sr. interjected in that cool, calm, and collected tone of voice, ready to steady the ship. "I may have a solution that could be of benefit to everyone."

"Oh?" Edel sank down on the edge of the couch beside her husband and placed a hand on his knee. "Do tell, love?"

Cool as a breeze, John squeezed his wife's hand affectionately before turning his attention to the many faces watching him. "You want to extend Joey's treatment under the guise of uncertainty around his ability to cope under the pressures facing him when he returns home to Ballylaggin." Turning to Darren, he added, "From what I'm gathering, one of your greatest concerns is your brother's lack of prospects."

"He doesn't have any qualifications," Darren replied with a grateful nod. "He hasn't even finished school. He doesn't have a trade. He doesn't have a well-paying job. Hurling is out of the question for him. They won't have him back. I've tried. Neither will BCS. They're standing firm on their decision. There isn't a school in the area who will consider taking him in."

"Like I give a fuck," I snorted.

"You should," Darren growled. "You've got a baby to look after — something you've been extremely vocal about telling everyone. How do you propose to do that on a minimum wage job. Because let's face it, Joe, with your record, you would be lucky to get a job stacking shelves."

"I'm a *good* worker."

"I never said you weren't," my brother argued. "But you have a record as long as your arm stacked up against you."

"What if there was an alternative?" John suggested calmly. "What if I could guarantee Joey a place in sixth year at the same school his siblings attend. Would that appease everyone's concerns?"

"The fuck?" I frowned. "What are you . . . ?"

"Tommen?" Darren's eyes widened. "They won't have him, John. Especially not after the spectacle back in May. Do you think I haven't tried? He was removed from the school by the Gards for physically assaulting pupils from Tommen."

"It's already done," John replied calmly, this time turning to me. "You have a place at Tommen College to complete your studies, Joey. It's yours for the taking." Shrugging, he added, "If you'll *take* it."

"Tommen." I stared blankly at him. "You want me to go to *Tommen*?"

"I want you to consider it."

"Are you serious?" Excitement filled my brother's voice. "How in God's name did you manage to pull that off?"

"How do you think, Darren?" I deadpanned. "Money."

"He'll take it," my brother answered for me.

"He won't," I was quick to argue, turning back to John. "I'm not going back to secondary school, John. I need to find work that brings home a steady paycheck at the end of the week."

"No, no, no, it makes sense," Edel hurried to say, turning to face me. "The new school term resumes on September 1st, Joey love. If you were to be enrolled at Tommen, then you would need to be discharged before . . . "

"Before the baby comes," I filled in, as my brain churned into gear.

"It would be a wonderful foundation to build your future on, Joey," Dr. B offered up her two cents. "Stability and friendship, and a solid education."

"I'll send you money," Darren blurted out. "Every week. Straight into your bank account. Whatever it takes."

"Pocket money?" I stared blankly. "Do you think I'm a little kid?"

"No, I think you're one of the smartest people I know, and the prospect of you having an actual shot at this – at an *education* – is too important to turn your nose up. I want this for you, Joe. Think about the job opportunities. Think about college. Your future, brother."

"I'm not going to college," I argued, feeling overwhelmed. "It's not on the cards for me."

"It *wasn't* on the cards for you before, but it *can* be now," he argued thickly. "Why shouldn't you have the same opportunities as the rest of us? You deserve this just as much as Shannon and Tadhg. He's starting first year there too, you know. At Tommen. You would be there to look out for him. To show him the way. Think about it, Joe. This could be lifechanging for you."

"Are you alright, Joey love?"

"No, Edel, I'm not," I admitted, knees bopping restlessly, as I sat opposite her and John at one of the picnic tables in the communal gardens after the meeting.

"You can thank Gerard for those," she said, pointing disapprovingly to the cigarette in my hand. "He smuggled three packets into the bags I packed for you today."

Good man, Gussie.

Taking a deep drag of my cigarette, I looked around the garden, feeling beyond agitated.

"I planted those," I decided to tell them, pointing to a bed of Black-Eyed Susans, standing alone amongst a flurry of pink Dahlias and Hydrangeas. "Those ones are mine."

"You've spent time working in the garden?"

"It's a part of the treatment," I explained, waving a hand around aimlessly. "We talk, we sit around in circles during group therapy and cry, we plant flowers, we paint shit." I took another drag of my smoke before saying, "It's all very woe-is-me around here. Just one big competition to see whose life is the most fucked up really."

John smirked. "Well then, I'm sure you're in the lead by a country mile."

I snorted. "You know it."

"Joey love," Edel began, tapping her perfectly manicured nails on the table. "About Tommen. I know your first instinct is to say no, but please don't do that. Just give yourself some time to mull it over before deciding."

"Okay," I replied, feeling overwhelmed at the prospect. "I'll think about it."

Call my girl

JOEY

"Fun fact of the day: I officially have udders."

"Udders?"

"Yep. That's right. I kid you not. Apparently, I produce milk now. By the bra full."

"You're leaking?"

"Like a faulty tap."

"Shit."

"Oh yeah, and fair warning, I haven't seen my vagina since June, so you know what that means, don't you?"

"No, Molloy, I really don't."

"It means you'll be returning to the Amazon Rainforest of vaginas."

"Jesus."

"Yep. Oh, and I have brown nipples."

"You've always had brown nipples."

"No, *you've* always had brown nipples," she argued. "I've always had rosy-pink ones."

"Well, a change is as good as a rest."

"Also, that spiel they give you about oiling your stomach to prevent stretchmarks is complete bullshit. I've been oiling, Joe. Three times a day, and your spawn still managed to bend me out of shape like a Stretch-Armstrong doll with varicose veins." She sighed dramatically before adding, "I fear I may never wear my yellow bikini again."

"Didn't you buy that bikini when we were in second year?"

"So?"

"So, maybe it doesn't matter if you can't fit into a bikini that you wore when you were fourteen?"

"Ugh, I hate it when you're so logical," she grumbled. "I think I liked you better when you were off your head and telling me whatever I wanted to hear."

I laughed down the line. "Molloy, you only ever hear what you want anyway, so that's a moot point."

"A moot point?" she teased down the line. "Get you, mister fancy pants. Practicing all the big words for Tommen, huh?"

"Don't," I groaned, resting my head against the wall. "I'm not doing it, Aoif."

"Oh yes you are," she argued back. "Come next month, my baby daddy is going to be a thoroughbred private school boy." Bursting into a fit of snickering laughter, she added, "Blazer and all."

"There is no fucking way that I am *ever* wearing a blazer to school," I growled, repressing a shiver. "I would rather shit in my hands and clap."

"Oh, smeared feces. How sexy."

"Give it a rest, will ya?"

"Hey now, you're the one threating to shit in your hands, drama queen," she teased.

"They want to change me, Molloy. Make me into a whole different person. It's not who I am. I'm me."

"They don't want to change you, Joe. They want to support you."

"I don't get it."

"I know you don't, and that makes me love you even more."

"You're a dope."

"You love me."

"Yeah." *I do.* I smiled to myself. "So, did you get your leaving cert results yet? They came out this morning, right?"

"Yeah," she sighed dramatically. "But I haven't been over to the school to collect them yet."

"Why the hell not?"

"Because I didn't want to miss your call."

"Molloy." Guilt sucker-punched me in the chest. "You need to go and get your results."

*

"I failed."

My heart sank.

"What do you mean you failed?"

"I mean I failed the leaving cert in spectacular fashion."

"Molloy."

"It's not all bad," she was quick to say. "Kev got six hundred points. So, he'll be heading off to his top choice university."

Like I gave a shit what her brother got.

"Let's see." I heard her sigh sadly as the sound of paper ruffling filled my ears. "D in Business. E in Irish. E in Maths. E in History. Oh, I got a C in Biology. D in English. Oh, and another D in Home Ec."

"I'm sorry, queen."

"Yep." Another heavy sigh. "Want some more crappy news?"

"What?"

"I didn't get in."

"To St. John's?"

"The rejection letter came yesterday."

Fuck.

"So, yeah, stud, it turns out you're not the only one heading back to school."

I frowned. "You're going back to school?"

"According to Mam and Dad, I have to repeat sixth year, which I am absolutely *not* doing." She released a frustrated growl. "I mean, it was hard enough last year. How the hell am I supposed to focus this time around with a baby to look after?"

"Aoif." Jesus, I could hardly speak I was so laden down with guilt. "I'm so fucking sorry, baby."

"It's not on you, Joe."

Yeah.

It was.

"Trish wants you to repeat, huh?" I knew it would be Trish, because Tony wasn't the school promotor type. In his mind, if you could read, write, count money, and had a good head on your shoulders, then you would make your way just fine in life. Trish, on the other hand, was the one gunning for her kids to make something of themselves.

"Yep," she replied. "Mam thinks it'll be good for me to get it done. She's been in contact with Mr. Nyhan, and he's been really good about it – all things considered. He told Mam the school will work with me, you know, sending homework and stuff, and that I don't have to attend in person until after the Halloween break."

"Jesus." I scrubbed my jaw, feeling overwhelmed *for* her.

"Mam offered to mind the baby for me if I go back to school, but I'm not doing it, Joe."

Anxiety filled me.

All these plans and decisions were being made without me.

"What about me?" I heard myself interject. "I can have the baby while you go to school. I'll find evening work that'll fit our schedule."

"And Tommen? Where does that fit in?"

"It doesn't."

"You're going to do this, Joe."

"No, Molloy. I'm going to take care of you and the baby."

"Yes, by finishing out school," she pushed. "At least that way our baby has one parent to be proud of."

Fuck, that stung.

"There's nothing about me to be proud of," I told her. "You're the good one, Aoif. You're the parent our kid will be proud of."

"Listen to you with all the compliments."

"Seriously, you do the whole school gig by day, and I'll have the baby, and then I'll work at night while you're with him."

"Yeah, because my dad's really going to go for that."

I rolled my eyes. "He can fire me, but he can't keep me from my kid."

"That's not it, Joe," she was quick to say. "He loves you. You know he does. He's just ... protective of me after everything that happened."

"You mean after I left you alone and pregnant."

"He knows you had to go."

"He might know it, but he doesn't accept it."

"Well, I do, and that's all that matters," she replied. "So, don't let it get you down. You and Dad will patch things up when you're home. You guys always do."

Yeah, somehow, I doubted that.

I'd overheard Tony ranting and raving the other night when she was on the phone to me.

He didn't want me going anywhere near his daughter, and I didn't blame him. Jesus, it was a miracle he hadn't confiscated her phone to stop me from calling. I sure as hell wouldn't blame him if he did. I'd put his daughter through hell.

"He'll give you back your job at the garage once he sees how well you're doing," Molloy said down the line. "Maybe not right away, but he will. Dad never replaced you. He never hired anyone else, Joe."

"I really fucking hope you're right, Molloy," I said honestly. Because they could talk about college degrees to me until the cows came home, but the only career I'd ever been interested in pursuing was under the bonnet of a car.

PART 11

Back to Ballylaggin

JOEY

After spending forever thinking it would never happen, it finally did.

The day I had been both living for and dreading since my mind came back to me had arrived.

August 29th 2005.

D day.

The first day of the rest of my life, or so I had been told.

Fuck.

The terms of my discharge came with stipulations though. Stipulations I'd agreed to in order to get out but could hardly bear thinking about now.

Stipulations that included blazers.

Standing outside the rehabilitation facility that had been my home since my own had burned to the ground, I dutifully ignored the elderly porter standing beside me.

The fuck was he going to do if I tried to escape? I had no plans on running and even if I had, my conscience would never allow. Poor bastard would probably keel over trying to chase me.

With a duffel bag thrown over one shoulder, and a folder clutched in the other hand, I watched as a shiny Range Rover pulled up beside the footpath.

Breathe.

Just breathe.

A not-so-little part of me was screaming at me to run for the hills, get the hell out of dodge and far away from these people. I didn't, I held firm, keeping my two feet locked in place as the tinted window rolled down and I was faced with a familiar blonde woman, who looked nothing like the woman who bore me.

"Hello, love." Edel beamed out the car window at me. "I would jump out and throw my arms around you, but I've been given strict instructions by John to lay off the hugging."

Thank Christ for that.

"Climb on in, love," she added, shifting her sunglasses onto the top of her head. "It's a long drive home, and the boys can't wait to see you."

Knowing that this woman held any future access I hoped to have with my siblings in the palm of her hand, I relented any notions of fleeing, and swung the car door open.

"Thanks again for coming to pick me up." Tossing my bag into the back seat, I climbed into the passenger seat beside her, feeling twitchy and off-kilter as fuck. "And, ah, for the rest of it."

"Anytime, Joey, love," Edel replied, as she pulled back onto the road. "How are you feeling?"

Ironically, Matchbox Twenty's 'Unwell' was playing on the car stereo, and for a brief moment, I debated telling her that I felt more than a little unwell, before settling on the standard, "I'm grand," instead.

Glancing sideways, Edel cocked a brow and gave me a 'don't bullshit me' look before turning her attention back to the road.

Behave, lad.

Don't fuck this woman off.

Knees bopping restlessly, I wiped my sweaty palms on my thighs, and blew out a breath, feeling both claustrophobic and agitated.

Life had moved on for everyone since I left Ballylaggin.

I no longer had a job, a team, a mother, or a fucking role to play.

I had to start from scratch, and regardless of the amount of counseling I had, I didn't know where *scratch* began for me.

The only arrow pointing the way for me now, was the one directing me straight towards Molloy.

"Shannon is just dying to see you," she continued, tone light. "She's been in the kitchen since the crack of dawn with Ollie and Sean – they're baking you a cake."

Jesus.

"How are they?" I forced myself to ask her before swallowing deeply. Feeling a white hot, scorching pain from the words, from the realization that I'd as good as abandoned my little brothers and sister when they needed me most.

She smirked before saying, "They're grand."

Reluctantly, my lips tipped up of their own accord. "I suppose I deserved that one."

"The boys are doing just fine, love." She smiled then, a huge, megawatt grin. "In fact, they're doing better than anyone could have hoped for, given the circumstances."

Thank Christ for small mercies.

"And Shannon?"

Grinning, Edel rolled her eyes. "Your sister is loved up to the hilt with my young fella. They're like an old married couple at this stage. Keeping them apart is the main challenge these days."

"I can imagine," I replied, all the while knowing that the very last thing that I ever wanted to do on this earth was imagine that particular scenario.

"Actually, I wanted to run something by you." Reaching for the radio, she turned the volume down. "I thought, with them both living together, that it would be safer for everyone involved to take Shannon to the doctor." She cast a nervous glance in my direction. "She's on the pill since June, love. I hope that's alright by you."

The fact that she was asking my permission did something to me.

She was treating me like an equal, *not* a child, and I was grateful.

"No, that's definitely a wise decision," I replied. "I mean, it's not bulletproof." I paused and gestured to myself. "*Clearly.* But it's good that she's protecting herself."

"I've warned them to keep their hands off," Edel continued. "But you know the way these things go. I can only do so much."

Yeah, I knew how it went.

Molloy and I had been plenty inventive back in the day.

"Listen." Clearing my throat, I rolled my sleeves up to my elbows, while I shifted around in discomfort, trying to form the words that would never come close to what needed to be said. "I can never repay you and John for what you've done for my family . . . " I paused and dragged in a pained breath, before adding, "For what you've done for me." Fuck, I hated this with every fiber of my being. "I'm still not sure why you did what you did – or why you continue to help us – but I think it's pretty clear that it takes a special sort of person to take in a family like you've done for us. I don't have anything to give you in return, I don't know if I ever will, but I'll do everything I can to pay you back for—"

"I love your family, Joey," she cut me off by saying, voice thick with emotion. "Each and every one of you." She winked. "Especially you."

Especially me.

Well shit.

I had nothing to say in return to that.

Because the truth was, I didn't love her.

My heart just didn't beat the same way as my siblings.

In fact, I was fairly certain that it didn't beat right at all.

In that moment, it felt like there was steel in my windpipe, blocking the air from escaping my lungs, and preventing the words that needed to be spoken from spilling from my lips.

Maybe it was just as well that I didn't love the woman in the driver's seat. After all, I had either let down or successfully ruined every woman that had managed to breach the walls around my cold, black heart.

My mother.

My sister.

My girlfriend.

Thinking about the girl I'd left behind in Ballylaggin at the beginning of the summer caused a swell of guilt so strong and severe to build up inside of me that I truly felt I might drown. The guilt made me itch and burn and fucking yearn to escape the confines of this woman's luxury car.

No, scratch that, it made me want to use.

Breathe, lad, just breathe.

No, don't breathe, just hold your breath until you pass the fuck out and stop feeling.

Turning to face my door window, I clenched my eyes shut and did just that.

Forcing my shoulders to relax, I allowed myself to absorb the feeling like I had been taught to.

I took it all in, while focusing on my breathing, the steady beat of my heart. Channeling in on my senses, I concentrated on the feel, and smell, and taste of fresh air.

Finally, it passed.

"I've been calling Aoife," I offered up out of thin air, surprising myself with the admission. "Every day since I earned my phone privileges."

"Oh?" Edel's eyes lit up. "And how's that been going for you?"

"Well, she's been answering every time."

"Psssh." Edel batted the air. "As if she wouldn't."

"It's more than I deserve," I admitted, angling myself to face her. "She's incredible."

"She's a little firecracker alright," Edel mused, smiling indulgingly. "She sure has her heart set on you, Joey love."

"Yeah." I shivered. "The feeling's mutual."

"I presume she doesn't know you're getting out today," Edel noted. "Otherwise, she would be in the car with me."

"No, I wanted to surprise her," I replied. "She thinks I'm not getting out until Wednesday." Grimacing, I added, "Before school starts back on Thursday."

"Ah, she'll be buzzing."

"Doubt her old man will be."

"Don't you worry about anyone else," she was quick to soothe. "You focus on your girlfriend and that little bundle about to arrive and everything else will fall into place."

"Do the kids know?" I asked. "About the baby? Did you tell them?"

"Apparently, Tadhg's known all along," she surprised me by saying.

I frowned. "What?"

"Uh-huh." She nodded. "That boy is as sharp as a razor."

"Well, shit."

"The rumors were rampant around town after you left, love, so I had to speak to the family about it."

"How did they take it?"

Edel grinned. "Ollie's thrilled to pieces. Tadhg's . . . Tadhg. Shannon's been non-stop shopping for baby clothes. Johnny and Gerard have been stocking up on preventative measures, and Seany? Well, he's a little young to grasp the concept of being an uncle."

"Really?"

"Really," she confirmed with a nod. "They're worried for their brother, but they're delighted that they're gaining a sister in Aoife, and a little niece or nephew."

"Nephew."

"It's a boy?" she squealed, almost crashing the car with excitement.

"Jesus Christ, eyes on the road, please," I strangled out. "And no, we don't know. It's just a hunch. But I can feel it in my bones."

"You know, funny you say that because your Nanny said the same thing."

I shrugged. "Yeah, she's fairly perceptive."

"She's clearly not the only one," Edel replied. "Right, when we get home, I'm putting a bet on with John. If your gut says boy, and Nanny's gut say boy, then I'm going with it."

"A wager for money?" I arched a brow. "Why?"

"I never said for money," she replied with a mischievous wink.

Jesus.

Forcing myself not to gag, I steered the conversation back to safer waters. "I thought they wouldn't take it well."

"Who, the kids?"

I nodded.

"Why so, Joey love?"

"Because despite my best efforts, I made the age-old mistake of following in our father's footsteps." Shaking my head, I looked at my siblings' foster mother and shook my head. "Because I turned my girl-friend into our mother."

"No, love, you didn't," she replied, reaching across the console to ruffle my hair affectionately. "Because Aoife is in no way similar to your mother, and you, my big-hearted boy, don't have a Teddy Lynch bone in your body."

"I already told you that I'm not interested in any of this," I reminded her, squirming in discomfort when she squeezed my cheek. "I'm not your boy."

"And I already told you that we're keeping you," she chuckled. "Finders keepers, Joey love. You're mine now."

Jesus.

Full term

AOIFE

"Well, good news, your cervix is favorable," the doctor said, tossing his gloves in the nearby bin. "The baby's head is engaged. That bloody show you experienced this morning. That was your mucus plug. I wouldn't be surprised if you delivered in the next twenty-four hours."

"Twenty-four hours?" Mam exclaimed. "That soon? But she's not due for another three weeks."

"Only 5% of babies are delivered on their due date, and this baby is measuring on the larger side, which aligns with why she's already two centimeters dilated," he replied. "It could take several more days. Another week, even. Babies are unpredictable, but in my experience, your daughter is a prime candidate to deliver sooner rather than later."

"Can you slow it down, doc?" Perched on the examination table, with my legs hanging open, and my dignity back in Ballylaggin, I pulled up on my elbows and pleaded with the man in green scrubs. "I'm not due for another three weeks and my boyfriend doesn't get back into town until Wednesday night."

"Aoife," Mam sighed. "It doesn't work that way, pet."

"Baby comes when baby is ready," the doctor replied. "And I'm hedging towards baby being ready, Aoife."

"Well, I don't care what either of you say," I grumbled, rolling off the examination table and adjusting my maxi-dress. "I'm not having the baby until Joe gets home."

"Hey, waddles," Casey called out, as she leaned against the side of my father's van in the hospital carpark, basking in the warm summer's afternoon. "How's our baby coming along?"

"Don't start," I grumbled, heaving my over-sized inmate across the carpark. "It's too damn hot and I'm suffering from a serious case of electric shocks to the fanny."

"Lightning crotch," Mam corrected, as she unlocked the van. "Please, love, I know you're cranky, but try not to be so vulgar."

"Lightning crotch." Casey grinned. "Oooh, sounds kinky."

"You know what's not kinky, Case? Having a geriatric obstetrician ram his entire hand inside of your fan—"

"Aoife!"

"Vagina," I amended with a huff.

"Are we talking an entire fist here?" my best friend asked, as she helped hoist me into the van.

"We're talking an entire fist, arm, and elbow!"

"I hope he wore a glove."

"Don't be so dramatic, Aoife," Mam chuckled, climbing into the driver's seat and starting the engine. "It was a standard internal, love, not calving season at old MacDonald's farm. If you think that was bad, just you wait until you're delivering. It'll be carnage down there."

"Old Macdonald's farm," Casey snorted. "Good one, Trish."

"Wow," I deadpanned. "I am so pleased that the impending demise of my vagina is so entertaining to you."

"Well, that'll teach you to let your boyfriend put his willy in there without protection."

"Yes, Mother," I drawled, tone laced with sarcasm. "I have indeed learned the error of my ways."

"She's already two centimeters dilated, Casey," Mam said excitedly. "The doctor thinks she'll have the baby by tomorrow."

"Chill, Mam," I cut in. "Nothing's coming out of me until Joey comes home."

"That's not technically true," Casey chimed in, pointing to damp circular stain on the front of my dress. "You're leaking a little there, babe."

"Oh, come on," wailed, throwing my hands up in dismay. "What the hell is wrong with that boob?"

"We should buy you a bell chain and rename you Daisy."

"Which one, love?"

"The left one," I grumbled, reaching for a tissue to stuff into my bra. "The right one always behaves herself, but the left one is an embarrassing bitch."

"Oh, come on," Casey chuckled, patting my big belly. "Ignore the leaks and let's go and get those swollen hooves a pedicure before baby daddy gets back."

"Hm," I grumbled, slightly mollified at the thought of seeing Joey again. "Do you think they have a hedge-trimmer at the beautician's?"

"Come on," Casey coaxed. "Give us a smile. You've only been waiting for this all summer."

She was right.

I *had* been waiting all summer.

Fifteen long weeks to be exact.

Joey was coming home.

Finally.

By Wednesday night, we would be together again.

"I'm nervous," I heard myself admit aloud for the first time, even though the feeling had been eating away at me for weeks now.

"What?" both Casey and Mam asked in unison. "Why?"

"Because look at me, guys." I gestured to my stomach. "I'm not exactly the Aoife he remembers."

"Aoife, you're about to have the boy's baby," Mam offered gently. "You are beautiful, sweetheart."

"Fuck beautiful, babe, you are *breathtaking* to look at," Casey chimed in supportively. "I don't know anyone else on this planet who could pull off a nine-month baby bump and still look completely fuckable! He's going to lose his shit when he sees you!"

"Casey," Mam chastised. "Please, love, can we not?"

"Sorry, Trish, but it's true," my best friend replied. "Our girl here is a MILF!" Grinning wickedly, she added, "And when Joey the DILF gets home, there's going to be explosions."

"Oh, sweet mother of mercy," Mam muttered, sounding pained.

"You have nothing to be insecure about, Aoif," Casey added. "But just to top up that glass of self-esteem, we're going to go all out on the pampering today, and it'll be Daddy T's treat." She looked to my mam before asking, "You swiped the credit card before we left the house this morning, didn't ya, Trish?"

"I sure did, girls."

"Yay." Clapping enthusiastically, my bestie draped her arm over my shoulder. "We're about to do some damage."

Thwarted reunions

JOEY

"Thanks for doing this," I said, several hours later, when we pulled up at Rosewood Estate. "I know the kids are waiting, but I just . . . "

"You have your priorities in order, love," Edel said when I climbed out. "Here, take this," she said, thrusting a sleek mobile phone into my hands. "It's fully charged with my number programed in. When you're ready to come home, just text me and I'll come get you."

"Will do." I pocketed the phone. "Thanks."

With a clear head and a heavy conscience, I pushed the rickety wooden gate inwards and made the familiar trek up the garden path, stepping over dogshit as I went.

Jesus, someone needed to start cleaning up after Spud.

When I reached the front door, I tapped lightly and then quickly lowered my hood and straightened up.

Swallowing my pride, if it even fucking existed anymore, I shoved my trembling hands deep into the pockets of my jeans and braced myself for the unknown.

When the front door swung open a few moments later, my heart sank into my ass.

"I thought you weren't coming back for another few days."

"I got back early," I replied, straightening my shoulders, as my heart gunned in my chest. "Is she here?"

Tony shook his head. "She's gone out with Trish and Casey for a girls' day. Won't be home until late."

My heart sank further.

"Are you clean?"

"Yeah, Tony, I am."

"How long?"

"One hundred and seven days," was my quiet response.

His eyes narrowed and I could see the disbelief written all over his face. "Show me."

"Tony."

"Show me, Joey."

"I'm clean." Exhaling heavily, I rolled up my sleeves and held out my hands for his inspection. "I promise."

"No offense, boyo, but any promises that come from your mouth don't inspire much confidence in me."

I deserved that.

Absorbing my old boss's disdain, I stood my ground, unwilling to turn around and walk away. Besides, feeling unwelcome wasn't anything new for me.

I'd felt it my whole life.

"So, you're clean and sober and back from the dead?" he said, eyes tracking the veins in my arms.

"I am."

"For now."

"Yeah."

"And tomorrow?" His accusatory gaze was hard to bear. "What happens tomorrow?"

"No clue." I shrugged, uttering my truth. "But I'm clean today."

"Yeah," he replied with a sniff, releasing my arms. "Good for you." And then he slammed the door in my face.

Rolling my eyes, I reached up and knocked again, and then I counted down from five, knowing full well that he was still behind the door, waiting to erupt on me.

I could take it.

I sure as fuck deserved everything this man could throw at me.

I'd put his entire family through hell.

I could see that now.

Five.

Four.

Three.

Two.

One . . .

"Jesus Christ, Joey!" he snarled the second the front door swung open again. "What were you thinking getting involved in that lifestyle?"

"I wasn't thinking," I admitted quietly. "I didn't want to think. That was the whole point."

"I gave you the benefit of the doubt," he strangled out. "I knew what you were about, but I saw a good lad underneath all of the trouble. I still do. But I . . . " His words broke off and he shook his head.

"Just say it, Tony," I said calmly. "Whatever you need to say. Get it off your chest. I can handle it."

"Can't do that," Tony grumbled. "According to my wife, I'm to mind my Ps and Qs around you. Since you're fragile and all that."

"Do I look fragile?"

"You look like a person I don't know anymore."

Ouch.

I kept my hands by my sides, willing to take whatever this man had to say – had to do. In a life of nothing, he'd been the only father figure I'd ever had, and I had ruined his daughter. I had robbed her of the future they'd hoped for her.

"I loved you," he finally roared, chest heaving. "Like you were my own flesh and blood."

"I know."

"You made my daughter a mother before she was a woman, and then you left her."

"I *had* to leave."

"Maybe you did, but that doesn't change anything in my head," he choked out, voice thick with emotion. "But I can't risk having you around her. Not in her condition. You let me down, Joey. You went spiraling down the rabbit hole and you took my daughter with you."

What could I say to that?

Nothing.

I couldn't change what I'd done.

I also couldn't change the fact that every word he was speaking was the absolute truth.

I *did* spiral out of control, I *did* lose myself, and I *did* take his daughter down with me.

"You dropped off the face of the planet for months. You left her on her own to clean up your bloody mess, Joey. Yours. And now you're back? For how long?"

"For good," I offered, forcing myself to meet his eyes. "I'm staying."

"You're staying," he repeated, tone laced with pain. "Can you do that, Joey? *Can* you stay?"

"Yeah, Tony, I can stay," I replied, full of emotion. "I won't leave her again."

"I hear you're heading to that fancy private school?" He sounded utterly disgusted. "Isn't it nice for some? To get such a prestigious second chance. Meanwhile, my daughter loses everything."

Again, I absorbed his anger, knowing full well that I had a huge role in his daughter failing her leaving cert. "I accepted the place at Tommen so I could get back to her," I heard myself say. "I'd gladly give it up if it meant that she could take my place instead, Tony. You *have* to know that."

"I don't know what to think anymore," he snapped, rubbing his jaw. "Right now, all I'm thinking is that I wished you never came back here."

"Well, I am back."

"You don't realize what you did to her," he tossed out. "How badly you hurt my daughter. If you did, you'd leave her alone, and let me take care of my family."

"I can't do that," I replied, desperately trying to keep the head. "Because your family is my family, too."

"She's my child."

"And she's the mother of my child." I countered hotly. "I can't walk away from her, Tony. That's my baby she's carrying."

"That's *my* grandchild, and I'll be damned if I stand back and let you hurt either one of them again."

"You can try to keep me from your child, but you won't be keeping me from mine."

I moved to leave then, but he reached out a hand and fisted the front of my hoodie. I stood my ground, hands at my sides, and waited for his fist to crush my face. It didn't come.

"Prove me wrong, Joey." His voice was thick with emotion, as he roughly pulled me into his arms and hugged me tightly. "Prove me wrong, son."

"Don't worry, Tony." Swallowing deeply, I hugged him back just as tightly. "I will."

An hour later, and still furious with the world and everyone in it, I folded my arms behind my head and lay on the ground beside the small wooden crucifix, staring up at a cloudless summer's sky. "Are you up there?" I asked and then mentally kicked myself. "Fuck, what am I saying? You're probably with him."

Death was all around me, peaceful and still, and I momentarily jealous.

The sun shone bright, and it felt like I was seeing it clearly for the first time in years.

What now?

What the fuck was I supposed to do now?

Go back and argue some more with Tony?

Drop to my knees and apologize?

Snatch Molloy up and steal her away?

Live?

Be happy?

Go home?

Where?

"You fucked me," I whispered, shifting one arm out from under my head to trail my fingers over the soil on her grave, disgusted when the echo of my own hollow voice reverberated in my ears.

Clenching my eyes shut, I forced myself to remember the sight of her.

How she looked.

What she smelled like.

Her voice.

Her pain.

Her screams.

Sniffing, I reached up and wiped my face with the back of my hand before climbing to my feet.

"I'll see ya soon, Mam." A tear trickled down my cheek and I was surprised I could still feel. "Stay out of my head now, ya hear?"

Dusting off the soil and grass on my jeans, I inhaled a few steadying breaths before making my trek across the graveyard, not stopping until I was standing at his headstone.

One time.

All through rehab, I had vowed to myself that I would only do this once.

And then I was done.

I had to be.

The notion was the only thing that seemed to keep me sane in the early days.

My spite and bitterness had given me something to live for.

Without a word, I collected every candle, wreath, and bouquet of flowers his family had left for him and tossed them over the nearby wall.

"How does it feel, old man?" I asked, returning to his graveside, and undoing the fly on my jeans. "To *finally* burn in hell?"

"Joey love." She placed a hand on my shoulder, and it hurt. The movement. The feeling. Absorbing the contact. The fucked-up gentleness of her touch. "I got your text message."

"I pissed on his grave."

"Is that all?" With a heavy sigh, she put her handbag down on the grass and knelt at my mother's grave beside me. "I'm impressed with your level of self-control. I wouldn't have been able to contain myself."

"Threw his flowers away, too," I muttered. "It wasn't enough."

"No." Sadness filled her voice. "And it probably never will be, love. At least, it won't feel that way."

"Thirty-eight," I whispered, inclining my head to the small crucifix with my mother's details engraved one. "She was only a baby, Edel."

"I know, love."

She reached for my hand.

I let her.

I absorbed the feel of her hand covering mine.

"I miss her," I admitted, clenching my eyes shut when the tears started to fall. "I miss her so fucking much." My voice cracked, and I choked out a sob. "I miss my mother."

"Your mother loved you, Joey," Edel vowed, as she pulled me into her arms. "I swear it, love." Tightening her arms around me, she stroked my hair with her hand. "She just forgot to show it."

When we drove through the gates of the manor, a million different thoughts and emotions were rushing through me. All of which fell out of my head as soon as we pulled up outside the house and I locked eyes on my siblings.

"Joey!"

"O-ee."

"He's back, guys. Look, it's really Joe!"

Shannon was holding a cake.

Sean was sitting on Kav's shoulders, clutching a bunch of balloons.

Ollie was holding one side of a homemade banner that read *Welcome Home, Joey*, while Gussie of all people held the other side.

All of them had party hats perched on their heads.

Jesus, even Nanny was there, sitting at a picnic table that had been decorated with streamers and more balloons, with John Sr. and Darren.

Fucking Darren.

"What the hell is this?" I muttered, unfastening my seatbelt, as I battled down a surge of emotion. "What's all this for?"

"I told you they were excited to see their big brother," Edel laughed, pushing her door open. "Welcome home, Joey Lynch."

The minute I climbed out of the car, I was caught up in a flurry of limbs as Shannon, Ollie, and Seany all dove for me.

"Oh my god, Joe," my baby sister was crying, as she practically climbed up my body, locking her arms around my neck so tight it was hard to breathe. "Joe, Joe, Joe." Peppering my cheek with kisses, Shannon laughed and cried and had a little emotional breakdown for herself, only releasing me when Ollie shoved her out of the way. "Hey, I wasn't finished!"

"I knew you'd do it," he said, beaming up at me with pride, as he tightened his hold on my waist. "I knew you'd come back for us, Joe."

"I'll always come back for you, Ols," I replied, voice thick and gravely as I tried to keep my emotions in check. "Look at how tall you've grown."

"O-ee." Pulling on the leg of my jeans, a pair of brown eyes looked up at me. "O-ee."

That did it.

Seeing Sean's little face had my heart cracking open in my chest.

This kid.

He was my brother, but it was different with him.

From birth, Sean had depended on me in a way the others hadn't.

I knew he wasn't mine, but it didn't stop my heart from beating for him in a paternal rather than brotherly way.

"Hey, Seany-boo." Sniffling back the lump in my throat, I sank to my knees in front of him. "How's my baby?"

"O-ee." He didn't hesitate to scramble onto my lap. "Seany loves O-ee," he whispered in my ear, as he stroked my cheeks with his chubby little hands. "O-ee make Seany happy."

"Joey loves Seany back," I replied, wrapping him up in my arms, overwhelmed by just how well his speech had come on since the beginning of summer. "Seany makes Joey the proudest brother in the world."

"Okay, okay, everyone back up and let your brother breathe," John instructed, when all three had thrown themselves on top of me – which wouldn't have been a problem if it wasn't for the big overgrown blond bastard who had decided to get in on the action.

"Jaysus, Gibs, can't you let them have their moment?" Kav growled, yanking his friend off the top of the pile before helping my sister to her feet. "I swear to god, you're like a bleeding puppy craving attention."

"Not attention, Johnny, just a little belly rub," Gibsie replied before turning his attention back to me. "Well, would you look at the comeback kid in all his glory." He winked. "Howdy, friend."

I narrowed my eyes. "It's you."

He beamed back at me. "It's me."

And then he had the gall to hug me.

He actually mother-fucking *hugged* me.

I was so taken aback from the sudden move that I didn't react.

I couldn't.

Not when he had my arms pinned to my sides in what I could only describe as the most uncomfortable bear hug of my life. "Believe it or not, Lynchy, I was half-lonesome for your big druggie head over the summer."

"Believe it or not, Gussie, I will take your rugby-ball shaped head clean off your shoulders if you don't let go."

"Oh no," Johnny sighed and covered his head. "Oh, sweet Jesus, here we go."

"I knew it!" Gibsie declared, yanking away from me and turning to Kav. "I fucking knew it. That's the second time someone has said that, Johnny." Clutching his head, he let out a pained wail. "Twice, Johnny. Two times. That's a pattern."

"That's a coincidence," Kav tried to reassure him. "I've already told ya a million times, Gibs, your head is in perfect symmetrical proportion."

"Symmetrical?" Gibsie blanched. "What in the name of Jesus are you bringing up maths at a time like this? When I'm having a fucking complex, Johnny!"

"You *are* a complex, Gibs." Rolling his eyes, Kav offered his buddy a sympathetic pat on the shoulder before stepping towards me with his hand outstretched. "Joey the hurler."

"Mister rugby," I replied, lips twitching up in a smirk that mirrored his, as I stepped forward and accepted his handshake. "Thank you."

With steel blue eyes full of unconcealed emotion, he offered me a stiff nod. "Anytime, brother."

And that was all that needed to be said between us.

He knew it and so did I.

The respect he directed towards me was returned in a handshake.

"Joe," Darren acknowledged with a smile when I approached the picnic table. "You look great."

"Darren," I forced myself to respond, offering him a clipped nod. "Thanks."

"This is Alex," he said then, gesturing to the man sitting beside him. "You met around the time of Mam's funeral, but I don't know if you remember . . . "

"It's good to see you again," I said, offering his boyfriend my hand. "And Darren's right; I have no recollection of us meeting."

"Aye, that's not a bother," he replied, with a thick northern accent. "You're looking well in yourself there, lad."

"Yeah." Clearing my throat, I turned my attention to the old woman, whose eyes were burning holes in the side of my face. "Hi, Nanny."

"Joseph." Her green eyes were full of unshed tears as she reached for my hand. "Our little Joseph."

Kneeling in front of my great-grandmother, I took her frail hand in mine and pressed a kiss to the back of it. "I'm so sorry, Nanny."

"What are you sorry for, pet?"

"For letting you down." I blew out a pained breath and shook my head. "For disappointing you."

"Look at my face," she instructed, cupping my cheeks between her tremor-racked hands. "Does this look like a face filled with disappointment?"

I couldn't answer her.

It hurt too much.

"I am so proud of you," she pushed, leaning forward and pressing a kiss to my brow. "And if Granda was here, he would tell you the same thing."

Fuck.

She hit me through the heart with that line.

"Before I go back to Beara, I have something for you," she whispered in my ear, so that Darren couldn't hear her. "I don't want you to show your brothers and sister." She slipped a folded-up envelope into the front pocket of my hoodie. "Granda only left it for you, but I couldn't give it to you at the time. Not while he was ... well, when you were in your father's house. I've been holding onto it for you. Until the time was right."

"Granda?" I frowned in confusion. "Left what for me?"

"The letter inside explains everything," she whispered, pressing a finger to her lips to silence me. "Not a word to the others, ya hear?"

I nodded cluelessly.

She smiled. "Now, be a good boy and enjoy your homecoming."

"Enough hoarding," Edel ordered, pushing her way into the action. "I'm sorry, Nanny, but I have to steal your grandson for a moment. Joey, I have a little present for you."

"We," John called over from where he was helping Gibsie untangle himself from the net of a goal post. "*We* have a present for him."

"Don't mind him," she said, rolling her eyes. "It was my idea."

"Actually, it was both of our—"

"Stop stealing my thunder, John," Edel huffed. "Come on, Joey, let me show you."

"It's so cool," Ollie chimed in, catching ahold of one of my hands, while Sean took hold of the other. "Dellie let us help."

"And you were the best little helper," she crooned, leading us around the side of the house to the back. "I couldn't have done it without you, my sweet boy."

"I'm super helpful," he agreed, blowing his own trumpet. "Sure I am, Dellie?"

"Yes, you are, pet," she mollified him by saying, as she led us through the backyard towards what looked like a recently renovated outbuilding. "Now, let's show Joey the annex."

"The annex?" I frowned. "What's that?"

"*That*," she teased, stopping at the door of a freshly painted outbuilding. "Is your abode." Reaching into her pocket, she retrieved a set of keys and dangled them in front of my face. "I figured as soon as you got home, you'd be on the hunt for somewhere for your little family to live, so I went out on a limb and made a preemptive strike." Grinning, she dropped the keys into my hand. "Like I said, welcome home, Joey Lynch."

"Huh?" I stood there, with the keys in my hand, and my brain on empty. "I mean ... *what?*"

Laughing, she pushed the door inwards and stepped inside, followed swiftly by Ollie who barreled into the annex after her. "Follow us."

"Well, Seany?" I muttered, hoisting him into my arms before stepping inside. "I guess we're doing this, aren't we?"

"The second bedroom is a little cozy," Edel explained, as she walked me around what looked I could only describe as a high-end duplex. "But the master is a decent size, with an en suite attached."

"Wow," Sean whispered in my ear, voicing my thoughts aloud, as I followed Edel and Ollie back down the staircase to an open plan kitchen-living area.

"Yeah, kid," I whispered back. "Wow."

"Of course, if you would prefer to stay in the main house, that is absolutely fine by me, Joey love. I'm not trying to push you out in any shape or form. I'm just trying to be sensitive to your little family's needs."

This woman.

Not only had she taken on my brothers and sister, but she was providing shelter for my little family.

My little family.

Fuck.

"Jesus, Edel," was all I could muster. "I don't know what to say to you."

My gut reaction was to refuse her offer.

To tell her no thank you.

To run for the hills from this woman.

But I couldn't.

I *couldn't*.

Because time in therapy had helped me to come to terms with the fact that I *couldn't* do this on my own.

That it was *okay* to ask for help.

More importantly, it was okay to *accept* it.

"I . . ." I shook my head, feeling at a complete loss. "One day, I will pay you back for everything."

"Joey love." Closing the space between us, she pressed her hand to my cheek and smiled up at me. "You being here is all the payment I need."

"Where's Tadhg?" I asked John later that evening, when we were alone in the kitchen of the main house. Darren and Alex had left to drop Nanny back to Alice's house in Beara, but the kids and Gussie were still in full-swing party mode outside.

It didn't settle well with me that Tadhg hadn't shown up.

I knew why, of course.

I'd hurt him the most.

His reaction to my leaving felt remarkably like my reaction to Darren leaving all those years ago.

"I suspect he's down the back field in the treehouse," John replied, as he cut the crusts off a chocolate spread sandwich for Sean before using a cookie cutter to make dinosaur shaped sandwiches. "He's thrilled you're home, Joey. He's just . . . Well, you know Tadhg better than anyone."

"He's pissed as hell is what you mean to say," I offered up, resting a hip against the counter, as I watched this hotshot barrister take great care in preparing snacks for my baby brother. "I get it, John. I don't blame him one bit. I checked out on him. He's going to hold onto that in his head." *It's what I taught him to do.*

"He has a couple of spare hurleys and sliotars stashed in the utility room," John told me. "Somehow, I have a feeling that he would enjoy a puck about a lot more with his brother than a bunch of rugby players."

My heart skipped a beat. "He's still hurling?"

"Like a demon," John replied with a smile. "He's hellbent on following in his big brother's footsteps."

"Jesus, that's a worrying concept," I muttered, rubbing my jaw, as I moved for the utility room to grab a couple of hurls.

"Good luck," John called over his shoulder. "Good luck and watch out for the cannon."

My brows furrowed in confusion. "The cannon?"

The *cannon* turned out to be Tadhg, perched on a stool on top of an impressive looking treehouse, with a hurley in hand, and an unlimited supply of sliotars at his disposal.

"I told ya before, fatty," he called out, lacing a sliotar full force in my direction. "Try and take over my fort again and I'll take the head clean off ya!"

"Jesus Christ," I hissed, narrowly avoiding a ball to the face.

"I can do this all night," my brother called out, letting another sliotar fly, clearly too busy taking fire to realize who he was firing at. "Pussy!"

"Little shit," I grunted when he got me in the nuts. "I'll give you pussy." Tossing down the hurley I'd brought with me for him, I quickly hooked up a rogue sliotar with the one I'd claimed as my own and fired back at him.

Clearly, my ability to puck a sliotar hadn't diminished one bit since my departure. In fact, it was a little too accurate. When the sliotar I pucked hit my brother square between the eyes, and he fell headfirst out of the tree, my heart stopped beating for a solid five seconds.

"Oh, shit," I choked out, tossing the hurley away, as I raced towards him. "Tadhg? Are ya dead?"

"No," he growled, scrambling onto his feet and lunging for me. "But you're about to be."

The guilt I was feeling for the steady stream of blood trickling from his nose was enough to make me stand there and take my beating.

"Fucker," he growled, wrestling me to the ground. "You broke my nose."

"You broke my nuts," I shot back, unable to stop myself from laughing at the outraged expression etched on his face as he attempted to pummel me into the grass. "You got big, kid."

"Yeah, and you got skinny," he countered, twisting and rolling around in the grass with me. "And I hope I did break your nuts."

"Me too," I agreed, rolling onto my back and letting him pin me. "On a scale of one to ten, how pissed are you?"

"Fourteen," he hissed, pulling on my hair. "And a half."

"What the fuck is this?" I laughed, bucking him off my lap. "Who taught you to pull hair? Shannon?"

"Actually, it was your girlfriend," he countered. "When she was screaming my name."

I narrowed my eyes in warning. "Tadhg."

"Yes, Tadhg, yes!" he mocked.

"I'm warning ya."

"Oh, *Tadhg*, you're so much better than Joey."

"You little shit."

"You deserved it," he chuckled, flopping onto his back beside me. "Asshole."

"Yeah," I panted. "I think we've already established I'm an asshole."

"So, you're back."

"I'm back."

He nudged my shoulder with his. "About fucking time."

"I know, kid." I nudged him back. "I missed you, too."

"Hey, Johnny?" Ollie asked, strolling into the living room later that evening. "Are you going to marry my sister?"

"Wait for it," Gibsie snickered, nudging my shoulder as he tapped away on his PlayStation controller in front of a giant TV in the living room. "He's going to start getting stroke symptoms."

Smirking, I paused our game with my controller and turned my attention to the terrified looking rugby player. "Good question, Ols."

Right on cue, Kav's breathing increased, and a bead of sweat trickled down his temple.

"Ollie!" Shannon squealed, turning the color of her crimson sundress. "You can't ask him that."

"But he bought balloons to play with you," Ollie offered innocently. "And Joe says you only use those special balloons with girls when you want to marry them."

"I *did* say that," I laughed, remembering back to a time when that awkward fucking conversation came up. In my defense, Ollie was eight at the time, and he'd caught me off guard.

"A lot he'd know about using balloons," Johnny muttered, looking rattled, as he pulled at the collar of his shirt. "Bareback bollocky-Bill."

"Balloons?" Shannon asked, tone laced with confusion, as she snuggled up on Kav's lap. "What are you—"

"Yeah, baby." He gave her a meaningful look that said *go with it.* "*Balloons.*"

"Oh." Shannon's eyes widened as awareness dawned on her. "*Balloons.*"

"Balloons." Gibsie choked out a laugh. "Ah, lad. I love this kid."

"Hold on." Frowning, Ollie turned to look at me. "Do you and Aoife play with balloons together?"

"Not nearly enough," Gibsie snickered.

"Ha-fucking-ha, lad." I rolled my eyes. "You're hilarious."

Ollie frowned in confusion. "Huh?"

"Joey burst his balloon," Johnny explained to number five.

"And now he can't play anymore games with Aoife because of his dodgy balloons," Gibsie laughed, thoroughly fucking enjoying himself at my expense.

"Oh no," Ollie said with a sad sigh. "Was it the needles? Does she not want to play with you anymore now?"

"Huh?"

"Did you burst her balloon with your needles?" His brown eyes were full of compassion. "Did you make her sad?"

Everyone fell quiet, the laughing stopped, and I felt another piece of me die inside.

"Yeah, Ols," I forced the words out. "I made her sad with my needles."

"Huh." Seeming mollified with that answer, Ollie skipped out of the living room, leaving behind a bad taste in my mouth.

"Well, *that* sure as hell went south fast," Gibsie declared, tossing his controller down and climbing to his feet. "Now, I feel like comfort eating."

"Stay out of the biscuit tin, Gibs," Johnny argued from his perch on the couch with my sister. "You're in training, lad, remember?"

"Yeah, well, you tell my emotions that, Johnny, because I'm feeling raw, lad. *Raw*, I tell you," he replied, swiping his car keys off the coffee table. "I'm going on a food run into town."

"There's plenty to eat in the kitchen."

"Grease, Cap," he snapped, moving for the door. "I need grease, lad. Not another boiled chicken fucking fillet."

"You disgust me."

"Not nearly as much as this healthy eating plan you've got me following disgusts me," he huffed before wagging his brows and grinning. "Now, who's up for a burger from the chipper?"

Kav said *no* and the same time Shannon said *yes*, and I swear I'd never seen a lad do a one-eighty faster. "You want something from the chipper, Shan?"

"Uh, maybe?" she replied. "If that's okay?"

"Anything," he replied gruffly. "You can anything you want, baby."

Beaming up at him, my sister reeled off her food order, while Kav hung on her every word.

"*Anything, Shannon like the river,*" Gibsie parroted in mocking tone, clutching his chest. "*You can have anything, baby.*"

"Gibs," Kav warned, climbing to his feet and pocketing his wallet. "Give it a bleeding rest, will ya?"

"*You can have my battered sausage,*" Gibs continued to gush mockingly. "*Like I said: anything for you, baby.*"

"I'll take a spin into town if it's going," I interrupted, deciding that it would be mentally less scarring to ignore the battered sausage jibe. "See if Aoife's back."

Maths is not my strong point, Mam!

AOIFE

"Where's Dad? Has he come back yet?"

"No, I presume he's still at the garage, love. I haven't seen him since we got home from town. How are you feeling, Aoife love?"

"Oh, I don't know, Mam," I called out from our bathroom later that night, as I stood under the steady spray of water pouring down on me. "Like I want to throttle Dad for getting rid of the bath."

"How are the pains?" Mam asked from the bathroom doorway. "Are they coming regular yet?"

"No, they're not coming regular," I snapped, having had quite enough of this whole damn ordeal. "Nothing about my life is regular, so why would my contractions be any different."

"Well, you heard what the midwife said on the phone," she parroted. "As soon as they start coming every five minutes, and last for a full minute consistently for over an hour, then we need to head to the hospital."

"Maths is not my strong point, Mam," I snapped, scrubbing myself down with a loofah, while I mentally warned my little intruder to stay the hell put for another night. "You do realize you're talking to the girl who failed leaving cert maths, don't ya?"

"Oh, Aoife," she laughed. "Only you could make a joke during a time like this."

"Who's joking?"

"Have you packed your bag for the hospital?"

"Yeah, it's in the back of my car," I called back. "That's why I was asking where Dad was. He took my car, remember?"

"Oh Jesus." I could hear the panic in her voice. "Let me go and phone him up. Tell him to get back with it."

"No need," I grunted, breathing through a particularly crippling tightening, as my belly turned to rock from the pressure. "I'm not having the baby tonight."

I waited until my mother had closed the bathroom door before releasing what I could describe as a low keening noise from my throat.

The pressure building up in my body was beyond intense.

Electrifying and assaulting my core.

"Jesus, I'm going to die," I wailed, biting down on my lip, as I tried to breathe through the pain. "This is going to take me out."

Wanting to stay under the steady spray of hot water, but *needing* to move more, I climbed out of the shower and hastily wrapped a towel around myself, squatting and lunging awkwardly, as I tried to ease the pressure in my pelvis.

"Don't kill me, kid," I begged, clutching the rim of the sink when another wave of heated pressure began to build. "Be gentle on Mammy."

This was it.

Dammit, it was happening.

I could feel it in my bones.

I could hear it in the feral noise my mouth continued to make.

"You've got this," I told the girl staring back at me in the bathroom mirror. "You've absolutely got this."

Riding out another contraction, while mentally wondering how the hell I was going to manage to dress myself in order to actually *go* to the hospital, I half-walked, half-waddled into my bedroom in search of something to throw on, puffing and panting like an injured animal.

When the words, "Nice legs," filled my ears, I froze in my bedroom doorway.

Froze *and* peed myself.

My breath hitched in my throat when I saw him.

There he was.

Covered in scars and drowning in secrets.

The self-inflicted ones, the bruising on his veins, the indents on his flesh from where he'd shot up, were harder to stomach than the ones he'd endured at the hands of his father.

But he was *here*.

He was *back*.

He was *home*.

He was *clean*.

Broken, bruised, and a little bent out of shape, Joey Lynch sat at the foot of my bed, with the sleeves of his hoodie rolled up to his elbows, and a wild-eyed expression etched on his face.

"Holy shit." Springing into action, Joey jerked to his feet. "Did you just . . ."

"Just wet myself?" I strangled out, chest heaving, as my emotions threatened to consume me. "Yeah, Joe, I think I did."

"I think that was your waters going, Molloy," he told me, closing the space between us. "Are you in *labor*?"

"Depends," I cried, throwing my arms around him when he reached me. "Are you really here?"

"I'm here, queen." His arms came around my body, and I felt myself grow limp against him, as my ability to be strong suddenly abandoned me.

Months.

I had kept up the act for *months*.

Holding on, keeping my head up, praying, hoping, willing, and manifesting this moment into existence.

And now it was *happening*.

He had come back for me.

"Then yeah, Joe," I sobbed, clutching onto him as another contraction started to build up inside of me. "I'm definitely in labor."

"Jesus, Mary, Joseph, and the donkey," Mam screeched when she returned to room and found my long-lost love standing there. "Where in the name of Jesus did you come from?"

"The window," Joey told my mother, as he knelt in front of me and pulled the biggest granny knickers I owned up my thighs.

Oh, the indignity.

"When did you get back, Joey love?"

"Today. Came straight here, but Tony told me to go fuck myself."

"Explains the window entrance."

"Do you have a bag, Molloy?" he asked, reaching for a pair of fluffy socks and slipping them on my feet. "If the contractions are coming that close together, then we need to get a shove on."

"Tony has her car. The bag is in the boot," Mam answered for me. "He's on a roadside call out – said he'd be another hour at the least before he gets back into town. And ah, well, I don't want to worry anyone, but I've just been out to the van and we've a flat tire."

"Is there a spare in the back?" I heard him ask. "I'll run down and change it."

"No."

"What the *fuck*, Trish!"

"I know, love! I know!"

"Aw crap," I groaned, leaning heavily against Joey as another contraction ricocheted through my body. "It feels like I'm splitting down the middle."

"You're grand," he was quick to soothe, reaching around to rub my back when a pained cry escaped me. "Just keep breathing. Nice and steady."

"Joe," I groaned, digging my chin into the crook of his neck when the pain threatened to rip me open. "I'm dying here."

"Keep breathing," he instructed, slipping a hand into his jeans pocket and withdrawing a mobile phone. "I can get us a spin to the hospital."

"Yeah, I'm going to need you to let me out of this car," Gibsie announced, dry heaving from the front seat, as he drove like a maniac towards the city. "Like right fucking now!"

"You're driving the bleeding car, ya bollox," Johnny barked, looking equally as distressed in the passenger seat. Putting his head in his hands, he rocked his oversized body back and forth. "It's grand, Gibs. It's perfectly normal. We can get through this together."

"All I wanted was a burger."

"I know, Gibs."

"Any maybe a curry chips. Is that too much to ask for? And now, after what we've just witnessed, I'll never eat again, Johnny."

"Would you two shut the fuck up," Joey snapped, flustered. "You're scaring her."

"She's scaring me!" Gibsie accused, reaching across the console to grab Johnny's hand.

"I know, lad," Johnny choked out, clutching his hand. "Me too."

"Stop panicking!" I screamed, lunging between the seats to clatter the pair of them. "You're making it worse."

"Calm down, boys," my mother commanded from the other side of me. "This is all very natural."

"There's nothing natural about the noises coming out of your daughter," Gibsie wailed, dodging a fist to the back of the head from Joey. "I want my mam."

"*When you approach the roundabout, take the third exit*," the Sat Nav in his car instructed in that mechanical robot voice. "*And continue southbound.*"

"Southbound? Where the hell is southbound?"

"Straight ahead, Gibs."

"Oh Jesus, Cap," Gibsie practically wept. "Not the roundabouts."

"You've got this, Gibs."

"You know I'm not good with roundabouts."

"*Veer left. Redirecting route*," the Sat Nav said when he took the wrong turn off. "*Redirecting route northbound.*"

"Would you listen to her?" Gibsie demanded, waving a hand around animatedly. "Talking down to me like she knows everything." Glaring at the Sat Nav attached to the dashboard of his car, he shouted, "What the fuck do you know about it? Huh? You're not even *from* Ireland!"

"It's a bot, Gibs, not an actual person," Johnny tried to explain. "Don't take it personal."

"Oh, don't let her fool you, Cap, she knows what she's doing," Gibsie argued. "Judging me from her little screen."

"I can't," I cried out, unable to hold it together a second longer, as the pressure in my pelvis became too much. "Fuck. I need to open my legs and I don't have enough room."

"Molloy, look at me."

"No, Joe, No. I don't want to do this! Please god … I've had enough—"

"*Aoife*, open your eyes!"

Panic-stricken, and for what had to be the first time in my life, I did as I was told.

"I'm here." Joey's voice was full of confidence. "Right here with ya." His eyes shone with clearness – with sobriety. "I'm going nowhere, okay? Never again. I won't leave your side." And then his steady hands were on my cheeks, forcing me to focus on his crystal-clear green eyes. "And I won't let anything bad happen to you."

Reunion 2.0

JOEY

When I climbed through Molloy's window tonight, the last thing I had expected to witness was her in full-blown labor, but that's exactly what happened.

Battling her mother when we got to the hospital was another event I hadn't anticipated. To be fair, I didn't blame Trish for wanting to be with her daughter.

It was a heated argument that resulted in me winning when Molloy stepped in and told the midwife that I was the one she wanted with her.

Several hours had passed since we were taken down to delivery, and while she was dilating and had reached seven centimeters according her last internal, it seemed to be dragging on forever.

Sucking on gas and air like it was going out of fashion, my best friend balanced on a birthing ball, rocking and rolling her hips, as the worst fucking noises I'd ever heard in my life escaped her.

I wanted to save her.

I wanted to put a goddamn stop to her suffering.

But I was completely helpless.

Contorting in pain, as her body tried to expel the baby I'd put in there, I never felt so fucking guilty in my life.

Even now, as she leaned against me in her delivery suite, in the throes of another contraction, all I wanted to do was apologize.

Jesus Christ.

"I need to go to the bathroom," she declared, twisting sideways on the ball to grip my shoulders. "Joe, I need to go right now."

"Okay," I replied, trying to remain calm when her face turned a deep shade of red. "I'll help you."

"What's that?" the midwife, who was lingering nearby, asked when

I moved for the adjoined bathroom with my girlfriend leaning heavily against me.

"She needs to use the bathroom," I explained. "I'm just taking her now."

"No, no, no," the midwife replied, ushering us towards the bed instead. "Climb on, Aoife pet, and let me examine you."

"No, you don't understand," Molloy groaned, climbing onto the bed, and then writhing in pain when the nurse stepped between her legs. "If you don't let me go to the bathroom right this second, I'm going to shit on you!"

"Just as I thought. You're fully dilated, Aoife," the midwife declared. "You're ready to deliver."

"A poo?"

"No, pet, a baby."

"Oh, Jesus, Joe." Crying out, she clutched my hand and pulled me close. "If I shit in front of you, please don't hold it against me."

"Molloy," I coaxed, brushing her hair off her clammy face. "You can do whatever you want in front of me, okay?"

"That's comforting, Joe," she cried out, hooking an arm around my neck and catching me up in a headlock Kav would be proud of. "Because I think you're about to see what I look like on the inside."

Something was wrong.

I could feel it.

Molloy had been pushing for over an hour and nothing was happening.

The concerned look in the midwife's eyes was enough to send my heartrate spiking, but it was the shrill sound of the bell ringing that put the fear of God into me.

"You're grand," I coaxed, keeping a death grip on her hand, as her panicked green eyes looked up at me from her hospital bed when the room filled with doctors and nurses. "This is all normal, Molloy."

It wasn't.

It couldn't be.

I'd been with my mother when she delivered Sean.

This was about as far from normal as you could get.

"Okay, Mom, the baby is starting to get very tired, sweetheart, so we're going to help you deliver, okay?" the midwife that had been with us since admission told us. "We're doing to take you down to theatre now."

Theatre?

Jesus Christ.

"Joe," Molloy cried out, as I was pushed aside for them to wheel her away. "Joe!"

"It's okay," I called out, feeling helpless as I watched them take her away from me. "Everything is grand, Molloy, I promise!"

"Dad will follow you down," the nurse holding her hand said, as they disappeared through the doors with my girlfriend. "He just needs to gown up first."

"What's happening?" I choked out, feeling like I was about to pass the hell out, as another nurse helped me into a blue operating gown and hair net. "What's wrong with her?"

"The baby is showing signs of shoulder dystocia," she explained calmly. "Mom needs intervention to deliver."

"What do you mean shoulder dystocia?" I demanded, following her over to the sink and scrubbing my hands raw before patting them dry on paper towels and masking up. "Does Aoife need a caesarian?"

"Baby's head is out, but baby's shoulders are stuck in the birth canal," she explained as she ushered me down a long corridor towards theatre. "Don't worry, Dad. Mom and baby are in great hands."

"Joe," Molloy was crying out when I was finally let into theatre. I could see her on the operating table, surrounded by the surgical team, as her hand flailed around wildly, searching for mine.

"I'm right here, Molloy," I called out, jumping into action as I moved straight for her, only to be herded towards the top end of the table by one of the surgical team. "I'm here, baby."

"Joe," she sobbed, snatching up my hand in hers, as she screamed in pain. "Joe, it hurts so bad."

"Can you give her something?" I demanded, feeling myself spiral as I watched them manhandle her like she didn't have feelings. "Jesus Christ, you can't do *that* to her without an epidural."

"No time for that now, Dad."

"Joe—"

"You're grand. You're grand, baby."

"Push, Aoife. We need you to push."

"I'm right here," I whispered in her ear, holding onto her head to stop us both from watching. "Just stay with me, Aoif. Stay with me, okay?"

Crying out in agony when they pushed on her stomach, she clung to my shoulders. "Make it stop!"

I wanted to.

More than anything I'd ever wanted in my life.

"Push, Aoife. Harder. Come on, baby needs to be delivered."

"Ahhhh." Her face was white to the point of grey, as she clung to me and pushed with all her might, panting and shaking violently. "I'm scared."

Me, too.

"Don't be," I tried to soothe, leaning in close so that she was only focusing on my face, and *not* what was happening around us. "I won't let anything happen to you."

"Ahhhh," she screamed again, face contorting in pain before suddenly growing limp in my arms.

Moments later, the sound of a baby screaming filled the room.

"You did it, Aoif," I choked out, trembling just as badly as she was, as the sound of our child filled the room. "You did it, baby."

"Yeah," she strangled out, nodding weakly, as her eyes rolled. "Oh, god . . ."

"Hey, hey hey." Leaning over the bed, I caught ahold of her face between my hands and tried to keep her focused, while the doctors continued to work on her. "You're okay." I pressed a kiss to her head. "Come on, Molloy, stay with me. Can you hear the baby?"

"Yeah." She was trembling and so was I.

I could hear the screaming baby in the background, I didn't even know what we had, but I didn't dare move from her side, as I focused on her face and ignored the way they were working on her body. "You're okay. Shh, shh, baby, you're okay."

"Joe . . ."

"Step aside, Dad," one of the nurses instructed. "Mom needs a little help right now."

I'd never seen so much blood.

But I wasn't about to tell her that.

"No, no, no," she slurred, pushing weakly at the oxygen mask they were placing over her mouth and nose. "Joe . . ."

They were all so calm when I felt like my world was slipping away from me. I was watching her body bleed out while, she was still conscious.

It was beyond terrifying.

Freaking the fuck out, a nurse led me over to where the baby was, as they worked on stemming the bleeding.

She's hemorrhaging.

She's bleeding out.

You killed her.

She's going to die.

Feeling faint, my gaze flicked between the operating table my girlfriend was lying on, and the baby in the incubator in front of me.

I didn't even know what it was.

I was too fucking panic stricken.

"Mom is *fine*," the nurse continued to coax. "Don't worry. She's in the best hands. She's going to be just *fine*. Now, come and meet your son."

"Son," I repeated, numb, as my attention flicked back to Molloy. "Aoif?"

I couldn't see her anymore.

Too many people in scrubs had taken up position around her for me to see.

"Molloy?" My heart gunned in my check. "Aoife!"

"Here you go, Dad."

Moments later, the screaming bundle was thrust into my arms.

"Congratulations, Dad. He's a beauty."

Struck fucking dumb, I stared down the baby in my arms.

He was roaring like a bull, with his tiny hands balled into fists, as he squirmed and stretched in my arms.

"Jesus," I breathed, cradling him in my arms, as my emotions got the better of me. "You're here."

And then he opened his eyes and looked at me.

And I was done.

My heart no longer beat for me.

For the rest of my days, it would beat entirely for the child in my arms.

Fuck.

Still draped in a blue gown and hairnet, I was removed from theatre, while my girlfriend and baby remained inside.

My heart was hammering.

My mind was reeling.

Breathing hard and fast, I sagged against the wall in a nearby corridor, feeling my heart thunder wildly in my chest.

What the fuck just happened?

It was all so fast.

My phone was ringing in my pocket, and I had to get a handle on myself and force myself to answer.

"Joey." That was Trish. "What's happening? Is she okay? Did she have the baby?"

"I, ah, yeah, she's okay," I croaked out, still completely reeling from the way it had all gone down. "The baby got stuck. They had to bring her down to theatre to deliver."

"She had a caesarean?"

"No." I shook my head, feeling rattled. "They got him out before that."

But the things they had to do to her.

The blood.

The pain on her face.

I flinched at the memory.

"Him?" Trish's voice hitched. "It's a boy?"

"Yeah." I exhaled a ragged breath, head nodding vigorously, as I tried to get my head around the lifechanging events that had just taken place. "He's huge, Trish. They told me he was 56 centimeters long and he weighs like 4.4 kilos."

"What's that in pounds and ounces?"

"9lbs 12oz according to the midwife."

"Oh Jesus, the poor girl."

"Yeah, I know." I flinched again. "What time is it?"

"It's half past three in the morning," she replied. "What time was the baby born?"

"A little over an hour ago," I replied. "Just after twenty-past two."

"Where are you now? Are you with Aoife? Can you put her on the phone?"

"No, I ah . . . " I swallowed deeply and pressed the heel of my hand to my head, fighting down the panic trying to claw its way out of me. "She was, ah, she was hemorrhaging, and they couldn't find the source of the bleeding. I heard them say something about a possible uterine rupture." Blowing out a pained breath, I strangled out, "She's still in theatre."

"No." The cry that tore from my girlfriend's mother's throat put the fear of God inside of me. "Oh Jesus no. She's in there alone?"

"They wouldn't let me stay," I strangled out, chest heaving, as the realization of how serious this was hit home. "I tried, Trish, but they put me out. Said I couldn't be in there when she was under general anesthetic."

"Oh, Joey love, don't panic," she choked out. "I'm sure she'll be fine."

"Yeah." I blinked back my tears. "Me, too."

PART 12

Mammy's a fighter

JOEY

After being put through the wringer, Molloy was wheeled into the recovery room ninety minutes later, hooked up to more wires and drips than I'd ever seen in my life.

When I was taken in to be with her, I felt faint.

She was grey in color.

Fucking *grey*.

All completely normal, I was continuously reassured of by the nurses and doctors still gathered around her, monitoring her vitals, as I remained by her side. My attention flicked between the girl asleep on the bed, and the baby that had been returned to me with his mother.

Baby boy Molloy, date of birth: 30/08/05, time of birth: 02:22 was scribbled on his little hand and ankle name tags, but I didn't think he needed any of that to be recognized.

He was every inch his mother's son with clumps of bloodied blond curls matted to his little head, and a pair of lungs he clearly inherited from his mother's side.

Even though Molloy lost a lot of blood after delivery, the team had managed to stop the postpartum hemorrhaging without having to operate, but the thought of *how* they managed to do that sent a shiver down my spine. I was grateful that they knocked her out, because nobody deserved to be put through that kind of physical manhandling.

Torture.

That was the only word for it.

For what I'd witnessed them do to save her and the baby's lives.

"You're amazing," I whispered, leaning over the bed, as I pressed a kiss to her clammy forehead. "You're a soldier, baby."

Repressing the urge to pull her sleeping frame into my arms and cling to her, I continued to hover anxiously. With our son in my arms, I needed her to wake up and stay asleep all in one breath.

"I'm so proud of you," I whispered, using one hand to adjust the blanket draped over her limp body. "You're a queen."

"We'll be moving her back up to the labor ward soon," one of the nurses told me, as he adjusted the flow of whatever the hell they had dripping from a bag into the IV line in her arm. "She's going to be in and out of it for a few more hours," he added. "All normal, so nothing to worry about. Her body has been through it, and she needs time to rest and recover. She has a catheter in, so no need to wake her, Dad."

"She'll be okay, though, won't she?"

"Absolutely," he reassured me, smiling down at the baby in my arms. "This little guy has a one heck of a fighter for a mammy."

Back on the ward early Tuesday morning, with Molloy sleeping off the drugs they gave her, I sat at her bedside, cradling the tiny bundle in my arms.

For the second time in my life, I was a father.

For the first time in my life, I had a child of my own.

It felt different now than it had with Ollie, Sean, and Tadhg.

It felt *deeper*.

There was something inside of me, an invisible cord of sorts, that went from my chest into his. I felt it every time I laid eyes on him.

Feeling his tiny body pressed to my chest when I fed him was the reality check I needed. I was responsible for this tiny person and his sleeping mother.

Anxiety thrummed through my body as my attention flicked between my son and his mother.

The two people that created me had destroyed each other.

My father killed my mother.

He tried to take the whole fucking lot of us out with him.

And now we were here.

Me and Aoife and this tiny little baby.

He was depending on me just the same as I had depended on my old man.

I just kept staring at him, wondering how *he* could do it to us, when every instinct inside of me was demanding I protect the infant in my arms and the girl who bore him.

They said he was huge, but he looked tiny to me.

He had a cute little button nose that reminded me of Shan, and puffy swollen lips just like the rest of us.

Mam's lips.

We all had them.

All six of us.

His fingers were freakishly long to match the rest of him, but Jesus did he have his mother's looks.

Honestly, I'd never seen a more beautiful baby in all my eighteen years on earth.

A little while later a nurse came in to check on the line in Molloy's arm, and to replace the bag of fluid on her drip.

"Is she okay?" I asked, instantly on edge, as I watched the nurse like a hawk. "She's been asleep for a long time."

"She's fine," the nurse replied with such certainty that it put me at ease. "Poor mite is exhausted." Turning to look at me, she offered me a sympathetic smile. "How's baby taking his feeds for you, Dad?"

"He took two ounces in theatre, and another two down in the recovery room, and he's after taking another three ounces now," I told her, gesturing to the half-empty bottle resting on the arm of the chair. "I don't know if I should give him any more formula until his mam wakes up." Feeling helpless, I shrugged before saying, "She mentioned something awhile back about wanting to breastfeed."

She gave me a sympathetic smile before asking, "Any dirty nappies?"

"Yeah, he's been wet and dirty."

"Fantastic."

"He had the, uh, the black poo. You know the first one they have?"

"Meconium."

"That's the name of it."

She gave me this strange smile. "Younger siblings?"

I nodded.

"How many?"

"Four."

"Uh-huh." Her smile deepened. "We could tell."

My brows furrowed. "We?"

"All of the nurses on the ward." She smiled again. "It's not often we see young boys on this ward taking to fatherhood like you."

"Oh."

I wasn't taking to anything.

I was fucking petrified.

But I *was* determined.

To be present.

To do right by this boy and his mother.

"Does your son have a name?"

"I, ah ... " Blowing out a breath, I shook my head. "I don't know what she wants to call him yet."

"Ah, mammy is making the decision."

"She did all the work," I replied, settling my son on my shoulder to wind him. "She can name the baby."

"Smart boy."

"Could that happen again?" Gently patting our son's back, I gestured to his mother. "What happened to Aoife after delivery? The bleeding. It won't come back, will it?"

After consoling me with a whole heap of medical terminology and lingo that went clean out of my head, the nurse stopped in the doorway and asked, "Do you need me to help you with anything?"

Yeah, I need you to make my girlfriend open her eyes.

"No," I replied gruffly. "I've got this."

I waited until the nurse left before setting my son back down in his bassinet and returning to my post of hovering over his mother.

"You've got this," I whispered, stroking her cheek. "Little fighter."

Remembering what the nurse said about letting her sleep, I reluctantly shoved my hands into the front pocket of my hoodie to stop myself from touching her, only to frown when my fingers grazed paper.

Nanny's letter.

Returning to my perch on the chair at her bedside, I withdrew the envelope my great-grandmother had given to me yesterday.

Christ, it felt like a million years ago.

Tearing open the envelope, I reached for the note inside only to halt in my tracks when my eyes landed on cash.

A *lot* of cash.

"Holy fuck," I strangled out, eyes widening as a thick wad of fifty-euro notes spilled onto my lap.

Panic -stricken, I looked around to make sure that I was alone before quickly counting the money up.

I broke into a cold sweat when I finished counting and had to re-count it another three times before my head registered what my brain was telling me.

Fifteen thousand euro.

Fifteen grand.

Fifteen fucking k.

"What the hell?" Beyond confused, I stuffed the cash back into my pocket and quickly unfolded the note.

Dear Joseph,

To know that I finally get to write this letter brings me both immense joy and sadness in equal measures.

Joy, because I know that you are thriving and most importantly finally free of that horrible man, but great sorrow because it came with such a high price.

I know you're probably wondering about the money, so I won't beat around the bush. When Granda passed away, he left you a few bob in his will, but with it came strict instructions to not hand it over to you until you were away from your father and out from under his roof.

I suppose Granda knew as well as I did that you would give it to your mother, who, in turn, would give it to him.

This money was meant for you, Joseph.

Granda wanted to do this for you.

For your future.

And by God do you have a bright one ahead of you, sweet boy.

I want you to take this money and look after your little family.

I like her very much, Joseph. Don't let her slip through your fingers. Trust old Nanny when I tell you that she's a keeper.

You'll make a wonderful father and a devoted husband in time.

I sleep well at night knowing that I have a grandson like you in the world.

All my love,

Nanny Murphy.

Say hi to Mammy

AOIFE

When I opened my eyes, I was bombarded with an array of feelings and emotions.

Pain came first.

Confusion followed swiftly after.

Licking my dry lips, I twisted my head from side to side, trying to shake the wave of dizziness off and make sense of what the hell was happening. It was only when I twisted sideways to my right that I saw him.

Joey.

He was sitting in a chair next to my bed, cradling something to his chest.

"Hey, stud," I mumbled, feeling groggy and hoarse, as I soaked in the sight of him.

Instantly, his focus snapped to me, and the emotion I saw in his crystal-clear green eyes was overwhelming.

He's here.

He's really here.

"Hey, queen." Dropping his feet from where they had been resting on the side of my bed, he straightened up. "How are you feeling?"

"Like I went ten rounds with Tyson."

"Well, you don't look it," he was quick to reply, as he stood up and closed the space between us. "Nice everything, Molloy."

"Joe." My voice was thick with emotion. My entire focus on the baby nestled in the crook of his arm. "Is the baby okay?"

"He's perfect," he replied, sinking down on the edge of my bed and then leaning in close to press a kiss to my brow. "You did such a good job, Aoif."

"He?" My heart bucked wildly in my chest, as I snaked a trembling hand out from under the blankets to touch his little pink hand. "We have a son?"

"We have a son, and he has a set of pipes on him just like his mam," he confirmed gruffly, carefully placing the small baby on my chest. "Say hi to Mammy."

Unable to stop the tears from spilling from my eyes, I attempted to cradle the baby in my arms, feeling completely overwhelmed.

"We did this?" Sniffling, I stared at his tiny little face, feeling too much in this moment to comprehend. "Oh my god." I choked out a half-laugh, half-sob. "He has Shannon's little nose."

"That's what I thought."

"He's got your curls."

"He's got your eyes."

"It's all you, Molloy." Pressing a few buttons on the remote attached to my bed, he raised the back of the bed into a semi-sitting position before removing the hairnet from my hair and pressing another kiss to my brow. "He's gorgeous like his mam."

"Yeah, well, his mam doesn't feel so gorgeous anymore," I mumbled, feeling vulnerable and weirdly exposed.

"His mam never looked more gorgeous than she does right now," Joey corrected. "Six years ago today, I locked eyes on you for the first time, sitting on the wall outside of school, and now we're sitting here with our son." Smiling, he leaned in close and kissed me again. "Thanks for my baby, queen. You still take the air clean out of my lungs."

That did it.

His words of affection broke the dam inside of me.

"Joe." Heaving out a pained sob, I heaved our baby closer to my chest and kissed his chubby cheek. "When they couldn't get him out, I thought he was going to—"

"He's right here," Joey was quick to coax, shifting closer, and wrapping an arm around my shoulders. "You're both here, and I'm going to take care of ye." Another kiss. "I won't let anything happen to either one of you, Molloy, I promise."

"Have you been here the whole time?"

"I told you that I wouldn't leave you." He gently lifted our son out of my arms and placed him in the bassinet next to the bed before returning to my side. "I'll never leave you again."

I didn't have the strength to be strong or put on a brave face in this moment.

I didn't have anything left in the tank.

I had spent so long being the brave one.

The strong one.

Now, all I wanted to do was fold into him.

Because I couldn't do this anymore.

I needed someone to lean on.

"I can't do this on my own," I admitted, fisting his hoodie as he carefully cradled me in his arms. "I'm so tired, Joe."

"I know you are," he replied, pushing my hair off my face, as he tucked me in closer.

"You can't get sick again," I cried, clinging to him for all I was worth. "You can't leave me on my own in this."

"I'll never leave you on your own again," he vowed, wrapping both of his arms around me. "I will *never* fail you again." I could hear the sincerity in his voice, and I needed so badly for him to be right about this. For him to *stay*. "It's my turn, Molloy." He kissed my hair. "To look after you."

I'll look after you

JOEY

Later that afternoon, the quiet bubble Molloy and I had been cocooned in while we came to terms with the squawking baby we co-created, was well and truly burst.

Barging into the hospital room, laden down with balloons, stuffed animals, and shopping bags came Trish and Casey, followed by a squeamish looking Tony.

"Aoife!" Trish and Casey both exclaimed, making a beeline for my girlfriend. "Oh, my poor baby."

"Hi, Mam. Hi, Case."

"Oh, look at your poor face. You look dead only to wash ya."

"Wow. Thanks, Mam."

"Don't mind your mam," Casey was quick to interject. "You're every inch the ridey you've always been. Minus the big belly."

Having the good sense to get out of the way, I stepped around the girls and moved for Tony.

"I see your father's still here," Tony noted, eyes locked on the baby in my arms. "That's a good start."

"I'm still here," I confirmed, readjusting my hold on my son. "Say hi to your grandfather, kid."

"Better not be calling any grandson of mine after the car in *Knight Rider*," Tony grumbled, eyes locked on the baby in my arms.

"Wash your ears out, Dad," Molloy called back. "He said kid, not Kit."

"Kid?" Tony blanched. "Jesus, that's worse."

"That's not his name," I chuckled, holding him out for Tony to hold. "Here."

"Ah Jesus, boyo, don't be giving him to me to hold," Tony strangled out, eyes locked on my son, as he quickly removed his coat and rolled up the sleeves of his shirt to the elbows. "Look at the size of him." Moving for the chair next to the bed, he sat down and blew out a shaky breath. "I haven't held a baby since the twins were small."

"Give him to me," Trish cut in, making a beeline for us. "I want the first squeeze."

"Don't mind her," Tony grumbled, gesturing me towards him with both hands. "Come here to me, boyo, and have a cuddle with Grandad."

"Oh my god," Casey crooned, leaning over Tony with a pink digital camera in her hands, as she snapped away like a mad woman. "He's absolutely divine, you guys."

"He's like a small man already," Trish cooed. "He's huge, Aoife."

"Yeah," Molloy mumbled, closing her eyes. "I can still feel how huge he was."

With all eyes on the baby, I returned to her side, "You good?"

"Mm-hm." She nodded, eyes still shut. "Just some tightening."

Yeah, they told us that would happen.

She'd been given a shit ton of medicine to help her uterus contract.

"So, mister reformed bad boy," Casey acknowledged, offering me a wink. "Still behaving yourself?" Waggling her brows, she added, "I hope you haven't been sneaking any gas and air on the sly."

"Casey!"

"Nah, I'm good," I chuckled, shaking my head. "Clean as a whistle."

"There's a first time for everything."

"Sure is."

"So, have you two given this little man an actual name yet?" she asked. "Or are we going by kid for the foreseeable."

Molloy looked to me, and I shrugged. "It's your call, baby."

"We have a name," she said, licking her lips. "We have two, actually."

"Oh?" Trish's eyes lit up. "Do tell."

"Joe's against it, but I want his middle name to be Joseph," she told them. "And his last name will be Lynch." Shivering, she added, "We're not married, so it's important to me that everyone knows our son has a father who claimed him."

I swallowed down my protests, refusing point blank to argue with the girl that had been through eight hours of hell to give me a son. Instead, I nodded in support when she looked to me for reassurance.

"And his first name?" Trish pushed.

"Anthony," Molloy said. "His name is Anthony Joseph Lynch." Smiling, she added, "AJ for short."

"But *I'm* Anthony," Tony squeezed out, turning the color of his daughter's Opal Corsa.

"Yeah, Dad." Molloy rolled her eyes. "We know."

"You've decided to name your son after the man who raised you," Trish said proudly, giving her daughter a huge smile. "Oh, Aoife, that's a lovely sentiment."

"Actually, we decided to name our son after the man who raised the both of us," I confirmed quietly. "Because, let's face it, the only man I ever had to show me the way was your husband."

Roughly clearing his throat, Tony looked down at AJ and sniffed. "I know exactly what that father of yours is trying to do, boyo," he told my son, voice thick with emotion. "He's trying to butter up old Grandad, isn't he?" He pressed a kiss to my son's forehead and smiled down at him. "Well, you can tell your father that it worked. Yes, you can. Tell your father that I expect his ass at the garage the minute your mother is home and back on her feet."

My heart stopped in my chest.

Molloy turned to gape at me.

"But tell that father of yours that he's on his last life," Tony continued to say, speaking to me through my son. "And tell your old fella that your grandad has a *Burdizzo* on hand if he gets any notions about giving you a brother or sister before he finishes his apprenticeship and puts a ring on your mother's finger."

"*Burdizzo?*" Casey frowned. "The hell is that?"

"It's what they use on farms to sever a bull's testicular cord," I strangled out, thinking back to something Podge once told me. "You can tell your grandfather that you're going to be an only child."

Tony smirked. "You can tell your father that's a wise decision."

"Oh my god, Dad," Molloy grumbled, waving a hand around. "Just kiss and make up already. Everyone knows you've been miserable all summer without your little sidekick at the garage."

"Well, it looks like I've a new little sidekick to keep me occupied," Tony mused, fighting off Trish, who was trying to coax the baby out of his arms.

"You feel like going to the bathroom yet?" I asked, turning my attention back to Molloy. They'd removed her catheter a while ago and encouraged her to get out of bed and use the bathroom, but Molloy hadn't budged an inch.

"Joe?"

"Yeah?"

Wide-eyed, she gestured for me to come closer so that she could whisper in my ear. "I'm scared to move." Shivering, she cupped my cheek, and whispered, "It feels like everything is going to fall out of me."

My heart cracked.

"That won't happen," I tried to reassure her, tucking her under my arm. "You've just given birth, baby. It's going to feel all kinds of fucked up, but I promise nothing bad going to happen to you."

"I'm covered in blood," she whispered, hand trembling, as she buried her face in my neck. "I'm disgusting."

"You're fucking beautiful," I corrected gruffly before turning my attention to her parents. "Aoife needs a shower. Can you watch the baby?"

"I can take you, Aoife love—"

"No, I'll take her," I cut Trish off and said when I felt her daughter's body stiffen in protest. "I've got this."

"My legs feel like concrete," Molloy mumbled as she gingerly climbed out of bed. "Nobody look, okay?"

"Okay," all three of her visitors dutifully chorused.

"Joe, the bed," she choked out when she was standing, eyes locked on the dried blood on the sheets.

"It's grand."

"But there's blood everywhere."

"It's okay."

"It's on my nightie and my legs – ugh, Joe, it's even on my socks."

"Molloy, I promise you it's *grand*," I coaxed, hooking one arm around her waist, while taking her elbow with the other. "Every other woman in this hospital is in the same boat. You've got nothing to be embarrassed about, okay? They see this kind of thing a dozen times a day here."

"But *you* saw it, Joe," she mumbled, lip wobbling.

"You think I care about that?" I shook my head. "I'm in fucking awe of you, baby. What you just did? Giving me a son? Christ, Molloy I'm punching so high right now it's ridiculous."

"Really?"

"Really, really."

"Oh, lovely." Sniffling, she nodded and leaned into my side. "I'm wearing a nappy."

She had those disposable knickers and socks on, and I felt so fucking guilty for doing this to her, because I was under no illusions as to who was responsible for this girl.

Me.

"That's it. Nice and slow." Taking it one step at a time, I helped her into the adjoining bathroom. "There's no rush, baby."

"Thanks, Joe," she said when we were safely inside the bathroom and away from prying eyes. "You can go out now."

Yeah, I wasn't going anywhere. Not when she looked like she was two seconds away from passing out on the floor. She'd been giving two units of blood and an iron transfusion for Christ's sake. She wasn't fit to be going anywhere on her own, much less showering alone.

"No, Molloy, stop, okay?" I coaxed, recapturing her arm when she tried to stand on her own. "Let me help you."

"No." Her lip wobbled again, and I watched as she tried to blink her tears away, as I helped her into the shower. "I don't want you to see me like this."

"Like what?"

"Like this," she cried, using her free hand to gesture to her stomach and legs. "It's disgusting."

"It's not disgusting," I corrected gruffly. When she made no move to, I reached for the hem of the bloodstained nightdress she'd been wearing during labor.

"No." She shook her head and twisted her body away. "Joe, no. I don't look like me anymore."

Fuck, that hurt.

Her vulnerability was soul shredding.

I was desperate to soothe her.

To make it right.

Her stomach was bruised and deflated, with deep purple stretch marks from where her body had housed and carried my son.

"You're so beautiful," I told her, voice cracking when my stupid fucking emotions threatened to get the better of me.

"No." Sniffling, she shook her head, refuting my words.

"Yes," I corrected gruffly, catching ahold of her chin with my hand. "*Yes*."

Green eyes stared up at me, so full of pain and vulnerability. "I missed you so bad." Clutching the back of my neck, she pulled my face down to hers. "I feel like I died this summer without you and I'm only coming back to life now."

"Yeah." Resting my brow against hers, I absorbed the moment, the feelings, the weight of my conscience, the future laid out before us. "I know the feeling."

It was her.

It always had been.

It always would be.

The girl from the wall.

"I'm going to take care of you," I told her. "Because I love you." She shivered violently when I pressed a kiss to her head. "Because I think you're sexy as fuck." Carefully reaching for the hem of her disposable underwear, I guided them off. "Because you're my queen." Disposing of everything she was wearing, I switched on the shower and held onto her trembling frame as she stood under the hot spray of water, not giving a damn that I was getting wet in the process. My entire focus was on the girl *still* looking at me like I hung the moon. "And because everything I have, everything I am, I owe to you."

"Aoife, love? How are you getting on in there?" Trish called out, moments before barreling into the bathroom.

"Mam, get out," Molloy hissed, giving her mother her back. "God!"

"What's that on your arse?"

"Nothing."

"Is that a tattoo?"

"No."

"Is that Joey's *name*?"

"Mam, get out!"

"Oh, Jesus, Tony."

"What's wrong, Trish?"

"No wonder that daughter of ours didn't want me helping her shower. She has that young fella's name tattooed on her arse!"

I can't do this.

AOIFE

Sleep deprivation made me a weak woman. It was the reason I had sent that dangerous text message in the middle of the night.

Exhaustion had well and truly set in, making it harder not to dwell on the feelings of confliction and regret raging inside of me.

It was the reason that Joey was sitting on the edge of my hospital bed at eight o'clock on Thursday morning.

Clad in a freshly ironed uniform, and with our son nestled in the crook of his elbow, he looked more natural at this parenting gig than I could ever dream to be.

"That's it," he coaxed, as he fed AJ his bottle.

His *bottle.*

Another pained sob escaped me.

I couldn't get him to latch.

I couldn't do anything right.

Night two with our son had been an even bigger disaster than night one, and I was beginning to think that AJ didn't like me.

"You're just tired," Joey said, setting down the empty bottle and reaching for my hand. "You've got this, Molloy."

"No, Joe, I really don't," I croaked out, trying my best not to give in to the overwhelming temptation to scream at the top of my lungs. "Everyone was right. I can't do this."

"Yes, you can," he corrected, releasing my hand to settle AJ against his shoulder. "I promise you can," he continued, shifting closer to tuck me under his free arm. "Everything's going to be fine."

"It won't be." I shook my head and wiped my nose with the sleeve of my hoodie. "I'm a shit mam." Another sob racked through my chest. "He h-hates me. He n-never c-cries for you. I c-can't even f-feed him p-properly."

"Bullshit." Standing up, I watched as he finished winding our son. "You're not a shit mam." Handling our son with as much skill as any of the midwives in the hospital, Joey set him down on the bed and went to work on changing him. "You're panicking and he can sense it," he explained gently, giving our baby a fresh nappy before popping his tiny body back into a clean onesie. "As soon as you relax, he will too." Lifting AJ into his arms, he cradled him for a moment, swaying from side to side, before settling him down in his bassinet and returning to me. "You're exhausted, Molloy. You're going through a lot right now, baby, and that little baby *adores* you, okay?" Sinking down on the bed, he carefully pulled me onto his lap. "And don't worry about how he's fed just as long as he's *fed*."

"But Mam said I sh-should be breastfeeding."

"I don't give a shit what your mother said," he countered, tightening his hold on me. "I'm his father, and I'm telling you now that he's fine. He's guzzling his bottles. He's clearly piling on the weight. There's not a bother on him, Molloy. He's thriving."

"I hate being here on my own," I admitted, burying my face in his new school jumper. "Nighttime is the worst."

"You know I would've stayed with you if I could've," he replied, sounding pained. "But they kick partners out at midnight."

"Yeah," I squeezed out, clinging to him. "I know."

"You're coming home today," he coaxed. "And I'll be over straight after school, okay? I'll bring a bag and stay at your place." He pressed a kiss to my head. "I'll do the night feeds tonight, okay? All I want you to do is *breathe* and take it handy until I get back. Your mam will be here in an hour. Let her help you."

Don't leave me.

Please don't leave me.

"I don't want to go," he said in a pained voice, clearly reading my thoughts. "But if I don't show up, I'll be in shit with my doctors—"

"It's okay," I quickly interrupted, needing to not have this conversation while I was feeling so on edge. "I'll see you after school."

"You will," he assured me. "And then we'll talk, okay? I actually have something I want to run by you and your parents." He leaned in and brushed his lips to mine. "We'll put a plan together." He kissed me again. "We'll make this work, Molloy."

Welcome to Tommen

JOEY

It was September 1st, 2005.

The first day of my second chance at sixth year, and the first day of my second chance at life – according to my therapist, that was.

The truth was my second chance was born two days ago, and being at this school instead of being with my son and girlfriend was killing me. When I stepped through the front doors of the school, the anxiety I was experiencing had little to do with my surroundings and everything to do with the girl I had left alone in the hospital.

I'd been in this position before.

I'd sat at the foot another woman's bed, watching as she crumbled under the mental anguish that came with giving birth.

I never understood it when it happened to my mother, and I was just as clueless now that it was happening to my girlfriend.

I wanted to make it right. I wanted to turn on my heels and go back to her, but we needed this little deal I had carved out.

It came with perks that I couldn't afford to turn down.

It came with freedom, and accommodation, and a future that I was banking on for my family.

My family that consisted of Molloy and AJ.

The principal of Tommen couldn't hide his distaste for me.

He made that perfectly clear.

His mistrust was potent, his wariness even more stifling, as he sat behind his desk and looked down his nose at me.

"Is he on a methadone program?" His question, while about me, was directed towards Edel and John who were sitting beside me. "Is he receiving regular counselling sessions? Attending an outpatient clinic?"

Swallowing my temper, I let John do the talking for me. After all, the man made a career out of it.

Instead, I balled my hands into fists at my sides and zoned out, only responding when the patriarch of my siblings' newfound family encouraged me to do so.

Unwelcome.

It was only one word, but the most accurate one I could think up to describe how I felt. I didn't belong here, not in this school, and not in this uniform.

Still, I held firm and allowed myself to be led by one of the few men in my life that I *actually* considered to be trustworthy.

In the end, I'd been sent on my way with a timetable and a warning to behave myself.

Like I hadn't heard that before.

"I've heard about him."

"He's bad news."

"He's constantly getting into fights over at BCS."

People whispered when I passed in the hallways.

"Apparently, he's got a big, fat chip on his shoulder."

I ignored them all. They couldn't hurt me. I'd been through too much and had come too damn far to let a few opinions throw me off track.

"That one has a seriously bad reputation."

"I heard he got a girl from his last school pregnant."

"I'm pretty sure he just got *me* pregnant by glaring at me."

"He's my brother," a familiar voice snapped, and I swung around to find Shannon of all people standing up to a group of girls in the hallway. "And you shouldn't believe everything you hear."

"Is he single?"

"You're not his type."

"What's his type?"

"His girlfriend."

I smirked to myself.

Well, this was a turn up for the books.

She was defending *me*.

Shaking off their remarks, I winked at my sister before making my way to my first class, arriving later than everyone else because this school was a fucking castle to navigate.

"Are they going to check his blood?" was the first snide comment I was dealt when I walked into Maths. "Because I don't want any druggies bleeding all over me."

"He's probably riddled with HIV," the girl beside him sneered.

"Trust me when I tell ya, Buckley, that the best part of you ran down your father's leg," a familiar voice shot back in defense, and I turned in the direction of where Gibsie was pulling out the empty chair beside him. "And as for your girlfriend, Miss fucking piggy," he added, narrowing his eyes at the girl snickering beside the prick running his mouth. "I think it's safe to say the tide wouldn't take her out."

"Fuck you, Gibsie."

"Fuck *you*?" He threw his head back. "I wouldn't ride you into battle."

The entire class erupted in laughter.

"Howdy, friend," Gibsie said with a grin when I dropped into the chair next to his.

Jesus.

"Gibs."

"Wahey! You got my name right."

"Yeah." I shrugged. "Well, I figured I better learn it off seeing as I'm stuck with ya until next June."

"That you are, my friend," he chuckled, nudging my shoulder with his. "That you are."

"So, where's your other half?"

"Claire-bear? She's in the year below us."

"No, asshole. Kav."

"Oh!" Gibsie laughed. "Oh, you mean my *other* other half. He's in honors maths." Frowning, Gibsie muttered, "Cap's in honors everything." He chuckled to himself, clearly amused with something he was thinking about, before shaking his head and adding, "Fair bit of a genius is your future brother-in-law."

Baby blues

AOIFE

I'd been home for three hours and I couldn't stop crying.

In floods of tears, I sat cross-legged on my bed, and stared down at the tiny human screaming his lungs out.

I couldn't do this.

I was stupid to even think that I was capable.

"Shh, shh, shh," I choked out through fits of tears, as I tried to rub his tiny belly and held the soother to his lips, praying for him to just stop crying.

"Aoife, love?" Mam hovered in the bedroom door, eyes laced with a mixture of sympathy and concern. "Would you like me to take AJ for an hour?"

"No," I choked out through fits of tears, as I sat cross-legged on my childhood bed, and stared down at the tiny human I was now responsible for. "I need to learn how to do this."

"Would you like me to call Joey?" she asked, still lingering. "See if he could come over a little sooner."

"He's at school, Mam!" I cried out, throwing my hands up. "He can't come any sooner. He has to stay until four!"

"Yes," she replied slowly. "I understand he's at school, but if he knew you were struggling like this, he would—"

"I'm not struggling," I choked out, burying my face in the crook of my arm as another wave of hysteria washed through me. "I'm just scared."

"Oh love." Closing the space between us, Mam sat at the edge of my bed and lifted AJ into her arms. "What are you scared of?"

"Being alone," I sobbed, beyond inconsolable now. "Having to do this without him."

"Aoife, pet, Joey's home," she tried to coax, as she rocked my son in her arms. "He's not going anywhere."

But he could.
He could relapse.
He could leave me.
Again.

"I'm still scared," I cried, wincing when I moved too quickly and caused a burning pain to shoot up through me. "He's over there and I'm here and I'm just . . . " I choked out a shuddering breath and reached for my son. "I'm just really scared, Mam."

"You know, it's completely normal to feel all over the place in the early days after giving birth." Mam wrapped an arm around my shoulders as I cradled AJ to my chest. "Your hormones are in disarray and your entire system is going through a reboot, so to speak."

"I'm just scared," I repeated, unable to repress the shivers racking through me. "I'm just . . . " Shaking my head, I leaned in close and pressed a kiss to AJ's head. "I'm scared."

"Of course you're scared," she soothed. "You've been through hell this year, and you're still only eighteen, sweetheart. It's okay to feel uncertain. It's very normal. I remember when I first brought you and Kev home. I cried for a solid three months."

"You did?"

"Absolutely," she replied, tightening her hold on me. "I was so out of my depth, and your father was working all the hours God gave him to put food on the table. Back in those early days, I genuinely thought I was losing my mind. But it gets better, love. It gets easier. I promise."

Change of plans

JOEY

"But he's a hurler, Gibs," Kav pointed out, voicing my thoughts aloud, as I sat at their lunch table, listening to his demented best friend spurt off his latest wild idea.

It turned out that Gibsie had a lot of wild ideas, and *I* would know, since I was the misfortunate bastard with a class timetable identical to his, meaning we'd spent the first six classes of the day together.

And oh yes, he saved a seat for me in *every* single one of those classes.

Apparently, Johnny was an even bigger egghead than Kev, and was primed for the illustrious 600 points leaving cert score in June that only the academically gifted snagged.

Meanwhile, I was destined for average, right alongside a lad who could never be accused of being average.

"True," Gibsie replied with a nod. "But Lynchy needs a change of scenery, and we need a winger. Tommen doesn't have a hurling team, but we *do* have a rugby team. A team that's running seriously low on quality players this year."

"Look at him," Hughie interjected. "He's too—"

"I'm too what?" I sneered, daring him with my eyes to finish that sentence.

"Nothing," he muttered, turning away. "Nothing at all."

"Yeah," I growled, still glowering. "That's what I thought."

"He's aggressive and argumentative, not to mention downright vicious at the best of times," Feely decided to throw his two cents into the conversation.

"The fuck would you know about it?" I snapped, glaring at him. "You don't know shit about me."

"Case in point," Feely replied calmly. "Plus, he's already a skilled athlete."

"True," Kav mused, scratching his chin, expression thoughtful.

"You've seen the lad," Gibsie continued, ignoring me entirely, and concentrating his attention on his teammates. "He's lightning on his feet."

Feely smiled. "He's perfect."

Turning to face me, Gibsie grinned widely. "So, are ya feeling me, Lynchy?"

"Like fuck I am," I deadpanned. "If you pricks even think or imagine that I'm going to join your—"

"You'll get to hit people," he cut me off by saying, "Repeatedly, legally, and without getting arrested. Consider it a physical form of therapy."

"I'm reformed," I replied with a sniff. "Besides, I'm a father now. I don't have time for sports."

"Yeah," all four laughed.

"What?" I snapped. "I fucking am!"

"A father, yeah," Kav agreed.

"Reformed?" Gibsie snickered. "Never."

Refusing to take the bait from who I could only compare to a wealthier version of Alec, I shook my head and leaned back in my seat. "Listen, while I appreciate the offer to join your team, I have a girl, a kid, and a job that come before everything. So, it's a pass."

"A job?" Kav's brows shot up. "Already?"

I nodded. "Got my old one back at the garage."

"Shite, lad." He smiled, looking genuinely happy for me. "Congrats."

"Cheers."

"Hey, guys," Shannon chirped, strolling into the canteen with her two pals in tow. Her eyes lit up the moment she saw me sitting at the table with them, she even bounced a little, but managed to school her features before reaching the table. "Hey, Joe," she said, trying to sound nonchalant as she moved to take up the vacant seat next to Kav.

"Shan," I acknowledged, watching as Kav pulled the chair out for her – the same chair he'd been guarding like a lion all lunch.

"Hi, Johnny."

"Hi, Shannon."

"That's her throne," Gibsie chuckled in my ear. "Nobody but Little Shannon sits next to the king of the jungle – or in our case, the king of Tommen."

I rolled my eyes, uninterested in social politics.

It did warm something inside of me, though, to see my baby sister find her feet.

To have her own circle.

To *finally* belong.

When Lizzie pushed past me, she offered me a sly wink and nothing else.

Not a hello.

Not a smile.

Not an anything, and I couldn't have been more grateful to her in this moment.

Keeping my eyes trained on her, I watched as she lowered herself down between Feely and another lad with a shaved head, directly opposite Hughie.

This girl. Messy as fuck or not, this girl had my unconditional support.

I had a girlfriend and a son to go home to that I wouldn't have if she hadn't taken a second to talk me down from the edge that night. The thought of what could have happened – what *would* have happened – if she hadn't intervened meant that I would be forever indebted to her. My son had a father because of her, and whenever the shit hit the fan for her, because it *would* hit the fan, then she would have my backing.

Yeah, for the rest of the school year, she would come under the same umbrella that Tadhg and Shannon did.

"Well, if it isn't the broken boy and the comeback kid," Claire Biggs chimed in as she strolled over to the lunch table and, seeing there weren't any free seats, dropped onto Gibsie's lap.

"Oh, Jesus," Gibs groaned, shifting around in discomfort. "I'm hardly a comeback kid, Claire-bear," he added as he concentrated really hard on something.

Not getting a stiffy, I presumed.

Yeah, we'd all been there.

Poor bastard.

"No, Gerard." Shaking her head, she hooked an arm around his shoulders and leaned in close enough to stroke his nose with hers. "*You're* the broken boy. *He's* the comeback kid."

"If I'm broken then what does that make you, Claire-Bear?"

"I don't know, Gerard," she teased. "What does it make me?"

"My it girl," he purred, arms coming around her, as he closed the space between their noses. "My everything girl."

"Claire!" Hughie barked. "Get off his lap. Now."

"Okay, he's definitely the annoying old bastard always ruining a moment," Gibsie huffed, turning to glower at his friend. "I was *having* a moment, Hugh!"

"Yeah," Hughie shot back, red-faced. "With *my* sister!"

"Fine!" Lizzie snapped then dragging my attention back to her, as she threw her hands up and glared at Feely. "Say it." Leaning back in her seat, she folded her arms across her chest and glared at him. "Give it your best bloody shot."

When he didn't respond, I thought she might scream.

She certainly looked like she was close to it.

"Dammit, Patrick, just say something."

"Okay." Setting his water bottle down, he turned in his seat and gave her his full attention. "I think you have the loneliest blue eyes I've ever seen, and looking at you hurts, but not nearly as much as being near you hurts. Your fractured pieces are sharp and jagged and cut anyone who gets too close."

"Well, shiiiit," Gibsie choked out a laugh when Lizzie stood up and stalked out of the lunch hall. "You told her, lad." He held his hand up for a high five. "You silenced the viper."

"Put your hand down, asshole," Hughie snapped, rising from his chair. "You're embarrassing yourself." Without saying another word, Hughie walked off in the same direction Lizzie went.

Arching a brow, I took a moment to watch their friends' reactions, and waited for the proverbial penny to drop for them.

It didn't.

Fucking clueless, the lot of them.

Something was happening there.

Maybe it was years of substance abuse that had made me so damn perceptive. Maybe I had spent too many years as the third wheel in Molloy's relationship with Ricey, and life had made me cynical.

I thought about it for a moment before shaking the thought off.

Nah, screw that, those two are definitely fucking.

"Shan?" Two girls approached the table then. "Is your little brother Tadhg Lynch?"

"Yeah," my sister replied, brows furrowing in confusion. "Why?"

"He's outside the girls bathroom getting into it with Ronan McGarry."

"Oh god," Shan mumbled, dropping her head in her hands.

"I'll sort it," Kav said, rising to his feet, but I was already on my feet, retracing my steps back towards the main hallway.

"Tadhg!" I snapped, pushing through the crowded corridor in search of my hot-headed baby brother. I could see his blond head at the far end of the hallway, clearly sizing up some older lad.

"Your kind don't belong in this school," the other lad taunted, and I knew his words would be like a red rag to a bull to my brother. "So, why don't you and the rest of your band of scumbag siblings go back where you belong."

"And where exactly do my kind belong?" Tadhg seethed, letting his school bag fall from his shoulders, as he stepped forward to shove the bigger lad in the chest. "Hmm? Come on, fuck face. Where do I belong?"

"Across town, in one of the council estates with the rest of your scummy kind." Grinning, the bigger lad added, "But you can leave your sister here with us, since she so willingly opens her legs for Cap—"

"You're a fucking dead man, McGarry!" came Tadhg's feral roar just as I shoved through the crowd and reached his side.

"Don't be thick," I warned, catching ahold of the arm my little brother had reared back. "He's not worth your time, kid. Walk away." ·

"But he called Shannon a—"

"He's a spoilt, entitled rugby prick, who's never seen a hard day in his life," I interjected. "We don't care about his opinion."

"Ah, would ya look at that," the prick sneered, tormenting Tadhg with a cruel smirk. "Big brother's here to bail you out." His gaze landed on me, and his grin deepened. "Heard all about you, junkie."

"Original," I deadpanned, entirely uninterested in wasting my energy on arguing with him. "Look at the ugly head on him," I continued, focusing on my brother. "Poor bastard's clearly never had the taste of pussy in his life. Walk away, kid."

Laughter erupted around us, all at the asshole's expense.

"I've seen plenty pussy," the lad snarled, face turning a bright shade of red.

"Coming out of your mother's hole doesn't count, lad," Tadhg shot back, as I pulled him away. "Sorry to disappoint ya."

"As opposed to you and that junkie brother of yours?" he countered. "Word around school is that big brother got a slut from BCS humped with his kid and—"

He didn't finish his sentence – couldn't if he wanted to, because I laid the bastard on the flat of his back.

A laugh tore from Tadhg's chest. "Thought we didn't care about his opinion?"

"Change of plans."

At least you made it to big lunch

JOEY

"Dellie, he called our sister a slut," Tadhg defended with a huff, climbing into the back seat of her Range Rover, after she'd been called to come collect us from the office. "Yeah, Joe threw the first slap, but he goaded it out of him by bringing up Aoife and my nephew. And listen, before you say it, I'm not apologizing for kicking him in the nuts when he was on the ground either. The prick had it coming."

"Well," she sighed heavily. "At least you made it to big lunch."

"I'm sorry," I muttered from the passenger seat. "I fucked it."

"No, you didn't," Tadhg argued, reaching a hand through the seats to pat my shoulder. "You turned his nose sideways, Joe. It was a solid right hook."

"Not helping, kid." I dropped my head in my hands, knowing that I was in deep shit for my outburst. "How long am I being suspended for?"

"For the next two weeks," Edel replied, pulling into traffic.

"Sweet," Tadhg hooted. "Talk about a result!"

"Not you, Rocky," she corrected. "You're back on Monday."

"Fuck my life," number four grumbled. "I *knew* I should have thrown the first punch."

"Hey," I snapped, twisting around to face him. "Stop acting like a little shit. I did the wrong thing back there."

"But you—"

"I did the wrong thing, Tadhg," I reinforced, giving him a stern look of warning. "I was *wrong*, okay? Don't copy me. It's *not* a good thing. Do better, Tadhg. *Be* better." *Than me.*

"Can we talk?" I asked, lingering in the kitchen doorway a little while later, watching as Edel Kavanagh mothered my youngest brother.

"Always, love," she replied.

"Nanny gave me money."

"Oh?" she mused, ruffling Sean's curls before turning her attention back to the pot of stew she was stirring.

"Yeah." I shrugged, still lingering. "A *lot* of money."

She turned to look at me then. "How much are we talking?"

"Fifteen grand." I reached into the gear bag I had packed for Molloy's house and showed her the envelope full of cash. "It's from my grandfather. He left it to me when he died."

Her brows shot up. "And you haven't touched it?"

I shook my head. "Not a penny."

"Have you been tempted?"

"I'm tempted every second of the day," I admitted. "But I'm not going back there."

She smiled. "Good boy."

"I guess, what I wanted to talk to you about was the matter of settling up with you and John. Obviously, I need to keep some of the money for Aoife and AJ, but Tony's after giving me back my job at the garage, so I'll be able to set up a payment plan—"

"Don't you dare finish that sentence," she cut in, spinning around to face me. "I mean it, Joey Lynch." Wiping her hands on her apron, she stalked towards me, not stopping until she had the envelope in her hands and was stuffing it back into my bag. "I will never take so much as a cent from you. Do you hear me, love? Not a brown brass penny, so put any notions of that out of your head."

"Edel." Sighing heavily, I rubbed my jaw. "I *have* to pay you back."

"You already are," she replied, reaching up to pat my cheek. "By staying clean and going to school."

"I got suspended on my first day at Tommen," I reminded her.

"Psssh. So did I." She waved a hand around aimlessly. "And I did it in epic fashion."

"You went to Tommen?"

"I was transplanted there," she replied with a smirk. "Same as you."

"I didn't know that."

"There's a lot you don't know, Joey love." Smirking, she patted my cheek once more before turning her attention back to her stew. "A *lot*."

Well shit.

"Do you, ah, think you could give me a spin into town?" I gestured to my bag. "I need to see Aoife."

"I can drop you into town in an hour or two, love, but if you need to go now, then just run upstairs and ask Johnny before he leaves for training. I'm sure he wouldn't mind dropping you off on his way."

Navigating my way through Tommen was one thing, but navigating my way through the maze that was the Kavanagh Manor was something entirely different. Wandering through the maze of corridors, I finally found my feet on the right wing of the house. Knowing my surroundings, I walked to the end of the hallway, stopping just outside the door that housed my sister's soft laughter.

When our mother was alive, I had been too high to hear her warnings about Shannon's relationship with Kav. Now, as I stood on my own two feet, with a clear head and my wits about me, I got it. I finally saw what my mother had been so afraid of.

This wasn't puppy love.

It wasn't a fleeting romance, either.

No, whatever was happening between these two was raw, real, and mixed with an undeniable air of permanence.

Smiling to myself, I knocked once and pushed the door inwards.

That was my first mistake.

My second mistake was . . . nope, it was gone.

I could focus on nothing but the image of my naked sister, bouncing on top of her equally naked boyfriend.

"Trigger," I roared, slapping a hand over my eyes two seconds too late. "Trigger, trigger, get-your-fucking-dick-out-of-my-baby-sister trigger!"

"Oh my god!" Shannon screamed, hands and legs flailing, as she scrambled off mister fucking rugby's lap and tried to hide behind his back. "Joey! Get the hell out!"

"Yeah," I roared, feeling faint, as I leaned against the door frame and resisted the overpowering urge to heave my guts up. "Get out of her, you big, overgrown bastard. You'll break her!"

"Not him – Johnny, don't move!" my sister screamed back, as she peeked over his shoulder, and pointed a finger at me. "You, Joe! Get out."

"I can't!"

"Why not?"

"Because I'm frozen to the fucking spot here, Shannon! I'm having an out of body experience here, and it's fairly traumatizing," I choked out. "Jesus Christ, have I taught you nothing?" I demanded, feeling faint. "Have you learned *nothing* from my mistakes?"

"I'm on the pill," my baby sister offered up.

"And I'm wearing a condom," the big bastard chimed in.

"Oh Jesus," I whimpered, gagging at the mental image.

"You need to learn how to knock," Shannon strangled out breathlessly. "Now go."

"Are you seriously going to keep going?" When she didn't deny it, I shuddered in repulsion. "I can't believe you're actually doing *that*."

"Joe, we've been doing '*that*' for months now."

"For fuck's sake, Shannon, why'd you have to tell me that?" I hissed, stomach churning in disgust, as I staggered blindly for the door. "I only wanted a spin to Aoife's place, not another reason to be in therapy."

"About what you saw back there," Kav finally addressed the elephant in the room, much to my dismay. "About me and Shan."

"Listen, lad, all I need from you is a spin to my girlfriend's house," I replied, still feeling queasy, as he drove me into town. "Not an explanation."

"I love her."

"I'm sure you do."

"No," he said, tone serious. "I *love* her, lad. I'm *in* love with her."

"Good for you," I muttered, unable to look at him anymore without seeing the image of . . . Jesus, I couldn't even think it. "I know you love her," I decided to add. "It's the only reason I'm not losing it right now."

He was quiet for a moment, clearly absorbing my words, before he spoke again.

"I'm going to take her with me, Joey," he said quietly. "When I leave Ballylaggin? Wherever I end up, I'm taking her with me."

"Good," I replied. "At least she'll have a fighting chance."

"She already has a fighting chance," he replied gruffly. "Because of you, lad. Not me."

My phone rang then, distracting me from our conversation, and I quickly snatched it out of my pocket and clicked accept. "Hello?"

"Hello? Joey love, it's me, Trish. I was just wondering what time you would be here?"

"Hey. I'm on the way over now."

"Oh, thank god." She sighed heavily down the line. "She's having a bad day, pet."

My heart sank. "I won't be long."

Daddy's here

JOEY

My heart was thundering in my chest the rest of the way to her house, and that thundering sensation only increased when Trish opened the door to me.

"How is she?"

Her mother's eyes were full of concern when she stepped aside and gestured for me to come in. "I think she could use her partner in crime."

I could hear AJ crying the minute I stepped inside, but that crying only intensified with every step I took to her bedroom door.

I didn't knock, because I didn't see the point. Instead, I quietly slipped inside and closed the door behind me.

Sitting on the bed, cradling the tiny blonde head of curls, Aoife rocked and sobbed. "Mam, I can do it."

"Hey, queen."

Her breath hitched and she turned to look at me. "Hey, stud."

Hands shaking, I closed the space between us and sat down on the edge of the bed beside her. "What's happening, baby?" I coaxed, reaching for the screaming baby. "Why are you crying?"

"I've done everything," she strangled out, hands hanging limply at her sides when I shifted the baby into my arms. "He's fed, changed, and winded, and he won't stop."

"Okay," I coaxed, settling him into the crook of my arm so that I could wrap my arm around her shoulders. "You're okay."

"I'm not, okay, Joe," she sobbed, twisting sideways and burying her face in my neck. "I'm not okay. I can't do this."

"Yeah, you can," I whispered. "All you need to do is sleep. Just lie down and get some sleep, Molloy. I'll handle everything."

"I need to be able to do it myself."

"You're already more than able," I coaxed. "You're just running on empty here. He needs you to sleep. That's the best thing you can do for the both of you right now."

Finally complying, she curled up in a small ball on her bed and closed her eyes, still sobbing as she slowly drifted to sleep.

With the baby cradled in my arms, I slipped out of her room, and padded down the stairs, moving to the kitchen to where the sterilizer was located.

"She's been trying to nurse, but it's not coming easily," Trish said when I stepped into the kitchen. "It's all getting on top of her."

"Trish, I know you have the best of intentions, but I need you to lay off the breastfeeding talk."

"I'm only trying to help my daughter."

"I get that, but she's exhausted," I replied evenly, trying not to step on toes, but needing to take control of this shitstorm before it got out of hand. "She can't do it right now, and quite frankly, her mental health is a hell of a lot more important to me than whether or not my son is breastfed. AJ will continue to thrive on formula, but Aoife won't, and I need you to tell her it's okay to do what's right for her."

She seemed to consider what I said before releasing a heavy sigh. "I suppose I have been championing her going down the nursing route."

"And that's grand," I assured her, as I one-handedly prepped a bottle. "But she's having a hard time getting through this, and we need to make it as easy as possible for her."

"I agree."

"Good." Nodding, I exhaled a relieved sigh. "Listen, Trish, I know you and Tony don't exactly trust me right now, and I don't blame you, but I can't leave the two of them here and just walk away. I can't do it. They need me."

"Yes, they do."

"I want them to come and live with me."

"Absolutely not," her mother replied, exactly as I predicted. "You're welcome to stay and help with the baby as much as you want, but they're staying with me."

Deciding now was not the time to poke the bear, I relented, content that I had planted the seed. "I'll take him in the sitting room for a bit, if that's okay. Let her get some sleep."

"Of course."

"Thanks."

Switching on the television for background noise, I settled down on the couch with AJ resting on my shoulder.

"You're grand," I coaxed, patting his back to break his wind. "But you need to steady up on the drama. Your poor mam is wrecked from ya."

He pulled his knees up and released another furious squawk.

"Yeah, I know," I coaxed, upping the pace of the patting. "You need to take a big shit, don't ya? Come on, big man. Get it out. Daddy's here."

Several minutes ticked by and then I felt a sudden flush of heat against my hand, along with an impressive five-second-long fart.

"That's my lad," I praised, pulling him back to look at me. "Did you leave me a present?"

Looking like butter wouldn't melt now that his pain was gone, AJ looked right at me, squinting and grimacing, as his pouty lips formed a perfect little o-shape.

"Where does your mammy keep your nappies down here?" I muttered more to myself than him, as I searched for supplies. Finding them in a changing bag at the side of the couch, I laid him down and set to work.

"You're a little pro at the nappy changing, aren't you?" Trish mused, strolling into the sitting room and setting a mug of coffee on the table beside me. "None of this is new to you, is it?"

"I've had a lot of practice," I replied, switching out nappies, as I cleaned and changed my baby son.

"Call me if you need anything."

I wouldn't.

Settling him back into the crook of my arm, I placed the teat of the bottle I had prepped to his lips and smirked when he sought it out, lips smacking wildly.

"Good job," I whispered, snuggling him in close. "Get your chops around that."

Thirty minutes later, AJ's bottle was drained dry and he was out for the count on my chest.

Setting to work on a task I honestly could do blindfolded, I went through the motions of winding my son before changing his nappy again and settling him back down to continue his snooze. With the sound of soft snuffling snores filling my ears, I stared down at him, feeling my heart hammer harder with every breath I took.

Fear channeled its way up inside of me and I instantly began to worry about his future.

Would he have the same failing – the same defected genes – as his father?

As his grandfather?

Did I curse this baby?

Was he going to grow up all fucked up in the head because I was his father?

Jesus, I hoped not.

The thought of him feeling about me the way I felt about my own father made it hard to breathe. It made me want to run and drown myself in whatever I could get my hands on.

I must have sat there for a solid hour, eyes glued to his blond head, praying to whatever was up there to skip over my child and give him a fair shot at life.

A fighting chance.

Vowing more than I could ever give, I offered it all up for this kid.

Promising the sun, the moon, and the stars for life to give him all the good in exchange for whatever was left inside of me.

When he stirred a little while later, I pressed a kiss to his hair and cuddled him closer to me.

Be like her, I mentally begged my sleeping son. *Please don't turn out like me.*

*

"Joey," Tony acknowledged later that night when I walked into the kitchen and found him and Trish sitting at the table for their nightly chat. "How's that grandson of mine?"

I'd spent enough time in this house to know that every night before bed, Molloy's parents shared a pot of tea at the kitchen table and dissected the day's events. It was a stark contrast to what happened at the kitchen table in the home I'd been raised in.

"No fear of him," I replied, adjusting my sleeping son in the crook of my arm. "Fed like a lord and out for the count."

"And my daughter?" he asked, gesturing towards a chair at the table.

"Overtired. Overworked," I replied, moving for the chair. "And really fucking overwhelmed."

"Come to Nana," Trish cooed, snatching AJ out of my arms and cuddling him to her chest.

"Jesus," Tony muttered, rubbing his jaw. "Never thought I'd say it after what you put her through, boyo, but I'm glad you're here."

"Yeah." I nodded, not taking his words to heart. "Me, too."

"It's just the baby blues," Trish interjected. "It'll pass."

"I don't know, Trish," Tony said, worrying his lip. "What if it's the other thing?"

"The other thing?"

"The depression after having a baby?"

"Tony, it's only been a few days since she gave birth, love. Give the girl a chance to adjust. She doesn't have postnatal depression," his wife tried to soothe. "She's just shattered."

"My mam had really bad postnatal depression after Sean," I decided to throw out there. "It was . . . not good."

"Is that what you think is happening here?" Tony asked, imploring me with his eyes to give him the answers. "With my daughter?"

"No, not right now," I replied, choosing my words carefully. "But I think we need to have a conversation about what needs to happen next."

"No." Trish, quick to catch on, shook her head. "I told you before, Joey, you're welcome to stay here, but she's not moving in with you."

Biting back my frustration, I focused on Tony. "I have my own place – an annex on the Kavanaghs' property. It's safe. It's secure. It's completely mine. If Aoife comes to live with me, I can be there for her to help with AJ. I can give her the support she needs."

"She already has support," Trish argued. "I'm right down the hall, for Christ's sake. I'm on call 24/7 if she needs me."

"It's not the same thing," I pushed, surprised with how even-toned I sounded. "I know you mean well, and I'm so fucking grateful for everything you've done for them, but I need to be with my family."

"Joey, I love you, but I'm not having this conversation," Trish growled. "My daughter is *not* moving in with you."

"I understand that—"

"You are *just* out of rehab," she spat. "You are barely three months clean. Now, don't get me wrong because I am absolutely rooting for you, but you are hardly the stable solution here."

"I fucked up," I held my hands up and admitted. "Spectacularly. I let your daughter down and I put her through hell. I'm not denying it, and I'm not excusing it. But I *am* standing over it." Repressing the urge to growl, I drummed my fingers on the table, willing her parents to just *hear* me. "I love your daughter, Trish. I always have. And yeah, I'm the first person to admit that I haven't always shown it in the ways she needed me to – in the ways *you* needed me to, but I fucking love her."

"Joey."

"I *can* do this," I continued to argue. "I can look after Aoife and AJ. I can, Trish, and what's more, I *will*. We're a family. We're going to be together, and that's not going to start when you decide that I'm stable enough. It starts *now*."

"And where does Tommen fit into this?" Tony asked. "You're at school by day. Aoife will be on her own in this annex with the baby until you get home in the evenings?"

"And what about when she goes back to BCS in a couple of months?" Trish interjected. "What do you propose then? With you two attending different schools? I'm going to mind AJ for her while she attends her classes. We have it all organized. How does that fit in with your plan?"

"That's another thing I wanted to talk about."

Trish narrowed her eyes in warning. "My daughter is finishing her education and I don't want to hear a word of protest."

"I couldn't agree more," I told her. "Aoife needs to finish school."

Trish visibly sagged in relief. "Good."

"Just not at BCS."

Her eyes narrowed again. "Joey Lynch, if you even think about putting notions in her head, I will—"

Her words broke off when I reached into my pocket and laid the cash on the table in front of them.

"What in the name of Jesus?"

"Where did you get that kind of money?"

"My grandmother."

"How much is there?"

"There's fifteen grand," I said calmly. "Four thousand of that is for Aoife's tuition for Tommen." I swallowed deeply and looked her parents in the eyes. "Let me do this for her."

"Joey." Trish's eyes were wild with panic. "She doesn't even want to go back to school. If you heard the fights we've had about her returning to BCS." She shook her head. "She's fighting me tooth and nail on this."

"I'll be with her at Tommen," I pushed, sensing her mother's resistance falter, and going in for the kill. "Nothing has to change regarding AJ's childcare. If you're willing to look after him for us while we're at school, then I would be so fucking grateful."

"You want her to go to Tommen?" That was Tony. "Private school?"

"I can't get back into BCS. If I could follow her there, I would," I told him. "But Tommen is the only school willing to take me."

"And she'll follow you anywhere," he answered for me.

"It's a good school," I added. "She would get the best education there."

"Well, shit." Leaning back in his chair, Tony rubbed his jaw. "You have this all thought out, don't ya, boyo?"

I shrugged, not bothering to deny it.

"And what about Aoife?" he asked then. "What is she saying about this?"

"I haven't spoken to her about it," I replied. "I wanted to run it by you first."

"Hm."

"No, Tony, I don't want her to move out," Trish was quick to protest. "It's not the right time."

"Trish," he sighed heavily. "It's not about what we want, love. Not anymore. She's over eighteen." His gaze flicked to AJ and emotion flashed in his eyes. "And the boy's right. They're a little family."

"And if he lets her down again?"

"I've a shovel in the backyard that we can use to bury him with."

Jerking awake in the middle of the night, Molloy sprang up in a panic, immediately seeking out our baby.

"AJ's fine," I whispered in the darkness, gently pulling her back down. "I just checked him. He's sleeping."

Sagging in relief, she twisted onto her side to face me and expelled a shaky breath. "Have you slept?"

I shook my head.

"Why not?"

"I'm sort of . . . battling something here."

"Her ghost?"

I nodded.

"Joe." Her hand was on my cheek then. "Tell me what's going on in that head of yours."

"It hurts."

"Where?"

"Everywhere."

She watched me and I watched her right back. I wanted to be closer to her than my own skin. The connection I felt to her was overwhelming when I was high but now that I was sober, it was so strong that I could hardly stand it.

After watching her give birth, after witnessing the inhuman strength she possessed, I knew I would never be worthy of the girl.

"Here?" she finally asked, reaching a hand out to trail over my chest. She pressed her palm to the skin covering my heart. "In here?"

I nodded slowly.

"And here?" she asked, trailing her fingertips over my temple. "In here?"

Shuddering, I moved to snatch her hand up, desperate for the physical contact.

"I'm proud of you, Joe."

"You are?"

Smiling softly, she trailed her fingers down my neck before placing her hand back down on my chest. "I am."

"I don't deserve it."

Wordlessly, she took my hand in hers and placed it to her chest. "Feel that?"

"Yeah." Her heart was hammering violently against my palm. "I feel it."

"That's you," she whispered. "That's what you do to me."

"Still?"

"Then. Still. Always."

"Aoif..."

"No more chances, Joe," she croaked out, eyes filling up with tears. "This is the last one, okay?"

"Yeah." Nodding, I blew out a ragged breath. "It's the last one I'll need."

"I mean it," she added. "You screw up again and we're done. One more time and I'm gone. I'm out of your life and there's no way back." She eyed me warily. "I can't risk his safety." A shiver rolled through her. "I won't put *us* before our son."

"I don't want you to," I strangled out, breathing hard and fast as the prospect of having her back in my life danced before my eyes. "He comes first."

"Before drugs?"

Swallowing the lump in my throat, I nodded stiffly. "You both come first."

"I know it won't be easy for you."

"No, it won't," I agreed. "But I'm making you and him my first priority."

"I don't want you to drink either," she blurted out. "If that's a hard limit for you then you need to say so now. I know you're not alcohol dependent, but I can't risk you losing your head. I—"

"I get it," I hurried to soothe. "And I agree. I won't drink. I know what's at stake."

"I want to keep you alive, Joe," she breathed, looking into my eyes. "I need you alive." Chewing on her bottom lip, she glanced at the bassinet next to her bed. "I don't want to do this on my own."

My heart cracked in my chest.

"You won't have to," I vowed, finding strength in having someone need me again.

I needed that, I suddenly realized.

I needed to be needed.

I was programed to take care of the people I loved.

Not having that made me feel off-balance.

Maybe that was unhealthy, but I'd take it over sticking needles in my veins any day of the week.

"Good," she sniffled. "Now kiss me and make it worth it."

Wholeheartedly complying with her wishes, I leaned in and brushed my lips against hers, shivering when I felt the familiar jolt of excitement shoot through me at the feel of her lips on mine.

Shivering, she wrapped her arms around my neck and whispered the words, "Ride or die, Joe."

My heart gunned ferociously in my chest, because I knew she meant it, and when I whispered the words, "Ride or die, Molloy," I knew I meant it, too.

More than anything.

Better days are coming

AOIFE

Secretly thrilled that Joey was handed a two-week suspension from Tommen, I soaked in every second of having him with me.

Because the truth was that I felt *better* when he was around.

More stable.

More supported.

More like *me*.

Unlike when I was with my mother, I didn't feel embarrassed or inadequate when I had to ask him a question about AJ. It was like Home Economics class all over again and I had the best partner. He was so patient with me, even when I didn't have any patience for myself. For the first week of his suspension, he rarely left our sides. By the second week, he managed to coax me out of the house with the prospect of hitting the shop. The boy knew my weakness and targeted it with unapologetic deviousness.

"How would you feel about taking a spin over to the manor?" Joey asked on Tuesday morning, as he drove us back from the doctor's office, after taking our son to his two-week checkup.

The Pogues' 'A Rainy Night In Soho' was playing on the radio, and the lyrics were curling around my heart like a little blanket of warmth.

"Everyone will be at school, so it'll just be Edel and Sean," he was quick to add, reaching across the console to give my thigh a reassuring squeeze. "Nothing too stressful, I promise."

"Of course, Joe," I replied, snatching his hand up in mine. "God, I'm sorry, I didn't even think that you would want to bring AJ over to see your family."

"I want to bring the both of you over," he corrected gruffly. "But it doesn't have to be today if you're not feeling up to it."

"Why wouldn't I feel up to it?"

"You've had a hard couple of weeks, Molloy."

"So have you."

He snorted. "Hardly."

"You've literally done every single night feed for the past seven nights."

"Because you've literally grown a human for the past nine months."

"You think I can do this, right, Joe?" I asked, looking back to check on AJ, who was nestled in his car seat in the back of my car. "You think I can be a good mam, right?"

"I don't think it, Molloy, I know it."

"I'm getting better at it, though, right?" I chewed out my lip, feeling another horrible wave of uncertainty. "It's just that I love him so much, Joe. Every time I look at him, I get completely overwhelmed thinking about all the things that could go wrong. All the things I *don't* know. The thought of doing something wrong or making a mistake with him makes the anxiety inside of me multiply until I can't breathe."

"I feel the exact same way," he replied, squeezing my hand.

"You do?"

He nodded. "With *you*, Molloy."

My breath hitched and my heart squeezed tight. "Joe."

"Listen to me, you are an unbelievable mam, and that kid is lucky to have you," he urged. "You don't need to second guess a damn thing you do, Aoif. You honestly don't, because you've got this, baby. You're the glue. The three of us are here together because of *you*." He squeezed my hand again. "AJ wouldn't be here without you, and neither would I. So, don't doubt yourself because you're temporarily out of steam. The only reason you've been running on fumes in the first place is because you've spent your entire pregnancy picking up the slack for me."

His words curled around my heart, and I shivered. "Joe, it's okay. I understand. You were sick."

"Yeah, I was," he agreed. "And I can't change that part of our story, but I *can* lighten the load for you now. I can step up now, Aoif, so let me do it, okay?" He cast a glance in my direction, imploring me with his clear green eyes to listen to him. "Let me take care of you."

"Joey?" Edel called out from behind the kitchen door. "Is that you, love?"

Standing in the utility room, I watched as my boyfriend fought an internal battle.

I could see it in his eyes.

I knew *exactly* what was happening in his brain.

Joe was willing himself not to run.

He was willing himself to *trust* the woman on the other side of the door.

"You've got this," I whispered, reaching out to trace his cheek with my thumb.

Finding that inner steel I adored so much, he took a steadying breath and nodded to himself before calling out, "Yeah, it's me." I watched as he tightened his hold on AJ's car seat and pushed the door open. "I brought a few people to see you."

Pride.

It roared to life inside of me.

When we stepped into the kitchen, I was too overwhelmed to speak.

"Look at you," Edel whispered, clasping the front of her apron with floury hands, as her tear-filled gaze flicked from me, to AJ, before settling on Joey. "Look at the man standing in my kitchen."

"Holy shit, Joe," I spluttered when he let me inside his new digs. "This entire place is yours?" I spun around with our son in my arms, taking in the huge open plan kitchen/living area. "Are these people fucking *millionaires*?"

"I think they are," he replied with a frown, as he set the empty car seat on the table. "It's fairly wild, huh?"

"I'd say," I replied, choking out a laugh. "Holy crap, this is *insane*."

"It sure beats that mouse-infested flat in Elk's Terrace we talked about, huh?"

"Yeah," I laughed and then quickly spun back to face him, when awareness smacked me upside the head. "Wait, *what?*"

"Move in with me."

I stood, unmoving, un-bloody-blinking, as I tried to absorb his words. "*Huh?*"

"Move in with me, Molloy," Joey repeated, closing the space between us. "Live with me."

"Here?"

"Here," he confirmed with a nod. "For now, at least."

My heart bucked wildly in my chest as my eyes roamed over his face, searching for the lie.

I didn't find it.

"You're serious," I breathed, feeling dizzy. "You're not joking."

"No, I'm not," he replied, clamping a hand down on my hip. "Be with me."

"I am with you, Joe."

"No." He shook his head. "*Be* with me, Molloy."

"In what way?"

"In every way."

Whoa.

"I love you." He reached a hand between us and stroked AJ's soft curls. "I've spent a third of my life loving you, Aoife Molloy, and I don't plan on stopping." Leaning in close, he pressed his brow to mine and exhaled a shaky breath. "I've made a lot of terrible decisions," he admitted quietly. "But the worst, by far, was hurting you and pushing you away."

"It's okay, Joe," I heard myself whisper, trembling now. "I forgive you."

"I don't deserve your forgiveness," he replied, voice thick and gruff. "But I *will* earn it. Because whatever comes our way, from here on out, I'll be right beside you." He nuzzled my nose with his before pressing a kiss to my lips. "Because in this version of forever, we get the happy ending, Molloy."

EPILOGUE

King of my heart

SHANNON

December 22nd, 2005

"Shannon, love," Edel called over her shoulder from her perch at the stove, while she balanced Sean on her hip. "You wouldn't pop next door and see if your brother needs a hand with the baby before school?"

"Mm-hmm." Nodding, I took one final bite of my chocolate spread on toast, munching it down, before hopping off the stool at the island. "Sure thing."

"Good girl," she called after me. "You're my rock, love."

Ignoring Tadhg and Ollie, who were battling it out in the kitchen doorway for dominion over a sliotar, while a frazzled looking John tried to talk them down, I skipped out of the kitchen.

The minute I stepped outside, the arctic December morning air hit my face and I smiled, reveling in the sensation of the light dusting of snow as it fell from the sky. It wouldn't stick, of course. At least not enough of it to make a snowman, but it sure was beautiful to look at.

Inhaling deeply, I took a moment to just breathe and take it all in.

The calmness.

The tranquility.

The contentment.

The Christmas spirit.

Today was our last day of school before winter break and I couldn't wait to spend two whole weeks at home with my family.

And Johnny.

Okay, so mostly Johnny.

It was closer to eighty/twenty in Johnny's favor.

Maybe ninety . . .

With my shoulders relaxed and a smile etched on my face, I tiptoed around a couple of ice-filled puddles leftover from yesterday's heavy downpour, and then broke into a run, desperate to get to the safety of the annex before Bonnie and Cupcake realized that I was outside. If they noticed me, then the perfectly ironed uniform I was donning would be toast.

Muddy toast.

"Joe?" I called out, hurrying inside without knocking when my foster mother's yellow-tailed demons came into sight, all muddy-pawed and ready to inflict affection on me. That wasn't to say that I didn't love Bonnie and Cupcake. I adored them, but those dogs gave Gibsie and Claire a run for their money in the boisterous stakes – and *that* was an impressive feat.

The minute I closed the door of my brother's glorified apartment, I heard a huge thud on the other side of it.

"Did one of those dopes crash into the door again?" Joey called down from upstairs.

"Yeah," I snickered, and then clamped my hand over my mouth, feeling bad for laughing at the poor thing's lack of coordination. After all, I didn't have room to talk. "I think it was Cupcake."

"Something seriously fucking wrong with that one," he called back. "Why can't they be like the good one?"

I grinned to myself. My brother was referring to my boyfriend's number one girl.

Well, number one dog, at least.

Sookie.

"It's cold outside," I called out, making a beeline for the Christmas tree. "Oh, and it's snowing."

"It won't stick."

"Yeah, I know."

"Having a good root around there, Shan?" Leaning against the upstairs railing, with his school shirt hanging open, and a toothbrush hanging out of his mouth, my brother arched a brow. "You're such a child."

"I was just ... checking." Cheeks flushed, I sprang back from the tree, and then hastily set the present I was holding back down before smiling sheepishly up at my brother. "Edel wants to know if you need help with AJ before school?"

"Nah, it's all good," he replied, resuming his brushing of his teeth as he disappeared inside what I knew what his gigantic bedroom.

"Speak for yourself," Aoife interjected, as she bolted past my brother, with my nephew on her hip, and only her school shirt covering her dignity. "Oh, look, AJ. It's your aunty Shan." Making a beeline for me, she hurried down the rustic-looking, spiral staircase that connected to the upper level of their little apartment. "Please take your nephew for a second so I can get dressed, will you?"

"Of course," I crooned, snatching AJ up in my arms. He was all blond curls and big green eyes like his parents. "How's my favorite nephew?"

"He's your only nephew," Aoife laughed, thundering back up the staircase like a woman on a mission.

"For now," Joey taunted, blocking the bedroom doorway with a mischievous glint in his eyes.

"If you even *think* about putting another baby in me after what that son of yours did to my fanny, then I hope you have the cash for genital corrective surgery."

"It wasn't that bad, Molloy," he laughed, staggering out of the doorway when his girlfriend shoved him with her ass. "You healed up perfectly."

"Not for me, asshole." She reappeared in the bedroom doorway, dragging a Tommen school skirt up her hips. "For you. Because if you put that weapon of mass temptation anywhere near me without a condom, I'll cut the damn thing off."

"Sounds like foreplay, Molloy," Joey purred, prowling after her when she raced back into the bedroom.

"Sounds like a stark warning, Lynch," I heard her warn, moments before the screams of laughter filled my ears. "Mercy, mercy, ah, stop. Fuck, Joe – ah, that tickles!"

"Your mammy and daddy are crazy," I cooed, blowing raspberries on his chubby little cheek. The move caused him to release a hearty chuckle and reveal a wide gummy smile. I knew I was biased, what with being his aunt and all, but AJ Lynch was, hands down, the most perfect baby in the world.

Yeah, my nephew was ridiculously adorable.

"How are you almost four months old already?" I mused, shaking my head in wonder.

So much had happened in such a short space of time, but it felt like an entire lifetime had passed since Joey returned from rehab. He'd barely been back two weeks when Aoife and AJ came for a sleepover. Clearly, it was an extended sleepover because they arrived in September and hadn't left since – much to our delight.

Having AJ living next door was a huge treat for the rest of us, but it paled in comparison to how *wonderful* it was to see our big brother *finally* happy.

Joe had been through so much that there was a point in time where I thought we might not get him back. But like a phoenix rising from the ashes, my brother was reborn the day his son took his first breath.

Joey was living for himself now.

For his little family.

And it gave me so much peace to know that he was finally at peace with *himself.*

When Aoife joined him at Tommen after Halloween break, it settled something inside of the both of them. I wasn't sure about soulmates, but if they existed, then my nephew's parents were a prime example. Joey Lynch and Aoife Molloy; both full of flaws and humanly imperfect and yet so undeniably perfect for one another.

I knew that my brother still struggled daily, and he probably always would, but he was so determined to get this right, to stay on track, that I didn't have a doubt in my heart that his sobriety would continue to flourish.

When Joey and Aoife finally emerged from their bedroom ten minutes later, the flushed look on both of their faces, not to mention their rumpled school uniforms, assured me that while they had no immediate plans to extend their brood, they had no problem with practicing the art of making a baby.

"You're disgusting," I scolded, handing AJ off to my brother, and then smacking his shoulder when he continued to shamelessly ogle his girlfriend's ass. "Seriously, Trish will be here any minute to collect AJ. What if she caught you two?"

"What if I caught those two doing what, Shannon love?" Aoife's mother asked from behind me, as she set her handbag down on the kitchen counter. "Actually, on second thoughts, don't tell me, pet. I think it's safer I don't know."

When I stepped outside a little later, I had to blink several times before my brain accepted what my eyes were seeing.

The snow that was falling earlier. Well, it was heavier now. And it was *sticking!*

Bubbling with excitement at the prospect of a snow day, I bolted back towards the big house at full speed, relieved when I spied Bonnie and Cupcake back in their impressive run. Seriously, they had a doghouse bigger than my bedroom back in Elk's Terrace.

I had almost made it inside the house when a huge snowball smacked me upside the head. Releasing the door handle, I staggered backwards from the force of the snowball before falling flat on my ass. "Ouch," I choked out a pained laugh, feeling both startled and amused. "Tadhg, that hurt!"

"Ah shite," a familiar voice called out. "Sorry, Shan. I thought you were Gibsie."

Twisting sideways, I watched as a sheepish looking Johnny peeked over the bonnet of his mother's Range Rover.

"Quick, baby," he whisper-hissed, disappearing behind the jeep, only to reappear a moment later, tumble-rolling towards me like a ninja. "Get into the den," Johnny instructed, tucking me under his arm as he pulled me back to where he had claimed sanctuary. "That bleeding assassin is on the loose with snowballs."

"Who?" I laughed, eyeing up the impressive stack of snowballs he had stored up. "Tadhg?"

"Shan, get down!" Throwing himself on top of me when a sliotar sized snowball came whizzing past my head, Johnny released a battle-cry growl. "You're a dead man, Gibs!"

"You'll have to face me to kill me, Cap!" I heard Gibsie call back as another snowball hurled past me and smashed into the side of Johnny's face. "And we both know you're too pussy-whipped to leave Little Shannon unprotected."

"Put your balls anywhere near my girlfriend and I'll kill ya," Johnny snarled, launching a snowball of his own. "Do ya hear me, Gibs? I'll take the bleeding face clean off ya!"

"I'm going to put my balls on her face."

"Gibs."

"My big wet balls all over her face – Jesus Christ, Johnny!" Appearing from behind the garage, Gibsie clutched his head. "There was a stone in that snowball."

"I know," Johnny shot back unapologetically. "I put it there."

"That *hurt*."

"*Good*!"

"I'm not playing anymore." Shaking off the snow dusting his hair, Gibsie threw one last snowball at my boyfriend before stalking off in a huff in the direction of the house. "I'm telling Mammy K."

"Who's the pussy now?" Johnny called after him. "Ya little rat."

"Johnny," I scolded, smacking his arm. "Don't be so mean. You know he's a sensitive soul deep down."

"Ah, he'll live," Johnny chuckled, turning his attention to me. Smiling, he leaned in close and tucked a strand of hair behind my ear. "Hi, Shannon."

Shivering, I beamed back at him. "Hi, Johnny."

"Sorry about the snowball earlier." He shrugged sheepishly. "Apparently, I have a thing for hitting you in the head with my balls."

"Yeah, well." I waggled my brows teasingly. "You could aim lower next time."

"Is that so?" Johnny purred, leaning in to brush a kiss to my lips. "How low?"

"My lips."

"Which lips?"

"You choose."

"Fuck." Johnny blew out an impressed breath and grinned. "Forget school." Catching ahold of my hand, he dragged me off in the direction of the back field. "Let's go down to the treehouse."

"Wait!" I laughed breathlessly, struggling to keep up with his rocket fast pace. "Don't you want to build a snowman?"

"Lips and balls first," he called over his shoulder. "Snowman after."

THANK YOU SO MUCH FOR READING!

Joey and Aoife's story has concluded, but the Boys of Tommen series is far from over.

For updates on release dates, check out **chloewalshauthor.com.**

Keep reading for an exclusive **bonus chapter** from *Redeeming 6*. Find out what happened just before the **Epilogue** on page 919!

Bonus Scene

AOIFE

November 7ᵗʰ, 2005

When I blinked awake the first Monday in November, the first thing I registered was the familiar sound of "Semi-Charmed Life" from Third Eye Blind as it echoed through the house.

"Jesus, again?" I mumbled to myself, as I grabbed my pillow and covered my face with it.

Since discovering one of my old mixtapes soothed AJ, we played it constantly.

Not a mixtape, I mentally corrected. *This song.*

The irony that the only song that settled our son was one about crystal meth didn't escape me, either.

Rolling onto my side, I took note of the empty bassinet for a brief second before bolting out of bed, feeling a combination of lethargy and sheer panic.

Lethargy because I hadn't slept properly in months, and panic because today was my first day at Tommen, which meant I would have to leave AJ with my mam for seven whole hours.

Naked as the day I was born, I grabbed a rogue t-shirt off the bedroom floor and went in search of my baby.

The jittery nervousness that had been steadily growing in my belly all week was temporarily set aside when I jumped off the bottom step of the staircase and took in the sight of both my baby and his daddy.

With his back to me, Joey swayed and shimmied to the music with AJ snuggled on his shoulder.

Clad in nothing but a pair of black boxers, I watched as he flipped a pancake in the pan, while humming along to the lyrics of the song playing on repeat.

Oh, dear Jesus.

Regular Joe was irresistible, but daddy Joey? Dear God, he was too much for my poor, barely recovered ovaries.

These past two months hadn't been easy, but we were doing it.

Together.

I had my best friend back, my partner in crime, in life, and parenthood.

"How much for a private show later?" I teased, thoroughly amused by his exhibition. "Nice moves, stud."

"You couldn't afford me," came Joey's smart-ass response, as he turned back to wink at me. "Morning, queen."

"Then it's a good thing I own you and don't have to pay," I replied, sidling up to him, eyes locked on AJ. "How's my baby?"

"That you do, Molloy." Leaning in, he pressed a kiss to my temple before handing AJ over to me and turning his attention back to the cooker. "You know, I'm sure he's cutting a tooth."

"Thank you!" Cradling my little pudge in my arms, I blew raspberries on his chubby cheek, causing AJ to grin up at me. "I've been saying this for days, but Mam and Casey said I was being daft because he's only a couple of months old."

"Well, Casey doesn't know shit because his gums are like rocks," Joey shot back. "And no offense to your mam, but she doesn't know AJ best. You do. You're his mam, and you're on the ball with him, baby."

"I am?"

"You are."

I beamed down at AJ's little face, feeling an immense amount of pride at being praised for my parenting skills. It meant a lot coming from Joe. Then again, he was always the first to praise me – not to mention the first to step in and back me up when Mam got a little overbearing.

My mind drifted back to the day I moved out of home and the epic showdown between my mother and my boyfriend . . .

"Who's AJ's mother here, Trish? You or Aoife? Because I'm sure as hell his father and, no offense, but I know for a fact, high or not, that I didn't climb on top of you nine months ago."

"Joey!"

"No, this overbearing grandmother shit has to stop," my boyfriend interrupted, taking our sleeping son out of my mother's arms and placing him back into mine – where he had been until Mam snatched him off me. "We appreciate everything you've done for us. More than can be said, but Aoife's his mam. And she's a fucking brilliant mam."

"I know she is—"

"Then let her be one, and stop undermining her," he snapped, while tossing my clothes into black bin liners. "Stop interfering and making her question everything she does for the kid, because she can do this."

"Am I undermining you, Aoife?" Mam asked, turning her attention to me. "Do you feel the same way as Joey?"

"Uh ... " Yes, absolutely. I cleared my throat and shrugged. "Maybe a tad."

Joey cut me a look that said coward before turning his attention back to my mother. "You know I'm mad about ya, Trish. You're like a second mother to me," he tried again. "And there's no one else I would trust to mind our son, but it's the little comments directed at Aoife and the constant running commentary when she's looking after our son that has to stop." Unrolling another bin liner from the pack, he shook it open and continued to empty my wardrobe. "I can take it because, quite frankly, I don't give a shit about what you think about my parenting, but Aoife does, it's not doing any good for her confidence, so I need you to cut the motherly apron strings and let your daughter breathe ... "

"Oh Jesus, your mother is here already," Joey announced, dragging me back to the present, as several enthusiastic knocks came from the other side of our little front door. "At half seven in the morning."

"She's excited," I offered, swallowing down my laughter. "It's her first day minding AJ."

"Yeah." Looking comically flustered, Joey pinched the bridge of his nose and muttered something unintelligible under his breath.

"She just wants to help me, Joe," I tried again, resting my hand on his forearm. "Don't be cranky."

"I get that," he agreed with a solemn nod. "But her version of helping you doesn't always help *you*, Molloy."

"And I get that," I agreed right back before heading towards the porch. "But she's doing a lot better lately, and besides, who else are we going to trust with AJ when we're both at school?"

Joey leaned a hip against the kitchen counter and shrugged. "Edel offered."

"Edel already has her hands full with your brothers."

"I just don't want anyone making you feel bad about yourself."

"That's really not what she's trying to do, Joe," I replied. "She loves me. Her version of loving me is trying to take away my worries."

"By taking your kid."

"Joe." I batted my eyes at him, knowing that this argument could go on forever, and we didn't have the time. "Please."

"Fine." Throwing his hands up in defeat, he shook his head and turned back to plating up the pancakes. "I won't say another word on the matter."

"Thank you."

"Unless she starts taking over again," he called after me. "And in that scenario, all bets are off."

"I wouldn't have it any other way," I called back to him before opening the door and welcoming my mother inside.

JOEY

Deep down inside, I knew I had lucked out in the mother-in-law department. Trish Molloy had a heart of gold. She had given birth to and raised the mother of my son and had forgiven me for my endless stream of misgivings against her daughter. Problem was, since AJ's birth the woman was driving me batshit crazy. She constantly wanted to be overly involved in every miniscule detail of her daughter and grandson's lives, which was a huge problem for me considering her involvement usually resulted in her daughter in tears.

Tony hadn't changed one bit since AJ's arrival. He was the same at work as he'd always been. In fact, our relationship had improved if anything, but Trish? Yeah, she was getting on my last nerve.

Maybe it was because of how I was raised that I had such a problem with her lack of boundaries and incessant intrusiveness on my little family, or maybe Trish and Molloy's relationship had always been this way and I had been too high to notice or care, but I was here now.

Clearheaded and present, and going out of my fucking mind.

According to Kav this was normal behavior, and his own mother was just as heavily a meddler in his life, but since Edel had been nothing but respectful of my boundaries, and my own mother had been mentally absent for most of my life, I had nothing to compare this motherly behavior to.

Retreating upstairs to our bedroom for the sake of both my sanity and sobriety, I stalked into the shower in the adjoining ensuite bathroom, praying that the water could somehow burn the agitation out of me.

A few minutes later, Molloy hurried into the bathroom, looking flustered and panicked. "Joe!"

"What, Jesus, what?" I demanded, equally panicked, as I turned around to face her. "You hurt?"

"It won't tie!"

"Come again?" I asked, wiping the condensation from the glass so that I could see her.

"My skirt," she cried dramatically, tossing a flimsy scrap of navy fabric on the sink. "It won't fucking tie, Joe!"

"What do you mean it won't tie?"

"I mean, you ruined my body with your big dick and your son ruined my body with his big head and now I can't fit into a size ten skirt!"

"A size ten?" I balked, repressing the urge to remind her that she had never been a size ten to begin with. My baby had always been a size twelve. I knew this because I had been dragged along on enough shopping trips down through the years. "Molloy, you literally had a baby two months ago. The fuck were you thinking buying a skirt size that Shannon would struggle to fit into?"

"Oh, please. Shannon's a size six."

"Molloy!"

"Because I had this whole healthy eating and exercise plan with Casey to lose the baby weight before I started at Tommen."

"And you did," I replied, before quickly following it up with, "Not that you had anything to lose to begin with." Clearing away the condensation once more, I took a slow appraisal of her body and blew out an impressed breath. "You look fucking amazing."

"That's it. It's a sign." She threw her hands up in defeat. "I'm not supposed to go back to school. I'll stay home with AJ. That's where I should be anyway, and I'll miss him too much if I have to leave him all day. Besides, it's not like I'm going to do wonders academically anyway. We both know that I'm no Kev."

"Like hell you're not going back." Switching off the shower, I stepped out and grabbed a towel. "You're going to school, Molloy."

"Well, I can't go now, can I?" she countered huffily. "Unless you want me to walk into Tommen with my bare ass on full display."

"You can absolutely do that," I replied, stalking towards her. "But just know that I won't be around to sit with you in class because I'll be too busy getting expelled for killing every bastard that ogles your ass."

"Be serious."

"I am," I told her. "Now, give me your skirt and I'll take it next door. I'm sure Edel can do something with it. Let it out an inch or whatever it needs."

"Edel?"

"Yeah, she does clothes and shit, remember?"

"No, you don't have to do that," she mumbled, cheeks reddening. "I have one in a bigger size in the wardrobe."

"Then what's the problem, Molloy?" I demanded. "Because you're not getting out of going to school, baby ... "

"Look at this, Joe," she cried, gesturing to the soft pouch of silvery, loose skin under her bellybutton. "I'm going to be the only girl at Tommen with a Joey pouch."

I cocked a brow. "A Joey pouch?"

"Yeah," she sniffled, nodding solemnly. "It's my own personal version of a mummy tummy. Except it's called a Joey pouch. You know," she paused to choke back another dramatic sob, "because you put it there."

Give me strength. "You listen to me." Backing her up against the far wall of the bathroom, I tilted her chin up to look at me, while adjusting the towel around my hips to hide the solid semi I was sporting at the mere sight of her. "You are fucking gorgeous, Aoife Molloy."

"Past tense."

"Past, present, future tense," I cut her off with a growl. "Infinity tense. There isn't a girl at Tommen – or BCS for that matter, that can hold a flame to you."

"Joe, I just want to be me again," she admitted with a sigh. "I want to be the me I used to be when you and I ... you know." Shaking her head, she released a heavy sigh and mumbled. "I just want to be like I was for you."

So, that was it.

She thought I didn't want her like before.

Because we hadn't been intimate since ... Jesus, since before my mother died.

"I want you," I said gruffly, reaching down to cup her cheek. "Desperately."

Her eyes widened in surprise. "You do?"

"At what point in time have I given you the impression that I'm not completely besotted with ya?"

My words were direct, straight to the point, and stunned her into a rare moment of silence. "You're besotted with me?" she finally asked, fumbling over her words in a very unlike-Molloy way. "I just ... it's been over two months, and I thought since you haven't tried to—"

"If I could have been with you the second I got home from rehab I would have," I hurried to interject, needing to fix this before it grew into something that festered between us. Needing to give her my truth. "I wanted to. More than life. I *still* want to. Morning, noon, and night, Molloy." Blowing out a frustrated breath, I said, "You're the mother of my child, Molloy. You're my best friend in the whole world. Christ, the only place I ever want to be is *inside* you."

"Then why haven't you, you know, initiated anything?"

"Because you were healing after giving birth," I admitted honestly. "Because you're still healing, and I won't be my father."

Her brows furrowed in confusion. "Your father?"

"I spent a lifetime listening to that man force himself into my mother's body. At times, seeing it happen, too." The words were a torn admission from somewhere deep within. Somewhere I didn't like to visit often. "After Tadhg he waited a few weeks for her to heal after giving birth, but after the rest of them, it was a matter of days or hours."

"Oh my god." She sucked in a sharp breath. "Joe ..."

"So, the reason I haven't initiated anything physical isn't because I don't want you, but because I won't be him, Molloy," I doubled down and reaffirmed both to her and myself. "And I won't ever turn you into her."

There was a long stretch of silence after that where no words were spoken between us. Instead, we just stood in the bathroom, eyes locked on each other, both taking the other's measure, as she absorbed my truth, and I grounded myself in her presence.

"Tonight," Molloy finally broke the silence by saying. "After AJ goes to sleep." Reaching a hand up, she pushed my hair off my forehead before leaning in to press a kiss to my shoulder. "I'm ready."

Instantly hard at the thought, but desperately trying to repress the carnage urge I had to take her against this wall, I swiped her hand up and pressed a kiss to the inside of her wrist. "It's a date."

"Condoms, stud."

"On it, queen."

Acknowledgements

I have so much to be grateful for and some many people to thank. People who, with their encouragement and undiluted support, made this book a reality.

Walshy: What can I say, lad? It's been whirlwind. I love you longtime, my old pal. Thanks for being my own personal Johnny. ♥

Kiddos: Well, lads? I suppose it's time to get the wellies out and make use of that annual pass. Lol. I love you so very much. It's my love for you that created Edel Kavanagh. Got your backs for life, my little crew. ♥

Sinead: I was eleven years old when you walked into my world, and I am so glad that you stayed. I couldn't have gotten through the last five months without you. You're one of the best people I know and I'm so proud to claim you as family.

Johnny Butt: The coffee man. The OG. Love you, Dad. Always. Thank you for being my rock.

Nikki, Bianca, Danielle, Rayna, Fiona, Chitra, Aleesha: girls, what would I do without you? Your support and friendship means the absolute world to me and I love you all so very much. Thanks for having my back, girls. Love your bones. Ride or die. ♥

Nicole & Inbal: Well, ladies, ye did it. Ye officially dragged Joey out of me, and I can't thank you enough. I told you before. You changed everything.

Shai: the kindest friend I never knew I needed. Thanks for putting up with me. I know I'm a full-blown Aoife at times haha. You're the best.

To all the people I've met on this journey: thank you so much for your support and friendship.

To my readers: Thank you for supporting me. Thank you for putting your faith in me. Thank you for reading my stories. Thank you. ♥

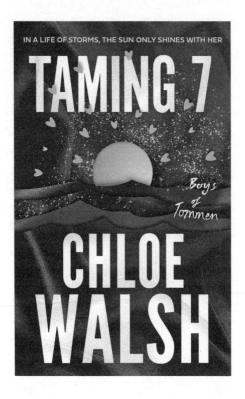

Epic, emotional and addictive . . .

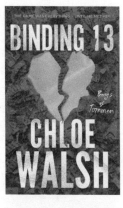 

The power and pain of first love has never been more deeply felt than in Chloe Walsh's extraordinary stories about the irresistible Boys of Tommen, which will give you the ultimate book hangover.

Collect them all!